Goody Two-Shoes
and other 18th-century British stories

Goody Two-Shoes
and other 18th-century British stories

edited by Henry M. Wallace

Universitas Press
Montreal

Universitas Press

Montreal

www.universitaspress.com

First published in December 2017

Library and Archives Canada Cataloguing in Publication

   Goody Two-Shoes and other 18th-century British stories / edited by Henry M. Wallace.

ISBN 978-1-988963-01-3 (softcover)

   1. Short stories, English. 2. English fiction--18th century.
I. Wallace, Henry M., 1970-, editor

PR1309.S5G66 2017   823'.010805   C2017-906858-X

To Don Neilson

TABLE OF CONTENTS

Introduction

There is an 18th century of the "rise of the novel," one of the poetry and another of the drama, all well established as fields of study, with their own instruments and their own debates. There is no 18th century of the short story, however; there are no "companions" to the 18th-century British short fiction and no anthologies (before this one) uniquely devoted to it. When the major works of 18th-century authors are being brought together into a single volume, a few of their short stories are sometimes included, but never in a special section which would identify them as such; rather, they can be found jumbled together with the nonfiction, in a section of "prose." When short stories appear in general anthologies of 18th-century British literature, they are often untitled, bearing simply the name of the periodical and the number of the issue in which they were first published; thus they remain unidentified as individual pieces of fiction and as belonging to a particular genre.

There are a few obvious reasons for this. First, 18th-century short stories appear to have been, for both authors and readers of the time, in a state of generic confusion: on the one hand, they were often confused with the longer fictions and were even named "novels" by their very practitioners; on the other, they were confused with nonfiction, being called "essays" or being published as part of what were, manifestly, essays. Second and third, because 18th-century writers do not seem to have taken the trouble to clarify this confusion, for example by publishing single-authored short-story collections (as it became customary in the 19th century); and because in the 1700s there are none of those obvious genre-building signs: manifestos of the short story like Poe's, identifiable models like Hawthorne, or authors clearly working to perfect the genre, like Maupassant and Chekhov.

We have been used to seeing the rise of the short story as a 19th-century phenomenon. What seems to be specific to the 18th century, on the other hand, is the rise of journalistic literature. However, it is precisely in newspapers and periodicals of all kinds that one finds the great majority of 18th-century short fiction: it was written by authors (like Daniel Defoe, Eliza Haywood, Oliver Goldsmith, or Henry Mackenzie) who also penned full-length novels and full-fledged essays and were well aware of the differences between genres. In the 18th century, periodicals included a "large quantity of fiction" (Boyce 95) and, if one were to count all the tales and anecdotes related in these journals, the number of these short pieces might be as high as 50,000 (Pitcher 360). Short stories, as this anthology will hopefully show, can help just as much, if not more, than novels and poems, to get a sense of the 18th century; they feature the same adventures of the body, the mind, or the soul that one finds in *Robinson Crusoe*, *Pamela*, or *Tristram Shandy*.

In literary history and in anthologies of British literature, the 1700s are often bundled together with the Restoration into a long 18th century of 140 years (1660-1800); or even, together with both the Restoration and the early 1800s, into a very long 18th century (1660-1837). The reasons for this are almost entirely non-literary and it can be easily argued that the literature of the Restoration and that of the Romantic era should be studied separately from the cultural products of the 1700s.[1] It is, indeed, around 1700 that a (new) change began in British cultural and literary history: with the lapse of the Licensing Act in 1695, the censorship of the press all but disappeared and scores of new publications (newspapers, magazines, pamphlets, chapbooks, essay serials, etc.) found their way to an ever increasing reading public; the English version of the quarrel of the ancients and the moderns, begun in 1690 in a scholarly environment, found literary expression in satires, poetry, drama, and the "modern" medium of literary criticism soon after 1700; and a change of generations sounded the real end of the 17th century with the arrival of Daniel Defoe, Tom Brown, Ned Ward, Jonathan Swift, and the younger Joseph Addison, Richard Steele and Alexander Pope. John Dryden (1631-1700), the most celebrated poet of the late 17th century, prophesied on his deathbed (in his 1700 "Secular Masque") that "'Tis well an Old Age is out/ And time to begin a New."

It seems at first sight that there is nothing unitary about the British literature of the 18th century and one reason for this is the absence of a sweeping, long-lasting, transnational movement like Romanticism or postmodernism, both of which manifested themselves in the arts, in historiography, in politics, etc. The most conventional perspective on the century has it divided into an Augustan Age (roughly from 1700 to 1740) and an Age of Johnson (from 1740 to 1780), followed by the beginnings of Romanticism. In fact, many of the cultural products of the 18th century, such as the sentimental novels, the discovery of the picturesque, the gothic, the poetry of ruins, Young's *Night Thoughts* and Macpherson's Ossian cycle, are often seen as pre-Romantic. Thus, much of the latter half of the 18th century is usually hijacked into a large-scale study of Romanticism, because the 18th century itself seems to lack a similar movement into whose gravitational pull all or most of its own decades may be brought and held together. However, the Enlightenment, or more exactly the British Enlightenment (since it manifested itself quite differently from one country to another) can be understood as exactly that unifying movement that can allow us to see the 18th century as a whole, at least until the *Lyrical Ballads* in 1798; a century going from the death of John Dryden to the death of William Cowper.

The Enlightenment

The most significant cultural change that occurred at the turn of the 18th century in England was the fact that, quite rapidly, the City replaced the Court

[1] There is also no reason why the general study of the 18th century should not have a more conventional beginning such as 1700 or 1701, rather than 1660, 1688, or 1690, since all the structural changes that are supposed to have been brought about by the Glorious Revolution were felt more strongly and more clearly at the turn of the century (see Claydon 101-106).

as patron and arbiter of the arts. Before 1700, most writers (but this was also true of musicians, actors, or painters) needed and sought social and financial protection from the rich and powerful. Only the aristocracy could provide the recognition (which in turn conferred status) to those involved in the production of cultural artefacts. Aristocrats organised private concerts, commissioned and bought paintings, offered grants and pensions to writers. In fact, many artists and even some scholars not associated with the universities often lived on the estate of a nobleman and became members of his household.

On the contrary, after the turn of the 18th century, when London with its heterogeneous public became the main hub for the production and consumption of printed commodities, writers had only to move to the capital in search of an audience,[1] even if it was only to join that much-maligned category of authors for hire ("hack writers") employed by the many publishers of the time to write whatever was asked of them. If not always financially rewarding (except for the booksellers), a writer's career in the 18th century unfolded with a degree of freedom that would have seemed unthinkable a few decades before. As Oliver Goldsmith put it, in one the letters of his *Citizen of the World* (1762):

> At present the few poets of England no longer depend on the Great for subsistence, they have now no other patrons but the public, and the public, collectively considered, is a good and a generous master. It is indeed, too frequently mistaken as to the merits of every candidate for favour; but to make amends, it is never mistaken long. . . . [The writer] may now refuse an invitation to dinner, without fearing to incur his patron's displeasure, or to starve by remaining at home. He may now venture to appear in company with just such clothes as other men generally wear, and talk even to princes, with all the conscious superiority of wisdom. Though he cannot boast of fortune here, yet he can bravely assert the dignity of independence. (II, 84)

Writers of the 18th century organised themselves in clubs or only met informally in cafés and taverns; they dialogued, often vehemently, in the pages of newspapers, pamphlets, and books, enjoying the autonomy of the republic of letters, in which symbolic status came from the inter-recognition of the community of authors.

Their discourse and ongoing dialogue played an important part in the constitution of the public sphere, which emerged in the early 18th century as a safe arena in which opinions could be exchanged and ideas take shape.[2] It was this arena that Voltaire discovered and described with envious admiration in the late 1720s. His *Philosophical Letters* (also known as *Letters Concerning the English Nation*), first published a few years later, in 1734, display a great deal of wishful thinking, both about religious freedom (epitomised by the free-for-all environment of the stock exchange) and supposed celebrity status enjoyed by

[1] This was also true of musicians, who often came to London from countries like Germany and Italy, because concerts in front of British middle-class audiences had become more financially rewarding than the support of their aristocratic patrons at home.

[2] The existence of a public sphere in the early 1700s was first suggested in 1962, in *The Structural Transformation of the Public Sphere* by Jürgen Habermas. Although his conclusions have been later deemed too optimistic, as the 18th-century public sphere included neither women nor most men, it remains true that at least its beginnings must be placed in that era.

men of letters. Nevertheless, much of what he reported about 18th-century Britain, including his flattering comparisons with contemporary France, holds true. Unlike other countries at the time, England and, after 1707, Great Britain was a constitutional monarchy, guaranteed by the Bill of Rights of 1689, which had secured the right for free elections and had limited the powers of the king.

Europe had entered a distinct era in the history of ideas, known as the Enlightenment, and in Britain, like everywhere else, it had a local specificity. In 1784, Friedrich Kant, who still understood the Enlightenment in terms of the quarrel of the ancients and the moderns (that is, he placed its beginnings at the turn of the century), defined it as both a phenomenon of political and intellectual progress (the modern man, according to Kant, had come of age) and as a *task*: one had to work hard to bring the "light" of this progress to as many people as possible.[1] When reduced to these two simple ideas, the Enlightenment can indeed appear as a pan-European movement; many of its ways of manifestation did not, however, reach all places or did not reach them at the same time. In Britain, specifically, the Enlightenment began with the very challenge against political absolutism mentioned above and with the creation of a modern public sphere. Clubs, cafés, and secret societies became widespread. The newly emerged public post allowed for the development of private correspondence (and, in the American colonies, to that of the "committees of correspondence") and assisted in the production and consumption of printed commodities, beginning with the public newspaper, which was delivered by the post. New institutions were created, such as the circulating library or the public museum. New genres emerged, including the encyclopaedia and the philosophical "system," both in an attempt to "systematise" knowledge for an expanding reading public. The novel was sometimes repurposed as a philosophical tale, sometimes as a scandalous chronicle exposing the sins of society, both in an attempt to draw attention to the task at hand.

Most 18th-century British writers, including the authors of short fiction selected here, were what we would call today "public intellectuals," interested in all aspects of the task of "enlightening," and practicing all genres. They produced poetry, drama, novels, short stories; they wrote on philosophy, ethics, politics, "the state of learning" and that of the English language. Perhaps the most salient feature of British Enlightenment is the journalistic revolution. Oliver Goldsmith, in an article published in *The Daily Advertiser* (31 March 1773), confessed that he had "always considered the press as the protector of our freedom, as a watchful guardian, capable of uniting the weak against the encroachments of power. What concerns the public, most properly admits of a public discussion" (Goldsmith IV, 428). Short stories of the 18th century were part and parcel of this "public discussion": directly or indirectly, their authors followed the task of improving human relationships and human lives. They were perhaps more honest (or more hopeful) than their successors in their longing for a reality that would match their ideals; for the respect of social values and norms; for intellectual and emotional soundness; for some kind of confirmation of their religious faith; for community, friendship, and love.

[1] Two centuries later, although he disagreed with many of Kant's views, Michel Foucault admitted that the task of the modern man still "requires work on our limits, that is, a patient labour giving form to our impatience for liberty" (50).

Ends

Voltaire's post-religious utopia of the London stock market in which men of all classes and creeds lived and let others live was nevertheless set in a world that had only recently bounced back from the scandal of the South Sea Bubble. Although the downfall of the South Sea Company was ultimately not as calamitous as originally assessed (and as it was reported well into the 19th century), the reputation of British financiers, already made dubious by the many "schemes" or "projects" of the early 1700s, took an extremely heavy blow in 1720. In the 1721 poem "The South Sea Project," his savage attack on the company's directors, Jonathan Swift speaks of "jugglers" and fairground magicians, relentlessly cheating people out of their money. His story of the following year, "The Wonder of All the Wonders that Ever the World Wonder'd at," which takes the form of an advertisement for the outrageously unrealistic stunts promised by a street performer, is clearly reminiscent of his opinions on the South Sea Company, but it is also, and especially, a powerful expression of one of the most important themes in 18th-century British short fiction: imposture.

In Defoe's 1720 version of the famous story about Diogenes's unsuccessful search for an honest man, "good men" are, surprisingly, everywhere, because collective representations are flawed and anything can be masqueraded as virtue: honesty, as the narrator concludes, has been taken out of the equation and replaced by whichever quality fits our utilitarian needs. It is no coincidence that the story begins among stockbrokers, for whom a "good man" is simply someone well-off and debt-free. In an early example of a satire of get-rich-quick schemes, Addison's narrator in "In Search of the Philosopher's Stone" (1713) is too naive to realise that he is being swindled by his "operator," busy as he is to make plans about spending his impending fortune. In Matthew Concanen's "A 'Novel'" (1726), different forms of imposture are pitted against each other: nobody is what he or she claims to be, and this time con artists are encouraged to take advantage of a hypocrite. In Thomas Warton's "Journal of a Fellow from College" (1758), imposture reigns supreme in the university which, instead of a place of learning, has become an extension of the outside world, and study has been replaced by the usual activities of men of leisure.

In "A Country Entertainment" (1718), Thomas Gordon does not criticise country manners, but the illusion that they might be somehow purer, less full of affectation and self-importance. Similarly, George Colman's "A Country Gentleman" (1775) attacks corruption and drunkenness which otherwise, thanks to the same illusion, would endure beyond scrutiny. Many 18th-century authors were concerned with the behaviour of gentlemen and their families, whether in the city or the country, because they were supposed to be models of polite manners, free of pretensions, affectation, and pomposity. The gentleman was being socially constructed as a man of honour, taste, and Christian virtue, but he had to exist at the same time (especially in the city) as a man of the world. The latter was supposed to be witty, fashionable, a good conversationalist who saw all the shows and who could hold a drink; of course, the same person was expected to be both. In what was arguably the most important book of conduct for men in the 18th century, Lord Chesterfield's posthumous *Letters to His Son on the Art of Becoming a Man of the World and a Gentleman* (1774), polite manners, including a little flattery and white lies, are paid constant tribute. With good reason, Chesterfield has been criticised for having showed "how easily civilised behaviour could be reduced to the lowest common denominator" (Rothblatt 31); in other words, to something much like dissimulation and hypocrisy. Appearances mattered, however, to Chesterfield and to many other 18th-century authors, who were ready to point at social upstarts, country bumpkins, and old-fashioned folk because of their lack of worldliness and good manners, whether these also concealed moral flaws or not. In this anthology, this is the case, for example, of Erasmus Philips's "Foul Weather" (1726), Samuel Johnson's "Story of Zosima" (1750), John Boyle's "Sir Josiah Pumpkin's Courage" (1753), George Colman and Bonnell Thornton's "Supper at Vaux-Hall" (1755), or Thomas Chatterton's "Tony Selwood" (1770). Polite manners were, in fact, the very fabric of society: before being a man of virtue, the gentleman needed to be a man of the world. As Samuel Johnson put it to James Boswell, his aristocratic amanuensis: "What is it but opinion, by which we have a respect for authority, that prevents us, who are the rabble, from rising up and pulling down you who are gentlemen from your places, and saying, 'We will be gentlemen in our turn?'" (II, 8). Opinion, appearances, perfectly rehearsed manners, kept Britain safe from revolutionary troubles like those in France. Well sheltered by manners, the gentleman was able to discover the virtues exclusively prepared for him in British schools (as suggested in Thomas Gordon's 1740 "Fashionable Education") or, like in Maria Edgeworth's "Tarlton" (1796), in the company of other gentlemen-in-the-making.

Outwardly polite manners (and not just their imperfect imitation by unsophisticated provincials) began being targeted, when spurious and insincere, in the latter half of the century, in the wake of sentimental literature calling for a "man of feeling" (as Henry Mackenzie entitled his 1771 novel) to replace the man of the world. The man of feeling listened to his heart more often than he did to his reason; he sought purity and authenticity of sentiments; he enjoyed the simplicity that he discovered in nature, in the country, and among the country people living close to nature. The narrator in Nathan Drake's "Agnes Felton" (1790) takes this kind of pure, unadulterated joy from his encounter with the simple, honest, and attractive inhabitants of the Lake District. So does Sir Edward, in Mackenzie's "Louisa Venoni" (1780), even though he only understands it when he has the opportunity to compare it to the disgust he feels when he returns to the company of polite society: "In their pretended attachments, he discovered only designs of selfishness; and their pleasures, he experienced, were as fallacious as their friendships. In the society of *Louisa* [on the contrary] he found sensibility and truth" (262, in this volume).

In the conclusion to his 1720 story, Defoe explained that, according to the definition in use at the time, "Honesty has a very small Share in the Composition of a good Man" (68, in this volume); others explored the honesty of feeling or, rather, the lack thereof. Of particular importance for many 18th-century authors seems to be the problem of the authenticity of romantic feelings, as they understood that most marriages of "persons of quality" were decided by the fortune and social position of the betrothed and matrimony was often little more than a financial and real-estate transaction in a time when the desire for monetary gain outweighed sheer love (which was relegated to fairy tales). The race for gold in the years of the South Sea scandal is a leitmotif in Eliza Haywood's roman à clef *Memoirs of a Certain Island, Adjacent to the Kingdom of Utopia* (1725-1726) and John O'Brien has suggested in a recent study that Haywood "explains the Bubble as the consequence of a national infatuation with money that had displaced the desire for romantic love" (88). The absence of love is, in fact, the other major theme in many of the short stories of the century. In Richard Steele's "The Civil Husband" (1709), the spouses have grown apart and make special arrangements to avoid each other, as long their wealth allows them to do so. In Mary Hays's "Melville and Serena" (1793), wealth only lasts for a while and the mismatched husband and wife have to bear insolvency as well as an oppressive union. Absence of love may sometimes lose the battle against love, as it happens in Haywood's "The Reclamation of Dorimon" (1744) and Edward Moore's "The Story of Mrs Wilson" (1753) but, when allied with the possibility of financial gain, it is utterly triumphant, like in Delarivier Manley's "Story of Samuel Slender" (1709), Richard Steele's "Inkle and Yarico" (1711), or Alexander Kellet's "The Man of Spirit" (1761).

Elizabeth Griffith's "An Affecting Instance of the Effects of Love" (1776) begins with an ironic statement about love being the exception to the rule. Her story comes to a sorrowful end, but love is ultimately triumphant, since not even Eliza's death can put an end to Richard's affection. A much sadder outcome is that of stories such as Ned Ward's "The Rise and Fall of Madam *Coming-Sir*" (1702), Eliza Haywood's "Fantomina" (1725) and Henry Fielding's "The Female Husband" (1746), despite their manifest moralising tones. "Fantomina" is not so much the story of a ruined reputation, as it is rather that of a young woman who multiplies herself in a desperate attempt to gain someone else's love, only to find out that, no matter how many personas she might embrace for the sake of her lover, he will ultimately grow bored of her; "The Female Husband" is not so much the story of a serial "perversion," but rather that of another young woman who offers her love over and over again, only to be each time rejected and eventually punished.

As men and women of the Enlightenment era, 18th-century British fiction writers do not shrink from sermonising, either directly, via the narratorial voice, or (mostly towards the end of the 1700s) through the voice of a wise character. They believed that both society and the individual could be improved. Especially in the first two thirds of the century, authors insisted that their characters *could* be healed or corrected and that society needed saving from the faults of individuals (unlike, for example, in 19th-century fiction, in which individuals need saving from the sins of society). In the satirical realism that is so characteristic of the British literature of the first half of the 18th century, characters ruin themselves and they ruin or pervert society; they are not afflicted by hubris or ancestral sin or a profound moral flaw (like in so many 19th-century stories); and they do not have to bear serious social adversity. The seducer (often identified as a "rake") who is rarely punished (an exception being the eponymous character in John Hawkesworth's 1752 "Story of Opsinous"), the prostitute (whose "origin story" is always carefully recounted), and the voiceless illegitimate child constitute an ever-present and pitiful trinity in the social imaginary of the 18th century. Fallen women, like the protagonists of Ned Ward's and C. E.'s stories in this volume, transgress because of their own weakness of character, at least until the late 1700s, when society as a whole began to be questioned. Bastard children were spared the blame, but it was understood that they could never become "persons of quality" (although, ironically, Chesterfield's treatise on how to be a gentleman was addressed to his illegitimate son).

In "The History of the Little Goody Two-Shoes" (1765), society is once again revealed as salvageable through the merits of the individual and against the sins of other individuals; however, the original tragedy affecting the eponymous girl is a sin of society: the deserted village. Other signs of change are noticeable in the early 1760s, with characters like Goldmith's ("The Disabled Soldier"), Kellet's ("The Man of Spirit"), and Bickerstaff's ("Ambrose Gwinett"), who are all innocents who suffer despite having no flaw or having committed no sin. Society becomes blameable in Leonard McNally's 1782 story "Fanny; or, The Fair Foundling of St George's Fields," in which the fallen woman is pushed into a life of poverty through a Jean-Valjean-like episode that leaves her an orphan; and she is capable (and deemed worthy) of redemption. Hannah More goes back to identifying individual sinners (Mrs Sponge), but the little girl (in "Betty Brown, the St Giles's Orange Girl") is saved by the magistrate's wife, who is an example of what society as a whole can do. Many 18th-century writers actively sought to improve both individuals and the society, mostly by correcting manners; but some went further, like Fielding who became a magistrate and established a police force (the Bow Street Runners). When reading the literature of the time, one has to understand that the authors' social involvement as well as their moralising effort came from the disturbing realities of the century: slavery, gallows and gibbets, deportation for the vagrant homeless (like Goldsmith's "disabled soldier," people could be found "guilty of being poor" and deported), workhouses, lack of welfare, little charity, pirates and highwaymen, and perhaps (see Cruickshank 138-139) as many as 80,000 prostitutes at any given time in London. The authors of the century of the Enlightenment were certainly more concerned than their ancestors with the many social problems of their own era. These problems, in turn, were instrumental in creating specific narrative techniques. As George Farquhar anticipated in his 1702 "A Discourse upon Comedy": "if our Utile, which is the End, be different from the Ancients, pray let our Dulce, which is the Means, be so too" (I, 98).

Means

Working on improving manners meant, for many of the authors of 18th-century Great Britain, using concrete examples of individuals that could be recognised by their readers. Much of the literature of the era, especially in the first half of the century, was a literature "à clef," in which characters were either supposed to be easily identified despite their made-up monikers, usually taken from Greek mythology; or they were simply mentioned by name. In the first case, a key was sometimes provided at the end of the book or the names were represented by initials (or by the first and last letters of the real names). In the second case, real names were provided because they belonged to individuals who had already been condemned by society and their lives had become cautionary tales. Authors themselves, especially in periodicals, hid behind an array of personas, which are usually identifiable as belonging to one writer or to several, while some will very likely remain anonymous.

Among the first such personas are the ones used to create collections of fictional letters, like the ones composed by Tom Brown and his collaborators in "Love-Letters by Several Hands" (1701), the anonymous "S. M.," author of *The Female Critick* (1701), or the unknown author of the *Letters from the Living to the Living* (1703). Each fictional letter-writer had his or her own style and preoccupations and sometimes they entered into dialogue with other correspondents. Tom Brown and Ned Ward, in *Amusements Serious and Comical, Calculated for the Meridian of London* (1700) and *The London Spy* (1698-1700), respectively, also introduced the so-called "ramble fiction," a sort of urban picaresque, which deeply influenced many later works of fiction. Both Brown and Ward used a fictional version of themselves (Ward's is identified simply as "the London spy") and fictional companions, with whom they travel trough the English capital, discovering engrossing characters, describing street tableaux, and usually finding trouble. When Defoe started his *Review* (1704-1713), he continued this tradition by interspersing news about the ongoing War of the Spanish Succession with little essays which, in turn, often included stories[1] in which a fictional version of the author rambled through London, meeting and discussing with its citizens. In 1709, when Richard Steele founded *The Tatler*, he chose Isaac Bickerstaff, a fictional astrologer created by Jonathan Swift, as the fictional editor and main author of his periodical. All his contributors used the same persona; Bickerstaff, however, was given not only a name and a style, but also a family and a set of friends, several of whom not only appeared as characters in rambles and conversations, but also contributed their own letters and essays (and these new personas were used both by Steele and his contributors). In Steele and Addison's later periodicals, the fictional editor gave his name to the publication (a persona called "the Spectator" was in charge of *The Spectator*, "the Guardian" edited *The Guardian*, etc.), but his family and friends (used by a large number of contributors), for instance the famous Sir Roger de Coverley, were just as popular among contemporary readership.

This model was followed throughout the 18th century, with periodicals produced by fictional editors like "Caleb d'Anvers" (*The Craftsman*), "Mrs Crackenthorpe" (*The Female Tatler*), or "Adam Fitz-Adam" (*The World*) or by eponymous personas, such as "The Idler" or "The Rambler." When these magazines appeared in volume format, an index of titles often (not always) identified the real authors of the pieces included. The persona adopted by the author(s), together with their friends and the numerous letter-writers (i.e.,

---

[1] As one biographer puts it, Defoe "almost never wrote anything without interspersing entertaining, illustrative stories" (Backsheider 17).

fictional readers) brought unity to the succession of fictional and nonfictional pieces. Robert D. Mayo has suggested for such a unitary cycle the terms "essay serial" (when the periodical consisted entirely of these pieces) and "essay-series" (when the cycle was identified via the fictional editor, but appeared, regularly or sporadically, in a different publication, usually a newspaper). For example, Samuel Johnson's *The Rambler* (1750-1752) was an independent bi-weekly (it appeared on Tuesdays and Saturdays), whereas his "The Idler" (1758-1760) appeared in the columns of *The Universal Chronicle*. The terms are justified by the fact that most of the pieces contributed by editors and contributors were, in fact, essays. Richard Cumberland's volume *The Observer* (1785), organised as an essay serial though never published periodically, never really leaps into the realm of fiction. Hugh Kelly's "The Babler" (1763-1766) is a good example of essays tottering on the edge of the short-story genre; but each of his essay-anecdotes is rather an illustrative situation worthy of sermonising. Most essays—and especially the letters from fictional readers—include, however, illustrative stories or anecdotes; others are full-fledged stories, from beginning to end.

The use of illustrative stories in nonfictional works has, of course, a long tradition, in English and any other language. Johnson had discovered, for example, in *Serious Call to a Devout and Holy Life* (1728), the sermons of William Law, a theologian he appreciated, many such stories (see, for instance, "Flavia and Miranda"). Characters in these stories are, however, mere prototypes of particular virtues, sins, worldviews, and so on—and this is also the case in most "oriental tales," self-styled "moral tales," or allegorical "visions" of the 18th century. The "real" short stories produced in the 1700s, on the other hand, are characterised by a particular kind of realism, stemming from their focus on everyday manners and on their preference for easily identifiable characters (sometimes in the *à clef* mode).[1] Even when they have been written as part of an essay, 18th-century fictions are true to their mission of enlightening a society that can see itself in them; and to the narrative device of the "ramble," which allows them to "discover" realistic characters. In 1750, in the fourth essay of his essay serial *The Rambler*, Johnson set out to explain "the task" of contemporary writers:

> it requires, together with that learning which is to be gained from books, that experience which can never be attained by solitary diligence, but must arise from general converse, and accurate observation of the living world. . . . [Writers] are engaged in portraits of which every one knows the original, and can detect any deviation from exactness of resemblance. Other writings are safe, except from the malice of learning, but these are in danger from every common reader. (I, 18)

When their characters and the events they narrate are based on the exploits of real people (whether their names are revealed or encoded), these short stories belong to the category of "factual fictions," usually more given

---

[1] A similar argument can be made about satirical pieces and parodies: as long as they aim at a general critique of the mores, they can be safely accepted as short stories (see Swift's and Smart's pieces in this anthology).

to unfettered imagination than the oxymoronic term[1] might seem to imply. Daniel Defoe's "The Apparition of Mrs Veal" (1706), the anonymous "A Letter from Mrs Jones" (1737), and Henry Fielding's "The Female Husband" (1746) narrate real occurrences and portray real people (with their real names), known to the reading public from other sources. Both Fielding and the anonymous "C. E." take liberties with the events and they invent secondary characters. But they both use the same device as Defoe, that of pretending they have obtained the story from their protagonists themselves (either through a letter or an interview). In Defoe's account, it is his artifice of creating a fictional version of himself as a reporter who calls on Mrs Veal to ask for her version of the story that, paradoxically, increases the degree of fictionality (albeit in hindsight, as this technique of the "real" document has become a staple of gothic fiction). This intense preoccupation with "facts" also means that, unlike 19th- and 20th-century fictions, 18th-century short stories are almost entirely unconcerned with descriptions: "Not until the end of the century did writers of fiction begin to learn what enrichment might come from a more imaginative attention to physical background" (Boyce 112). The discovery of the picturesque is, indeed, a late-18th-century phenomenon, as Nathan Drake's early romantic "Agnes Felton" (1790), included here, shows (see also Mary Hays's 1793 "Melville and Serena," in which the husband is displeased with his wife's failure to appreciate the beauties of nature). However, earlier "rambles" already demonstrate an interest in creating "tableaux"—see the counterexample of Oliver Goldsmith's "City Night Piece" from 1759.

Many short stories of the century seem difficult to classify because of a certain association with nonfiction, especially when authors themselves have labelled them "essays." However, one should take into account that the term "short story" was not yet in use. Some authors do use the term "tale," but this remains ambiguous, as it applies sometimes to fabulous accounts[2] and very often to poems. On the other hand, some 18th-century short stories were designated "novels," because there was no clear limit as to the length of such a work of fiction (like the one established in the 20th century by E. M. Forster, according to whom a novel has 40,000 words or more); and because short stories developed from Renaissance models called "novella" in Italian and "nouvelle" in French.[3] In fact, short-story writers often followed the familiar model of longer fictions, by summarising all or most of their protagonists' lives in only a few pages. It would be wrong, however, to think that 18th-century authors were not aware of the differences in length between short stories and novels, even though they may have been confused by the differences between novels and what we would call today novellas. Many of the latter appeared in the 18th century under the *novel* denomination when they were not longer than 40 pages.

---

[1] Lennard J. Davis, who suggested the term in his 1983 study *Factual Fictions: The Origins of the English Novel,* is less concerned with short stories, although several of the novelists he discusses (e.g., Defoe and Fielding) also wrote shorter fictions.

[2] Oriental and fairy tales have been avoided in this selection. The supernatural is, however, present in two more highbrow subgenres: the gothic fragment (John Aikin's "Sir Bertrand") and the Romantic "art tale" (Robert Burns's "Three Witch Stories").

[3] A 1702 edition of Boccaccio's *Decameron* bears the title: "One hundred ingenious novels written by John Boccacio."

Some of this confusion of genres, of fiction and nonfiction, has found its way into the critical assessment of 18th-century British stories. One gets from these studies a very complicated picture of something both minor and chaotic. The main reason for this is, very likely, the representation that we have of the short story as being founded on 19th-century models. Short stories of the 18th century, on the other hand, thrived on chaos and on the freedom to experiment, which should make them more appealing to today's readers. As one commentator has recently argued, "In many ways, our culture of upheaval has more in common with the eighteenth century than the somewhat better-remembered Victorian era" (Powell 2).

Works cited

Backsheider, Paula R. *Daniel Defoe: His Life*. Baltimore: The Johns Hopkins University Press, 1989.

Boswell, James. *The Life of Samuel Johnson*. Ed. Alexander Napier. London: George Bell and Sons, 1884.

Boyce, Benjamin. "English Short Fiction in the Eighteenth Century: A Preliminary View." *Studies in Short Fiction* 5.2 (Winter 1968): 95-112.

Claydon, Tony. "When Did the 'Long Eighteenth Century' Begin?" *Les âges de Britannia. Repenser l'histoire des mondes britanniques*. Rennes: Presses Universitaires de Rennes, 2015. 99-106.

Cruickshank, Dan. *London's Sinful Secret: The Bawdy History and Very Public Passions of London's Georgian Age*. New York: St Martin's Press, 2009.

Davis, Lennard J. *Factual Fictions: The Origins of the English Novel*. New York: University of Pennsylvania Press, 1983.

Farquhar, George. *Works*. In Two Volumes. Ninth Edition. London: J. Clarke, John Rivington, James Rivington and James Fletcher, S. Crowder and Co., T. Caslon, T. Lownds, H. Woodgate and S. Brookes, 1760.

Foucault, Michel. "What Is Enlightenment?" *The Foucault Reader*. Ed. Paul Rabinow. New York: Pantheon, 1984. 32-50.

Goldsmith, Oliver. *The Citizen of the World; or Letters from a Chinese Philosopher, Residing in London, to His Friends in the East*. Volume the Second. London: Printed for the Author, 1762.

Goldsmith, Oliver. *Works*. In Four Volumes. Ed. Peter Cunningham. London: John Murray, 1854.

Johnson, Samuel. *The Rambler. In Four Volumes*. London: A. Millar, J. Hodges, J. and J. Rivington, R. Baldwin, and B. Collins, 1756.

Mayo, Robert D. *The English Novel in the Magazines, 1740-1815*. Evanston: Northwestern University Press, 1962.

O'Brien, John. *Literature Incorporated. The Cultural Unconscious of the Business Corporation, 1650-1850*. Chicago: The University of Chicago Press, 2016.

Pitcher, Edward W. *Discoveries in Periodicals, 1720-1820: Facts and Fictions*. Lewiston, NY: Edwin Mellen Press, 2000.

Powell, Manushag N. *Performing Authorship in Eighteenth-Century English Periodicals*. Lewisburg: Bucknell University Press, 2012.

Rothblatt, Sheldon. *Tradition and Change in English Liberal Education*. London: Faber, 1976.

NOTE ON THE TEXTS

The following stories have been selected, inasmuch as it has been possible, from textual versions corrected by the authors themselves. When their access to later versions of the texts could not be established, the earliest versions have been preferred. Fortunately, many of the authors in this anthology were also editors of the periodicals in which their stories were published; and some, though not all, also saw to the publication of the volume format of their periodicals. In many other cases, however, it was printers who exerted complete control over the artistic product, because they were legally liable for the content.

Due to the chronological order of the texts, one can follow the evolution of the language, including peculiarities of grammar, quaint vocabulary, and the volatility of spelling preferences. In an essay published on 28 November 1754 in the 100th issue of *The World*, Lord Chesterfield noted that "It must be owned that our language is at present in a state of anarchy." This anarchy has been preserved in the following texts, even in cases when the same author oscillates between one form and another. With the exception of the spelling "goal" for "gaol" (which could have seemed too ambiguous), all alternative forms have been preserved and are explained in footnotes. Everything else of interest concerning the texts and the language is included in the introductory notes to each story.

NED WARD

The Rise and Fall of Madam *Coming-Sir* (1703)

The author: Edward (Ned) Ward (1667-1731) was one of the most prolific English writers at the turn of the 18th century. He probably did a series of hack jobs for various London printers after 1691, when he published his first poem. He lived in poverty, decided to emigrate, and left England for the West Indies. He soon returned disappointed and, in 1698, he recorded his first success with *A Trip to Jamaica*, very critical of the agents who were persuading Englishmen to settle in the New World. Towards the end of the same year, he began publishing the work for which he is best known, *The London Spy* (1698-1699), a serialised account of the colourful life of the English capital. He continued publishing prose fictions, poems, and essays, mostly in a satirical vein, but in 1712 he opened a tavern and wrote much less. He came out of semi-retirement in the late 1720s and wrote two pamphlets in answer to Alexander Pope's misrepresentation of him in *The Dunciad*.

The text: The story appeared under the full title of *The Rise and Fall of Madam* Coming-Sir*: or, An Unfortunate Slip from the* Tavern-Bar *into the* Surgeons Powdering-Tub (London: J. How, 1703). Ward then published his collected works in two volumes in 1703, with a second edition coming out the following year (still with his friend John How, a printer turned publisher). The third edition of 1706 included a third volume. The following text is from *The Second Volume of the Writings of the Author of the* London-Spy. The Third Edition (London: Printed and Sold by *J. How*, at the *Seven-Stars*, in *Talbot-Court*, in *Grace-Church-Street*, 1706), 364-401.

Further reading: Fritz-Wilhelm Neumann. "Ned Ward's 'The Rise and Fall of Madam Coming-Sir': the Evolution of Character Writing." *RANAM* 26 (1993): 51-61.

Howard William Troyer. *Ned Ward of Grub Street. A Study of Sub-Literary London in the Eighteenth Century*. Cambridge, MA: Harvard University Press, 1946.

I Shall not use the Accustomary Policy of my own Sex, and endeavour to strengthen the Readers Appetite, to a short Entertainment (which as yet lies behind the Curtain) by keeping him in suspence with a tedious Preamble; but like a true good Humour'd *Prostitute*, who, at the Expence of a Bottle Resigns her Ultimate, I will open the Secret, and give you leave to enter the Premises without any further Hesitation or Delay: So I shall look back into my first *State of Innocence*, and present the Gentleman

Reader with a Virgin about Fourteen Years of Age, and Question not but the pretty Damsel will be thought worth Embracing.

My Father was a *Kentish Farmer*, my Elder Brother a *Vintner* in *London*, and my self, poor Girl, Educated in the Country, to the Innocent stroaking of a Cows Teat, and, with a Bountiful Hand, to replenish the Hog-Trough with such a Compound of Filthiness, as Providence had ordain'd for the Succour of those Swine that had their Dependance on our Family. But my Brother in *London*, being a Jolly Young Fellow, had got the length of his Mistresses Foot,[1] who was a Brisk Widow, that had sent her Husband to poke his way into another World with his Horns, and being left without Issue, like a Provident Relict, she had entirely secur'd his Effects to herself, by perswading the *Dying Cuckold*, to appoint her in his Will his Sole *Executrix*, that she might Reward her *Living Gallant* with the Industrious Gleanings of her Dead Husband, which I have observ'd of late is become such an accustomary piece of Gratitude in our Sex, that when ever the *Cuckold-Maker* survives the *Cuckold*, the Generous Widow commonly gives the former the spending of what the latter got.

Under this very Circumstance had my Brother put himself, and became at once, by the Assistance of a *Priest*, his Mistresses Master, and his Masters Successor both in Trade and Riches; and having call'd into his Remembrance the many little Presents he had receiv'd from the Fair Hand of his *Co-Partner*, before she was his *Bride*, which he had just Reason to suspect were *Clandestinely* intercepted in their passage to the Money-Box, and converted to that use which was not consistent to his Masters Interest as it ought to be; but was given for the Reward of such *Secret Services*, as the Injur'd *Pricket*[2] had but little Reason to Recompence, which occasion'd my Brother to have a Jealous Eye towards the *Bar*, and to be very Circumspect in his Business, lest the same Trick should be put upon himself, which had pass'd Current for several Years upon his Predecessor—therefore, as soon as he had enter'd into this Conjugal Obligation, to prevent the Evil which he suspected might happen, he Writes a Perswasive Letter to my Father, to send me to Town with all Expedition, that I might become his *Bar-Keeper*.

Thus of a sudden was I taken up from serving of Hogs, leasing of Corn, and howing of Turnips,[3] and being Dizen'd up in my best *Paragon* Gown and Red Petticoat,[4] which had stood the Attack of many a *Turky-Cock*, I was appointed *Super-Cargo* over a Basket of *Kentish Pippins*,[5] which were sent as a Present to my unknown Sister-in-Law, that her new Relation might have the kinder Reception.

[1] To find or know (etc.) the length of someone's foot means to get to know a person very well or to identify someone's weakness, especially in order to influence them.
[2] A two-year-old male deer; but here: a young man, a boy.
[3] To "lease" meant to pick, gather, collect; "how" or "howe" is one of the many alternative spellings of "hoe," which became common in the mid-18th century.
[4] To dizen meant to dress, but it was already archaic and used mostly humorously; paragon was a thick fabric usually made of wool, used both for clothing and upholstery; women either wore outer skirts and underskirts (petticoats) one on top of each other, or, if they wore a dress (gown), had a petticoat (a decorative underskirt) showing underneath the dress.
[5] Supercargo (used here in jest) is an officer in charge of the cargo on a merchant ship; Kentish pippin is an old variety of apple, very appreciated at the time.

When all things were in a Readiness for me to begin my Journey, by the help of a *Buffet-Stool*,[1] I was mounted into a *Butter-Cart*, where I sat wedg'd in between *Hand-Baskets* and *Hampers*, Litter'd up to the Shoulders with clean Straw, and cover'd with a *Sack-Cloth Canopy*, to defend my Prettiness from the Sun, and my best Cloaths from wet Weather. In this Travelling Condition, Chearful as a Smitten Maid to meet her Lover, but Innocent as *Eve* before Corruption, I jog'd on towards the great *Sodom* of the Kingdom, whilst my Rural Charioteer Entertain'd my Ears with the Melancholly Whistle of a Psalm Tune, and at once Encourag'd his Teem,[2] and Seranaded his Passenger; and that which added something to the Harmony, was the Incessant Melody of the Horses Bells, which kept such a confused Tinkling in my poor Persecuted Ears, that I had much ado to forbear thinking I was drawn along by a Set of *Morice Dancers*.

By that time I had Nibbled up about half a six Pounder of *Plumb-Cake*,[3] with an answerable Quantity of *Cheese*, and empty'd a large Leathern Bottle of my Fathers *March-Beer*, Brew'd to Fuddle the *Reapers* at the Feast of *Harvest Home*,[4] we were got upon *Southwark* Stones, which jumbled me about after so terrible a manner, that I was afraid every Joint of my Body would have been Dislocated before I could get to the Inn, where my Brother was to meet me.[5]

This severe Pennance I under-went for about a quarter of an Hour, dreading every Kennel[6] as much as a *Vagabond* does a *Whipping-Post*[7]; being Jolted about from Side to Side, like a *Horse-Bean* in a *Childs-Rattle*, till my Flesh was all over as Tender, as if I had been Persecuted a Week together by a whole Family of *Fairies*, for some unusual piece of *Sluttishness*,[8] and had also such a Noise in my Head, from the Rumbling

1703

---

[1] A buffet-stool, or simply a buffet, was a low stool (originally three-legged), like in the nursery rhyme: "Little Miss Muffet/ Sat on a buffet" (where it also appears as "tuffet").
[2] This alternative spelling of "team" survived until the mid-18th century.
[3] Then (and now), a plum cake did not have plums in it, but rather raisins and currants.
[4] Strong beer, brewed in spring. Harvest-home is a festival of the end of the harvesting; today it is celebrated towards the end of September, but at the turn of the 18th century it was rather at the beginning of the month.
[5] The Southwark road was the road to Kent. Today, Southwark is in Central London, but at the time it was a suburb in Surrey, albeit a very culturally active one. She is describing entering the paved area. To this day, there is a Stones End Street in Southwark, named after the outskirts, the "stones' end."
[6] Old term for a type of gutter that carried the water on both sides of the street, but without draining it underground.
[7] Vagrancy (of which were accused the homeless and/or the unemployed) was illegal in England. Around 1700, the first offense was punishable by being stripped down to the waist and flogged at a public "whipping post." At the beginning of the century, vagrants were often flogged and immediately imprisoned, but soon each county began to employ the services of a private "vagrant contractor," who was supposed to gather all "vagabonds" and send them to America as indentured servants.
[8] Fairies, who were traditionally seen as unpredictable and vengeful, were especially supposed to punish the lack of neatness. "Slut" meant a slovenly, untidy, girl or woman (it also meant bold, impudent girl; and it was also used as a term of endearment).

of *Carts*, and Rattling of *Coaches*, that had every Shop-keepers Wife been a *Drum*, and her Husband Beating her, the frightful Sound could not have been more Ingrateful to the Ears of a Stranger, than the hideous Noise I at first met with. At last, Heavens be praised, I got pretty safe, without Dis-joynting a Member, to my Journeys End, where my Brother sat waiting in the *Top-House*, to receive his New *Rural* and *Unpolish'd Bar-Keeper*. When a *Filial Joy* was Reciprocally exprest on both sides, he order'd a *Coach* to be call'd, and away he hurry'd me to a Private Lodging, where he kept me for a Week, till he had strip'd my *Innocence* of its *Rustick Ornaments*, in which *Unstudy'd Decencies*, *Vertue* keeps it *Natural Air*, and *Youth* and *Beauty* look the most *Inviting*.

The *Silk-worm* now supply'd the *Sheeps Product*, and my Gown of *Stubborn Stuff*, was turn'd into a *Soft* and *Pliable Silk* one; my *Flaxen Shifts* were chang'd into *Holland-Smocks*, and my *Country Coifs*, into a *Lofty Head-Dress*.[1] When I was thus Metamorphiz'd for the Honour of our Family, had shifted off all the Signs of *Country Drudgery*, and had effectually Transform'd Poor *Country Jugg* to *Madam*, or at least Mistress *Johanna*[2]; and after I had received Nice Instructions how to behave my self, I was Conducted by my Brother Home to his House, in all my *Gaity*,[3] as if I was just come to Town; and made such a Topping Figure, that whoever beheld me, could conceive me to be any thing less than a *Country Justices* Daughter. Thus, in a Weeks time, by the help of a new Fashionable Apparel, was I chang'd from a *Home-bred Country Housewife*, to the near Resemblance of a *Lazy Gentlewoman*, exactly qualified for the New *Occupation* I was now design'd for.

From the first time that I shifted off my *Country Habiliments*, the good Effects of my own *Industry*, I found all those *Housewifely Inclinations*, which carry'd me, with *Pleasure*, thro' my *Rural Labour*, were quite vanish'd, and had no sooner Deck'd up my Person with these *Splendid Ornaments*, which I had no share in the Earning of; but the Spirit of *Prodigality*, which, till now, had lain *Dormant* in my *Youthful Breast*, awaken'd from its long Sleep, and grew so Powerful in me of a sudden, that methoughts I was willing to forget I had ever Sweated at a *Chirm*, or Broil'd in a *Hay-Harvest*, at the spreading of a *Cock*:[4] And began (instead of *Bread* and *Cheese*, and the *Leathern-Bottle*) to Dream of nothing but *Lac'd Shoes*, *Furbelo'd Scarfs*, and fine *Top Knots*.[5]

---

[1] "Supply," here, means replace, substitute; "stuff" could be any kind of woven fabric, but the term was used especially for one made of worsted wool; "shift(s)" and "smock(s)" were synonyms, both referring to a woman's undergarments; "Holland" cloth is linen and, as such, made of flax, but we are to understand that it was better quality than her former "flaxen" shifts; the coif was a close-fitting cap, usually tied under the chin.

[2] "Jug" was a pet name for Joan or Joanna, often used disparagingly to refer to a maidservant or a homely girl; "mistress" was used for a woman who had authority over others, but also as a form of address preceding the name of an unmarried woman or girl, especially when her mother had died.

[3] "Gaiety," here, means "showy clothes."

[4] "Chirm" means sing (like a bird); a "cock" is a conical heap of hay.

[5] A furbelow (alteration of French and Italian "falbala") is a piece of fabric pleated onto clothes, a ruffle or frill; a "topknot" was a bow or knot of ribbon worn on top of the hat.

When Pretty Miss was thus Gloriously Equip'd, that I might be no Disgrace to my New Married Brother, I was presented with abundance of *Formality* to my Fine Sister-in-Law, who kindly receiv'd me according to the Rules of *Court-Breeding*, and Usher'd me in behind the Bar, with all seeming *Alacrity*.

The *Pippins* were handed out of the *Coach*, which I presented to my Sister, as a Token of my Father's *Affection*, which she received with an Humble Acknowledgement of her Duty to her unknown Parents; and express'd, in a great deal of *Florid Tittle-Tattle*, all the *Thankful Submission*, becoming of a Daughter in Law. A Fat Fowl of the first Quality, was now laid down for Supper, and a Glass of *Primitive Canary*, that never had committed Adultery with Lean *White-Wine*, or the Whites of *Eggs*,[1] was brought me by the Hand of the Eldest *Drawer*,[2] to refresh me after my Journey; for my Sister knew no other but that I had just taken my Leave of the *Rochester* Coach[3]; her Belief of which I was to manage with all Caution, according to my Brothers Instructions. My Sister seem'd wonderfully pleas'd, and my Brother not a little Proud of his New Assistant; and every Favourite Customer had the Honour to be Invited in behind the Bar to take a View and a Salute of my Pretty Ladiship.

Supper was soon ready, and nothing less than *Unsophisticated French*[4] was suffer'd to come near the Table, such as the best Customers never tasted Neat, tho' they doubled the Price to gratifie their Pallats. I could not forbear Blessing Providence at this happy Alteration, especially when I consider'd the vast difference I found betwixt such a Heavenly Banquet as was now before me, and a Mess of *Skim'd-Milk*, stuff'd with *Brown-Crust* that had been Cupboarded a Fortnight. When I cast an Eye upon my new Finery, and saw my self thus seated in the midst of Plenty, I had much Difficulty to perswade my self I was the same *Individual Creature*, that us'd to run a Mile thro' the Dirt to fetch up the *Cows*, ride five Miles to Market to Sell a Fat *Pig*, or half a Dozen Pound of *Butter*, Sweat two Hours together with hunting *Hogs* out of the *Corn*, then return Home and Scrape *Trenchers*[5] for the *Ploughmen*; but rather fancy'd I had been all my Life time in a Dream, and that I never till now had been thoroughly awaken'd.

When Supper was over, my Sister, to show her *Filial Care* and *Affection*, began to send me a little of her good Advice, and Caution'd me against being too Familiar with the Lazy Baggages,[6] her *Maids*; also that

---

[1] Canary wine is a sweet fortified wine from the Canary Islands; the adjective "primitive" indicates that it was unfermented; this wine was often used at the time in combination with other drinks (including milk) and egg whites to produce "possets" and other beverages, consumed either cold or hot, mostly for medicinal purposes.
[2] The drawer was the one who "drew" beer from a cask for the consumption of customers. By extension, any waiter could be called a drawer.
[3] Rochester, Kent, is 30 miles southeast of London.
[4] "Unsophisticated," here, means genuine, unadulterated
[5] A trencher is a flat piece of wood, often circular, sometimes in the form of a flat plate with wide edges, on which food was served, cut up, and eaten.
[6] An either playful (similar to "wench" or "minx") or derogatory (like "strumpet," "harlot") term for a young girl or a woman.

I should be Careful how I look'd with too Favourable an Eye upon any of the *Drawers*, but to keep them at such a distance, that might make them both Respectful to my Person, and Obedient to my Commands; for that it became a *Bar-Keeper* to have an Ascendency over all the Servants.

This kind Advice was not at all Disagreeable with that Proud Spirit which my fine Apparel had now possess'd me with; for I confess I was so Exalted in my own Thoughts, upon this sudden Revolution of my Circumstances, that tho' I was assur'd of the contrary, yet I had much struggling with my self, sometimes, to forbear thinking I had Ten Thousand Pounds to my Portion, and that I was at least Daughter to some Topping Quality.[1]

When I was thus enter'd into my Brother's *Tipling Habitation*,[2] where *Sobriety* and *Good Husbandry* were as much out of Fashion, as *Honesty* amongst *Lawyers*, or *Charity* amongst *Clergymen*, and all the Examples of *Extravagancy* imaginable were daily put in practice, to encourage those who were Customers, in their *Luxury* and *Profuseness*: My Station was appointed in the Bar, where I was first to sit and learn of my Sister-in-Law how to Magnifie a Reckoning,[3] and Score double to a Drunken Company; how to Ogle a *Beau* into a Spirit of *Generosity*, and keep in hopes of what he was never likely to obtain; that when I had made my self an Absolute Mistress of these Necessary Acquirements, I might take the whole Trust of the Bar upon my self, under pretence of easing my Sister, tho' the main Design was to secure my Brother from those little Female Encroachments which he knew his Wife had formerly been liable to; so that he had some Reason to fear she might fall into a Relapse of the same Distemper, which highly became his Prudence to prevent. Being a Pert Young Baggage, I had soon qualified my self for my Post, and was accordingly admitted Sole Auditor of the Bar-Accounts, by that time I had spent a full Month as a Deputy.

Besides the keeping of the Bar, I had now Learn'd the Modish way of *Dressing*, and had made my self an Absolute Mistress of all the little Chamber Practices that heighten *Female Charms*, and set off *Beauty* to the best Advantage; insomuch that all the *Young Students* of the *Law*, and *Shop-keeping Batchelors* that us'd our House, admir'd my Prettiness, and thought me a Delicious Creature, none of them could pass the Bar, but, to be sure, a kind *Word* or *Complement* was the least Favour that was bestow'd upon me; and if Opportunity presented fair, a *Loving Kiss* and an *Amorous Hug*, were given me as Convincing Testimonies of their loose *Affections*; for every Body talk'd to me of *Love*, but no Body of *Matrimony*; so that I found they all wanted me for a *Mistress*, but none of them cared to take me for a *Wife*: Yet all the *Amorettoes* in the Neighbourhood express'd such Violent Passions for me, that their Words were enough to have perswaded such a Poor Innocent Creature as I to have believ'd not a Man of them, in a Weeks time, would have escap'd Hanging

---

[1] A person of high rank was a person "of quality;" but "quality" could also be used in a concrete sense to refer to the actual person or to high society in general ("the quality").

[2] An ale-house, a tavern; "to tipple" meant either sell or drink liquor.

[3] The "reckoning" was the bill.

or Drowning, if I had not Mercifully bestow'd my Realing Favours upon them; which I had Wit enough to know was both my Interest and Security to keep from them.

Not a *Pheasant* or a *Partridge* could be Cook'd for a Beaus Supper, but I was as sure of a Leg and a Wing, as a Parson is of his Tythes; and as certain as he pass'd the Bar, I was Honour'd with a Bow and a Languishing Look, as if he was just Dying for me: If he Kiss'd but my Hand, 'twas like a Cordial to a Sick Man,[1] he would appear so suddenly reviv'd upon it, that I could not but fancy he took the Favour as a present Earnest of his future Happiness, which he would tell me depended upon my Kindness. Old *Leachers* us'd to come and whet their *Colts-Teeth*[2] by looking at me, and stand Quarrelling half an Hour at the Bar about their Reckoning, on purpose to gratifie their Itch in Ogling of me: Admirers of all Ages us'd to swarm about me, and please themselves under the Influence of my *Youth* and *Beauty*, as *Flies* does in the *Sun-shine*. And because some of the Amorous Number were as singular in their Persons, as they were in their Courtship, I shall Concisely entertain the Reader first with some of their Characters, and next with a few of their Letters, which I hope will prove as Pleasant as Remarkable.

The first Spark that laid close Siege to *Loves* little Fortress, and shot whole Volleys of *Affection* at me, every time he saw me, was a Young Student of the *Temple*, whose Nimble Tongue, like an *Aspen Leaf*, was always wagging, but to no purpose. The *Law* was his Profession, but *Poetry* his Study, *Love* was the Sphere he mov'd in, and *Fornication* the Center of all his Happiness. His Books were of no other use but to Adorn his Study; and he never thought of Pleading at any other Bar but a *Vintner*'s: The Morning he spent in *Dressing*, the Afternoon in *Courtship*, and the most part of the Night in *Debauchery*: The greatest of his Knowledge consisted in a New Fashion, of which he was an Absolute Judge; and the most diligent of his Enquiries, were after the best *Taylor*, and a new Face: He admir'd every Woman he saw, but had a better Opinion of himself than he had of any of them. He talk'd mightily of Great Lords and Ladies; but never had the Honour to be nearer them, than as they pass'd by him in their Coaches. He had the *Wits* in the Town by their Nick-Names; but never was admitted into any of their Companies, except it was to Treat 'em. He was Proud of a few *French* Phrases he had got by Heart, which he Repeated as a *Magpye* does *What's a Clock*, upon all occasions. He was a great Visiter of a *Fencing-School*, and talk'd mightily among Cowards of *Tiers, Cart,* and *Secoon*[3]; but would sooner draw a Dozen of his Teeth, than a Sword, tho' in Defence of his Mistress. He set himself up for a Man of Honour, and was very cautious how he Affronted a Gentleman; but would suffer himself to be call'd Twenty *Block-Heads*, rather than his Skin should once run the hazard of an Ilet-hole:[4] His Amours were

[1] Cordials were medicinal beverages, the recipes of which usually included alcohol, spices, and sweetening ingredients, used especially as restoratives.
[2] Youthful and/or sensual desires (also: "colt's tooth").
[3] Actually, "quarte," "tierce," "seconde," three of the basic positions in fencing.
[4] Usually spelled "eyelet," i.e., a small round hole; a "blockhead," i.e., a foolish person, was originally a wooden head used for holding wigs.

more fulsome than a *Poets* Dedication; and every Attack was but the dull Repetition of his former Addresses. His Person was a moving Machine of *Prodigality*, his Dress the Extravagant purchase of *Fools Pence*,[1] his Face a Register of *Folly*, and his Ridiculous Deportment a meer Antidote against *Love*; his way of Courtship was to write Letters, and bring them himself, under a pretence of wanting an Opportunity to Express his Mind otherwise, or else that he could write better than he could speak. And that the Reader may Judge of his *Penman-ship*, I have here presented him with a true Copy of one of his Amorous Epistles, which I hope will prove Diverting.

Most Seraphick Angel,

The Power of your Beauty, and the Pregnancy of your Wit, like a huge pair of Bellows, with two Nossels,[2] *have puff'd up a Flame in the Breast of your Humble Servant, more Fierce than Ætna; which, except suddenly Corrected, or Extinguish'd by the Cooling Engine of your Compassion, will positively Consume, in a little time, my whole Fabrick of Mortality. O that there was an* Insurance-Office *against the Fire of Love; but, who Alas! Upon Earth, is able to Repair that Noble Structure, if once Defac'd, which was Built alone by the inimitable Artifice of Heaven. Could any Humane Society indemnifie a Lover from the sad Effects of this dangerous* Ignis Fatuus,[3] *for certain every Man, like an Insur'd House, would wear a* Phoenix *or a* Salamander, *as a Token of his Security; but since it is not to be done, Madam, I must only depend upon your Favours, as my safest Refuge in this time of Extremity; and therefore Humbly Beg you to cast an Eye of Pity on the most Combustible of your*

Humble Servants,

I. M.

This Allegorical piece of Singularity was thrust into my Hand, as I was stepping into the Bar, which I was under an Obligation of receiving, lest I should otherwise do my Brother an Injury by hazarding the loss of a good Customer. I never in my Life was much Merrier at *Questions* and *Commands*, or *Cross-Purposes*, than I was over my Sparks[4] *Love-Letter*, and kept it by me, on purpose to now and then stir up my Blood by an Extravagant Fit of Laughter. I had an Itching Mind to Answer it, only to carry on the Jest; but upon due Deliberation thought it would be Construed an Encouragement not Consistent with a Maids Modesty, and be apt to Flush him with new Hopes of Effecting his Ends, which I had

---

[1] "Fools' pence," "fool's penny," etc. was used mostly in reference to the money spent on alcohol; by extension, any money badly spent.
[2] Variant of "nozzle," a spout or pipe through which gas or liquid is discharged.
[3] Latin phrase (literally, "foolish fire") for will-o'-the-wisp.
[4] Although sometimes used in a deprecating manner, the term "spark" usually described a young man, especially a beau, a suitor.

sufficient Reasons to mistrust were not at all Honourable; so Prudently forbore to gratifie my Whim, lest my Hand, (as is every *Fops* Custom) should be shown to all his Brother *Block-heads* in prejudice of my Reputation.[1]

Another Spark I had, who was always Hovering about the Bar, like a Cricket about a Bakers Oven, and fancy'd he receiv'd as much Benefit from my Smiles, as the other does from the comfortable Blaze of a Brushwood Faggot. This most Humble and Obliging Servant, was a Young *Physician*, just come from the *University*, who had as much Conjuration in his Head, as ever had Fryar *Bacon*, and was so deeply Learn'd in Natural Magick, that he could do any thing in the World, by the help of Sir *Kellum Digby*,[2] but make me Love him: If a Slovenly Drunkard had Manur'd the Door, my Lover, by the help of a Red-Hot poker applied to the Unsavory Drippings of his unmannerly Bumfiddle, could make the Offender Roar, tho' at Twenty Miles distance, worse than a Groaning-Board.[3]

Besides the wonderful Knowledge he had in *Physick*,[4] he was an Excellent *Sympathetick Surgeon*; and if he had but the Cudgel a Mans Head was Broke with, by Dressing the Plant that had done the Mischief, he would make the Patients Noddle as sound as if he had been a Month for his Cure in St. *Bartholomews-Hospital*.[5] He had always abundance of Projects in his Head to get Money, yet he commonly wanted it; and had a Universal *Nostrum* that would Cure all Distempers but *Poverty*.

He had Invented a Subterranean Conveyance for *Hampstead* Air to be brought into *London*, for the better Preservation of the Health of the Inhabitants, that every House-Keeper should have had it laid into his Cellar, at as small an Expence, as they have the *New-River* Water:[6] And that every *Smith* and *Founder* should be supply'd with a pair of Mathematical Bellows, that should Work without any Hands, and continue Blowing Everlastingly.

[1] A "fop" was a dandy, a man whose vain pursuit of fancy dress and manners was often satirised in the literature of the time.
[2] Roger Bacon (c.1220-c.1292), today recognised as a major medieval philosopher, was still known at the time mostly for building a "magical" automaton, a "talking brazen head," which figures prominently in Robert Greene's Elizabethan comedy *Friar Bacon and Friar Bungay*; Sir Kenelm Digby (1603-1665) was an alchemist and adventurer, founding member of the Royal Society, also famous for his experiments in "sympathetic magic," whereby a remedy applied to the weapon which had caused a wound was supposed to heal the wound itself; his name was sometimes misspelled as "Kellum" even during his lifetime.
[3] "Bumfiddle" was a euphemism for a person's bum; the "groaning board" was a famous plank of elm wood, presented to the king in 1682: when touched with a hot iron, it produced a deep sound (this was repeatedly done by many others over the following decades, with mixed results and, despite scientific explanations provided at the time, the boards were thought by some to be possessed and the sounds to be premonitory); the "groaning board" was talked about all through the 18th century.
[4] This was either the medical profession (like here) or medicines in general.
[5] See two notes above about Digby's "sympathetic magic"; a "noddle" was originally the back of the head, before designating the entire head; St Bartholomew's Hospital, founded in 1123, is in Smithfield, City of London.
[6] The New River was a man-made channel conveying fresh water to London from nearby springs between 1613 and 1990.

9

Many Advertisements were put into the News-Papers, to amuse the Publick, insomuch that some *Fools* were afraid to walk in the Fields, for fear of an Eruption. He was mighted Proud of this Windy Projection,[1] and was highly pleas'd that, at his own Expence, he could make other People like him. He was always as Pert as if he had the World in a String; and was as Prodigal of his Eloquence as an Ape is of Mimickry. He was as Lavish of his *Latin*, as an *Irishman* is of his *Bulls*; and *Ovid* or *Virgil* must be call'd to the Justification of every Sentence that he spoke. He us'd more hard Words in his common Talk than there are Knots in a *Crab-Tree*; and always made such unintelligible Courtship to me, that it was hard for a Woman to distinguish whether he Talked *English* or *Arabick*.

His Person was of a Diminutive Size, as if Nature had design'd him, by his Dapper Stature, for a *New-Market* Rider[2]; yet he Strutted as he Walked as if he had swell'd himself to a Giant in his own fancy. He commonly wore *Black*, as most agreeable to his Profession; and always look'd as Neat, and as Japan,[3] as a piece of *Polish'd Ebony*. He was mighty Complaisant, especially to the Female Sex; and was so very Officious, Fawning, and Subservient, that he would become a Ladies Chamber much better than a Lap-Dog.

When *Pleasure*, more than *Business*, had drawn him into the Country, his Head being a little Troubled with *Love* Megrims,[4] he Honour'd me with the following Letter, as a Token of his Affections.

Dear Lady,

The Magick Power of your Eyes, tho' at this distance, has put my Hearts Blood into so Violent an Ebullition, that nothing but a Cordial Assurance of your Salutiferous[5] Affections, can Reduce it to its Natural Disposition: Your Killing Beauty has made me your Patient, *and no* Physician *but your self, can Administer a Cure. I Protest, Madam, I Love you much better than I do* Gallen *or* Hippocrates; *and could Heartily forsake my Books to Study Nature in your Admirable Perfections: Your Eyes, to me, are like a couple of Actual Cautries,[6] which, every Look, applies a fresh to my Wounded Breast, to the Terror of my Vitals. Had I Purgatory in my Heart, and Hell in my Conscience, I could not be more Terrified than I am with that Igniferous[7] Passion which your Charms have Kindled: Awake you are the Subject of my Muse; and Asleep the Object of my Dream.*

Besides the Fever in my Breast, I have a Frenzy in my Brains, both owing to the Enchantments of your bewitching Beauty. I am

[1] "Projection" usually meant a plan or scheme, especially an economic or financial one; "windy" meant extravagant, vainglorious, conceited.
[2] A jockey; Newmarket is a town in Suffolk, famous for its horse races.
[3] A black varnish (known also as "japan lacquer" or "japan black").
[4] Headache or migraine (the last syllable remodelled after the adjective "grim").
[5] Conducive to either good health or salvation.
[6] "Actual" cautery (cauterisation), executed with a heated instrument, is different from "potential" cautery, produced by medicine.
[7] Fire-bearing; capable of producing fire.

neither *Easie when I am Up, nor can I Rest when I'm in Bed but Rise at Midnight, in the Moon-Shine, and Dance about the Room, in Search of you. In short, Madam, I am so Disorder'd with the Extravagant Passion I have for your Dear Person, that I do every thing like a Bedlamite, Stare like a Dead Pig, and Run about like a Wild-Cat; and except you restore me to my Senses, by the kind Administration of one Dose of your Favours, when I come next to Town, the Blind Conquerour, Love, will certainly Trip up my Heels, and send me out of the World a Raving Madman; therefore, if you are Qualified with that Pity, which becomes the Tenderness of your Fair Sex, I desire you would make it Manifest to your*

> Languishing Lover
> *and*
> Humble Servant,
> *T.H.*

My Innocency hitherto had not suffer'd me to form any Idea of the Happiness of *Love*, so that none of their Rhetorical Bombast could as yet kindle the least Spark of Affection in me towards my Admirers, so that their Letters and Addresses were as wholly Ineffectual as an Application to a *Courtier*, without *Money*, for a Place: Serving me only now and then to Divert me at a Leisure Minute instead of an Academy of Complements; and to please me with bringing into my remembrance that I had something in my Power worth such abundance of Solicitation.

Another Amourist I had whose Figure and Disposition was quite different from the former. This was a *Swordless* City Beau, and the Eldest Prentice of a *Linnen Draper*, Heir to a good Estate, which he could no ways loose the Certainty of, but by Disobliging his Father. His Amorous Proceedings were very well approved on by my Brother, who would have been glad to have had it a Match, and therefore gave him those Opportunities of Courtship behind the Bar, which his Rivals wanted; but notwithstanding he was a Young *Citizen*,[1] yet he was no such *Chub* to fasten himself upon the *Hook* for all his Nibbling, but only wanted, like the rest of my Suitors, to entertain his *Lust* with that Delicious Curiosity a *Maiden-Head*,[2] that he might have the Satisfaction of Boasting amongst his Brother *Libertines*, that he had the Honour of being the first Man that had brought a Young Creature to Ruin: Many kind Words, Kisses, and close Hugs were dayly bestow'd upon me, in order to warm my Heart, beget *Vitious Inclinations*, and by gentle Degrees to bring me at last to a Compliance. I must confess, I began now upon Kissing and Toying to find an unusual Disorder in me, and should sometimes be Seized with such a Shortness of Breath, and Tremulation in my Limbs, that I was almost ready to Die away without knowing what was the matter with me: A Desire of Male-Conversation I found was now quicken'd in me;

[1] A citizen of London, that is a merchant or his apprentice after 7 years of training. He was thus a freeman of the City, but not yet a liveryman; also, because he was not a gentleman, he did not have the right to carry a sword.
[2] A chub is a river fish from the carp family, but the word was also used at the time with the meaning of "lad," "fellow"; "maidenhead" means virginity.

and methoughts every little Love Dallience, which before I esteem'd but a Trifle, was now become the highest Satisfaction I had ever tasted; not that I alone found this Pleasure in his Company, but I began to behold Man in General with other Eyes, tasted their Kisses with New Lips; and all the little pleasing Familiarities which before seem'd Troublesome and Impertinent, now render'd their Conversation the more Delightful to me. This was the second Revolution my unsettled Disposition had been Subject to, and now I shall proceed to give a Character of the Spark, in whose Company I was first made Sensible of this pleasing Alteration in me.

His Person was very Tolerable, tho' not half so Handsome as he thought himself; he was not Silly enough to be deem'd a Fool, nor had he Sense enough to be though Wise, except in his own Conceit. He was always as Neat about the Feet, as a *Dancing-Master*, using two Black *Spanish* Balls, to one Whit Wash-Ball,[1] and never needed any other Looking-Glass, than his Shining-Shoes, to Wash his Face by; his Buckles were adorn'd with *Bristol*-Stones,[2] to the Terrible Discomfort of all Sore Eyes, that met him in the Sun-shine. He wore his own Hair, under the Management of *Sedgwick*, and every Lock stood as formally in Curl, as a Deal-Shaving, just plain'd from a Plank.[3] His Cloaths were always well made, and his Linnen at all times very Neat; yet any Body would have guess'd him a *Citizen* by his Formality, and a *Linnen-Draper* by the Profuseness of his Neck-Cloth. He was very Facetious in his Carriage,[4] and as Obliging in his Words; but had practic'd so much Lying on the other-side of the Counter, that he knew not how to speak Truth, when he was out of the Shop. He was a very great Country Dancer, and valu'd himself mightily upon the Nimbleness of his Legs, and rather than sit still, would take a Chair for his Partner. If he wanted Company, he was very Liberal of his Money in Treating of those who would be at the Trouble of Humouring him, and was always Fondest of their Company that made him the greatest *Bubble*.[5] He was a mighty Admirer of a New Song, and he thought it requir'd more Wit to make a pretty Ballad, than a good Sermon. He was a great Lover of Riding, and valu'd himself much upon a little Horsemanship; and a Journey out of Town to see some Villain Hang in Chains, was his Holiday Recreation. His Spurs were kept in Cotton to prevent their Rustying; and his Boots, to preserve their Blackness, were kept close in a Case, as Nicely as a *Beau* keeps his best Periwig.[6] He was

1703

---

[1] A black ball was made of a waxy substance and was used to give shoes a shiny black appearance; the young man added a tiny amount ("one whit") of wash ball, i.e., soap.

[2] Bristol-stones (sometimes called "Bristol diamonds") were a popular variety of quartz.

[3] A "deal" is a slice of wood sawn from a plank; the shavings are obtained when the wood is being "planed," i.e., smoothed with a tool called "plane." Sedgwick was a family of London barbers. At the turn of the 18th century, a simple haircut there cost 1 shilling.

[4] "Carriage" meant behaviour, demeanour; at the time, "facetious" meant agreeable or agreeably humorous.

[5] "Bubble" was a slang word for a dupe, a gullible person.

[6] Periwigs were the highly elaborate wigs worn in the 17th and 18th centuries.

very Ambitious of being thought a Gentleman, and would he Curse his Parents for putting him to a Trade, because it hinder'd him from wearing a Sword. He was mighty forward to lay Wagers, and very apt to lose them, and was a very Talkative Companion over a Bottle, from the time of Shutting up of Shop to the Ringing of *Bow* Bell.[1]

In the height of his Amours, his Father heard of his Courtship; upon which he was fore-warn'd my Brothers House, and my Company, upon the Penalty of Dis-Inheritance; so that my Brothers Hopes and my Lovers Intrigue were at once Baffled, and my self Disappointed, and set at Liberty for the next fair Bidder. But, that the Reader may see he took his Leave like a Man of Honour, I have made a Recital of a Farewel Letter, which he sent me after his Father had Enjoyn'd him to a Renunciation of my Company.

Dear Madam,

Of all the Old Rogues in Suffolk, *that ever got an Estate by Fatting Cattle with Turnips, and Cheating* London *with Rotten Sheep, and Ill Fed Oxen, my Father, for certain, is the most Hard Hearted; for, upon some Intelligence he has met with of the Passionate Affection your Charms and Vertue have oblig'd me to bear to your sweet self, he has serv'd me with such an Injunction by the Post, to forbear your Company, that Threatens me with nothing less than a Threadbear-Coat, and Empty Pockets, and as many more Curses as the most Undutiful of Sons can possibly deserve from an Unforgiving, Offended and Implacable Father. He Swears by all the Oxen in his Ground, the Fatted Swine in his Hogsties, and all the rest of Gods Blessings about him, that if I do not desist in my Addresses to you, if a Sheeps-Turd off his Uplands would save me from Hanging, he would not spare me one as big as his Wastcoat Button; and that when he Dies his Estate should sooner go to the Building an Alms-House to maintain Decay'd Sheep-Stealers and House-Breakers, than he would leave me as much Land as I could stand upon on Tip-Toe; and that he will never own me for his Child, but Swear to all the World that I am an Undutiful Bastard. Under these Difficulties how shall I be able to behave my self? I want your Advice, but dare not come to ask it, and if I did, I fear it would Puzzle you to direct me Right; all my Hopes are, if you have any Respect for me, that you will still continue it, tho' I do not see you till the present Scene of Affairs be alter'd, which, by the help of Providence, may happen much sooner than expected; for the Old Gentleman, God be Praised, has been Dropsical this Ten Years, by denying himself Strong-Beer when he Sweats, and Guzzling down such small Rat Gut with his Tobacco, that his Hogs would scarce Thank him for. These are Hopeful Signs, that, in a little time, if I do but Oblige him, Good Luck will befall me; and those Seven Hundred Fat Acres, of which he has Cozen'd the Publick, may descend into his Hands who will do the World Justice with them.*

[1] The bells of St Mary-le-Bow in Cheapside were used to sound the curfew or, at the time, simply the beginning of the night (the Bow Bell was also known as "night-bell").

I assure you, Madam, the Love I have hitherto profess'd to you, shall be always kept Sacred, and all my Promises remain inviolable; and as soon as the Old Grizzle Beard drops into the other World, and the Estate into my Hands, you shall find I will propose such Terms as shall make both you and my self Happy; till which time I must Beg your Pardon that I do not wait upon you: For to run the hazard of losing an Estate for the Pursuit of a Mistress, whose Favours or Affections I am in no measure assur'd of, would render me such a Reprobate to my Father, and such a Block-head to my self, that when you found my Angry Dad had given away the Estate from me, you'd be apt to follow his Example, and Dispose of your Person after the like manner; so that I think it the best way to secure the Estate first, and then there will be no great danger of losing my Mistress, if she be not otherwise Dispos'd on, to the great Dissatisfaction of him, who Remains, between Hawk *and* Buzzard,[1]

Your most Affectionate,

Humble Servant,

G. S.

This Letter I must confess, Nettl'd me a little at first Reading on't, appearing to me by its Stile to be downright Banter, and nothing of Truth in't, but sent purely in Ridicule to Affront me, which, in as little time as Runnet[2] turns Milk into Cheese-Curd had so alter'd the Temper of my Body, and Disposition of my Mind, that the little Respect which once I had for him, was now turn'd into such a Revengeful Agony, that I could think of nothing but his speedy Ruin and Destruction, to compleat which I had soon projected a Method; for Women, the World knows, in such Cases, are always very quick of Invention; but it happen'd in two Days time (before I had put my Design in Execution) to be fully satisfied that what he Writ to me concerning his Fathers severe Edict, was Matter of Fact; and that he would utterly lose the Paternal Affection of his Parents, as well as a good Estate, should he be known to continue his Amour; so that I was a little better satisfied, or else I had fully resolv'd to have convey'd my Lovers Letter to the Hand of his Father, that the Old Gentleman might have seen what a wonderful deal of Reverence and Respect his hopeful Son had for his Grey Hairs, and how heartily he pray'd, the backward way, for his long Life and Happiness; which Dutiful Expressions would, without doubt, have so Oblig'd the Old Man, that if a Hens Egg would have sav'd him from Starving, he would sooner have suffer'd it to have been Suck'd by a Weasle, than a Miserable Death should not have Rewarded his Disobedience: But upon a right Understanding of Matters, I consider'd better, subdued the Tyrant *Revenge*, pacified my restless Bosom, and depended on the Conduct of Providence for the future Issue of our interrupted Love.

[1] A phrase which came to mean "be in a tight place, unable to choose between two equally bad things;" its earlier meaning, however, was "to be between a bad and a good thing, in transition or expectation." A third meaning is "at twilight."
[2] Alternate spelling of "rennet" (substance found in the stomach of calves or lambs and used in curdling and in the separation of milk into cheese and whey).

Gratitude, the Punctual Register of all Kindness, had so deeply Scor'd the Amorous Hugs, Indearing Words, and Pleasant Kisses of my last Lover in my Memory; that before I could rub them out of my Thoughts with the Spunge of Oblivion, (Remember my Station, and forgive me that I speak like a *Bar-Keeper*) I had a fresh Attack made upon me, by a Young Officer who was as Vigorous in his On-set, as if he design'd, when Opportunity stood fair, to attempt Loves Cittadel by Storm. He had a new Air in his Courtship and Deportment, with which before I had ne'er been acquainted, and so very Complaisant, and yet so very Confident, that at once his Carriage was both Surprizing and Obliging; by his forward Application, and familiar way of Exhibiting his Passion, he had gain'd more Ground, and made himself better acquainted with me in two Days time, than his Predecessors had done in two Months: I began to approve mightily of his Martial way of Proceeding, and in a very little time was so hugely Enamour'd with a Red Coat, that tho' I had always hated a *Lobster* as bad as Measly Swines-Flesh, I now began to take a wonderful liking to the Meat purely for the Shells sake; so that I reconciled my self to a thing that I hated, because a Man that I lik'd happened to be of the same Colour. I had not been Besieged above Eight and Forty Hours by my new Knight-Errant, but he had Chas'd all my former Admirers out of my Thoughts, as if I had never known 'em, finding my self as forgetful as the Good Woman, who having been Marry'd a Fortnight to a Second Husband, and being ask'd what the Name of her First Husband was, and truly she had utterly forgot it.

Till now I never had a thorough Sense of Love, and must acknowledge 'twas *Mars*, not *Cupid*, that was the God that Wounded me; all the short Momentory Warmths I had hitherto felt, were no more than the Effects of some Provoking Freedoms that Ruffles Nature for the present, and Ripens our Inclinations to that Lushious Familiarity, to which my self, amongst the rest of the Number of true Maids, was as yet a Stranger, as Kisses, Squeezes, Hugs, and such Dalliance, that raise Wanton Thoughts, beget Loose Desires, warm the Breasts, and a pleasing *Titillation* both to the Veins and Fancies of Young Creatures, tho' never so Innocent and Ignorant; but now, all of a sudden, I found my self in such a Condition, that had he been no more than a *Powder-Monkey*,[1] methoughts I could have Travelled with him round the Universe, and have carry'd a Snap-Sack at his Heels, as a *Tinkers* Dog does his Budget:[2] Nay, as Modest and Undefiled, as Young and Innocent as I was, had I seen Mischief approach him, I could have hid him under my Petticoats to have preserv'd him from Danger: I was never Easie when he was out of the House, and never Contented when he was in't; except he was behind the Bar, where I could now and then have a Kiss from him, or a Peep at him, which to me were Pleasures I had never before Experienc'd. His Visits and Pretensions were as often renew'd as my Brothers Absence would afford him Opportunity; for my Brother, as I suppose, knowing him to be a true Son of *Mars*, that

---

[1] Also a "powder boy"; he carried gunpowder to the guns, especially on a ship.
[2] "Snap-sack" was a preferred version of "knapsack"; a "budget" was a leather bag: itinerant tinkers often had a dog carry it for them.

15

us'd to Attack a Hundred Petticoats to the Storming of one Town, thought it necessary to caution me against him, that I should not be Deluded by that Insinuating Tongue, that had Conquer'd more Women than his Sword had Enemies; but my Brothers Care was all in vain, for like a *Bat* about a *Torch*, there was no beating me off till I had Burn'd my self.

It being Vacation time, and our Trade depending much upon the *Inns-of-Court* and *Chancery*,[1] we had but little to do at this Juncture; so that my Sister-in-Law was sent into the Country, and my Brother was often Abroad, which gave my *Lover* large Opportunities of Tickling my Ears with his *Campaign Eloquence*; and giving me strange Notions at a distance, of those *Love Enjoyments*, which I had never Tasted. These kind of pleasing Hints, and Intimations, still nourish'd my *Affections*, and made him every Day, a further Conqueror of my Heart, than other: Tho' his Designs were Vicious, as the Consequence made Manifest; yet he never all this while offer'd any such Rank *Immodesty*, but what an *Overfond*, tho' *Honourable Lover*, in an *Extasie* might be apt to commit; and a very *Vertuous Maid* be willing enough to Pardon; tho' I have since Reason to suspect the cause of his Civility was owing to the want of Opportunity; for the Room behind the Bar lay so expos'd to the Servants, that nothing could be done there Private enough to escape their Discovery; which Prudent Considerations, I suppose, deter'd him from an Attempt, and kept him to a forbearance, till all things should be convenient for his Enterprize.

Thus he continued his *Amours*, till he had made as compleat a Conquest over me, as ever did Heroe over the Heart of a Fair Lady; and tho' he had not pierc'd me with his Launce, and laid me Sprawling upon my Back, as St. *George* did the *Dragon*, yet I don't know what he might have done, if he had but had a clear Stage; for I believe he would scarce have wanted my Favour to have gain'd an Absolute Mastership; for I fear I should have been too ready to have become his Victim: And to let you know how Handsome a Gentleman, and how Formidable a Champion in *Love* I thought him, (not as after I found him) I shall here Picture him in Black and White, as he appear'd to me thro' *Loves* Dim Eyes, that discovers Objects but Imperfectly.

He had Ten Thousand *Handsome Fieldings* in every Feature,[2] and was always as Brisk as a Young Heir that had just Buried his Father. Many Notable Exploits he had done in *Flanders*;[3] and to hear him talk of his Bravery, was enough to make any Man *Fear* him, and every Woman *Love* him: There had been no Battle since he had been in the Army, but he was always in the midst on't, where Men fell as thick to the

[1] The Inns of Court are the four associations of barristers in England: Lincoln's Inn, the Inner Temple, the Middle Temple, and Gray's Inn. The Court of Chancery was a court of equity, the jurisdiction of which covered much of what had traditionally been known as natural law. It existed concurrently with (and tried to remedy) common law.
[2] Robert Fielding (c.1651-1712), known as Beau Fielding or Handsome Fielding, was a popular courtier of Charles II. In 1706 he was arrested for bigamy.
[3] The English fought in Flanders both in the Nine Years' War (1688-1697) and the War of the Spanish Succession (1701-1714).

Ground, as Ripe Plumbs from a shaken Tree; yet he had always the good Fortune to come off Shot-Free. The General and he us'd often to lay their Heads together; and no considerable Design was ever Form'd, but he had always a Hand in it.

He never talk'd of any Body less than Quality; and the Duke of O—nd and he were as great as two Inkle-makers.[1] The King had such a Kindness for him, that he might have any thing for Asking; but he scorn'd to beg a higher Post, till he had done his King and Country some Signal Service to Deserve it. He was never uncivil to an Enemy, when he had him in his Power, but always dealt by his Prisoner like a Man of Honour. He was Born under the Influence of *Mars*, with a wonderful Inclination to Fighting, insomuch that he would often Swear he had rather be in a Battle against the *French*, than at a good Dinner with a keen Appetite. He had kill'd, perhaps, many a Brave Fellow in his Time; but (God be thank'd) he never did any Man a Mischief in Cold Blood. He was very Affable in his Deportment, and extreamly Complaisant in all Company, and would sooner take an Affront at any time, than to Revenge it with Bloodshed. He was a great Lover of a well Bred Gentleman, but hated a Book Learn'd Blockhead, much worse than a *French* Coward. He was a Mortal Enemy to a *Papist*; and, D—n him, he would stand by the *Protestant* Religion whilst he had a drop of Blood in his Body. He shifted his Wigs as often as a *Barbers* Block, and would not, like an *Owl*, be seen two Hours together in the same *Ivy-Bush*.[2] His Body was like a Wax-Work Figure,[3] and his Cloaths the very Perfection of *Taylorism*: His Tongue was the Oracle of *Love*, and his Dear Self the very Jewel of a *Lover*.

When the Fire of *Love* had almost Consum'd my Senses, and Burn'd my poor Heart to a *Cinder*, my dear Captain was Order'd to change his Town-Quarters, and return into the Country, upon which he sent the following Letter, wherein he made himself a Plain Dealer, and in down right Terms, told me what I had to trust to.

Dear Madam,

Tho' Love *is as* Natural *to a* Soldier *as* Oats *to a* Game-Cock, *or* Raw Flesh *to a* Lion; *yet* Matrimony, *that terrible piece of* Priest Craft, *which every Wise Man dreads, as much as an* Ape *does a* Whip, *or a* Seaman *a* Cat-of-Nine-Tails, *is more disagreeable to a* Martial Constitution, *than*

---

[1] James Butler, 2nd Duke of Ormonde (1665-1745) was an English general in both the Nine Years' War and the War of the Spanish Succession; inkle (a type of linen ribbon) weavers had to work closely together and the phrase above was a proverb; for "quality" see note 1 on page 6.

[2] The last part of this sentence is a complex play on words: "to look like an owl in an ivy-bush" meant to look ridiculous – a saying much played upon, among others, by Shakespeare; an "ivy bush" also meant a hiding place but, especially, a tavern, often advertised by the sign of an ivy bush placed outside; for "barber's block," see note 4 on page 7.

[3] A reference to the wax figures of monarchs and courtiers at Westminster Abbey.

Fighting to a Dutchman.[1] *Tho' I cannot but acknowledge that I Admire your* Beauty, *Dote upon your Dear Person, and always think my self Blest when I am Honour'd with your Company; yet* Marriage *that dulls the Edge of* Loves *Appetite, and Over-ballances the Enjoyment with* Cares, Crosses, *and* Vexations, *is not a State fit for a Man who gets his Living by the Sword, and must, upon occasion, if Commanded, wander into Foreign Countries, and cut his way thro' his Enemy to come at a good Dinner.* Seamen, *I must confess, are mighty fond of entering themselves into this double Condition, and will have* Wives, *tho' they see them but seldom, if it were only to be Honour'd with the Venerable Names of* Husband, *and* Father; *but if there had been a Married* Seaman *in the Fleet ever since the Building of* Noah's Ark *but what has been a* Cuckold, *I'll be bound to Drink the Fat of* Rhenish *at* Heidleburg *for a Whet, and as soon as I have done, Eat up all* Leadenhall-Market *for a Breakfast:*[2] *Therefore we* Landmen *of the* Soldiery, *are very Timerous of entering into the* Church Noose, *for fear of falling under the same* Predicament: *But if I have so prevail'd upon your Compassionate Heart, as to have any share in your* Affections, *and you will make me happy with your Dear Company whilst I stay in* England, *you shall find me as* Just *and as* Loving *a* Confident *as ever Woman trusted her* Honour *with, or* Innocent Maid *bestow'd the first Fruits of her* Virginity *upon: And after we have had the Experience of one anothers Embraces, and we both agree in a Mutual Approbation, I will endeavour by all possible means, to reconcile my self to that abominable Bugbear, which, as yet, I am very much afraid of. If you dare trust your self under my Care, I assure you, Madam, you shall find me a Man of Honour; for I will treat you Lovingly while you are with me, and provide for you when I am from you, which is all the Justice a Man can do, or a Woman reasonably expect. I have this Day received Orders to March with my Troop to* Northampton; *I shall begin my March on* Friday Morning; *therefore if you are willing to comply with the Terms I have propos'd, I desire you will meet me to Morrow Night, about Seven a Clock, at the* Three-Tun-Tavern, *in* Shandois-Street, Covent-Garden,[3] *and I shall be ready, with open Arms, to give you a Joyful Reception; and to consider of such*

1703

[1] A cat-o'-nine-tails was a whip with nine lashes (all full of knots), used in the British navy as instrument of punishment; because of their rivalry with the Dutch, the English often used them as an example of anything cowardly or harebrained.

[2] The "fat" or "vat" (i.e., a big barrel) of Heidelberg had been built in 1591 and was supposed to contain the equivalent of 212,400 bottles of Rhenish wine. It was, however, destroyed by French soldiers in 1688 and only replaced by an even bigger one, known as the "Heidelberg Tun" in 1751 (preserved today in the Heidelberg Castle). Leadenhall Market (today covered), in the City of London, was originally a poultry market, but after the Great Fire of 1666, meat, cheese, fish, and vegetables were also sold there.

[3] There were many taverns with this name (because the three tuns were the emblem of the Vintners' Livery Company). The one on Chandos Street (today, Chandos Place) had been in place for several decades. It had a famous balcony and an infamous history of drunken altercation, murder, and attempted murder.

Preparations for your Journey into the Country along with me, as shall be Necessary, therefore, if you have any Respect for me, you cannot Manifest it more, than in thus Obliging your

> Faithful Friend,
> *and* Admirer,
> *P. H.*

This surprising Letter was like a Thunder-Bolt to my Breast, and struck me Backwards into a Chair for a few Minutes, as Dead as a *Herring*;[1] but at last recovering Breath enough to Pump up a deep Sigh, I began to recollect my self, and consider what little Reason I had to afflict my self with such an Insupportable Passion, since there was nothing hindered me of enjoying all the Happiness I could wish for, but my insisting upon that *Ecclesiastical Ceremony*, which ought to License us to our Liberty: So that I found I had nothing left to do but to set them together by the Ears, and, like a Politick Coward, submit my self to that which should prove the strongest side.[2] I let them Battle fairly in my Breast, till *Love*, upon the Trial of Skill, got a compleat Victory, and Insinuated Marriage was but a Tyrannical Embargo, laid upon the Natural Freedom of Humane Race, by the Cunning of the Priests, who had always Wit enough, till of late Days, to exempt themselves from the Confinement. *Love* prompting me to consider further, that as long as he Lov'd me, he would be kind and obliging to me, and when-ever he was tir'd with my Company, and grew Morose and Slighting, it was my Advantage to be at Liberty to leave him; for the Meat which has Surfeited one Man, may go down with a fresh Appetite, be thought a Dainty; and that it was one of the highest Cures imaginable for a Woman to be Chained to a Man that cares not a Fart for her, who, if she were at Liberty, might have a thousand Admirers. Besides, I had often heard from Men of Wit, that Liberty and Variety are the two Parents of Delight: These, and a hundred such Whimsical Notions *Love* had partially possest me with, till at last the mighty Conqueror had fully prevail'd upon me to comply with the desires of my *Lover.*

Accordingly at the time prefix'd, having Equip'd my self in my best Apparel, and furnish'd my self with all profitable necessaries for my Amorous Expedition, I made an Elopement from the Bar with all imaginable Privacy, and posted to the Arms of my *Lover*, who, in a Dispairing Condition, sat ready to receive me, knowing not what to think because I had neglected to dispatch to him any Intelligence of my Resolution.

To express the Joy he seem'd Transported with at my coming, lies not within the Power of Female Eloquence; but his Extasie was so great, and his Desires so ungovernable, that he had much difficulty to forbear

---

[1] A popular saying, especially in the late 17th century.

[2] The adjective "politick" means "prudent" or "shrewd." In 1702, Tom Brown wrote that "a politick coward often passes for a brave man for want of being try'd [i.e., tested]."

Sacrificing my Innocence to his Passion, the first moment I had blest him with so fair an Opportunity; and indeed I had much Struggle to defend my self from the Attack. When with a Throbbing Heart, and Blushing Cheeks, I had acknowledged my Female Weakness, and made him truly sensible he had brought my Heart into an Absolute Subjection, and that I was thoroughly resolv'd to commit my self to his Mercy, as a Victim to a Conqueror; and he with a deep Sigh of Gratitude, as the Obligation could require, had exprest his Thanks for that inesteemable Treasure, as he deem'd it, which I had Generously promis'd to confer upon him; he first entertain'd me with a Supper suitable to the Enterprize then in Hand, and then remov'd me in a Coach to a Lodging in St. *James*'s, where I suffer'd that to be spoil'd in one Minute, which had been Eighteen Years in Nursing to a Perfection. To set forth the Felicity of the Nights Adventure, would be a Description too Lushious for a Maids Perusal, and those who are acquainted with the Joys of *Love*, are already far more Wise in Fact, than Words can make them: Such was the Enjoyment, that none can be taught to truly know, except by sweet Experience.

Now I had taken leave of my Virginity, and so had Gratify'd my keen Appetite with a plentiful Meal of *Loves* Delicious Food, before the Feast was Consecrated, we began next Day to prepare for our Journey to *Northampton*; my Love and I went down in the Coach, and the Marching down of the Troop was left to the Lieutenant. I was now honour'd with the Title of the Captains Lady; and all the accustomary Formalities of Man and Wife, pass'd mutually between us. All the Honey Moon Words that a couple of Fond Fools could think on; our Loving Dialect consisted of, *My Dear, My Love, My Honey*, or *My Jewel*, was the beginning and end of every Amorous Expression, and nothing but Love Toys, and provoking Dalliance were the Pastimes of the Day, and Pleasures unexpressible the Recreations of the Night.

But as all the Satisfactions in this Transitory World are but short Liv'd, and the greatest Felicities on this side Heaven have always the quickest Expirations; so the happy Paradice, wherein I had Tasted the Forbidden Fruit, soon vanish'd from my Sight, and left me amidst a Thousand Sorrows, as great as those Falacious Joys which had trapan'd[1] me into 'em: For e'er the Revolving *Moon* had once Travel'd thro' the Twelve Signs,[2] and Curs'd the World with her Fickle Influence, the Pleasing Smiles that used to sit upon his Brow, and all the kind Engaging Air with which he us'd to Illustrate his Deportment, were now all Vanish'd, and the Soldier had flung off the Disguise and Flattery of a Courtier, and put on the Stern Behaviour of a Robust Heroe, looking as if he had a greater Appetite to Eat an Enemy, than he had to Treat a Mistress with Civility. This sudden Alteration in him, work'd an answerable Change in me; and made me grow as Sullen, as he was Morose. Thus after he had been a meer Glutton in *Love*, and Surfeited himself with Excess of what should have

---

[1] "Trapan" or "trepan" means to entrap, ensnare or to lure, inveigle.
[2] Astrology was a common pastime and the contemporary reader would have understood that the narrator means a couple of months; the Moon passes through all 12 signs of the zodiac in 2 to 3 months, although sometimes in only 1 month.

been us'd with Moderation, I found the Sight of the Lushious Fruit which he once long'd so much for, was become as Nauseous to his Squeamish Stomach, as a Bumper to a Drunkard that is already over charg'd.

Fortune to favour my Gallant just according to his Desires, had so order'd the Affairs of *Europe* that he was Commanded into Foreign Service, which gave him a fairer Opportunity to shake off his Bundle of *Rue*,[1] than otherwise he would have had; which so pleas'd him, that he began again to Clear up a little, and show some small Glimmerings of Good Nature, thro' his Cloudy Uneasiness; thinking it would look more Honourable to come fairly off by Pleading the Necessity of his Command, than it was willfully to break all his Vows and Promises, without the least Occasion or Provocation on my side, to furnish him with an Excuse.

Tho' the shortness of his Stay made him thus dissemble an Affable out-side, yet I was not such a Child but I could discern a great Abatement in his Kindness, and thought it high time to put him in mind of making some Provision or other for me, in his Absence, or at least put me into some sort of Condition, that I might be able to provide for my self: When an Opportunity sat fair, and I judg'd by his Looks he was in a Complying Temper, I put on the best Begging Countenance I could, and sprinkled my Rosie Cheeks, with a few Mollifying Tears, first expressing an unextinguishable Passion for his Person; secondly, an unfeigned Sorrow that I must so soon lose him; and at last, in the softest Language I could use, to move him to Compassion, I touch'd upon the hardships of my own Circumstances, and how Wretched I was like to be, when I was Rob'd, not only of every thing that was Dear to me, but left Destitute of Support.

I thank my Stars, I manag'd this my last Point so feelingly, that I melted his Stubborn Heart into a Generous Compliance of giving me Thirty Guineas; which, for a Soldier to part with to a Mistress, under the Declension of his Love, I must confess, was like a Man of Honour. After I had thankfully receiv'd his Present, finding him in great Hurry to put things in order for his Voyage, and being willing, as I plainly discover'd, to be rid of me, I told him I could think no less, than that a Womans Company to a Gentleman at such a Juncture, when his Head and his Heart must be both taken up with the Fatigue of Business, could neither be at all pleasant or convenient; therefore, if it would be any ease to him, I would remove to *London*, and, by my self, bewail the Thoughts of his Departure. He made a faint Apology for his being so taken up about the Regulation of his Troop, that he could not give that Attention, and show that respect to me that he ought to do; but hop'd I would acquaint him where I fix'd in Town, that he might take his leave of me before he went to *Flanders*; which I promis'd I would do accordingly: So waiting on me to the Stage-Coach, where he Kiss'd me with as much Indifference as if I had been his Sister; and looking as if he wish'd his Thirty Guineas again

---

[1] "Rue" means "sorrow" and it is also a medicinal plant with multiple uses, which allowed many authors to insert facile double entendres. Ned Ward's is more complex: he clearly alludes to a particular use of the plant, recommended by Constantinus Africanus in his 11th-century popular treatise *De Coitu*: that of extinguishing sexual desire.

in his Pocket, he gave me Two or Three Campaign Cringes,[1] wish'd me a good Journey, and took his last Farewel; for, notwithstanding I was as good as my Word, I never saw him after.

I.

Thus Woman, when she's once Resign'd,
*   What Crowns her other Graces,*
Has nothing left, that long can bind
*   Her Spark to her Embraces.*

II.

For Lovers, as Ingrateful Men,
*   Their Benefactors use us;*
Our Friendship in Distress obtain,
*   And when they're serv'd abuse us.*

Having thus, to my great Sorrow, unhappily Tasted of the Forbidden Fruit, and being utterly forsaken of my Relations, as well as my Lover; when I came to Town I began to seriously consider what an Uncomfortable Condition I was now left in, having very Authentick Reasons to believe, I had Metamorphos'd my self from an Innocent Virgin, into a Four Leg'd Animal,[2] which I found in a little time so Substantially true, that I felt Loves sweet Remains kindled into a Troublesome *Hansen-Kelder*,[3] that grew so unruly in his narrow Confines, that I thought sometimes, to enlarge his Dominions, he was endeavouring to kick my Guts out. Notwithstanding the unhappiness of my Circumstances, the Imprudence of my Youth was such, that I had not that due Regard to my Misfortune, as was necessary; but Squander'd away my Sparks Benevolence in Rich Commodes,[4] and Splendid Ornaments, forgetting the Time of Trouble and Adversity was drawing on, against which an unthinking Wretch, in my Condition, ought to have been well provided.

By this time I was so far Thriven under my Pregnancy, that I was forc'd to let out my Stays; and lengthen my Petticoats; and was so mightily swelled about the Bouge, that any Body might easily discern

[1] Like the "campaign eloquence" above, these "cringes" (bows) are martial, soldierlike. "Campaign" (understood as the military operations in which troops are engaged for a period of time) was a relatively new word.
[2] Another one of Ward's complex allusions, it probably refers both to sexual intercourse and to pregnancy; while the latter becomes obvious in the following lines, the former should be read in conjunction with the equally obvious reference to one of Ovid's *Metamorphoses* (X, 667-823; it is also recounted by Hesiod), that of Atalanta, who took an oath of virginity and kept it by challenging her suitors to a footrace, which she always won. She was finally defeated by Hippomenes, who subsequently took her virginity in a shrine of the goddess Cybele, who punished them by turning them both into lions.
[3] "Hans en kelder" (often anglicised as "hans in kelder") is a Dutch expression meaning "Jack in the cellar" (though often assumed to mean "jack-in-the-box") and used as an euphemism for a child in the womb. In Restoration and early-18th-century England, it was used especially as a toast to the unborn child.
[4] The commode was a tall head-dress made of wire framework covered with lace.

22

what sort of Poison I had been medling with.[1] When I was near my time, my Money was near Exhausted, without so much as a Swaddling Clout in readiness to cover my Shame, which was almost ready to start Naked into the World, and begin the Race of Life from the Womb to the Devouring Grave:[2] But, by chance, having crept into the Acquaintance of an Old Experienc'd Lady, whose *Wrinkled Brows, Hypocritical Eloquence, and Puritanical Deportment*, seem'd to show she had run thro' all the Changeable Conditions incident to the Complying Nature of the Female Sex, and looking upon her Grave Ladyship, to be a proper Confident for a Sinner in my Circumstances, I dealt plainly with her, and acquainted her with the particulars of my Misfortunes, and entreated her not only to give me her Advice, but to lend me her Assistance, for that I wanted both Money and Management to Steer my self clear of those Parochial Dangers that attend us Ladies, without a License from the *Clergy*;[3] she Faithfully promised me her Friendship, and told me she would undertake to convey me too thro' all my approaching Difficulties, provided I would afterwards comply with such Conditions, as she should propose, to make her amends for that Trouble and Expence she must of Necessity be at in digging the Fruits of my Labour out of the Parsley Bed:[4] Which Articles of Agreement were as follow, *viz. That as soon as I was discharged of my Troublesome Burthen, and all things were reduc'd to their Primitive Condition, and were again render'd capable of Humane Use, I should surrender up my whole Body from Head to Heel to be at her Disposal, without Exception, for the full space of one Year; and to readily submit, upon all Occasions, to all such Bodily Exercise and Occupation, that she, or any Friend of hers (according to a Womans Reason and Conscience) should require of me; she being oblig'd to find me, during the Time aforesaid, such Decent Apparel, Meat, Drink, Washing, Lodging, and Physick, as should be Judged Necessary.*

The Miserable Calamities I had brought my self under, were attended with so Dreadful a Prospect of further *Shame* and *Poverty*, that I was Foolishly glad to comply with any thing, that I might be subsisted in the time of my Pennance, and secur'd from the Mercenary Rage of a parcel of Parish Cormorants.

In a little time after we had thus Settled the Preliminaries, an Old Holland Sheet, and a Thin cast-off-Smock, which, I suppose had been long Privy to abundance of *Fornication* and *Adultery*, were given me to go to Work upon, that I might have a few Necessaries in readiness to Accommodate my New-Born Off-spring upon his Arrival out of Natures Dark Dungeon, into the Land of the Living: But before I had quite finish'd

---

[1] Stays is an older term for a corset; "bouge" is an old version of "bulge."

[2] The original text reads here "from the Womb *of* the Devouring Grave," which must be a mistake; "clout" is a piece of cloth, a rag.

[3] At least until the mid-18th century, unwed mothers were often subjected to punishment from the clergy, having to stand in front of the church dressed in sackcloth; in many cases, they also had to do hard labour and daily penance for a long time.

[4] "Out of the parsley bed" was the traditional answer to children's question "where do babies come from?"; "parsley bed" was also, at the time, a euphemism for the vagina.

one Suite of Linnen, for my Poppet, which lay as yet Obscur'd in the doubtful Gender, I began to find such an unusual Griping of the Guts, that I presently conjectur'd my little *Itinerate* (being grown weary of his close Quarters) was making his passage out of the *Straights Mouth*, into the *Wide World*; so that I thought it was high time to discover my Condition to my Confident, who being an *Amphibious Necessary*, between *Bawd* and *Midwife*,[1] began presently to Examine the Garden of *Venus*, and finding the Fruit to be full Ripe, sent immediately for a couple of her Trusty Familiars to help shake the Tree. I now began to Clinch my Hands, and make as many wry Faces, as a *Mumper* in a Fit of his Falling Sickness; continuing, for a few Hours, in as true a Humour of Repentance, as ever was a poor *Rogue* at the *Gallows*, or a *Jilt* in a *Salivation*.[2] Every now and then my Pains put me into the *Vocative Case*, and made me express the Sign *O* with such an Emphasis,[3] that had they not stood ready to apply a Pillow to my Mouth, I should have loudly Proclaim'd, what we had been doing, to the whole Neighbourhood; from about Catterwauling time of Night, to the Hour of Hot Bak'd Wardens, the next Evening,[4] I remain'd upon the Rack of Delivery, till it was greatly fear'd, that *Man* who had first the Tillage of the Ground, must have been call'd in to have Reap'd the Harvest;[5] but at last, *Nature*, the best *Midwife*, lending her Powerful Assistance, the little Author of my Pains, at the end of one long Squeak, shot the Gulph of *Venus*, and made his Entrance into the Wicked World, to my great Ease and the Companies Satisfaction; which he had no sooner done, but the poor Babe, to show its good Nature, first Cry'd, to think it had put the Mother to so much Misery, and before Morning gave back that Life he had so Dishonestly come by. Now the pretty Mortal was Defunk'd,[6] the greatest Care of my Confident was to Bury the Unchristian Clay, so as to avoid the Kings Tax, and the Parish Duties, which, like a Thrifty Old Gentlewoman, she very savingly accomplish'd after the following manner. She happen'd among the scanty Number of her Old Houshold Goods, to spy an Earthen Vessel, in which many an Ox Cheek, and Shin of Beef had formerly been Stewed to an Edible Condition; but, like the Pitcher that is carry'd often to the Well, that had been so often at the Oven, that it came Home crack'd at last, and being render'd unfit for Domestick Service, she made choice of this for the Babes Urn, that it might be Bury'd after the *Roman* Fashion: When she had thus Potted up the Dead Infant, with the rest of the Appurtenances, she made herself the Sexton, her Cellar the Church-Yard, and by the help of Fire-Shovel

1703

[1] "Itinerate" is an old variant of "itinerant"; "amphibious" was often used with the meaning of "having two lives"; a "bawd" was a procuress of prostitutes.

[2] A "mumper" was a beggar; the "falling sickness" is epilepsy; a "jilt" is used here in the original meaning of a strumpet, a harlot; "salivation" is a euphemism for syphilis (mercury, which was the current treatment, produced salivation).

[3] The vocative is one of the cases of nouns, adjectives, and pronouns in Latin; by extension, it referred to excessive use of interjections in English.

[4] The time of "caterwauling," which Ward borrows from Shakespeare's *Twelfth Night*, is late at night, towards morning; "wardens" are a type of pears, baked and sold in the London streets especially on winter evenings.

[5] In other words, the women were afraid they might have to call for a physician.

[6] Misspelling of "defunct."

and Poker, dug a very Commodious Grave for the Interment of the poor short-Liv'd Squab. Thus she became herself Sole Funeral-Undertaker, and Bury'd the little Corps without the Expence of a Penny.

Now her greatest Trouble was over, she began, I suppose, to think she had a good Bargain of it; and began to Cherish me up, with Caudle and Boil'd Chickens, till I was almost Surfeited; so that I was grown so Lusty in a Fortnights time, that the Old *Beldam*[1] would have Merrily insinuated, I had gathered Strength enough for Humane Consolation.

Notwithstanding the Violence of my Pain, and the Prolixity of my Labour, which, during the time of my Extremity, were enough to make *Lucifer* Renounce his Pride, or a Don *John* of *Austria* resolve against *Libertinism*; yet the prevalency of Stubborn Nature, and the Lascivious Insinuations of my Bawdy Governess, in a Months time, had so far Corrupted me, that I had Buried all my past Miseries in Oblivion, and was fallen into as deep a Relapse of my Love-Inclinations as ever, and was fit for any Lewd Expedition that my Wicked Matron could Project for me. When I was thoroughly Recovered of my Strength and Health, and was in an Airy Condition of going Abroad to scatter my Mice,[2] my Old Inductress carried me into a Wardrobe, where as many Changeable Fine Dresses were hung up in Order, as are to be seen in a *Theater*; and thus, upon her Tempting Plumes,[3] she began to Entertain me with the following Lecture. *viz. In this Strawberry-Colour'd Gown and Petticoat the Fair* Althea *Surrender'd her Virginity upon a Chair to the Lord* Biglook; *and in this Crimson Night-Gown and* India-*Sattin Petticoat, the Czar of* Muscovy *Embrac'd the Black-Ey'd* Phanny, *Thrice in one Morning before Dinner-Time. In this Furbelow'd Smock and Lac'd Night-Cloaths, the Witty* Celinda *Bedded with a Young Knight, who afterwards Play'd the Fool and Married her; and what is more worthy of Remark, in that Plain Lute-String Hood and Scarf,*[4] *and this Green Apron, Demure* Rachel, *a Famous Lady of this Town, Pick'd up a Presbyterian Parson, and Pox'd him at the* Salutation-Tavern.[5] When she had thus ended the History of her Sinful Apparel, she told me, *If I would prove but a good Girl, and deal Honestly by her, all, or any or those Ornaments should be at my Service, to carry on an Intrigue; for that Fine Dressing would be a great heightning to my Charms, and would render my Person the more Acceptable; besides it would be a means of Recommending me to*

[1] A "beldam" was either an old woman or a hag; "caudle" is a drink made of gruel, wine, sugar, and spices, recommended at the time for women during or after childbirth.
[2] "To scatter (one's) mice" was an expression used for a woman's first visit to her neighbours after her confinement (probably originating from the proverb "when cats prowl, mice will scatter").
[3] In the plural form, "plumes" could mean feathers, but also any flashy ornaments.
[4] Lutestring or lustring is a silk fabric with a sheen. It was manufactured both black and coloured and the plain, black version was used especially for mourning clothes.
[5] To "pox" meant to infect someone, especially with syphilis. The Salutation Tavern was in Newgate Street, and in the following decades it became very popular with literati.

the *Esteem of better Company, which would be more for her Advantage, and my own Credit*. This Scene being over, she then proceeded to give me Instructions how to behave my self, and after what manner I should Treat the several Tempers, Ages, Degrees, and Qualities of such Men that I should be liable to Converse with; concluding her Discourse with a necessary Caution against *Bullies*[1] and Bad Company; telling me, *Alas! 'Twas a Wicked World we Liv'd in, and that Man was a Treacherous Creature to Woman, and never to be Trusted*: Advising therefore, by all Means to be sure of my Wages before I did my Work.

When she thought by these, and such other Pious Instructions, she had thoroughly Qualified me for the Business she design'd me; then every Day she Jumbled me about Town in a Coach, to one Gentlemans Chamber or other, till before the Expiration of Six Months, there was not an *Inns-of-Court*, or *Chancery*, or indeed any other part of the Town, but where I had very Plentifully scatter'd my Favours; insomuch that by her Management, and my own Indefatiguable Industry, she had acquir'd Money enough, in a little time, to Take and Furnish a great House in *Pell mell*,[2] where she had the Honour to keep one of the most Eminent *Brothels* that ever stood between the two Famous Palaces, *White-Hall* and St. *James*'s.

By this time I had the Misfortune of becoming a known Face, she having Trapan'd several Fresh Country Lasses into her Service, whom she adorn'd (being new Faces) with her best Apparel, and plac'd 'em over my Head; so that the chief of my Business was to Dress the *Ladies*, and now and then to Oblige some *Courtiers Valet*, or *Lords Footman*. In this Sinful Servitude was I forc'd to remain, till at last my too frequent Debauch'd Practices had kindled in my Youthful Veins such a Venereal Fire, that *Scabs, Itch, Nodes, Nocturnal-Pains*, and all the Miseries that could at once attend a Wicked Life, Punish'd me for that Base Inconvenience, to which I had so Foolishly and Shamefully Submitted; and in this Condition the Vile *Beldam*, to show the Gratitude of a Superanuated Prostitute, strip'd me of my Plumes; Excluded me her House in Scandalous Apparel, and with Empty Pockets; that had I not sought Relief at *Kingsland*-Hospital,[3] I had Perish'd in the Streets, for want of *Food* as well as *Physick*.

These are the Comforts of a *Vicious Life*; therefore let *Youth* and *Beauty* stand upon their Guard, lest they are unhappily Seduc'd to share the same Fate, and be brought to a *Sorrowful Repentance* under the same Miseries.

---

[1] "Bully" was an ambiguous term in the early 18th century: it meant either someone who was cocky and a macho; or one who protected prostitutes, a "pimp."
[2] Pall Mall was one of the most fashionable streets in London.
[3] Located in Islington and administered by St Bartholomew's Hospital, Kingsland received incurables, especially those afflicted with syphilis.

DANIEL DEFOE

The Apparition of Mrs. Veal (1706)

The author: Daniel Defoe (1660-1731) was born in London, the son of a tallow chandler. Being a Presbyterian (and thus, a Nonconformist, i.e., worshipping outside the Church of England), Defoe could not study in a university, pursue a career in the army, or run for office. He was educated at the Newington Green academy in London and became a merchant, with disastrous results: he ran up huge debts, declared bankruptcy, and was more than once arrested and sent to debtors' prison. He acted as an agent or spy for Robert Harley, one of the prominent English statesmen at the turn of the 18th century, supporting in writing and by personal contacts the proposed Act of Union with Scotland. He was arguably the most prolific English author of that or any time, but he was middle-aged by the time he recorded his first success, in 1701, with the publication of a poem, *The True-Born Englishman*. The following year, he published the misunderstood pamphlet *The Shortest-Way with the Dissenters*, for which he was accused of libel, arrested, and pilloried. In 1704, he wrote *The Storm*, a nonfictional account of the Great Storm of 1703, and began the publication of *A Review of the Affairs of France* (thus entitled because of the war against France that had been raging since 1702). The paper appeared three times a week until 1713 and was entirely written by Defoe. *A True Relation of the Apparition of one Mrs. Veal*, which came out in pamphlet form in July 1706, is a "factual fiction," based as it is on a phenomenon recounted by several contemporary witnesses. It was not signed then or in any of the many editions it had throughout the 18th century. George Chalmers, in his *Life of Daniel De Foe* (London: John Stockdale, 1790), first spoke of "The tradition among the Booksellers . . . That when *Drelincourt's Consolations against the Fears of Death* first appeared, the book would not sell. De Foe said he would make it sell, and he made *the Apparition* recommend Drelincourt's Book of Death, as the best on that subject ever written" (74). This statement, though questionable, as well as an earlier hint by Defoe's son in *The Gentleman's Magazine*, has convinced most commentators that Defoe is, indeed, the author of *A Relation*. When his authorship is doubted, it is on account of his 1727 *An Essay on the History and Reality of Apparitions*, in which he denies the existence of ghosts, and suggests instead that only angels and demons can "appear" to humans. However, as J.M. Coetzee has keenly observed in his review of a new edition of that essay, "Whether Mrs. Bargrave was visited by a supernatural messenger or haunted by a ghost or was simply dreaming the early Defoe does not venture to guess." Defoe never uses the term "ghost," but only "apparition," which keeps the ambiguity intact.

The text: The first edition is "A True Relation of the Apparition of one Mrs. Veal, the next Day after Her Death: To one Mrs. Bargrave at *Canterbury*. The 8th of *September*, 1705" (London: Printed for B. *Bragg*, at the *Black Raven* in *Pater-Noster-Row*, 1706). Later editions (beginning with the third) had the following addition to the title: "Which Apparition recommends the Perusal of *Drelincourt*'s Book of

27

Consolations against the Fears of Death" and changes in spelling and punctuation. The new translation of Drelincourt, by Marius D'Assigny, was published by J. Robinson and others, not by Benjamin Bragg, who published Defoe's story. If Defoe agreed with the promotion of Drelincourt's book, which is very likely, since he had such appreciative terms for it in the text of the story, there is no proof that he had any other say in the possible understanding between Bragg and Robinson and in the form the text took after 1706, when much of Defoe's idiosyncratic capitalisation and punctuation was altered. The following is from the first edition.

Further reading: Manuel Schonhorn (ed.). *Accounts of the Apparition of Mrs. Veal by Daniel Defoe and Others.* Los Angeles: Augustan Reprint Society, Pub. No. 115, 1965.

George R. Wasserman. "John Norris and the Veal-Bargrave Story." *Modern Language Notes* 75.8 (December 1960): 648-665.

Kathleen "Kid" Kincade. "The Twenty Years' War: The Defoe Bibliography Controversy." *Textual Studies and the Enlarged Eighteenth Century: Precision as Profusion.* Eds. Kevin L. Cope and Robert C. Leitz III. Lewisburg: Bucknell University Press, 2012. 133-168.

Sasha Handley. "A New Canterbury Tale." *Visions of an Unseen World: Ghost Beliefs and Ghost Stories in Eighteenth-Century England.* New York: Routledge, 2016. 80-107.

The PREFACE.

This relation is Matter of Fact, and attended with such Circumstances, as may induce any Reasonable Man to believe it. It was sent by a Gentleman, a Justice of Peace, at Maidstone *in* Kent, *and a very Intelligent Person, to his Friend in* London, *as it is here Worded; which Discourse is attested by a very sober and understanding Gentlewoman, a Kinswoman of the said Gentlemans, who lives in* Canterbury, *within a few Doors of the House in which the within named Mrs.* Bargrave *lives; who believes his Kinswoman to be of so discerning a Spirit, as not to be put upon by any Fallacy, and who positively assured him, that the whole Matter, as it is here Related and laid down, is what is really True; and what She herself had in the same Words (as near as may be) from Mrs.* Bargraves *own Mouth, who she knows had no Reason to invent and publish such a Story, nor any Design to forge and tell a Lye, being a Woman of much Honesty and Virtue, and her whole Life a Course as it were of Piety. The use which we ought to make of it is, to consider, That there is a Life to come after this, and a Just God, who will retribute to every one according to the Deeds done in the Body; and therefore, to reflect upon our Past course of Life we have led in the World; That our Time is Short and Uncertain, and that if we would escape the Punishment of the Ungodly, and receive the Reward of the Righteous, which is the laying hold of Eternal Life, we ought for the time to come, to return to God by a speedy Repentance, ceasing to do Evil and Learning to do Well: To seek after God Early, if happily he may be found of us, and lead such Lives for the future, as may be well pleasing in his sight.*

1706

A Relation of the Apparition of Mrs. Veal.

This thing is so rare in all its Circumstances, and on so good Authority, that my Reading and Conversation has not given me any thing like it; it is fit to gratifie the most Ingenious and Serious Enquirer. Mrs. *Bargrave* is the Person to whom Mrs. *Veal* Appeared after her Death; she is my Intimate Friend, and I can avouch for her Reputation, for these last fifteen or sixteen Years, on my own Knowledge; and I can confirm the Good Character she had from her Youth, to the Time of my Acquaintance. Tho' since this Relation, she is Calumniated by some People, that are Friends to the Brother of Mrs. *Veal* who Appeared; who think the Relation of this Appearance to be a Reflection, and endeavour what they can to Blast Mrs. *Bargrave*'s Reputation; and to Laugh the Story out of Countenance. But by the Circumstances thereof, and the Chearful Disposition of Mrs. *Bargrave*, notwithstanding the unheard of ill Usage of a very Wicked Husband, there is not the least sign of Dejection in her Face; nor did I ever hear her let fall a Desponding or Murmuring Expression; nay, not when actually under her Husbands Barbarity; which I have been Witness to, and several other Persons of undoubted Reputation.

Now you must know, that Mrs. *Veal* was a Maiden Gentlewoman[1] of about 30 Years of Age, and for some Years last past, had been troubled with Fits; which were perceived coming on her, by her going off from her Discourse very abruptly, to some impertinence: She was maintain'd by an only Brother, and kept his House in *Dover*. She was a very Pious Woman, and her Brother a very Sober Man to all appearance: But now he does all he can to Null or Quash the Story. Mrs. *Veal* was intimately acquainted with Mrs. *Bargrave* from her Childhood. Mrs. *Veals* Circumstances were then Mean; her Father did not take care of his Children as he ought, so that they were exposed to Hardships: And Mrs. *Bargrave* in those days, had as Unkind a Father, tho' She wanted neither for Food nor Cloathing, whilst Mrs. *Veal* wanted for both: So that it was in the Power of Mrs. *Bargrave* to be very much her Friend in several Instances, which mightily endear'd Mrs. *Veal*; insomuch that she would often say, Mrs. *Bargrave you are not only the Best, but the only Friend I have in the World; and no Circumstances of Life, shall ever dissolve my Friendship.* They would often Condole each others adverse Fortune, and read together, *Drelincourt upon Death*,[2] and other good Books: And so like two Christian Friends, they comforted each other under their Sorrow.

---

[1] Until the end of the 18th century, "Mrs." (followed by the maiden name) was a title used for unmarried women or girls (married women, also called "Mrs," bore their husband's family name).

[2] Charles Drelincourt (1595-1669) was a French Protestant minister, author of a popular book on the *Christian Defense against the Fears of Death* (1651), translated by Marius d'Assigny and published in English in several editions before and after 1706.

29

Sometime after, Mr. *Veals* Friends got him a Place in the Custom-House at *Dover*, which occasioned Mrs. *Veal* by little and little, to fall off from her Intimacy with Mrs. *Bargrave*, tho' there was never any such thing as a Quarrel; but an Indifference came on by degrees, till at last Mrs. *Bargrave* had not seen her in two Years and a half; tho' above a Twelve Month of the time, Mrs. *Bargrave* hath been absent from *Dover*, and this last half Year, has been in *Canterbury* about two Months of the time, dwelling in a House of her own.

In this House, on the Eighth of *September* last, *viz.* 1705, She was sitting alone in the Forenoon, thinking over her Unfortunate Life, and arguing her self into a due Resignation to Providence, tho' her condition seem'd hard. And said she, *I have been provided for hitherto, and doubt not but I shall be still, and am well satisfied, that my Afflictions shall end, when it is most fit for me*: And then took up her Sewing-Work, which she had no sooner done, but she hears a Knocking at the Door; she went to see who it was there, and this prov'd to be Mrs. *Veal*, her Old Friend, who was in a Riding Habit: At that Moment of Time, the Clock struck Twelve at Noon.

Madam, says Mrs. *Bargrave*, I am surprized to see you, you have been so long a stranger, but told her, she was glad to see her, and offer'd to Salute her, which Mrs. *Veal* complied with, till their Lips almost touched, and then Mrs. *Veal* drew her hand cross her own Eyes, and said, *I am not very well*, and so waved it. She told Mrs. *Bargrave*, she was going a Journey, and had a great mind to see her first: But says Mrs. *Bargrave, how came you to take a Journey alone? I am amaz'd at it, because I know you have so fond a Brother*. O! says Mrs. *Veal, I gave my Brother the Slip, and came away, because I had so great a Mind to see you before I took my Journey*. So Mrs. *Bargrave* went in with her, into another Room within the first, and Mrs. *Veal* sat her self down in an Elbow-chair, in which Mrs. *Bargrave* was sitting when she heard Mrs. *Veal* Knock. Then says Mrs. *Veal, My Dear Friend, I am come to renew our Old Friendship again, and to beg your Pardon for my breach of it, and if you can forgive me you are one of the best of Women*. O! says Mrs. *Bargrave, don't mention such a thing, I have not had an uneasie thought about it, I can easily forgive it*. What did you think of me says Mrs. *Veal*? Says Mrs. *Bargrave, I thought you were like the rest of the World, and that Prosperity had made you forget your self and me*. Then Mrs. *Veal* reminded Mrs. *Bargrave* of the many Friendly Offices she did her in former Days, and much of the Conversation they had with each other in the time of their Adversity; what Books they read, and what Comfort in particular they received from *Drelincourt's Book of Death*, which was the best she said on that Subject, was ever wrote. She also mentioned Dr. *Sherlock*, and two *Dutch* Books which were Translated, Wrote upon Death,[1] and several others: But *Drelincourt* she said, had

---

[1] William Sherlock (c. 1641-1707) wrote a very popular *Practical Discourse concerning Death* (1689). There were, however, no translated Dutch books on the subject, but Defoe is, as always, guilty of pro-Dutch bias.

the clearest Notions of Death, and of the Future State, of any who have handled that Subject. Then she asked Mrs. *Bargrave*, whether she had *Drelincourt*; she said yes. Says Mrs. *Veal* fetch it, and so Mrs. *Bargrave* goes up Stairs, and brings it down. Says Mrs. *Veal*, Dear Mrs. *Bargrave*, *If the Eyes of our Faith were as open as the Eyes of our Body, we should see numbers of Angels about us for our Guard: The Notions we have of Heaven now, are nothing like what it is, as* Drelincourt *says. Therefore be comforted under your Afflictions, and believe that the Almighty has a particular regard to you; and that your Afflictions are Marks of Gods Favour: And when they have done the business they are sent for, they shall be removed from you.* And believe me my Dear Friend, believe what I say to you, *One Minute of future Happiness will infinitely reward you for all your Sufferings. For I can never believe,* (and claps her Hand upon her Knee, with a great Earnestness, which indeed ran through all her Discourse) *that ever God will suffer you to spend all your Days in this Afflicted State: But be assured, that your Afflictions shall leave you, or you them in a short time.* She spake in that Pathetical and Heavenly manner, that Mrs. *Bargrave* wept several times; she was so deeply affected with it. Then Mrs. *Veal* mentioned Dr. *Hornecks Ascetick*,[1] at the end of which, he gives an account of the Lives of the Primitive Christians. *Their Pattern she recommended to our Imitation*; and said, *their Conversation was not like this of our Age. For now* (says she) *there is nothing but frothy vain Discourse, which is far different from theirs. Theirs was to Edification, and to Build one another up in the Faith: So that they were not as we are, nor are we as they are*[2]; *but* said she, *We might do as they did. There was a Hearty Friendship among them, but where is it now to be found?* Says Mrs. *Bargrave*, 'tis hard indeed to find a true Friend in these days. Says Mrs. *Veal*, Mr. *Norris* has a Fine Copy of Verses, called *Friendship in Perfection*, which I wonderfully admire, have you seen the Book says Mrs. *Veal*? No, says Mrs. *Bargrave*, *but I have the Verses of my own writing out.*[3] *Have you*, says Mrs. *Veal*, *then fetch them*; which she did from above Stairs, and offer'd them to Mrs. *Veal* to read, who refused, and wav'd the thing, saying, *holding down her Head would make it ake*, and then desired Mrs. *Bargrave* to read them to her, which she did. As they were admiring Friendship, Mrs. *Veal* said, Dear Mrs. *Bargrave*, I shall love you for ever: In these Verses there is twice used the Word *Elysium*. Ah! says Mrs. Veal, *These Poets have such Names for Heaven.* She would often draw her Hand cross her own Eyes; and say, Mrs. *Bargrave Don't you think I am mightily impaired by my Fits?* No, says Mrs. *Bargrave*, I think you look as well as ever I knew you.

[1] Anthony Horneck (1641-1697) was a popular preacher of German origin, one of the chaplains of King William III. His *The Happy Ascetick* is from 1681.
[2] Later editions have this corrected: "nor are we as they were"; however, as she seems to have experienced heaven, Mrs. Veal may see its dwellers (including the "primitive Christians") as present, not past, references.
[3] "Damon and Pythias. Or, Friendship in Perfection," which Mrs. Bargrave has copied by hand, is a poem by John Norris (1657-1712), first published in 1681.

After all this discourse, which the Apparition put in much finer Words than Mrs. *Bargrave* said she could pretend to, and was much more than she can remember (for it cannot be thought, that an hour and three quarters Conversation could all be retained, tho' the main of it, she thinks she does) She said to Mrs. *Bargrave, she would have her write a Letter to her Brother, and tell him, she would have him give Rings to such and such; and that there was a Purse of Gold in her Cabinet, and that she would have Two Broad Pieces given to her Cousin Watson.* Talking at this Rate, Mrs. *Bargrave* thought that a Fit was coming upon her, and so placed her self in a Chair, just before her Knees, to keep her from falling to the Ground, if her Fits should occasion it; for the Elbow Chair she thought would keep her from falling on either side. And to divert Mrs. *Veal* as she thought, she took hold of her Gown Sleeve several times, and commended it. Mrs. *Veal* told her, it was a Scower'd Silk,[1] and newly made up. But for all this Mrs. *Veal* persisted in her Request, and told Mrs. *Bargrave* she must not deny her: and she would have her tell her Brother all their Conversation, when she had an opportunity. Dear Mrs. *Veal*, says Mrs. *Bargrave, this seems so impertinent, that I cannot tell how to comply with it; and what a mortifying Story will our Conversation be to a Young Gentleman?* Well, says Mrs. *Veal, I must not be deny'd.* Why, says Mrs. *Bargrave, 'tis much better methinks to do it your self.* No, says Mrs. *Veal; tho' it seems impertinent to you now, you will see more reason for it hereafter.* Mrs. *Bargrave* then to satisfie her importunity, was going to fetch a Pen and Ink; but Mrs. *Veal* said, *let it alone now, and do it when I am gone; but you must be sure to do it*: which was one of the last things she enjoin'd her at parting; and so she promised her.

Then Mrs. *Veal* asked for Mrs. *Bargraves* Daughter; she said she was not at home; but if you have a Mind to see her says Mrs. *Bargrave*, I'le send for her. *Do*, says Mrs. *Veal*. On which she left her, and went to a Neighbours, to send for her; and by the Time Mrs. *Bargrave* was returning, Mrs. *Veal* was got without the Door in the Street, in the face of the *Beast-market*, on a Saturday (which is Market day) and stood ready to part, as soon as Mrs. *Bargrave* came to her. She askt her, *why she was in such hast?* she said, *she must be going; tho' perhaps she might not go her journey till Monday.* And told *Mrs.* Bargrave *she hoped she should see her again, at her Cousin* Watsons before she went whether[2] she was a going. Then she said, *she would take her Leave of her*, and walk'd from Mrs. *Bargrave* in her view, till a turning interrupted the sight of her, which was three quarters after One in the Afternoon.

Mrs. *Veal* Dyed the 7th of *September* at 12 a Clock at Noon, of her Fits, and had not above four hours Senses before her Death, in which time she received the Sacrament. The next day after Mrs. *Veals*

[1] Scoured silk is silk cleaned of all impurities before dyeing.
[2] Alternate spelling of "whither," just as, two lines above, "hast" is a version of "haste."

appearing, being *Sunday*, Mrs. *Bargrave* was mightily indisposed with a Cold, and a Sore Throat, that she could not go out that Day; but on Monday morning she sends a Person to Captain *Watsons* to know if Mrs. *Veal* was there. They wondered at Mrs. *Bargraves* enquiry, and sent her Word, that she was not there, nor was expected. At this Answer Mrs. *Bargrave* told the Maid she had certainly mistook the Name, or made some blunder. And tho' she was ill she put on her Hood, and went her self to Captain *Watsons*, tho' she knew none of the Family, to see of Mrs. *Veal* was there or not. They said, they wondered at her asking, for that she had not been in Town; they were sure, if she had, she would have been there. Says Mrs. *Bargrave, I am sure she was with me on Saturday almost two hours.* They said it was impossible, for they must have seen her if she had. In comes Captain *Watson*, while they were in Dispute, and said that Mrs. *Veal* was certainly Dead, and her Escocheons were making.[1] This strangely surprised Mrs. *Bargrave*, who went to the Person immediately who had the care of them, and found it true. Then she related the whole Story to Captain *Watsons* Family, and what Gown she had on, and how striped. And that Mrs. *Veal* told her it was Scowred. Then Mrs. *Watson* cry'd out, *you have seen her indeed, for none knew but* Mrs. *Veal and my self, that the Gown was Scowr'd*; and Mrs. *Watson* own'd that she described the Gown exactly; for, said she, *I helpt her to make it up.* This, Mrs. *Watson* blaz'd all about the Town, and avouch'd the Demonstration of the Truth of Mrs. *Bargraves* seeing Mrs. *Veal's* Apparition. And Captain *Watson* carried two Gentlemen immediately to Mrs. *Bargraves* House, to hear the Relation from her own Mouth. And when it spread so fast, that Gentlemen and Persons of Quality, the Judicious and Sceptical part of the World, flock't in upon her, which at last became such a Talk, that she was forc'd to go out of the way. For they were in general, extreamly satisfyed of the truth of the thing; and plainly saw, that Mrs. *Bargrave* was no Hypochondriack,[2] for she always appears with such a chearful Air, and pleasing Mien, that she has gain'd the Favour and esteem of all the Gentry. And its thought a great favor if they can but get the Relation from her own Mouth. I should have told you before, that Mrs. *Veal* told Mrs. *Bargrave*, that he Sister and Brother in Law, were just come down from *London* to see her. Says Mrs. *Bargrave, how came you to order matters so strangely? it could not be helpt said* Mrs. *Veal*; and her Sister and Brother did come to see her, and entred the Town of *Dover*, just as Mrs. *Veal* was expiring. Mrs. *Bargrave* asked her, whether she would not drink some Tea. Says Mrs. *Veal, I do not care if I do: But I'le Warrant this Mad Fellow* (meaning Mrs. *Bargraves* Husband) *has broke all your Trinckets.* But, says Mrs. *Bargrave, I'le get something to Drink in for all that*; but Mrs. *Veal* wav'd it, and said, *it is no matter, let it alone*, and so it passed.

[1] Funeral escutcheons, or hatchments, are panels bearing the arms of the dead, fastened onto the walls of their house during the period of mourning and later in a church.

[2] In the old sense of "depressed," or suffering from a morbid form of melancholy.

All the time I sat with Mrs. *Bargrave*, which was some Hours, she recollected fresh sayings of Mrs. *Veal*. And one material thing more she told Mrs. *Bargrave*, that old Mr. *Breton* allowed Mrs. *Veal* Ten pounds a Year, which was a secret, and unknown to Mrs. *Bargrave*, till Mrs. *Veal* told it her. Mrs. *Bargrave* never varies in her Story, which puzzles those who doubt of the Truth, or are unwilling to believe it. A Servant in the Neighbours Yard adjoining to Mrs. *Bargraves* House, heard her talking to some body, an hour of the Time Mrs. *Veal* was with her. Mrs. *Bargrave* went out to her next Neighbours the very Moment she parted with Mrs. *Veal*, and told her what Ravishing Conversation she had with an Old Friend, and told the whole of it. *Drelincourt's Book of Death* is, since this happened, Bought up strangely. And it is to be observed, that notwithstanding all this Trouble and Fatigue Mrs. *Bargrave* has undergone upon this Account, she never took the value of a Farthing, nor suffer'd her Daughter to take any thing of any Body, and therefore can have no Interest in telling the Story.

But Mr. *Veal* does what he can to stifle the matter, and said he would see Mrs. *Bargrave*; but yet it is certain matter of fact, that he has been at Captain *Watsons* since the Death of his Sister, and yet never went near Mrs. *Bargrave*; and some of his Friends report her to be a great Lyar, and that she knew of Mr. *Breton*'s Ten Pounds a Year. But the Person who pretends to say so, has the Reputation of a Notorious Lyar, among persons which I know to be of undoubted Repute. Now Mr. *Veal* is more of a Gentleman, than to say she Lyes; but says, a bad Husband has Craz'd her. But she needs only to present her self, and it will effectually confute that Pretence. Mr. *Veal* says he ask'd his Sister on her Death Bed, whether she had a mind to dispose to any thing, and she said, No. Now what the things which Mrs. *Veal*'s Apparition would have disposed of, were so Trifling, and nothing of Justice aimed at in their disposal, that the design of it appears to me to be only in order to make Mrs. *Bargrave*, so to demonstrate the Truth of her Appearance, as to satisfie the World of the Reality thereof, as to what she had seen and heard: and to secure her Reputation among the Reasonable and understanding part of Mankind. And then again, Mr. *Veal* owns that there was a Purse of Gold; but it was not found in her Cabinet, but in a Comb-Box. This looks improbable, for that Mrs. *Watson* own'd that Mrs. *Veal* was so very careful of the Key of her Cabinet, that she would trust no Body with it. And if so, no doubt she would not trust her Gold out of it. And Mrs. *Veals* often drawing her hand over her Eyes, and asking Mrs. *Bargave*, whether her Fits had not impair'd her; looks to me, as if she did it on purpose to remind Mrs. *Bargrave* of her Fits, to prepare her not to think it strange that she should put her upon Writing to her Brother to dispose of Rings and Gold, which lookt so much like a dying Persons Bequest; and it took accordingly with Mrs. *Bargrave*, as the Effect of her Fits coming upon her; and was one of the many Instances of her Wonderful Love to her, and Care of her, that she should not be affrighted: which indeed appears in her whole management; particularly in her coming to her in the day time, waving the Salutation, and when she was alone; and then the manner of her parting, to prevent a second attempt to Salute her.

Now, why Mr. *Veal* should think this Relation a Reflection, (as 'tis plain he does by his endeavouring to stifle it) I can't imagine, because the Generality believe her to be a good Spirit, her Discourse was so Heavenly. Her two great Errands were to comfort Mrs. *Bargrave* in her Affliction, and to ask her Forgiveness for her Breach of Friendship, and with a Pious Discourse to encourage her. So that after all, to suppose that Mrs. *Bargrave* could Hatch such an Invention as this from *Friday-Noon*, till *Saturday-Noon*, (supposing that she knew of Mrs. *Veals* Death the very first Moment) without jumbling Circumstances, and without any Interest too; she must be more Witty, Fortunate, and Wicked too, than any indifferent Person I dare say, will allow. I asked Mrs. *Bargrave* several times, *If she was sure she felt the Gown*. She answered Modestly, *if my Senses be to be relied on, I am sure of it*. I asked her, *If she heard a Sound, when she clapt her Hand upon her Knee*: She said, *she did not remember she did*: And she said, *she Appeared to be as much a Substance as I did, who talked with her. And I may* said she, *be as soon persuaded that your Apparition is talking to me now, as that I did not really see her; for I was under no manner of Fear, I received her as a Friend, and parted with her as such. I would not*, says she, *give one Farthing to make any one believe it, I have no Interest in it; nothing but trouble is entail'd upon me for a long time, for ought I know; and had it not come to Light by Accident, it would never have been made Publick*. But now she says, *she will make her own Private Use of it, and keep her self out of the way as much as she can*. And so she has done since. She says, *she had a Gentleman who came thirty Miles to her to hear the Relation; and that she had told it to a Room full of People at a time*. Several particular Gentlemen have had the Story from Mrs. *Bargraves* own Mouth.

This thing has very much affected me, and I am as well satisfied, as I am of the best grounded Matter of Fact. And why should we dispute Matter of Fact, because we cannot solve things, of which we can have no certain or demonstrative Notions, seems strange to me: Mrs. *Bargrave*'s Authority and Sincerity alone, would have been undoubted in any other Case.[1]

---

[1] After the word "Finis," the text was followed by an "Advertisement":
"Drelincourt's Book of the Consolations against the Fears of Death, *has been four times Printed already in* English, *of which many Thousands have been Sold, and not without great Applause: And its bearing so great a Character in this Relation, the Impression is near Sold off.*"

RICHARD STEELE
The Civil Husband (1709)

The author: Richard Steele (1672-1729) was born in Dublin and was educated at Oxford, but chose a military career, from which he retired with the rank of captain in 1705. While still in the army, he had his first successes on the stage. Thanks to his reputation as a playwright, he was able to join the Kit-Cat Club, an influential group of Whig grandees and authors, who helped him to get appointed Gentleman-Waiter to Prince George, Queen Anne's husband, and Gazetteer (editor of the government's official paper, *The London Gazette*). In the spring of 1709, Steele founded *The Tatler*, a newspaper purportedly written by Isaac Bickerstaff, a fictional author first used by Jonathan Swift. It began on 12 April 1709 and came

out three times a week, on Tuesday, Thursday, and Saturday (the days when the post left London for the country). The various types of articles (most of which were written by Steele himself) were associated with actual meeting places from the British capital: "all accounts of gallantry, pleasure and entertainment shall be under the article of White's Chocolate House; poetry, under that of Will's Coffee-house; learning, under the title of the *Grecian*; foreign and domestic news, you will have from St. James's Coffee-house; and what else I have to offer on any other subject shall be dated from my own apartment."

The text: First published in *The Tatler* no. 53 (Thursday 11 August 1709), it is one of the first texts in *The Tatler* to have a title. Although set in "White's Chocolate-house, August 10," it has no reference to the Bickerstaff universe and the narrative voice is completely hidden until the conclusion, although the narrator remains unidentifiable as one of Steele's authorial personas. The following has been taken from *The Lucubrations of Isaac Bickerstaff, Esq; Revised and Corrected by the Author* (London: E. and R. Nutt, J. Knapton, J. and B. Sprint, D. Midwinter, B. and S. Tooke, R. Gosling, W. Taylor, W. and J. Innys, J. Osborn, and R. Robinson, 1723), Vol. II, 14-18.

Further reading: Nicola Parsons. "Lucubrating London: The *Tatler* and the *Female Tatler*." *Reading Gossip in Early Eighteenth-Century England*. London: Palgrave Macmillan, 2009. 92-118.

The Fate and Character of the inconstant *Osmyn*, is a just Excuse for the little Notice taken by his Widow, of his Departure out of this Life, which was equally troublesome to *Elmira* his faithful Spouse, and to himself. That Life passed between them after this Manner, is the Reason the Town has just now received a Lady with all that Gaiety, after having been a Relict but three Months, which other Women hardly assume under fifteen after such a Disaster.[1] *Elmira* is the Daughter of a rich

---

[1] A "relict" was a widow.

and worthy Citizen, who gave her to *Osmyn* with a Portion which might have obtained her an Alliance with our noblest Houses, and fixed her in the Eye of the World, where her Story had not been now to be related: For her good Qualities had made her the Object of universal Esteem among the polite Part of Mankind, from whom she has been banish'd and immur'd till the Death of her Gaoler. It is now full fifteen Years since that beauteous Lady was given into the Hands of the happy *Osmyn*, who in the Sense of all the World received at that Time a Present more valuable than the Possession of both the *Indies*. She was then in her early Bloom, with an Understanding and Discretion very little inferior to the most experienced Matrons. She was not beholden to the Charms of her Sex, that her Company was preferable to any *Osmyn* could meet with abroad; for were all she said considered, without Regard to her being a Woman, it might stand the Examination of the severest Judges. She had all the Beauty of her own Sex, with all the Conversation-Accomplishments of ours: But *Osmyn* very soon grew surfeited with the Charms of her Person by Possession, and of her Mind by Want of Taste; for he was one of that loose Sort of Men, who have but one Reason for setting any Value upon the Fair Sex, who consider even Brides but as new Women, and consequently neglect 'em when they cease to be such. All the Merit of *Elmira* could not prevent her becoming a meer Wife within few Months after her Nuptials; and *Osmyn* had so little Relish for her Conversation, that he complained of the Advantages of it.[1] My Spouse (said he to one of his Companions) is so very discreet, so good, so virtuous, and I know not what, that I think her Person is rather the Object of Esteem than of Love; and there is such a Thing as a Merit, which causes rather Distance than Passion. But there being no *Medium* in the State of Matrimony, their Life began to take the usual Gradations to become the most irksome of all Beings. They grew in the first Place very complaisant; and having at Heart a certain Knowledge that they were indifferent to each other, Apologies were made for every little Circumstance which they thought betray'd their mutual Coldness. This lasted but few Months, when they shewed a Difference of Opinion in every Trifle; and, as a Sign of certain Decay of Affection, the Word *perhaps* was introduced in all their Discourse. *I have a Mind to go the Park*, says she; *but* perhaps, *my Dear, you will want the Coach on some other Occasion.* He *would very willingly carry her to the Play; but* perhaps *she had rather go to Lady* Centaure's *and play at* Ombre.[2]

---

[1] In his 1822 edition of *The Tatler*, Chalmers (ii, 25) (taking a suggestion from the contemporary French translator of the periodical) writes that Osmyn is based on James Butler, 2nd Duke of Ormond[e] (1665-1745) who fought in the War of the Spanish Succession and in 1711 replaced Marlborough as Captain-General of the British army. He was accused of treason in 1715 and chose to live in exile and join the Jacobite cause. His second wife was Lady Mary Somerset (1665-1733). Steele's father had been private secretary of the first Duke of Ormond.

[2] Lady Centaure is the name of a character in Ben Jonson's 1610 play *Epicœne, or The Silent Woman*. Steele alluded to the play in *The Tatler* 16 and called it an "admirable play" in *The Tatler* 130. He had seen it staged at the Drury Lane Theatre (Katherine Baker played Lady Centaure) and it was reprinted in 1709. Ombre was a popular card game of Spanish origin (called "hombre," i.e., "man").

They were both Persons of good Discerning, and soon found that they mortally hated each other, by their Manner of hiding it. Certain it is, that there are some Genio's[1] which are not capable of pure Affection, and a Man is born with Talents for it as much as for Poetry or any other Science.

Osmyn began too late to find the imperfection of his own Heart, and used all the Methods in the World to correct it, and argue himself into Return of Desire and Passion for his Wife, by the Contemplation of her excellent Qualities, his great Obligations to her, and the high Value he saw all the World except himself did put upon her. But such is Man's unhappy Condition, that tho' the Weakness of the Heart has a prevailing Power over the Strength of the Head, yet the Strength of the Head has but small Force against the Weakness of the Heart. *Osmyn* therefore struggled in vain to revive departed Desire; and for that Reason resolved to retire to one of his Estates in the Country, and pass away his Hours of Wedlock in the noble Diversions of the Field; and in the Fury of a disappointed Lover, made an Oath, to leave neither Stag, Fox, or Hare living, during the Days of his Wife. Besides, that Country Sports would be an Amusement, he hoped also, that his Spouse would be half killed by the very Sense of seeing this Town no more, and would think her Life ended as soon as she left it. He communicated his Design to *Elmira*, who received it, (as now she did all Things) like a Person too unhappy to be relieved or afflicted by the Circumstance of Place. This unexpected Resignation made *Osmyn* resolve to be as obliging to her as possible; and if he could not prevail upon himself to be kind, he took a Resolution at least to act sincerely, and communicate frankly to her the Weakness of his Temper, to excuse the Indifference of his Behaviour. He disposed his Houshold in the Way to *Rutland*,[2] so as he and his Lady travelled only in the Coach for the Convenience of Discourse. They had not gone many Miles out of Town, when *Osmyn* spoke to this Purpose:

My Dear, I believe I look quite as silly now I am going to tell you I do not love you, as when I first told you I did. We are now going into the Country together, with only one Hope for making this Life agreeable, Survivorship: Desire is not in our Power; mine is all gone for you. What shall we do to carry it with Decency to the World, and hate one another with Discretion?

The lady answered without the least Observation on the Extravagance of the Speech:

My Dear, You have lived most of your Days in a Court, and I have not been wholly unacquainted with that Sort of Life. In Courts, you see Good-will is spoken with great Warmth, Ill-will covered with great Civility. Men are long in Civilities to those they hate, and short in Expressions of Kindness to those they love. Therefore, my Dear, let us be well-bred still, and it is no matter, as to all who see us, whether we love or hate: And to let you see how much you are beholden to me for my

[1] A "genio" is a person's distinctive character or genius.
[2] Rutland is the smallest historic county of England, 100 miles north of London.

*Conduct, I have both hated and despised you, my Dear, this half Year;
and yet neither in Language or Behaviour has it been visible but that I
loved you tenderly. Therefore, as I know you go out of Town to divert
Life in Pursuit of Beasts, and Conversation with Men just above 'em; so,
my Life, from this Moment, I shall read all the learned Cooks who have
ever writ, study Broths, Plaisters, and Conserves, till from a fine Lady I
become a notable Woman. We must take our Minds a Note or two lower,
or we shall be tortur'd by Jealousy or Anger. Thus I am resolved to kill
all keen Passions by employing my Mind on little Subjects, and lessening
the Easiness of my Spirit; while you, my Dear, with much Ale, Exercise,
and ill Company, are so good, as to endeavour to be as contemptible as
it is necessary for my Quiet I should think you.*

To *Rutland* they arrived, and lived with great, but secret Impatience
for many successive Years, till *Osmyn* thought of an happy Expedient to
give their Affairs a new Turn. One Day he took *Elmira* aside, and spoke
as follows:

*My Dear, You see here the Air is so temperate and serene, the
Rivulets, the Groves, and Soil, so extremely kind to Nature, that we are
stronger and firmer in our Health since we left the Town; so that there
is no Hope of a Release in this Place: But if you will be so kind as to go
with me to my Estate in the Hundreds of Essex,*[1] *it is possible some
kind Damp may one Day or other remove us. If you will condescend to
accept of this Offer, I will add that whole Estate to your Jointure*[2] *in
this County.*

Elmira, who was all Goodness, accepted the Offer, removed
accordingly, and has left her Spouse in that Place to rest with his Fathers.

This is the real Figure in which *Elmira* ought to be beheld in this
Town, and not thought guilty of an *Indecorum*, in not professing the
Sense, or bearing the Habit of Sorrow, for one who robbed her of all
the Endearments of Life, and gave her only common Civility, instead
of Complacency of Manners, Dignity of Passion, and that constant
Assemblage of soft Desires and Affections which all feel who love, but
none can express.[3]

---

[1] A hundred was a subdivision of a county, administrated by a local council, for
judicial and taxation purposes. However, the phrase "the hundreds of Essex" was
used especially for those (e.g., Rochford and Dengie) situated close to the sea and
the Thames, consisting mainly of marshy grounds and often blamed for seasonal
diseases.
[2] Originally, a "jointure" was property held jointly by the husband and wife,
but the term also came to mean an estate that the latter would inherit from the
former for her sole benefit.
[3] Coincidentally, Isaac Bickerstaff(e), the playwright of the 1760s and early
1770s (present in this anthology with a story from 1768), is the author of a farce
in two acts called *The Sultan; or, a Peep in the Seraglio*, performed by Garrick
after Bickerstaff went into exile. Two of the main characters are Elmira, the
"sultana," and Osmyn, chief of the eunuchs. The play, however, is an adaptation
of a French comedy in three acts by Charles Simon Favart (1710-1792), *Les
Trois Sultanes, ou Soliman Second*, first performed in Paris on 9 April, 1761. In
Favart's play, the same characters are called "Osmin" and "Elmire."

DELARIVIER MANLEY

Story of Sir Samuel Slender (1709)

1709

The author: Delarivier (also: Delariviere or De la Rivière) Manley was born either in 1663 or around 1670, probably in Jersey, as the daughter of Sir Roger Manley, a royalist historian and governor of Landguard Fort during the reign of James II, author of *The History of the Rebellions in England, Scotland and Ireland*. Delarivier first wrote plays, but became famous with her *romans à clef*: *The New Atalantis* (1709), *Memoirs of Europe* (1710) and *The Adventures of Rivella* (1714). Despite her initial friendship with Steele, a notorious Whig, Manley was a fierce Tory and, in the early 1710s, she edited *The Examiner*, an important Tory journal founded by Jonathan Swift. *The Female Tatler*, her answer to Richard Steele's *Tatler*, began its publication on 8 July 1709. The first 18 numbers were printed by Benjamin Bragg but, starting with number 19, while Bragg continued to print the newspaper (probably edited by Thomas Baker and other male authors), Manley edited a rival publication with the same title, printed by Ann Baldwin. The two periodicals were printed simultaneously until they both reached number 44, when Bragge gave up and only Baldwin's continued. However, beginning with number 51, *The Female Tatler* lost its editor, as Delarivier Manley was arrested for libel in *The New Atalantis*. The persona chosen here by Manley and other possible contributors is that of "Mrs. Crackenthorpe, a Lady that knows everything." Whereas Steele's *Tatler* usually has the stories set in various cafes, Mrs. Crackenthorpe's originate in her apartment, where she discusses with several female friends. After Manley's arrest, Phoebe Crackenthorpe was replaced by "a society of ladies" (possibly Susannah Centlivre and Bernard Mandeville). "We do not know to what extent the paper is a *periodical a clef*" (Italia 55). Delarivier Manley died on 24 July 1724.

The text: It appeared untitled in Baldwin's *The Female Tatler* 28 (Wednesday, 7 September, to Friday, 9 September, 1709), from which the following has been taken. It is here divided into paragraphs, something that the editor or the printer of *The Female Tatler* constantly avoids, most likely because of the scarcity of space (the paper was printed on a single leaf). Inconsistencies such as "show/shew," "her self/ himself" belong to the author; as elsewhere, "goal" has been spelled "gaol" when it means "prison."

Further reading: Iona Italia. "'The Conversation of my Drawing-Room': The female editor and the public sphere in the *Female Tatler*." *The Rise of Literary Journalism in the Eighteenth Century: Anxious Employment*. London and New York: Routledge, 2005. 49-65.

Tedra Osell. "Tatling Women in the Public Sphere: Rhetorical Femininity and the English Essay Periodical." *Eighteenth-Century Studies* 38: 2 (Winter 2005). 283-300.

Lady *Termigant*,[1] who is so violent an Advocate for her own Sex, that she interests her self in ev'ry Lady's Misfortunes, feels her Wrongs, and is as impatient for Revenge, as if they were immediately her own, came raving to me this Morning, more like a Fury than a Rational Creature; she had all the Agonies and Convulsions of an Enrag'd Lunatick, her Words were so many Claps of Thunder, she blasted with her Eyes, and her Looks and Motion show'd her impetuously resolute on some fatal Enterprize; she's a Lady of a right Understanding, strict Morals and unshaken Friendship, but as none are without Failings, her ungovern'd Zeal sometimes carries her beyond Reason, as a Faith too implicite often breeds Enthusiasm;[2] however, Passion, which rising to a Storm, blows soon over, is a Temper better to be indur'd than a peevish, fretful Disposition, which gives a whole Family the Spleen, without telling 'em Why; and when I heard the Cause of her Ladyship's disorder, I was not so much surpriz'd at it.

It seems, a certain Gentleman, now a Baronet, and whom we must call Sir *Samuel Slender*, about Sixteen Years past, made his Addresses to a very fine young Lady, a Relation of Lady *Termigant*'s, whose Perfections of Mind as well as Body, had attracted an infinite number of Admirers; she had a Gentlewoman's Fortune, Two Thousand Pounds, but Lovers blush'd at People's naming Worldly Pelf to 'em; she was an Angel of her self, and had prodigious offers, but Sir *Samuel* being her first Suitor, she thought Honour oblig'd her to shew particular Regard to him, and by his insinuating Behaviour and Amorous Protestations, he became her Favourite; he visited her at all Seasons, she admitted his Pretences, appeared Abroad with him, received Treats and Presents from him, and the Town concluded it a Match: But as the Tyranny of Doting Relations often prevents, or delays the Consummation of reciprocal Love, Sir *Samuel* had an extraordinary Old Uncle, whose Estate he impatiently waited for, *whose Deity was Money,* and whose obstinacy *unparallel'd,* and shou'd his Nephew have marry'd the most accomplish'd Nymph with a moderate Fortune, he would certainly have disinherited him. This Obstacle was no small damp to our enamour'd Knight, who, though he believ'd the present Sincerity of *Catherina*'s Flame, yet, as her Beauty was always wounding, Lovers eternally pressing, and Youth calling for Injoyment, he doubted the Constancy of her Mind; for his Circumstances wavering in an old Man's Breast, he cou'd not entertain the hopes of Matrimony till his Uncle's Death: But the Lady having more sublime *Platonick* Notions of Love than the generality of her Sex, and her Passion not proceeding chiefly from sensual Inclinations, but being grounded on the more substantial Comforts of Life, thought Sir *Samuel*'s Welfare

---

[1] Usually spelled "termagant," the term denoted an overbearing woman, a shrew (the word comes from the name of a fictional heathen god in medieval epics).
[2] In the early 18th century, it usually referred to the belief of some that they had a direct line with God or, as Dr. Johnson defines it, a "vain confidence of divine favour or communication."

equally concern'd her self, resolv'd patiently to wait the Event of Fortune, and they were *Contracted* in the most solemn manner imaginable.[1]

Catherina then led a most reserv'd Life, was deny'd to former Pretenders, Sir *Samuel* visited her hourly, and his Conversation was to her the summ of all Gallantries; her *Female* Friends, who generally meet to do a *little Work and have a great deal of Tittle-tattle*, were often levelling at her their malicious Artillery of—*mutual Bliss, Extatick Joys, Fading Charms*, and such Stuff, whom she heard with Temper and rally'd with Modesty; and tho' the Old Fellow had the Conscience to grunt out twice Seven Years, she kept her Faith inviolate with a most miraculous ease and inimitable Abstinence; at last the Infernal Powers wondering he staid so long, demanded his appearance, and the Nephew possess'd himself of a fine Seat, a large Estate, and a very ancient Title, all too little a Reward for *Catherina*'s Constancy: He continued his Visits to her, but *Business now multiplying upon him*, was his pretence, that they were not so frequent as formerly; he sometimes mention'd the *Contract*, but with unusual Coldness; *her Fortune he knew to be but small, and his Uncle was ever against the Match*: In short, he slited her by degrees, and at last most inhumanly threw her off.

Before the disconsolate *Catherina* let us draw a Veil, her Griefs must be inexpressible, tho' she ought to raise 'em to Resentments; and as she has Power yet left to prostrate Millions at her Shrine, she ought to summon ev'ry Charm, point ev'ry Glance, and pursue 'em with the Coquetry of *Smiles, Frowns, Complaisancy and Disdain, all the Crocadile Arts of designing Woman, and the inveterate Malice of neglected Beauty*, till she has reveng'd the Injuries done her by the perfidious *Strephon*[2] on his whole hated Race. But as the tenderness of her Sex rather supposes her dissolv'd in Tears, we ought to soften her Afflictions, Reason her into Calmness, and muster all our Forces to punish such unheard of Perjuries. Lady *Termigant* wou'd have had him flea'd alive, Mrs. *Romance* was for *exposing the Monster in an Iron Cage like the Tyrant* Bajazet, and Mrs. *Postscript* wou'd have had the Match made an *Article of the Peace*;[3] however, *Catherina* thus abandoned, Sir *Samuel* runs a *Fortune Hunting*, but Mrs. *Townly* had so told it in *Gath*, and published it in the Streets of *Askelon*,[4] that the *Court Ladies* were

[1] An engagement or act of betrothal was also called "contract" (noun and verb).
[2] Strephon was a common name in (pastoral) poetry for a young man in love. In Greek mythology, Strephon was an Arcadian shepherd who mourned the loss of his beloved.
[3] Bayezid I, Ottoman Sultan (1389-1403) was captured by Tamerlane at the Battle of Ankara in 1402 and exhibited in a cage. Introducing articles of the peace means making a formal civil complaint to a justice of the peace (so that the contract be respected).
[4] In the Bible, King David says to Saul and Jonathan: "The beauty of Israel is slain upon thy high places: how are the mighty fallen! Tell it not in Gath, publish it not in the streets of Askelon; lest the daughters of the Philistines rejoice, lest the daughters of the uncircumcised triumph" (2 Samuel 1:19-20). "Tell it not in Gath" is a saying used to discourage references to something disgraceful or discreditable.

1709

as apprehensive of him, as some People are of *a Cat*; the *City Ladies* jeer'd him, and the *Country Ladies* spit at him.

The Knight was not the least daunted at these Repulses, *Ill Principles must be supported with a good Assurance*; and pursuing his fantastick Adorations, at last fix'd upon *Blowzabella*[1] in *Charter-house Yard*, a Creature of that Pride, that she cou'd away with any thing to be a Baronet's Lady; her Family was perfectly cut out for such an Alliance; her Father was an Apothecary, the most *Crabbed, Crafty, Covetous* and *Fallacious* of his Trade, who, when he had once perswaded People they were Sick, gave 'em Medicines which really made 'em so; he less concern'd himself with the Patient's Death, than whether there were *Assids*[2] to pay his Bill; was ever making out his unreasonable unintelligible Scrawls, impatient for the Money, and implacable at an excuse, yet refus'd to pay the least Family Debt he ow'd others. The World knowing him to be a substantial Man, tho' a *Humourist*,[3] gave him unlimited Credit for ev'ry thing; and as his Receipts were numerous and his Disbursements few, his Coffers swell'd to a mighty height; but a long Series of Time making People grow impatient for their Money, which his Soul cou'dn't part with, and his Creditors finding Threats and Intreaties were to the same Purpose, at last threw himself into a Gaol; during his many Years' Confinement, his Wife and Daughters appear'd very mournful, both in Habit and Countenance, and their Father, to give eternal Proof of his Probity, dy'd in Prison, rather than he wou'd pay his Debts. Mrs. *Julip* soon dissipated her Tears, and chang'd the Melancholy Scene. She was now a rich Widow, her Daughters great Fortunes,[4] and they soon display'd themselves in their glaring Equipage; 'tis true, the baffl'd World may rail a little, but the ratling of the Charriot Wheels drowns the disagreeable Noise, and those that keep Coaches despise the petty Reflections of Creatures that walk a foot.

Sir *Samuel* was received here with all the Ceremony of City Affectation; *Preliminaries* soon adjusted, the Parties being eager on both sides, and they were *tack'd* together about three Weeks past. *The Bridegroom* having abandon'd Truth, Honour and Honesty, *Breeding, Gentility, and ev'ry agreeable Air* have fled from him, and he appears a most *Awkard, Tawdry, Tinsy old Fop of Fifty in White and Gold, Cherry and Silver Wastcoat, and Facings,*[5] and only wants *a Sword-knot, Shoulder-knot, and Cravat-string,*[6] to make him a compleat Sight. Lady

---

[1] Blowzabella is a character in Thomas d'Urfey 1699 tragedy *Massaniello*, the rude wife of a fisherman who makes ridiculous attempts to pass for a lady.

[2] Assets; the word comes from the French "assez" (sufficient), but it was sometimes mistakenly assumed to come directly from a Latin root.

[3] Dr. Johnson's dictionary defines "humorist" as "One who conducts himself by his own fancy; one who gratifies his own humour" or (with an older meaning) "One who has violent and peculiar passions."

[4] That is, great matches.

[5] Tins(e)y (related to "tinsel") means gaudy; facings were the cuffs and collar of a jacket or, by extension, ornaments.

[6] All three were ornamental ribbons placed on the sword's hilt, on the shoulder or around the tie; they could be enriched by jewels.

Bride is perfectly *the Queen of Diamonds*; her *Necklace, Pendants* and *Sparkling Nosegay*, the product of her Father's *Cozenage*, show her to be *Aesop's Jay deck'd with borrow'd Plumes*,[1] ev'ry Bird ought to seize his own, and leave her *Paramour*, who has shown his Judgment in Beauty, and how much he prefers it to Gold, by slighting the Fair, the charming *Catherina* with no despicable Fortune for the *ill-turn'd Blowzabella*, who has a larger supply, tho' of unprosperous Wealth, to new rig her[2] according to his manifest Generosity.

1709

---

[1] Conventionally known as "The Bird in Borrowed Feathers," the fable was known at the time as Aesop's "The Jay and the Peacock"; "cozenage" means cheating, fraud.

[2] The phrase, more frequently used by sailors, could also mean to change one's outfit entirely. In the prose commentary to his own *The Fable of the Bees* (1714; the poem had been published alone in 1705), Bernard Mandeville speaks of "A highwayman having met with a considerable booty, gives a poor common harlot, he fancies, ten pounds to new rig her from top to toe." In *The History of Charlotte Summers*, Sarah Fielding uses it as follows: "He was much out of repair in clothes and linen, and looked monstrous shabby, but she found means to new rig him very handsomely."

JOSEPH ADDISON

The Great Newsmonger (1710)

The author: Joseph Addison (1672-1719) was born in Wiltshire and grew up in Lichfield, where his father was dean of the cathedral. He was seven weeks younger than his friend Richard Steele, whom he met both at Charterhouse School and at Oxford. He wrote Latin poetry and received a travelling grant from King William, which allowed him a lengthy stay in Europe until 1704. When he returned, he published a well-received travelogue, *Remarks on Several Parts of Italy* (1705). His poem "The Campaign," celebrating Marlborough's victory at Blenheim, helped him start a career in politics. A devoted Whig and member of the Kit-Cat Club, he held several government jobs in the early 18th century. When Steele started *The Tatler*, Addison was in Dublin, as Chief Secretary to the Marquis of Wharton, Lord-Lieutenant of Ireland, and Keeper of the Irish Records. He soon became a trusted contributor, and Steele later acknowledged his worth: "This good office he performed with such force of genius, humour, wit and learning, that I fared like a distressed Prince, who calls in a powerful neighbour to his aid; I was undone by my auxiliary; when I had once called him in, I could not subsist without dependance on him."

The text: Addison was likely inspired by the personality of a real-life upholsterer, the father of Thomas Arne (1710-1778), the musician. The character of the upholsterer reappeared in No 160 of *The Tatler* (another text by Addison), as one of several people who disturb Bickerstaff's sleep with news from abroad, and then in Steele's essay on Don Quixote (no 178). Finally, in No 232 (3 October 1710), Steele inserted a letter from the upholsterer, with comments on the foreign news and the way they are reported in different newspapers. In 1757, Arthur Murphy (1727-1805) adapted the story into a farce in two acts: *The Upholsterer, or, What News?* (with Richard Yates and David Garrick in the main roles, it was one of the successes of 1758 at the Covent Garden).

It first appeared unsigned and untitled in *The Tatler* 155 (Thursday 6 April 1710). In the Index to Steele's revised edition of *The Tatler*, it is thrice identified as: "Upholsterer, Mr. Bickerstaff's Neighbour, a great Newsmonger," "Upholsterer Broke," and "Upholsterer His Conversation with Mr. Bickerstaff in the Park." In later reprints, it appears in the table of contents as "Character of the Upholsterer—A great Politician." It was introduced by a quote from Horace (3 Sat. ii, 19): "Aliena negotia curat,/Excussus propriis." ("When he had lost all business of his own,/ He ran in quest of news through all the town.") The following is taken from *The Lucubrations of Isaac Bickerstaff, Esq; Revised and Corrected by the Author* (London: E. Nutt, at *Middle Temple Gate*, in *Fleetstreet*, 1716), Vol. III, 201-205.

Further reading: Brian William Cowan. "Mr. Spectator and the Coffeehouse Public Sphere." *Eighteenth-Century Studies* 37.3 (Spring 2004): 345-366.

From my own apartment, April 5.

There lived some Years since within my Neighbourhood a very grave Person, an Upholsterer, who seemed a Man of more than ordinary Application to Business. He was a very early Riser, and was often abroad Two or Three Hours before any of his Neighbours. He had a particular Carefulness in the knitting of his Brows, and a kind of Impatience in all his Motions, that plainly discovered he was always intent on Matters of Importance. Upon my Enquiry into his Life and Conversation, I found him to be the greatest Newsmonger in our Quarter, that he rose before Day to read the *Post Man*; and that he would take Two or Three Turns to the other End of the Town before his Neighbours were up, to see if there were any *Dutch* Mails come in.[1] He had a Wife and several Children; but was much more inquisitive to know what passed in *Poland* than in his own Family, and was in greater Pain and Anxiety of Mind for King *Augustus*'s Welfare than that of his nearest Relations.[2] He looked extremely thin in a Dearth of News, and never enjoyed himself in a Westerly Wind.[3] This indefatigable kind of Life was the Ruin of his Shop; for about the Time that his Favourite Prince left the Crown of *Poland*, he broke and disappeared.

This Man and his Affairs had been long out of my Mind, till about Three Days ago, as I was walking in St. *James*'s Park, I heard some body at a Distance hemming after me: And who should it be but my old Neighbour the Upholsterer? I saw he was reduced to extreme Poverty, by certain shabby Superfluities in his Dress: For notwithstanding that it was a very sultry Day for the Time of the Year, he wore a loose great Coat and a Muff, with a long Campaign-Wig out of Curl;[4] to which he had added the Ornament of a Pair of black Garters buckled under the Knee. Upon his coming up to me, I was going to enquire into his present Circumstances; but was prevented by his asking me, with a Whisper, Whether the last Letters brought any Accounts that one might rely upon from *Bender*?[5] I told him, None that I heard of; and asked him, Whether he had yet married his eldest Daughter? He told me, No. But pray, says he, tell me sincerely, What are your Thoughts of the King of *Sweden*?

1710

[1] The mail from France and Holland arrived on Tuesdays and Fridays.
[2] Augustus II the Strong (1670-1733) was king of Poland from 1697 to 1706, when he was deposed by the invading Swedish troops of Charles XII, but he was restored in 1709, after Peter the Great defeated Charles XII at the Battle of Poltava.
[3] A westerly wind is not favourable to ships coming from the continent and, as Addison said elsewhere, it "keeps the whole town in suspence, and puts a stop to conversation."
[4] A campaign wig (or travelling wig) had bobs on each side and a curled fore-head.
[5] Bender (originally, the Moldavian city of Tighina) was at the time a fortress controlled by the Ottoman Empire, where Charles XII found refuge after Poltava.

For tho' his Wife and Children were starving, I found his chief Concern at present was for this great Monarch. I told him That I looked upon him as one of the first Heroes of the Age.[1] But pray, says he, do you think there is any Thing in the Story of his Wound?" And finding me surprised at the Question, Nay, says he, I only propose it to you. I answered, That I thought there was no Reason to doubt of it. But why in the Heel, says he, more than in any other Part of the Body? Because, says I, the Bullet chanced to light there.

This extraordinary Dialogue was no sooner ended, but he began to launch out into a long Dissertation upon the Affairs of the *North*; and after having spent some Time on them, he told me, He was in a great Perplexity how to reconcile the *Supplement* with the *English-Post*, and had been just now examining what other Papers say upon the same Subject. The *Daily Courant*, says he, has these Words, *We have Advices from very good Hands, That a certain Prince has some Matters of great Importance under Consideration.* This is very mysterious; *but the Post-Boy* leaves us more in the Dark, for he tells us, *That there are private Intimations of Measures taken by a certain Prince, which Time will bring to Light.* Now the *Post-Man*, says he, who uses to be very clear, refers to the same News in these Words; *The late Conduct of a certain Prince affords great Matter of Speculation.* This certain Prince, says the Upholsterer, whom they are all so cautious of naming, I take to be ———. Upon which, tho' there was no Body near us, he whispered something in my Ear, which I did not hear, or think worth my while to make him repeat.

We were now got to the upper End of the *Mall*,[2] where were Three or Four very odd Fellows sitting together upon the Bench. These I found were all of them Politicians, who used to Sun themselves in that Place every Day about Dinner-Time. Observing them to be Curiosities in their Kind, and my Friend's Acquaintance, I sat down among them.

The chief Politician of the Bench was a great Asserter of Paradoxes. He told us, with a seeming Concern, That by some News he had lately read from *Muscovy*, it appeared to him that there was a Storm gathering in the Black Sea, which might in Time do Hurt to the Naval Forces of this Nation. To this he added, That for his Part, he could not wish to see the Turk driven out of *Europe*, which he believed could not but be prejudicial to our Woollen Manufacture. He then told us, That he looked upon those extraordinary Revolutions which had lately happened in these Parts of the World, to have risen chiefly from Two Persons who were not much talked of; and those, says he, are Prince *Menzikoff*, and the Dutchess of

---

[1] Charles XII (1682-1718), King of Sweden (1697-1718) was the central figure of the Great Northern War (1700-1721), fought especially between the rival empires of Russia and Sweden. He was widely seen at the time as a new Alexander the Great.

[2] The Mall is a road in Westminster, created in the first years of the reign of Charles II as part of the improvements brought to St James's Park. It was the most fashionable street in London in the first half of the 18th century.

47

Mirandola.[1] He back'd his Assertions with so many broken Hints, and such a Show of Depth and Wisdom, that we gave our selves up to his Opinions.

The Discourse at length fell upon a Point which seldom escapes a Knot of true born *Englishmen,* Whether in Case of a Religious War, the Protestants would not be too strong for the Papists? This we unanimously determined on the Protestant Side. One who sat on my Right Hand, and, as I found by his Discourse, had been in the *West-Indies,* assured us, That it would be a very easy Matter for the Protestants to beat the Pope at Sea; and added, That whenever such a War does break out, it must turn to the Good of the *Leeward* Islands.[2] Upon this, one who sat at the End of the Bench, and, as I afterwards found, was the Geographer of the Company, said, that in case the Papists should drive the Protestants from these Parts of *Europe,* when the worst came to the worst, it would be impossible to beat them out of *Norway* and *Greenland,* provided the Northern Crowns hold together, and the Czar of *Muscovy* stand Neuter.

He further told us for our Comfort, That there were vast Tracts of Land about the Pole, inhabited neither by Protestants nor Papists, and of greater Extent that all the *Roman* Catholick Dominions in *Europe.*

When we had fully discussed this Point, my Friend the Upholsterer began to exert himself upon the Present Negotiations of Peace, in which he deposed Princes, settled the Bounds of Kingdoms, and Ballanced the Power of *Europe,* with great Justice and Impartiality.

I at length took my Leave of the Company, and was going away; but had not been gone Thirty Yards, before the Upholsterer hemm'd again after me. Upon his advancing towards me, with a Whisper, I expected to hear some secret Piece of News, which he had not thought fit to communicate to the Bench; but instead of that, he desired me in my Ear to lend him Half a Crown. In Compassion to so needy a Statesman, and to dissipate the Confusion I found he was in, I told him, if he pleased, I would give him Five Shillings, to receive Five Pounds of him when the Great Turk was driven out of *Constantinople,* which he very readily accepted, but not before he had laid down to me the Impossibility of such an Event, as the Affairs of *Europe* now stand.

This Paper I design for the particular Benefit of those worthy Citizens who live more in a Coffee-house than in their Shops, and whose Thoughts are so taken up with the Affairs of the Allies, that they forget their Customers.

[1] Prince Alexander Danilovich Menshikov (1673-1729) was a Russian general and close friend of Peter the Great. The Duchess of Mirandola, on the other hand, is a reference to Brigida Pico (1633-1720), regent of the duchy of Mirandola, in Italy, from 1691 to 1706. Addison suggests here that the upholsterer is also a conspiracy theorist.
[2] The Leeward Islands are the northern Lesser Antilles (Antigua, Barbuda, Montserrat, Saint Christopher, Nevis, Anguilla, and the Virgin Islands), a British colony after 1671.

1710

JOSEPH ADDISON
Adventures of a Shilling
(1710)

The author: Soon after the commencement of *The Tatler*, Addison became an Irish MP for Cavan, but he divided his time between Dublin and London. In September 1710, he started his first periodical, *The Whig Examiner*; in October he became MP for Malmesbury, a UK constituency. All this time, he continued writing for his friend's journal: of the 271 numbers of *The Tatler*, Steele was directly responsible for 188, Addison for 41 (but he contributed to another 28).

The text: First published, untitled, in *The Tatler* 249 (Saturday, 11 November 1710), it appeared in the contents of the volume format as "Adventures of a Shilling." It had a motto from Virgil: "Per varios casus, per tot discrimina rerum,/ Tendimus——" ("Through so many crises and calamities/ We make for——"; the missing destination is Latium in Virgil's poem, but here it remains unnamed). The following is from *The Lucubrations of Isaac Bickerstaff, Esq; Revised and Corrected by the Author* (London: E. Nutt, at the Middle Temple Gate, in *Fleetstreet*, 1716), Vol. IV, 261-265.

Further reading: Aileen Douglas. "Britannia's Rule and the It-Narrator." *Eighteenth-Century Fiction* 6.1 (October 1993): 65-82.

Mark Blackwell, Ed. *The Secret Life of Things: Animals, Objects, and It-Narratives in Eighteenth-Century England*. Lewisburg: Bucknell UP, 2007.

THE

LUCUBRATIONS

OF

Iſaac Bickerſtaff Eſq;

Reviſed and Corrected by the Author.

VOL I.

'Οὐ χρὴ παννύχιον εὕδειν βουληφόρον ἄνδρα.
Homer.

LONDON,

Printed by *John Nutt*, and ſold by *John Morphew*, near *Stationers-Hall.* MDCCXII.

1710

From my own Apartment, Nov. 10.

I was last Night visited by a Friend of mine who has an inexhaustible Fund of Discourse, and never fails to entertain his Company with a Variety of Thoughts and Hints that are altogether new and uncommon. Whether it were in Complaisance to my Way of Living, or his real Opinion, he advanced the following Paradox, That it required much greater Talents to fill up and become a retired Life, than a Life of Business. Upon this Occasion he rallied very agreeably the busie Men of the Age, who only valued themselves for being in Motion, and passing through a Series of trifling and insignificant Actions. In the Heat of his Discourse, seeing a Piece of Money lying on my Table, I defie (says he) any of these active

49

Persons to produce half the Adventures that this Twelvepenny-Piece has been engaged in, were it possible for him to give us an Account of his Life.

My friend's Talk made so odd an Impression upon my Mind, that soon after I was a-Bed I fell insensibly into a most unaccountable *Resverie*, that had neither Moral nor Design in it, and cannot be so properly called a Dream as a Delirium.

Methoughts the Shilling that lay upon the Table reared it self upon its Edge, and turning the Face towards me, opened its Mouth, and in a soft Silver Sound gave me the following Account of his Life and Adventures:

I was born, says he, on the Side of a Mountain, near a little Village of *Peru*, and made a Voyage to *England* in an Ingot, under the Convoy of Sir *Francis Drake*. I was, soon after my Arrival, taken out of my *Indian* Habit, refined, naturalized, and put into the *British* Mode, with the Face of Queen *Elizabeth* on one Side, and the Arms of the Country on the other. Being thus equipped, I found in me a wonderful Inclination to ramble, and visit all the Parts of the new World into which I was brought. The People very much favoured my natural Disposition, and shifted me so fast from Hand to Hand, that before I was Five Years old, I had travelled into almost every Corner of the Nation. But in the Beginning of my Sixth Year, to my unspeakable Grief, I fell into the Hands of a miserable old Fellow, who clapped me into an Iron Chest, where I found Five Hundred more of my own Quality who lay under the same Confinement. The only Relief we had, was to be taken out and counted over in the fresh Air every Morning and Evening. After an Imprisonment of several Years we heard some Body knocking at our Chest, and breaking it open with an Hammer. This we found was the old Man's Heir, who, as his Father lay a dying, was so good as to come to our Release: He separated us that very Day. What was the Fate of my Companions, I know not: As for my self, I was sent to the Apothecary's Shop for a Pint of Sack.[1] The Apothecary gave me to an Herb-Woman, the Herb-Woman to a Butcher, the Butcher to a Brewer, and the Brewer to his Wife, who made a Present of me to a Nonconformist Preacher. After this Manner I made my Way merrily through the World; for, as I told you before, we Shillings Love nothing so much as travelling. I sometimes fetched in a Shoulder of Mutton, sometimes a Play-Book, and often had the Satisfaction to treat a Templer at a Twelvepenny Ordinary,[2] or carry him with Three Friends to *Westminster Hall*.

In the Midst of this pleasant Progress which I made from Place to Place, I was arrested by a superstitious old Woman, who shut me up in a greasy Purse, in Pursuance of a foolish Saying, That while she kept a Queen *Elizabeth*'s Shilling about her, she should never be without Money. I continued here a close Prisoner for many Months, till at last I was exchanged for Eight and Forty Farthings.

---

[1] "Sack" was any kind of dry white wine imported from Spain (though the name is from the French for dry: "sec").

[2] An ordinary was an inn or a tavern where meals came with a fixed price (here, 12 pence) and gambling was de rigueur. A Templer (or Templar) was a barrister from the Inner or the Middle Temple.

I thus rambled from Pocket to Pocket till the Beginning of the Civil Wars, when (to my Shame be it spoken) I was employed in raising Soldiers against the King: For being of a very tempting Breadth, a Sarjeant made Use of me to inveigle Country Fellows, and list them in the Service of the Parliament.

As soon as he had made one Man sure, his Way was to oblige him to take a Shilling of a more homely Figure, and then practise the same Trick upon another. Thus I continued doing great Mischief to the Crown, till my officer chancing one Morning to walk Abroad earlier than ordinary, sacrificed me to his Pleasures, and made Use of me to seduce a Milk-Maid. This Wench bent me, and gave me to her Sweetheart, applying more properly than she intended the usual Form of, *To my Love and from my Love*. This ungenerous Gallant marrying her within few Days after, pawned me for a Dram of Brandy, and drinking me out next Day, I was beaten flat with an Hammer, and again set a running.

After many Adventures, which it would be tedious to relate, I was sent to a young Spendthrift, in Company with the Will of his deceased Father. The young Fellow, who I found was very extravagant, gave great Demonstrations of Joy at the receiving the Will; but opening it, he found himself disinherited and cut off from the Possession of a fair Estate, by Vertue of my being made a present to him. This put him into such a Passion, that after having taken me in his Hand, and cursed me, he squirred me away from him as far as he could fling me. I chanced to light in an unfrequented Place under a dead Wall, where I lay undiscovered and useless, during the Usurpation of *Oliver Cromwell*.

About a Year after the King's Return, a poor Cavalier that was walking there about Dinner-time fortunately cast his Eye upon me, and, to the great Joy of us both, carried me to a Cook's-Shop, where he dined upon me, and drank the King's Health. When I came again into the World, I found that I had been happier in my Retirement than I thought, having probably by that Means escaped wearing a monstrous Pair of Breeches.[1]

Being now of great Credit and Antiquity, I was rather looked upon as a Medal than an ordinary Coin; for which Reason a Gamester laid hold of me, and converted me into a Counter, having got together some Dozens of us for that Use.[2] We led a melancholy Life in his Possession, being busy at those Hours wherein Current Coin is at rest, and partaking the Fate of our Master, being in a few Moments valued at a Crown, a Pound, or a Sixpence, according to the Situation in which the Fortune of the Cards placed us. I had at length the good Luck to see my Master break, by which Means I was again sent Abroad under my primitive Denomination of a Shilling.

I shall pass over many other Accidents of less Moment, and hasten to that fatal Catastrophe when I fell into the Hands of an Artist who conveyed me under Ground, and with an unmerciful Pair of Sheers cut

[1] There were two shields on the shillings minted in Cromwell's time, but it was generally considered that they resembled breeches.

[2] A "counter" was a token used in gambling instead of real money.

off my Titles, clipped my Brims, retrenched my Shape, rubbed me to my inmost Ring, and, in short, so spoiled and pillaged me, that he did not leave me worth a Groat.[1] You may think what a Confusion I was in to see my self thus curtailed and disfigured. I should have been ashamed to have shown my Head, had not all my old Acquaintance been reduced to the same shameful Figure, excepting some few that were punched through the Belly. In the midst of this general Calamity, when every Body thought our Misfortune irretrievable, and our Case desperate, we were thrown into the Furnace together, and (as it often happens with Cities rising out of a Fire) appeared with greater Beauty and Lustre than we could ever boast of before. What has happened to me since this Change of Sex which you now see, I shall take some other Opportunity to relate. In the mean Time I shall only repeat Two Adventures, as being very extraordinary, and neither of them having ever happened to me above once in my Life. The First was, my being in a Poet's Pocket, who was so taken with the Brightness and Novelty of my Appearance, that it gave Occasion to the finest Burlesque Poem in the *British* Language, entituled from me, *The Splendid Shilling*.[2] The Second Adventure, which I must not omit, happened to me in the Year 1703, when I was given away in Charity to a blind Man; but indeed this was by Mistake, the Person who gave me having heedlessly thrown me into the Hat among a Pennyworth of Farthings.

1710

---

[1] A four-penny coin discontinued in 1662; the word still referred to anything of little value.
[2] John Philips (1676-1709) published *The Splendid Shilling* in 1705.

RICHARD STEELE
Inkle and Yarico (1711)

The author: On 2 January 1711, *The Tatler* ended: Steele admitted he had grown tired with the editorship of a tri-weekly and, when he realised that all the issues of the periodical fitted perfectly into four volumes, he decided to stop. However, when his friend Joseph Addison, who had helped edit *The Tatler*, started *The Spectator*, a daily publication, on 1 March 1711, he returned the favour: of the 555 numbers of the magazine's original run (until 6 December 1712), Steele contributed at least 257 texts. Addison, Steele, and the other contributors, used the persona of "Mr Spectator," a narrator who moved around, covering the social, political, and artistic life of London. *The Spectator* became the most successful essay-serial of the century and it was still widely read 200 years later. In 1713, Steele started another publication, *The Guardian*, and became MP for Stockbridge, but he was expelled because of a pamphlet issued in favour of the Hanoverian succession. When George I became king the following year and the Hanover dynasty began, Steele was knighted and he returned to Parliament. He was made governor of the Royal Company of Comedians in 1721 and, in 1722, he produced his fourth (and last) sentimental comedy, *The Conscious Lovers*. In 1726 he withdrew to Carmarthen, in Wales, his deceased wife's birthplace, where he died in 1729.

The text: The story of Inkle and Yarico is based on a passage from Richard Ligon's *A True & Exact History of the Island of Barbadoes* (1657; 2nd edition, 1673). Steele's version inspired *Inkle and Yarico*, a very successful opera written by Samuel Arnold with a libretto by George Colman the Younger, first staged in 1787. The original music has not survived and the opera was reconstructed several times in the late 20th and early 21st centuries. In Felsenstein's reader (see below), there are 20 versions of the story, almost all from the 18th century. Steele's story was first published, untitled, in *The Spectator* 11 (Tuesday, 13 March 1711), with an epigraph from Juvenal: "Dat veniam corvis, vexat censura columbas" ("The censor forgives the ravens but harasses the doves"). The following text reproduces that of *The Spectator*. The Ninth Edition (London: J. Tonson, at *Shakespear's-Head*, over-against *Katharine-street* in the *Strand*, 1728), Vol. I, 47-51.

Further reading: Frank Felsenstein, Ed. *English Trader, Indian Maid: Representing Gender, Race, and Slavery in the New World. An Inkle and Yarico Reader*. Baltimore: The Johns Hopkins UP, 1999.

Nicole Horejsi. "'A Counterpart to the Ephesian Matron': Steele's 'Inkle and Yarico' and a Feminist Critique of the Classics." *Eighteenth-Century Studies* 39:2 (Winter 2006). 201-226.

Lawrence Marsden Price, Ed. *Inkle and Yarico Album*. Berkeley: U of California P, 1937.

Arietta is visited by all Persons of both Sexes, who have any Pretence to Wit and Gallantry. She is in that time of Life which is neither affected with the Follies of Youth, or Infirmities of Age; and her Conversation is so mixed with Gaiety and Prudence, that she is agreeable both to the Young and the Old. Her Behaviour is very frank, without being in the least blameable; as she is out of the Tract of any amorous or ambitious Pursuits of her own, her Visitants entertain her with Accounts of themselves very freely, whether they concern their Passions or their Interests. I made her a Visit this Afternoon, having been formerly introduced to the Honour of her Acquaintance, by my friend WILL. HONEYCOMB,[1] who has prevail'd upon her to admit me sometimes into her Assembly, as a civil inoffensive Man. I found her accompanied with one Person only, a Common-Place Talker, who, upon my Entrance, arose, and after a very slight Civility set down again; then turning to *Arietta*, pursued his Discourse, which I found was upon the old Topick of Constancy in Love. He went on with great Facility in repeating what he talks every Day of his Life; and with the Ornaments of insignificant Laughs and Gestures, enforced his Arguments by Quotations out of Plays and Songs, which allude to the Perjuries of the Fair, and the general Levity of Women. Methought he strove to shine more than ordinarily in his Talkative Way, that he might insult my Silence, and distinguish himself before a Woman of *Arietta*'s Taste and Understanding. She had often an Inclination to interrupt him, but could find no Opportunity, till the Larum[2] ceased of it self; which it did not till he had repeated and murdered the celebrated Story of the *Ephesian* Matron.[3]

Arietta seemed to regard this Piece of Raillery as an Outrage done to her Sex; as indeed I have always observed that Women, whether out of a nicer Regard to their Honour, or what other Reason I cannot tell, are more sensibly touched with those general Aspersions which are cast upon their Sex, than Men are by what is said of theirs.

When she had a little recovered her self from the serious Anger she was in, she replied in the following manner.

Sir, When I consider how perfectly new all you have said on this Subject is, and that the Story you have given us is not quite two Thousand Years old, I cannot but think it a Piece of Presumption to dispute with you: But your Quotations put me in Mind of the Fable of the Lion and the Man. The Man walking with that noble Animal, shewed him, in the

[1] The "Gallant Will. Honeycomb" is one of The Spectator's circle of friends; he is "a Gentleman who according to his Years should be in the Decline of his Life, but having ever been very careful of his Person, and always had a very easie Fortune, Time has made but very little Impression, either by Wrinkles on his Forehead, or Traces in his Brain" (No 2, 2 March 1711).
[2] Clamour, tumult; originally, battle cry (alteration of "alarm").
[3] The "Matron of Ephesus" is an episode in Petronius's *Satyricon* (later retold in many variants) in which a widow mourning her husband while he is being buried is nevertheless ready to flirt with the first man passing by the tomb.

Ostentation of Human Superiority, a Sign of a Man killing a Lion. Upon which the lion said very justly, *We Lions are none of us Painters, else we could shew a hundred Men killed by Lions, for one Lion killed by a Man.* You Men are Writers, and can represent us Women as Unbecoming as you please in your Works, while we are unable to return the Injury. You have twice or thrice observed in your Discourse, that Hypocrisie is the very Foundation of our Education; and that an Ability to dissemble our Affections is a professed Part of our Breeding. These, and such other Reflections, are sprinkled up and down the Writings of all Ages, by Authors, who leave behind them Memorials of their Resentment against the Scorn of particular Women, in Invectives against the whole Sex. Such a Writer, I doubt not, was the celebrated *Petronius*, who invented the pleasant Aggravations of the Frailty of the *Ephesian* Lady; but when we consider this Question between the Sexes, which has been either a Point of Dispute or Raillery ever since there were Men and Women, let us take Facts from plain People, and from such as have not either Ambition or Capacity to embellish their Narrations with any Beauties of Imagination. I was the other Day amusing my self with *Ligon*'s Account of *Barbadoes*; and, in Answer to your well-wrought Tale, I will give you (as it dwells upon my Memory) out of that honest Traveller, in his fifty fifth page,[1] the History of *Inkle* and *Yarico*.

Mr. *Thomas Inkle*, of *London*, aged twenty Years, embarked in the *Downs*[2] on the good Ship called the *Achilles*, bound for the *West-Indies*, on the 16th of *June*, 1647, in order to improve his Fortune by Trade and Merchandize. Our Adventurer was the third Son of an eminent Citizen, who had taken particular Care to instil into his Mind an early Love of Gain, by making him a perfect Master of Numbers, and consequently giving him a quick View of Loss and Advantage, and preventing the natural Impulses of his Passions, by Prepossession towards his Interests. With a Mind thus turned, young *Inkle* had a Person every way agreeable, a ruddy Vigour in his Countenance, Strength in his Limbs, with Ringlets of fair Hair loosely flowing on his Shoulders. It happened, in the Course of the Voyage, that the *Achilles*, in some Distress, put into a Creek on the Main of *America*, in Search of Provisions: The Youth, who is the Hero of my Story, among others went ashore on this Occasion. From their first Landing they were observed by a Party of *Indians*, who hid themselves in the Woods for that Purpose. The *English* unadvisedly marched a great distance from the Shore into the Country, and were intercepted by the Natives, who slew the greatest Number of them. Our Adventurer escaped among others, by flying into a Forest. Upon his coming into a remote and pathless Part of the Wood, he threw himself, tired, and breathless, on a little Hillock, when an *Indian* Maid rushed from a Thicket behind him: After the first Surprize, they appeared mutually agreeable to each

[1] Arietta clearly read the 2nd edition of Richard Ligon's *A True & Exact History of the Island of Barbadoes* (London: Peter Parker, 1673), rather than the first edition of 1657.
[2] The area between the Strait of Dover and the estuary of the Thames.

other. If the *European* was highly Charmed with the Limbs, Features and wild Graces of the Naked *American*; the *American* was no less taken with the Dress, Complexion, and Shape of an *European*, covered from Head to Foot. The *Indian* grew immediately enamoured of him, and consequently sollicitous for his Preservation: She therefore conveyed him to a Cave, where she gave him a delicious Repast of Fruits, and led him to a Stream to slake his Thirst. In the midst of these good Offices, she would sometimes play with his Hair, and delight in the Opposition of its Colour to that of her Fingers: Then open his Bosom, then laugh at him for covering it. She was, it seems, a Person of Distinction, for she every Day came to him in a different Dress, of the most beautiful Shells, Bugles and Bredes.[1] She likewise brought him a great many Spoils, which her other Lovers had presented to her, so that his Cave was richly adorned with all the spotted Skins of Beasts, and most Party-coloured Feathers of Fowls, which that World afforded. To make his Confinement more tolerable, she would carry him in the Dusk of the Evening, or by the favour of Moon-light, to unfrequented Groves and Solitudes, and shew him where to lye down in safety, and sleep amidst the Falls of Waters, and Melody of Nightingales. Her part was to watch and hold him awake in her arms, for fear of her Country-men, and wake him on Occasions to consult his Safety. In this manner did the Lovers pass away their Time, till they had learned a Language of their own, in which the Voyager communicated to his Mistress, how happy he should be to have her in his Country, where she should be cloathed in such Silks as his Wastecoat was made of, and be carried in Houses drawn by Horses, without being exposed to Wind or Weather. All this he promised her the Enjoyment of, without such Fears and Alarms as they were there tormented with. In this tender Correspondence these Lovers lived for several Months, when *Yarico*, instructed by her Lover, discovered a Vessel on the Coast to which she made Signals; and in the Night, with the utmost Joy and Satisfaction, accompanied him to a Ship's-Crew of his Country-men, bound for *Barbadoes*. When a Vessel from the Main arrives in that Island, it seems the Planters come down to the Shore, where there is an immediate Market of the *Indians* and other Slaves, as with us of Horses and Oxen.

To be short, Mr. *Thomas Inkle*, now coming into *English* Territories, began seriously to reflect upon his loss of Time, and to weigh with himself how many Days Interest of his Money he had lost during his Stay with *Yarico*. This Thought made the young Man very pensive, and careful what Account he should be able to give his Friends of his Voyage. Upon which Considerations, the prudent and frugal young Man sold *Yarico* to a *Barbadian* Merchant; notwithstanding that the poor Girl, to incline him to commiserate her Condition, told him that she was with Child by him: But he only made use of that Information, to rise in his Demands upon the Purchaser.

[1] Archaic: ornamental embroidery or braiding.

I was to touch'd with this Story (which I think should be always a Counterpart to the *Ephesian* Matron) that I left the Room with Tears in my Eyes; which a Woman of *Arietta*'s good Sense, did, I am sure, take for greater Applause, than any Compliments I could make her.

N.B. The passage used by Steele actually begins on page 54 in Ligon's account and some details are differently related: "We had an *Indian* woman, a slave in the house, who was of excellent shape and colour, for it was a pure bright bay; small breasts, with the nipples of a porphyrie colour, this woman would not be woo'd by any means to wear Cloaths. She chanc'd to be with child, by a Christian servant, and lodging in the *Indian* house, amongst other [page 55] women of her own Country, where the Christian servants, both men and women came; and being very great, and that her time was come to be delivered, loath to fall in labour before the men, walk'd down to a Wood, in which was a Pond of water, and there by the side of the Pond, brought her self abed; and presently washing her Child in some of the water of the Pond, lap'd it up in such rags, as she had begg'd of the Christians; and in three hours time came home, with her Child in her arms, a lusty Boy, frolick and lively.

This *Indian* dwelling near the Sea-coast, upon the Main, an *English* ship put in to a Bay, and sent some of her men a shoar, to try what victuals or water they could find, for in some distress they were. But the *Indians* perceiving them to go up so far into the Country, as they were sure they could not make a safe retreat, intercepted them in their return, and fell upon them, chasing them into a Wood, and being dispersed there, some were taken, and some kill'd: but a young man amongst them stragling from the rest, was met by this *Indian* Maid, who upon the first sight fell in love with him, and hid him close from her Country-men (the *Indians*) in a Cave, and there fed him, till they could safely go down to the shoar, where the ship lay at anchor, expecting the return of their friends. But at last, seeing them upon the shoar, sent the long-Boat for them, took them aboard, and brought them away. But the youth, when he came ashoar in the *Barbadoes*, forgot the kindness of the poor maid, that had ventured her life for his safety, and sold her for a slave, who was as free born as he: And so poor *Yarico* for her love, lost her liberty."

JOSEPH ADDISON

In Search of the Philosopher's Stone (1713)

The author: In the spring of 1713, Addison was mostly preoccupied with the performance of his most famous play, *Cato, a Tragedy* (written in 1712, but first staged on 14 April 1713). Yet, he found time, as usual, to contribute to *The Guardian*, the new publishing venture of his good friend Richard Steele, which was started on 12 March of that year and folded on 1 October, after only five months and a half. Addison wrote for another two of Steele's projects: *The Reader* and *The Lover*, both from 1714. He edited himself *The Freeholder* (1715-1716) and *The Old Whig* (1719), the latter as a response to Steele's *The Plebeian*. The old friends were now at odds with each other and they may have reconciled, but Addison, now Secretary of State for the Southern Department (the equivalent of today's Foreign Office), was in poor health and died on 17 June 1719.

The text: First published, with no title, in *The Guardian* 166 (Monday, 21 September 1713). It was later anthologised with the title "On Charity—The Guardian in search of the Philosopher's Stone." The following text is reproduced from *The Guardian* (London: J. Tonson, at *Shakespear's-Head*, over-against *Catherine-Street* in the *Strand*, 1714), Vol. II, 308-311. It had an epigraph from Ovid's *Metamorphoses*: "aliquisque malo fuit usus in illo" ("let us derive some use or benefit from that evil"), which was not translated in the magazine, but which Addison later translated as "Some comfort from the mighty mischief rose." Interestingly, it was Richard Steele of whom it was rumoured that he had dabbled in alchemy and tried to discover "the philosopher's stone."

Charity is a Virtue of the Heart, and not of the Hands, says an old Writer. Gifts and Alms are the Expressions, not the Essence of this Virtue. A Man may bestow great Sums on the Poor and Indigent without being Charitable, and may be Charitable when he is not able to bestow any thing. Charity is therefore a Habit of good Will, or Benevolence, in the Soul, which disposes us to the Love, Assistance and Relief of Mankind, especially of those who stand in need of it. The poor Man who has this excellent frame of Mind, is no less intitled to the Reward of this Virtue than the Man who founds a College. For my own part, I am Charitable to an Extravagance this way. I never saw an Indigent Person in my Life, without reaching out to him some of this imaginary Relief. I cannot but Sympathise with every one I meet that is in Affliction; and if my Abilities were equal to my Wishes, there should be neither Pain nor Poverty in the World.

To give my Reader a right Notion of my self in this Particular, I shall present him with the secret History of one of the most remarkable Parts of my Life.

I was once engaged in search of the Philosophers Stone. It is frequently observ'd of Men who have been busied in this Pursuit, that tho' they have failed in their principal Design, they have however made such Discoveries in their way to it, as have sufficiently recompenced their Inquiries. In the same manner, tho' I cannot boast of my Success in that Affair, I do not repent of my engaging in it, because it produced in my Mind, such an habitual Exercise of Charity, as made it much better than perhaps it would have been, had I never been lost in so pleasing a Delusion.

As I did not question but I should soon have a new *Indies* in my Possession, I was perpetually taken up in considering how to turn it to the Benefit of Mankind. In order to it I employed a whole Day in walking about this great City, to find out proper Places for the Erection of Hospitals. I had likewise entertained that Project, which has since succeeded in another Place, of building Churches at the Court end of the Town, with this only difference, that instead of Fifty, I intended to have built a Hundred, and to have seen 'em all finished in less than one Year.[1]

St Paul's Cathedral being rebuilt under Christopher Wren's supervision.

I had with great Pains and Application got together a List of all the *French* Protestants; and by the best Accounts I could come at, had calculated the Value of all those Estates and Effects which every one of them had left in his own Country for the Sake of his Religion, being fully determined to make it up to him, and return some of them the double of what they had lost.

[1] Allusion to the Commission for Building Fifty New Churches, established in 1710 by an Act of Parliament. In the end, 12 new churches were built (the last one was finished in 1733), and the Commission also funded the reconstruction of five other churches. The "court end" of London is the West End, including Westminster.

As I was one Day in my Laboratory, my Operator, who was to fill my Coffers for me, and used to foot it from the other End of the Town every Morning, complain'd of a Sprain in his Leg, that he had met with over-against St. *Clement*'s Church. This so affected me, that as a standing Mark of my Gratitude to him, and out of Compassion to the rest of my Fellow-Citizens, I resolved to new Pave every Street within the Liberties,[1] and entered a *Memorandum* in my Pocket-book accordingly. About the same time I entertained some Thoughts of mending all the Highways on this side the *Tweed*,[2] and of making all the Rivers in *England* Navigable.

But the Project I had most at Heart was the settling upon every Man in *Great Britain* three Pounds a Year (in which Sum may be comprised, according to Sir *William Pettit*'s Observations, all the Necessities of Life) leaving to 'em whatever else they could get by their own Industry to lay out on Superfluities.[3]

I was above a Week debating in my self what I should do in the matter of *Impropriations*; but at length came to a Resolution to buy them all up, and restore 'em to the Church.[4]

As I was one Day walking near St. *Paul*'s I took some time to Survey that Structure, and not being entirely satisfied with it, though I could not tell why, I had some Thoughts of pulling it down, and building it up anew at my own Expence.

For my own part, as I have no Pride in me, I intended to take up with a Coach and six,[5] half a dozen Footmen, and live like a private Gentleman.

It happened about this time that publick Matters looked very gloomy, Taxes came hard, the War went on heavily, People complained of the great Burthens that were laid upon them: This made me resolve to set aside one Morning, to consider seriously the State of the Nation. I was the more ready to enter on it, because I was obliged, whether I would or no, to sit at home in my Morning Gown, having, after a most

[1] The "Liberties" represented the political and legal limits of the power of city government. The bounds of the "Liberties" were, roughly, the Tower of London to the east, and the Temple Bar, on Fleet Street, to the west. Beyond these Liberties were Westminster and the suburbs. Poverty and crime were high in the Liberties. They were hit by the plague in 1665, but largely spared by the Great Fire, which meant that the area was not rebuilt; so, at the time, it was one the most squalid areas of London. St Clement Danes is in Westminster, outside the Royal Courts of Justice on the Strand.

[2] The flow of the Tweed is part of the historic boundary between Scotland and England.

[3] William Petty (1623-1687), famous economist. Boswell quotes Samuel Johnson's remark in 1763 that, as times had changed, the sum of six pounds seemed more appropriate then. However, he also notes that he has been unable to find the passage where Petty fixes the allowance at 3 pounds. Perhaps Johnson found it in Addison.

[4] Impropriation, very controversial throughout the 17th century, was former church property that had come into lay hands after the Dissolution of the Monasteries.

[5] A "coach and six" was a coach drawn by six horses.

1713

incredible Expence, pawned a new Suit of Cloaths, and a Full-bottomed Wig,[1] for a Sum of Mony which my Operator assured me was the last he should want to bring all our Matters to bear. After having considered many Projects, I at length resolved to beat the common Enemy at his own Weapons, and laid a Scheme which would have him blown up in a Quarter of a Year, had things succeeded to my Wishes. As I was in this golden Dream some-body knocked at my Door. I opened it, and found it was a Messenger that brought me a Letter from the Laboratory. The Fellow looked so miserably poor, that I was resolved to make his Fortune before he deliver'd his Message: but seeing he brought a Letter from my Operator, I concluded I was bound to it in Honour, as much as a Prince is to give a Reward to one that brings him the first News of a Victory. I knew this was the long-expected Hour of Projection, and which I had waited for, with great Impatience, above half a Year before. In short, I broke open my Letter in a transport of Joy, and found it as follows.

"SIR,
After having got out of you every thing you can conveniently spare, I scorn to trespass upon your generous Nature, and therefore must ingenuously confess to you, that I know no more of the Philosophers Stone than you do. I shall only tell you for your Comfort, that I never yet could bubble a Blockhead out of his Mony. They must be Men of Wit and Parts who are for my Purpose. This made me apply my self to a Person of your Wealth and Ingenuity. How I have succeeded you your self can best tell.
Your humble Servant to command,
Thomas White.
I have locked up the Laboratory, and laid the Key under the Door."

I was very much shocked at the unworthy Treatment of this Man, and not a little mortified at my Disappointment, tho' not so much for what I my self, as what the Publick suffered by it. I think however I ought to let the World know what I designed for them, and hope that such of my Readers who find they had a Share in my good Intentions, will accept of the Will for the Deed.[2]

---

[1] A wig with a large lower portion; today worn only by judges on formal occasions.
[2] Variant of the proverbial phrase "to take the will for the deed," i.e., give credit for one's good intentions, similar to the phrase "it is the thought that counts."

THOMAS GORDON

A Country Entertainment (1718)

The author: Thomas Gordon was probably born in 1691 somewhere in Kirkcudbright, Scotland. He almost surely went to one of the Scottish universities, but very little is certain about his life in general and his youth in particular. He was a government spy, like Defoe, only more secretive, working first for Robert Harley (the de facto chief minister of Queen Anne) and then for Robert Walpole. When he was in his mid-twenties, Gordon became close to John Trenchard (1662-1723) and it is especially due to his collaboration with the older writer that he is remembered today.

The text: First published in *The Weekly Packet* No 339 (Saturday, 27 December 1718 – Saturday, 3 January, 1719, 1-2) as the fourth instalment of Gordon's essay-series "The Humourist." When the series was collected in book format, this piece was entitled "Of a Country Entertainment." The following text is from *The Humourist: Being Essays upon Several Subjects* (London: W. Boreham at the *Angel* in *Paternoster Row*, 1720) [Vol. I], 18-24. More than a century later, William Thackeray admired this story as a model of humorous depiction of country manners.

Further reading: J. M. Bulloch. *Thomas Gordon: The "Independent Whig."* Aberdeen: At the University Press, 1918.

I am led by the Regard which I bear to the Ladies and the *Christmass-Holidays*, to divert my Readers with the History of an Entertainment, where I made one, at the House of a Country 'Squire, this Time Twelve-month.

When I went in, I found the Dining-Room full of Ladies, to every one of whom I made a profound Bow, and was repaid in a whole Circle of Court'sies; but whether out of Respect to my Person, or my Lac'd Hat, I cannot say. Having, after some Ceremony, taken a Seat amongst them, we had profound Silence for near half a Minute, notwithstanding the Number of Ladies present. For my Part, I had fix'd my Eyes upon the Fire, meditating with myself what I had best to say. While I was in this Study, I could hear one of them whisper to another, *I believe he thinks we smoak Tobacco*; for, my Reader must know, I had omitted the Country Fashion, and not kiss'd one of them.

At last, says one of them to me, *Sir, it is very fine Weather. Mighty fine Weather, Madam*, says I to her again. Says another, *Dr. Partridge*[1]

[1] John Partridge (1644-1715), popular astrologer, made (in)famous in a 1708 hoax perpetrated by Jonathan Swift who pretended to be a rival astrologer called "Isaac Bickerstaff" (a name later borrowed by Richard Steele for his *Tatler*) and first predicted and then "confirmed" Partridge's death. Partridge spent the last years of his life trying to prove he was still alive. His almanac, the *Merlinus Liberatus*, continued to appear after 1715 (under the care of his wife), with the epigraph "Etiam mortuus loquitur" ("He, being dead, yet speaks").

has guess'd well this Bout. *Hang Dr. Partridge*, cries a little smart Widow in the Company, *he has prophesy'd the Downfal of the poor Pope I know not how often; but, God be thank'd,— Marry hang the Pope*, replies a jolly red-fac'd Woman, with a great Wart upon her Nose, *the Pope! Heaven keep us from that filthy Fellow and all his Family. Did you never read of that Popish Heathen Queen* Mary, *how she made Bonfires of all the poor Folk, that would not go to her bloody Mass, and fall down on their Knees to a Piece of rotten Wood? No, no, any Thing but the Pope as you love me: Boy, give me a Glass of Wine, and fill it up, for I am dry with Talking. Aye, aye,* quoth one that had not spoke before, *the Pope is a hopeful one, you may read enough of him and his Harlots in the* Revelations.—She was just going to tell us the Chapter and Verse, when up came a Fellow groaning under a great Chine of Bacon, and an overgrown two Year old Turkey, which put an End to this edifying Dialogue.

At Dinner we had many Excuses from the Lady of the House *for our indifferent Fare*, and she had as many Declarations from us, her Guests, that *all was very good*. And the 'Squire gave us the History and Extraction of every Fowl that came to the Table: He assur'd us, that his Poultry had neither Kindred nor Allies any where on this Side the Channel, except in his own Backside.

As soon as we were risen from Table, our great Parliament of Females presently resolv'd themselves into Committees of Twos and Threes all over the Dining-Room; and I perceiv'd that every Party was upon a different Subject.

In one Corner there was a learned Gentlewoman, who talk'd much of Steel-Waters,[1] and I think she said something about opening a Vein in the Ankle. Upon casting my Eyes that Way, I saw a pale-fac'd Girl of Eighteen list'ning to her with great Attention.

Another Knot of them were lamenting, in their Way, an unhappy young Woman, whose Name I could not hear: *Poor unfortunate Wretch*, cries one, *she fainted away at Church last* Sunday. *Aye*, says a second, *and well she might, she girds herself so strait in her Stays. And yet*, answers a third, *she can't hide it neither. Hide it*, says a fourth, *that's impossible; why, she has been Squeamish this Quarter's Year, and fainted the other Day at the Sight of a Lobster. And yet, let me tell you*, says the first, *they say he wont marry, her after all*. Much more was said on this Affair; but all the four happening to talk at the same Time, I could not, in that Confusion of Tongues, distinguish any other Particulars.

A Cabal under the Window seem'd to be more secret than all the rest, and from them I could only bring away the following Whisper.— *'Tis certainly so; he was seen come out of her Window at Two in the Morning, and in half an Hour her Husband came Home: But Murder will out one time or other.*

A Detachment of the Sex, that besieg'd the Fire, were exceeding severe upon one Mrs. *Bulkey*, who had not one Advocate among them:

1718

---

[1] Popular medicines containing iron included steel drops, steel water, and steel wine.

Every Limb, every Feature of her was faulty; she had nothing about her that was not monstrous and frightful. *She, a Coach!* cry'd Mrs. *Meagre, a Lumber-Cart is fitter for the great Mortar-Piece;"* and to this they all agreed. By which I perceiv'd that this same Coach was the great Grievance and Offence, and added extreamly to the poor Gentlewoman's Deformity. *I saw,* continu'd Mrs. *Meagre, the great greasy Thing the other Night at a Christ'ning in the Close!*[1]*—but such a tawdry unweildy Porpoise! well! She had on Bridles as clumsy as Cable-Ropes, and they stood staring half a Mile from her Chaps,*[2] *as if they had been afraid of her fiery Nose: And then that oily Face of hers!—it shin'd with its own native Liquor like a new-open'd Oyster; but I'll swear it did not smell half so sweet: And yet,* says another, *her Husband is extreamly fond of her,—Civil to her, you mean,* says the next, *I suppose he puts her Head in a Pillow-Bear.*[3] At which they all sneer'd.

Being naturally tender-hearted, I could hear no more of this unmerciful Treatment of poor Mrs. *Bulkey,* and therefore stole towards a Cluster of Wives, who, I observ'd, were calling for a Bible to decide a Dispute they had enter'd into, *whether Minc'd-Pies or Plum-Porridge were the properest Food on Christmas-Day.* A devout old Lady argu'd against Plumb-Porridge, *which being a kind a Broth or Jelly, was,* she said, *a carnal Repast, apt to stir up Concupiscence and ill Thoughts, and consequently unfit for that holy Time.* You cannot imagine with what Warmth this abstemious old Woman was answer'd by a couple of Ladies thirty Years younger than herself. *What!* cry'd they, *an unfit Repast for that holy Time! Why, 'tis a Festival Time, in which we ought to be merry ourselves, and endeavour to make those who belong to us so: For my part,* said one of them, *I hope to go to Bed with a chearful and willing Heart every Night in the Holy-days, and I hope the same of Mr.——* here she nam'd her Husband. The old Woman smil'd, and shaking her Head and Sighing, as if Age had been her greatest Grief, was falling into a Discourse about Husbands, Capons, and Marrow-Bones; but, to my great Sorrow, a Call to the Tea-Table put a Stop to this delightful Controversy.

They went into one Parlour to their Tea, and we Men into another to our Bottle; over which I was entertain'd with many ingenious Remarks on the Price of Barley, on Dairies, and the Sheepfold. But as the most engaging Conversation is, when too long, sometimes cloying, having smoak'd my Pipe in due Silence and Attention, I took a Trip to the Ladies, who had sent to know whether I would drink some Tea. Before I enter'd their Door, I halted a little, to know what they were upon; and, to my Surprize, heard them mention myself. They said I was a meer Mum-chance;[4] for that I had not spoke six Words since I came in. I would

[1] An enclosed space, especially beside or surrounding a cathedral or other building.
[2] "Bridles" or "brides" were bonnet strings, usually of lace; the "chaps" are the cheeks.
[3] Also "pillow-bere": a pillowcase.
[4] "Mumchance" means tongue-tied; a person that has nothing to say.

have evesdropp'd them a while longer, but that I was jealous they might call in Question my other Abilities, as well as that of Speaking, so in I bolted. When I made my Entrance, the Topic they were on was Religion; in their Sentiments about which they were terribly divided, and debated with such Agitation and Fervour, that I grew in Pain for the *China* Cups. But they happily departed from this warm Point, and unanimously fell a backbiting their Neighbours, which instantly qualify'd all their Heat, and heartily reconcil'd them to one another, insomuch, that all the Time the Business of Scandal was handling, there was not one dissenting Voice to be heard in the whole Assembly.

By this Time the Musick was come, and happy was the Woman that could first wipe her Mouth, and be soonest upon her Legs. In the Dance some mov'd very becomingly, but the Majority made such a Rattle on the Boards, as quite drown'd the Musick. This made me call to Mind your mettlesome Horses, that dance on a Pavement to the Musick of their own Heels.

We had among us the 'Squire's eldest Son, a Batchelor and Captain of the Militia. This honest Gentleman believing, as one would imagine, that good Humour and Wit did consist in Activity of Body, and Thickness of Bone, was resolv'd to be very witty, that's to say, very strong: he therefore not only threw down most of the Women, and with abundance of Wit hawl'd them round the Room, but gave us several farther Proofs of the Sprightliness of his Genius, by a great many Leaps he made about a Yard high, always remembering to fall on somebodies Toes. This ingenious Fancy was applauded by every one, except the Person that felt it, who never happen'd to have Complaisance enough to fall in with the general Laugh that was rais'd on that Occasion. For my own part, who am an occasional Conformist to common Custom, I was asham'd to be singular, so I e'en extended my Mouth into a Smile, and put my Face in a laughing Posture too. His Mother observing me to look pleas'd with her Son's Activity and gay Deportment, told me in my Ear, *he was never worse Company than I saw him*: To which I answer'd, *I vow, Madam, I believe you.*

Illustration to "A Country Entertainment" by
William Makepeace Thackeray.

DANIEL DEFOE

Good Men (1720)

The author: In the 1710s, Defoe wrote for and edited several publications, including *The Commentator*. He also went to prison for debt several times. Then, in 1719, he reinvented himself as a novelist, by publishing his first long fiction, *Robinson Crusoe*, which was quickly followed by *Captain Singleton, Moll Flanders, Colonel Jack, Roxana*, as well as many nonfiction books. Even though his earnings from journalism and fiction writing were quite impressive, he never managed to repay his debts and when he died, in 1731, he was hiding from his creditors.

The text: First published in *The Commentator* 28 (Monday, 4 April 1720), p. 1-2, from which this has been taken. It had an epigraph from Horace: "Vir bonus est Quis?" ("Who is a good man?"). *The Commentator* (printed in London for J. Roberts, "near the *Oxford-Arms* in *Warwick-Lane*") was written entirely by Defoe, whose editorial notices were untitled and followed one another, being only separated by a blank line. The following story is preceded by a very brief notice in response to *The Freethinker*, a newspaper edited by Ambrose Philips.

Further reading: P.N. Furbank and W. R. Owens. "The Return of the Prodigal." *A Political Biography of Daniel Defoe*. London: Routledge, 2016. 172-185.

I happen'd t'other Day to be wedg'd in among the *Stock-jobbing* Assembly at *Jonathan's*;[1] and the Two who were next to me having struck up a Bargain, *Come*, says one of 'em, *let me see your List; let me see if I like my Men*. Accordingly the other pulls out a Paper of Names, and begins with reading *A. B.* to which the first Nodded, and cry'd, *a good Man*; and the same to the Second; to a Third likewise, who was a *Jew*, the *Broker* replied, *very well, a very good Man*; so they went through a great Part of the List, and all were very good Men. At last, when they came to a certain Name, that shall be Nameless, *Hold*, says he, *I don't like him, he is not worth a Groat*; to another he cried, *he is a Beggar*; he stopp'd at a Third; but after having paused a while, *D——n him*, says he, *he's a great Rogue, but however, let him go among the rest; he's a very good Man: Read on*. The Stream of the Multitude carried me away to t'other end of the Room, before they got over the rest of the Names; however, I had heard enough to incite my Curiosity to know what this Jargon of a *good Man* meant. I was not so ignorant of the Language of the Place, but

---

[1] Jonathan's Coffee House was the meeting place of speculators at the time of the South Sea Bubble of 1720.

I could easily comprehend, that a good Man there must be a Responsible Man; however, I was willing to enter farther into the Explanation of it, as a Term of Art, and to have it from those who were Dealers and upon the Spot. But the Crowd was so great, and every body besides my self was so intent upon Gain, that I could not get a civil Answer to any Question I ask'd; so that I found I was out of my Element, and made the best of my way to t'other End of the Town. There happen'd at that Time to be a remarkable Contest about Politicks, upon which they fell to telling of Noses,[1] and the Lists were look'd over, as in the City. There was Sir *Thomas, a good Man*; Sir *John, a very good Man*, Sir *Richard, O! an extraordinary good Man*: Sir *William, I don't like him*, Mr. *S—he has left us*, Mr. *T—— he is bought off, and* Mr. *G—— is a Whimsical.*

I found there was as many good and bad Men stirring here, as in the City; and though they were of very different Kinds, they went all under the same common Appellative. I might run this Parallel through almost all Orders and Degrees of Men; so that one might, among People of all Employments and Professions, meet with an infinite Number of *good Men*, and scarce find among them one *good Christian*. The same Piece of Cant has obtained in the Country; and this makes me recollect a Discourse I had some time ago with a Farmer, who was running out in Praise of his Landlord, as the best and honestest Man upon Earth, though I knew him to be a very idle worthless Fellow, and withal a Rogue to the utmost of his Ability. *Your Landlord*, says I to him, *may be a very good Man, as a Landlord; but what he may be in other Respects, I don't know; for I am told he never is himself: so that there is no judging of a Man who is always in Liquor. O Sir*, says he, *that's a small Matter. My Landlord loves his Bottle indeed, and will take a hearty Glass sometimes. But that does not become him as a Magistrate*, I replied; *he is not the better qualified for it to act in the Commission of the Peace. Why, that's true*, says my Man again, *he will be overtaken a little now and then; but he is a very good Man for all that. Very well, Friend*, says I: *But how comes your Landlord to swear so bitterly, and to set so ill an Example in the Country? Why, yes, truly*, replied he, *my Landlord is a passionate Man, and when he is angry, he will rap 'em out pretty thick; but that's only a way that he has got; he comes to again presently; and he is a good Man for all that, a very good Man, I'll assure you. But hark you*, proceeded I, *your Landlord, I think, is pretty much in Debt; he pays no body, and his poor Workmen cry out shame upon him. I can't deny*, says he, *but there's something in it; but all the Gentlefolks now-a-days do the same Thing, and I hope my Landlord means honestly for all that; for indeed he is a very honest Gentleman, and a very good Man, Sir, upon my Word.* Then I added, *your Landlord has, if I mistake not, turned away his Wife too, and taken a Whore home in her Stead. Pray is it not so? Does not your good Man live in open Adultery? And has not he turned an honest Wife*

---

[1] An expression that meant "counting heads" or "counting votes."

out of Doors? Why truly, says he, *they had some Words, and my Lady is gone away; I don't know how it is, but they are parted; and as to the Gentlewoman that is there now, I can't say, it may be my Landlord and she may do bad Things together sometimes; but look ye, Sir, that's but a Trick of Youth, he'll leave it off when he grows older; he is a very good Man for all that. Very well, Friend*, says I; *and so at your Rate, many a good Man has been hang'd this last Year.* There stood an honest Countryman by, whilst we had this Parley; and seeing him smile at what pass'd between us, I ask'd him what he thought of his Neighbour, and his good Man. *O, Sir*, says he, *my Neighbour is in the right all this while; and if he would but speak plain, you would understand all he says of his Landlord in Two Words. How so*, said I? *why, Sir*, replies he, *my Neighbour should have said it thus; he is a good Man, and good to me. O, your Servant*, said I, *then I understand you. But then there can be no such Thing as a bad Man; for there is scarce any such Monster in the World, but he is good to somebody or other; as they say, the Devil is good, when he is pleased.*

Upon the whole, I find, that a good Man, according to the present Acceptation of it, is not a good Man with regard to the Community, but only with regard to the particular Persons he has to do with; and he who is a good Man in one Part of the World, may not be so in another. This good Man is one Sort of Man with the Tradesman, another with the Gentry, and another with the Clergy; he is one kind of Man in the City, another at Court, and another in the Countrey; and yet every body will allow there is really but one good sort of Man in the World. In the Way of Dealing, whether it be in Trade of Stock, or any Sort of Money-Contract, the good Man is the good Pay-master; in the Countrey 'tis the Landlord; in the Court 'tis Party; in Religion 'tis Opinion; in the Army 'tis Courage; and in Law and Physick it is Skill: So that People are good or bad only as they do well or ill in the Way of their Employments and Professions; and according to this Definition, Honesty has a very small Share in the Composition of a good Man; and is only a Word made use of, as a Term of Art, to denote how far he may be relied on in his proper Sphere of Action; whether the Business he is employed about be good or bad, lawful or unlawful.

JONATHAN SWIFT

The Wonder of All the Wonders, that Ever the World Wonder'd at (1722)

The author: Jonathan Swift (1667-1745) is perhaps the greatest satirist in the English language. He was born in Dublin, of parents originally from the Midlands. Educated at Trinity College in Dublin and then at Oxford, Swift had high hopes of receiving a bishopric in the Church of England, but in 1713 he accepted the position of Dean of St Patrick's Cathedral in Dublin and, to the end of his life, he was known as Dean Swift. His career as a writer began in 1704 with the publication of two satires, *A Tale of a Tub* and *The Battle of the Books*. In the following years, he contributed to several journals and wrote especially satires, such as his famous *A Modest Proposal* (1729), and political pamphlets like *Drapier's Letters* (1724-1725), while his best-known work, *Gulliver's Travels* appeared in 1726.

The text: The following text is reproduced from *The Wonder of all the Wonders, that Ever the World Wonder'd at. By the Author of* the Art of Punning, Benefit of Farting, &c. (London: Printed from the Original Copy from *Dublin*, and sold by A. Moore, near *St. Paul's*, 1722), which sold for 3 pence. The pamphlet had the following epigraph: "Quae Majora putes Miracula?" The quote is from an epigram of Martial and should read "quae maiora putas miracula" ("which do you think the greater miracle"). The pamphlet has usually been interpreted as a satire against bank "projecting," in the wake of the South Sea scandal, more exactly against the bill presented in the Irish parliament in 1721 to establish a national bank in Ireland. It has been called an "Irish tract" and even a "bank tract." However, as it has also been noted, and can be seen in the text below, there is nothing about a bank here (see Ryder 559n8). In later editions, Swift (or the publisher) added the phrase "Written in 1721" and the beginning of the first sentence appeared as "Newly arrived at this City of *Dublin*," which further encouraged the association between this text and the scheme for a national bank in Ireland. All this notwithstanding, the pamphlet is clearly about a quack performing artist and parodies advertisements for a fictional performance. The anonymous editor of *The Parlour Portfolio*, published a century later, may be right in suggesting that Swift "ridiculed" the style of advertisements for someone like Isaac Fawkes (c. 1675-1732), perhaps the most famous showman of the era, also satirised by Hogarth in his 1724 print *The Bad Taste of the Town*.

Further reading: *The Parlour Portfolio; or Post-Chaise Companion: Being A Selection of the Most Amusing and Interesting Articles and Anecdotes that Have Appeared in the Magazines, Newspapers, and Other Daily and Periodical Journals, from the Year 1700, to the Present Time*. Vol. I (London: Matthew Iley, 1820), 299-300.

Michael Ryder, "The Bank of Ireland, 1721: Land, Credit and Dependency" (*The Historical Journal* 25.3, September 1982, 557-582).

For all Persons of Quality, and Others;

Newly arrived at this City, the Famous Artist, *John Emanuel Schoitz*; who, to the great Surprize and Satisfaction of all Spectators, does the following wonderful Performances, the like before never seen in this Kingdom.

He heats a Bar of Iron red-hot, and thrusts it into a Barrel of Gunpowder, before all the Company; and yet it shall not take fire.

He lets any Gentleman charge a Blunderbuss with the same Gunpowder, and twelve Leaden-Bullets; which Blunderbuss the said Artist discharges full in the Face of the said Company, without the least Hurt, the Bullets sticking in the Wall behind them.

He takes any Gentleman's own Sword, and runs it through the said Gentleman's Body, so that the Point appears bloody at the back, to all the Spectators; then he takes out the Sword, wipes it clean, and returns it to the Owner, who receives no manner of hurt.

He takes a Pot of scalding Oil, and throws it by great Ladles full directly at the Ladies, without spoiling their Clothes, or burning their Skins.

He takes any Person of Quality's Child, from two Years old to six, and lets the Child's own Father or Mother take a Pike in their Hands; then the Artist takes the Child in his Arms, and tosses it upon the Point of the Pike, where it sticks, to the great Satisfaction of all Spectators; and is then taken off, without so much as a Hole in his Coat.

He mounts upon a Scaffold, just over the Spectators, and from thence throws down a great Quantity of large Tiles and Stones, which fall like so many Pillows, without so much as discomposing either Perukes or Head-dresses.

He takes any Person of Quality up to the said Scaffold, which Person pulls off his Shoes, and leaps nine Foot directly down on a Board, prepared on Purpose, full of sharp Spikes, six Inches long, without hurting his Feet, or damaging his Stockings.

He places the said Board on a Chair, upon which a Lady sits down, with another Lady in her Lap, while the Spikes, instead of entring into the under Lady's Flesh, will feel like a Velvet Cushion.

He takes any Person of Quality's Footman, ties a Rope about his bare Neck, and draws him up by Pullies to the Cieling, and there keeps him hanging as long as his Master, or the Company pleases; the said Footman, to the Wonder and Delight of all Beholders, with a Pot of Ale in one Hand, and a Pipe in the other: and when he is let down, there will not appear the least Mark of the Cord about his Neck.

He bids a Lady's Maid put her Finger into a Cup of clear Liquor, like Water; upon which her Face and both her Hands are immediately withered like an old Woman of Fourscore, her Belly swells, as if she were within a Week of her Time, and her Legs are as thick as Mill-posts: but upon putting her Finger into another Cup, she becomes as young and handsome as she was before.

He gives any Gentleman leave to drive forty Twelvepenny Nails up to the head, in a Porter's Back-side; and then places the said Porter on a Loadstone Chair,[1] which draws out every Nail, and the Porter feels no Pain.

He likewise draws the Teeth of half a dozen Gentlemen, mixes and jumbles them in a Hat, gives any Person leave to blindfold him, and returns each their own, and fixes them as well as ever.

With his Fore-Finger and Thumb he thrusts several Gentlemens and Ladies Eyes out of their Heads, without the least Pain, at which time they see an unspeakable Number of beautiful Colours; and after they are entertained to the full, he places them again in their proper Sockets, without any Damage to the Sight.

He lets any Gentleman drink a Quart of hot melted Lead, and by a Draught of prepared Liquor, of which he takes Part himself, he makes the said Lead pass through the said Gentleman before all the Spectators, without any Damage: After which it is produced in a Cake to the Company.

With many other wonderful Performances of Art, too tedious here to mention.

The said Artist has performed before most Kings and Princes in *Europe*, with great Applause.

He performs every Day (except *Sundays*) from Ten of the Clock in the Forenoon to One; and from Four till Seven in the Evening, at the New Inn in *Smithfield*.[2]

The first Seat a *British* Crown, the Second a *British* Half Crown, and the Lowest a *British* Shilling.[3]

N.B. The best Hands in Town are to play at the said Show.

1722

---

[1] Lodestone is a naturally-occurring magnet.
[2] Both Dublin and London have a marketplace called Smithfield.
[3] A crown was worth 5 shillings; a half-crown, 2 shillings 6 pence.

ELIZA HAYWOOD

Fantomina (1725)

The author: Despite being one of the most prolific English authors of the 18th century, Eliza Haywood was very parsimonious with information about her own life. She was probably born in 1693, in either London or Shropshire; her maiden name was probably Fowler and she probably married and was widowed of a man named Haywood. The first mention of her name appears in 1714, when she was an actress in Dublin; she debuted on the London stage in 1717. She soon reinvented herself as a professional author and in 1719 she had her first success with the novel *Love in Excess*. In the 1720s she published about 50 titles, mostly of original fiction.

The text: The following text is reproduced from *Secret Histories, Novels, and Poems, Written by Mrs. Eliza Haywood* (London: Printed for Dan. Browne *jun.* at the *Black-Swan* without *Temple-Bar*; and S. Chapman at the *Angel* in *Pallmall*, 1725), Vol. III, 257-291. The full title of this first edition of the story was "Fantomina: or, Love in a Maze." The story had the following epigraph: "In Love the Victors from the Vanquish'd fly:/ They fly that wound, and they pursue that die" (Waller): the last two lines of "To a friend, on the different success of their loves" by Edmund Waller (1606-1687).

Further reading: Tiffany Potter. "The Language of Feminised Sexuality: Gendered Voice in Eliza Haywood's *Love in Excess* and *Fantomina*." *Women's Writing* 10.1 (2003): 169-186.

Patricia Comitini. "Imaginative Pleasures: *Fantomina*, Ideology, and Aesthetics." *Studies in Eighteenth-Century Culture* 43 (2014): 69-187.

A young Lady of distinguished Birth, Beauty, Wit, and Spirit, happened to be in a Box one Night at the Playhouse; where, though there were a great Number of celebrated Toasts,[1] she perceived several Gentlemen extremely pleased themselves with entertaining a Woman who sat in a Corner of the Pit,[2] and, by her Air and Manner of receiving them, might easily be known to be one of those who come there for no other Purpose, than to create Acquaintance with as many as seem desirous of it. She could not help testifying her Contempt of Men, who, regardless either of the Play, or Circle, threw away their Time in such a Manner, to some Ladies that sat by her: But they, either less surprised by being more accustomed to such Sights, than she who had been bred for the most part in the Country, or not of a Disposition to consider any Thing

---

[1] A "toast" was a famous beauty, in whose honour men often raised their glasses.
[2] The aristocracy sat in boxes (like the "young lady of distinguished birth"), but the audience in the pit were mixed.

very deeply, took but little Notice of it. She still thought of it, however; and the longer she reflected on it, the greater was her Wonder, that Men, some of whom she knew were accounted to have Wit, should have Tastes so very depraved.——This excited a Curiosity in her to know in what Manner these Creatures were address'd:——She was young, a Stranger to the World, and consequently to the Dangers of it; and having no Body in Town, at that Time, to whom she was oblig'd to be accountable for her Actions, did in every Thing as her Inclinations or Humours render'd most agreeable to her: Therefore thought it not in the least a Fault to put in practice a little Whim which came immediately into her Head, to dress herself as near as she cou'd in the Fashion of those Women who make sale of their Favours, and set herself in the Way of being accosted as such a one, having at that Time no other Aim, than the Gratification of an innocent Curiosity.——She no sooner design'd this Frolick, than she put it in Execution; and muffling her Hoods over her Face, went the next Night into the Gallery-Box,[1] and practising as much as she had observ'd, at that Distance, the Behaviour of that Woman, was not long before she found her Disguise had answer'd the Ends she wore it for:——A crowd of Purchasers of all Degrees and Capacities were in a Moment gather'd about her, each endeavouring to out-bid the other, in offering her a Price for her Embraces.——She listen'd to 'em all, and was not a little diverted in her Mind at the Disappointment she shou'd give to so many, each of which thought himself secure of gaining her.——She was told by 'em all, that she was the most lovely Woman in the World; and some cry'd, *Gad, she is mighty like my fine Lady Such-a-one,*——naming her own Name. She was naturally vain, and receiv'd no small Pleasure in hearing herself prais'd, tho' in the Person of another, and a suppos'd Prostitute; but she dispatch'd as soon as she cou'd all that had hitherto attack'd her, when she saw the accomplish'd *Beauplaisir* was making his Way thro' the Crowd as fast as he was able, to reach the Bench she sat on. She had often seen him in the Drawing-Room, had talk'd with him; but then her Quality and reputed Virtue kept him from using her with that Freedom she now expected he wou'd do, and had discover'd something in him, which had made her often think she shou'd not be displeas'd, if he wou'd abate some Part of his Reserve.——Now was the Time to have her Wishes answer'd:——He look'd in her Face, and fancy'd, as many others had done, that she very much resembled that Lady whom she really was; but the vast Disparity there appear'd between their Characters, prevented him from entertaining even the most distant Thought that they cou'd be the same.——He address'd her at first with the usual Salutations of her pretended Profession, as, *Are you engag'd, Madam?*——*Will you permit me to wait on you home after the Play?*——*By Heaven, you are a fine Girl!*——*How long have you us'd this House?*——And such like Questions; but perceiving she had a Turn of Wit, and a genteel Manner in her Raillery, beyond what is frequently to be found among those Wretches, who are

1725

---

[1] The gallery is the highest and the cheapest part of the auditorium in a theatre.

for the most part Gentlewomen but by Necessity, few of 'em having had an Education suitable to what they affect to appear, he chang'd the Form of his Conversation, and shew'd her it was not because he understood no better, that he had made use of Expressions so little polite.——In fine, they were infinitely charm'd with each other: He was transported to find so much Beauty and Wit in a Woman, who he doubted not but on very easy Terms he might enjoy; and she found a vast deal of Pleasure in conversing with him in this free and unrestrain'd Manner. They pass'd their Time all the Play with an equal Satisfaction; but when it was over, she found herself involv'd in a Difficulty, which before never enter'd into her Head, but which she knew not well how to get over.——The Passion he profess'd for her, was not of that humble Nature which can be content with distant Adorations:——He resolv'd not to part from her without the Gratifications of those Desires she had inspir'd; and presuming on the Liberties which her suppos'd Function allow'd of, told her she must either go with him to some convenient House of his procuring, or permit him to wait on her to her own Lodgings.——Never had she been in such a *Dilemma*: Three or four Times did she open her Mouth to confess her real Quality; but the Influence of her ill Stars prevented it, by putting an Excuse into her Head, which did the Business as well, and at the same Time did not take from her the Power of seeing and entertaining him a second Time with the same Freedom she had done this.——She told him, she was under Obligations to a Man who maintain'd her, and whom she durst not disappoint, having promis'd to meet him that Night at a House hard by.[1]——This Story so like what those Ladies sometimes tell, was not at all suspected by *Beauplaisir*; and assuring her he wou'd be far from doing her a Prejudice, desir'd that in Return for the Pain he shou'd suffer in being depriv'd of her Company that Night, that she wou'd order her Affairs, so as not to render him unhappy the next. She gave a solemn Promise to be in the same Box on the Morrow Evening; and they took Leave of each other; he to the Tavern to drown the Remembrance of his Disappointment; she in a Hackney-Chair[2] hurry'd home to indulge Contemplation on the Frolick she had taken, designing nothing less on her first Reflections, than to keep the Promise she had made him, and hugging herself with Joy, that she had the good Luck to come off undiscover'd.

A SEDAN CHAIR.

---

[1] In close proximity.

[2] Also called a sedan chair, it was a type of litter or palanquin, carried by two men, one on each end. "Hackney" meant that it was for hire. A hackney chair was cheaper than a hackney coach, drawn by horses.

But these Cogitations were but of a short Continuance, they vanish'd with the Hurry of her Spirits, and were succeeded by others vastly different and ruinous:——All the Charms of *Beauplaisir* came fresh into her Mind; she languish'd, she almost dy'd for another Opportunity of conversing with him; and not all the Admonitions of her Discretion were effectual to oblige her to deny laying hold of that which offer'd itself the next Night.——She depended on the Strength of her Virtue, to bear her safe thro' Tryals more dangerous than she apprehended this to be, and never having been address'd by him as Lady,——was resolv'd to receive his Devoirs[1] as a Town-Mistress, imagining a world of Satisfaction to herself in engaging him the Character of such a one, and in observing the Surprise he would be in to find himself refused by a Woman, who he supposed granted her Favours without Exception.——Strange and unaccountable were the Whimsies she was possess'd of,——wild and incoherent her Desires,——unfix'd and undetermin'd her Resolutions, but in that of seeing *Beauplaisir* in the Manner she had lately done. As for her Proceedings with him, or how a second Time to escape him, without discovering who she was, she cou'd neither assure herself, nor whither or not in the last Extremity she wou'd do so.——Bent, however, on meeting him, whatever shou'd be the Consequence, she went out some Hours before the Time of going to the Playhouse, and took Lodgings in a House not very far from it, intending, that if he shou'd insist on passing some Part of the Night with her, to carry him there, thinking she might with more Security to her Honour entertain him at a Place where she was Mistress, than at any of his own chusing.

The appointed Hour being arriv'd, she had the Satisfaction to find his Love in his Assiduity: He was there before her; and nothing cou'd be more tender than the Manner in which he accosted her: But from the first Moment she came in, to that of the Play being done, he continued to assure her no Consideration shou'd prevail with him to part from her again, as she had done the Night before; and she rejoic'd to think she had taken that Precaution of providing herself with a Lodging, to which she thought she might invite him, without running any Risque, either of her Virtue or Reputation.——Having told him she wou'd admit of his accompanying her home, he seem'd perfectly satisfy'd; and leading her to the Place, which was not above twenty Houses distant, wou'd have order'd a Collation to be brought after them. But she wou'd not permit it, telling him she was not one of those who suffer'd themselves to be treated at their own Lodgings; and as soon she was come in, sent a Servant, belonging to the House, to provide a very handsome Supper, and Wine, and every Thing was serv'd to Table in a Manner which shew'd the Director neither wanted Money, nor was ignorant how it shou'd be laid out.

This Proceeding, though it did not take from him the Opinion that she was what she appeared to be, yet it gave him Thoughts of her, which he had not before.——He believ'd her a *Mistress*, but believ'd her to

---

[1] Respects, addresses.

be one of a superior Rank, and began to imagine the Possession of her would be much more expensive than at first he had expected: But not being of a Humour to grudge any Thing for his Pleasures, he gave himself no farther Trouble, than what were occasioned by Fears of not having Money enough to reach her Price, about him.

Supper being over, which was intermixed with a vast deal of amorous Conversation, he began to explain himself more than he had done; and both by his Words and Behaviour let he know, he would not be denied that Happiness the Freedoms she allow'd had made him hope.——It was in vain; she would have retracted the Encouragement she had given:—— In vain she endeavoured to delay, till the next Meeting, the fulfilling of his Wishes:——She had now gone too far to retreat:——*He* was bold;—— he was resolute: *She*, fearful,——confus'd, altogether unprepar'd to resist in such Encounters, and rendered more so, by the extreme Liking she had to him.——Shock'd, however, at the Apprehension of really losing her Honour, she struggled all she could, and was just going to reveal the whole Secret of her Name and Quality, when the Thoughts of the Liberty he had taken with her, and those he still continued to prosecute, prevented her, with representing the Danger of being expos'd, and the whole Affair made a Theme for publick Ridicule.——Thus much, indeed, she told him, that she was a Virgin, and had assumed this Manner of Behaviour only to engage him. But that he little regarded, or if he had, would have been far from obliging him to desist;——nay, in the present burning Eagerness of Desire, 'tis probable, that had he been acquainted both with who and what she really was, the Knowledge of her Birth would not have influenc'd him with Respect sufficient to have curb'd the wild Exuberance of his luxurious Wishes, or made him in that longing,——that impatient Moment, change the Form of his Addresses. In fine, she was undone; and he gain'd a Victory, so highly rapturous, that had he known over whom, scarce could he have triumphed more. Her Tears, however, and the Destraction she appeared in, after the ruinous Extasy was past, as it heighten'd his Wonder, so it abated his Satisfaction:——He could not imagine for what Reason a Woman, who, if she intended not be a *Mistress*, had counterfeited the Part of one, and taken so much Pains to engage him, should lament a Consequence which she could not but expect, and till the last Test, seem'd inclinable to grant; and was both surpris'd and troubled at the Mystery.——He omitted nothing that he thought might make her easy; and still retaining an Opinion that the Hope of Interest had been the chief Motive which had led her to act in the Manner she had done, and believing that she might know so little of him, as to suppose, now she had nothing left to give, he might not make that Recompense she expected for her Favours: To put her out of that Pain, he pulled out of his Pocket a Purse of Gold, entreating her to accept of that as an Earnest of what he intended to do for her; assuring her, with ten thousand Protestations, that he would spare nothing, which his whole Estate could purchase, to procure her Content and Happiness.

1725

This Treatment made her quite forget the Part she had assum'd, and throwing it from her with an Air of Disdain, Is this a reward (*said she*) for Condescentions, such as I have yeilded to?——Can all the Wealth you are possess'd of, make a Reparation for my Loss of Honour?——Oh! no, I am undone beyond the Power of Heaven itself to help me!——She uttered many more such Exclamations; which the amaz'd *Beauplaisir* heard without being able to reply to, till by Degrees sinking from that Rage of Temper, her Eyes resumed their softning Glances, and guessing at the Consternation he was in, No, my dear *Beauplaisir*, (*added she*,) your Love alone can compensate for the Shame you have involved me in; be you sincere and constant, and I hereafter shall, perhaps, be satisfy'd with my Fate, and forgive myself the Folly that betray'd me to you.

Beauplaisir thought he could not have a better Opportunity than these Words gave him of enquiring who she was, and wherefore she had feigned herself to be of a Profession which he was now convinc'd she was not; and after he had made her a thousand Vows of an Affection, as inviolable and ardent as she could wish to find in him, entreated she would inform him by what Means his Happiness had been brought about, and also to whom he was indebted for the Bliss he had enjoy'd.——Some Remains of yet unextinguished Modesty, and Sense of Shame, made her blush exceedingly at this Demand; but recollecting herself in a little Time, she told him so much of the Truth, as to what related to the Frolick she had taken of satisfying her Curiosity in what Manner *Mistresses*, of the Sort she appeared to be, were treated by those who addressed them; but forbore discovering her true Name and Quality, for the Reasons she had done before, resolving, if he boasted of this Affair, he should not have it in his Power to touch her Character: She therefore said she was the Daughter of a Country Gentleman, who was come to Town to buy Cloaths, and that she was call'd *Fantomina*. He had no Reason to distrust the Truth of this Story, and was therefore satisfy'd with it; but did not doubt by the Beginning of her Conduct, but that in the End she would be in Reality, the Thing she so artfully had counterfeited; and had good Nature enough to pity the Misfortunes he imagin'd would be her Lot: But to tell her so, or offer his Advice in that Point, was not his Business, at least, as yet.

They parted not till towards Morning; and she oblig'd him to a willing Vow of visiting her the next Day at Three in the Afternoon. It was too late for her to go home that Night, therefore contented herself with lying there. In the Morning she sent for the Woman of the House to come up to her; and easily perceiving, by her Manner, that she was a Woman who might be influenced by Gifts, made her a Present of a Couple of Broad Pieces,[1] and desir'd her, that if the Gentleman, who had been there the Night before, should ask any Questions concerning her, that he should be told, she was lately come out of the Country, had lodg'd there

---

[1] A name for the one-pound coin, so called after the introduction of the smaller guinea.

about a Fortnight, and that her Name was *Fantomina*. I shall (*also added she*) lie but seldom here; nor, indeed, ever come but in those Times when I expect to meet him: I would, therefore, have you order it so, that he may think I am but just gone out, if he should happen by any Accident to call when I am not here; for I would not, for the World, have him imagine I do not constantly lodge here. The Landlady assur'd her she would do every Thing as she desired, and gave her to understand she wanted not the Gift of Secrecy.

Every Thing being ordered at this Home for the Security of her Reputation, she repaired to the other, where she easily excused to an unsuspecting Aunt, with whom she boarded, her having been abroad all Night, saying, she went with a Gentleman and his Lady in a Barge, to a little Country Seat of theirs up the River, all of them designing to return the same Evening; but that one of the Barge-men happ'ning to be taken ill on the sudden, and no other Waterman to be got that Night, they were oblig'd to tarry till Morning. Thus did this Lady's Wit and Vivacity assist her in all, but where it was most needful.——She had Discernment to foresee, and avoid all those Ills which might attend the Loss of her *Reputation*, but was wholly blind to those of the Ruin of her *Virtue*; and having managed her Affairs so as to secure the *one*, grew perfectly easy with the Remembrance she had forfeited the *other*.——The more she reflected on the Merits of *Beauplaisir*, the more she excused herself for what she had done; and the Prospect of that continued Bliss she expected to share with him, took from her all Remorse for having engaged in an Affair which promised her so much Satisfaction, and in which she found not the least Danger of Misfortune.——If he is really (*said she, to herself*) the faithful, the constant Lover he has sworn to be, how charming will be our Amour?——And if he should be false, grow satiated, like other Men, I shall but, at the worst, have the private Vexation of knowing I have lost him;——the Intreague being a Secret, my Disgrace will be so too:——I shall hear no Whispers as I pass,——She is Forsaken:——The odious Word *Forsaken* will never wound my Ears; nor will my Wrongs excite either the Mirth or Pity of the talking World:——It will not be even in the Power of my Undoer himself to triumph over me; and while he laughs at, and perhaps despises the fond, the yeilding *Fantomina*, he will revere and esteem the virtuous, the reserv'd Lady.——In this Manner did she applaud her own Conduct, and exult with the Imagination that she had more Prudence than all her Sex beside. And it must be confessed, indeed, that she preserved an Œconomy in the management of this Intreague, beyond what almost any Woman but herself ever did: In the first Place, by making no Person in the World a Confident in it; and in the next, in concealing from *Beauplaisir* himself the Knowledge who she was; for though she met him there of four Days in a Week, at that Lodging she had taken for that Purpose, yet as much as he employ'd her Time and Thoughts, she was never miss'd from any Assembly she had been accustomed to frequent.——The Business of her Love has engross'd

1725

her till Six in the Evening, and before Seven she has been dress'd in a different Habit, and in another Place.——Slippers, and a Night-Gown loosely flowing, has been the Garb in which he has left the languishing *Fantomina*;——Lac'd, and adorn'd with all the Blaze of Jewels, has he, in less than an Hour after, beheld at the Royal Chapel, the Palace Gardens, Drawing-Room, Opera, or Play, the Haughty Awe-inspiring Lady.——A thousand Times has he stood amaz'd at the prodigious Likeness between his little Mistress, and this Court Beauty; but was still as far from imagining they were the same, as he was the first Hour he had accosted her in the Playhouse, though it is not impossible, but that her Resemblance to this celebrated Lady, might keep his Inclination alive something longer than otherwise they would have been; and that it was to the Thoughts of this (as he supposed) unenjoy'd Charmer, she ow'd in great measure the Vigour of his latter Caresses.

But he varied not so much from his Sex as to be able to prolong Desire, to any great Length after Possession: The rifled Charms of *Fantomina* soon lost their Poinancy, and grew tastless and insipid; and when the Season of the Year inviting the Company to the *Bath*, she offer'd to accompany him, he made an Excuse to go without her. She easily perceiv'd his Coldness, and the Reason why he pretended her going would be inconvenient, and endur'd as much from the Discovery as any of her Sex could do: She dissembled it, however, before him, and took her Leave of him with the Shew of no other Concern than his Absence occasion'd: But this she did to take from him all Suspicion of her following him, as she intended, and had already laid a Scheme for.——From her first finding out that he design'd to leave her behind, she plainly saw it was for no other Reason, than that being tir'd of her Conversation, he was willing to be at liberty to pursue new Conquests; and wisely considering that Complaints, Tears, Swoonings, and all the Extravagancies which Women make use of in such Cases, have little Prevailance over a Heart inclin'd to rove, and only serve to render those who practise them more contemptible, by robbing them of that Beauty which alone can bring back the fugitive Lover, she resolved to take another Course; and remembring the Height of Transport she enjoyed when the agreeable *Beauplaisir* kneel'd at her Feet, imploring her first Favours, she long'd to prove the same again. Not but a Woman of her Beauty and Accomplishments might have beheld a Thousand in that Condition *Beauplaisir* had been; but with her Sex's Modesty, she had not also thrown off another Virtue equally valuable, tho' generally unfortunate, *Constancy*: She loved *Beauplaisir*; it was only he whose Solicitations could give her Pleasure; and had she seen the whole Species despairing, dying for her sake, it might, perhaps have been a Satisfaction to her Pride, but none to her more tender Inclination.——Her Design was once more to engage him, to hear him sigh, to see him languish, to feel the strenuous Pressures of his eager Arms, to be compelled, to be sweetly forc'd to what she wished with equal

Ardour, was what she wanted, and what she had form'd a Stratagem to obtain, in which she promis'd herself Success.

She no sooner heard he had left the Town, than making a Pretence to her Aunt, that she was going to visit a Relation in the Country, went towards *Bath*, attended but by two Servants, who she found Reasons to quarrel with on the Road and discharg'd: Clothing herself in a Habit she had brought with her, she forsook the Coach, and went into a Waggon, in which Equipage she arriv'd at *Bath*. The Dress she was in, was a round-ear'd Cap, a short Red Petticoat, and a little Jacket of Grey Stuff; all the rest of her Accoutrements were answerable to these, and join'd with a broad Country Dialect, a rude unpolish'd Air, which she, having been bred in these Parts, knew very well how to imitate, with her Hair and Eye-brows black'd, made it impossible for her to be known, or taken for any other than what she seem'd. Thus disguis'd did she offer herself to Service in the House where *Beauplaisir* lodg'd, having made it her Business to find out immediately where he was. Notwithstanding this Metamorphosis she was still extremely pretty; and the Mistress of the House happening at that Time to want a Maid, was very glad of the Opportunity of taking her. She was presently receiv'd into the Family; and had a Post in it, (such as she would have chose, had she been left at her Liberty) that of making the Gentlemen's Beds, getting them their Breakfasts, and waiting on them in their Chambers. Fortune in this Exploit was extremely on her side; there were no others of the Male-Sex in the House, than an old Gentleman, who had lost the Use of his Limbs with the Rheumatism, and had come thither for the Benefit of the Waters, and her belov'd *Beauplaisir*; so that she was in no Apprehensions of any Amorous Violence, but where she wish'd to find it. Nor were her Designs disappointed: He was fir'd with the first Sight of her; and tho' he did not presently take any farther Notice of her, than giving her two or three hearty Kisses, yet she, who now understood that Language but too well, easily saw they were the Prelude to more substantial Joys.——Coming the next Morning to bring his Chocolate, as he had order'd, he catch'd her by the pretty Leg, which the Shortness of her Petticoat did not in the least oppose; then pulling her gently to him, ask'd her, how long she had been at Service?——How many Sweethearts she had? If she had ever been in Love? and many other such Questions, befitting one of the Degree she appear'd to be: All which she answer'd with such seeming Innocence, as more enflam'd the amorous Heart of him who talk'd to her. He compelled her to fit in his Lap; and gazing on her blushing Beauties, which, if possible, receiv'd Addition from her plain and rural Dress, he soon lost the Power of containing himself.—— His wild Desires burst out in all his Words and Actions; he call'd her little Angel, Cherubim, swore he must enjoy her, though Death were to be the Consequence, devour'd her Lips, her Breasts with greedy Kisses, held to his burning Bosom her half-yielding, half-reluctant Body, nor suffer'd her to get loose, till he had ravaged all, and glutted each rapacious Sense with the sweet Beauties of the pretty *Celia*, for that was the Name she bore in

1725

this second Expedition.——Generous as Liberality itself to all who gave him Joy this way, he gave her a handsome Sum of Gold, which she durst not now refuse, for fear of creating some Mistrust, and losing the Heart she so lately had regain'd; therefore taking it with an humble Curtesy, and a well counterfeited Shew of Surprise and Joy, cry'd, O Law, Sir! what must I do for all this? He laughed at her Simplicity, and kissing her again, tho' less fervently than he had done before, bad her not to be out of the Way when he came home at Night. She promis'd she would not, and very obediently kept her Word.

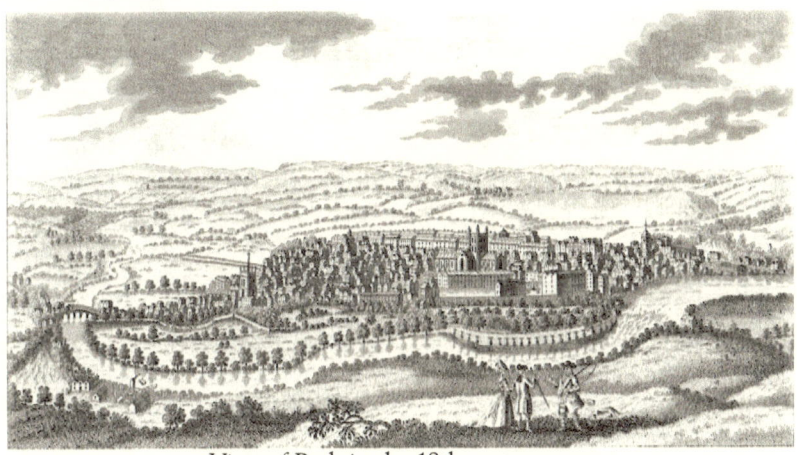

View of Bath in the 18th century

His Stay at *Bath* exceeded not a Month; but in that Time his suppos'd Country Lass had persecuted him so much with her Fondness, that in spite of the Eagerness with which he first enjoy'd her, he was at last grown more weary of her, than he had been of *Fantomina*; which she perceiving, would not be troublesome, but quitting her Service, remained privately in the Town till she heard he was on his Return; and in that Time provided herself of another Disguise to carry on a third Plot, which he inventing Brain had furnished her with, once more to renew his twice-decay'd Ardours. The Dress she had order'd to be made, was such as Widows wear in their first Mourning, which, together with the most afflicted and penitential Countenance that ever was seen, was no small Alteration to her who us'd to seem all Gaiety.——To add to this, her Hair, which she was accustom'd to wear very loose, both when *Fantomina* and *Celia*, was now ty'd back so strait, and her Pinners[1] coming so very forward, that there was none of it to be seen. In fine, her Habit and her Air were so much chang'd, that she was not more difficult to be known in the rude Country *Girl*, than she was now in the sorrowful *Widow*.

She knew that *Beauplaisir* came alone in his Chariot to the *Bath*, and in the Time of her being Servant in the House where he lodg'd, heard

[1] Pinner was a woman's close-fitting cap or, like here, each of the flaps of such a cap.

nothing of any Body that was to accompany him to *London*, and hop'd he wou'd return in the same Manner he had gone: She therefore hir'd Horses and a Man to attend her to an Inn about ten Miles on this side *Bath*, where having discharg'd them, she waited till the Chariot should come by; which when it did, and she saw that he was alone in it, she call'd to him that drove it to stop a Moment, and going to the Door saluted the Master with these Words:

The Distress'd and Wretched, Sir, (*said she,*) never fail to excite Compassion in a generous Mind; and I hope I am not deceiv'd in my Opinion that yours is such:——You have the Appearance of a Gentleman, and cannot, when you hear my Story, refuse that Assistance which is in your Power to give to an unhappy Woman, who without it, may be render'd the most miserable of all created Beings.

It would not be very easy to represent the Surprise, so odd an Address created in the Mind of him to whom it was made.——She had not the Appearance of one who wanted Charity; and what other Favour she requir'd he cou'd not conceive: But telling her, she might command any Thing in his Power, gave her Encouragement to declare herself in this Manner: You may judge, (*resumed she,*) by the melancholy Garb I am in, that I have lately lost all that ought to be valuable to Womankind; but it is impossible for you to guess the Greatness of my Misfortune, unless you had known my Husband, who was Master of every Perfection to endear him to a Wife's Affections.—— But, notwithstanding, I look on myself as the most unhappy of my Sex in out-living him, I must so far obey the Dictates of my Discretion, as to take care of the little Fortune he left behind him, which being in the Hands of a Brother of his in *London*, will be all carry'd off to *Holland*, where he is going to settle, if I reach not the Town before he leaves it, I am undone for ever.——To which End I left *Bristol*, the Place where we liv'd, hoping to get a Place in the Stage at *Bath*, but they were all taken up before I came; and being, by a Hurt I got in a Fall, render'd incapable of travelling any long Journey on Horseback, I have no Way to go to *London*, and must be inevitably ruin'd in the Loss of all I have on Earth, without you have good Nature enough to admit me to take Part of your Chariot.

Here the feigned Widow ended her sorrowful Tale, which had been several Times interrupted by a Parenthesis of Sighs and Groans; and *Beauplaisir*, with a complaisant and tender Air, assur'd her of his Readiness to serve her in Things of much greater Consequence than what she desir'd of him; and told her, it would be an Impossibility of denying a Place in his Chariot to a Lady, who he could not behold without yielding one in his Heart. She answered the Compliments he made her but with Tears, which seem'd to stream in such abundance from her Eyes, that she could not keep her Handkerchief from her Face one Moment. Being come into the Chariot, *Beauplaisir* said a thousand handsome Things to perswade her from giving way to so violent a Grief, which, he told her, would not only be distructive to her Beauty, but likewise her Health. But all his Endeavours for Consolement appear'd ineffectual, and he began to think he should have but a dull Journey, in the Company of one who seem'd so obstinately devoted to the Memory of her dead Husband, that there was no getting a Word from her on any other Theme:—But bethinking himself of the celebrated Story of the *Ephesian* Matron, it came into his Head to make Tryal, she who seem'd equally susceptible of *Sorrow*, might not also be so too of *Love*; and having began a Discourse on almost every other Topick, and finding her still incapable of answering, resolv'd to put it to the Proof, if this would have no more Effect to rouze her sleeping Spirits:——With a gay Air, therefore, though accompany'd with the greatest Modesty and Respect, he turned the Conversation, as though without Design, on that Joy-giving Passion, and soon discover'd that was indeed the Subject she was best pleas'd to be entertained with; for on his giving her a Hint to begin upon, never any Tongue run more voluble than hers, on the prodigious Power it had to influence the Souls of those possess'd of it, to Actions even the most distant from their Intentions, Principles, or Humours.——From that she pass'd to a Description of the Happiness of mutual Affection;——the unspeakable Extasy of those who meet with equal Ardency; and represented it in Colours so lively, and disclos'd by the Gestures with which her Words were accompany'd, and the Accent of her Voice so true a Feeling of what she said, that *Beauplaisir*, without being as stupid, as he was really the contrary, could not avoid perceiving there were Seeds of Fire, not yet extinguish'd, in this fair Widow's Soul, which wanted but the kindling Breath of tender Sighs to light into a Blaze.——He now thought himself as fortunate, as some Moments before he had the Reverse; and doubted not, but, that before they parted, he should find a Way to dry the Tears of this lovely Mourner, to the Satisfaction of them both. He did not, however, offer, as he had done to *Fantomina* and *Celia*, to urge his Passion directly to her, but by a thousand little softning Artifices, which he well knew how to use, gave her leave to guess he was enamour'd. When they came to the Inn where they were to lie, he declar'd himself somewhat more freely, and perceiving she did not resent it past Forgiveness, grew more encroaching still:——He now took the Liberty of kissing away her Tears, and catching the Sighs as they issued from her Lips; telling her if Grief was infectious, he was resolv'd to have his Share; protesting he would gladly exchange Passions with her, and be content to bear her Load of *Sorrow*, if she would as willingly ease the Burden of his *Love*.——She said little in answer to the strenuous Pressures with which at last he ventur'd to enfold her, but not thinking it Decent, for the Character she had assum'd, to yeild so suddenly, and unable to deny both his and her own Inclinations, she counterfeited a fainting, and fell motionless upon his Breast.——He had no great Notion that she was in a real Fit, and the Room they supp'd in happening to have a Bed in it, he took her in his

Arms and laid her on it, believing, that whatever her Distemper was, that was the most proper Place to convey her to.——He laid himself down by her, and endeavour'd to bring her to herself; and she was too grateful to her kind Physician, at her retuning Sense, to remove from the Posture he had put her in, without his Leave.

It may, perhaps, seem strange that *Beauplaisir* should in such near Intimacies continue still deceiv'd: I know there are Men who will swear it is an Impossibility, and that no Disguise could hinder them from knowing a Woman they had once enjoy'd. In answer to these Scruples, I can only say, that besides the Alteration which the Change of Dress made in her, she was so admirably skill'd in the Art of feigning, that she had the Power of putting on almost what Face she pleas'd, and knew so exactly how to form her Behaviour to the Character she represented, that all the Comedians at both Play-houses[1] are infinitely short of her Performances: She could vary her very Glances, tune her Voice to Accents the most different imaginable from those in which she spoke when she appear'd herself.——These Aids from Nature, join'd to the Wiles of Art, and the Distance between the Places where the imagin'd *Fantomina* and *Celia* were, might very well prevent his having any Thought that they were the same, or that the fair *Widow* was either of them: It never so much as enter'd his Head, and though he did fancy he observed in the Face of the latter, Features which were not altogether unknown to him, yet he could not recollect when or where he had known them;——and being told by her, that from her Birth, she had never remov'd from *Bristol*, a Place where he never was, he rejected the Belief of having seen her, and suppos'd his Mind had been deluded by an Idea of some other, whom she might have a Resemblance of.

They pass'd the Time of their Journey in as much Happiness as the most luxurious Gratification of wild Desires could make them; and when they came to the End of it, parted not without a mutual Promise of seeing each other often.——He told her to what Place she should direct a Letter to him; and she assur'd him she would send to let him know where to come to her, as soon as she was fixed in Lodgings.

She kept her Promise; and charm'd with the Continuance of his eager Fondness, went not home, but into private Lodgings, whence she wrote to him to visit her the first Opportunity, and enquire for the Widow *Bloomer*.——She had no sooner dispatched this Billet, than she repair'd to the House where she had lodg'd as *Fantomina*, charging the People if *Beauplaisir* should come there, not to let him know she had been out of Town. From thence she wrote to him, in a different Hand, a long Letter of Complaint, that he had been so cruel in not sending one Letter to her all the Time he had been absent, entreated to see him, and concluded with subscribing herself his unalterably Affectionate *Fantomina*. She received in one Day Answers to both these. The first contain'd these Lines:

---

[1] The two theatres at Covent Garden and Drury Lane had exclusive rights to represent spoken drama in London since the times of Charles II.

To the Charming Mrs. BLOOMER,

It would be impossible, my Angel! for me to express the thousandth Part of that Infinity of Transport, the Sight of your dear Letter gave me.——Never was Women form'd to charm like you: Never did any look like you,——write like you,——bless like you;——nor did ever Man adore as I do.——Since Yesterday we parted, I have seem'd a Body without a Soul; and had you not by this inspiring Billet, gave me new Life, I know not what by To-morrow I should have been.——I will be you this Evening about Five:——O, 'tis an Age till then!——But the cursed Formalities of Duty oblige me to Dine with my Lord—— who never rises from Table till that Hour;——therefore Adieu till then sweet lovely Mistress of the Soul and all the Faculties of

Your most faithful,
BEAUPLAISIR.

The other was in this Manner:

To the Lovely FANTOMINA.

If you were half so sensible as you ought of your own Power of charming, you would be assur'd, that to be unfaithful or unkind to you, would be among the Things that are in their very Natures Impossibilities.——It was my Misfortune, not my Fault, that you were not persecuted every Post with a Declaration of my unchanging Passion; but I had unluckily forgot the Name of the Woman at whose House you are, and knew not how to form a Direction that it might come safe to your Hands.——And, indeed, the Reflection how you might misconstrue my Silence, brought me to Town some Weeks sooner than I intended.——If you knew how I have languish'd to renew those Blessings I am permitted to enjoy in your Society, you would rather pity than condemn

Your ever faithful,
BEAUPLAISIR.

P.S. *I fear I cannot see you till To-morrow; some Business has unluckily fallen out that will engross my Hours till then.——Once more, my Dear,* Adieu.

Traytor! (*cry'd she,*) as soon as she had read them, 'tis thus our silly, fond, believing Sex are serv'd when they put Faith in Man: So had I been deceiv'd and cheated, had I like the rest believ'd, and sat down mourning in Absence, and vainly waiting recover'd Tendernesses.—— How do some Women (*continued she*) make their Life a Hell, burning in fruitless Expectations, and dreaming out their Days in Hopes and Fears, then wake at last to all the Horror of Dispair?——But I have outwitted even the most Subtle of the deceiving Kind, and while he thinks to fool me, is himself the only beguiled Person.

She made herself, most certainly, extremely happy in the Reflection on the Success of her Stratagems; and while the Knowledge of his Inconstancy and Levity of Nature kept her from having that real Tenderness for him she would else have had, she found the Means of gratifying the Inclination she had for his agreeable Person, in as full a Manner as she could wish. She had all the Sweets of Love, but as yet had tasted none of the Gall, and was in a State of Contentment, which might be envy'd by the more Delicate.

When the expected Hour arriv'd, she found that her Lover had lost no part of the Fervency with which he had parted from her; but when the next Day she receiv'd him as *Fantomina*, she perceiv'd a prodigious Difference; which led her again into Reflections on the Unaccountableness of Men's Fancies, who still prefer the last Conquest, only because it is the last.——Here was an evident Proof of it; for there could not be a Difference in Merit, because they were the same Person; but the Widow *Bloomer* was a more new Acquaintance than *Fantomina*, and therefore esteem'd more valuable. This, indeed, must be said of *Beauplaisir*, that he had a greater Share of good Nature than most of his Sex, who, for the most part, when they are weary of an Intreague, break it entirely off, without any Regard to the Despair of the abandon'd Nymph. Though he retain'd no more than a bare Pity and Complaisance for *Fantomina*, yet believing she lov'd him to an Excess, would not entirely forsake her, though the Continuance of his Visits was now become rather a Penance than a Pleasure.

The Widow *Bloomer* triumph'd some Time longer over the Heart of this Inconstant, but at length her Sway was at an End, and she sunk in this Character, to the same Degree of Tastlesness, as she had done before in that of *Fantomina* and *Celia*.——She presently perceiv'd it, but bore it as she had always done; it being but what she expected, she had prepar'd herself for it, and had another Project in *embrio*, which she soon ripen'd into Action. She did not, indeed, compleat it altogether so suddenly as she had done the others, by reason there must be Persons employ'd in it; and the Aversion she had to any *Confidents* in her Affairs, and the Caution with which she had hitherto acted, and which she was still determin'd to continue, made it very difficult for her to find a Way, without breaking thro' that Resolution to compass what she wish'd.——She got over the Difficulty at last, however, by proceeding in a Manner, if possible, more extraordinary than all her former Behaviour:——Muffling herself up in her Hood one Day, she went into the Park about the Hour when there are a great many necessitous Gentlemen, who think themselves above doing what they call little Things for a Maintenance, walking in the *Mall*, to take a *Camelion* Treat, and fill their Stomachs with Air instead of Meat.[1]

---

[1] Chameleons had long been reputed to survive on nothing but air.

Two of those, who by their Physiognomy she thought most proper for her Purpose, she beckon'd to come to her; and taking them into a Walk more remote from Company, began to communicate the Business she had with them in these Words: I am sensible, Gentlemen, (*said she,*) that, through the Blindness of Fortune, and Partiality of the World, Merit frequently goes unrewarded, and that those of the best Pretensions meet with the least Encouragement:——I ask you Pardon, (*continued she,*) perceiving they seem'd surpris'd, if I am mistaken in the Notion, that you two may, perhaps, be of the Number of those who have Reason to complain of the Injustice of Fate; but if you are such as I take you for, have a Proposal to make you, which may be of some little Advantage to you. Neither of them made any immediate Answer, but appear'd bury'd in Consideration for some Moments. At length, We should, doubtless, Madam, (*said one of them,*) willingly come into any Measures to oblige you, provided they are such as may bring us into no Danger, either as to our Persons or Reputations. That which I require of you, (*resumed she,*) has nothing in it criminal: All that I desire is *Secrecy* in what you are intrusted, and to disguise yourselves in such a Manner as you cannot be known, if hereafter seen by the Person on whom you are to impose.——In fine, the Business is only an innocent Frolick, but if blaz'd abroad, might be taken for too great a Freedom in me:——Therefore, if you resolve to assist me, here are five Pieces to drink my Health, and assure you, that I have not discours'd you on an Affair, I design not to proceed in; and when it is accomplish'd fifty more lie ready for you Acceptance. These Words, and, above all, the Money, which was a Sum which, 'tis probable, they had not seen of a long Time, made them immediately assent to all she desir'd, and press for the Beginning of their Employment: But Things were not yet ripe for Execution; and she told them, that the next Day they should be let into the Secret, charging them to meet her in the same Place at an Hour she appointed. 'Tis hard to say, which of these Parties went away best pleas'd; *they*, that Fortune had sent them so unexpected a Windfall; or *she*, that she had found Persons, who appeared so well qualified to serve her.

Indefatigable in the Pursuit of whatsoever her Humour was bent upon, she had no sooner left her new-engag'd Emissaries, than she went in search of a House for the compleating her Project.——She pitch'd on one very large, and magnificently furnished, which she hir'd by the Week, giving them the Money before-hand, to prevent any Inquiries. The next Day she repaired to the Park, where she met the punctual 'Squires of low Degree; and ordering them to follow her to the House she had taken, told them they must condescend to appear like Servants, and gave each of them a very rich Livery. Then writing a Letter to *Beauplaisir*, in a Character vastly different from either of those she had made use of, as *Fantomina*, or the fair Widow *Bloomer*, order'd one of them to deliver it into his own Hands, to bring back an Answer, and to be careful that he sifted out nothing of the Truth.——I do not fear, (*said she,*) that you should discover to him who I am, because that is a Secret, of which you yourselves are ignorant; but I would have you be so careful in your Replies, that he may not think the Concealment springs from any other Reasons than your great Integrity to your Trust.——Seem therefore to know my whole Affairs; and let your refusing to make him Partaker in the Secret, appear to be only the Effect of your Zeal for my Interest and Reputation. Promises of entire Fidelity on the one Side, and Reward on the other, being past, the Messenger made what haste he could to the House of *Beauplaisir*; and being there told where he might find him, perform'd exactly the Injunction that had been given him. But never Astonishment exceeding that which *Beauplaisir* felt at the reading this Billet, in which he found these Lines:

To the All-conquering BEAUPLAISIR,

I imagine not that 'tis a new Thing to you, to be told, you are the greatest Charm in Nature to our Sex: I shall therefore, not to fill up my Letter with any impertinent Praises on your Wit or Person, only tell you, that I am infinite in Love with both, and if you have a Heart not too deeply engag'd, should think myself the happiest of my Sex in being capable of inspiring it with some Tenderness.——There is but one Thing in my Power to refuse you, which is the Knowledge of my Name, which believing the Sight of my Face will render no Secret, you must not take it ill that I conceal from you.——The Bearer of this is a Person I can trust; send by him your Answer; but endeavour not to dive into the Meaning of this Mystery, which will be impossible for you to unravel, and at the same Time very much disoblige me:——But that you may be in no Apprehensions of being impos'd on by a Woman unworthy of your Regard, I will venture to assure you, the first and greatest Men in the Kingdom, would think themselves blest to have that Influence over me you have, though unknown to yourself acquir'd.——But I need not go about to raise your Curiosity, by giving you any Idea of what my Person is; if you think fit to be satisfied, resolve to visit me To-morrow about Three in the Afternoon; and though my Face is hid, you shall not want sufficient Demonstration, that she who takes these unusual Measures to commence a Friendship with you, is neither Old, nor Deform'd. Till then I am,

Yours,

INCOGNITA.

He had scarce come to the Conclusion, before he ask'd the Person who brought it, from what Place he came;——the Name of the Lady he serv'd;——if she were a Wife, or Widow, and several other Questions directly opposite to the Directions of the Letter; but Silence would have avail'd him as much as did all those Testimonies of Curiosity: No *Italian Bravo*,[1] employ'd in a Business of the like Nature, perform'd

[1] A "bravo" was either a hired assassin or a swashbuckler.

his Office with more Artifice; and the impatient Enquirer was convinc'd, that nothing but doing as he was desir'd, could give him any Light into the Character of the Woman who declar'd so violent a Passion for him; and little fearing any Consequence which could ensue from such an Encounter, resolv'd to rest satisfy'd till he was inform'd of every Thing from herself, not imagining this *Incognita* varied so much from the Generality of her Sex, as to be able to refuse the Knowledge of any Thing to the Man she lov'd with that Transcendency of Passion she profess'd, and which his many Successes with the Ladies gave him Encouragement enough to believe. He therefore took Pen and Paper, and answer'd her Letter in Terms tender enough for a Man who had never seen the Person to whom he wrote. The Words were as follows:

To the Obliging and Witty
INCOGNITA,

Though to tell me I am happy enough to be lik'd by a Woman, such, as by your Manner of Writing, I imagine you to be, is an Honour which I can never sufficiently acknowledge, yet I know not how I am able to content myself with admiring the Wonders of your Wit alone: I am certain, a Soul like yours must shine in your Eyes with a Vivacity, which must bless all they look on.——I shall, however, endeavour to restrain myself in those Bounds you are pleas'd to set me, till by the Knowledge of my inviolable Fidelity, I may be thought worthy of gazing on that Heaven I am now but to enjoy in Contemplation.——You need not doubt my glad Compliance with your obliging Summons: There is a Charm in your Lines, which gives too sweet an Idea of their lovely Author to be resisted.——I am all impatient for the blissful Moment, which is to throw me at your Feet, and give me an Opportunity of convincing you that I am,

Your everlasting Slave,
BEAUPLAISIR.

Nothing could be more pleas'd than she, to whom it was directed, at the Receipt of this Letter; but when she was told how inquisitive he had been concerning her Character and Circumstances, she could not forbear laughing heartily to think of the Tricks she had play'd him, and applauding her own Strength of Genius, and Force of Resolution, which by such unthought-of Ways could triumph over her Lover's Inconstancy, and render that very Temper, which to other Women is the greatest Curse, a Means to make herself more bless'd.——Had he been faithful to me, (*said she, to herself,*) either as *Fantomina*, or *Celia*, or the Widow *Bloomer*, the most violent Passion, if it does not change its Object, in Time will wither: Possession naturally abates the Vigour of Desire, and I should have had, at best, but a cold, insipid, husband-like Lover in my Arms; but by these Arts of passing on him as a new Mistress whenever the

89

Ardour, which alone makes Love a Blessing, begins to diminish, for the former one, I have him always raving, wild, impatient, longing, dying.— —O that all neglected Wives, and fond abandon'd Nymphs would take this Method!——Men would be caught in their own Snare, and have no Cause to scorn our easy, weeping, wailing Sex! Thus did she pride herself as if secure she never should have any Reason to repent the present Gaiety of her Humour. The Hour drawing near in which he was to come, she dress'd herself in as magnificent a Manner, as if she were to be that Night at a Ball at Court, endeavouring to repair the want of those Beauties which the Vizard[1] should conceal, by setting forth the others with the greatest Care and Exactness. Her fine Shape, and Air, and Neck, appear'd to great Advantage; and by that which was to be seen of her, one might believe the rest to be perfectly agreeable. *Beauplaisir* was prodigiously charm'd, as well with her Appearance, as with the Manner she entertain'd him: But though he was wild with Impatience for the Sight of a Face which belong'd to so exquisite a Body, yet he would not immediately press for it, believing before he left her he should easily obtain that Satisfaction.— —A noble Collation being over, he began to sue for the Performance of her Promise of granting every Thing he could ask, excepting the Sight of her Face, and Knowledge of her Name. It would have been a ridiculous Piece of Affection in her to have seem'd coy in complying with what she herself had been the first in desiring: She yeilded without even a Shew of Reluctance: And if there be any true Felicity in an Amour such as theirs, both here enjoy'd it to the full. But not in the Height of all their mutual Raptures, could he prevail on her to satisfy his Curiosity with the Sight of her Face: She told him that she hop'd he knew so much of her, as might serve to convince him, she was not unworthy of his tenderest Regard; and if he cou'd not content himself with that which she was willing to reveal, and which was the Conditions of their meeting, dear as he was to her, she would rather part with him for ever, than consent to gratify an Inquisitiveness, which, in her Opinion, had no Business with his Love. It was in vain that he endeavour'd to make her sensible of her Mistake; and that this Restraint was the greatest Enemy imaginable to the Happiness of them both: She was not to be perswaded, and he was oblig'd to desist his Solicitations, though determin'd in his Mind to compass what he so ardently desir'd, before he left the House. He then turned the Discourse wholly on the Violence of the Passion he had for her; and express'd the greatest Discontent in the World at the Apprehensions of being separated;——swore he could dwell for ever in her Arms, and with such an undeniable Earnestness pressed to be permitted to tarry with her the whole Night, that had she been less charm'd with his renew'd Eagerness of Desire, she scarce would have had the Power of refusing him; but in granting this Request, she was not without a Thought that he had another Reason for making it besides the Extremity of his Passion, and had it immediately in her Head how to disappoint him.

[1] A mask for disguise or protection.

The Hours of Repose being arriv'd, he begg'd she would retire to her Chamber; to which she consented, but oblig'd him to go to Bed first; which he did not much oppose, because he suppos'd she would not lie in her Mask, and doubted not but the Morning's Dawn would bring the wish'd Discovery.——The two imagin'd Servants usher'd him to his new Lodging; where he lay some Moments in all the Perplexity imaginable at the Oddness of this Adventure. But she suffer'd not these Cogitations to be of any long Continuance: She came, but came in the Dark; which being no more than he expected by the former Part of her Proceedings, he said nothing of; but as much Satisfaction as he found in her Embraces, nothing ever long'd for the Approach of Day with more Impatience than he did. At last it came; but how great was his Disappointment, when by the Noises he heard in the Street, the Hurry of the Coaches, and the Crys of Penny-Merchants, he was convinc'd it was Night no where but with him? He was still in the same Darkness as before; for she had taken care to blind the Windows in such a Manner, that not the least Chink was left to let in Day.——He complain'd of her Behaviour in Terms that she would not have been able to resist yielding to, if she had not been certain it would have been the Ruin of her Passion:——She, therefore, answered him only as she had done before; and getting out of the Bed from him, flew out of the Room with too much Swiftness for him to have overtaken her, if he had attempted it. The Moment she left him, the two Attendants enter'd the Chamber, and plucking down the Implements which had skreen'd him from the Knowledge of that which he so much desir'd to find out, restored his Eyes once more to Day:——They attended to assist him in dressing, brought him Tea, and by their Obsequiousness, let him see there was but one Thing which the Mistress of them would not gladly oblige him in.—— He was so much out of Humour, however, at the Disappointment of his Curiosity, that he resolv'd never to make a second Visit.——Finding her in an outer Room, he made no Scruple of expressing the Sense he had of the little Trust she reposed in him, and at last plainly told her, he could not submit to receive Obligations from a Lady, who thought him uncapable of keeping a Secret, which she made no Difficulty of letting her Servants into.——He resented,——he once more entreated,——he said all that Man could do, to prevail on her to unfold the Mystery; but all his Adjurations were fruitless; and he went out of the House determin'd never to re-enter it, till she should pay the Price of his Company with the Discovery of her Face and Circumstances.——She suffer'd him to go with this Resolution, and doubted not but he would recede from it, when he reflected on the happy Moments they had pass'd together; but if he did not, she comforted herself with the Design of forming some other Stratagem, with which to impose on him a fourth Time.

She kept the House, and her Gentlemen-Equipage for about a Fortnight, in which Time she continu'd to write to him as *Fantomina* and the Widow *Bloomer*, and received the Visits he sometimes made to each; but his Behaviour to both was grown so cold, that she began to

grow as weary of receiving his now insipid Caresses as he was of offering them: She was beginning to think in what Manner she should drop these two Characters, when the sudden Arrival of her Mother, who had been some Time in a foreign Country, oblig'd her to put an immediate Stop to the Course of her whimsical Adventures.——That Lady, who was severely virtuous, did not approve of many Things she had been told of the Conduct of her Daughter; and though it was not in the Power of any Person in the World to inform her of the Truth of what she had been guilty of, yet she heard enough to make her keep her afterwards in a Restraint, little agreeable to her Humour, and the Liberties to which she had been accustomed.

But this Confinement was not the greatest Part of the Trouble of this now afflicted Lady: She found the Consequences of her amorous Follies would be, without almost a Miracle, impossible to be concealed:—— She was with Child; and though she would easily have found Means to have skreen'd even this from the Knowledge of the World, had she been at liberty to have acted with the same unquestionable Authority over herself, as she did before the coming of her Mother, yet now all her Invention was at a Loss for a Stratagem to impose on a Woman of her Penetration:——By eating little, lacing prodigious strait, and the Advantage of a great Hoop-Petticoat, however, her Bigness was not taken notice of, and, perhaps, she would not have been suspected till the Time of her going into the Country, where her Mother design'd to send her, and from whence she intended to make her escape to some Place where she might be deliver'd with Secrecy, if the Time of it had not happen'd much sooner than she expected.——A Ball being at Court, the good old Lady was willing she should partake of the Diversion of it, as a Farewel to the Town.——It was there she was seiz'd with those Pangs, which none in her Condition are exempt from:——She could not conceal the sudden Rack which all at once invaded her; or had her Tongue been mute, her wildly rolling Eyes, the Distortion of her Features, and the Convulsions which shook her whole Frame, in spite of her, would have reveal'd she labour'd under some terrible Shock of Nature.——Every Body was surpris'd, every Body was concern'd, but few guessed at the Occasion.——Her Mother griev'd beyond Expression, doubted not but she was struck with the Hand of Death; and order'd her to be carried Home in a Chair, while herself follow'd in another.——A Physician was immediately sent for: But he presently perceiving what was her Distemper, call'd the old Lady aside, and told her, it was not a Doctor of his Sex, but one of her own, her Daughter stood in need of.——Never was Astonishment and Horror greater than that which seiz'd the Soul of this afflicted Parent at these Words: She could not for a Time believe the Truth of what she heard; but he insisting on it, and conjuring her to send for a Midwife, she was at length convinc'd of it.——All the Pity and Tenderness she had been for some Moments before possess'd of, now vanish'd, and were succeeded by an adequate Shame and Indignation:——She flew to the Bed where her

1725

Daughter was lying, and telling her what she had been inform'd of, and which she was now far from doubting, commanded her to reveal the Name of the Person whose Insinuations had drawn her to this Dishonour.——It was a great while before she could be brought to confess any Thing, and much longer before she could be prevailed on to name the Man whom she so fatally had lov'd; but the Rack of Nature growing more fierce, and the enraged old Lady protesting no Help should be afforded her while she persisted in her Obstinacy, she, with great Difficulty and Hesitation in her Speech, at last pronounc'd the Name of *Beauplaisir*. She had no sooner satisfy'd her weeping Mother, than that sorrowful Lady sent Messengers at the same Time, for a Midwife, and for that Gentleman who had occasion'd the other's being wanted.——He happen'd by Accident to be at Home, and immediately obey'd the Summons, though prodigiously surpris'd what Business a Lady so much a Stranger to him could have to impart.——But how much greater was his Amazement, when taking him into her Closet, she there acquainted him with her Daughter's Misfortune, of the Discovery she had made, and how far he was concern'd in it?—— All the Idea one can form of wild Astonishment, was mean to what he felt:——He assur'd her, that the young Lady her Daughter was a Person whom he had never, more than at a Distance, admir'd:——That he had indeed spoke to her in publick Company, but that he never had a Thought which tended to her Dishonour.——His Denials, if possible, added to the Indignation she was before inflam'd with:——She had no longer Patience; and carrying him into the Chamber, where she was just deliver'd of a fine Girl, cry'd out, I will not be impos'd on: The Truth by one of you shall be reveal'd.——*Beauplaisir* being brought to the Bed side, was beginning to address himself to the Lady in it, to beg she would clear the Mistake her Mother was involv'd in; when she, covering herself with the Cloaths, and ready to die a second Time with the inward Agitations of her Soul, shriek'd out, Oh, I am undone!——I cannot live, and bear this Shame!—— But the old Lady believing that now or never was the Time to dive into the Bottom of this Mystery, forcing her to rear her Head, told her, she should not hope to Escape the Scrutiny of a Parent she had dishonour'd in such a Manner, and pointing to *Beauplaisir*, Is this the Gentleman, (*said she,*) to whom you owe your Ruin? or have you deceiv'd me by a fictitious Tale? Oh! no, (*resum'd the trembling Creature,*) he is, indeed, the innocent Cause of my Undoing:——Promise me your Pardon, (*continued she,*) and I will relate the Means. Here she ceas'd, expecting what she would reply; which, on hearing *Beauplaisir* cry out, What mean you, Madam? I your Undoing, who never harbour'd the least Design on you in my Life, she did in these Words, Though the Injury you have done your Family, (*said she,*) is of a Nature which cannot justly hope Forgiveness, yet be assur'd, I shall much sooner excuse you when satisfied of the Truth, than while I am kept in a Suspence, if possible, as vexatious as the Crime itself is to me. Encouraged by this she related the whole Truth. And 'tis difficult to determine, if *Beauplaisir*, or the Lady, were most surpris'd at what they

heard; he, that he should have been blinded so often by her Artifices; or she, that so young a Creature should have the Skill to make use of them. Both sat for some Time in a profound Resvery; till at length she broke it first in these Words: Pardon, Sir, (*said she,*) the Trouble I have given you: I must confess it was with a Design to oblige you to repair the supposed Injury you had done this unfortunate Girl, by marrying her, but now I know not what to say:——The Blame is wholly her's, and I have nothing to request further of you, than that you will not divulge the distracted Folly she has been guilty of.——He answered her in Terms perfectly polite; but made no Offer of that which, perhaps, she expected, though could not, now inform'd of her Daughter's Proceedings, demand. He assured her, however, that if she would commit the new-born Lady to his Care, he would discharge it faithfully. But neither of them would consent to that; and he took his Leave, full of Cogitations, more confus'd than ever he had known in his whole Life. He continued to visit there, to enquire after her Health every Day; but the old Lady perceiving there was nothing likely to ensue from these Civilities, but, perhaps, a renewing of the Crime, she entreated him to refrain; and as soon as her Daughter was in a Condition, sent her to a Monastery in *France*, the Abbess of which had been her particular Friend. And thus ended an Intreague, which, considering the Time it lasted, was as full of Variety as any, perhaps, that many Ages has produced.

1725

MATTHEW CONCANEN

A "Novel" (1726)

The author: Matthew Concanen (1701-1749) was born in Ireland, where he studied law. He came, however, to London in the early 1720s to become a professional writer. He quickly established his reputation thanks to his poems (his early "A Match at Football" remains his best-known work) and journalism. He supported the government of Robert Walpole and entered into a polemic against Alexander Pope. In 1732 he was named attorney general of Jamaica. He spent the next 16 years in the West Indies; then he returned to London, where he died of consumption.

The text: It was published in the *British Journal* 180 (Saturday 19 February 1726), 1-2. The letter was dated 18 February 1726. Concanen collected his essays from the *London* and the *British Journal*, as he writes in the "Advertisement" to his collection, "not . . . from any Opinion of their Excellence, but to refute the Calumny of a rancorous and foul-mouth'd Railer who has asserted in print that the Author of them wrote *several Scurrilities* in those Papers." That "foul-mouth'd Railer" was Alexander Pope, who had referred to Concanen's "Speculatist" as "several dull and dead scurrilities." The text is taken from this collection: *The Speculatist. A Collection of Letters and Essays, Moral and Political, Serious and Humorous: Upon Various Subjects* (London: Printed by J. Watts, for the Author, 1730). 60-68. Like many of the newspaper essays of the era, it was conceived in the form of a letter to the editor, or, in this case, to the author of the essay-series entitled "The Speculatist." The word "novel" in the title did not have quotation marks, but it was printed in a different style (with a different slope) than the indefinite article. What it first appeared it bore no title, but began with the address "To the Author of the *British Journal*."

Sir,

Hypocrisy is one of the vilest as well as one of the commonest Vices of Humanity; the fair Sex seems the most tainted with it, and it is not much to the Honour of human Nature, that the greatest Proficients in this ungenerous Frailty should be the most agreeable Part of our Species. Instead of bringing elaborate Arguments to prove this, give me leave to present the World with an Instance of the Truth of it, in a faithful Narrative of an Adventure which I am well assured happened lately at *Paris*, and which made so great a Noise there, as to give occasion to a Comedy written upon the Groundwork of this Story.

A Widow Lady, who was neither overstocked with Youth nor Beauty, but whose Estate could more than supply those Wants, and whose Family was considerable enough to make her proud, had, by Means of these Charms, drawn about her an Army of Lovers, who continually laid Siege to her Person, in hopes of reducing her to the Necessity of surrendering her Fortune. She put on the Appearance of Piety and Devotion, affected to be scrupulously nice in the most trifling Matters; Sanctity and Religion were her continual Topicks, her Confessor was her chief Minister, and she found out Scruples of Conscience almost enough to turn his Brain, if he attended to them. In short, she repented of the Pleasures she had formerly received in the Marriage-Bed, and determined to atone for them by a most austere Chastity for the future: She gave Alms in abundance, comforted the Sick in Hospitals, and, as Mr. *Pope* expresses it,

> *Visits to every Church she daily paid;*
> *And march'd in every holy Masquerade.*[1]

Upon these specious Appearances she founded so fair a Reputation, that, by the help of a little Flattery from her Favourites, the Priests and Friars, she was universally known by the Name of the *Holy Widow*; but lest her true Name should be necessary, through the Course of this Story, I take this Opportunity of informing my Readers, that she was called *Maria*.

Her Lovers were Men of Courage, not a whit dishearten'd by all this: Some of them, in order to be always at hand, pursued her from Church to Church, from Hospital to Hospital, and underwent for her sake, what they would never have done for their Souls, all the Fatigues of her Devotion and Charity; while others brib'd the Confessor to assure her, that her Soul might as well be saved in Matrimony as Widowhood; but all to little Purpose. There was only one of them that was wise enough to foresee the Success of their Wild-Goose-Chase, or honest enough to despise such sinister Means of carrying his Point, and therefore discontinued his Visits; his Name was *Lysander*: But our Widow had not an Admirer the less for his Absence; for just about this Time arrived in Town *Sylvio*, a younger Brother of a genteel, but decayed Family: Miserably poor was *Sylvio*, but he had a well-made Person, a fine Face, some Wit, and a good Address.

Fortune threw him into the Neighbourhood of the Widow, where he had not been long, before he heard so much of her Estate, and her Piety, that he long'd to know more of her: He soon found out her Haunts, followed and observed her, and from thence made a shrewd Guess at her Constitution: He saw Vanity in her Devotion, and Ostentation in her Charity; those shock'd him not; but the Number of her Suitors, that puzzled him: Ordinary Methods he saw would not do; well then, extraordinary must be used: He knew, as I said, her Constitution, that she was more in love with Reputation than Virtue, and less afraid of Sin than Shame; from which he concluded, that if he could procure Access to her, and at the same Time baffle Suspicion, his Point was as good as gained.

In order to this, he left the Part of the Town she lived in, and retired to the most obscure Corner of it; and, by the Help of a little Money, soon found Means to procure a Licence to beg, with an Attestation of his being deaf and dumb from his Birth. Our new Beggar, thus equipped, knowing *Maria*'s Haunts, though perfectly unknown to her, took Care to appear at all the Churches where there was any Likelihood of her coming: His good Presence, in a little time, attracted her Eyes, she read

[1] From Alexander Pope's *Wife of Bath* (1714), an imitation of Chaucer's tale; in the first line, the original reads "we daily paid."

the Licence and Certificate, appeared concern'd at his Case, and gave him a bountiful Alms. *Sylvio* thank'd her with a Bow so graceful, that, turning to her Maid surpriz'd, she cried, What Pity it is so likely a Fellow should be so unfortunate. *Sylvio* was pleased with his Success, and therefore constantly gave his Attendance at one Church or other, where he never failed to find her, and never found her in vain. He constantly drained her Purse, which he as generously distributed among the real Beggars, as soon as her Back was turned. *Lucy*, her Woman, one Day observed this, and reported it to the Widow, who was so struck with the Generosity of the Action, that she made it the Pretence for putting in Practice a Resolution she had before made in favour of *Sylvio*, which was to take him home to her House, cloath, feed him, and provide him an Apartment, out of pure Charity: However, she would neither do this nor any thing else, without consulting her Confessor: The good Man, charm'd with the Charity of the Widow, gave his Consent joyfully. *Sylvio*, though he counterfeited so well as to make it hard for them to communicate the Design to him, yet, when it was proper for him to understand, thankfully accepted the Favour, and was in effect brought home, new cloathed, well lodged, and the Widow made it her own Task to attend him.

Pleasure and Reputation, when they can be enjoy'd together, are the greatest Comforts in Life. These *Maria* had in view; *Sylvio*'s Form gave her Hopes of one, and his Infirmities of the other. But *Lucy*, who was as wanton and hypocritical as her Mistress, got before-hand with her; being more amorous, and less nice, she sooner found Means to make herself understood by *Sylvio*; who, from an Opinion that she might be of use to him in his Design, administred to her all the Happiness in his Power.

While Things went on thus, an Accident happen'd which gave the Widow's Wantonness a Tincture of Love, and added to her Desire of his Person, an Esteem for the Merits of *Sylvio*. One of the briskest of her Admirers, but the least in her good Graces, who remember'd the old Rule of wooing a Widow, was resolved to put it in practice; and accordingly took the Opportunity of being alone with her for making an attack upon her Chastity; she resisted and cry'd out, and did all that was in the Power of a poor weak Woman; but had nevertheless been deflower'd, if *Sylvio* (who wandered up and down the House like a tame Bird, or any other domestick Animal, and had Access every where, went in and came out as he pleased, and was known by all Visitors, for the Widow's Mute) had not bounc'd into the Room at the Instant when her Virtue was at the last Gasp; he quickly snatch'd up a Sword he saw in the Room, and, by his stern Aspect and Posture, gave the Ravisher to know, it was proper to defend himself: He presently took the Hint, left the Widow, and made an Attack of a different nature upon her Champion, who soon disarmed and laid him at her Feet: Thus was the House cleared of one troublesome Rival.

The Widow's Friends and Visitants were soon acquainted with the Story, and the Address and Dexterity of *Sylvio* was the Widow's constant Theme; she affirmed it was marvellous, and the flattering Friars assured her, it was a Miracle wrought by God to reward her Charity to the Mute.

To be as concise as possible: The Widow ever after this burned for the Enjoyment of *Sylvio*, till her Woman, who was more learn'd than she, put her in the way of satisfying her Appetite: If she lov'd *Sylvio* before, now she doated on him; she thought of nothing but how to secure the Continuance of her Happiness, and began to entertain groundless Fears for the loss of it: For this Reason, she held frequent Conferences with *Lucy* how to keep the Mute for ever in her House, in spite of his Friends, if he should have any, or his own Inclinations, if they should prompt him to wander. These, and many other Discourses, were always in the Presence of *Sylvio*, who still behaved so properly that he gave no Suspicion.

Lucy, who was a cunning Baggage, and knew how to make her own Advantage of every thing, answered the Widow, that to oblige her, and secure her Happiness, she was willing to give up her own Hopes, and marry *Sylvio*. This *Maria* did not entirely approve of; but as she was in her Woman's Power, could not absolutely reject it: But the Question was put to the Mute by Bits of Drawings, as all their Love Questions were, which he very gallantly answered, to the Widow's Satisfaction. This, if possible, encreased her good Liking towards him; and all Things went on very happily, till she found herself, by God's Blessing on their Endeavours, in a way of being shortly detected by a growing Belly. This occasioned several private Conferences (still in the Presence of *Sylvio*) between her and *Lucy*: Matters were strangely perplexed: *Sylvio* was offered as a Husband by *Lucy*, but refus'd with the utmost Abhorrence and Detestation: In short, after several vain fruitless Projects concerted, it was agreed to send to *Lysander*, and offer him that Happiness upon his own Terms, which he had for some time past neglected to pursue: So said, so done. Her Confessor was employ'd to break the Matter to *Lysander*, and assure him, that, in regard to his Probity, *Maria* had pitched upon him, among her Admirers, to be the happy Man. He, tho' absolutely void of Tenderness for her Person, yet had a great Esteem for her Estate, and not thinking it proper, when Fortune knocked at his Door, to enquire the Way she came, quickly consented; and a Day was appointed accordingly.

Sylvio was now in a distracted Condition. He saw all his Endeavours lost, his Hopes ready to vanish, and he himself unable to prevent them: But something must be done. He presently writ to his elder Brother a pressing Letter, assuring him, that his Rise or Ruin depended upon his being in Town on a Day, which was to be a Week before the Marriage: When he had done this, he went to *Lucy*'s Apartment, and, taking her by the Hand, spoke to her: She, with surprize to hear him, swoon'd; which, when he had recover'd her from, and comforted her a little, he addressed her in this manner. "Don't be surpriz'd, my dear *Lucy*, to hear me speak now; my All is at Stake, and a longer Silence might lose it: Be in no Fear; for what has passed between us, it shall be as secret as if I was really dumb; make use of this Knowledge to assist me in my Design on your Mistress; assure her, that if she marries me, she marries a Man that can speak, a Man of Honour, and a Gentleman: If you can succeed, as my Fortune will be made, so, I promise you, shall yours. Farewel, and use Dispatch."

Lucy went to her Mistress, and *Sylvio* posted himself so as to overhear them: *Maria* received the Proposal with the utmost Indignation; and, upon Assurance of *Sylvio*'s having the Use of his Tongue, vow'd his Death, either by Poison of Assassination. *Lucy* urged the Marriage as a mild Revenge; but in vain: Her Answer was, "Shall the filthy World discover what were the Motives of my Charity to the Villain?"

Sylvio knew enough from this, to think it advisable to provide for his own Safety, which he did by retiring to his own obscure Lodging, and there waiting his Brother's Arrival, who was exactly punctual. He acquainted him with the History, and sent him presently to *Lysander*; who, upon examining Circumstances, found Reason to believe that he was made a Dupe: But *Lucy*, who was brought to him, by her Testimony, put Matters beyond Doubt. He therefore came to an Interview with *Sylvio*; where it was agreed to divide the Widow's Fortune between them, two thirds and the Lady to *Sylvio*, and one third to *Lysander*; who, being of a revengeful Temper, could not forgive the Affront put upon him, but made it part of his Bargain to have Liberty of resenting it publickly, which was agreed to, and done in this manner.

On the Day appointed, *Lysander* and the Widow, with a number of their Friends and Relations, went to the Parish-Church as Bride and Bridegroom, in order, as was thought, to be publickly married. *Sylvio* and his Brother paid their Attendance also among the Crowd: When the Couple stood before the Priest to have the Ceremony perform'd, *Lysander* suffered all, till this Question was asked, Wilt thou take *Maria* to Wife? &c. to which he answered aloud, "No. But perhaps this Gentleman may, (pointing to *Sylvio*.) I don't care for trespassing upon another's Ground; and he that sow'd the Corn shall reap the Harvest for me." Here he told the Audience the whole History, while the Widow stood in the utmost Confusion, which *Sylvio* took Advantage of, to speak to her. He pressed her to Marriage, that the Company might not be disappointed; and she, to make the best of a bad Market, struck up a Bargain. They were married, her Hypocrisy blown up, and her Fortune divided according to the Agreement. *Lysander* had enough to live happily without her, and *Sylvio* to repair the Ruin of his Family with her. *Lucy* was sufficiently provided for soon after by *Sylvio*, who, I am told, lives happily and pleasantly with his Widow to this Day.

Thus, Sir, have I told you as succinctly as possibly, the History and Fall of this Piece of Hypocrisy. I am satisfy'd that several Circumstances in it, were I inclined to play the *Frenchman*, and dwell upon them, might be wrought up to more Entertainment, and the Whole make an agreeable Novel: But I was tied down to the Limits of a Letter, which, I fear, in spite of my Caution, I have exceeded, and therefore beg Pardon for.

I am, Sir,
Your Humble Servant, &c.

ERASMUS PHILIPS
Foul Weather (1726)

The author: Although he was one of the most important British economists of the first half of the 18th century, almost nothing is known about Erasmus Philips. He started publishing in 1720 and collected his works in a volume in 1751, which can give us an idea about the span of his life, but when and where he was born and died remains a mystery. His best-known work is *The State of the Nation, in Respect to her Commerce, Debts, and Money* (1725). In 1726, he started a periodical called *The Country Gentleman*, which folded a year later. William Pulteney and Viscount Bolingbroke authored one of the numbers (37), in which they foreshadowed their own journal, the very successful *The Craftsman* (1727-1753). Like them, Philips had intended to criticise Robert Walpole's government, but in the end decided that did not offer him enough material, so he turned his attention to the mores. He is not to be confused with Sir Erasmus Philipps (1699-1743), MP for Haverfordwest.

The text: It first appeared, untitled, in Philips's magazine, *The Country Gentleman* 39 (Friday, July 22, 1726) and it was later reprinted in his last known publication, *Miscellaneous Works Consisting of Essays Political and Moral* (London: Printed for Mr. Waller, over-against *Fetter-Lane, Fleet-street*; Mr. Lewis, near *Tom's Coffee-House, Covent-Garden*; Mr. Jackson, and Mr. Joliffe, in *St. James's-Street*, 1751), 302-307, from which this has been taken. It was introduced by a line from Virgil: "Multum ille & terris jactatus & alto" ("much tossed on sea and land by violence from above"), which is the third line from the *Aeneid*. Unlike in the original, the text is here divided into paragraphs.

1726

Will. Testy call'd upon me t'other Day to go along with him as far as *Hammersmith*,[1] to dine with an old Acquaintance of ours, who lives near the *Thames* side. As *Will* happens to be a Man of that delicate Constitution, that his Mind seems to be govern'd by the good or evil Impressions of the Weather, he always chuses a Sun-shiny Day, when he goes to visit his Friends, and indeed, when we took Water at *Whitehall* Stairs,[2] the *Sun* spread all his Glories over the Horizon, with so clear a Light, and so agreeable a Warmth, that I fancied myself, for a Time, in *Campania*, or *Naples*.

The Whitehall Stairs in the first half of the 18th century.

---

[1] The westernmost of London's inner boroughs, then in the parish of Fulham.
[2] The Whitehall Stairs, originally a public right of way through the palace buildings of Whitehall, gave their name to an embarkation point on the Thames.

We had not been long in this agreeable Situation, before a Cloud appear'd in the *West*, which the Watermen affirm'd was a Sign of Change of Weather. This put us a little out of Humour, because it defeated those great Hopes we had raised in our Minds of spending that Day in an uninterrupted Satisfaction. Whilst we were bewailing our Disappointment, and putting on our Cloaks to prevent being surprized by the Rain, we were overtaken by a Boat with two Ladies in it, who attack'd us in a familiar Language, peculiar to the Inhabitants of that Element where we travelled, and cryed out, *Where are those two old Prigs agoing?* But without staying for an Answer, one of them continued, *I suppose, these are a Couple of old Fornicators, that are stealing out of Town to see a Wench. Don't you think* Fanny (says one to the other) *these queer Fellows look like the two Elders in the Picture, that hangs in our Parlour at* Putney? As great an Enmity as *Will* professes for that Sex, yet he can't forbear pratling to them whenever they come in his Way; *I believe* (says he) *Ladies, it would be for your Advantage, if the Character of* Susanna *fitted either of you half so well.*[1] *D'ye hear* Molly (reply'd the other) *the Thing can speak! Well Dad, how do you pay, by the Week, or by the Quarter? O! by the Week you may be sure* (says the other) *these old Curmudgeons never trust a Girl with a Quarter's Pay at a Time. Heark'ee you old Toast in the Camblet*[2] *Cloak?* (addressing herself to me) *do you think any Body can like that Weather-beaten Face of yours? I had rather kiss a Peruke Block.*[3] *What a sapless Stick of Wood is there? I'll be hang'd* Fanny, says she, *if you were to put a Candle to him, if he did not burn like a Billet.* I was resolv'd not to speak a Word, believing Silence the best Way to put an End to this Impertinence, but unfortunately for poor *Will Testy,* their Boat approaching still nearer us, one of them burst out a Laughing, as if she would split her Sides, and bawl'd out, Fanny, *what d'ye think? That's old Squire* Testy, *that kept the famous Mrs.——* here, she had as much good Manners, which I did not expect, as to whisper the Name in her Ear; *What,* says she, *will you never have done? Surely thou art the most impudent old Sinner that ever was born. Pray Sir, what's become of that fine Lady, that equipp'd you so handsomely?* Here poor *Will* could not contain himself, but bid her *hold her Tongue, for an impertinent Hussy.* I could easily perceive he was stung with this Part of the Discourse, therefore I ordered the Watermen to feather their Oars, by which Means we got rid of our new Acquaintance, but however, I found this foolish Adventure had put my Friend very much

1726

---

[1] Susanna and the Elders, a story from the Book of Daniel, often represented in painting, about two lustful elders who discover a young woman bathing and try to blackmail her into having sex with them. She refuses, is arrested when the two men accuse her of having lain in waiting for a tryst, and sentenced to death. Daniel intervenes, interrogates the men separately, proves their misdeed and has them executed instead.

[2] Camblet, camlet or camelot, an "Oriental" type of woven fabric, originally made of goat's hair, later replaced by sheep' wool. In the 18th century, England was the main manufacturer of camlet in Europe.

[3] Wig head, also called "block head."

out of Humour, by certain broken Sentences that fell from him (as if he were talking to himself) whenever he is under this Circumstance.

We were now arrived as high as *Battersea*,[1] when the Wind began to rise, and thick Clouds obscured the Heavens, and gave us certain Symptoms of an approaching Shower; in a few Minutes the Rain fell in a most violent Manner, and being driven furiously by the Wind we were hardly able to defend ourselves with our Cloaks. I comforted my Companion as well as I could, but he broke out every now and then; and said, Well, *if there is any Thing more deceitful than Women, it is the Weather? If they ever catch me upon the Water again, I'll give them leave to pickle me.*[2]

At last, with a great deal of Difficulty we arrived at *Hammersmith*, where getting as fast as we could to our Friend's House, we were received with all the Kindness and good Manners imaginable. As much as *Will* was out of Humour at the Disappointment of his Voyage, yet at the Sight of his old Acquaintance, he put on Air of Cheerfulness and Pleasure, and after some Time spent in an agreeable Raillery upon the former Transactions of their Lives, we were interrupted by the Approach of some young Ladies who came in upon us, upon Notice that Dinner was ready. After our Friend had presented us to his Wife, and the rest of the Company, we sat down to Table. I forgot to mention, that this Gentleman's Wife was a Stranger to us, he having lately married her. I could not help observing, that these young Creatures look'd upon us with a great deal of Contempt, and when *Will* tucked his Napkin into his Collar, they all burst out a Laughing. The Gentleman of the House seem'd to be out of Countenance at their Behaviour, but *Will* with a great deal of Gallantry turn'd off the Ridicule, by saying, *That it was his greatest Happiness, to think, that in all Parts of his Life, he should contribute to the Pleasure and Entertainment of the Fair Sex.*

We had not been long in this Situation, before our Company increased upon us prodigiously, and every Person had the Head of a large Spaniel or Greyhound at his Elbow; besides these, there were three or four Perroquets, that flew about the Room, and scream'd most hideously. While *Will* was deliberating in directing the Wing of a *Chicken* to his Mouth, one of these Domestick *Hawks* stoop'd at it, and carry'd it off his Fork in an Instant. This Disappointment was attended with a worse soon after, for when he was going to drink the Lady of the House's Health in a Bumper of Claret, one of the Spaniels sprung up upon his Arm, and made him spill all the Liquor upon his Cloaths. It is impossible to look grave, when these trifling Accidents happen, and a very hard Matter for the Sufferer to keep his Temper under this Circumstance; in short, poor *Will* could preserve his Equanimity, but resented it by giving the Dog a Box on the Ear. The Lady of the House colour'd immediately, and cry'd out,

[1] District on the south bank of the River Thames.
[2] Allusion to the common punishment of flogging and "pickling," i.e., rubbing salt, brine, or vinegar into the back of the victim.

Law Sir, how could you be so barbarous? The Dog snarl'd, and seem'd resolv'd to revenge the Affront, the rest of his Brethren began to bark and animate him to the Combat, in a Minute there was nothing but Noise and Confusion, the Birds scream'd, the Dogs bark'd, the Mistress scolded, the Ladies laugh'd, the Master and Servants rose up and storm'd to put an End to the Fray. There could not possibly be more Noise in a Sea Fight.

In some Time, when the Dogs were turned out of the Room, and all was quiet, the Gentleman of the House spoke to his Lady, *Madam, how often have I desired, that these Creatures should not be admitted here at Dinner Time? Sir*, says she very warmly, *I don't see what Harm they do; if People are so indiscreet to provoke them, they must take what follows, I think.* I could perceive by this Answer, that my Friend liv'd under a Female Government, and when Dinner was over, the Lady's Looks shew'd, that we had not been welcome Guests, for she went away without taking any Notice of us. As for the Gentleman himself, he was so much out of Countenance, that he could hardly speak a Word, but the Weather continuing still very foul, *Will* desired him to lend him his Coach to *London*, which was immediately got ready, and we took our Leave. As we were on the Road, I could not help reflecting on our ill Fortune, which had disappointed us in every Part of the most pleasing Expectation, but *Will* interrupted me and said, *He could not account for it any Way, but that he had observ'd some Men were so unhappy thro' almost the whole Course of their Lives, as to meet with cross Accidents in all their Undertakings. I am one of those unlucky Wretches myself*, says he, *and I should not wonder to see the Coach overturn'd before we get to* London; but, however, we got Home without any farther Accident.

The river front at Hammersmith in the 18th century.

ELIZABETH SINGER ROWE
Friendship in Death (1728)

The author: Elizabeth Singer was born in 1674 in a dissenting family. Her poetry made her famous in the early 18th century and she was admired, among others, by Alexander Pope, Matthew Prior, Isaac Watts, and John Dunton. She married poet Thomas Rowe (1687-1715) in 1710; after his death, she retired to her family farm in Frome, Somerset, from where she continued to send her poetry, fiction, and essays to London booksellers. *Friendship in Death* was arguably the best-selling English-language work in prose for more than a century. Rowe died in 1737, after she sent farewell letters to friends.

The text: This is the first piece in her *Friendship in Death. In Twenty Letters from the Dead to the Living* (London: T. Worrall, 1728), 1-8. The following is from the fourth edition "corrected with Additions" (London: T. Worrall, at the Judge's Head, over-against St. *Dunstan's* Church in *Fleet-Street*, 1736), 1-5. With few exceptions, Rowe's corrections concern spelling: she wrote out all the contractions of the first edition and replaced most of the capitalisations. Like the other pieces in the volume, it is numbered rather than titled and it appears in all editions as "Letter I."

Further reading: Paula R. Backsheider. *Elizabeth Singer Rowe and the Development of the English Novel*. Baltimore: The Johns Hopkins UP, 2013.

Melanie Bigold. "Elizabeth Rowe's Fictional and Familiar Letters: Exemplarity, Enthusiasm, and the Production of Posthumous Meaning." *Journal for Eighteenth-Century Studies* 29.1 (March 2006): 1-14.

To the Earl of R——, from Mr.——, who had promised to appear to him after his Death.

This will find you, my Lord, confirmed in your Infidelity, by your late disappointment. It was not in my power to give you the evidence of a future state, which you desired, and I had rashly promised; but since this engagement was a secret to every mortal but ourselves, you must be assured that this comes from your deceased friend, whose friendship you see has reached beyond the grave.

In my last sickness, we fixed on the time and place of my appearance; you was punctual to the appointment: for though I was not permitted to make myself visible, I had the curiosity to know if you had the resolution to attend the solemnity of a visit from the dead. The hour was come, the clock from a neighbouring steeple struck *one*, no human voice was heard to break the awful silence; the moon and stars shone clear in their midnight splendour, and glimmered through the trees, which in lofty rows led to the center of a grove, where I was engaged to meet you.

I saw you enter the walks, with a careless incredulous air, not the least concern or expectation appeared in your looks; as if you came there only in regard to your own word, and a sort of respect to my memory: However, the calmness of the night induced you to walk 'till the morning began to break, when you retired, singing an idle song you had got out of the *Fairy Tales*.[1] By the gayety of your temper you seemed pleased, my Lord, with a new proof against a future life, and happy to find yourself (as you concluded) on a level with the beasts that perish.—A glorious advantage! and worthy of your triumph!

But we have so often discoursed on this subject, that I would not tire you with the repetition of any thing past; only once more to make way to your reason, by moving your passions, in recollecting the manner of your brother's death, which was all a demonstration of the immortality of the Soul, and to what heights of fortitude that prospect could raise the heart of man, at the hour of terror, and in the jaws of death.

With what a ready composure did he endure the violence of his distemper! with what conviction and full assurance expect the reward of his piety! with what calmness, with what a graceful resignation, did he receive the sentence of death, when (at his importunity) the physicians told him there was no hopes of his recovery! *Then I have but a few weary steps*, he replied, *and the Journey of life will be finished.*

This was not a time for affectation, all was open undissembled goodness, and a true greatness of mind: Nothing else could have supported him, when every circumstance of life conspired to allure him back to life, to deepen the shadows of the grave, and make the King of Terrors more terrible.

There was not, my Lord, among the race of men, a more lovely and agreeable person than your brother; his marriage was just concluded with the charming *Cleora*, he had just finished a noble seat and fine gardens to receive her. When he was near death, she came at his request to take a last and sad farewell; Angels might have sorrowed to see tears in the brightest eyes on earth, while her tenderness for him would have disguised her anguish: This, with the sight of a fond young sister, fainting in her woman's arms; your aged father sitting near, silent and stupid with his grief: what could support the mind of man in such complicated distress! The accomplished youth, who had all that was gentle and humane in his disposition, must have betrayed some weakness, if he had not been assisted by a Power superior to Nature. But how equal, how steady was his mind! how becoming, how graceful his whole behaviour! Never was the last, the closing part of life, performed with more decency and grandeur: His reason was clear and elevated, and his Words were the very language of immortality, and excited at the same time both *pity* and *envy* in those that were near him.

When the cold sweats hung on his brows, and his breath and speech failed, joy struggled thro' the decay of nature, and a heavenly smile sate on his face; a smile that at once compelled our tears, and accused us of weakness in them.

[1] The reference here is probably to Madame d'Aulnoy's fairy tales (first translated in 1691), which Rowe admired, and which included songs.

You, my Lord, attended him to the last moment of life; and when I pressed this argument of a future state, you confessed, that though you thought Religion a delusion, it was the most agreeable delusion in the world, and that men who flattered themselves with those gay visions, had much the advantage of those that saw nothing before them but a gloomy uncertainty, or the dreadful hope of an annihilation.

From this Uncertainty I was very sollicitous to draw you, while I was in a mortal state; but I have now a more ardent desire to convince you, though I cannot obtain the permission to give you that Evidence you requested: However, this Letter may satisfy you that I am in a state of existence; nor is an apparition from the dead a greater miracle than a variety of objects that daily surround you, and owe the loss of their effect to your familiarity with them.

Happy minds in this superior state are still concerned for the welfare of mortals, and make a thousand kind visits to their friends; to whom, if the laws of the immaterial worlds did not forbid, it would be easy to make themselves visible, by the splendor of their own vehicles, and the command they have on the powers of material things, and the organs of sight: It often seems a miracle to us that you do not perceive us; for we are not absent from you by *places*, but by the different conditions of the *states* we are in.

You'll find this in your Closet, and may be assured it comes from
Your constant

And immortal Friend

CLERIMONT.

1728

106

THOMAS GORDON

Inconstancy and Fickleness of Man (1732)

The author: By the time he published his essay-series "The Humourist" in volume format, Thomas Gordon had already begun the brief collaboration with John Trenchard (1662-1723), which remains his main claim to fame. Together, they wrote two important essay-series: *The Independent Whig* and *Cato's Letters* (the latter, especially, deeply influenced 18th-century political thought in Britain and the United States). After Trenchard's death, Gordon was appointed commissioner of the wine licenses and produced a well-received translation of Tacitus (1728). He then started his collaboration with *The Universal Spectator* in late 1730, and in 1733 became the magazine's editor, replacing Defoe's son-in-law Henry Baker (but keeping the latter's persona, Henry Stonecastle).

The text: In *The Universal Spectator*, Gordon published two stories with similar plot and title. After 1733, when he was the magazine's editor, he was able to republish, in slightly modified form, some of the "Humourist" essays from 1718-1720, including a reworking of "Of the Fickleness of Human Nature" in number 316 (26 October 1734). In 1730-1732, when he was only a contributor, he simply borrowed subject matter from *The Humourist* (for another example, see number 131) and that is why another story, with the same topic, but different character sketches, had already appeared, untitled, in *The Universal Spectator and Weekly Journal* 199 (29 July

1732), 1-2. An abridgment of this story (published here) also appeared in *The London Magazine; or, Gentleman's Monthly Intelligencer* (July 1732), reprinted in volume (London: Ackers, Wilford, Cox, Clarke and Astley) with the title "Inconstancy and Fickleness of Man" (Vol. I, 196). The following is the original version of this story, as published in *The Universal Spectator* 199.

There are some People who may be called meer Nothings of themselves, being never long any Thing: They take the Impression of their Company as Wax does that of a Seal; but their Inclinations are as soon chang'd by the next agreeable Idea, as the Impression on Wax by a Second Melting. Every Thing new is engaging, and they are impatient 'till they have experienc'd what they imagine capable of giving them Pleasure, but by their Ir-resolution never go farther than a Design. I knew, last War,[1] a young Gentleman of this Stamp, who was so delighted with the Account

[1] The most recent war in which Britain had been involved was the War of the Quadruple Alliance (1718-1720), although only the Royal Navy took active part in the conflict. The ground troops had fought numerous battles in the War of the Spanish Succession (1702-1714).

given of a Campaign, that he resolv'd nothing should hinder his making one the next Summer. Unluckily a Captain of a Man of War extolling a Sea Life as much more honourable, since they had both the Enemy and an inexorable Element to battle, and had no back Doors, no Hopes to escape but by their Bravery and Conduct, though he acknowledg'd they were not expos'd to tedious Marches and wet Trenches, but quietly took their Rest in warm Cabbins and good Beds. This Captain, I say, put my Friend WHIRL, for that was his Name, quite out of Conceit with the Land Service, and made him resolve upon taking a Voyage with the Captain, who was order'd to the *West-Indies*. A grave old Gentleman at Table, asked Mr. WHIRL, if he thought Heaven had been too indulgent to him, that he must needs go in search of Misfortunes because he was not subject to them? "Pray Squire WHIRL," said he, "do you imagine you will either walk better, or look one jot the handsomer for a wooden Leg, or an armless Coat Sleeve dangling as you go? Do you want for any Thing? Do you imagine a foreign Country, where you are a Stranger, will afford you more delightful Prospects than your own? That you will be better receiv'd than at your own Seat, or more respected and caress'd than in your own Neighbourhood? There you are at home, and may command; abroad you will be look'd upon as a Man of desperate Fortune, who hires out his Limbs and Life for scanty Bread. Would any Man of your easy Fortune, and in his Senses, change a wholesome Air for the sickly Climate you propose to go to, where, if you escape the Enemy, 'tis a Million to one you die by the Dry Gripes, or lose the Use of your Limbs? Is there not more Satisfaction to be found in a Country Life, which affords such Number of innocent Diversions; you can Fish, Hunt, Set and Shoot in your own Manors, you have Nobody to contradict you, all the lower Sort are in a Manner your Vassals, they are overjoy'd to be employ'd by you, take it as an Honour if you speak to them, and never approach you but with a respectful Distance in their Behaviour; the Gentry round are all pleas'd when you favour them with a Visit, and not a Man of Distinction round the Country but values you. Can't you then be quiet, and enjoy the Blessings Providence (I may say) has shower'd down upon you? Are you weary of them? Are you tir'd of Life, that you go in Search of Fatigues and Death? Take my Advice, go down to your Seat, look into your Affairs, don't trust the Management of your Estate to Stewards and Baillifs, who commonly make Fortunes for their own, by beggaring the Families of their Masters; and like your Fathers, live cheerfully and belov'd, and you may hope, like them, to see your Children fit to manage the Estate transmitted to you, thro' many brave Ancestors, when good Old Age shall give Happiness to you, and Grief to all your Acquaintance."

Mr. WHIRL was so affected with the old Gentleman's Discourse, that he resolved to leave the Town the very next Morning, and give himself up to a Country Life. BOB SAUNTER hearing this Resolution, ask'd him, "What Diversions he could propose to himself in the Country; which to him was as dangerous as a Campaign or a *West-India* Voyage; for what Soldier runs more Risque of his Life than a Country Sportsman, who every Day

1732

108

ventures his Limbs and Life in the Pursuit of a Fox, which when kill'd is thrown away; or in that of a Hare, which is not worth Half a Crown? If a Country Squire gets no Harm, he gets no Credit; whereas, the Soldier may not only come off as well, but he is sure of Glory; he is look'd upon at his Return, as a Bulwark of the Nation; and every Man, who sees him, pays him Respect, as he is conscious, he owes his Safety, his Liberty, and every Thing that's dear, to the Bravery of the Soldier. But suppose there was no Danger in leaping Ditches; how much is it below a Man of Sense, to be running all his Life after a Kennel of Hounds, in pursuit of a poor, frighted, innocent Animal! nay, how cruel is it to exult in the putting to Death, after the most cruel Manner, one of the most harmless Creatures of the whole Creation! Then, for our Evening Diversions; is the dry Belly-ach more dangerous than the drinking Bumpers of Ale like Brandy, and being in a Cloud of Smoak of stinking Tobacco? Death from a Cannon Ball is not more sure, tho' somewhat more rapid. But let us, for Argument Sake, allow, your Constitution will bear this Way of Life, how can you answer it to your good Sense? Where's the Edification from such Company? You may, indeed, learn the Diseases incident to Dogs and Horses, to halloo a Pack of Hounds, to make Flies for Rates, to knit Nets for Setting and Fishing, to take a Gun Lock to Pieces, and perhaps, to be Jockey enough to over-reach an honest Gentleman in selling a Horse upon your Word: And would any Man bury himself in the Country, who can live in Town, to attain to such useful Qualifications as these? Consider, you change sparkling generous Wine, for heavy stupifying Ale; the Drawing-Room for a Dog-kennell; for a well accomplish'd Country 'Squire must delight in the Smell of Carrion; the Playhouse, Assemblies, Balls, Masquerades, rich Dress, fine Equipage, beautiful Women, and Men of Wit; for now and then a Company of Strollers in the Barn, a Country Sessions, a Game of Romps with a Parcel of Miss Hoydens, a Fustian Jockey Frock,[1] and greasy Leather Breeches, a hard trotting Hunter, or Road Nag, Dairy Maids, and which is worst of all, Country Squires, or Purse-proud Farmers. JACK WHIRL, I speak as a Friend, and have not exaggerated; you were born for Pleasure; Wine and Women, Musick and Wit, are the only Pleasures in Life; Shew and Equipage are subservient to these, they are but Instruments. Examine your own Conscience, and determine from her Dictates, like an unbias'd Judge. I allow, the Military Men are an Honour to their Country, as well as a Safeguard; and I would rather see you bravely knock'd o' the Head at Scaling a Town, than ignominiously drown'd in an Ale Vatt. But name me one Thing a Country Squire is good for, except to furnish a Theme for the Theatre, for us Men of Taste to laugh at?" "Egad," reply'd WHIRL, "and that's true! Not the Country; I don't want to save; my Estate will answer my Way of Living, and why should I be always a poring over Accounts and Leases, like a miserly old Money-Scrivener?" "Or (said BOB) a Hackney Writer; you have resolved like a Man of Spirit."

---

[1] Miss Hoyden, the daughter of a country gentleman, in William Vanbrugh's comedy *The Relapse; or, Virtue in Danger;* fustian was a coarse cotton fabric.

This Resolution was scarcely taken, when Mr. PLAINLY ask'd BOB, to what End his Reason was given him? "Why," said SAUNTER, "to distinguish Good from Bad." "And do you do it?" "No Doubt," reply'd the other. "And your Reason tells you, you were born to gratify your Passions? Let me tell you, Sir, I am scandaliz'd at your Discourse, and more so, at your endeavouring to propagate such infamous Tenets. I will allow you, our Reason admits our Pursuits of Pleasure; but then 'tis not the Brutal Pleasure you have been crying up; for to that, sound Reason denies the Epithet. No Action leaving a Remorse after the Commission, however pleasing it may be to the Sense, can be the Choice of Reason: Knowledge and Virtue are her Favourites, and 'tis they which administer an unallay'd Satisfaction; the Pleasure of a good Action is as great, as the Torments of Remorse after an ill one; and you, I am satisfy'd, are a very proper Man to judge from the Comparison, that a good Man must be as happy, as you have found your self tortur'd by Reflection.

"You, Sir, are a Man of Wit and Taste; pray tell me, Where's the Wit of being the Laughing-Stock of even your Companions; for there is not one of you Men of Wit, but will sacrifice his Friend, as you call your Bottle-Companions, to the Ridicule of the next Company, and I myself have heard, Mr. Whirl, laugh at your being incapable of as great Brutalities as your Inclinations prompt you to. Pray tell me, in what consists your  refin'd Taste? I fear in Wine and Ragouts only. Do you know anything of yourself, anything of this Universe? Have you enquir'd what you are, or how you came to have Existence? Have you ever examin'd into the Nature of the Deity; are you acquainted with his Attributes; have you any Notion of Eternity? No, I see by your Looks you have glory'd in your Ignorance; like a Swine you find your Wash in your Trough, and never consider how it came there, but suck it up, and lie down again to wallow. Endeavour to learn that you are a Man, and be asham'd to act longer like a Brute. Rouze from this Lethargy: Experience may have convinced you, that you hunt Pleasure by the backward Track. You see your Senses are not capable to give it you, at least but a momentary one, which you pay for with great Interest of Pain. Your Taste is soon vitiated, and your Stomach soon loaths the greatest Delicacies. In like Manner, every other Sense is presently disgusted with Repetition; but Knowledge and Virtue afford an inexhaustible Fund of Pleasure: None were ever tir'd with knowing, who once had tasted the Sweets of Knowledge; and the Love and Thirst after Virtue increase in Proportion to our Progression in her Ways."

WHIRL cry'd out, 'twas very true, he had often paid dear for a Debauch; that he was sensible he must ruin his Constitution, if he long led that Course of Life; and had often been asham'd of his Ignorance, when among Men of Letters, and heard them talk of the Stars, the Tides, the World going round the Sun, and a great many other abstruse Points; but he was resolved he would no longer lie bury'd in such gross Ignorance, he would apply himself to Study, learn the meaning of *Rationales* and *Antipodes*. Tho' he at present knew only their Names, he was resolved to get some ingenious Man to teach him; buy a Study of Books, and lock himself up in his House in the Country, 'till he was so far improv'd as to be fit to travel; then he'd make the Tour of *Europe*, and come home qualify'd to serve his Country in Parliament.

This is not the only Person I have met with of his fickle Temper, which is entirely owing to what all Follies spring from, Want of Consideration; which makes us immediately give into every pleasing Idea, without examining either what it is in itself or Consequences. But as these People never go farther than designing, so there are their Antipodes, if I may so say, who can never be diverted from a Resolution, when once taken, by the most powerful Remonstrances; who are as little considerate in making their Resolutions as the others; but who persist in them from a blameable Bashfulness, or an obstinate Pride. WILL. SAUNTER made a Resolution to go to *Rome*; his Uncle, on whom he had a Dependance, dissuaded him as much as possible: No, he had resolv'd, and would go, whatever was the Consequence: Had his Uncle been as resenting, as WILL positive, he might have smarted for his Obstinacy. When Men will once allow themselves Time to consider before they act, I shall be eas'd of the Trouble of my Post, as I shall have neither Vice nor Folly to censure, and Virtue will be so well known, it will want no Pen to recommend it.

1732

111

C. E.

A Letter from Mrs. Jane Jones (1737)

The Author: He or she was probably acquainted with Pope (the poet is alluded to in flattering terms and mentioned by name in the preface; and the publisher of the story is the same as that of the *Dunciad*). The anonymous author re-imagines the life of the real Jenny Diver (c. 1700-1741), a famous thief who inspired the character of that name in John Gay's *The Beggar's Opera* (1728), and turns her into a prostitute (although other misdeeds are hinted at) and has her meet famous people of the age. The story is introduced under the conceit of the "found manuscript": when the addressee's belongings were sold, according to the preface (not included here), "a small Cabinet fell into the Hands of Mr.——, at the *Ditch-side*. He being a Man of little Curiosity, set it to Sale unexamin'd; and it was my good Fortune to purchase it. In a little Drawer, among other Curiosities, was concealed the soul Copy of this Epistle."

The Text: The following is from the first edition, whose full title was *A Letter from Mrs. Jane Jones, Alias Jenny Diver, in Drury-Lane, to Mrs. Arabella B—wl—s, near Wine-Office Court, Fleetstreet. Interspers'd with Reflections, Humorous and Moral, Pious and Political*. London: Printed for A[nne]. Dodd; and sold at all the Pamphlet Shops in Great Britain, Ireland, and Town of Berwick upon Tweed. 1737. [Price 6d.] It opened with a prefatory epistle from "The Editor to the Reader," signed "C.E.," which mostly summarised the story itself.

Further reading: Anonymous, "Rogues and Clerics." *Times Literary Supplement* 3,526 (25 September 1969), 1105-1106;

Charles Andrews, "Jenny Diver." *Lives of Twelve Bad Women*. Ed. Arthur Vincent. London: T. Fisher Unwin, 1897. 137-161.

Oct. 3, 1736.

Dear BELL,

It is some Time since I had the Pleasure of your agreeable Conversation. Indeed, of late I have been in so unhappy a Situation, that I could as little wish you to favour it with your Company, as I could bring my self to be tolerably easy in it. And this Uneasiness I have found increase so strongly upon me within these few Days since the Gin-Act's

112

taking Place,[1] that I find a Life, attended with the Inconveniences ours is continually subject to, is not to be borne, without the Assistance of Liquor, to animate our Spirits, and dissipate our Thought. This wretched State of ours I have long felt in a slighter Manner; but now perceive it so intolerable, that I have Thoughts of leaving the Kingdom, and retiring to a *religious House* beyond Sea; where Father *B*——, (who now, I hear, favours you with his Company, and who wants to be rid of me,) promises I shall be admitted suitably to the imaginary Title I formerly bore;[2] and for which he engages to procure me *proper Testimonials*. I am now 35, having lived much longer than most of my Profession; my first Acquaintance, both Men and Women, being long since gone off. My *Natural Mother* dy'd before I had any Knowledge of her; nor was I much sensible of the good Lady who took care of me in my Infancy. From about my tenth year Mrs. NEEDHAM, (to whom you owe your Education, tho' much later,) directed my Behaviour, and gave me Instructions for her future Purposes; and this only Comfort I have in my Reflections, that I never had the Opportunity of being rescued from her Designs, nor the least Sentiment that they were improper, till they were impossible to be prevented. After this, what has been my Condition? Shall I review it?— Dear ARABELLA! What are Men! shall I describe them to you; or do you already think of them as I do? I will however, as you are so much younger, and have not yet *been Common-Hackney'd in the Ways of Men*, just give you a Sketch of some of the Occurrences of the many Years I have been subjected to their Pleasure.

The Noble Lord who first possess'd me, tho' a Man of Genius, and whom I could have lov'd for the Agreeableness of his Person, (with which, I own, I was soon charm'd,) had scarce enjoy'd me, when I was treated by him with a Coolness I had till then no Sentiment of; and in less than three Weeks after he had taken me from Mrs. NEEDHAM's, he left me in the Lodgings he had provided for me in *King-street, Covent-Garden.* He had the Humanity indeed, not to leave me entirely destitute; but his Fortune and Extravagancies were such, that I never saw more of his Money than 30 Guineas, which he sent me with his Farewel Letter. Thus was I in Lodgings of two Guineas a Week, a Maid and a Black, left with this small Pittance, without a Friend in the World: For Mrs. NEEDHAM, to whom I would have return'd, would not so much as suffer me to enter her Doors.

[1] Parliament was concerned about the so-called "gin craze" which started in the last decade of the 17th century and amplified in the early 18th century. The first Gin Act of 1729 restricted the sale of gin to licensed operators. The Gin Act of 1736, mentioned here, raised the cost of these licenses to 50 pounds a year and also increased the duty on gin. The Gin Act of 1743 repealed these provisions.
[2] According to the Editor's foreword, when she was fifteen, "the D[uke] of — was then favour'd with her Maidenhead, for which Mrs. NEEDHAM [her first matron] is said to have had a Note for 200*l.* which was never paid, [and] she afterwards bore the Title of my *Lady Dutchess.*" Father B. is supposed to provide the documents necessary for her to be admitted in a monastery under false name and the title of duchess.

I was just leaving these Lodgings, having turn'd off my Black, and about to dismiss my Maid, when one Evening, taking the Air in the Garden, a Gentleman, famed for his Humanity and his Writings, seeing me disconsolate, join'd Company with me; and was not long, before he had artfully got from me my unhappy Story. He ask'd my Lodgings; which I having told him, he desir'd he might have the Liberty to drink a Dish of Tea with me on the Morrow; and taking me by the Hand at parting, slipt a Bank Note of 20*l.* into it. I was so confounded at this Generosity in an entire Stranger, that I could only acknowledge it by my Confusion: Which he perceiving, immediately withdrew. I had the Pleasure of seeing him the next Morning, according to his Appointment: Which was the greater Favour, as it was a Circumstance he was always too regardless of; and nothing could have made him so punctual at that Time, but the compassionate Sentiments I always discover'd him to have for the Unfortunate. You may be sure, I was not a little happy in such an Acquaintance; so much Wit! such an agreeable Turn of Conversation! the Pleasure of being favour'd by a Man, beloved by Women, and esteem'd and honour'd by every Man of Sense. Dear ARABELLA, the Remembrance is Transport, as his Loss made me quite inconsolable: For I lost him long before his Death; tho' I was often favour'd with his Bounty.

HARRIS's LIST

O F

Covent-Garden Ladies:

O R

MAN OF PLEASURE's

KALENDAR,

For the YEAR 1773.

CONTAINING

An exact Defcription of the moft celebrated Ladies of Pleafure who frequent COVENT-
GARDEN, and other parts of this Metropolis.

THE SECOND EDITION.

LONDON.

Printed for H. RANGER, Temple Exchange
Paffage, Fleet-Street.

M DCCLXXIII.

A popular yearly guide to London's prostitutes listing their name, address, and characteristics.

1737

Upon finding myself forsaken, I was at first almost distracted, and soon totally regardless of myself and Conduct: And, like one abandon'd, car'd not who had my Person, while my dear, inconstant, witty, generous K——t alone posses'd my Mind; till after a Succession of Wretches, between whom I perceiv'd no Difference, I found myself constantly visited, (tho' my Lodgings were then much below what I had ever before been reduc'd to,) by One, who I have observed since was far from being the only one of his Character among the Sex. He was admitted to all my Favours; which he was no sooner in Possession of, than he exerted the Tyrant, instead of the Lover. I was kept poor; always suspected; and dared not to stir out without Permission. I had yielded at first to this, being in infinite Perplexity about my lost Favourite, and indifferent what became of me; and when I at last found this Condition intolerable, and would have freed myself, it was then impossible. Every Attempt for Liberty, was a fresh Ground for Suspicion and ill Usage; and tho' I was maintain'd, it was barely a Maintenance, and that literally in a Prison. This insupportable Jealousy of his, as I afterwards discover'd, proceeded from his having acquir'd, and maintain'd in his Writings, the Character of the *Just*, the *Chaste*,

114

and the *Good*, (without which Epithets he was seldom mention'd,) and of which he was too tenacious to be agreeable to one in our Way of Life: For who should this be, but the most intimate Friend of my Favourite. But, sure never, never were two Men of such different Dispositions join'd together under that Denomination; I remember, he once downright quarrel'd with me, because, upon the Mention of his Friend's Name, I sigh'd, and told him, I was one of his *Band of Pensioners*.[1] You may guess, my dear ARABELLA, how irksome such a Confinement with such a Man (tho' possess'd of the most sprightly Genius, the most natural Turn of Humour in Conversation, and the most inexhaustible Fund of polite Learning,) must be to a Woman of my free and unconfin'd Manner of Thinking. However his Marriage soon deliver'd me from my disagreeable Keeper; and Chance threw me into the Arms of the famous Col. C—s.[2] He had view'd me by Accident one Morning dressing at my Window, with my Hair dishevel'd; and the natural Bloom, and the Delicacy and Tenderness of my Features, rais'd in him a Passion to be better acquainted with them. To this End he had bribed my Maid a few Weeks before the Marriage of my last Gallant; and she took her Opportunity to communicate and forward his Purpose soon after. He was so much a Brute, that tho' he was at first very liberal; yet I soon took so great a Disgust to him, that I had no Means of making my Situation tolerable, but by Drinking; into which indeed my late Keeper had initiated me, as it was privately his Practice; and which at this Time I fell into too inordinately. But I cannot sincerely repent of it at this Time, as it was the Occasion of my Colonel's leaving me; for tho' he was so much a Brute himself, he could not bear to see me so; and upon that took such an Antipathy, that he soon left me, as my Beauty was inclining to do, by the Practice of strong Liquors.

But from this I was happily recover'd by a Gentleman, whose Memory is yet dear to me. It was the witty, the gay, the polite J— C—s, Esq; I caught him by a Conversation at the Masquerade.[3] He was so struck with my Prattle, that tho' he was then in a very important Post, and was press'd with a publick Misfortune, which was too soon after his Death, his chief Felicity, as he often told me, and I could easily discover, was with me. How often has he been lost to his high Station, and his most intimate Friends, to toy and chat with his Darling JENNY! for such he always consider'd me. He entertain'd so high an Opinion of my Understanding, that, contrary to the general Maxims of the World, he favour'd me with his inmost Sentiments, and all his Thoughts were open'd to my View. In this he was never betray'd. I esteem'd this Compliment to my good Sense

[1] The ironical reference is to the gentlemen attending the King and who received an allowance; they were often called the "Band of Pensioners." The narrator indicates that both the generous and the jealous lovers were writers. The former has been identified as William Congreve (1670-1729), the satirical playwright (see "Rogues and Clerics"), while the latter seems to be a religious author.
[2] Colonel Francis Charteris (1675-1732), a Scottish adventurer and infamous rake. He was found guilty of rape in 1730 but was pardoned by the king.
[3] A likely reference to James Craggs the Younger (1686-1721), a politician who in the last years of his life was Secretary of State for the Southern Department.

and Confidence in my Discretion, infinitely beyond the finest Things that could be said or thought of my Person; nor could any Art or Violence ever have extorted from me what he at any Time intrusted: It was an Honour not to be rated too high, to be the Confident of a Man of his distinguished Abilities. But he had too great a Spirit, to be indifferent to strong Injuries; and such were the Circumstances of the Times, that popular Clamour, added to a private Distress, threw him into a Fever, of which he dy'd in a few Days. You know, Dear ARABELLA, what a Character is given him by the finest Genius now living. I who knew and loved him well, feel the Truth of each Part of the Description—[1] But I must endeavour to forget him.

During this Time, I lived in all the Splendor of a Woman of Fortune. My Dress and Equipage were suited to such a Character; and a Chair was always attending my Commands. But all the outward Ornaments of which our Sex are too fond, were unattended to by me, farther than to render myself more agreeable to the kind Bestower: My Happiness resulted from the Esteem of such a Man; and I never once thought of the Prudence of a Reserve, till his Death, shew'd me the Want of it. For as his Illness was sudden, and I had no Opportunity of seeing him, I was deprived at once of the dear Man I loved, and all the Means of my Support.

I continued in a retired Way for some Months, and lived by converting what was most valuable into ready Money; when I grew acquainted with the afterwards famous CHARLOTTE M—R. She was wild and witty, and of an extravagant Taste. Her Beauty was then in its Prime; and as her good Nature was her great Foible, she conceived a Friendship for me, that brought on the most disagreeable Part of my Life. She could not bear my retired Manner, as she called it; but would force me into the World. There was now no Medium in my Fortunes. She led me from one Set of her Acquaintance to another, till I had lost all Sense of Reserve; and was at last, through Necessity and Inattention, as profligate as herself: Not omitting often to frequent the publick Streets. What a Wild of Distress and Irregularity does this Scene open to my View! What Creatures are the general Herd of Mankind! Bad as I was now grown, I could not have supported myself under this State of Ignominy and Subjection, had I not destroy'd all Reflection by strong Liquors. To be the Instrument of Pleasure to Drunkards, Fools and Idiots, to the lowest Baseness, Ingratitude, and Brutality; to be subject to weak and wanton Humour, and to be ill treated for all Endeavours to be agreeable: It is a State, greatly to be pitied, and devoutly to be shun'd.

Dear ARABELLA! 'tis the Thought of this unhappy Condition of the poor Creatures about Town, that drew this Epistle from me. I knew it in its worst Shape; and cannot but pity those who are in it, as I would guard

[1] Probable allusion to Alexander Pope's epigraph, engraved on the memorial to Craggs in Westminster Abbey: "Statesman, yet friend to Truth, of Soul sincere/ In Action faithful and in Honour clear/ Who broke no promise, serv'd no private end/ Who gain'd no Title, and who lost no Friend/ Ennobled by Himself, by all approv'd/ Prais'd, wept, and honour'd by the Muse he lov'd."

all I had the least Regard to from falling into it. You have hitherto pretty well escaped it; shun the very Possibility of it. Mrs.——, with whom you now live, as I hear you have done since the Death of Sir C——s B——s, has too selfish a Character, not to expose you to Usage you are yet a Stranger to; and I must own to you, I was extremely sorry you were got into her House. Retire with me, my Dear, into a Land unknown; and prevent, by a timely Escape, all the Evils I have pass'd thro'; if you are not destroy'd long before you come to my Age. You, when you lived with a Character and Reputation, favour'd me with your Friendship and Assistance, in the lowest State of my Prostitution; as you said you discover'd in me something worthy of better Fate: Let me repay those Obligations, by guarding you from the same distressful Circumstances. Consider, there are few Men like some I have named to you, and your late Sir CHARLES, who continued your Friend for Years. Such good Fortune is not to be expected twice; at least by living with Mrs.—— you are not in the Way of meeting with it. Think of me, my Dear, as one you always profess'd an Esteem for, reflecting on the Ways of Life I have pass'd thro'; and let my Experience prevent your ever making such unhappy Reflections. My Thoughts are now cool, and free from all the intoxicating Powers I have been long inured to; and should you fly to them for Aid in your future Distress, you will find them too ineffectual to prevent the painful Result of your good Sense.

I am now within a few Days of leaving the Kingdom, but not entirely on a Religious Account: For tho' I have convers'd much with Father B——, who has labour'd my Conversion to the *Roman Catholick* Church, with a Zeal as if he thought thereby to extinguish all his Sins, yet he has not reconciled me to any of the *Absurdities* of that Religion. Indeed, I must do him the Justice to own, he never attempted it: And I am so far from charging any thing of that Kind to his Account, that I question much if he himself believes them. This Opinion is founded on the slight Manner in which he has always in Conversation treated *Protestant Mysteries*; some of which he never fail'd to equal to any in his Church. His real Sentiments I take to be in Favour of Deism: Of which he always spoke with great Respect; at the same Time he acknowledged his own Conduct as contrary to *natural* as *revealed Religion*. For this Reason, he said, he could not but wish, tho', he own'd, he could not hope, that the Absolutions of Holy Church would be effectual to extirpate all Offences: But of these Things he avoided Converse with every one, and said, he dared not permit himself often to think of them. He assures me, I shall find a very agreeable Reception in the House he recommends me to, and meet every Thing suitable to a Person of Condition. What had I to do, but to accept this Offer, with the greatest Readiness? I have seen Life for these 20 Years past in all its Variety; and there is nothing now to invite my Stay. A new Climate, and a different Scene, may yield something entertaining; but the main Point, as I have told you, is a Subsistence. To obtain which, were it in my Power, I would not chuse to go over the same Track I have already trod. But, alas! that is impossible, were it my Will: All my boasted Beauty is now no more; and I have only the varying Remains of the agreeable Face which once was so engaging.

I consider the Difficulty, my Dear, of spending Time in such a Recluse State. Tho' I have much natural Tenderness, yet, I believe, I shall not readily fall into the Joys of a *Mystick*, and feel the Raptures that attend the heated *Pietist*. Such a Disposition might have been form'd in me, when I ran from Mrs. NEEDHAM with Earl——; but my Passions are now too much allay'd and too settled, to turn them to such a Purpose; and I must freely own to you, that were this less practicable from Nature, my Judgment, ever since I have thought upon this Subject, has greatly disapprov'd this spiritualiz'd Wantonness. Shall I tell you the Occasion? When my dear Favourite Mr. C—— dy'd, and left me in the Condition I have mention'd; a venerable Clergyman who lodged over-against me, I supposed perceiving me disconsolate, came to visit me; and as he consider'd me an unhappy Woman, who had lost a good Friend and near Relation, (for I put on Mourning for his Death,) he endeavour'd to turn my Thoughts from the Pleasures of This World, by acquainting me, as he said, with those of Another. He furnish'd me with several religious Books to this End; *Meditations* and *Ejaculations*, full of elevated Rapture and passionate Affection. My young Mind was soon caught with the new Transport which my pious Instructer had initiated me into; till, from a heated Contemplation of invisible and inconceivable Objects, the Scale was easily turn'd, and I found myself, as I mention'd before, engag'd in the most dissolute Course that I ever knew: And I am fully persuaded, my Dear, that heating my Imagination in that unreasonable Manner, without informing my Judgment, only render'd me more capable of my former Flame, and of worse and baser Methods to support it. I recollect now, my Dear ARABELLA, (and with greater Uneasiness than I do any Part of my Conduct,) that it was in this Interval I acquir'd, by my Dexterity in the basest, meanest Arts in the World, the Nick-Name of JENNY DIVER,[1] by which I was deservedly made infamous ever after.

Well, this is past and cannot be recall'd; nor, I fear, forgotten. Another Country, other Customs, other Scenes of Gallantry, may put other Thoughts into my Head. You think this is not talking like a *Recluse.*—Come, I will lay my whole Heart before you. I am not without Hopes of making a Captive in *France*, that will surprize the whole World. While I was at *Paris* one Summer with my dear *Witty, Gay and Polite*, I contracted a Friendship with Mademoiselle——, whom the C—d—l M——r,[2] I hear now visits. To her am I now really going. Beauty, my Dear, is but of short Date here in *England*; yet a British Face of 35, with a little *Art*, will make as good a *French* 18, as any in *Paris*. If, with all the

[1] To "dive" was a slang word for "steal." Jenny Diver in Gay's *The Beggar Opera* is a pickpocket rather than a prostitute.

[2] The real Jenny Diver was deported (although she managed to return). The mademoiselle and the cardinal may be imaginary and the entire letter may be supposed to conceal rather than reveal her destination.

Charms I am Mistress of; with Gentility, Wit, Ease of Conversation, and my Remains of Beauty, (which I flatter myself, when properly aided, will appear not of the smallest,) I can but make a Conquest of that *Great Man*, and be an *English* R——t of the *F—ch* Affairs; then—But whither does my Fancy lead me? I will have done. But be assured, whatever Station I am in, I shall always be, my dearest ARABELLA,

> *Most Affectionately Yours,*
> J. JONES.

POSTSCRIPT.

Before I leave the Kingdom, I shall send you all my Manuscripts; as I know you are a Girl of good Sense, and capable of perfecting what I have left unfinish'd. You'll see, I had gone a good way in a Scheme for incorporating the Women of our Profession; and had laid down some Rules for their better Management. There are a few Political Pamphlets, half finish'd; Love Songs, without the last Stanza; and a new Design, just enter'd upon, of *Dialogues* between some worthless Living Characters, whom Imagination was to place in the Shades. What an inexhaustible Fund, is here for such a Genius as yours to work on. —How many Authors has my necessitous Muse at Times created! Both Patriots and Courtiers have father'd my Prose, and great Ladies taken the Credit of my Poetical Pieces. The Epistle to Lady *B. G.* burn, when you have read it; but use the others in any Way most to your Advantage. Once more Farewel.[1]

---

[1] The editor's foreword tells us that "The unhappy Lady, to whom this Epistle was address'd, dy'd a few Days ago at Mother ——'s in ——*Square*; (whence we gather, that she did not follow the good Advice given her by our Authoress)."

THOMAS GORDON

Fashionable Education (1740)

The author: Gordon remained the editor of *The Universal Spectator* for a long time and contributed essays and short fiction, often on the same topics he had covered two decades before. The following story appeared anonymously, but it can be easily identified as Gordon's, since it contains ideas (e.g., the superiority of British universities, and parents' unrealistic confidence in their children) which first appeared in some of his essays from 1718-1720, such as "Of Education" and "Of Travelling, Misapply'd." Sometimes called "Tacitus" Gordon because of his successful translation of 1728, Thomas also published a version of Sallust in 1745 and many anti-Jacobite pamphlets. For about a decade, he worked on a history of England, which remained unfinished (it has recently appeared in a critical edition by Giovanni Tarantino). He died in 1750.

The text: First published, unsigned and untitled, in *The Universal Spectator* 596, 8 March 1740. The following is from the magazine's book version, *The Universal Spectator. By Henry Stonecastle, of Northumberland, Esq;* (London: A. Ward, J. Clarke, D. Browne, R. Nutt, T. Astley, A. Millar, and H. Pemberton, 1747), vol. IV, 92-95 (the 1740 original has not survived on microfilm). The title "Fashionable Education" was given by the editors of *The London Magazine*, where it was reprinted in number 9 (March 1740). It is introduced by a short essay on education, in which the author argues that it is not manners, as most of his contemporaries are purported to believe, but indeed education that "makes the man." Only the last paragraph of that essay has been kept here, since the story is a direct illustration only of the last lines of the essay.

There has been a Maxim of late Years too much inculcated, which is, to let Youth have an *early Knowledge of the World*; and hence it is that we have Boys and Girls at fourteen and fifteen have gain'd, according to this modern Phrase, *a Knowledge of the World*, who, through their whole Lives, will never know one necessary Qualification of Life: They became instructed in the Vices and Follies of *Rakes* and *Coquets*, at an Age when the Principles of true Knowledge and Virtue should be establish'd.

I saw the other Day a Proof of what I have advanced in a domestick Scene of private Life, which I will venture to relate. I was intreated by an old Acquaintance, whom I shall call WILL AIRY, to take a Family Dinner with him; which Invitation I accepted with the more Pleasure, as he told me I should be very agreeably entertain'd, in seeing the *finest Boy* and *Girl* in *Christendom*: I made Allowance for the zealous Fondness of a Father in giving such a Description of his own Children, and expected to be very agreeably entertain'd, as *Miss*, I understood, was turn'd of *thirteen*, and *Master* about *fifteen*. I have naturally a particular Satisfaction in observing the Progressions of human Nature and Understanding, and was therefore highly delighted to think that in my Friend's Children I should see human Nature in its most *amiable Stage*; for at those Years *Beauty* and *Knowledge* are rising with great Speed to *Perfection*, and that *uncorrupted Simplicity* which they should then enjoy renders them charming.—As soon as I was conducted into the Dining-Room, I enquir'd of my Friend for the young Gentleman and Lady; but it seems *Miss* was gone with *Mamma* to an *Auction*, and *Master* to take a Turn into the *Mall*.—They all came home much about when the Dinner was spoilt; and, after a little genteel Bickering between WILL and his *Lady*, we sat down: The little gloomy Chagrin which at first appear'd, was soon dissipated by this Address of *Miss* to her Father.—*O, Papa! we have seen the most charming Things at the Auction, so neat and so cheap—There is an* India *Skreen, you must let my* Mamma *have—it comes but to—to—I forget how many Guineas—but you must let* Mamma *have it.*—My dear, says her Father, we don't want one.—*Why truly, Mr.* Airy, (replies his Wife) *ours is not in Taste, and if you make me a Present of this you will oblige me.*—My Friend began to look a little grave, but before he could reply, his Daughter accosted him again.—*Why, Papa, Miss* Polly Squander's *Mamma has one, and why should not we?—You'll have my* Mamma *vex herself sick about it,—and I am sure I shall fret myself almost dead if you deny it us.*—On *Will*'s seeming Compliance the young Lady and her Mamma appear'd more compos'd, and he with much Satisfaction whisper'd me—*Cou'd you have thought a Girl of her Age had so much Knowledge?*—I made Answer with a Smile, which seem'd to give him great Pleasure, and he was therefore resolv'd to shew me the *Genius* of the Boy.—*Well, Sir*, says he, *how have you dispos'd of yourself since your Masters left you in the Morning?—When I had dress'd myself* (replies my Spark) *I took a Turn in the* Mall, *where I met young Master* Flutter, *who last Week was made an Officer in the Marines, and, Sir, he has made me promise to go to the Play with him to Night.*—And do you intend to go, says the Father.—To which Question his Son, with some Warmth, answer'd—*Pray, Sir, when I have engaged in a Party, how can I in Honour get off?*—My Friend rising up with some Emotion, alarm'd me a little; but his Speech much more, *Sir,* (cry'd he) *keep your Honour for ever sacred, and when I know you lose your Honour, you lose your Father's Affection.—There's a Guinea for your Pocket.*—Then turning to me—*Such generous Principles and Knowledge of Mankind ought to be encourag'd, Mr.* Stonecastle.—When the Cloth was taken away, I had a Mind to converse a little with this knowing Youth, and unfortunately ask'd him what School he went to.—*School, Sir*, says he, with some Indignation; wherefore I imagin'd he might, as he was so forward a Genius, have been lately taken from one, and made an Apology, in asking him whether he had left *Westminster*, or *Eton*, or *Winchester*, or— *Sir,* replies he, with an Air of Pride, *I was never at any of those Schools—I was educated at home.*—But you intend for *Oxford* or *Cambridge.*—*No*

1740

121

Sir, said he, *I am to go to a Foreign University, and so have the Benefit of Travelling and University Learning at the same Time.*—I was going to speak to my Friend on this Subject, when he himself thus spoke to me—*I see, Mr.* Stonecastle, *you are surpriz'd at this, but the People of Fashion all come into this Way of Education; it shews young People the World, and brings them early to a just Knowledge of Mankind: I don't care if my Son has not so much* Greek *and* Latin; *I don't intend him for any Ecclesiastical Preferment; therefore there is no Necessity to send him to one of our Universities, where his Morals will be rather corrupted than improv'd, for I hear they learn nothing there but to drink Ale and smoak Tobacco.*—I attempted to corrected this false Notion they entertain'd, but soon they were too bigotted to their *fashionable Education* to be convinced; and, besides, our Discourse was interrupted by two or three young Ladies, of about Miss's Age, who were come to pay her a Visit. My young Spark, whose *Morals* were not to be *corrupted* by a *University Education,* took his Leave to meet his *Party* and go to the Play; and at his Departure my Friend said to me with some Passion—*Is not that Boy, Mr.* Stonecastle, *a perfect Man?*—The young Ladies and Mrs. *Airy* were now retir'd to another Room, and *Will* and I had half an Hour's Chit-chat by ourselves: I again endeavour'd to shew him the Error of his educating his Children; but he smil'd at me with a genteel Kind of Contempt. Just as I was going to take my Leave, *Miss* came running in to make a Request to her Papa—*Dear Papa,* says she, *Miss* Lucy Forward *goes next Monday to the Masquerade, and you said I shou'd go soon: Pray, Papa, let me go now; and I know Mamma goes, because she bespoke a Habit this Morning.*—I must own that my Friend had Prudence enough to deny this Request; but with a Promise she should certainly go *next Season:* Miss retired in the Dumps, and I took my Leave with Amazement at such a fashionable Education of Children. I cannot omit another Circumstance before I conclude: I accidentally dropp'd into the Play-house that Evening, and saw my *young Man* of *Morals* in one of the Gallery Boxes, with two other young Sparks, and two noted *Courtezans* of the Town.

I need make no Reflections on this Kind of Education, the Misconduct must be evidently seen; I could wish it was less practis'd, and that Parents, instead of learning their Children to *know* the *World,* wou'd teach them to know *themselves.*

ELIZA HAYWOOD

The Reclamation of Dorimon (1744)

The author: Eliza Haywood remained a prolific novelist until very close to her death in 1756, but one of the most successful works in the latter part of her career was a periodical: *The Female Spectator*, published in 24 monthly "books" between April 1744 and May 1746. In the following years, it was translated in German, French, Italian, and Dutch (as *Die Zuschauerin*, *La Spectatrice*, *La Spettatrice*, and *De Engelsche Spectatrice*).

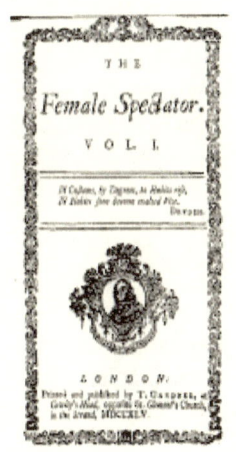

The text: First published in *The Female Spectator*, Book 6, September 1744. The text is taken from the subsequent publication in book format, (London, Printed for T[homas]. Gardner, at *Cowley's-Head*, near *St. Clement's-Church* in the *Strand*, 1745), Vol. I, 356-383. Like most of the stories in *The Female Spectator*, it was untitled. It was named "The Reclamation of Dorimon" by Gabrielle M. Firmager in her 1993 selection of *The Female Spectator*.

Further reading: Chris Roulston. *Narrating Marriage in Eighteenth-Century England and France*. London: Routledge, 2016. 30-33.

Dorimon and *Alithea* were married almost too young to know the Duties of the State they enter'd into; yet both being extremely good-natur'd, a mutual Desire of obliging each other appear'd in all their Words and Actions; and tho' this Complaisance was not owing to those tender Emotions which attract the Heart with a resistless Force, and bear the Name of Love, yet were the Effects so much the same as not to be distinguish'd.

The first Year of their Marriage made them the happy Parents of an Heir to a plentiful Estate.—The Kindred on both Sides seem'ed to vye with each other, which should give the greatest Testimonies of their Satisfaction.—All their Friends congratulated this Addition to their Felicity; and for a Time, the most perfect joy and Tranquility reigned, not only in their own Family, but in all those who had any Relation to them.

Alithea after she became a Mother began to feel, by Degrees, a greater Warmth of Affection for him that made her so; and having no Reason to doubt an equal Regard from him, thought herself as happy as Woman could be, and that there were Joys in Love greater than before she had any Notion of.

Quite otherwise was it with *Dorimon*; the Time indeed was now arrived, which taught him what it was to love.—The Hopes, the Fears, the Anxieties, the Impatiences, all the unnumber'd Cares which are attributed to that Passion, now took Possession of his Heart:—He pin'd, he languish'd, but alas! not for his Wife.—He had unhappily seen a young Lady at the Opera, who had Charms for him, which he had never found in the whole Sex before.—As he happen'd to sit in the same Box with her, he had an Opportunity of speaking to her, which tho' only on ordinary Subjects, every Answer she made, to what he said, seem'd to him to discover a Profusion of Wit, and gave him the most longing Desire to be acquainted with her.

Fortune, favourable to his Wishes, presented her to him the next Day in the Park, accompany'd with a Lady and a Gentleman, the latter of whom he had a slight Knowledge of:—he only bow'd to them the first Turn, but gather'd Courage to join Company with them on the second; and perceiving that it was to the other Lady that the Gentleman seem'd most attach'd, he was at the greater Liberty to say a thousand gallant Things to her, who was the Object of his new Flame.

Melissa, for so I shall call her, was vain, gay, and in every respect one of those modish Ladies, of which a former Spectator[1] has given a Description: She receiv'd the Compliments he made her in a Manner, that made him see his Conversation was not disagreeable to her; and some mention happening to be made of a Masquerade that Night, she told him, as if by Chance, that she was to be there, and that her fair Companion and herself were going to bespeak Habits at a Warehouse she mention'd, as soon as they left the Park.

The Hint was not lost upon him, and thinking that it would seem too presuming to ask leave to wait on her at her House, the first Time of being in her Company, he resolved to make it his Business to find out, if possible, what Habit she made choice of, to go to the Masquerade, where the Freedom of the Place might give him a better Opportunity of testifying the Desire he had of improving an Acquaintance with her.

Accordingly, after their quitting him at the Park-Gate, he followed at a Distance the two Chairs that waited for them, and placing himself near enough to the Habit-Shop, to see whoever went in or out, found his Adorable had not deceiv'd him in what she said.—The Ladies having dispatch'd what they came about, went again into their Chairs.—They were no sooner gone than he went into the Shop, and on a pretence of ordering a *Domine*[2] for himself, fell into Discourse with the Woman behind the Counter, whom he easily prevail'd on to let him know, not only what Habits the Ladies who had just left her had bespoke, but also

[1] In Book V of *The Female Spectator*, Haywood described the "truly modish lady [who] looks now, by turns, every thing—but a gentlewoman."

[2] A domino (also called "domine" in the first half of the 18th century) was a cloak with a small mask (covering the upper half of the face) worn at masquerades by people without a costume representing specific historical or mythological characters.

of what Condition and Character they were.—She informed him that *Melissa* had a large Fortune, and her Parents being dead was under the Care of Guardians, whom, notwithstanding, she did not live with, but had Lodgings herself near *Grosvenor* Square[1]: That she kept a great deal of Company, was what the world call'd a *Coquet,* but had hitherto preserv'd her Reputation: That the Lady who was with her was the Daughter of a Country Gentleman somewhat related to her, how nearly she could not tell, but heard she was on the point of Marriage with a Person of Rank.

Dorimon was transported at this Intelligence, as it seem'd to promise him an easy Access to her Acquaintance, and the Privilege of visiting her; which, probably, in these early Days of his Passion, was all he aim'd at: Or if he thought on any thing further, the Difficulties in accomplishing his Desire seem'd less formidable than they would have done, had she been of a more reserv'd Temper, were already married, or under the Direction of Parents.

Never did Time appear so tedious as that before the Hour of going to the Masquerade: His Impatience brought him there the very first, and by that means he had an Opportunity of observing every one as they came in.—*Melissa,* he was told, would be in the Habit of a Nun; and tho' there were several drest in that manner, yet he distinguish'd her from the others by her Tallness the Moment she appear'd.

He accosted her with the usual Phrases of—*Do you know me?*— and—*I know you!*—but was not long before he made her sensible of his more particular Attachment; and told her, that having lost his Heart that Morning in the *Park,* it now directed him how to discover the lovely Thief, tho' disguised, and amidst so numerous an Assembly.

This, and some other Expressions of the same nature, convincing her that he was the Gentleman who had made her so many Compliments in the Morning, immediately flatter'd her Vanity with a new Conquest; and as she found him a Man of Wit, and doubted not of his being a Person of Condition by his Appearance, resolv'd to omit nothing that might secure him: Accordingly, as all true *Coquets* do at first, she affected to listen with a pleas'd Attention to the Assurances he gave her of his Passion, and frequently let fall some Words, as if they escaped her inadvertently, that might make him think she would not be ungrateful if he persisted in giving her Testimonies of a constant Flame. Ladies of her Character have always this Maxim at heart,

Kindness has resistless Charms,
All Things else but faintly warms:
It gilds the Lover's servile Chain,
And makes the Slave grow pleas'd and vain.[2]

---

[1] To this day one of the most prestigious addresses to have in London, Grosvenor Square (a typical London "garden square," i.e., open space surrounded by houses) was very recent at the time, having been built in the 1720s. Very high prices had forced many of its original inhabitants to declare bankruptcy.
[2] Paraphrase of lines from a poem by the Earl of Rochester (these are lines 1-2 and 7-8 of an octave, with lines 3-6 missing).

But the Misfortune is, that such a Behaviour for the most part proves fatal to themselves in the End:—They toy so long with the Darts of Love, that their own Bosoms are frequently pierced when they little think of it; and the deluding She, who has made Numbers languish, becomes a Prey perhaps to one who least merits or regards the Victory he gains.

Dorimon, however, was transported to find the Offer he had made her of his Heart so well received, and made so good Use of the Opportunity she gave him of entertaining her the whole Time of the Masquerade, that he obtained her Permission to attend her home, and as it was then too late for them to continue their Conversation, to visit them the next Day in the Afternoon.

This quite established an Acquaintance between them; he went every Day to see her; she admitted him when all other Company were denied; he had always the Preference of waiting on her to the Park, the Opera, the Play, and, in fine, wherever she went; and when some of her more prudent Friends took notice of their being so frequently together, and had heard that he was a married Man, she only laughed at their Remonstrances, and replied, that as she had no farther Concern with him than merely to gallant her about to public Places, she had no Business to enquire into his private Circumstances;—that if he were married, his *Wife* only had to do with it; and as for her own Part, she thought him a very pretty Fellow, and quite fit for the Use she had made of him; adding, that if she were Mistress of his *Heart*, it was indifferent to her who had his *Hand*.

Melissa, 'tis probable, had indeed no other View in entertaining *Dorimon*, and receiving his Addresses, than the same she had in treating with a like Behaviour Numbers before him, merely for the sake of hearing herself praised, and giving Pain, as she imagined, to others of her Admirers, who were less frequently admitted.

But how dangerous a Thing it is to have too great an Intimacy with a Person of a different Sex, many of a greater Share of Discretion than *Melissa* have experienced.—This unwary lady, in meditating new Arts, the more to captivate her Lover, became ensnared herself;—in fine, she liked, she loved as much as any Woman of that airy and volatile Disposition can be said to love:—What she felt for him, however, had all the Effects which the most serious Passion in one of a different Temper could have produced, and *Dorimon* had as ample a Gratification of his Desires, as his most sanguine Hopes could have presented him an Idea of.

Alithea all this while lost Ground in his Affection;—she every Day seemed less fair, and whatever she said or did had in it a kind of Aukwardness, which before he was far from discovering in her; every thing was displeasing in her;—if endearing, her Fondness was childish and silly; and if she was more reserved, sullen and ill-natured.—One Moment he was out of Humour is she spoke, the next offended at her Silence.—He was continually seeking some Pretence to find Fault with the most justifiable Conduct that ever was, and even vexed that he had nothing in reality to condemn.—Unhappy, but certain Consequence of a new Attachment, which not content with the Injury it does, also adds to it by Ill-Humour, and a Wish of some Occasion to hate the Object we no longer love.

The poor Lady could not but observe this Alteration in his Behaviour; but as she was far from guessing the real Motive, imputed it to some unlucky Turn in his Affairs, tho' of what Nature she could not imagine, he having a large Fortune settled on him at their Marriage, beside the Reversion of what his Father should die possessed of, and was in the Power of nobody to deprive him of.

On the first notice she took of his Discontent, she asked him, as became a tender and affectionate Wife, if any thing had happen'd either from her Family or his own to give him Subject of Complaint? But he answering with Peevishness, she desisted from any further Enquiry, judging, as he did not think proper to trust her with the Secret, it would but add to his Disquiets to testify a Desire of knowing it.

For more than a whole Year did she combat his Ill-Humour with Sweetness, Gentleness, and the most obliging Behaviour; and tho' she began to think herself lost to his Affection, bore even that afflicting Reflection with the most submissive Patience, till flattering herself that, if it were even so, he would one Day consider she deserved not her ill Fortune.

Jealousy was, however, a Passion she was wholly unacquainted with: Many very beautiful Ladies often visited at her House, and she had never seen the least Propensity in him to Gallantry with any of them;—he rather behaved to them with a greater Reserve than was consistent with the good Breeding and Complaisance which might have been expected from a Man of his Years: So that she imagined rather a Disgust to the whole Sex was growing on him, than any particular Attachment to one.

Thus did her Innocence and unsuspecting Nature deceive her, till one Day a Female Friend, more busy than wise, open'd her Eyes to the true Reason of her Husband's Coldness.

This Lady, by means of a Servant Maid she had lately entertained, and who had lived with *Melissa* long enough to know the whole Secret of her Amour with *Dorimon*, and was dismissed on some Dislike, was made acquainted with all that passed between that guilty Pair.—She learned from this unfaithful Creature, that *Melissa* had been made a Mother by *Dorimon*, and that the Child was disposed of to a Person, who, for a Present of fifty Guineas, had taken the sole Charge of it, so as it should never appear to the Disgrace of the unnatural Parents.—Not the most minute Circumstance relating to the Affair but was betrayed by this Wretch, partly in Revenge for her having been discarded by her former Lady, and partly to gain Favour with the present, who, she easily perceived, loved to hear News of this kind.

Alithea would fain have treated this Account as fabulous, and have perswaded her Friend to regard it only as a Piece of Malice in the Reporter; but the other was positive in her Assertion, and told her, that it was utterly impossible for such a Creature to dress up a Fiction with so

1744

many Particulars, and such a Shew of truth;—*besides*, added she, *if there were nothing in it, we might easily disprove all she has said, by going to the Woman who has the Care of the Child, and whose Name and Place of Abode she has told me.*

Compelled at last to believe her Misfortune but too certain, a-while she gave a loose to Tears, and to Complainings, but her good Sense, as well as good Nature, soon got the better of this Burst of Passion; and when her Friend asked her in what Manner she would proceed in order to do herself Justice?—*What can I do*, reply'd this charming Wife, *but endeavour to render myself more obliging, more pleasant, more engaging if possible than my Rival, and make* Dorimon *see, he can find nothing in* Melissa *that is wanting in me.*

O Heaven! cried the Lady, *can you forgive such an Injury?—Yes*, resumed *Alithea*, stifling her Sighs as much as she was able, *Love is an involuntary Passion.—And will you not upbraid him with his Ingratitude, and expose* Melissa? said she.—*Neither the one, nor the other*, answered *Alithea* coldly; *either of these Methods would indeed render me unworthy of a Return of his Affection; and I conjure and beseech you*, added she, *by all the Friendship I flatter myself you have for me, that you will never make the least Mention of this Affair to any one in the World.*

This Moderation was astonishing to the Person who was Witness of it; however, she promised to be entirely silent, since it was requested with so much Earnestness: But how little she was capable of keeping her Word, most of her Acquaintance could testify, to whom not only the Fault of *Dorimon*, but the Manner in which his Wife received the Account of it, was not three Days a Secret.

Alithea was no sooner left alone, and at Liberty to meditate more deeply on the shocking Intelligence she had received, than she again began to fancy there was a Possibility of its being false:—the Suspence, however, seeming more uneasy to her than the Confirmation could be, resolved to be more fully convinced of the Truth, if there was any means of being so.

Accordingly she made an old Woman, who had been her Nurse in her Infancy, and whose Fidelity and Discretion she could depend upon, her Confidante in this Affair; and it was concluded between them, that a Spy should be employed to follow *Dorimon* at a Distance wherever he went, and also make a private Enquiry into the Behaviour and Character of *Melissa* among the Neighbours who lived near her.

A very little Search served to unravel the Mystery, and corroborate all that had been said to her concerning it.—The Emissary soon learned that *Dorimon* failed not one Day in his Visits to this Engrosser of his Heart;—that they were often seen to go out together in a Hackney-Coach in the beginning of the Evening, and that the Lady returned not till near Morning;—that she had been observed some Months past to be more gross than usual, and had affected to wear a loose Dress;—that she

1744

had been absent from her Lodgings three or four Days, came home very much indisposed, and kept her Bed for more than a Week, yet had neither Physician nor Apothecary to attend her; and on the whole it was believed by every body, that she had been in that Time delivered of a Child.

The unhappy Wife of *Dorimon*, now as much assured of his Perfidy as she could be without ocular Demonstration, set herself to bear it with as much Patience as she was able; which was indeed sufficient to render her Behaviour such as made him certain in his own Mind, that she had not the least Suspicion of the wrong he did her, and also compelled him very often to accuse himself for being guilty of what he could not answer to his Reason, yet had not Strength enough of Resolution to refrain, even tho' the Conduct of *Melissa*, who could not help coquetting with others even before his Face, occasioned him to have many Quarrels with her, and made him see, in spite of the Passion he still continued to have for her, the Difference between a Mistress and a Wife.

Whenever *Alithea* reflected on this Change in her Husband, as she had little else in her Mind, there was no Part in the Adventure appeared more strange to her, than that a Lady born and educated in the manner she knew *Melissa* was, and who had so far yielded to the Temptations of her Passion, as to throw off all Modesty and Honour for the Gratification of it, should have so little Regard for the innocent Babe, the Produce of her guilty Flame, as to abandon it to Miseries of she knew not what kind.—This was a Barbarity she thought exceeded the Crime to which it owed its Birth, and she more readily forgave the Injury done to herself, than that to the helpless Infant.

The more she reflected the more she was astonished, that Womankind could act so contrary to Nature; and by often picturing to herself the Woes to which this poor deserted Child might probably be exposed, became at length so dissolved in soft Compassion, as to form a Resolution which, I believe, few beside herself was ever capable of.

She had been inform'd, by her officious Friend, both of the Name and Habitation of the Woman with whom this poor little Creature had been left; and without making any one Person privy to her Design, muffled herself up in her *Capuchin*,[1] and went in a Hackney-Chair to her House: The other received her with a great deal of Respect and Kindness, imagining she was come on the same Business *Melissa*; and many besides her, who love the Crime, but hate the Shame of being detected in it, had done.—She was immediately conducted into a private Room, and told, that she might be free in communicating any thing to her, for she was a Person who had been entrusted by those who would not be thought guilty of a false Step for the World.

The virtuous *Alithea* blushed, even at being suspected by this Woman to be guilty of an Act her Soul shuddered at the Thoughts another could commit, and soon put an end to the Harangues she was making on her own Care, Skill, and Fidelity:—*I come not*, said the Wife of *Dorimon*, *on the Business you seem to think, yet which no less requires your*

---

[1] A fashionable kind of hooded cloak, worn by women in the 18h century.

Secrecy:—I have no happy Infant to leave with you; but to ease you of one whom you have lately taken charge of.

The Midwife looked very much surprized to hear her speak in this Manner, and knew not well what Answer to make; but *Alithea* soon put an End to her Suspence, by telling her that she was in the Secret of the Lady who was delivered of a Child at her House such a Time, which she mentioned exactly to her, and who had given fifty Guineas to be eased for ever of the Trouble of it.—*I am*, said *Alithea, a near Relation of that Gentleman to whom the little Wretch owes its Being, and who cannot consent that any Thing which does so, tho' begot in an unwarrantable Way, should be deserted and exposed in the Fashion such Children often are;—I therefore desire that, if alive, you will let me see it, that I may provide for it in a different Way than it can be expected you should do for the poor Pittance left you by the Mother.*

The woman then began to expatiate on the Impossibility of her taking the Care she could wish to do of Children left with her on those Terms; but that Heaven knew she did all she could, and often laid out more than she received.—She assured her that the Child she enquired after was alive, and a fine Boy; and that he was with a Person who indeed nursed for the Parish, but was a very good Woman, and did her Duty.—

That may be, said *Alithea, but I must have him removed; and if you can provide another who may be depended on, I have Orders from the Father to satisfy you for your Trouble, in a more ample Manner than you can desire: In the mean time*, continued she, putting five Guineas into her Hand, *take this as an Earnest, and let the Child be brought here To-morrow about this Time, and a new Nurse whom you can recommend, and I will give them a Meeting.*

A great deal of farther Discourse past between them on this Affair, on the Conclusion of which the Woman agreed to do whatever was required of her; and was doubtless no less rejoiced at the Offer made by this unknown Lady, than she was that by accepting of it she should preserve from Misery an innocent Creature, who tho' she had not seen she felt a kind of natural Affection for, as being *Dorimon's*.

This excelling Pattern of Good-Nature and Conjugal Love, took with her the next Day every Thing befitting a Child to wear whom she was determined to make her own by Adoption; and no sooner saw him in his new Nurse's Arms, than she took him, embraced and kiss'd him with a Tenderness little less than maternal; and having agreed upon Terms for him, made him be dress'd in her Presence in the Things she had brought, which were very rich and had belonged to her own Son at his Age; and every thing being settled highly to the Satisfaction of all Parties concerned, returned home with a secret Contentment in her Mind which no Words are able to express.

Nor was this a sudden Start of Goodness and Generosity, which I have known some People to have manifested for a Time, and afterwards repented of: The more she reflected on what she had done, the more Pleasure she felt in it.—She never let a Week pass over without going

to see her Charge, and how the Person entrusted with him behaved.—
Had he been in reality her own, and Heir of the greatest Possessions, her
Diligence in looking over the Management of him could not have been
more.

Dorimon all this while persisted in his Attachment to *Melissa*, tho'
her ill Conduct gave him such frequent Occasions of quarrelling with
her, that they were several times on the point of seeing each other no
more.—The long Intimacy between them, however, gave sufficient room
for Censure:—Those least inclined to judge the worst of things could not
help saying, that it looked ill for a married Man to appear in all publick
Places without his Wife, and in Company with a Lady whom she was not
even acquainted with; but others there were who were informed of their
more guilty Meetings in private, and talked with so little reserve on the
Occasion, that what was said reached the Ears of the Kindred of them
both:—Those of *Alithea's* were extremely troubled and incensed at the
Indignity offered to a Woman, whose Behaviour not Envy itself could
traduce;—but desirous of being better informed of the Truth than by
common Fame, they asked her many Questions concerning the Conduct
of her Husband towards her; and gave some Hints, plain enough to be
understood, that the World had but an ill Opinion of him on that Head.

To all which this excellent Wife replied, with an Air that shewed
how little she was pleased with any Discourses of that nature,—telling
them, that the idle Scandal of Persons, who made it their Business to pick
Meanings out of nothing, ought to be despised, not listen'd to;—that she
herself, who must be allowed the best Judge, found nothing in *Dorimon's*
manner of living with her to complain of; and that she should never
believe that Person wished her well, who endeavoured to fill her Mind
with any Suspicions on that Score.

These Answers at length silenced all who took an Interest in her
Happiness; her Friends wisely reflecting, that tho' all they had heard of
Dorimon were true, the greatest Addition that could be to her Misfortune,
was to be convinced of it.

But the Father of *Dorimon*, who was a Person of great Sobriety,
and to whom the Virtues of *Alithea* had rendered her extremely dear,
was less easily put off than those of her own Blood.—He chid his Son in
the severest Manner; and on his denying what he was accused of, and
throwing out some Insinuations as if he imagined his Wife had uttered
some Complaints against him.—*No*, said the old Gentleman, *she bears
the Wrong you do her but with too much Patience; and either not sees,
or pretends not to see, what is obvious to the whole Town beside.* He
then ran into many Encomiums on the Sweetness of her Disposition;
said, that whether her Complaisance toward him were owing either to an
unsuspecting Nature, or to her Prudence in aiming to regain his Love by
such ways as were most likely to succeed; either of these Qualities ought
not to lose their Merit with a Man of Understanding; *and methinks,*
added he, *should make you ashamed, as often as you reflect that you
have acted so as to oblige her to exert all her Love and Virtue to forgive.*

131

These kind of Discourses lost not all their Effect on *Dorimon*:—
He had often been astonished that all the Rumours which had been
spread concerning his Amour with *Melissa*, and which seemed to him
next to an Impossibility not to have reached the Ears of his Wife, had
never occasioned her to let fall some Hints at least, as if she feared a
Rival in his Heart.—He very well knew she wanted not a great Share of
Discernment in other things, and to be blind to that alone, wherein she
had the most Concern, he never could account for.—He had often heard
from his Acquaintance, and sometimes been a Witness of the Behaviour
of Women to their Husbands on the Subject of Jealousy, and found that
of *Alithea* so widely different from all he had been told of others, that he
could not help being extremely puzzled what Motive to ascribe it to; but
was obliged to acquiesce in his own Mind with the Remonstrance made
by his Father, that whether it were owing to her own Innocence, which
would not suffer her to think another could be guilty, or to the Strength
of Resolution and Discretion which enabled her to bear the Injury done
to her; he was however either way more fortunate than any Husband he
knew of in the like Circumstance, and in spite of his faulty Inclination for
Melissa, presented her to his cooler Thoughts in the most amiable Light.

'Tis highly probable, that in maturely balancing the solid Merits of
the *Wife*, against the light and trifling Allurements of the *Mistress*, he
would in Time have brought himself to do Justice to the *one*, and entirely
ceased to have any Regard for the *other*; but the Virtues of *Alithea* had
already sustained a sufficient Trial, and Heaven thought fit to reward
them, when she, so long inured to Suffering, least expected a Relief.

By accustoming herself to perform the Duties of a Mother to the
Child of *Melissa*, she grew really to love him as such; and what at first was
only Pity, converted by degrees into a tender Affection.—When *Dorimon*
was abroad she would often order him to be brought to her, and sending
for her own at the same time, diverted herself with observing the little
Grimaces which the two Infants would make at each other.—She was one
Day employed in this manner when *Dorimon* unexpectedly returned, and
came directly into the Room where they were:—Whatever Indifference
he had for his Wife, he had always shewn the greatest Tenderness to her
Son; and he now took him in his Arms and kiss'd him, as was his Custom
to do.—*Here is another little One*, said *Alithea* smiling, *who claims some
Portion of your Kindness too*, and at the same time presented *Melissa's*
Child to him. *By what Right, Madam?* replied *Dorimon*, in the same
gay Tone.—*As he is mine*, resumed his Wife.—*Yours!* cried he.—*Yes,*
answered she, *he is mine by Adoption; and I must have you look upon
him as your's also.—My Complaisance for you may carry me great
Lengths*, said he; *but as I know you do nothing without being able to
give a Reason, should be glad to learn the Motive of so extraordinary
a Request.*

One of the Children beginning to whimper a little, *Alithea* ordered
the Nurses to take them both into another Room; and finding *Dorimon*

in an exceeding good Humour, was pushed on by an irresistible Impulse, to speak to him in the following Manner.

The Infant you saw, said she, in a more serious Tone than before, *and whom I have in Reality taken under my Care, owes its Being to two Persons of Condition; but being illegally begot, the Care of Reputation prevailed above Nature; and this innocent Produce of an inconsiderate Passion I found abandoned, a wretched Cast-away, either to perish, or, surviving, survive but to Miseries much worse than Death.—The Thought was shocking to me, and I resolved to snatch him from the threatened Woes, and provide for him out of my private Purse, in such a Manner as may not make Life hateful to him.*

An Action truly charitable, said *Dorimon*, a little perplexed; *but this is not the Reason I expected, since by the same Rule your Pity might be extended to Hundreds, whom doubtless you may find exposed in the like Manner. It must therefore be some Plea more forcible than mere Compassion that attaches you particularly to this Child.*

Alithea, who had foreseen what Answer he Husband would make, was all the Time he was speaking debating within herself, whether it would be best for her to evade or to confess the Truth of this Affair; and not being able to determine as yet, appeared no less confused and disordered than she would have done, if about to make an Acknowledgment for some great Offence:—At last, *A Plea there is indeed*, said she, *but—* here her Voice and Courage failed her, and she was utterly unable to give him the Satisfaction he had asked.

Dorimon was confounded beyond Measure, and not knowing what to think of a Behaviour so new, and which seemed to denote she laboured with some Secret of great Importance, he looked stedfastly on her for some Minutes, and perceiving that she changed Colour, and had her Eyes fixed on the Earth, grew quite impatient for the Certainty of what, as he has since confessed, he then began to conceive, cried out, *What Plea?— What Mystery?*

A Mystery, replied she, *which I had much rather you would guess at than oblige me to unravel.—Oh* Dorimon! continued she, after a Pause, *is there no Instinct in Nature that can inform you; my Affection for the Father makes his Offspring, of whomsoever born, dear to me?—I cannot hate* Melissa *so much as I love* Dorimon; *and while I am performing the Offices of a Mother to this Child, forget the Share she has in him, to remember what I owe to him as yours.*

The Reader's own Imagination must here supply the Place of Description.—Impossible it is for any Words to give a just Idea of what a Husband, circumstanced like *Dorimon*, must feel!—To have his Fault thus palpably made known to her, whom he most desired should be ignorant of it;—to receive the highest Obligations, where he could have expected only Resentment;—and to hear the Detection of what he had done discovered to him by the injured Person, in such a manner as if herself, not he, had been the Criminal, so hurried his Thoughts, between Remorse, Astonishment, and Shame, as left him not the Power of making

133

the least Reply to what she said:—He walked several Turns about the Room in a disordered Motion, endeavouring to recover a Presence of Mind, which seemed so necessary on this Occasion, but in vain; and at last, throwing himself into an easy Chair, just opposite to that in which his Wife was sitting, *Good God!* cried he, *am I awake!—Can it be possible there is such a Woman in the World!*

The sweet tempered *Alithea* could not see him in these Agitations without a Concern, which made her almost repent her having occasioned them:—She ran hastily to him, and throwing her Arms about his Neck, *My dear, dear* Dorimon, said she, *let it not trouble you that I am in Possession of a Secret which I neither sought after, nor, when in a manner forced upon me, ever divulged to any Person in the World.— Consider me as I am—your Wife,—Part of yourself,—and you will then be assured you can be guilty of no Errors, which I shall not readily excuse, and carefully conceal.—Judge of my Sincerity,* continued she, renewing her Embraces, *by my Behaviour, which you are sensible has not the least been changed by my Knowledge of this Affair.*

O Alithea, cried he, pressing her tenderly to his Bosom, *I am indeed sensible how little I have deserved such Proofs of your amazing Goodness;—my Soul overflows with Gratitude and Love:—Yet how can I attone for my past Crime?—By mentioning it no more,* interrupted she, *and to let me share in that Heart my Want of Charms denies me the Hopes of filling wholly.*

To these endearing Words he answered only in broken Sentences, but such as more testified what she wished to find in him towards her than the most eloquent Speeches could have done.—She now was convinced that the Victory she had gained over him was perfect and sincere, and would have known a Transport without Alloy, but for the tender Pain it gave her to find so much Difficulty in perswading him to forgive himself.

He held her sitting on his Knee, with his Arms round her Waist, while she related to him the means by which she was made acquainted with his Crime; concealing no Part either of what she heard, the Steps she took after the Knowledge of her Misfortune, and the various Emotions which passed in her Soul, during the long Series of his Indifference to her: In all which he found something to admire, and the more he saw into the Greatness, as well as Sweetness of her mind, the more his Love and Astonishment increased.

The first Proof he gave her, that she should have nothing for the future to apprehend on the Score of *Melissa*, was to write a Letter to that Lady; wherein he acquainted her, that, sensible of the Injury he had done the best of Wives and Women, he was determined to pursue no Pleasures in which she did not participate.—He represented to her the Shame and Folly of carrying on an Intrigue of the Nature theirs had been in the most pathetick Terms, and advised her to think of living so as to regain that Reputation in the World which, he was obliged to confess, he had contributed to make her lose;—assured her that the Resolution he had now made, of seeing her no more, was not to be shaken by any Arguments

1744

in her Power to make use of; therefore begged she would endeavour to follow his Example, and forget all that had passed between them.

This, he shewing to *Alithea*, gave her a new Opportunity of exerting her Good-Nature.—She made him write it over again, in order to soften some Expressions in it, which she would have it were more harsh than was becoming in him, to a Woman he had once loved; and perhaps would have rendered it at last too gentle for the Purpose it was intended, could she have prevailed on him to alter it according to the Dictates of her own compassionate and forgiving Soul. But he best knew the Temper of the Person he had to deal with, and would not bid her Adieu in such a Manner as should give her the least room to flatter herself it would not be his last.

Tho' he desired no Answer he received one, filled with the most virulent Reproaches on himself, and mingled with many contemptuous Reflections on his Wife.—The first he was unmoved at, but the other totally destroyed all the Remains of Regard and Consideration he had for her.—He tore the Letter into a thousand Pieces, and, to shew this injurious Lady the Contempt and Resentment with which he had treated what she said, gathered up the scattered Fragments, and sent them back to her and a sealed Cover, but without writing a Word.

After this he was entirely easy, *Melissa* made no Efforts to regain him, but contented herself with railing against him and the innocent *Alithea* wherever she went; but, most People knowing the Motive, her Malice had no other Effect than to make herself laughed at:—She soon, however, entered into a new Amour, and in the Noise that made, all Talk of her former Engagement was laid aside; while the happy *Alithea* enjoyed the Recompense of her Virtue in the continued Tenderness of a Husband, who never could have loved her half so well had he not loved elsewhere, because he never could have had an Opportunity of being so well acquainted with those Virtues in her, which were the Ground of his Affection.

The Compassion she had shewn for the Child of *Melissa* was not a temporary Start of Goodness,—she persisted in the most tender Care of him,—had him educated in the same manner with her own,—and to alleviate the Misfortune of his Birth, engaged *Dorimon* to set apart a considerable Sum of Money, in order to put him into a Business, which, when he grows of Years to undertake, it will, according to all human Probability, be his own Fault if he does not succeed in.

I have been the more tedious in this Narrative, because I think there is no Particular in the Conduct of the amiable *Alithea* that ought to be omitted, or may not serve to shew how much a perfect Good-Nature may enable us to sustain, and to forgive.

I would have no Husband, however, depend on this Example, and become a *Dorimon* in Expectation of finding an *Alithea* in his Wife:—It is putting the Love and Virtue of a Woman to too severe a Test, and the more he thinks her capable of forgiving the less ought he to offend.

1744

135

HENRY FIELDING

The Female Husband (1746)

The author: Henry Fielding was born in 1707 near Glastonbury, in Somerset (where *The Female Husband* is partially set), but his family moved to Dorset in 1710, where his sister, the novelist Sarah Fielding (1710-1768) was born. His mother died in 1718 and his father, General Edmund Fielding, remarried and had six more sons, one of whom, John Fielding (1721-1780) became Henry's close friend and business partner. After finishing his studies at Eton, he published his first poems, had his first comedy performed at Drury Lane (1728), but then enrolled at the University of Leiden to study literature. Sued for debts in 1729, he returned to London, where he soon became a very successful playwright. He also published anonymous articles and essays, and in 1739 he started his own publication, *The Champion*. In 1741 he published his first work of prose fiction, *Shamela Andrews*, a parody of Samuel Richardson's bestselling *Pamela*, followed in 1742 by *Joseph Andrews* and in 1743 by *Jonathan Wild*. In 1748, Fielding (who had taken the bar eight years before), became justice of the peace and established his offices at Bow Street, Covent Garden. With the help of his half-brother John (blind from the age of 19), he formed what is considered the first professional police force, the so-called Bow Street Runners. In 1749, he published his most famous novel, *The History of Tom Jones, a Foundling*, followed in 1751 by his last novel, *Amelia*. He died in Lisbon in 1754.

The text: Taken from the first edition, published under the title *The Female Husband: or, The Surprising History of Mrs. Mary, Alias Mr. George Hamilton, who was convicted of having married a YOUNG WOMAN of WELLS and lived with her as her HUSBAND. Taken from Her own MOUTH since her Confinement* (London: Printed for M. Cooper, at the Globe in Pater-noster-Row, 1746). It bore the following epigraph: "Quodque id mirum magis esset in illo;/ Faemina natus erat. Monstri novitate moventur,/ Quisquis adest: narretque rogant" from the 12th Book of Ovid's *Metamorphoses*. This should read, however, "'quoque id mirum magis esset in illo,/ femina natus erat.' Monstri novitiate moventur/ quisquis adest, narretque rogant." Nestor begins to tell the story of the hero Caeneus of Thessaly, ending with the words: "'and what was even more marvellous about him was that he had been born a woman.' All who heard were astonished at this and begged him to tell the tale." The story was published anonymously, but Fielding's authorship has been universally acknowledged since the turn of the 20th century.

Further reading: Sheridan Baker, "Henry Fielding's 'The Female Husband': Fact and Fiction" (*PMLA* 74:3, June 1959, 213-224).

Terry Castle, "Matters Not Fit to Be Mentioned: Fielding's 'The Female Husband'" (*ELH* 49: 3, Autumn 1982, 602-622).

Bonnie Blackwell, "'An Infallible Nostrum': Female Husbands and Greensick Girls in Eighteenth-Century England" (*Literature and Medicine* 21:1, Spring 2002, 56-77).

Caroline Derry, "Sexuality and Locality in the Trial of Mary Hamilton, 'Female Husband'" (*King's Law Journal* 19:3, 2008, 595-616).

Misty G. Anderson, "The New Man: Desire, Transformation, and the Methodist Body" (*Imagining Methodism in Eighteenth-Century Britain*: Baltimore, The Johns Hopkins UP, 2012, 70-99).

Sarah Nicolazzo, "Henry Fielding's 'The Female Husband' and the Sexuality of Vagrancy" (*The Eighteenth Century* 55:4, January 2014, 335-353).

That propense inclination which is for very wise purposes implanted in the one sex for the other, is not only necessary for the continuance of the human species; but is, at the same time, when govern'd and directed by virtue and religion, productive not only of corporeal delight, but of the most rational felicity.

But if once our carnal appetites are let loose, without those prudent and secure guides, there is no excess and disorder which they are not liable to commit, even while they pursue their natural satisfaction; and, which may seem still more strange, there is nothing monstrous and unnatural, which they are capable of inventing, nothing so brutal and shocking which they have not actually committed.

Of these unnatural lusts, all ages and countries have afforded us too many instances; but none I think more surprising than what will be found in the history of Mrs. *Mary*, otherwise Mr. *George Hamilton*.

This heroine in iniquity was born in the Isle of *Man*, on the 16th Day of *August*, 1721. Her father was formerly a serjeant of grenadiers in the Foot-Guards, who having the good fortune to marry a widow of some estate in that island, purchased his discharge from the army, and retired thither with his wife.

He had not been long arrived there before he died, and left his wife with child of this *Mary*; but her mother, tho' she had not two months to reckon, could not stay till she was delivered, before she took a third husband.

As her mother, tho' she had three husbands, never had any other child, she always express'd an extraordinary affection for this daughter, to whom she gave as good an education as the island afforded; and tho' she used her with much tenderness, yet was the girl brought up in the strictest principles of virtue and religion; nor did she in her younger years discover the least proneness to any kind of vice, much less give cause of suspicion that she would one day disgrace her sex by the most abominable and unnatural pollutions. And indeed she hath often declared from her conscience, that no irregular passion ever had any place in her mind, till she was first seduced by one *Anne Johnson*, a neighbour of hers, with whom she had been acquainted from her childhood; but not with such intimacy as afterwards grew between them.

This *Anne Johnson* going on some business to *Bristol*, which detained her there near half a year, became acquainted with some of the people called *Methodists*, and was by them persuaded to embrace their sect.

At her return to the Isle of *Man*, she soon made an easy convert of *Molly Hamilton*, the warmth of whose disposition rendered her susceptible enough of Enthusiasm, and ready to receive all those impressions which her friend the *Methodist* endeavoured to make on her mind.

These two young women became now inseparable companions, and at length bed-fellows: For *Molly Hamilton* was prevail'd on to leave her mother's house, and to reside entirely with Mrs. *Johnson*, whose fortune was not thought inconsiderable in that cheap country.

Young Mrs. *Hamilton* began to conceive a very great affection for her friend, which perhaps was not returned with equal faith by the other. However Mrs. *Hamilton* declares her love, or rather friendship, was totally innocent, till the temptations of *Johnson* first led her astray. This latter was, it seems, no novice in impurity, which, as she confess'd, she had learnt and often practiced at *Bristol* with her methodistical sisters.

As *Molly Hamilton* was extremely warm in her inclinations, and as those inclinations were so violently attached to Mrs. *Johnson*, it would not have been difficult for a less artful woman, in the most private hours, to turn the ardour of enthusiastic devotion into a different kind of flame.

Their conversation, therefore, soon became in the highest manner criminal, and transactions not fit to be mention'd past between them.

They had not long carried on this wicked crime before Mrs. *Johnson* was again called by her affairs to visit *Bristol*, and her friend was prevail'd on to accompany her thither.

Here when they arrived, they took up their lodgings together, and lived in the same detestable manner as before; till an end was put to their vile amours, by the means of one *Rogers*, a young fellow, who by his extraordinary devotion (for he was a very zealous *Methodist*) or by some other charms, (for he was very jolly and handsome) gained the heart of Mrs. *Johnson*, and married her.

This amour, which was not of any long continuance before it was brought to a conclusion, was kept an entire secret from Mrs. *Hamilton*; but she was no sooner informed of it, than she became almost frantic, she tore her hair, beat her breasts, and behaved in as outrageous a manner as the fondest husband could, who had unexpectedly discovered the infidelity of a beloved wife.

In the midst of these agonies she received a letter from Mrs. *Johnson*, in the following words, or as near them as she can possibly remember:

"DEAR MOLLY,

I know you will condemn what I have now done; but I condemn myself much more for what I have done formerly: For I take the whole shame and guilt of what hath passed between us on myself. I was indeed the first seducer of your innocence, for which I ask GOD's pardon and yours. All the amends I can make you, is earnestly to beseech you, in the name of the Lord, to forsake all such evil courses, and to follow my example now, as you before did my temptation, and enter as soon as you can into that holy state into which I was yesterday called. In which, tho' I am yet but a novice, believe me, there are delights infinitely surpassing the faint endearments we have experienc'd together. I shall always pray for you, and continue your friend."

This letter rather increased than abated her rage, and she resolved to go immediately and upbraid her false friend; but while she was taking this resolution, she was informed that Mr. *Rogers* and his bride were departed from *Bristol* by a messenger, who brought her a second short note, and a bill for some money from Mrs. *Rogers*.

As soon as the first violence of her passion subsided, she began to consult what course to take, when the strangest thought imaginable suggested itself to her fancy. This was to dress herself in mens cloaths, to embarque for *Ireland*, and commence Methodist teacher.

Nothing remarkable happened to her during the rest of her stay at *Bristol*, which adverse winds occasioned to be a whole week, after she had provided herself with her dress; but at last having procured a passage, and the wind becoming favourable, she set sail for *Dublin*.

As she was a very pretty woman, she now appeared a most beautiful youth. A circumstance which had its consequences aboard the ship, and had like to have discovered her, in the very beginning of her adventures.

There happened to be in the same vessel with this adventurer, a Methodist, who was bound to the same place, on the same design with herself.

These two being alone in the cabin together, and both at their devotions, the man in the extasy of his enthusiasm, thrust one of his hands into the other's bosom. Upon which, in her surprize, she gave so effeminate a squawl, that it reached the Captain's ears, as he was smoaking his pipe upon deck. Hey day, says he, what have we a woman in the ship! and immediately descended into the cabin, where he found the two Methodists on their knees.

Pox on't, says the Captain, I thought you had had a woman with you here; I could have sworn I had heard one cry out as if she had been ravishing, and yet the Devil must have been in you, if you could convey her in here without my knowledge.

I defy the Devil and all his works, answered the He Methodist. He has no power but over the wicked; and if he be in the ship, thy oaths must have brought him hither: for I have heard thee pronounce more than twenty since I came on board; and we should have been at the bottom before this, had not my prayers prevented it.

Don't abuse my vessel, cried the Captain, she is as safe a vessel, and as good a sailer as ever floated, and if you had been afraid of going to the bottom, you might have stay'd on shore and been damn'd.

The Methodist made no answer, but fell a groaning, and that so loud, that the Captain giving him a hearty curse or two, quitted the cabbin, and resumed his pipe.

He was no sooner gone, than the Methodist gave farther tokens of brotherly love to his companion, which soon became so importunate and troublesome to her, that after having gently rejected his hands several times, she at last recollected the sex she had assumed, and gave him so violent a blow in the nostrils, that the blood issued from them with great Impetuosity.

Whether fighting be opposite to the tenets of this sect (for I have not the honour to be deeply read in their doctrines) or from what other motive it proceeded, I will not determine; but the Methodist made no other return to this rough treatment, than by many groans, and prayed heartily to be delivered soon from the conversation of the wicked; which prayers were at length so successful, that, together with a very brisk gale, they brought the vessel into *Dublin* harbour.

Here our adventurer took a lodging in a back-street near *St. Stephen's Green*,[1] at which place she intended to preach the next day; but had got a cold in the voyage, which occasioned such a hoarseness that made it impossible to put that design in practice.

There lodged in the same house with her, a brisk widow of near 40 Years of age, who had buried two husbands, and seemed by her behaviour to be far from having determined against a third expedition to the land of matrimony.

To this widow our adventurer began presently to make addresses, and as he at present wanted tongue to express the ardency of his flame, he was obliged to make use of actions of endearment, such as squeezing, kissing, toying, &c.

These were received in such a manner by the fair widow, that her lover thought he had sufficient encouragement to proceed to a formal declaration of his passion. And this she chose to do by letter, as her voice still continued too hoarse for uttering the soft accents of love.

A letter therefore was penned accordingly in the usual stile, which, to prevent any miscarriages, Mrs. *Hamilton* thought proper to deliver with her own hands; and immediately retired to give the adored lady an opportunity of digesting the contents alone, little doubting of an answer agreeable to her wishes, or at least such a one as the coyness of the sex generally dictates in the beginning of an amour, and which lovers, by long experience, know pretty well how to interpret.

But what was the gallant's surprize, when in return to an amorous epistle, she read the following sarcasms, which it was impossible for the most sanguine temper to misunderstand, or construe favourably.

"SIR,

I was greatly astonished at what you put into my hands. Indeed I thought, when I took it, it might have been an Opera song, and which for certain reasons I should think, when your cold is gone, you might sing

---

[1] St Stephen's Green is a garden square in Dublin, founded in 1664. Several nonconformist meeting houses existed in the area.

as well as *Farinelli*,[1] from the great resemblance there is between your persons. I know not what you mean by encouragement to your hopes; if I could have conceived my innocent freedoms could have been so misrepresented, I should have been more upon my guard: but you have taught me how to watch my actions for the future, and to preserve myself even from any suspicion of forfeiting the regard I owe to the memory of the best of men, by any future choice. The remembrance of that dear person makes me incapable of proceeding farther.—"

And so firm was this resolution, that she would never afterwards admit of the least familiarity with the despairing Mrs. *Hamilton*; but perhaps that destiny which is remarked to interpose in all matrimonial things, had taken the widow into her protection: for in a few days afterwards, she was married to one *Jack Strong*, a cadet in an *Irish* regiment.

Our adventurer being thus disappointed in her love, and what is worse, her money drawing towards an end, began to have some thoughts of returning home, when fortune seemed inclined to make her amends for the tricks she had hitherto played her, and accordingly now threw another Mistress in her way, whose fortune was much superior to the former widow, and who received Mrs. *Hamilton*'s addresses with all the complaisance she could wish.

This Lady, whose name was *Rushford*, was the widow of a rich cheese-monger, who left her all he had, and only one great grand-child to take care of, whom, at her death, he recommended to be her Heir; but wholly at her own power and discretion.

She was now in the sixty eighth year of her age, and had not, it seems, entirely abandoned all thoughts of the pleasures of this world: for she was no sooner acquainted with Mrs. *Hamilton*, but, taking her for a beautiful lad of about eighteen, she cast the eyes of affection on her, and having pretty well outlived the bashfulness of her youth, made little scruple of giving hints of her passion of her own accord.

It has been observed that women know more of one another than the wisest men (if ever such have been employed in the study) have with all their art been capable of discovering. It is therefore no wonder that these hints were quickly perceived and understood by the female gallant, who animadverting on the conveniency which the old gentlewoman's fortune would produce in her present situation, very gladly embraced the opportunity, and advancing with great warmth of love to the attack, in which she was received almost with open arms, by the tottering citadel, which presently offered to throw open the gates, and surrender at discretion.

In her amour with the former widow, Mrs. *Hamilton* had never any other design than of gaining the lady's affection, and then discovering

---

[1] Farinelli (1705-1782) was the most famous castrato opera singer. He lived and performed in London between 1734 and 1737.

herself to her, hoping to have had the same success which Mrs. *Johnson* had found with her: but with this old lady, whose fortune only she was desirous to possess, such views would have afforded very little gratification. After some reflection, therefore, a device entered into her head, as strange and surprizing, as it was wicked and vile; and this was actually to marry the old woman, and to deceive her, by means which decency forbids me even to mention.

The wedding was accordingly celebrated in the most public manner, and with all kind of gaiety, the old woman greatly triumphing in her shame, and instead of hiding her own head for fear of infamy, was actually proud of the beauty of her new husband, for whose sake she intended to disinherit her poor great-grandson, tho' she had derived her riches from her husband's family, who had always intended this boy as his heir. Nay, what may seem very remarkable, she insisted on the parson's not omitting the prayer in the matrimonial service for fruitfulness; drest herself as airy as a girl of eighteen, concealed twenty years of her age, and laughed and promoted all the jokes which are usual at weddings; but she was not so well pleased with a repartee of her great-grandson, a pretty and a smart lad, who, when somebody jested on the bridegroom because he had no beard, answered smartly: There should never be a beard on both-sides: For indeed the old lady's chin was pretty well stocked with bristles.

Nor was this bride contented with displaying her shame by a public wedding dinner, she would have the whole ceremony compleated, and the stocking was accordingly thrown with the usual sport and merriment.[1]

During the three first days of the marriage, the bride expressed herself so well satisfied with her choice, that being in company with another old lady, she exulted so much in her happiness, that her friend began to envy her, and could not forbear inveighing against effeminacy in men; upon which a discourse arose between the two ladies, not proper to be repeated, if I knew every particular; but ended at the last, in the unmarried lady's declaring to the bride, that she thought her husband looked more like a woman than a man. To which the other replied in triumph, he was the best man in *Ireland*.

This and the rest which past, was faithfully recounted to Mrs. *Hamilton* by her wife, at their next meeting, and occasioned our young bridegroom to blush, which the old lady perceiving and regarding as an effect of youth, fell upon her in a rage of love like a tygress, and almost murdered her with kisses.

One of our *English* Poets[2] remarks in the case of a more able husband than Mrs. *Hamilton* was, when his wife grew amorous in an unseasonable time.

[1] The throwing of the stocking (or of the garter) in the direction of male guests (the one who caught it was supposed to get married next) was often criticised at the time as indecent.

[2] Here, the author has inserted a brief note indicating the name of the poet: "Prior." The lines are, indeed, from the 1707 verse tale "Paulo Purganti and His Wife" by Matthew Prior (1664-1721).

1746

The doctor understood the call,
But had not always wherewithal.

So it happened to our poor bridegroom, who having not at that time *the wherewithal* about her, was obliged to remain meerly passive, under all this torrent of kindness of his wife; but this did not discourage her, who was an experienced woman, and thought she had a cure for this coldness in her husband, the efficacy of which, she might perhaps have essayed formerly. Saying therefore with a tender smile to her husband, I believe you are a woman, her hands began to move in such direction, that the discovery would absolutely have been made, had not the arrival of dinner, at that very instant, prevented it.

However, as there is but one way of laying the spirit of curiosity, when once raised in a woman, *viz.* by satisfying it, so that discovery, though delayed, could not now be long prevented. And accordingly the very next night, the husband and wife had not been long in bed together, before a storm arose, as if drums, guns, wind and thunder were all roaring together. Villain, rogue, whore, beast, cheat, all resounded at the same instant, and were followed by curses, imprecations and threats, which soon waked the poor great-grandson in the garret; who immediately ran down stairs into his great-grandmother's room. He found her in the midst of it in her shift, with a handful of shirt in one hand, and a handful of hair in the other, stamping and crying, I am undone, cheated, abused, ruined, robbed by a vile jade, impostor, whore.— What is the matter, dear Madam, answered the youth; O child, replied she, undone! I am married to one who is no man. My husband? a woman, a woman, a woman. Ay, said the grandson, where is she?—Run away, gone, said the great-grandmother, and indeed so she was: For no sooner was the fatal discovery made, than the poor female bridegroom, whipt on her breeches, in the pockets of which, she had stowed all the money she could, and slipping on her shoes, with her coat, waiste-coat and stockings in her hands, had made the best of her way into the street, leaving almost one half of her shirt behind, which the enraged wife had tore from her back.

As Mrs. *Hamilton* well knew that an adventure of that kind would soon fill all *Dublin*, and that it was impossible for her to remain there undiscovered, she hastened away to the Key, where by good fortune, she met with a ship just bound to *Dartmouth*,[1] on board which she immediately went, and sailed out of the harbour, before her pursuers could find out or overtake her.

She was a full fortnight in her passage, during which time, no adventure occurred worthy remembrance. At length she landed at *Dartmouth*, where she soon provided herself with linnen, and thence went to *Totness*,[2] where she assumed the title of a doctor of physic, and took lodgings in the house of one Mrs. *Baytree*.

---

[1] "Key" is an alternate spelling for "quay." Dartmouth is a port in Devon.
[2] Totnes (as it is spelled today) is a market town in Devon, 12 miles north of Dartmouth.

Here she soon became acquainted with a young girl, the daughter of one Mr. *Ivythorn*, who had the green sickness;[1] a distemper which the doctor gave out he could cure by an infallible *nostrum*.

The doctor had not been long intrusted with the care of this young patient before he began to make love to her: for though her complexion was somewhat faded with her distemper, she was otherwise extreamly pretty.

This Girl became an easy conquest to the doctor, and the day of their marriage was appointed, without the knowledge, or even suspicion of her father, or of an old aunt who was very fond of her, and would neither of them have easily given their consent to the match, had the doctor been as good a Man as the niece thought him.

At the day appointed, the doctor and his mistress found means to escape very early in the morning from *Totness*, and went to a town called *Ashburton* in *Devonshire*,[2] where they were married by a regular Licence which the doctor had previously obtained.

Here they staid two days at a public house, during which time the Doctor so well acted his part, that his bride had not the least suspicion of the legality of her marriage, or that she had not got a husband for life. The third day they returned to *Totness*, where they both threw themselves at Mr. *Ivythorn*'s feet, who was highly rejoic'd at finding his daughter restor'd to him, and that she was not debauched, as he had suspected of her. And being a very worthy good-natur'd man, and regarding his true interest and happiness of his daughter more than the satisfying his own pride, ambition, or obstinacy, he was prevailed on to forgive her, and to receive her and her husband into his house, as his children, notwithstanding the opposition of the old aunt, who declared she would never forgive the wanton slut, and immediately quitted the house, as soon as the young couple were admitted into it.

The Doctor and his wife lived together above a fortnight, without the least doubt conceived either by the wife, or by any other person of the Doctor's being what he appeared; till one evening the Doctor having drank a little too much punch, slept somewhat longer than usual, and when he waked, he found his wife in tears, who asked her husband, amidst many sobs, how he could be so barbarous to have taken such advantage of her ignorance and innocence, and to ruin her in such a manner? The Doctor being surprized and scarce awake, asked her what he had done. Done, says she, have you not married me a poor young girl, when you know, you have not—you have not—what you ought to have. I always thought indeed your shape was something odd, and have often wondred that you had not the least bit of beard; but I thought you had been a man for all that, or I am sure I would not have been so wicked to marry you for the world. The Doctor endeavoured to pacify her, by every kind of promise, and telling her she would have all the pleasures of marriage without the

---

[1] Also called "chlorosis" (and today, "hypochromic anemia"); paleness is the most common symptom. At the time, it was considered associated with virgin girls.
[2] A small town, some 10 miles north of Totnes.

inconveniences. No, no, said she, you shall not persuade me to that, nor will I be guilty of so much wickedness on any account. I will tell my Papa of you as soon as I am up; for you are no husband of mine, nor will I ever have any thing more to say to you. Which resolution the Doctor finding himself unable to alter, she put on her cloaths with all the haste she could, and taking a horse, which she had bought a few days before, hastened instantly out of the town, and made the best of her way, thro' bye-roads and across the country, into *Somersetshire*, missing *Exeter*, and every other great town which lay in the road.

And well it was for her, that she used both this haste and precaution: For Mr. *Ivythorn* having heard his daughter's story, immediately obtained a warrant from a justice of peace, with which he presently dispatch'd the proper officers; and not only so, but set forward himself to *Exeter*, in order to try if he could learn any news of his son-in-law, or apprehend her there; till after much search being unable to hear any tidings of her, he was obliged to set down contented with his misfortune, as was his poor daughter to submit to all the ill-natured sneers of her own sex, who were often witty at her expence, and at the expence of their own decency.

The Doctor having escaped, arrived safe at *Wells* in *Somersetshire*, where thinking herself at a safe distance from her pursuers, she again sat herself down in quest of new adventures.

She had not been long in this city,[1] before she became acquainted with one *Mary Price*, a girl of about eighteen years of age, and of extraordinary beauty. With this girl, hath this wicked woman since her confinement declared, she was really as much in love, as it was possible for a man ever to be with one of her own sex.

The first opportunity our Doctor obtain'd of conversing closely with this new mistress, was at a dancing among the inferior sort of people, in contriving which the Doctor had herself the principal share. At that meeting the two lovers had an occasion of dancing all night together; and the Doctor lost no opportunity of shewing his fondness, as well by his tongue as by his hands, whispering many soft things in her ears, and squeezing as many soft things into her hands, which, together with a good number of kisses, &c. so pleased and warmed this poor girl, who never before had felt any of those tender sensations which we call love, that she retired from the dancing in a flutter of spirits, which her youth and ignorance could not well account for; but which did not suffer her to close her eyes, either that morning or the next night.

The Day after that the Doctor sent her the following letter.

"My Dearest Molly,

Excuse the fondness of that expression; for I assure you, my angel, all I write to you proceeds only from my heart, which you have so entirely conquered, and made your own, that nothing else has any share in it; and,

[1] Thanks to the presence there, since the Middle Ages, of the Cathedral Church of Saint Andrew, Wells is considered not a town, but a "city" (England had only 24 "cities" in the 18th century).

my angel, could you know what I feel when I am writing to you, nay even at every thought of my *Molly*, I know I should gain your pity if not your love; if I am so happy to have already succeeded in raising the former, do let me have once more an opportunity of seeing you, and that soon, that I may breathe forth my soul at those dear feet, where I would willingly die, if I am not suffer'd to lie there and live. My sweetest creature, give me leave to subscribe myself

> You fond, doating,
> Undone SLAVE."

This letter added much to the disquietude which before began to torment poor *Molly*'s breast. She read it over twenty times, and, at last, having carefully survey'd every part of the room, that no body was present, she kissed it eagerly. However, as she was perfectly modest, and afraid of appearing too forward, she resolved not to answer this first letter; and if she met the Doctor, to behave with great coldness towards him.

Her mother being ill, prevented her going out that day; and the next morning she received a second letter from the Doctor, in terms more warm and endearing than before, and which made so absolute a conquest over the unexperienc'd and tender heart of this poor girl, that she suffered herself to be prevailed on, by the intreaties of her lover, to write an answer, which nevertheless she determin'd should be so distant and cool, that the woman of the strictest virtue and modesty in *England* might have no reason to be asham'd of having writ it; of which letter the reader hath here an exact copy:

"SUR,

I haf recevd boath your too litters, and sur I ham much surprise hat the loafe you priten to haf for so pur a garl as mee. I kan nut beleef you wul desgrace yourself by marring sutch a yf as mee, and Sur I wool nut be thee hore of the gratest man in the kuntry. For thof mi vartu his all I haf, yit hit is a potion I ham rissolv to kare to mi housband, soe noe moor at presant, from your humble savant to cummand."

The Doctor received this letter with all the ecstasies any lover could be inspired with, and, as Mr. *Congreve* says in his *Old Batchelor*, Thought there was more eloquence in the false spellings, with which it abounded, than in all *Aristotle*.[1] She now resolved to be no longer contented with this distant kind of conversation, but to meet her mistress face to face. Accordingly that very afternoon she went to her mother's house, and enquired for her poor *Molly*, who no sooner heard her lover's voice than she fell a trembling in the most violent manner. Her sister who opened the door informed the Doctor she was at home, and let the impostor in; but *Molly* being then in dishabille, would not see him till she had put on

[1] *The Old Bachelor* (1693) is the first play by William Congreve (1670-1729). In the first scene, Bellmour speaks of a letter from Sylvia: "There's more Elegancy in the false Spelling of this Superscription than in all *Cicero*."

clean linnen, and was arrayed from head to foot in as neat, tho' not in so fine a manner, as the highest court lady in the kingdom could attire herself in, to receive her embroider'd lover.

Very tender and delicate was the interview of this pair, and if any corner of *Molly*'s heart remain'd untaken, it was now totally subdued. She would willingly have postponed the match somewhat longer, from her strict regard to decency; but the earnestness and ardour of her lover would not suffer her, and she was at last obliged to consent to be married within two days.

Her sister, who was older than herself, and had over-heard all that had past, no sooner perceiv'd the Doctor gone, than she came to her, and wishing her joy with a sneer, said much good may it do her with such a husband; for that, for her own part, she would almost as willingly be married to one of her own sex, and made some remarks not so proper to be here inserted. This was resented by the other with much warmth. She said she had chosen for herself only, and that if she was pleased, it did not become people to trouble their heads with what was none of their business. She was indeed so extremely enamoured, that I question whether she would have exchanged the Doctor for the greatest and richest match in the world.

And had not her affections been fixed in this strong manner, it is possible that an accident which happened the very next night might have altered her mind: for being at another dancing with her lover, a quarrel arose between the Doctor and a man there present, upon which the other seizing the former violently by the collar, tore open her wastecoat, and rent her shirt, so that all her breast was discovered, which, tho' beyond expression beautiful in a woman, were of so different a kind from the bosom of a man, that the married women there set up a great titter; and tho' it did not bring the Doctor's sex into an absolute suspicion, yet caused some whispers, which perhaps might have spoiled the match with a less innocent and less enamoured virgin.

It had however no such effect on poor *Molly*. As her fond heart was free from any deceit, so was it entirely free from suspicion; and accordingly, at the fixed time she met the Doctor, and their nuptials were celebrated in the usual form.

The mother was extremely pleased at this preferment (as she thought it) of her daughter. The joy of it did indeed contribute to restore her perfectly to health, and nothing but mirth and happiness appeared in the faces of the whole family.

The new married couple not only continued, but greatly increased the fondness which they had conceived for each other, and poor *Molly*, from some stories she told among her acquaintance, the other young married women of the town, was received as a great fibber, and was at last universally laughed at as such among them all.

Three months past in this manner, when the Doctor was sent for to *Glastonbury*[1] to a patient (for the fame of our adventurer's knowledge in

[1] A town in Somerset, about 6 miles southwest of Wells.

physic began now to spread) when a person of *Totness* being accidentally present, happened to see and know her, and having heard upon enquiry, that the Doctor was married at *Wells*, as we have above mentioned, related the whole story of Mr. *Ivythorn*'s daughter, and the whole adventure at *Totness*.

News of this kind seldom wants wings; it reached *Wells*, and the ears of the Doctor's mother before her return from *Glastonbury*. Upon this the old woman immediately sent for her daughter, and very strictly examined her, telling her the great sin she would be guilty of, if she concealed a fact of this kind, and the great disgrace she would bring on her own family, and even on her whole sex, by living quietly and contentedly with a husband who was in any degree less a man than the rest of his neighbours.

Molly assured her mother of the falsehood of this report; and as it is usual for persons who are too eager in any cause, to prove too much, she asserted some things which staggered her mother's belief, and made her cry out, O child, there is no such thing in human nature.

Such was the progress this story had made in *Wells*, that before the Doctor arrived there, it was in every body's mouth; and as the Doctor rode through the streets, the mob, especially the women, all paid their compliments of congratulation. Some laughed at her, others threw dirt at her, and others made use of terms of reproach not fit to be commemorated. When she came to her own house, she found her wife in tears, and having asked her the cause, was informed of the dialogue which had past between her and her mother. Upon which the Doctor, tho' he knew not yet by what means the discovery had been made, yet too well knowing the truth, began to think of using the same method, which she had heard before put in practice, of delivering herself from any impertinence; for as to danger, she was not sufficiently versed in the laws to apprehend any.

In the mean time the mother, at the solicitation of some of her relations, who, notwithstanding the stout denial of the wife, had given credit to the story, had applied herself to a magistrate, before whom the *Totness* man appeared, and gave evidence as is before mentioned. Upon this a warrant was granted to apprehend the Doctor, with which the constable arrived at her house, just as she was meditating her escape.

The husband was no sooner seized, but the wife threw herself into the greatest agonies of rage and grief, vowing that he was injured, and that the information was false and malicious, and that she was resolved to attend her husband wherever they conveyed him.

And now they all proceeded before the Justice, where a strict examination being made into the affair, the whole happened to be true, to the great shock and astonishment of every body; but more especially of the poor wife, who fell into fits, out of which she was with great difficulty recovered.

The whole truth having been disclosed before the Justice, and something of too vile, wicked and scandalous a nature, which was found in the Doctor's trunk, having been produced in evidence against her, she was committed to *Bridewell*,[1] and Mr. *Gold*, an eminent and learned counsellor at law, who lives in those parts, was consulted with upon the occasion, who gave his advice that she should be prosecuted at the next sessions, on a clause in the vagrant act, *for having by false and deceitful practices endeavoured to impose on some of his Majesty's subjects.*[2]

Bridewell in the first half of the 18th century.

As the Doctor was conveyed to *Bridewell*, she was attended by many insults from the mob; but what was more unjustifiable, was the cruel treatment which the poor innocent wife received from her own sex, upon the extraordinary accounts which she had formerly given of her husband.

Accordingly at the ensuing sessions of the peace for the county of *Somerset*, the Doctor was indicted for the abovementioned diabolical fact, and after a fair trial convicted, to the entire satisfaction of the whole court.

At the trial the said *Mary Price* the wife, was produced as a witness, and being asked by the council, whether she had ever any suspicion of the Doctor's sex during the whole time of the courtship, she answered positively in the negative. She was then asked how long they had been married, to which she answered three months; and whether they had cohabited the whole time together? to which her reply was in the affirmative. Then the council asked her, whether during the time of this cohabitation, she imagined the Doctor had behaved to her as a husband ought to his wife? Her modesty confounded her a little at this question; but she at last answered she did imagine so. Lastly, she was asked when it was that she first harboured any suspicion of her being imposed upon? To which she answered, she had not the least suspicion till her husband was carried before a magistrate, and there discovered, as hath been said above.

The prisoner having been convicted of this base and scandalous crime, was by the court sentenced to be publickly and severely whipt four several times,[3] in four market towns within the county of *Somerset*, to wit, once in each market town, and to be imprisoned, &c.

[1] Bridewell was a women's prison in London, but similar houses of correction, bearing the same name, had been built in other places in England.
[2] The many "vagrant acts" condemned "idle" and "disorderly" people.
[3] She was to be whipped four different times.

These whippings she has accordingly undergone, and very severely have they been inflicted, insomuch, that those persons who have more regard to beauty than to justice, could not refrain from exerting some pity toward her, when they saw so lovely a skin scarified with rods, in such a manner that her back was almost flead: yet so little effect had the smart or shame of this punishment on the person who underwent it, that the very evening she had suffered the first whipping, she offered the goaler money,[1] to procure her a young girl to satisfy her most monstrous and unnatural desires.

But it is to be hoped that this example will be sufficient to deter all others from the commission of any such foul and unnatural crimes: for which, if they should escape the shame and ruin which they so well deserve in this world, they will be most certain of meeting with their full punishment in the next: for unnatural affections are equally vicious and equally detestable in both sexes, nay, if modesty be the peculiar characteristick of the fair sex, it is in them most shocking and odious to prostitute and debase it.

In order to caution therefore that lovely sex, which, while they preserve their natural innocence and purity, will still look most lovely in the eyes of men, the above pages have been written, which, that they might be worthy of their perusal, such strict regard hath been had to the utmost decency, that notwithstanding the subject of this narrative be of a nature so difficult to be handled inoffensively, not a single word occurs through the whole, which might shock the most delicate ear, or give offence to the purest chastity.

1746

[1] "Flead" is an alternate spelling of "flayed: and "goaler" of "gaoler."

SAMUEL JOHNSON
History of Zosima (1750)

The author: Born in Lichfield, Samuel
Johnson (1709-1784) went to Oxford for a while,
but lack of funds forced him to leave without
a degree. He opened an unsuccessful school in
Lichfield, but one of his pupils was the future
famous actor David Garrick (1717-1779). Together,
they left in 1737 for London, where Johnson
soon became factotum for Edward Cave's *The
Gentleman's Magazine*. In 1738, he published
his first successful work, *London*, a poem praised
by Pope. After a series of short biographies, he
announced his plan for a dictionary of the English
language in 1747. The following year, he published
his first short story, "The Vision of Theodore,
the Hermit of Teneriffe, Found in his Cell" (in
The Preceptor, Robert Dodsley's anthology of
educational texts). In the winter of 1748-1749,

Johnson formed the Ivy Lane Club, with meetings at the King's Head, a beef-steak
house near St. Paul's; other members included Richard Bathurst, John Hawkesworth,
Samuel Dyer, and the publisher John Payne. It was Payne (first together with Joseph
Bouquet, then alone for the collected editions) who, on 20 March 1750, assumed the
publication of *The Rambler*, an essay serial of which Johnson (with the exception
of 4 issues) was the sole author until its end on 17 March 1752. *The Rambler* was
printed (by Edward Cave) twice a week in 500 copies; each issue cost 2 pence. It
was reprinted by many national and provincial papers and, although it was not
commercially successful at first, it was soon acknowledged by many as the best
journal since *The Spectator* and it established Johnson's reputation as a leading man
of letters in England.

    The text: First published as a letter signed "Zosima" in number 12 of *The
Rambler* (Saturday, April 28, 1750), it was later named "The History of a Young
Woman That Came to London for a Service" in the contents of all subsequent volume
editions. Johnson made several changes post-1750, and other changes appeared in
other editions published during his lifetime, but, as C.B. Bradford shows, the last time
Johnson had control over the text was in the fourth edition, which appeared in 1756,
when the copyright had changed hands. In the journal as well as in the volume version,
the story was introduced by a quote from Lucan. It was not translated in 1750; James
Elphinson, an Edinburgh editor who reprinted *The Rambler* in Scotland, provided a
translation, also published in 1752 in *The Gentleman's Magazine*. However, Johnson
later came up with his own translation, which first appeared in 1753:

> Unlike the ribald whose licentious jest
> Pollutes his banquet and insults his guest;
> From wealth and grandeur easy to descend,
> Thou joy'st to lose the master in the friend:
> We round thy board the cheerful menials fee,
> Gay with the smile of bland equality;
> No social care the gracious lord disdains;
> Love prompts to love, and rev'rence rev'rence gains.

The text provided here comes from *The Rambler. In Four Volumes* (London: Printed
for A. Millar, in the Strand; J. Hodges; J. and J. Rivington; R. Baldwin; and B. Collins,
1756), Vol. I, 61-68.

Further reading: C.B. Bradford. "Johnson's Revision of *The Rambler*." *The Review of English Studies* 15.59 (July 1939), 302-331.

Chance David Pahl. "Samuel Johnson, Periodical Publication, and the Sentimental Reader: Virtue in Distress in *The Rambler* and *The Idler*." *Lumen* XXXXVI, hors série (2017): 21-35.

To the RAMBLER.

S I R ,

As you seem to have devoted your labours to virtue, I cannot forbear to inform you of one species of cruelty, with which the life of a man of letters perhaps does not often make him acquainted; and which, as it seems to produce no other advantage to those that practise it than a short gratification of thoughtless vanity, may become less common when it has been once exposed in its various forms, and its full magnitude.

I am the daughter of a country gentleman, whose family is numerous, and whose estate, not at first sufficient to supply us with affluence, has been lately so much impaired by an unsuccessful law-suit, that all the younger children are obliged to try such means as their education affords them, for procuring the necessaries of life. Distress and curiosity concurred to bring me to London, where I was received by a relation with the coldness which misfortune generally finds. A week, a long week, I lived with my cousin, before the most vigilant enquiry could procure us the least hopes of a place, in which time I was much better qualified to bear all the vexations of servitude. The first two days she was content to pity me, and only wish'd I had not been quite so well bred, but people must comply with their circumstances. This lenity, however, was soon at an end; and, for the remaining part of the week, I heard every hour of the pride of my family, the obstinacy of my father, and of people better born than myself that were common servants.

At last, on Saturday noon, she told me, with very visible satisfaction, that Mrs Bombasine, the great silk-mercer's lady, wanted a maid, and a fine place it would be, for there would be nothing to do but to clean my mistress's room, get up her linen, dress the young ladies, wait at tea in the morning, take care of a little miss just come from nurse, and then sit down to my needle. But madam was a woman of great spirit, and would not be contradicted, and therefore I should take care, for good places were not easily to be got.

With these cautions, I waited on madam Bombasine, of whom the first sight gave me no ravishing ideas. She was two yards round the waist, her voice was at once loud and squeaking, and her face brought to my mind the picture of the full-moon. Are you the young woman, says she, that are come to offer yourself? It is strange when people of substance want a servant, how soon it is the town-talk. But they know they shall have a belly-full that live with me. Not like people at the other end of the town, we dine at one o'clock. But I never take any body without a character; what friends do you come of? I then told her that my father was a gentleman, and that we had been unfortunate.—A great misfortune, indeed, to come to me and have three meals a-day!—So your father was a gentleman, and you are a gentlewoman I suppose—such gentlewomen!— Madam, I did not mean to claim any exemptions, I only answered your enquiry— Such gentlewomen! people should set their children to good trades, and keep them off the parish. Pray go to the other end of the town, there are gentlewomen, if they would pay their debts: I am sure we have lost enough by gentlewomen. Upon this, her broad face grew broader with triumph, and I was afraid she would have taken me for the pleasure of continuing her insult; but happily the next word was, Pray, Mrs gentlewoman, troop down stairs. You may believe I obeyed her.

I returned and met with a better reception from my cousin than I expected; for while I was out, she had heard that Mrs Standish, whose husband had lately been raised from a clerk in an office, to be commissioner of the excise, had taken a fine house, and wanted a maid.

To Mrs Standish I went, and, after having waited six hours, was at last admitted to the top of the stairs, when she came out of her room, with two of her company. There was a smell of punch. So young woman, you want a place, whence do you come?—From the country, madam.—Yes, they all come out of the country. And what brought you to town, a bastard? Where do you lodge? At the Seven-Dials?[1] What, you never heard of the foundling house? Upon this, they all laughed so obstreperously, that I took the opportunity of sneaking off in the tumult.

I then heard of a place at an elderly lady's. She was at cards; but in two hours, I was told, she would speak to me. She asked me if I could keep an account, and ordered me to write. I wrote two lines out of some book that lay by her. She wonder'd what people meant, to breed up poor girls to write at that rate. I suppose, Mrs Flirt, if I was to see your work, it would be fine stuff!—You may walk. I will not have love-letters written from my house to every young fellow in the street.

Two days after, I went on the same pursuit to Lady Lofty, dressed, as I was directed, in what little ornaments I had, because she had lately got a place at court. Upon the first sight of me, she turns to the woman that showed me in, Is this the lady that wants a place? Pray what place wou'd you have, miss? a maid of honour's place? Servants now a days!— "Madam, I heard you wanted— Wanted what? Somebody finer than myself! A pretty servant indeed—I should be afraid to speak to her—I suppose, Mrs Minx, these fine hands cannot bear wetting—A servant indeed! Pray move off—I am resolved to be the head person in this house—You are ready dress'd, the taverns will be open.

I went to enquire for the next place in a clean linen gown, and heard the servant tell his lady, there was a young woman, but he saw she would not do. I was brought up, however. Are you the trollop that has the impudence to come for my place? What, you have hired that nasty gown, and are come to steal a better.— Madam, I have another, but being obliged to walk—Then these are your manners, with your blushes and your courtesies, to come to me in your worst gown. Madam, give me

[1] In the 18th and 19th centuries, Seven Dials was a slum.

leave to wait upon you in my other. Wait on me, you saucy slut! Then you are sure of coming—I could not let such a drab come near me—Here, you girl that came up with her, have you touch'd her? If you have, wash your hands before you dress me.—Such trollops! Get you down. What, whimpering? Pray walk.

I went away with tears; for my cousin had lost all patience. However she told me, that having a respect for my relations, she was willing to keep me out of the street, and would let me have another week.

The first day of this week I saw two places. At one I was asked where I had lived? And upon my answer, was told by the lady, that people should qualify themselves in ordinary places, for she should never have done if she was to follow girls about. At the other house, I was a smirking hussy, and that sweet face I might make money of— For her part, it was a rule with her, never to take any creature that thought herself handsome.

The three next days were spent in lady Bluff's entry, where I waited six hours every day for the pleasure of seeing the servants peep at me, and go away laughing—Madam will stretch her small shanks in the entry; she will know the house again—At sun-set the two first days I was told, that my lady would see me to-morrow; and on the third, that her woman staid.

My week was now near its end, and I had no hopes of a place. My relation, who always laid upon me the blame of every miscarriage, told me that I must learn to humble myself, and that all great ladies had particular ways; that if I went on in that manner, she could not tell who would keep me; she had known many that had refused places, sell their cloaths, and beg in the streets.

It was to no purpose that the refusal was declared by me to be never on my side; I was reasoning against interest, and against stupidity; and therefore I comforted myself with the hope of succeeding better in my next attempt, and went to Mrs Courtly, a very fine lady, who had routs at her house, and saw the best company in town.

I had not waited two hours before I was called up, and found Mr Courtly and his lady at piquet, in the height of good humour. This I looked on as a favourable sign, and stood at the lower end of the room in expectation of the common questions. At last Mr Courtly call'd out, after a whisper, Stand facing the light, that one may see you. I chang'd my place, and blush'd. They frequently turn'd their eyes upon me, and seem'd to discover many subjects of merriment; for at every look they whisper'd, and laugh'd with the most violent agitations of delight. At last Mr Courtly cried out, Is that colour your own, child? Yes, says the lady, if she has not robb'd the kitchen hearth. This was so happy a conceit, that it renew'd the storm of laughter, and they threw down their cards in hopes of better sport. The lady then called me to her, and began with an affected gravity to enquire what I could do? But first turn about, and let us see your fine shape; Well, what are you fit for, Mrs Mum? You would find your tongue, I suppose, in the kitchen. No, no, says Mr Courtly, the girl's a good girl yet, but I am afraid a brisk young fellow, with fine tags on his shoulder—Come, child, hold up your head; what? you have

154

stole nothing—Not yet, says the lady, but she hopes to steal your heart quickly.—Here was a laugh of happiness and triumph, prolonged by the confusion which I could no longer repress. At last the lady recollected herself: Stole? no—but if I had her, I should watch her; for that downcast eye—Why cannot you look people in the face? Steal? says her husband, she would steal nothing but, perhaps, a few ribbands before they were left off by her lady. Sir, answer'd I, why should you, by supposing me a thief, insult one from whom you have received no injury? Insult, says the lady; are you come here to be a servant, you saucy baggage, and talk of insulting? What will this world come to, if a gentleman may not jest with a servant? Well, such servants! pray be gone, and see when you will have the honour to be so insulted again. Servants insulted—a fine time.— Insulted! Get down stairs, you slut, or the footman shall insult you.

The last day of the last week was now coming, and my kind cousin talked of sending me down in the waggon to preserve me from bad courses. But in the morning she came and told me that she had one trial more for me; Euphemia wanted a maid, and perhaps I might do for her; for, like me, she must fall her crest, being forced to lay down her chariot upon the loss of half her fortune by bad securities, and with her way of giving her money to every body that pretended to want it, she could have little beforehand; therefore I might serve her; for, with all her fine sense, she must not pretend to be nice.

I went immediately, and met at the door a young gentlewoman, who told me she had herself been hired that morning, but that she was order'd to bring any that offered up stairs. I was accordingly introduced to Euphemia, who, when I came in, laid down her book, and told me, that she sent for me not to gratify an idle curiosity, but lest my disappointment might be made still more grating by incivility; that she was in pain to deny any thing, much more what was no favour; that she saw nothing in my appearance which did not make her wish for my company; but that another, whose claims might perhaps be equal, had come before me. The thought of being so near to such a place, and missing it, brought tears into my eyes, and my sobs hinder'd me from returning my acknowledgements. She rose up confused, and supposing by my concern that I was distressed, placed me by her, and made me tell her my story: which when she had heard, she put two guineas in my hand, ordering me to lodge near her, and make use of her table till she could provide for me. I am now under her protection, and know not how to shew my gratitude better than by giving this account to the RAMBLER.

ZOSIMA.

CHRISTOPHER SMART

A Very Curious Petrifaction (1751)

The author: Christopher Smart (1722-1771) studied at Pembroke College, Cambridge, where he remained as a fellow until 1750 and wrote his first prose pieces for *The Student*. In 1751 he started a new periodical, *The Midwife*, in which he signed his texts "Mrs. Mary Midnight" (a persona he also used in *The Student* and elsewhere, including on stage). Under controversial circumstances, Smart was confined to a lunatic asylum from 1757 to 1763. While there, he wrote his best poems, *A Song to David* (published in 1763) and *Jubilate Agno* (first published posthumously, in 1939). He died in the debtors' prison.

 The text: First published in *The Midwife, or The Old Woman's Magazine* 4 (17 January 1751). The following is from *The Midwife, or The Old Woman's Magazine* (London: Printed for Mary Midnight and sold by T. Carnan in St. Pauls Church Yard, [1751]) [Vol. I], 151-154. Its full title was "A Letter from Mrs. *Mary Midnight*, to the Society of *Antiquarians*, giving them an Account of a very curious Petrifaction found near *Penzance*, in the County of *Cornwal*."

 Further reading: Min Wild, *Christopher Smart and Satire: "Mary Midnight" and the* Midwife (Aldershot: Ashgate, 2008), 49-72.

1751

GENTLEMEN,

Superfluous and absurd wou'd an Apology be from me to you, for any Address which I can make to you, since doubtless I have a Right to your Acquaintance, and a Property in your Protection; being myself a most extraordinary Piece of venerable Antiquity. But shou'd I wave this Priviledge, the singular Curiosity I am about to present you, in the Formation of which, Nature, Time and Art have been employ'd would sufficiently plead my Excuse. As my worthy Friend Mr. *Powallis* of *Penzance*, was taking an Evening's Walk in the Fields, he accidentally trod upon something, which having all the Appearance of an human Excrement, made him immediately congratulate himself upon his good Luck. But upon a stricter Scrutiny it appeared to be a Pebble, which both in Shape and Colour perfectly resembled what he at first took it for. He carried it Home to his Lady, who at first Sight cry'd out, my Dear, you have brought Home a ——— mentioning a Word, which I am sorry shou'd ever drop from a Woman of her Decency and Discretion. However, upon handling it she was pacify'd, and diverted herself by now and then depositing it in the Parlour, to the Confusion of the House-Maid,

156

and sometimes dropping it in Company, for the Entertainment and Astonishment of her Friends. At length a Gentleman who was an excellent Antiquarian, and likewise profoundly learn'd in Minerals and Fossils, happen'd to pay Mr. *Powallis* a Visit; and upon Inspection declar'd with Transport, that it was the greatest Curiosity in *Europe*. "This (says he) is really and *bonâ fide*, a petrified Excrement, and as it was found in the Fields, is a valuable Monument of ancient Simplicity; when our Fathers (how unlike the Effeminacy of our Moderns!) used to *do their Business* in the most pastoral and unaffected Manner, and (as the Divine *Milton* sings)

> Every Shepherd *laid his Tail*
> Under the Hawthorne in the Vale."[1]

This Gentleman is now in Possession of the Petrifaction which he obtain'd from Mr. *Powallis*, who (because he was his very intimate Friend) let him have it at the easy Expence of Fifty Pound. I wish, Gentlemen of the Society, it was mine to bestow, I declare I should not hesitate a Moment about the Disposal of it. But, as it is, you will be content with a Description of it, which I shall attempt in as brief a Manner, as I may: This Rarity then, which you may either call an artificial Piece of Nature, or a natural Piece of Art, is about seven Inches long, and about three and a half diameter; (I mean in the Centre) for, towards the End, it's taper, and is (as a certain Poet says by a Lady's Shape)

> *"Fine by Degrees and beautifully less."*[2]

It resembles a Rainbow in its Curvature, but not in Colour; for in that Respect it is uniform to a surprizing Exactness, which Dr. *Bolus* assures us is a strong Proof that the Ancients lived upon a Milk and Vegetable Diet, and were free from those luxurious Compositions that discolour the Excrements of this degenerate Age. Mr. *Fondledust*, (who, tho' he has not the Honour to be of your Society is yet a Man of great Penetration and Curiosity) declares, he is absolutely certain that in a few Years Study he could find out the Age, Condition, Sex, Situation, Country and Constitution of the Person who generously bequeath'd this remarkable Relict to Posterity.—Nay, he still goes farther—and most confidently (tho' I think somewhat rashly) declares, that he can find out whether it is a Jewish, Pagan, or Mahometan Business. I intended to have given you a Figure of this Petrifaction; but my Engraver is such a Coxcomb that he refused the Job; and swore he wou'd not draw the Picture of a damn'd ――― for any Man; speaking disrespectfully of that Thing which with us is in such Esteem, that, by the Courtesy of the Kingdom, it has obtain'd the

---

[1] The narrator misquotes from Milton's pastoral poem *L'Allegro* (1645), which reads: "And ev'ry shepherd tells his tale/ Under the hawthorn in the vale."
[2] From Prior's *Henry and Emma* (1709), where it refers to the lady's waist.

Order of Knighthood, under the Style and Title of Sir Reverence.[1] Now, Gentlemen, having laid before you this Matter in as plain and succinct a Manner as I was capable of, I humbly take my Leave, but not without most sincerely promising you, that if any of *this Sort* shou'd occur to me hereafter, I will not fail to communicate it to you as a Testimony of that Esteem with which I remain

Your most humble Servant,

M. MIDNIGHT.

1751

---

[1] An old euphemism for excrement; a corruption of "save reverence," from the Latin phrase "*salva reverentia*" ("saving regard or respect"), it was originally used as an apology before mentioning anything discourteous, then it connoted specifically the unrefined word or phrase, and it finally came to be used especially for the feces.

SAMUEL JOHNSON
The Revolutions of a Garret (1751)

The author: Until 25 March 1752, Johnson was busy with *The Rambler*, which came out twice a week. He still had financial problems: in 1751 he asked his publisher (John Newbery) at least three times for a small loan. At the same time, his wife became seriously ill (she died three days after the publication of the last *Rambler*).

The text: First published in *The Rambler* number 161 (Tuesday, October 1, 1751). Originally untitled, it soon appeared in the indexes of volume versions with the title "The Revolutions of a Garret." The following is from *The Rambler. In Four Volumes*. The Fourth Edition. (London: Printed for A. Millar, in the Strand; J. Hodges; J. And J. Rivington; R. Baldwin; and B. Collins, 1756), Vol. IV, pp. 5-10. The story was preceded by an epigraph from Homer, translated by Johnson as "Frail as the leaves that quiver on the sprays/ Like them man flourishes, like them decays."

Mr. RAMBLER,

S I R ,

You have formerly observed that curiosity often terminates in barren knowledge, and that the mind is prompted to study and enquiry rather by the uneasiness of ignorance, than the hope of profit. Nothing can be of less importance to any present interest than the fortune of those who have been long lost in the grave, and from whom nothing now can be hoped or feared. Yet to rouse the zeal of a true antiquary little more is necessary than to mention a name which mankind have conspired to forget; he will make his way to remote scenes of action thro' obscurity and contradiction, as *Tully* sought amidst bushes and brambles the tomb of *Archimedes*.[1]

It is not easy to discover how it concerns him that gathers the produce or receives the rent of an estate, to know through what families the land has passed, who is registered in the conqueror's survey as its possessor,[2] how often it has been forfeited by treason, or how often sold by prodigality. The power or wealth of the present inhabitants of a country cannot be much increased by an enquiry after the names of those

[1] In his *Tusculan Disputations*, Marcus Tullius Cicero (usually called Tully in the 18th century), relates his discovery of the tomb in Syracuse, in Sicily. Today, the location of the tomb is unknown.
[2] William the Conqueror's 1086 Great Survey, known as the Domesday Book, includes the names of all those who held land at the time. Not everybody can trace one's ancestry all the way to the Domesday Book.

barbarians, who destroyed one another twenty centuries ago, in contests for the shelter of woods or convenience of pasturage. Yet we see that no man can be at rest in the enjoyment of a new purchase till he has learned the history of his grounds from the ancient inhabitants of the parish, and that no nation omits to record the actions of their ancestors, however bloody, savage and rapacious.

The same disposition, as different opportunities call it forth, discovers itself in great or little things. I have always thought it unworthy of a wise man to slumber in total inactivity only because he happens to have no employment equal to his ambition or genius; it is therefore my custom to apply my attention to the objects before me, and as I cannot think any place wholly unworthy of notice that affords a habitation to a man of letters, I have collected the history and antiquities of the several garrets in which I have resided.[1]

> *Quantulacumque estis, vos ego magna voco.*
> How small to others, but how great to me![2]

Many of these narratives my industry has been able to extend to a considerable length; but the woman with whom I now lodge has lived only eighteen months in the house, and can give no account of its ancient revolutions; the plaisterer, having, at her entrance, obliterated, by his white-wash, all the smoky memorials which former tenants had left upon the ceiling, and perhaps drawn the veil of oblivion over politicians, philosophers, and poets.

When I first cheapened[3] my lodgings, the landlady told me, that she hoped I was not an author, for the lodgers on the first floor had stipulated that the upper rooms should not be occupied by a noisy trade. I very readily promised to give no disturbance to her family, and soon dispatched a bargain on the usual terms.

I had not slept many nights in my new apartment before I began to enquire after my predecessors, and found my landlady, whose imagination is filled chiefly with her own affairs, very ready to give me information.

Curiosity, like all other desires, produces pain as well as pleasure. Before she began her narrative, I had heated my head with expectations of adventures and discoveries, of elegance in disguise, and learning in distress; and was somewhat mortified when I heard that the first tenant was a taylor, of whom nothing was remembered but that he complained of his room for want of light; and, after having lodged in it a month, and

[1] A garret was a room or an apartment on the uppermost floor of a house; often, an apartment occupying the entire attic.
[2] A more literal translation would be "However small you are, I call you great." It is from the last poem of Ovid's *Amores*. Christopher Marlowe had famously translated Ovid's elegies, and his version reads "How small soe'er, I'll you for greatest praise." In *The Rambler*, the first word was misprinted as "quantulacunque" from one edition to the next, but it has been corrected here.
[3] In the old sense of "bargaining for, offering a price for," or even "asking the price of" something.

paid only a week's rent, pawned a piece of cloth which he was trusted to cut out, and was forced to make a precipitate retreat from this quarter of the town.

The next was a young woman newly arrived from the country, who lived for five weeks with great regularity, and became by frequent treats very much the favourite of the family, but at last received visits so frequently from a cousin in *Cheapside*, that she brought the reputation of the house into danger, and was therefore dismissed with good advice.

The room then stood empty for a fortnight; my landlady began to think that she had judged hardly, and often wished for such another lodger. At last an elderly man of a grave aspect, read the bill, and bargained for the room at the very first price that was asked. He lived in close retirement, seldom went out till evening, and then returned early sometimes chearful, and at other times dejected. It was remarkable, that whatever he purchased, he never had small money in his pocket, and tho' cool and temperate on other occasions, was always vehement and stormy till he received his change. He paid his rent with great exactness, and seldom failed once a week to requite my landlady's civility with a supper. At last, such is the fate of human felicity, the house was alarm'd at midnight by the constable, who demanded to search the garrets. My landlady assuring him that he had mistaken the door, conducted him up stairs, where he found the tools of a coiner[1]; but the tenant had crawled along the roof to an empty house, and escaped; much to the joy of my landlady, who declares him a very honest man, and wonders why any body should be hanged for making money when such numbers are in want of it. She however confesses that she shall for the future always question the character of those who take her garret without beating down the price.

The bill was then placed again in the window, and the poor woman was teazed for seven weeks by innumerable passengers, who obliged her to climb with them every hour up five stories, and then disliked the prospect, hated the noise of a publick street, thought the stairs narrow, objected to a low cieling, required the walls to be hung with fresher paper, asked questions about the neighbourhood, could not think of living so far from their acquaintance, wished the windows had looked to the south rather than the west, told how the door and chimney might have been better disposed, bid her half the price that she asked, or promised to give her earnest the next day, and came no more.

At last, a short meagre man, in a tarnish'd waistcoat, desired to see the garret, and when he had stipulated for two long shelves and a larger table, hired it at a low rate. When the affair was completed, he looked round him with great satisfaction, and repeated some words which the woman did not understand. In two days he brought a great box of books, took possession of his room, and lived very inoffensively, except that he frequently disturbed the inhabitants of the next floor by unseasonable noises. He was generally in bed at noon, but from evening to midnight he sometimes talked aloud with great vehemence, sometimes stamped as

[1] A counterfeiter.

in rage, sometimes threw down his poker, then clattered his chairs, then set down in deep thought, and again burst out into loud vociferations; sometimes he would sigh as oppressed with misery, and sometimes shake with convulsive laughter. When he encountered any of the family, he gave way or bowed, but rarely spoke, except that as he went up stairs he often repeated,

—Ὃς ὑπέρτατα δώματα νάιει.
This habitant th'aerial regions boast,[1]

hard words, to which his neighbours listened so often, that they learned them without understanding them. What was his employment she did not venture to ask him, but at last heard a printer's boy enquire for the author.

My landlady was very often advised to beware of this strange man, who, tho' he was quiet for the present, might perhaps become outrageous in the hot months; but as she was punctually paid, she could not find any sufficient reason for dismissing him, till one night he convinced her by setting fire to his curtains, that it was not safe to have an author for her inmate.

She had then for six weeks a succession of tenants, who left the house on Saturday, and instead of paying their rent, stormed at their landlady. At last she took in two sisters, one of whom had spent her little fortune in procuring remedies for a lingering disease, and was now supported and attended by the other: she climbed with difficulty to the apartment, where she languished eight weeks, without impatience or lamentation, except for the expence and fatigue which her sister suffered, and then calmly and contentedly expired. The sister followed her to the grave, paid the few debts which they had contracted, wiped away the tears of useless sorrow, and returning to the business of common life, resigned to me the vacant habitation.

Such, Mr. *Rambler*, are the changes which have happened in the narrow space where my present fortune has fixed my residence. So true is it that amusement and instruction are always at hand for those who have skill and willingness to find them; and so just is the observation of *Juvenal*, that a single house will shew whatever is done or suffered in the world.[2]

I am, SIR, &c.

---

[1] From the beginning of Hesiod's *Works and Days*, in which the formula is about Zeus. Here, it is clearly intended to speak for the "lofty" areas in which authors live and work. In one of his essays from 1784, French writer Louis Sébastien Mercier (1740-1814) reworks this passage and has a printer's boy go up to a garret to meet a "Mr Author." Mercier then inserts the Greek quote (which he believes to be Homer's) and explains that it refers to philosophers, because they always live "in the uppermost apartments."

[2] A reference to Juvenal's *Satires* (13.159-160), although the "house" there is a courthouse in which one can find all mankind's vices.

JOHN HAWKESWORTH
Story of Opsinous (1752)

The author: John Hawkesworth was probably born in 1715, as his epitaph indicates (though 1719 has also been suggested, and parish records show he was only baptised in 1720) in a dissenting family. He was apprenticed as a lawyer's clerk, but chose a literary career and, for most of his life, he was an editor and contributor of *The Gentleman's Magazine*, in the rooms of which he met Samuel Johnson. A few years later, Johnson assisted him in the publication of *The Adventurer* (1752-1754), in which most of Hawkesworth's short fiction was published. In his later life, he edited the works of Jonathan Swift and Captain Cook (the latter in the year of his death, 1773).

The text: Somewhat autobiographical, the following story was first published in *The Adventurer* 12 (Saturday, December 16, 1752), 13 (Tuesday, 19 December 1752), and 14 (Saturday, 23 December 1752). Originally untitled, it soon appeared in the indexes of volume versions with the title "Story of Opsinous." The following text is reproduced from *The Adventurer* (London: Printed for J. Payne, at Pope's Head in Pater-Noster-Row, 1753), Vol. I, 67-84. The first instalment was introduced by an epigraph from Horace: "Magnum pauperies opprobrium jubet/ Quidvis aut facere aut pati" (literally: "poverty compels many men to perpetrate crimes, and to subject themselves to great disgrace") translated by Hawkesworth as: "He whom the dread of want ensnares,/ With baseness acts, with meanness bears." The other epigraphs will be signalled in footnotes. "Opsi" means "late," and "nous" means "knowledge," in Greek.

Further reading: Nathan Drake. "The Literary Life of Dr. Hawkesworth." *Essays, Biographical, Critical, and Historical, Illustrative of the Rambler, Adventurer, and Idler*. London: Printed by J. Seeley, Buckingham, for W. Suttaby, Stationers Court, London, 1810. Vol. II, 1-34.

To the ADVENTURER.

SIR,

Of all the expedients that have been found out to alleviate the miseries of life, none is left to despair but complaint: and though complaint, without hope of relief, may be thought rather to increase than mitigate anguish, as it recollects every circumstance of distress, and imbitters the memory of past sufferings by the anticipation of future; yet, like weeping, it is an indulgence of that which it is pain to suppress, and sooths with the hope of pity the wretch who despairs of comfort. Of this number is he who now addresses you: yet the solace of complaint and the hope of pity, are not the only motives that have induced me to communicate the series of events, by which I have been led on in an insensible deviation from felicity, and at last plunged in irremediable calamity: I wish that others may escape perdition; and am, therefore, solicitous to warn them of the path, that leads to the precipice from which I have fallen.

I am the only child of a wealthy farmer, who as he was himself illiterate, was the more zealous to make his son a scholar; imagining that there was in the knowledge of Greek and Latin, some secret charm of perpetual influence, which as I passed through life would smooth the way before me, establish the happiness of success, and supply new resources to disappointment. But not being able to deny himself the pleasure he found in having me about him, instead of sending me out to a boarding school, he offered the curate of the parish ten pounds a year and his board to become my tutor.

This gentleman, who was in years, and had lately buried his wife, accepted the employment, but refused the salary: the work of education, he said, would agreeably fill his intervals of leisure, and happily coincide with the duties of his function: but he observed that his curacy, which was thirty pounds a year, and had long subsisted him when he had a family, would make him wealthy now he was a single man; and therefore he insisted to pay for his board: to this my father, with whatever reluctance, was obliged to consent. At the age of six years I began to read my Accidence[1] under my preceptor; and at fifteen had gone through the Latin and Greek Classics. But the languages were not all that I learned of this gentleman; besides other science of less importance, he taught me the theory of Christianity by his precepts, and the practice by his example.

As his temper was calm and steady, the influence which he had acquired over me was unlimited: he was never capriciously severe; so that I regarded his displeasure not as an effect of his infirmity, but of my own fault: he discovered so much affection in the pleasure with which he commended, and in the tender concern with which he reproved me, that I loved him as a father: and his devotion, though rational and manly, was yet so habitual and fervent, that I reverenced him as a saint. I found even my passions controuled by an awe which his presence impressed; and by a constant attention to his doctrine and his life, I acquired such a sense of my connexion with the invisible world, and such a conviction of the consciousness of DEITY to all my thoughts, that every inordinate wish was secretly suppressed, and my conduct regulated by the most scrupulous circumspection.

My father thought he had now taken sufficient care of my education, and therefore began to expect that I should assist in over-looking his servants, and managing his farm, in which he intended I should succeed him: but my preceptor, whose principal view was not my temporal advantage, told him, that, as a farmer, great part of my learning would be totally useless; and that the only way to make me serviceable to mankind, in proportion to the knowledge I had acquired, would be to send me to the university, that at a proper time I might take orders: but my father, besides that he was still unwilling to part with me, had probably many reasons against my entering the world in a cassock: such, however, was the deference which he paid to my tutor, that he had almost implicitly

1752

[1] Today called usually inflection, it is the study of the way in which words change their form via declension and conjugation.

submitted to his determination, when a relation of my mother's, who was an attorney of great practice in the Temple, came to spend part of the long vacation at our house, in consequence of invitations which had been often repeated during an absence of many years.

My father thought that an opportunity of consulting how to dispose of me with a man so well acquainted with life, was not to be lost; and perhaps he secretly hoped, that my preceptor would give up his opinion as indefensible, if a person of the lawyer's experience should declare against it. My cousin was accordingly made umpire in the debate; and after he had heard the arguments on both sides, he declared against my becoming a farmer: he said it would be an act of injustice to bury my parts and learning in the obscurity of rural life; because, if produced to the world, they would probably be rewarded with wealth and distinction. My preceptor imagined the question was now finally determined in his favour; and being obliged to visit one of his parishioners that was sick, he gave me a look of congratulation as he went out, and I perceived his cheek glow with a flush of triumph, and his eye sparkle with tears of delight.

But he had no sooner left the room, than my cousin gave the conversation another turn: he told my father, that though he had opposed his making me a farmer, he was not an advocate for my becoming a parson; for that to make a young fellow a parson, without being able to procure him a living, was to make him a beggar: he then made some witty reflections on the old gentleman who was just gone out; "Nobody," he said, "could question his having been put to a bad trade, who considered his circumstances now he had followed it forty years." And after some other sprightly sallies, which though they made my father laugh, made me tremble; he clapped him upon the shoulder, "If you have a mind your boy should make a figure in life, old gentleman," says he, "put him clerk to me: my lord chancellor King[1] was no better than the son of a country shopkeeper; and my master gave a person of much greater eminence many a half crown when he was an attorney's clerk in the next chambers to mine. What say you? shall I take him up with me or no?" My father, who had listened to this proposal with great eagerness, as soon as my cousin had done speaking, cried, "A match;" and immediately gave him his hand, in token of his consent. Thus the bargain was struck, and my fate determined before my tutor came back.

It was in vain that he afterwards objected to the character of my new master, and expressed the most dreadful apprehensions at my becoming an attorney's clerk, and entering into the society of wretches who had been represented to him, and perhaps not unjustly, as the most profligate upon earth: they do not, indeed, become worse than others, merely as clerks; but as young persons, who with more money to spend in the gratification of appetite, are sooner than others abandoned to their own conduct: for though they are taken from under the protection of a parent, yet being scarce considered as in a state of servitude, they are not sufficiently restrained by the authority of a master.

[1] Peter King, 1st Baron King (1669-1734), Lord Chancellor from 1725 to 1733.

My father had conceived of my cousin as the best natured man in the world; and probably was intoxicated with the romantic hope, of living to see me upon the Bench in Westminster-hall, or of meeting me on the circuit lolling in my own coach, and attended by a crowd of the inferior instruments of justice. He was not therefore to be moved either by expostulation or intreaty; and I set out with my cousin on horseback, to meet the stage at a town within a few miles, after having taken leave of my father, with a tenderness that melted us both; and received from the hoary saint his last instructions and benediction, and at length the parting embrace, which was given with the silent ardor of unutterable wishes, and repeated with tears that could no longer be suppressed or concealed.

When we were seated in the coach, my cousin began to make himself merry with the regret and discontent that he perceived in my countenance, at leaving a cowhouse, a hogstye, and two old grey-pates,[1] who were contending whether I should be buried in a farm or a college: but I who had never heard either my father or my tutor treated with irreverence, could not conceal my displeasure and resentment: but he still continued to rally[2] my country simplicity with many allusions which I did not understand, but which greatly delighted the rest of the company. The fourth day brought us to our journey's end, and my master, as soon as we reached his chambers, shook me by the hand, and bid me welcome to the Temple.

Temple Bar in the early 18th century. This gateway to the City led to the Inner Temple and the Middle Temple, two of the Inns of Court.

He had been some years a widower, and his only child a daughter being still at a boarding school, his family consisted only of a man and maid servant and myself; for though he had two hired clerks, yet they lodged and boarded themselves. The horrid lewdness and profaneness of these fellows terrified and disgusted me; nor could I believe that my master's property and interest could be safely intrusted with men, who in every respect appeared to be so destitute of virtue and religion: I, therefore, thought it my duty to apprise him of his danger; and accordingly one day when we were at dinner, I communicated my suspicion, and the reason upon which it was founded. The formal solemnity with which I introduced this conversation, and the air of importance which I gave to my discovery, threw him into a violent fit of laughter, which struck me dumb with confusion and astonishment. As soon as he recovered himself,

[1] The top of the head (the term was used humorously and it is now archaic).
[2] To tease, make fun of. The noun, "raillery" (see next paragraph) is closer to the French origin, "railler."

he told me, that though his clerks might use some expressions that I had not been accustomed to hear, yet he believed them to be very honest; and that he placed more confidence in them, than he would in a formal prig, of whom he knew nothing but that he went every morning and evening to prayers, and said grace before and after meat; that as to swearing they meant no harm; and as he did not doubt but that every young fellow liked a girl, it was better they should joke about it than be hypocritical and sly: not that he would be thought to suspect my integrity, or to blame me for practices, which he knew to be merely effects of the bigotry and superstition in which I had been educated, and not the disguises of cunning or subterfuges of guilt.

I was greatly mortified at my cousin's behaviour on this occasion, and wondered from what cause it could proceed, and why he should so lightly pass over those vices in others, from which he abstained himself; for I had never heard him swear; and as his expressions were not obscene, I imagined his conversation was chaste; in which, however, my ignorance deceived me, and it was not long before I had reason to change my opinion of his character.

II[1]

There came one morning to enquire for him at his chambers, a lady who had something in her manner which caught my attention and excited my curiosity: her cloaths were fine, but the manner in which they were put on was rather flaunting than elegant; her dress[2] was not easy nor polite, but seemed to be a strange mixture of affected state and licentious familiarity; she looked in the glass while she was speaking to me, and without any confusion adjusted her tucker;[3] and she seemed rather pleased than disconcerted at being regarded with earnestness. Being told that my cousin was abroad, she asked some trifling questions, and then making a slight curtsey, took up the side of her hoop with a jerk that discovered at least half her leg, and hurried down stairs.

I could not help enquiring of the clerks, if they knew this lady; and was greatly confounded when they told me with an air of secrecy, that she was my cousin's mistress, whom he had kept almost two years in lodgings near Covent-garden. At first I suspected this information, but it was soon confirmed by so many circumstances, that I could no longer doubt of its truth.

As my principles were yet untainted, and the influence of my education was still strong, I regarded my cousin's sentiments as impious

[1] The second instalment was introduced by a Latin epigraph from Virgil, accompanied in later editions by Dryden's translation: "Thus all below, whether by nature's curse,/ Or fate's decree, degen'rate still to worse./ So the boat's brawny crew the current stem,/ And, slow advancing, struggle with the stream:/ But if they slack their hands, or cease to strive,/ Then down the flood with headlong haste they drive."
[2] In an old sense of "appearance, guise." It appeared as "address" in later editions, which is, of course, a different quality.
[3] A piece of muslin or lace worn by women around the top of the bodice.

and detestable; and his example rather struck me with horror, than seduced me to imitation: I flattered myself with hopes of effecting his reformation, and took every opportunity to hint the wickedness of allowed incontinence;[1] for which I was always rallied when he was disposed to be merry, and answered with the contemptuous sneer of self-sufficiency when he was sullen.

Near four years of my clerkship were now expired, and I had never yet entered the lists as a disputant[2] with my cousin: for tho' I conceived myself to be much his superior in moral and theological learning, and though he often admitted me to familiar conversation, yet I still regarded the subordination of a servant to a master, as one of the duties of my station, and preserved it with such exactness, that I never exceeded a question or a hint when we were alone, and was always silent when he had company; tho' I frequently heard such positions advanced, as made me wonder that no tremendous token of the divine displeasure immediately followed: but coming one night from the tavern, warm with wine, and, as I imagined, flushed with polemic success, he insisted upon my taking one glass with him before he went to bed; and almost as soon as we were seated, he gave me a formal challenge, by denying all divine revelation, and defying me to prove it.

I now considered every distinction as thrown down, and stood forth as the champion of religion, with that elation of mind which the hero always feels at the approach of danger. I thought myself secure of victory; and rejoicing that he had now compelled me to do what I had often wished he would permit, I obliged him to declare that he would dispute upon equal terms, and we began to debate. But it was not long before I was astonished to find myself confounded by a man, whom I saw half drunk, and whose learning and abilities I despised when he was sober; for as I had but very lately discovered that any of the principles of religion, from the immortality of the soul to the deepest mystery, had been so much as questioned, all his objections were new. I was assaulted where I had made no preparation for defence; and having not been so much accustomed to disputation, as to consider that in the present weakness of human intellects, it is much easier to object than answer, and that in every disquisition difficulties are found which cannot be resolved, I was overborne by the sudden onset, and in the tumult of my search after answers to his cavils, forgot to press the positive arguments on which religion is established: he took advantage of my confusion, proclaimed his own triumph, and because I was depressed, treated me as vanquished.

As the event which had thus mortified my pride, was perpetually revolved in my mind, the same mistake still continued: I inquired for solutions instead of proofs, and found myself more and more entangled in the snares of sophistry: in some other conversations which my cousin

---

[1] Inability to contain sexual appetite; unchastity.
[2] "To enter the lists" is a phrase meaning "to enter into a place or scene of combat or contest." The "lists" (from "list" = margin) were an enclosed space where tournaments were held in the Middle Ages.

1752

was now eager to begin, new difficulties were started, the labyrinth of doubt grew more intricate, and as the question was of infinite moment,[1] my mind was brought into the most distressful anxiety. I ruminated incessantly on the subjects of our debate, sometimes chiding myself for my doubts, and sometimes applauding the courage and freedom of my inquiry.

While my mind was in this state, I heard by accident that there was a club at an alehouse in the neighbourhood, where such subjects were freely debated, to which every body was admitted without scruple or formality: to this club in an evil hour I resolved to go, that I might learn how knotty points were to be discussed, and truth distinguished from error.

Accordingly on the next club night I mingled with the multitude that was assembled in this school of folly and infidelity: I was at first disgusted at the gross ignorance of some, and shocked at the horrid blasphemy of others; but curiosity prevailed, and my sensibility by degrees wore off. I found that almost every speaker had a different opinion, which some of them supported by arguments, that to me who was utterly unacquainted with disputation, appeared to hold opposite probabilities in exact equipoise; so that, instead of being confirmed in any principle, I was divested of all; the perplexity of my mind was increased, and I contracted such a habit of questioning whatever offered itself to my imagination, that I almost doubted of my own existence.

In proportion as I was less assured in my principles, I was less circumspect in my conduct: but such was still the force of education, that any gross violence offered to that which I had held sacred, and every act which I had been used to regard as incurring the forfeiture of the divine favour, stung me with remorse. I was indeed still restrained from flagitious[2] immorality, by the power of habit: but this power grew weaker and weaker, and the natural propensity to ill gradually took place; as the motion that is communicated to a ball which is struck up into the air, becomes every moment less and less, till at length it recoils by its own weight.

Fear and hope, the great springs of human action, had now lost their principal objects, as I doubted whether the enjoyment of the present moment was not all that I could secure; my power to resist temptation diminished with my dependance upon the grace of GOD, and regard to the sanction of his law; and I was first seduced by a prostitute, in my return from a declamation on the *beauty* of virtue and the strength of the *moral sense*.

I began now to give myself up intirely to sensuality, and the gratification of appetite terminated my prospects of felicity: that peace of mind, which is the sunshine of the soul, was exchanged for the gloom of doubt, and the storm of passion; and my confidence in GOD and hope of everlasting joy, for sudden terrors and vain wishes, the loathings of satiety and the anguish of disappointment.

---

[1] Here: momentum, significance, importance.
[2] Wicked, heinous, villainous.

I was indeed impatient under this fluctuation of opinion, and therefore I applied to a gentleman who was a principal speaker at the club, and deemed a profound philosopher, to assists the labours of my own mind in the investigation of truth, and relieve me from distraction by removing my doubts: but this gentleman, instead of administering relief, lamented the prejudice of education, which he said hindered me from yielding without reserve to the force of truth, and might perhaps always keep my mind anxious, though my judgment should be convinced: but as the most effectual remedy for this deplorable evil, he recommended to me the works of Chubb, Morgan, and many others,[1] which I procured and read with great eagerness; and though I was not at last a sound deist, yet I perceived with some pleasure that my stock of polemic knowledge was greatly increased; so that, instead of being an auditor, I commenced a speaker at the club: and though to stand up and babble to a crowd in an alehouse, till silence is commanded by the stroke of a hammer, is as low an ambition as can taint the human mind; yet I was much elevated by my new distinction, and pleased with the deference that was paid to my judgment. I sometimes, indeed, reflected, that I was propagating opinions by which I had myself become vicious and wretched: but it immediately occurred, that though my conduct was changed, it could not be proved that my virtue was less; because many things which I avoided as vicious upon my old principles, were innocent upon my new. I therefore went on in my career, and was perpetually racking my invention for new topics and illustrations; and among other expedients, as well to advance my reputation, as to quiet my conscience and deliver me from the torment of remorse, I thought of the following.

Having learned that all error is innocent, because it is involuntary, I concluded, that nothing more was necessary to quiet the mind, than to prove that all vice was error: I therefore formed the following argument; "No man becomes vicious, but from a belief that vice will confer happiness: he may, indeed, have been told the contrary; but implicit faith is not required of reasonable beings: therefore, as every man ought to seek happiness, every man may lawfully make the experiment; if he is disappointed, it is plain that he did not intend that which has happened: so that every vice is an error; and therefore no vice will be punished."

I communicated this ingenious contrivance to my friend the philosopher, who, instead of detecting the difference between ignorance and perverseness, or stating the limitations within which we are bound to seek our own happiness, applauded the acuteness of my penetration, and the force of my reasoning. I was impatient to display so novel and important a discovery to the club, and the attention that it drew upon me gratified my ambition, to the utmost of my expectation: I had indeed some opponents; but they were so little skilled in argumentation, and so ignorant of the subject, that it only rendered my conquest more signal and important; for the chairman summed up the arguments on both sides, with so exact and scrupulous an impartiality, that as I appeared not

1752

[1] Thomas Chubb (1679-1747) and Thomas Morgan (d.1743) were English Deists.

to have been confuted, those who could not discover the weakness of my antagonists, thought that to confute me was impossible; my sophistry was taken for demonstration, and the number of proselytes was incredible. The assembly consisted chiefly of clerks and apprentices, young persons who had received a religious though not a liberal education; for those who were totally ignorant, or wholly abandoned, troubled not themselves with such disputations as were carried on at our club: and these unhappy boys, the impetuosity of whose passions was restrained chiefly by fear, as virtue had not yet become a habit, were glad to have the shackles struck off which they were told priestcraft had put on.

But however I might satisfy others, I was not yet satisfied myself; my torment returned, and new opiates became necessary: they were not indeed easily to be found; but such was my good fortune, that an illiterate mechanic afforded me a most seasonable relief, *by discussing the importing question, and demonstrating that the soul was not nor could be immortal.* I was, indeed, disposed to believe without the severest scrutiny, what I now began secretly to wish; for such was the state of my mind, that I was willing to give up the hope of everlasting happiness, to be delivered from the dread of perpetual misery; and as I thought of dying as a remote event, the apprehension of losing my existence with my life, did not much interrupt the pleasures of the bagnio[1] and the tavern.

They were, however, interrupted by another cause; for I contracted a distemper, which alarmed and terrified me, in proportion as its progress was swift, and its consequences were dreadful. In this distress I applied to a young surgeon, who was a speaker at the club, and gained a genteel subsistance by keeping it in repair: he treated my complaint as a trifle; and to prevent any serious reflections in this interval of pain and solitude, he rallied the deplorable length of my countenance, and exhorted me to behave like a man.

My pride, rather than my fear, made me very solicitous to conceal this disorder from my cousin; but he soon discovered it rather with pleasure than anger, as it compleated his triumph, and afforded him a new subject of raillery and merriment. By the spiritual and corporeal assistance of my surgeon, I was at length restored to my health, with the same dissolute morals, and a resolution to pursue my pleasures with more caution: instead, therefore, of hiring a prostitute, I now endeavoured to seduce the virgin, and corrupt the wife.

III[2]

In these attempts my new principles afforded me great assistance: for I found that those whom I could convert, I could easily debauch; and that to convert many, nothing more was necessary than to advance my

---

[1] Originally a bathing house (especially one with hot baths), but used in the 18th century mostly as a euphemism for brothels.

[2] A third and final epigraph, from Virgil's *Aeneid*, is inserted here and translated by Hawkesworth as "Ev'n yet his voice from hell's dread shades we hear—/ 'Beware, learn justice, and the Gods revere.'"

principles, and allege something in defence of them, by which I appeared to be convinced myself; for not being able to dispute, they thought that the argument which had convinced me, would, if they could understand it, convince them; so that, by yielding an implicit assent, they at once paid a compliment to their own judgments, and smoothed the way to the indulgence of appetite.

While I was thus gratifying every inordinate desire, and passing from one degree of guilt to another, my cousin determined to take his daughter, who was now in her nineteenth year, from school; and as he intended to make her mistress of his family, he quitted his chambers and took a house.

This young lady I had frequently seen and always admired; she was therefore no sooner come home than I endeavoured to recommend myself by a thousand assiduities, and rejoiced in the many opportunities that were afforded me to entertain her alone; and perceived that she was not displeased with my company, nor insensible to my complaisance.

My cousin, though he had seen the effects of his documents[1] of infidelity in the corruption of my morals, yet could not forbear to sneer at religion in the presence of his daughter; a practice in which I now always concurred, as it facilitated the execution of a design that I had formed of rendering her subservient to my pleasures. I might, indeed, have married her, and perhaps my cousin secretly intended that I should: but I knew women too well to think that marriage would confine my wishes to a single object; and I was utterly averse to a state, in which the pleasure of variety must be sacrificed to domestic quiet, or domestic quiet to the pleasure of variety; for I neither imagined that I could long indulge myself in an unlawful familiarity with many women, before it would by some accident be discovered to my wife; nor that she would be so very courteous or philosophical, as to suffer this indulgence without expostulation and clamour: and besides, I had no liking to a brood of children, whose wants would soon become importunate, and whose claim to my industry and frugality would be universally acknowledged; though the offspring of a mistress might be abandoned to beggery, without breach of the law, or offence to society.

The young lady on the contrary, as she perceived that my addressed exceeded common civilities, did not question but that my view was to obtain her for a wife, and I could discern that she often expected such a declaration, and seemed disappointed that I had not yet proposed an application to her father: but imagining, I suppose, that these circumstances were only delayed till the fittest opportunity, she did not scruple to admit all the freedoms that were consistent with modesty; and I drew every day nearer to the accomplishment of my design by insensible approaches, without alarming her fear, or confirming her hopes.

I knew that only two things were necessary; her passions were to be inflamed, and the motives from which they were to be suppressed, removed. I was therefore perpetually insinuating, that nothing which

1752

---

[1] In the old sense of "teaching, instructions."

was natural could be ill; I complained of the impositions and restrains of priestcraft and superstition; and, as if these hints were casual and accidental, I would immediately afterwards sing a tender song, repeat some seducing verses, or read a novel.

But henceforward, let never insulted beauty admit a second time into her presence the wretch, who has once attempted to ridicule religion, and substitute other aids to human frailty, for that love of GOD *which is better than life*, and that fear *which is the beginning of wisdom*: for whoever makes such an attempt, intends to betray; the contrary conduct being without question the interest of every one whose intentions are good, because even those who profanely deny religion to be of divine origin, do yet acknowledge that it is a political institution well calculated to strengthen the band of society, and to keep out the ravager by intrenching innocence and arming virtue. To oppose these corrupters by argument rather than contempt, is to parley with a murderer, who may be excluded by shutting a door.

My cousin's daughter used frequently to dispute with me, and these disputes always favoured the execution of my project: though, lest I should alarm her too much, I often affected to appear half in jest; and when I ventured to take any liberty, by which the bounds of modesty was somewhat invaded, I suddenly desisted with an air of easy negligence; and as the attempt was not persued, and nothing farther seemed to be intended than was done, it was regarded but as waggery,[1] and punished only with a slap or a frown. Thus she became familiar with infidelity and indecency by degrees.

I once subtily engaged her in a debate, whether the gratification of natural appetites was in itself innocent; and whether, if so, the want of external ceremony could in any case render it criminal. I insisted that virtue and vice were not influenced by external ceremonies, nor founded upon human laws, which were arbitrary, temporary and local: and that as a young lady's shutting herself up in a nunnery was still evil, though enjoined by such laws; so the transmitting her beauty to posterity was still good, though under certain circumstances it had by such laws been forbidden. This she affected utterly to deny, and I proposed that the question should be referred to her papa, without informing him of our debate, and that it should be determined by his opinion; a proposal to which she readily agreed. I immediately adverted to other subjects, as if I had no interest in the issue of our debate; but I could perceive that it sunk deep into her mind, and that she continued more thoughtful than usual.

I did not however fail to introduce a suitable topic of discourse the next time my cousin was present, and having stated the question in general terms, he gave it in my favour, without suspecting that he was judge in his own cause; and the next time I was alone with his daughter, without mentioning his decision, I renewed my familiarity, I found her resistance less resolute, persued my advantage, and compleated her ruin.

[1] Mischievous jesting or practical joke.

Within a few months she perceived that she was with child; a circumstance that she communicated with expressions of the most piercing distress: but instead of consenting to marry her, to which she had often urged me with all the little arts of persuasion that she could practice, I made light of the affair, chid her for being so much alarmed at so trivial an accident, and proposed a medicine which I told her would effectually prevent the discovery of our intercourse, by destroying the effect of it before it could appear. At this proposition she fainted, and when she recovered, opposed it with terror and regret, with tears, trembling and entreaty; but I continued inflexible, and at length, either removed or over ruled her scruples by the same arguments, that had first seduced her to guilt.

The long vacation was now commenced, and my clerkship was just expired: I therefore proposed to my cousin that we should all make a visit to my father, hoping that the fatigue of the journey would favour my purpose, by increasing the effect of the medicine, and accounting for an indisposition which it might be supposed to cause.

The plan being thus concerted, and my cousin's concurrence being obtained, it was immediately put in execution. I applied to my old friend the club surgeon, to whom I made no secret of such affairs, and he immediately furnished me with medicaments, which he assured me would answer my purpose: but either by a mistake in the preparation, or in the quantity, they produced a disorder which, soon after the dear injured unhappy girl arrived at her journey's end, terminated in her death.

My confusion and remorse at this event are not to be expressed, but confusion and remorse were suddenly changed into astonishment and terror; for she was scarce dead before I was taken into custody, upon suspicion of murder. Her father had deposed, that just before she died, she desired to speak to him in private; and that then, taking his hand and intreating his forgiveness, she told him that she was with child by me, and that I had poisoned her under pretence of preserving her reputation.

Whether she made this declaration, or only confessed the truth, and her father, to revenge the injury had forged the rest, cannot now be known; but the coroner having been summoned, the body viewed, and found to have been pregnant, with many marks of a violent and uncommon disorder, a verdict of wilful murder was brought in against me, and I was committed to the county gaol.

As the judges were then upon the circuit,[1] I was within less than a fortnight convicted and condemned by the zeal of the jury, whose passions had been so greatly inflamed by the enormity of the crime with which I had been charged, that they were rather willing that I should suffer being innocent, than that I should escape being guilty: but it appearing to the judge in the course of the trial that murder was not intended, he reprieved me before he left the town.

1752

[1] Judges travelled through certain appointed areas for the purpose of holding court.

I might now have redeemed the time, and, awakened to a sense of my folly and my guilt, might have made some reparation to mankind for the injury which I had done to society, and endeavoured to rekindle some spark of hope in my own breast, by repentance and devotion. But alas! in the first transports of my mind, upon so sudden and unexpected a calamity, the fear of death yielded to the fear of infamy, and I swallowed poison: the excess of my desperation hindered its immediate effect; for, as I took too much, great part of it was thrown up, and only such a quantity remained behind, as was sufficient to insure my destruction, and yet leave me time to contemplate the horrors of the gulph into which I am sinking.

In this deplorable situation I have been visited by the surgeon who was the immediate instrument of my misfortune, and the philosopher who directed my studies: but these are friends who only rouze me to keener sensibility, and inflict upon me more exquisite torment. They reproach me with folly, and upbraid me with cowardice; they tell me too, that the fear of death has made me regret the errors of superstition: but what would I now give for some erroneous hopes, and that credulous simplicity, which, though I have been taught to despise them, would sustain me in the tremendous hour that approaches, and avert from my last agony the horrors of despair.

I have indeed a visitor of another kind, the good old man who first taught me to frame a prayer, and first animated me with the hope of heaven: but he can only lament with me that this hope will not return, and that I can pray with confidence no more: he cannot by a sudden miracle re-establish the principles which I have subverted: my mind is all doubt, and terror, and confusion; I know nothing but that I have rendered ineffectual the clemency of my judge, that the approach of death is swift and inevitable, and that either the shades of everlasting night, or the gleams of unquenchable fire are at hand. My soul in vain shrinks backward; I grow giddy with the thought: the next moment is distraction! Farewell.

OPSINOUS.

175

EDWARD MOORE
The Story of Mrs. Wilson
(1753)

The author: Edward Moore (1712-1757), son, grandson, and nephew of Presbyterian ministers, was born in Abingdon, which at the time was the county town of Berkshire. After studies at a dissenting academy, he became apprentice to a linen draper in London and, in 1734, he was admitted to the Freedom of the Company of Glovers. The same year he published his first poem (a song) in *The Gentleman's Magazine*. More songs and a "serenata" followed and, in 1744, he published his first book of poetry, *Fables for the Female Sex*. His first play (*The Foundling*) was produced in 1748, but his greatest success on stage came in 1753, with *The Gamester*, a prose tragedy. He befriended David Garrick and Henry Fielding and, in 1749, he quit the linen business to concentrate on writing drama and song lyrics. That same year, Robert Dodsley, the publisher of Johnson's *Dictionary*, invited Moore to edit an essay-journal; Dodsley came up with the title, Moore with the persona of "Adam Fitz-Adam," the fictional editor; *The World* began on 4 January 1753 and appeared weekly for four years and 209 issues, 62 of which were written by Moore. Each issue was printed in 2,500 copies, five times more than *The Rambler* and more even than *The Spectator*, making of Moore and Dodsley's enterprise the most successful essay-journal of the half-century. Moore and Dodsley divided between themselves the profits for the collected editions, while Dodsley retained the profits for the original weeklies, Moore being paid 3 guineas for each contribution, whether written by him or received from a contributor. Lord Lyttelton, whose protégé Moore was, arranged for many upper-class contributors who did not need to be paid for their work. Thus, very shortly, *The World* became, as John Duncombe (one of the contributors) put it, "the bow of Ulysses, in which it was the fashion for men of rank and genius to try their strength" and, at the same time, it was acknowledged as a more elitist paper than any before or after. Moore died while the last issue of *The World*, in which the fictional Fitz-Adam also dies, was in press.

The text: The story first appeared untitled in two numbers (4-5) of *The World* (Thursday, 25 January, and Thursday, 1 February, 1753). It was subsequently identified in the contents and indices of various editions as either "Story of Mrs. Wilson" or "Story of Mr. and Mrs. Wilson." In one 19th-century anthology by Richard Griffin, it was entitled "A Domestic Story." The following text is reproduced from *The World. By Adam Fitz-Adam* (London, Printed for R. and J. Dodsley, in Pall-mall, 1755), Vol. I, 25-42.

Further reading: Robert Moore. "The Life of Moore." *The Poetical Works of Edward Moore*. London: C. Cooke, 1797, 3-18.

1753

To the entertainment of my fair readers, and to recommend to them an old-fashioned virtue, called prudence, I shall devote this and a following paper.[1] If the story I am going to tell them should deserve their approbation, they are to thank the husband and wife from whom I had it; and who are desirous, this day, of being the readers of their own adventures.

An eminent merchant in the city, whose real name I shall conceal under that of Wilson, was married to a lady of considerable fortune and more merit. They lived happily together for some years, with nothing to disturb them but the want of children. The husband, who saw himself richer every day, grew impatient for an heir; and as time rather lessened than increased the hopes of one, he became by degrees indifferent, and at last, averse to his wife. This change in his affections was the heaviest affliction to her; yet so gentle was her disposition, that she reproached him only with her tears; and seldom with those, but when upbraidings and ill-usage made her unable to restrain them.

It is a maxim with some married philosophers, that the tears of a wife are apt to wash away pity from the heart of a husband. Mr. Wilson will pardon me if I rank him, at that time, among these philosophers. He had lately hired a lodging in the country, at a small distance from town, whither he usually retired in the evening, to avoid (as he called it) the persecutions of his wife.

In this cruel separation, and without complaint, she passed away a twelvemonth; seldom seeing him but when business required his attendance at home, and never sleeping with him. At the end of which time, however, his behaviour, in appearance, grew kinder; he saw her oftener, and began to speak to her with tenderness and compassion.

One morning, after he had taken an obliging leave of her, to pass the day at his country lodgings, she paid a visit to a friend at the other end of the town; and stopping in her way home at a thread shop in a by-street near St. James's, she saw Mr. Wilson crossing the way, and afterwards knocking at the door of a genteel house over-against her, which was opened by a servant in livery, and immediately shut, without a word being spoken. As the manner of his entrance, and her not knowing he had an acquaintance in the street, a little alarmed her, she enquired of the shop-woman if she knew the gentleman who lived in the opposite house. "You have just seen him go in, madam," replied the woman. "His name is Roberts, and a mighty good gentleman, they say, he is. His lady"—At these words Mrs. Wilson changed colour; and interrupting her—"His lady, madam!—I thought that—Will you give me a glass of water? This walk has so tired me—Pray give me a glass of water—I am quite faint with fatigue." The good woman of the shop ran herself for the water, and by the additional help of some hartshorn[2] that was at hand, Mrs. Wilson became, in appearance, tolerably composed. She then looked

[1] The story was published in two instalments, the second of which begins with the words "I return now to Mrs. Wilson."
[2] An extract from the horn of the male red deer, containing ammonia, used as smelling salts.

over the threads she wanted, and having desired a coach might be sent for, "I believe," said she, "you were quite frightened to see me look so pale; but I had walked a great way, and should certainly have fainted if I had not stept into your shop.—But you were talking of the gentleman over the way—I fancied I knew him; but his name is Roberts, you say. Is he a married man, pray?" "The happiest in the world, madam (returned the thread-woman) he is wonderfully fond of children, and to his great joy, his lady is now lying in of her first child, which is to be christened this evening; and as fine a boy, they say it is, as ever was seen." At this moment, and as good fortune would have it, for the saving a second dose of hartshorn, the coach that was sent for came to the door; into which Mrs. Wilson immediately stept, after hesitating an apology for the trouble she had given; and in which coach we shall leave her to return home, in an agony of grief which herself has told me she was never able to describe.

The readers of this little history have been informed that Mr. Wilson had a country lodging, to which he was supposed to retire almost every evening since his disagreement with his wife; but in fact, it was to his house near St. James's that he constantly went. He had indeed hired the lodgings above-mentioned, but from another motive than merely to shun his wife. The occasion was this.

As he was sauntering one day through the bird-cage walk in the park,[1] he saw a young woman sitting alone upon one of the benches, who though plainly, was neatly dressed, and whose air and manner distinguished her from the lower class of women. He drew nearer to her without being perceived, and saw in her countenance, which innocence and beauty adorned, the most composed melancholy that can be imagined. He stood looking at her for some time; which she at last perceiving, started from her seat in some confusion, and endeavoured to avoid him. The fear of losing her gave him courage to speak to her. He begged pardon for disturbing her, and excused his curiosity by her extreme beauty, and the melancholy that was mixed with it.

It is observed by a very wise author, whose name and book I forget, that a woman's heart is never so brim-full of affliction, but a little flattery will insinuate itself into a corner of it; and as Wilson was a handsome fellow, with an easy address, the lady was soon persuaded to replace herself upon the bench, and to admit him at her side. Wilson, who was really heart-struck, made her a thousand protestations of esteem and friendship; conjuring her to tell him if his fortune or services could contribute to her happiness, and vowing never to leave her, till she made him acquainted with the cause of her concern.

Here a short pause ensued; and after a deep sigh and a stream of tears, the lady began thus.

"If, sir, you are the gentleman your appearance speaks you to be, I shall thank heaven that I have found you. I am the unfortunate widow of an officer who was killed at Dettingen.[2] As he was only a lieutenant, and

[1] A walk running on the south edge of St. James's Park, so named after Charles II's birds (the "Aviary") that used to be kept there.
[2] The battle of Dettingen was fought on 27 June 1743 and it was a victory of the British, Austrian and Hanoverian allies against the French.

178

his commission all his fortune, I married him against a mother's consent, for which she has disclaimed me. How I loved him, or he me, as he is gone forever from me, I shall forbear to mention, though I am unable to forget. At my return to England (for I was the constant follower of his fortunes) I obtained, with some difficulty, the allowance of a subaltern's widow, and took lodgings at Chelsea.

"In this retirement I wrote to my mother, acquainting her with my loss and poverty, and desiring her forgiveness for my disobedience; but the cruel answer I received from her determined me, at all events, not to trouble her again.

"I lived upon the slender allowance with all imaginable thrift, till an old officer, a friend of my husband, discovered me at church, and made me a visit. To this gentleman's bounty I have long been indebted for an annuity of twenty pounds, in quarterly payments. As he was punctual in these payments, which were always made me the morning they became due, and yesterday being quarter-day, I wondered I never saw him nor heard from him. Early this morning I walked from Chelsea to enquire for him at his lodgings in Pall-Mall;[1] but how shall I tell you, sir, the news I learnt there!—This friend! this generous and disinterested friend! was killed yesterday in a duel in Hyde-park." She stopt here to give vent to a torrent of tears, and then proceeded. "I was so stunned at this intelligence that I knew not whither to go. Chance more than choice brought me to this place; where if I have found a benefactor—and indeed, sir, I have need of one—I shall call it the happiest accident of my life."

The widow ended her story, which was literally true, in so engaging and interesting a manner, that Wilson was gone an age in love in a few minutes. He thanked her for the confidence she had placed in him, and swore never to desert her. He then requested the honour of attending her home, to which she readily consented, walking with him to Buckingham gate,[2] where a coach was called, which conveyed them to Chelsea. Wilson dined with her that day, and took lodgings in the same house, calling himself Roberts, and a single man. These were the lodgings I have mentioned before; where by unbounded generosity, and constant assiduities, he triumphed in a few weeks over the honour of this fair widow.

I shall stop a moment here, to caution those virtuous widows who are my readers, against too hasty a disbelief of this event. If they please to consider the situation of this lady, with poverty to alarm, gratitude to incite, and a handsome fellow to inflame, they will allow, that in a world near six thousand years old,[3] one such instance of frailty, even in a young and beautiful widow, may possibly have happened. But to go on with my story.

The effects of this intimacy were soon visible in the lady's shape; a circumstance that greatly added to the happiness of Wilson. He

---

[1] A street in Westminster, running from St. James's Street to Trafalgar Square parallel to The Mall (the latter being the northern edge of St. James's Park).
[2] Street in Westminster, south of St. James's Park, leading into Birdcage Walk.
[3] According to the largely accepted chronology proposed by Archbishop James Ussher (1581-1656), the Creation of the world by God had occurred in 4004 BC.

determined to remove her to town; and accordingly took house near St. James's,[1] where Mrs. Wilson had seen him enter, and where his mistress, who passed in the neighbourhood for his wife, at that time lay in.

II

I return now to Mrs. Wilson, whom we left in a hackney coach, going to her own house, in all the misery of despair and jealousy. It was happy for her that her constitution was good, and her resolution equal to it; for she has often told me, that she passed the night of that day in a condition little better than madness.

In the morning her husband returned; and as his heart was happy, and without suspicions of a discovery, he was more than usually complaisant to her. She received his civilities with her accustomed chearfulness; and finding that business would detain him in the city for some hours, she determined, whatever distress it might occasion her, to pay an immediate visit to his mistress, and to wait there till she saw him. For this purpose she ordered a coach to be called, and in her handsomest undress,[2] and with the most composed countenance, she drove directly to the house. She enquired at the door if Mr. Roberts was within; and being answered no, but that he dined at home, she asked after his lady, and if she was well enough to see company; adding that as she came a great way, and had business with Mr. Roberts, she should be glad to wait for him in his lady's apartment. The servant ran immediately up stairs, and as quickly returned with a message from his mistress, that she would be glad to see her.

Mrs. Wilson confesses that at this moment, notwithstanding the resolution she had taken, her spirits totally forsook her, and that she followed the servant with her knees knocking together, and a face paler than death. She entered the room where the lady was sitting, without remembering on what errand she came; but the sight of so much beauty, and the elegance that adorned it, brought every thing to her thoughts, and left her with no other power than to fling herself into a chair, from which she instantly fell to the ground in a fainting fit.

The whole house was alarmed upon this occasion, and every one busied in assisting the stranger; but most of all the mistress, who was indeed of a humane disposition, and who, perhaps, had other thoughts to disturb her than the mere feelings of humanity. In a few minutes, however, and with the proper applications, Mrs. Wilson began to recover. She looked round her with amazement at first, not recollecting where she was; but seeing herself supported by her rival, to whose care she was so much obliged, and who in the tenderest distress was enquiring how she did, she felt herself relapsing into a second fit. It was now that she exerted all the courage she was mistress of, which, together with a flood of tears that came to her relief, enabled her (when the servants were withdrawn) to begin as follows.

[1] St. James's Park, in Westminster, lying east of Buckingham Palace.
[2] Casual clothing.

"I am indeed, madam, an unfortunate woman, and subject to these fits; but will never again be the occasion of trouble in this house. You are a lovely woman, and deserve to be happy in the best of husbands. I have a husband too; but his affections are gone from me. He is not unknown to Mr. Roberts, though unfortunately I am. It was for his advice and assistance that I made this visit; and not finding him at home, I begged admittance to his lady, whom I longed to see and to converse with." "Me, madam!" answered Mrs. Roberts, with some emotion, "had you heard any thing of Me?" "That you were such as I have found you, madam," replied the stranger, "and had made Mr. Roberts happy in a fine boy. May I see him, madam? I shall love him for his father's sake." "His father, madam!" returned the mistress of the house, "his father did you say? I am mistaken then; I thought you had been a stranger to him." "To his person, I own," said Mrs. Wilson, "but not to his character; and therefore I shall be fond of the little creature. If it is not too much trouble, madam, I beg to be obliged."

The importunity of this request, the fainting at first, and the settled concern of this unknown visitor, gave Mrs. Roberts the most alarming fears. She had, however, the presence of mind to go herself for the child, and to watch without witnesses the behaviour of the stranger. Mrs. Wilson took it in her arms, and bursting into tears, said, "'Tis a sweet boy, madam; would I had such a boy! Had he been mine, I had been happy!" With these words, and in an agony of grief and tenderness, which she endeavoured to restrain, she kissed the child, and returned it to its mother.

It was happy for that lady that she had an excuse to leave the room. She had seen and heard what made her shudder for herself; and it was not till some minutes, after having delivered the infant to its nurse, that she had resolution enough to return. They both seated themselves again, and a melancholy silence followed for some time. At last Mrs. Roberts began thus.

"You are unhappy, madam, that you have no child; I pray heaven that mine be not a grief to me. But I conjure you, by the goodness that appears in you, to acquaint me with your story. Perhaps it concerns Me; I have a prophetic heart that tells me it does. But whatever I may suffer, or whether I live or die, I will be just to You."

Mrs. Wilson was so affected with this generosity, that she possible had discovered herself, if a loud knocking at the door, and immediately after it the entrance of her husband into the room, had not prevented her. He was moving towards his mistress with the utmost chearfulness, when the sight of her visitor fixed him to a spot, and struck him with an astonishment not to be described. The eyes of both ladies were at once rivetted to his, which so increased his confusion, that Mrs. Wilson, in pity to what he felt, and to relieve her companion, spoke to him as follows. "I do not wonder, sir, that you are surprized at seeing a perfect stranger in your house; but my business is with the master of it; and if you will oblige me with a hearing in another room, it will add to the civilities which your lady has entertained me with."

Wilson, who expected another kind of greeting from his wife, was so revived at her prudence, that his powers of motion began to return; and quitting the room, he conducted her to a parlour below stairs. They were no sooner entered into this parlour, than the husband threw himself into a chair, fixing his eyes upon the ground, while the wife addressed him in these words.

"How I have discovered your secret, or how the discovery has tormented me, I need not tell you. It is enough for you to know that I am miserable for ever. My business with you is short; I have only a question to ask, and to take a final leave of you in this world. Tell me truly then, as you shall answer it hereafter, if you have seduced this lady under false appearances, or have fallen into guilt by the temptations of a wanton?" "I shall answer you presently," said Wilson; "but first I have a question for You. Am I discovered to her? And does she know it is my wife I am now speaking to?" "No, upon my honour," she replied; "her looks were so amiable, and her behaviour to me so gentle, that I had no heart to distress her. If she has guessed at what I am, it was only from the concern she saw me in, which I could not hide from her." "You have acted nobly then," returned Wilson, "and have opened my eyes at last to see and to admire you. And now, if you have patience to hear me, you shall know all."

He then told her of his first meeting with this lady, and of every circumstance that had happened since; concluding with his determinations to leave her, and with a thousand promises of fidelity to his wife, if she generously consented, after what had happened, to receive him as a husband.—"She must consent," cried Mrs. Roberts, who at that moment opened the door, and burst into the room; "she must consent. You are her husband, and may command it. For me, madam," continued she, turning to Mrs. Wilson, "he shall never see me more. I have injured you through ignorance, but will atone for it to the utmost. He is your husband, madam, and you must receive him. I have listened to what has passed, and am now here to join my entreaties with his, that you may be happy for ever."

To relate all that was said upon this occasion would be to extend my story to another paper. Wilson was all submission and acknowledgment; the wife cried and doubted, and the widow vowed an eternal separation. To be as short as possible, the harmony of the married couple was fixed from that day. The widow was handsomely provided for, and her child, at the request of Mrs. Wilson, taken home to her own house; where at the end of a year she was so happy, after all her distresses, as to present him with a sister, with whom he is to divide his father's fortune. His mother retired into the country, and, two years after, was married to a gentleman of great worth; to whom, on his first proposals to her, she related every circumstance of her story. The boy pays her a visit every year, and is now with his sister upon one of these visits. Mr. Wilson is perfectly happy in his wife, and has sent me, in his own hand, this moral to his story.

"That though prudence and generosity may not always be sufficient to hold the heart of a husband, yet a constant perseverance in them will, one time or other, most certainly regain it."

JOHN BOYLE, EARL OF CORK

Sir Josiah Pumpkin's Courage (1753)

The author: John Boyle (1707-1762) was born in his father's house on Glasshouse Street, Westminster. He was tutored in English and Latin by Elijah Fenton (1683-1730), who assisted Alexander Pope in the translation of the *Odyssey*. He was educated at Westminster School and at Christ Church (Oxford). He succeeded his father as 5th Earl of Orrery in 1731 and his third cousin Richard Boyle as 5th Earl of Cork in 1753. In the House of Lords, he unsuccessfully opposed the long-lived ministry of Robert Walpole. He was usually called "Orrery" by his friends. Elizabeth Singer Rowe (1674-1737), one of the most successful English authors of the time, was his neighbour in Somersetshire and Orrery became a close friend of hers in the last years of her life. Some of his first attempts at poetry were contained in letters sent to Mrs. Rowe. He befriended Jonathan Swift and Alexander Pope. In the mid-18th century, he was known almost exclusively as Jonathan Swift's first biographer. His less than flattering *Remarks on the Life and Writings of Jonathan Swift* (1752) provoked countless vituperative reactions. It was translated into French the following year. It was published in a critical edition by Joao Froes in 2000 (Newark: U of Delaware P). He also published a two-volume translation of the letters of Pliny the Younger (1751) and an edition of the *Memoirs* of Robert Cary, Earl of Monmouth (1759), while his *Letters from Italy* were published posthumously in 1773. In the late 1730s and early 1740s, he had published occasional poetry and two short volumes consisting of imitations of Horace's *Odes*. His shorter writings in prose appeared in the early 1750s in three periodicals: *The World*, *The Connoisseur* (where he signed "G.K."), and Frances Brooke's *The Old Maid* (1755-1756).

The text: The following short story appeared anonymously in the form of a letter to the editor of *The World* (47), "Mr. Fitz-Adam" (Edward Moore) on Thursday, 22 November 1753. In the original form, the story was untitled, but in the contents of subsequent volume editions it appears as "Courage of Sir Josiah Pumpkin – Remarkable Duel in Moorfields." When anthologised, it was given other titles, e.g., "Mrs. Muzzy on Duelling" in Vol. 1 of Charles A. Read's 1879 *The Cabinet of Irish Literature* (the last time it was anthologised). It was a favourite of William Makepeace Thackeray, who drew three illustrations for it on the margins of his own copy of *The World*. In number 68 of *The World* (18 April 1754), Boyle published a sequel to this story. The following is reproduced from *The World. By Adam Fitz-Adam* (London, Printed for R. and J. Dodsley in Pall-mall, 1755), Vol. II, p. 108-115.

Further reading: Countess of Cork and Orrery [Emily-Charlotte de Burgh], ed. *The Orrery Papers*. Vol. 1-2. London: Duckworth and Company, 1903.

Duncombe, John. "Preface." *Letters from Italy in the Years 1754 and 1755 by the Late Right Honourable John Earl of Corke and Orrery*. London: B. White, 1773. i-xxxvii.

[Grego, Joseph.] *Thackerayana: Notes & Anecdotes Illustrated by nearly Six Hundred Sketches by William Makepeace Thackeray*. London: Chatto and Windus,

1875.

Sir,

Dim-sighted as I am, my spectacles have assisted me sufficiently to read your papers. Permit me, as a recompense for the pleasure I have received from them, to send you an anecdote in my family, which till now has never appeared in print.

I am the widow of Mr. Solomon Muzzy; I am the daughter of Ralph Pumpkin, Esq; and I am the grandaughter of Sir Josiah Pumpkin, of Pumpkin-hall, in South-Wales. I was educated, with my two elder sisters, under the care and tuition of my honoured grandfather and grandmother, at the hall-house of our ancestors. It was the constant custom of my grandfather, when he was tolerably free from the gout, to summon his three grandaughters to his bedside, and amuse us with the most important transactions of his life. I took particular delight in hearing the good old man illustrate his own character, which he did, perhaps not without some degree of vanity, but always with a strict adherence to truth. He told us, he hoped we would have children, to whom some of his adventures might prove useful and important.

Sir Josiah was scarce nineteen years old, when he was introduced at the court of Charles the second, by his uncle Sir Simon Sparrowgrass, who was at that time Lancaster herald at arms, and in great favour at Whitehall. As soon as he had kissed the king's hand, he was presented to the duke of York,[1] and immediately afterwards to the ministers, and the mistresses. His fortune, which was considerable, and his manners, which were extremely elegant, made him so very acceptable in all companies, that he had the honour to be plunged at once into every polite party of wit, pleasure and expence, that the courtiers could possibly display. He danced with the ladies; he drank with the gentlemen; he sung loyal catches, and broke bottles and glasses in every tavern throughout London. But still he was by no means a perfect fine gentleman. He had not fought a DUEL. He was so extremely unfortunate, as never to have had even the happiness of a RENCOUNTER.[2] The want of opportunity, not of courage, had occasioned this inglorious chasm in his character. He appeared not only to the whole court, but even in his own eye, an unworthy and degenerate PUMPKIN, till he had shewn himself as expert in opening a vein with a sword, as any surgeon in England could be with a lancet. Things remained in this unhappy situation till he was near two and twenty years of age. At length his better stars prevailed, and he received a most egregious affront from Mr. Cucumber, one of the gentlemen-ushers of the Privy-chamber.[3] Cucumber, who was in waiting at court, spit inadvertently into the chimney, and as he stood next to Sir Josiah Pumpkin, part of the spittle rested upon Sir Josiah's shoe. It was then that the true Pumpkin honour arose in blushes upon his

---

[1] James II (1685-1688), who was Duke of York before 1685.
[2] Hand to hand combat, brawl.
[3] Part of the royal household, whose gentlemen served the king directly in various everyday activities.

cheeks. He turned upon his heel, went home immediately, and sent Mr. CUCUMBER a challenge. Captain DAISY, a friend to each party, not only carried the challenge, but adjusted the preliminaries. The heroes were to fight in Moor-fields,[1] and to bring fifteen seconds on a side. Punctuality is a strong instance of valour upon these occasions. The clock of St. Paul's struck seven, just when the combatants were marking out their ground, and each of the two and thirty gentlemen was adjusting himself into a posture of defence against his adversary. It happened to be the hour for breakfast in the hospital of Bedlam.[2] A small bell had rung to summon the Bedlamites into the great gallery. The keepers had already unlocked the cells, and were bringing forth their mad folks, when the porter of Bedlam, OWEN MACDUFFY, standing at the iron-gate, and beholding such a number of armed men in the midst of the fields, immediately roared out, "fire, murder, swords, daggers, bloodshed!" OWEN's voice was remarkably loud, but his fears had rendered it still louder and more tremendous. His words struck a pannic into the keepers; they lost all presence of mind; they forgot their prisoners, and hastened most precipitately down stairs to the scene of action. At the sight of naked swords, their fears increased, and at once they stood open-mouthed and motionless. Not so the lunatics; freedom to madmen, and light to the blind are equally rapturous. RALPH ROGERS the tinker began the alarm. His brains had been turned with joy at the Restoration, and the poor wretch imagined that this glorious set of combatants were Roundheads and Fanatics,[3] and accordingly he cried out, "Liberty and property, my boys! down with the Rump! CROMWELL and IRETON[4] are come from hell to destroy us. Come, my Cavalier lads, follow me, and let us knock out their brains." The Bedlamites immediately obeyed, and with the tinker at their head, leaped over the ballistres of the great stair-case, and ran wildly into the fields. In their way, they picked up some staves and cudgels, which the porter and the keepers had inadvertently left behind, and rushing forward with amazing fury, they forced themselves outrageously into the midst of the combatants, and in one unlucky moment, destroyed all the decency and order with which this most illustrious DUEL had begun.

It seemed, according to my grandfather's observation, a very untoward fate, that two and thirty gentlemen of courage, honour, fortune and quality, should meet together in hopes of killing each other, with all that resolution and politeness which belonged to their stations, and should at once be routed, dispersed, and even wounded by a set of madmen, without sword, pistol, or any other more honourable weapon

---

[1] Although situated in the City of London, near Moorgate, it was still very much open land during the reign of Charles II.

[2] Bethlehem Royal Hospital, known as Bedlam, had been rebuilt in the Moorfields area in the 17th century. Today, it is in Croydon, south London.

[3] The Roundheads (so called because of the closely cropped haircut of many Puritans) were supporters of the Parliament against Charles I in the English Civil War (1642-1651). They were also called "fanatics," especially when they rejected the authority of the crown over the church and sympathised with republican ideas. Supporters of the king were known as Cavaliers.

[4] Henry Ireton (1611-1651), a general in the Parliamentary army, was son-in-law of Oliver Cromwell (1599-1658), leader of the Roundheads.

than a cudgel.

The madmen were not only superior in strength, but numbers. Sir JOSIAH PUMPKIN and Mr. CUCUMBER stood their ground as long as possible, and they both endeavoured to make the lunatics the sole objects of their mutual revenge; but the two FRIENDS were soon over-powered, and no person daring to come to their assistance, each of them made as proper a retreat as the place and circumstances would admit.

Many of the other gentlemen were knocked down, and trampled under foot. Some of them, whom my grandfather's generosity would never name, betook themselves to flight in a very inglorious manner. An earl's son was spied clinging submissively round the feet of mad POCKLINGTON the taylor. A young baronet, although naturally intrepid, was obliged to conceal himself at the bottom of PIPPIN KATE's apple stall. A Shropshire squire of three thousand pounds a year, was discovered chin deep, and almost stifled in Fleet-ditch.[1] Even Captain DAISY himself was found in a milk cellar, with visible marks of fear and consternation. Thus ended this inauspicious day. But the madmen continued their outrages many days after. It was near a week before they were all retaken and chained down in their cells. During that interval of liberty, they committed many offensive pranks throughout the cities of London and Westminster; and my grandfather himself had the misfortune to see mad ROGERS come into the Queen's drawing room, and spit in a duchess's face.

Such unforeseen disasters occasioned some prudent regulations in the laws of honour. It was enacted that from that time, six combatants (three on a side) might be allowed and acknowledged to contain such a quantity of blood in their veins, as should be sufficient to satisfy the highest affront that could be offered.

Afterwards, upon the maturest deliberation, as my grandfather assured me, the number six was reduced to four; two principals and two seconds; each second was to be the truest and best-beloved friend that his principal had in the world: and these seconds were to fight, provided they declared upon oath, that they had no manner of quarrel to each other: for the canons of honour ordained, that in case the two seconds had the least heat or animosity one against the other, they must naturally become principals, and therefore ought to seek out for seconds to themselves.

Having told you a very remarkable event in my grandfather's life, almost in his own words, and finding that the story has carried me perhaps into too great a length of letter, I shall not mention some curious facts relating to my father, and to poor dear Mr. SOLOMON MUZZY, of whom I am the unfortunate and mournful relict. But I have at least the honour and consolation to be,

SIR,

Your constant reader, and
most humble servant,
MARY MUZZY.

---

[1] The subterranean Fleet River flowing through London was already becoming a sewer in the late 17th century.

GEORGE COLMAN THE ELDER & BONNELL THORNTON

Supper at Vauxhall (1755)

The authors: George Colman (1732-1794) and Bonnell Thornton (1725-1768) edited and, for the most part, wrote *The Connoisseur* between 1754 and 1756. It was intended to be a more youthful and playful version of the other essay serials of the 1750s. Thornton, a Londoner and the son of a wealthy apothecary, had already edited *The Student* with Christopher Smart while at Oxford and *The Drury Lane Journal* by himself. He took his M.A. in 1750, but his father insisted he get a physician's degree so he went back to school, where he found his younger collaborator. Colman was born in Florence as the son of Thomas Colman, the British Resident at the court of the Duke of Tuscany. *The Connoisseur* was projected by the two Oxonians and there has been some debate about the roles played by each of them in planning and executing the journal. Their own confession (in the last issue) seems quite trustworthy: "We have not only joined in the work taken together, but almost every single paper is the joint product of both: and, as we have laboured equally in erecting the fabric, we cannot pretend that any one particular part is the sole workmanship of either. An hint has perhaps been started by one of us, improved by the other, and still further heightened by an happy coalition of sentiment in both."

Bonnell Thornton was also the leader of the Nonsense Club, which met every Thursday in the late 1750s and early 1760s and which included Colman, William Cowper, Charles Churchill, and Robert Lloyd. In 1761, Colman and Thornton founded one the most important newspapers of the time, *The St. James's Chronicle*. The following year, Thornton organised in his rooms in Bow Street a controversial "Grand Exhibition" of London's sign painters, which gathered about 110 inn and shop signs from all over the city. In his late life, Thornton was praised by Dr. Johnson for his burlesque poetry and, when he died, he was working on a translation of Plautus. George Colman switched his interest to the theatre and became one the most successful playwrights of the 1760s and 1770s. In the 1780s, he began to be known as "the Elder," because his son George Colman (1762-1836) also became active in the theatre and replaced his father as manager of the Haymarket theatre in 1789.

The text: First published in *The Connoisseur* 68 (Thursday, 15 May 1755), untitled; when published in volume form, it was identified as "On the Public Gardens. Dearness of Provisions there. Description and Conversation of a Citizen, with his Wife and two Daughters, at Vaux-Hall." It was introduced by an epigraph from Horace (*Odes* I. 9, 18-20): "Nunc et campus et areae,/ Lenesque sub noctem susurri/ Composita repetantur hora": "Now [that spring has come] let soft whispers be resumed in both the Field [of Mars] and the public walks [*areae*, i.e., the unenclosed parts of the city of Rome] before night-time at the appointed hour." An "Irish" edition was published the same year in Dublin by George Faulkner, in which the translation by Philip Francis (his Horace had recently come out) was inserted. In the second edition, Colman and Thornton responded by providing a "modernised" translation, more adapted to the realities of mid-18th-century London: "Now *Venus* in *Vaux-Hall* her altar rears,/ While fiddles drown the music of the spheres:/ Now girls hum out their loves to ev'ry tree,/ 'Young *Jockey* is the lad, the lad for me.'" The following text reproduces the version published in *The Connoisseur. By Mr. Town, Critic and Censor*-General. The Second Edition (London: Printed for R. Baldwin, at the *Rose* in *Pater-Noster Row*, 1755), Vol. II, p. 249-259. It was translated in the Parisian *Journal étranger* under the title "Les Jardins de Londres" in April 1758.

Further reading: Alexander Chalmers. "Historical and Biographical Preface to *The Connoisseur." The British Essayists* (London: Nichols, Son, and Bentley, 1817). Vol. 30, xi-xxxv.

Shaun Regan. "Updating Addison: Culture, Appropriation and *The Connoisseur." Forum for Modern Language Studies* 51.1 (2015): 1-14.

The various seasons of the year produce not a greater alteration in the face of nature, than in the polite manner of passing our time. The diversions of winter and summer are as different as the dog-days and those at *Christmas*; nor do I know any genteel amusement, except Gaming, that prevails during the whole year. As the long days are now coming on, the theatrical gentry, who contribute to dissipate the gloom of our winter evenings, begin to divide themselves into strolling companies; and are packing up their tragedy wardrobes, together with a sufficient quantity of thunder and lightning, for the delight and amazement of the country. In the mean time, the several public Gardens near this metropolis are trimming their trees, levelling their walks, and burnishing their lamps, for our reception. At *Vaux-Hall* the artificial ruins are repaired; the cascade is made to spout with several additional streams of block-tin; and they have touched up all the pictures, which were damaged last season by the fingering of those curious *Connoisseurs*, who could not be satisfied without *feeling* whether the figures were alive. The magazine at *Cuper's*,[1] I am told, is furnished with an extraordinary supply of gunpowder, to be shot off in squibs and sky-rockets, or whirled away in blazing suns and *Catherine* wheels: And it is not to be doubted, in case of a war, but that *Neptune* and all his *Tritons* will assist the *British* navy; and as we before took *Porto-Bello* and *Cape-Breton*,[2] we shall gain new victories over the *French* fleet every night, upon that canal.[3]

Happy are they, who can muster up sufficient, at least to hire tickets at the door, once or twice in a season! Not that these pleasures are confined to the rich and the great only: for the lower sort of people have their *Ranelaghs* and their *Vaux-Halls*, as well as the quality. *Perrot's* inimitable Grotto may be seen for only calling for a pot of beer; and the royal diversion of duck-hunting may be had into the bargain, together

[1] Cuper's Gardens, like the more famous Vauxhall and Ranelagh, was a pleasure garden (offering the public dinner, music, and fireworks) in Southwark, south of the Thames, lying opposite the City. It lost its licence in 1753, but remained open as a "tea garden" and, in 1755, the music and fireworks resumed for subscribers only. It was closed in 1760.
[2] The Battle of Porto Bello (1739) was a British naval victory against Spain. The Siege of Louisbourg (1745), on Cape Breton Island, was a victory against France.
[3] Re-enactments of British naval victories were a popular attraction.

with a decanter of *Dorchester*, for your six-pence at *Jenny's Whim*.[1] Every skettle-alley[2] half a mile out of town is embellished with green arbours and shady retreats; where the company is generally entertained with the melodious scraping of a blind fiddler. And who can resist the luscious temptation of a fine juicy ham, or a delicious buttock of beef stuffed with parsley, accompanied with a foaming decanter of sparkling home-brew'd, which is so invitingly painted at the entrance of almost every village ale-house?

Our Northern climate will not, indeed, allow us to indulge ourselves in all those pleasures of a garden, which are so feelingly described by our poets. We dare not lay ourselves on the damp ground in shady groves, or by the purling stream; but are obliged to fortify our insides against the cold by good substantial eating and drinking. For this reason the extreme costliness of the provisions at our public Gardens has been grievously complained of by those gentry, to whom a supper at these places is as necessary a part of the entertainment, as the singing or the fire-works. Poor Mr. *John* sees with an heavy heart the profits of a whole week's card-money devoured in tarts and cheese-cakes, by Mrs. House-keeper or Mrs. Lady's Own Woman; and the substantial cit,[3] who comes from behind the counter two or three evenings in the summer, can never enough regret the thin wafer-like slices of beef and ham, that taste of nothing but the knife.

I was greatly diverted last saturday evening at *Vaux-Hall* with the shrewd remarks made on this very head by an honest citizen, whose wife and two daughters had, I found, prevailed on him to carry them to the Garden. As I thought there was something curious in their behaviour, I went into the next box to them, where I had an opportunity of seeing and over-hearing every thing that past.

After some talk,—"Come, come, (said the old don[4]) it is high time, I think, to go to supper." To this the ladies readily assented; and one of the misses said, "Do let us have a chick, papa." "Zounds[5] (said the father) they are half a crown a-piece, and no bigger than a sparrow." Here the old lady took him up—"You are so stingy, Mr. *Rose*, there is no bearing you. When one is out upon pleasure, I love to appear like somebody: and what signifies a few shillings once and away, when a body is about it?" This reproof so effectually silenced the old gentleman, that the youngest miss had the courage to put in a word for some ham likewise: Accordingly the waiter was called, and dispatched by the old lady with an order for a

[1] Jenny's Whim was another tea garden, located in Pimlico (Westminster), which included a "grotto" associated with a Samuel Perrot. Dorchester, a pale ale made in Dorset, was one of the most popular beers.
[2] Skittles is a game similar to bowling.
[3] A citizen; the term "cit" rather contemptuously referred to someone from the city as opposed to someone from the country, and especially to a shopkeeper or a tradesman as opposed to a gentleman.
[4] An important man (this Spanish title was thus used humorously in the 18th century).
[5] Old minced oath, an abbreviation of "by God's wounds."

chicken and a plate of ham. When it was brought, our honest cit twirled the dish about three or four times, and surveyed it with a very settled countenance; then taking up the slice of ham, and dangling it to and fro on the end of his fork, asked the waiter, "how much there was of it." "A shilling's worth, Sir," said the fellow.—"Prithee, said the don, how much dost think it weighs?—An ounce?—A shilling an ounce! that is sixteen shillings *per* pound!—A reasonable profit truly!—Let me see—suppose now the whole ham weighs thirty pounds:—At a shilling *per* ounce, that is, sixteen shillings *per* pound, why your master makes exactly twenty-four pounds of every ham; and if he buys them at the best hand, and salts them and cures them himself, they don't stand him in ten shillings a-piece." The old lady bade him hold his nonsense, declared herself ashamed for him, and asked him if people must not live: then taking a coloured handkerchief from her own neck, she tucked it into his shirt-collar, (whence it hung like a bib) and helped him to a leg of the chicken. The old gentleman, at every bit he put into his mouth, amused himself with saying,—"There goes two-pence—there goes three-pence—there goes a groat.—Zounds a man at these places should not have a swallow so wide as a tom-tit."[1]

This scanty repast, we may imagine, was soon dispatched; and it was with much difficulty our citizen was prevailed on to suffer a plate of beef to be ordered. This too was no less admired, and underwent the same comments with the ham: At length, when only a very small bit was left, as they say, for manners in the dish, our don took a piece of an old news-paper out of his pocket, and gravely wrapping up the meat in it, placed it carefully in his letter-case. "I'll keep thee as a curiosity to my dying day; and I'll shew thee to my neighbour *Horseman*, and ask him if he can make as much of his stakes."[2] Then rubbing his hands, and shrugging up his shoulders—"Why now (says he) to-morrow night I may eat as much cold beef as I can stuff in any tavern in *London*, and pay nothing for it." A dish of tarts, cheese-cakes, and custards next made their appearance at the request of the young ladies, who paid no sort of regard to the father's remonstrance, "that they were four times as dear as at the pastry-cook's."

Supper being ended, madam put her spouse in mind to call for wine.—"We *must* have some wine, my dear, or we shall not be looked upon, you know." "Well, well, says the don, that's right enough. But do they sell their liquor too by the ounce?—Here, drawer, what wine have you got?" The fellow, who by this time began to smoke[3] his guests, answered—"We have exceeding good *French* wine of all sorts, and please your honour. Would your honour have a bottle of Champagne, or Burgundy, or Claret, or"—"No, no, none of your wishy-washy outlandish rot-gut for me:" interrupted the citizen.—"A tankard of the Alderman beats all the red Claret wine in the *French* king's cellar.—But come, bring us a bottle of sound old Port: And d'ye hear? let it be good."

[1] Name often given to the blue tit (Cyanistes caerulus), a small forest bird.
[2] Alternative spelling for "steaks."
[3] To have an inkling about, to understand.

While the waiter was gone, the good man most sadly lamented, that he could not have his pipe; which the wife would by no means allow, "because (she said) it was ungenteel to smoke, where any ladies were in company." When the wine came, our citizen gravely took up the bottle, and holding it above his head, "Aye, aye, said he, the bottom has had a good kick.—And mind how confoundedly it is pinched on the sides.—Not above five gills,[1] I warrant.—An old soldier at the *Jerusalem*[2] would beat two of them.—But let us see how it is brewed." He then poured out a glass; and after holding it up before the candle, smelling to it, sipping it twice or thrice, and smacking with his lips, drank it off: but declaring that second thoughts were best, he filled another bumper; and tossing that off, after some pause, with a very important air, ventured to pronounce it drinkable. The ladies, having also drank a glass round, affirmed it was very good, and felt warm in the stomach: and even the old gentleman relaxed into such good humour by the time the bottle was emptied, that out of his own free will and motion he most generously called for another Pint, but charged the waiter "to pick out an honest one."

While the glass was thus circulating, the family amused themselves with making observations on the Garden. The citizen expressed his wonder at the number of lamps, and said it must cost a great deal of money every night to light them all: The eldest miss declared, that for her part she liked the Dark Walk best of all, because it was *solentary*: Little miss thought the last song mighty pretty, and said she would buy it, if she could but carry home the tune: And the old lady observed, that there was a great deal of good company indeed; but the gentlemen were so rude, that they perfectly put her out of countenance by staring at her through their spy-glasses. In a word, the tarts, the cheese-cakes, the beef, the chicken, the ounce of ham, and every thing, seemed to have been quite forgot, 'till the dismal moment approached, that the reckoning was called for. As this solemn business concerns only the gentlemen, the ladies kept a profound silence; and when the terrible account was brought, they left the pay-master undisturbed, to enjoy the misery by himself: only the old lady had the hardiness to squint at the sum total, and declared "it was pretty reasonable *considering*."

Our citizen bore his misfortunes with a tolerable degree of patience. He shook his head as he run over every article, and swore he would never buy meat by the ounce again. At length, when he had carefully summed up every figure, he bade the drawer bring change for six-pence: then pulling out a leathern purse from a snug pocket in the inside of his waistcoat, he drew out slowly, piece by piece, thirteen shillings; which he regularly placed in two rows upon the table. When the change was brought, after counting it very carefully, he laid down four half-pence in the same exact order; then calling the waiter,—"There, says he, there's your damage—thirteen and two-pence—And hearkye, there's three-pence over for yourself." The remaining penny he put into his coat-pocket; and chinking

[1] A measure for liquids: one fourth of a pint.
[2] Old tavern in Clerkenwell, in central London.

191

it—"This, says he, will serve me to-morrow to buy a paper of tobacco."

The family now prepared themselves for going; and as there were some slight drops of rain, madam buttoned up the old gentleman's coat, that he might not spoil his laced waistcoat; and made him flap his hat, over which she tied his pocket handkerchief, to save his wig: And as the coat itself (she said) had never been worn but three Sundays, she even parted with her own Cardinal,[1] and spread it the wrong side out over his shoulders. In these accoutrements he sallied forth, accompanied by his wife with her upper petticoat thrown over her head, and his daughters with the skirts of their gowns turned up, and their heads muffled up in coloured handkerchiefs. I followed them quite out of the Garden: and as they were waiting for their hack to draw up, the youngest miss asked, "When shall we come again, papa?" "Come again? (said he) What a pox would you ruin me? Once in one's life is enough; and I think I have done very handsome. Why it would not have cost me above four-pence half-penny to have spent my evening at *Sot's Hole*:[2] and what with the cursed coach-hire, and all together, here's almost a pound gone, and nothing to shew for it."—"Fye, Mr. *Rose*, I am quite ashamed for you," replies the old lady. "You are always grudging me and your girls the least bit of pleasure; and you cannot help grumbling, if we do but go to *Little Hornsey* to drink tea.[3] I am sure, now they are women grown up, they ought to see a little of the world;—and they *shall*." The old don was not willing to persue the arg... ...an enc... ...ife; or ... ...out aga...

The Chinese Pavilion in Vauxhall Gardens.

---

[1] A short hooded cloak worn by ladies, originally of scarlet cloth.
[2] The reference here is to the *Black Prince*, a public house on Princes' Road on the corner of Sot's Hole (an adjacent lane) in Kennington, central London.
[3] This is a reference to Hornsey Wood House, a tea-house in north London.

THOMAS WARTON
Journal of a Fellow from College (1758)

The author: Known as Thomas Warton the Younger (1728-1790), he was an acclaimed poet from an early age. He studied at Oxford, where he was a fellow, and became Professor of Poetry, like his father (Thomas Warton the Elder). He is best remembered for his *The History of English Poetry* (3 volumes, 1774-1781). In the last 5 years of his life, he was Poet Laureate of England.

The text: "Journal of a Fellow from College" was first published in Samuel Johnson's essay-series "The Idler" 33 (Saturday 2 December 1758). The title appeared only in the contents of the volume format. The following text reproduces the version published in *The Idler. In two Volumes*. (London: Printed for J. Newbery, at the *Bible* and *Sun* in *St. Paul's Church-Yard*, 1761), Vol. I, p. 182-189. The story is introduced by a brief note within brackets: "I hope the Author of the following letter will excuse the omission of some parts, and allow me to remark, that the Journal of the Citizen in the *Spectator*[1] has almost precluded the attempt of any future Writer." An untranslated epigraph from Horace follows: "Non ita Romuli/ Praescriptum, & intonsi Catonis/ Auspiciis, veterumque norma" ("Not thus was the rule of Romulus and the unshaven Cato, nor the standard when under the authority of men of old.")

Further reading: Graham Midgley. *University Life in Eighteenth-Century Oxford*. New Haven: Yale University Press, 1996. 39-74.

Sir,

You have often solicited Correspondence. I here send you the *Journal* of a *Senior Fellow*, or *Genius Idler*, just transmitted from *Cambridge* by a facetious Correspondent, and warranted to have been transcribed from the Common-place book of the Journalist.

Monday, Nine o'clock. Turned off my Bed-maker[2] for waking me at eight. Weather rainy. Consulted my weather-glass.[3] No hopes of a ride before dinner.

---

[1] Allusion to Addison's "[Journal of a Citizen]" from *The Spectator* 317 (4 March 1712).

[2] "Every set of rooms is under the care of a 'bed-maker,' who is generally a female, but sometimes a man and his wife are attached to each staircase. At the Colleges where there is only a female 'bed-maker,' the attendance of a man-servant (called a gyp) may be had if desired. The payment for a bedmaker varies from £1 to £2 a term. A gyp usually receives £1 per term" (*The Student's Guide to the University of Cambridge* [Cambridge: Deighton, Bell & Co., 1863] 68).

[3] Barometer.

Ditto, Ten. After breakfast, transcribed half a Sermon from Dr. *Hickman. N. B.* Never to transcribe any more from *Calamy;*[1] Mrs. *Pilcocks*, at my Curacy, having one volume of that author lying in her parlour window.

Ditto, Eleven. Went down into my cellar. *Mem.* My *Mountain* will be fit to drink in a month's time.[2] *N.B.* To remove the five-year-old Port into the new bin on the left hand.

Ditto, Twelve. Mended a pen. Looked at my weather glass again. Quicksilver very low. Shaved. Barber's hand shakes.

Ditto, One. Dined alone in my room on a soal.[3] *N.B.* The shrimp-sauce not so good as Mr. *H.* of *Peterhouse*[4] and I used to eat in *London* last winter at the *Mitre* in *Fleet-street*.[5] Sat down to a pint of *Madeira*. Mr. *H.* surprized me over it. We finished two bottles of Port together, and were very chearful. *Mem.* To dine with Mr. *H.* at *Peterhouse*, next *Wednesday*. One of the dishes a leg of pork and pease by my desire.

Ditto, Six. News-paper in the common-room.

Ditto, Seven. Returned to my room. Made a tiff of warm punch, and to bed before nine; did not fall asleep till ten, a young Fellow-commoner[6] being very noisy over my head.

Tuesday, Nine. Rose squeamish. A fine morning. Weather-glass very high.

Ditto, Ten. Ordered my horse, and rode to the five miles stone on the *New Market* Road. Appetite gets better. A pack of hounds, in full cry, crossed the road, and startled my horse.

Ditto, Twelve. Drest. Found a letter on my table to be in *London* the 19th inst. Bespoke a new wig.

Ditto, One. At dinner in the hall. Too much water in the soup. Dr. *Dry* always orders the beef to be salted too much for me.

Ditto, Two. In the common-room. Dr. *Dry* gave us an instance of a Gentleman who kept the gout out of his stomach by drinking old *Madeira*. Conversation chiefly on the Expeditions.[7] Company broke up at four. Dr. *Dry* and myself played at Back Gammon for a brace of Snipes. Won.

Ditto, Five. At the Coffee-house. Met Mr. *H.* there. Could not get a sight of the *Monitor*.[8]

---

[1] Henry Hickman (1629-1692) and Edmund Calamy the Elder (1600-1666), English divines.
[2] Wine of Malaga, known in England at the time as "Mountain wine," which oenophiles recommended to be bottled 18 months after vintage.
[3] Old spelling of "sole" (the fish).
[4] The oldest college of the University of Cambridge.
[5] The Mitre in Fleet street was, according to Boswell, Dr. Johnson's favourite tavern.
[6] Below noblemen but above commoners, a fellow commoner was a student who paid double the tuition and the commons (the dining hall).
[7] The two expeditions (1757 and 1758) against the fortress of Louisbourg, the latter of which brought Atlantic Canada under British dominion.
[8] A newspaper in the 1750s, in which, apart from news of the war, military "essays" were more likely to appear.

Ditto, Seven. Returned home, and stirred my fire. Went to the Common-room, and supped on the snipes with Dr. *Dry*.

Ditto, Eight. Began the evening in the Common-room. Dr. *Dry* told several stories. Were very merry. Our new Fellow, that studies physic, very talkative toward twelve. Pretends he will bring the youngest Miss——to drink tea with me soon. Impertinent blockhead!

Wednesday, Nine. Alarmed with a pain in my ancle. Q. The gout? Fear I can't dine at *Peterhouse*; but I hope a ride will set all to rights. Weather-glass below FAIR.

Ditto, Ten. Mounted my horse, though the weather suspicious. Pain in my ancle entirely gone. Catched in a shower coming back. Convinced that my weather-glass is the best in *Cambridge*.

Ditto, Twelve. Drest. Sauntered up to the *Fishmongers-Hill*. Met Mr. *H.* and went with him to *Peterhouse*. Cook made us wait thirty six minutes beyond the time. The company some of my *Emanuel* friends.[1] For dinner a pair of soals, a leg of pork and pease, among other things. *Mem.* Pease-pudding not boiled enough. Cook reprimanded and sconced[2] in my presence.

Ditto, after dinner. Pain in my ancle returns. Dull all the afternoon. Rallied for being no company. Mr. *H*'s account of the accommodations on the road in his *Bath* journey.

Ditto, Six. Got into spirits. Never was more chatty. We sat late at Whist. Mr. *H.* and self agreed at parting to take a gentle ride, and dine at the old house on the *London* road to-morrow.

Thursday, Nine. My Sempstress. She has lost the measure of my wrist. Forced to be measured again. The baggage[3] has got a trick of smiling.

Ditto, Ten to Eleven. Made some rappee-snuff.[4] Read the magazines. Received a present of pickles from Miss *Pilcocks*. *Mem.* To send in return some collared eel, which I know both the old Lady and Miss are fond of.

Ditto, Eleven. Glass very high. Mounted at the gate with Mr. *H.* Horse skittish, and wants exercise. Arrive at the old house. All the provisions bespoke by some rakish Fellow-Commoner in the next room, who had been on a scheme to *Newmarket*.[5] Could get nothing but mutton chops, off the worst end. Port very new. Agree to try some other house to-morrow.——

Here the Journal breaks off: For the next morning, as my friend informs me, our genial Academic was waked with a severe fit of the gout; and, at present, enjoys all the dignity of that disease. But I believe we have lost nothing by this interruption: Since, a continuation of the

[1] Another college of the University of Cambridge.
[2] Sconcing (also, skoncing) meant exacting a fine, usually in the form of a huge tankard of beer or other beverage.
[3] Cheeky girl.
[4] Grated tobacco (from French "râpé," grated).
[5] Town near London, famous for its horse races.

remainder of the Journal, thro' the remainder of the week, would most probably have exhibited nothing more, than a repeated relation of the same circumstances of *Idling* and Luxury.

I hope it will not be concluded, from this specimen of Academic Life, that I have attempted to decry our Universities. If Literature is not the essential requisite of the modern Academic, I am yet persuaded, that *Cambridge* and *Oxford*, however degenerated, surpass the fashionable *Academies* of our metropolis, and the *Gymnasia* of foreign countries. The number of learned persons in these celebrated seats, is still considerable, and more conveniences and opportunities for study still subsist in them, than in any other place. There is at least one very powerful incentive to Learning; I mean the GENIUS *of the place*. 'Tis a sort of inspiring Deity which every youth of quick sensibility and ingenious disposition creates to himself, by reflecting, that he is placed under those venerable walls, where a HOOKER and a HAMMOND, a BACON and a NEWTON, once pursued the same course of science, and from whence they soared to the most elevated heights, of Literary Fame. This is that incitement, which, *Tully*, according to his own testimony, experienced at *Athens*, when he contemplated the porticos where *Socrates* sate, and the Laurel-Groves where *Plato* disputed. But there are other circumstances, and of the highest importance, which render our Colleges superior to all other places of Education. Their Institutions, although somewhat fallen from their primæval simplicity, are such as influence, in a particular manner, the moral conduct of their youth; and in this general depravity of manners and laxity of principles, pure Religion is no where more strongly inculcated. The *Academies*, as they are presumptuously stiled, are too low to be mentioned; and foreign Seminaries are likely to prejudice the unwary mind with Calvinism. But *English* Universities render their Students virtuous, at least by excluding all opportunities of Vice; and by teaching them the principles of the *Church of England*, confirm them in those of true Christianity.

1758

196

SAMUEL JOHNSON
Marvel's Journey (1759)

The author: After *The Rambler*, Johnson poured his energy into his famous *A Dictionary of the English Language* (1755). In 1756, he was briefly imprisoned for debt, but the novelist Samuel Richardson paid to have him released. The same year he started *The Literary Magazine* and began work on an edition of Shakespeare's plays. In early 1758, he was arrested again for debt, but this time his publisher paid the outstanding amount. On 15 April of that year, he began an essay-series called "The Idler," which ran for 2 years in *The Universal Chronicle*. In the meantime, he published his philosophical novella *Rasselas* (1759). In 1763, he met James Boswell, who was to become his biographer and amanuensis, and he formed "The Club" with Joshua Reynolds, Edmund Burke, David Garrick, Oliver Goldsmith, and others. He went on writing until the end of his life, in 1784, his last major work being the *Lives of the Poets* (1779-1781).

The text: "Marvel's Journey" was first published in "The Idler" 49 (Saturday 24 March 1759). The title appeared first in the contents of the volume format. The following text reproduces the version published in *The Idler. In two Volumes*. (London: Printed for J. Newbery, at the *Bible* and *Sun* in *St. Paul's Church-Yard*, 1761), Vol. I, p. 273-279.

Further reading: Francis R. Hart. "Johnson as Philosophic Traveler: The Perfecting of an Idea." *ELH* 36.4 (December 1969): 679-695.

I supped three nights ago with my friend *Will Marvel*. His affairs obliged him lately to take a journey into *Devonshire*, from which he has just returned. He knows me to a very patient hearer, and was glad of my company, as it gave him an opportunity of disburthening himself by a minute relation of the casualties of his expedition.

Will is not one of those who go out and return with nothing to tell. He has a story of his travels, which will strike a home-bred citizen with horror, and has in ten days suffered so often the extremes of terror and joy, that he is in doubt whether he shall ever again expose either his body or mind to such danger and fatigue.

When he left *London* the morning was bright, and a fair day was promised. But *Will* is born to struggle with difficulties. That happened to him, which has sometimes, perhaps, happened to others. Before he had gone more than ten miles it began to rain. What course was to be taken! His soul disdained to turn back. He did what the King of *Prussia* might have done,[1] he flapped his hat, buttoned up his cape, and went forwards, fortifying his mind, by the stoical consolation, that whatever is violent will be short.

[1] Frederick II, King of Prussia (1740-1786) was Britain's greatest ally in the Seven Years' War (1756-1763). Johnson alludes to his campaign of 1757, when he rallied his forces after the defeat at Kolin and won two more battles.

His constancy was not long tried; at the distance of about half a mile he saw an inn, which he entered wet and weary, and found civil treatment and proper refreshment. After a respite of about two hours he looked abroad, and seeing the sky clear, called for his horse, and passed the first stage without any other memorable accident.

Will considered, that labour must be relieved by pleasure, and that the strength which great undertakings require must be maintained by copious nutriment; he therefore ordered himself an elegant supper, drank two bottles of claret, and passed the beginning of the night in sound sleep; but waking before light, was forewarned of the troubles of the next day, by a shower beating against his windows with such violence as to threaten the dissolution of nature. When he arose he found what he expected, that the country was under water. He joined himself, however, to a company that was travelling the same way, and came safely to the place of dinner, tho' every step of his horse dashed the mud into the air.

In the afternoon, having parted from his company, he set forward alone, and passed many collections of water of which it was impossible to guess the depth, and which he now cannot review without some censure of his own rashness; but what a man undertakes he must perform, and *Marvel* hates a coward at his heart.

Few that lie warm in their beds, think what others undergo, who have perhaps been as tenderly educated, and have as acute sensations as themselves. My friend was now to lodge the second night almost fifty miles from home, in a house which he never had seen before, among people to whom he was totally a stranger, not knowing whether the next man he should meet would prove good or bad; but seeing an inn of a good appearance, he rode resolutely into the yard, and knowing that respect is often paid in proportion as it is claimed, delivered his injunction to the hostler with spirit, and entering the house, called vigorously about him.

On the third day up rose the sun and Mr. *Marvel*. His troubles and his dangers were now such, as he wishes no other man ever to encounter. The ways were less frequented, and the country more thinly inhabited. He rode many a lonely hour thro' mire and water, and met not a single soul for two miles together with whom he could exchange a word. He cannot deny that, looking round upon the dreary region, and seeing nothing but bleak fields and naked trees, hills obscured by fogs, and flats covered with inundations, he did for some time suffer melancholy to prevail upon him, and wished himself again safe at home. One comfort he had, which was to consider, that none of his friends were in the same distress, for whom, if they had been with him, he should have suffered more than for himself; he could not forbear sometimes to consider how happily the *Idler* is settled in an easier condition, who, surrounded like him with terrors, could have done nothing but lie down and die.

Amidst these reflections he came to a town and found a dinner, which disposed him to more chearful sentiments: but the joys of life are short, and its miseries are long; he mounted and travelled fifteen miles more thro' dirt and desolation.

At last the sun set, and all the horrors of darkness came upon him. He then repented the weak indulgence by which he had gratified himself at noon with too long an interval of rest: yet he went forward along a path which he could no longer see, sometimes rushing suddenly into water, and sometimes incumbered with stiff clay, ignorant whither he was going, and uncertain whether his next step might not be the last.

In this dismal gloom of nocturnal peregrination his horse unexpectedly stood still. *Marvel* had heard many relations of the instinct of horses, and was in doubt what danger might be at hand. Sometimes he fancied that he was on the bank of a river still and deep, and sometimes that a dead body lay across the track. He sat still awhile to recollect his thoughts; and as he was about to alight and explore the darkness, out stepped a man with a lantern, and opened the turnpike. He hired a guide to the town, arrived in safety, and slept in quiet.

The rest of his journey was nothing but danger. He climbed and descended precipices on which vulgar mortals tremble to look; he passed marshes like the *Serbonian bog, where armies whole have sunk;*[1] he forded rivers where the current roared like the *Egre* of the *Severn;*[2] or ventured himself on bridges that trembled under him, from which he looked down on foaming whirlpools, or dreadful abysses; he wandered over houseless heaths, amidst all the rage of the Elements, with the snow driving in his face, and the tempest howling in his ears.

Such are the colours in which *Marvel* paints his adventures. He has accustomed himself to sounding words and hyperbolical images, till he has lost the power of true description. In a road through which the heaviest carriages pass without difficulty, and the post-boy every day and night goes and returns, he meets with hardships like those which are endured in *Siberian* deserts, and misses nothing of romantic danger but a giant and a dragon. When his dreadful story is told in proper terms, it is only, that the way was dirty in winter, and that he experienced the common vicissitudes of rain and sunshine.

[1] According to Herodotus, a deceptive lake in Egypt, which appears as solid land to travellers, because of the sand blown onto it by winds.
[2] The "egre" is a violent current produced by high tide near the mouth of rivers such as the Trent or the Severn.

OLIVER GOLDSMITH
A City Night-Piece (1759)

The author: Oliver Goldsmith's year of birth is a matter of controversy: he was born in Ireland, where his father was an Anglican curate, in 1728, 1730, or 1731. He graduated from Trinity College, Dublin, in 1750, and from 1752 to 1755 he studied medicine at Edinburgh and Leyden. After a year of travel through France, Germany, and Italy, he came to London, where he worked as a journalist and translator and where he befriended Samuel Johnson. His first book was *An Enquiry into the Present State of Learning in Europe* (1759).

The text: "A City Night-Piece" was first published in *The Bee* 4 (27 October 1759), then (without the final paragraph) as Letter 114 in *The Citizen of the World* (1761), although it also appears in subsequent editions as Letter 112 or Letter 117. The following text reproduces the version published in *The Citizen of the World; or, Letters from a Chinese Philosopher, Residing in London, to his Friends in the East* (London: Printed for the Author; and sold by J. Newbery and W. Bristow, in St. Paul's Church-yard; J. Leake and W. Frederick, at Bath; B. Collins, at Salisbury; and A.M. Smart and Co. at Reading, 1762), Vol. II, p. 209-212.

Further reading: Richard C. Taylor. "The Politics of Goldsmith's Journalism." *Philological Quarterly* 69.1 (Winter 1990): 71-89.

David McCracken. "Goldsmith and the 'Natural Revolution of Things.'" *The Journal of English and German Philology* 78.1 (January 1979): 33-48.

The clock just struck two, the expiring taper rises and sinks in the socket, the watchman forgets the hour in slumber, the laborious and the happy are at rest, and nothing wakes but meditation, guilt, revelry, and despair. The drunkard once more fills the destroying bowl, the robber walks his midnight round, and the suicide lifts his guilty arm against his own sacred person.

Let me no longer waste the night over the page of antiquity, or the sallies of contemporary genius, but pursue the solitary walk, where vanity, ever changing, but a few hours past, walked before me, where she kept up the pageant, and now, like a froward child, seems hushed with her own importunities.

What a gloom hangs all around! the dying lamp feebly emits a yellow gleam, no sound is heard but of the chiming clock, or the distant watchdog. All the bustle of human pride is forgotten, an hour like this may well display the emptiness of human vanity.

There will come a time when this temporary solitude may be made continual, and the city itself, like its inhabitants, fade away, and leave a desart in its room.

What cities, as great as this, have once triumphed in existence, had their victories as great, joy as just, and as unbounded, and with short-sighted presumption, promised themselves immortality. Posterity can hardly trace the situation of some. The sorrowful traveller wanders over the awful ruins of others; and as he beholds, he learns wisdom, and feels the transience of every sublunary possession.

Here, he cries, stood their citadel, now grown over with weeds; there their senate-house, but now the haunt of every noxious reptile; temples and theatres stood here, now only an undistinguished heap of ruin. They are fallen, for luxury and avarice first made them feeble. The rewards of state were conferred on amusing, and not on useful, members of society. Their riches and opulence invited the invaders, who, though at first repulsed, returned again, conquered by perseverance, and at last swept the defendants into undistinguished destruction.

How few appear in those streets, which but some few hours ago were crowded; and those who appear, now no longer wear their daily mask, nor attempt to hide their lewdness or their misery.

But who are those who make the streets their couch, and find a short repose from wretchedness at the doors of the opulent? These are strangers, wanderers, and orphans, whose circumstances are too humble to expect redress, and whose distresses are too great even for pity. Their wretchedness excites rather horror than pity. Some are without the covering even of rags, and others emaciated with disease; the world has disclaimed them; society turns its back upon their distress, and has given them up to nakedness and hunger. These poor shivering females have once seen happier days, and been flattered into beauty. They have been prostituted to the gay luxurious villain, and are now turned out to meet the severity of winter. Perhaps, now lying at the doors of their betrayers, they sue to wretches whose hearts are insensible, or debauchees who may curse, but will not relieve them.

Why, why was I born a man, and yet see the sufferings of wretches I cannot relieve! Poor houseless creatures! the world will give you reproaches, but will not give you relief. The slightest misfortunes of the great, the most imaginary uneasinesses of the rich, are aggravated with all the power of eloquence, and held up to engage our attention and sympathetic sorrow. The poor weep unheeded, persecuted by every subordinate species of tyranny; and every law, which gives others security, becomes an enemy to them.

Why was this heart of mine formed with so much sensibility! or why was not my fortune adapted to its impulse! Tenderness, without a capacity of relieving, only makes the man who feels it more wretched than the object which sues for assistance.

Adieu.

OLIVER GOLDSMITH
The Disabled Soldier (1760)

The author: From January 1760 to August 1761, Oliver Goldsmith contributed his "Chinese Letters" to *The Public Ledger*, later republished as *The Citizen of the World*. In 1763, he was in the debtors' prison, but was freed when Dr Johnson persuaded John Newbery to purchase a share of Goldsmith's future novel, *The Vicar of Wakefield*, published only in 1766. His two comedies, *The Good Natured Man* and *She Stoops to Conquer*, were produced in 1768 and 1773, respectively. In 1770, he published his most famous poem, *The Deserted Village*. He died in 1774.

The text: It was first published in the June 1760 issue of *The British Magazine, or Monthly Repository for Gentlemen & Ladies* 6 (June 1760), edited by Tobias Smollett. It was anonymous and bore the title: "The Distresses of a Common Soldier." One year later, it appeared as Letter 119 in *The Citizen of the World* (1762), when it was subtitled "On the Distresses of the Poor; Exemplified in the Life of a Private Sentinel." Another four years afterwards, it appeared, with several changes, as "Essay XXIV" in *Essays. By Mr. Goldsmith*. It was subsequently anthologised many times in the following century, under various titles, usually including variations on the phrase "disabled soldier." The following is the version published in *Essays. By Mr. Goldsmith* (London: Printed for W. Griffin in Fetter Lane, 1765), 214-223.

Further reading: David Turner. *Disability in Eighteenth-Century England: Imagining Physical Impairment*. London: Routledge, 2012. 74-76.

ESSAYS.

BY

Mʳ GOLDSMITH.

Collecta revirescunt

LONDON.
Printed for W. GRIFFIN in Fetter Lane.
MDCCLXV.

No observation is more common, and at the same time more true, than That one half of the world are ignorant how the other half lives. The misfortunes of the great are held up to engage our attention; are enlarged upon in tones of declamation; and the world is called upon to gaze at the noble sufferers: the great, under the pressure of calamity, are conscious of several others sympathizing with their distress; and have, at once, the comfort of admiration and pity.

There is nothing magnanimous in bearing misfortunes with fortitude, when the whole world is looking on: men in such circumstances will act bravely even from motives of vanity; but he who, in the vale of obscurity, can brave adversity; who, without friends to encourage, acquaintances to pity, or even without hope, to alleviate his misfortunes, can behave with tranquillity and indifference, is truly great: whether peasant or courtier, he deserves admiration, and should be held up for our imitation and respect.

While the slightest inconveniences of the great are magnified into calamities; while tragedy mouths out their sufferings in all the strains of eloquence, the miseries of the poor are entirely disregarded; and yet some of the lower ranks of people undergo more real hardships in one day, than those of a more exalted station suffer in their whole lives. It is inconceivable what difficulties the meanest of our common sailors endure without murmuring or regret; without passionately declaiming against Providence, or calling their fellows to be gazers on their intrepidity. Every day is to them a day of misery, and yet they entertain their hard fate without repining.

With what indignation do I hear an Ovid, a Cicero, or a Rabutin,[1] complain of their misfortunes and hardships, whose greatest calamity was that of being unable to visit a certain spot of earth, to which they had foolishly attached an idea of happiness. Their distresses were pleasures, compared to what many of the adventuring poor every day endure without murmuring. They ate, drank, and slept; they had slaves to attend them, and were sure of subsistence for life; while many of their fellow-creatures are obliged to wander, without a friend to comfort or assist them, and even without a shelter from the severity of the season.

I have been led into these reflections from accidentally meeting, some days ago, a poor fellow, whom I knew when a boy, dressed in a sailor's jacket, and begging at one of the outlets of the town, with a wooden leg. I knew him to be honest and industrious when in the country, and was curious to learn what had reduced him to his present situation. Wherefore, after giving him what I thought proper, I desired to know the history of his life and misfortunes, and the manner in which he was reduced to his present distress. The disabled soldier, for such he was, though dressed in a sailor's habit, scratching his head, and leaning on his crutch, put himself into an attitude to comply with my request, and gave me his history as follows:

"As for my misfortunes, master, I can't pretend to have gone thro' any more than other folks; for, except the loss of my limb, and my being obliged to beg, I don't know any reason, thank Heaven, that I have to complain; there is Bill Tibbs, of our regiment, he has lost both his legs, and an eye to boot; but, thank Heaven, it is not so bad with me yet.

"I was born in Shropshire, my father was a labourer, and died when I was five years old; so I was put upon the parish. As he had been a wandering sort of a man, the parishioners were not able to tell to what parish I belonged, or where I was born, so they sent me to another parish, and that parish sent me to a third. I thought in my heart, they kept sending me about so long, that they would not let me be born in any parish at all; but, at last, however, they fixed me. I had some disposition to be a scholar, and was resolved, at least, to know my letters; but the master of the work-house put me to business as soon as I was able to handle a mallet; and here I lived an easy kind of a life for five years. I only wrought ten hours in the day, and had my meat and drink provided for my labour. It is true, I was not suffered to stir out of the house, for fear,

[1] Marie de Rabutin-Chantal, marquise de Sévigné, known as Madame de Sévigné (1626-1696), famous for her letters to her daughter.

as they said, I should run away: but what of that, I had the liberty of the whole house, and the yard before the door, and that was enough for me. I was then bound out to a farmer, where I was up both early and late; but I ate and drank well, and liked my business well enough, till he died, when I was obliged to provide for myself; so I was resolved to go and seek my fortune.

"In this manner I went from town to town, worked when I could get employment, and starved when I could get none: when happening one day to go through a field belonging to a justice of peace, I spy'd a hare crossing the path just before me; and I believe the devil put it in my head to fling my stick at it:—Well, what will you have on't? I killed the hare, and was bringing it away in triumph, when the justice himself met me: he called me a poacher and a villain; and collaring me, desired I would give an account of myself: I fell upon my knees, begged his worship's pardon, and began to give a full account of all that I knew of my breed, feed, and generation; but, though I gave a very good account, the justice would not believe a syllable I had to say; so I was indicted at sessions, found guilty of being poor, and sent up to London to Newgate, in order to be transported as a vagabond.

"People may say this and that of being in jail; but, for my part, I found Newgate as agreeable a place as ever I was in all my life. I had my belly full to eat and drink, and did no work at all. This kind of life was too good to last for ever; so I was taken out of prison, after five months, put on board a ship, and sent off, with two hundred more, to the plantations. We had but an indifferent passage, for, being all confined in the hold, more than a hundred of our people died for want of sweet air; and those that remained were sickly enough, God knows. When we came a-shore we were sold to the planters, and I was bound for seven years more. As I was no scholar, for I did not know my letters, I was obliged to work among the negroes; and I served out my time, as in duty bound to do.

"When my time was expired, I worked my passage home, and glad I was to see Old England again, because I loved my country. I was afraid, however, that I should be indicted for a vagabond once more, so did not much care to go down into the country, but kept about the town, and did little jobbs when I could get them.

"I was very happy in this manner for some time, till one evening, coming home from work, two men knocked me down, and then desired me to stand. They belonged to a press-gang:[1] I was carried before the justice, and, as I could give no account of myself, I had my choice left, whether to go on board a man of war, or list for a soldier. I chose the latter; and, in this post of a gentleman, I served two campaigns in Flanders, was at the battles of Val and Fontenoy,[2] and received but one wound, through the breast here; but the doctor of our regiment soon made me well again.

[1] A group of soldiers or sailors who forced civilians to join the army or the navy by kidnapping them (a practice known today as shanghaiing).
[2] The battles of Fontenoy (1745) and Lauffeld, also known as Val (1747) were both French victories against the British, Dutch, Austrian, and Hanoverian allies in the War of the Austrian Succession (1740-1748).

"When the peace came on I was discharged; and, as I could not work, because my wound was sometimes troublesome, I listed for a landman[1] in the East-India company's service. I here fought the French[2] in six pitched battles; and I verily believe, that, if I could read or write, our captain would have made me a corporal. But it was not my good fortune to have any promotion, for I soon fell sick, and so got leave to return home again with forty pounds in my pocket. This was at the beginning of the present war,[3] and I hoped to be set on shore and to have the pleasure of spending my money; but the government wanted men, and so I was pressed for a sailor before ever I could set foot on shore.

"The boatswain found me, as he said, an obstinate fellow: he swore he knew that I understood my business well, but that I shammed Abraham, merely to be idle;[4] but God knows, I knew nothing of sea-business, and he beat me without considering what he was about. I had still, however, my forty pounds, and that was some comfort to me under every beating; and the money I might have had to this day, but that our ship was taken by the French, and so I lost all.

"Our crew was carried into Brest,[5] and many of them died, because they were not used to live in a jail; but, for my part, it was nothing to me, for I was seasoned. One night, as I was sleeping on the bed of boards, with a warm blanket about me, for I always loved to lie well, I was awakened by the boatswain, who had a dark lanthorn in his hand; 'Jack,' says he to me, 'will you knock out the French centry's brains?' I don't care, says I, striving to keep myself awake, if I lend a hand. 'Then follow me,' says he, 'and I hope we shall do business.' So up I got, and tied my blanket, which was all the cloaths I had, about my middle, and went with him to fight the Frenchmen. I hate the French because they are all slaves, and wear wooden Shoes.

"Though we had no arms, one Englishman is able to beat five French at any time; so we went down to the door, where both the centries were posted, and rushing upon them, seized their arms in a moment, and knocked them down. From thence, nine of us ran together to the quay, and, seizing the first boat we met, got out of the harbour and put to sea. We had not been here three days before we were taken up by the Dorset privateer,[6] who were glad of so many good hands; and we consented to run our chance. However, we had not as much luck as we expected.

---

[1] Landman or landsman was a seaman during his first year of service.
[2] The British East India Company fought the French East India Company in three conflicts known as the Carnatic Wars (1744-1763) for supremacy in India.
[3] The Seven Years' War (1756-1763).
[4] A "sham Abraham" (used here as a verb) was a term used especially by sailors for someone who pretended to be sick in order to avoid duty (and, by extension, any kind of work).
[5] Major port in Brittany, France.
[6] Here, "privateer" means a privateering ship. This first appeared as "an English privateer" in *The Citizen of the World*. The *Dorset* was a real ship, of 28 guns. It was boarded and destroyed by a French privateer, the *Mélampe*, of either 36 or 40 guns. Between 70 and 80 of its men were killed or wounded.

In three days we fell in with the Pompadour privateer, of forty guns, while we had but twenty-three; so to it we went, yard-arm and yard-arm. The fight lasted for three hours, and I verily believe we should have taken the Frenchman, had we but had some more men left behind; but, unfortunately, we lost all our men just as we were going to get the victory.

"I was once more in the power of the French, and I believe it would have gone hard with me had I been brought back to Brest: but, by good fortune, we were retaken by the Viper.[1] I had almost forgot to tell you, that, in that engagement, I was wounded in two places; I lost four fingers of the left hand, and my leg was shot off. If I had had the good fortune to have lost my leg and use of my hand on board a king's ship, and not a-board a privateer, I should have been entitled to cloathing and maintainance during the rest of my life; but that was not my chance: one man is born with a silver spoon in his mouth, and another with a wooden ladle. However, blessed be God, I enjoy good health, and will for ever love liberty and Old England. Liberty, property, and Old England, for ever, huzza!"

Thus saying, he limped off, leaving me in admiration at his intrepidity and content; nor could I avoid acknowledging, that an habitual acquaintance with misery serves better than philosophy to teach us to despise it.

1760

---

[1] There was a 10-gun sloop-of-war at the time called HMS *Viper*.

ALEXANDER KELLET
The Man of Spirit (1761)

The author: Alexander Kellet (sometimes spelled Kellett) is one of the more obscure authors of 18th-century England. He may have been from the Christchurch parish in South London, perhaps the son of another Alexander Kellet, merchant and "one of the proprietors of the New River water," as he appears mentioned in 1727. The little we know about Kellet is that he went to the American colonies and, in 1754, he became one of the councillors of Governor John Reynolds of Georgia. In 1755, he co-authored a bill seeking to legalise the independent economic activities of married women and another "for the ease of Persons who have Scruples about the form of taking Oaths" (that is, in favour of Dissenters, Catholics, and Jews). On 16 January 1756, he was granted "Lot no. 182 in the Town of Hardwicke." However, in the spring of 1756, he left for England, and, in July of the same year, he presented to the Commissioners of Trade and Plantations a report, very critical of Reynolds's activities in Georgia (Reynolds was recalled, but not before replacing Kellet as provost marshal). Back in London, he wrote essays, stories, and poems, some inspired by his American adventures. His obituary notice reported his death at Bath, "at his lodgings," on 17 June, 1788. Kellet's only claim to (some) fame was his "A true Relation of the unheard of Sufferings of David Menzies, Surgeon, among the Cherokees, and of his surprising Deliverance," often believed to be factual at the time, and sometimes reprinted or at least mentioned among contemporary captivity stories.

The text: It was first published in *The London Chronicle: or, Universal Evening Post* Vol. X, no. 760 (Thursday, 5 November – Saturday, 7 November, 1761), as "The Cottager No. 26" (Kellet's essay-series, consisting of political essays, poems, odd thoughts, and a few tales, some presented as factual), and it subsequently appeared in the volume format of the newspaper (London: sold by J. Wilkie, at the Bible, in St. Paul's Church-Yard, 1761), 443. It was anonymous, untitled, and introduced by an epigraph from Virgil: "Quicquid erit, superanda omnis Fortuna ferendo est" ("Happen what will, every fortune is to be surmounted by patience"). It was republished, in a revised version (unlike in his other stories, which were modified and expanded, here only one word was dropped, but the spelling and the punctuation were modernised), and without the epigraph, in Kellet's anthology, *A Pocket of Prose and Verse: Being a Selection from the Literary Productions of Alexander Kellet, Esq.* (Bath: R. Cruttwell; sold by E. and C. Dilly, in the Poultry, London, 1778), 134-147. In the "Contents," it was included among the author's "Papers," under the title "Narrative of Good Spirits," while in the body of the book it appears as "Paper II. Alacer; or, An History of Good-Spirits." This volume was reprinted 5 years later by a London publisher, without changes, but under a different title: *The Mental Novelist, and Amusing Companion, A Collection of Histories, Essays, & Novels . . . with many other curious Literary Productions of Alexander Kellet, Esq.* (London: W. Lane, Leadenhall-Street, 1783). Although the interior is identical with that of the Bath edition, the London version lists the titles of the stories on the title page, including "The Man of Spirit; or History of *Alacer*." Eight years later, Rev. John Adams (c.1750-1814) republished it without acknowledging the source, in his *Elegant Tales, Histories, and Epistles of a Moral Tendency* (London: G. Kearsley, 1791). He renamed the protagonist Hilaris, gave his wife the name of Speciosa, and re-titled the story "Hilaris and Speciosa; or, Magnanimity and Cheerfulness Exemplified" (179-186). The following is Kellet's corrected version from 1778.

The birth of Alacer,[1] through the unskilfulness of a favourite midwife, cost his mother her life; and the negligence of her substitutes marked him with the curvature of deformity, and superinduced the sickly constitution its natural consequence. His father died while Alacer was yet at school, of an intemperance occasioned by wetting a commission, in the purchase of which he had exhausted his estate.[2] As he possessed all the military prejudice for flat backs and fine figures, he held his son in necessary dislike, and had designed him, contemptuously, for a parson. Alacer was therefore disposed rather to consider his father's death as an emancipation from parental despotism, than as an irreparable misfortune; of the over-early loss of his mother he was altogether insensible. Alacer was gifted with lively parts, which he had cultivated as far as opportunity permitted; he was so fortunate too, as to be in constant possession of that happy state of nerves, which is meant by *good-spirits*; accompanied with which no calamity can be insufferably grievous, and without which affluence, influence, and health itself, are petty enjoyments.

The undismayed orphan collects then the wreck of his fortune, and comes to town, full of hopes, in order to solicit personally his pretensions with his father's great friends. After experiencing for a patience-killing time the difficulty of access, the tedious attendance, the pompous accueil, and the ineffectual promises, that are become no inconsiderable part of the business of greatness, Alacer was glad to accept of, what alone he seemed likely to obtain, a pair of colours in a newly-raised regiment. He joined this corps a sanguine candidate for preferment and glory; not discountenanced by his approximation to deformity, he remembered that Cocles and Hannibal were blinkards,[3] and (which was still more to his purpose) that Richard the Third, and the Third William, were crook-backed.[4] Unluckily this regiment misbehaved so much in its noviciate, in conjunction with other raw troops, that it was judged expedient to break one corps by way of terrific example; and the lot fell on that to which Alacer belonged.[5] Alacer, though by no means particularly faulty, applied for permission to serve out the remainder of the campaign, as a volunteer, in an old regiment of horse. The day of general action now arrives, the squadrons form the dreadful line, the troopers put on their serious countenances, the trumpets play undistinguishable tunes, and the hostile artillery presently entertain the brigade with a spirited cannonade. Alacer's left-hand man soon lost his horse; he on his right, ere long, his

[1] Alacer is a Latin masculine adjective meaning "lively, eager, quick" but also "happy, cheerful" (it has given "alacrity" in English and "allegro" in Italian).
[2] When navy officers received (or purchased) a "commission," it was traditional to "wet" it, that is to entertain one's shipmates with a big party.
[3] "Blinkard" meant "with bad eyesight," but here it clearly means one-eyed (as were both the Roman hero Horatius, called "Cocles," i.e., "one-eyed," and the Carthaginian general Hannibal), probably because Andrew Marvell's famous line "Among the blind the one-eyed blinkard reigns."
[4] Both Richard III (1483-1485) and William III (1689-1702) were hump-backed.
[5] "Breaking" meant disbanding a regiment.

head; but Alacer suppresses his apprehensions, and manfully maintains the rank, till the bound of a ricochet ball mashes his arm to pieces; when he is carried into the rear, and the surgeons, before he well knows what they are about, inspect, condemn, and amputate it. He returns home, in chearful expectation of an honourable reward, and with great difficulty gets appointed a lieutenant in an independent company of invalids, and is roster'd to perform, for life, the moping rotation of Sheerness, Upnor, and Tilbury.[1] Alacer's constancy was not proof against such duty; he desired (and really thought it a favour) leave to resign, and was once in his life readily gratified; and having now nothing else to do, he fell in love.

The authoress of this passion was not respectable on account of her family, breeding, or riches; but she was confessedly handsome, and appeared good-natured: Alacer marries her then in a hurry, and conveys his prize to a cottage, there to live luxuriously on love. The spouse of Alacer had neither an enthusiastic, nor constitutional, attachment to him; she had married him to become a gentlewoman, of which condition the frugality he was obliged to observe admitted her to enjoy very few of the privileges: she had therefore no other comfort left but to give way, without regard to his consequential unhappiness, to the natural bent of her uncivilized temper. She gradually deposited all submission, all condescension, all compliance; she exerted an exclusive power in most branches of their menage, litigated an equality in every other, and, when she could find no personal cause of quarrel, engaged him heroically as champion for her sex; she assumed a new look, she altered the soft tone of her voice, she *maunder'd* in a dialect of her own; she warned away Alacer's favorite servants, she affronted away his friends; she stunned him with a din[2] of weeks, she spoke nothing for days; in a word, she *beshrewed him*. The hapless lover was all astonishment at first, and endeavoured unsuccessfully to reason or fondle his wife into another conduct; he then submitted to this torture, with varying degrees of patience, as long as any remains of fondness yet throbbed in his heart: but he was at last worried into so cordial an hatred of her, as to buy a separation at the price of the better part of his small income; declaring at the same time, that "though he had made an extravagant, yet was it an important, purchase; for he could now eat a meal in peace, and sleep for the future in the middle of his own bed."

By this abridgment of his finances, Alacer was entirely disabled from living at his ease in this opulent nation; and very judiciously turned his eyes on an object, to which all Englishmen in similar circumstances could then direct their views with the most promising prospect of success. Though incapacitated to abide in England, he determined to live under the English government nevertheless; though disqualified from mixing with cockneys, he resolved to consort with Britons notwithstanding: having pitched therefore on a province whose climate and produce

[1] Small towns in Kent and Essex.
[2] "Maunder" means "babble;" "din" means to make a loud noise, especially repetitively.

suited his constitution and plan, Alacer equipped and provided himself accordingly, crossed the Atlantic, and applied to the administration of a North-American colony, for the proportion of land his substance entitled him to.

But his ill-luck pursued him hither; for the governor of this province, through whatever incitement or caprice, conceived a dislike to Alacer, and set himself in evident opposition to his interests; in which he was seconded diligently by his dirty creatures. Alacer, who considered himself still on English ground, nor was aware of his being in the power of a petty Phalaris,[1] (who every day did what a King of England never dares do) impoliticly widened the breach by public complaints and private threats, until he determined his excellency to get rid of so troublesome a subject, in a legal manner. Returning home one evening, the new colonist found his house beset by a mob, and the officers of justice in possession; who informed him, they were there in virtue of a search-warrant, to look for a negro that he had stolen, whom they accordingly soon produced, to the surprise and terror of Alacer; who had, however, presence of mind enough to tell them, "that it was very easy for those who hid to find." The same night a provincial, commiserating Alacer's incautious innocence, came secretly and advised him, not to neglect to enter himself passenger in a schooner that would sail at day-break for England, or he would the next day be held to bail on an action brought against him for large damages by the proprietor of the negro which had been conveyed into his house, or be imprisoned perhaps on a charge of felony at the suit of the crown. The affrighted settler (settler now no more) did not hesitate about embracing this salutary counsel, he precipitated himself aboard the ship, saw with delight the inhospitable shore astern, and made the port of London; less concerned for his disappointment, and the diminution of his effects, than overjoyed at his escape from ignominy, and his planting the foot once more on a land of liberty.

Alacer afterward formed a succession of schemes, of which the major part proved impracticable, and the rest unsuccessful: meanwhile distress advanced imperceptibly upon him thus occupied; his debts increasing, and his credit diminishing, till such time as he was arrested for a sum he could not readily bail, by a tradesman who was worth a plumb, and had always made a liberal self-allowance in the price of his goods for bad debts.

He has now been years in jail, where the curiosity of an old acquaintance lately carried him to visit Alacer; he surprised him at chess, in the triumph of victory, after a well-contested game, and laid hold of the occasion to compliment him on his spirits. Alacer turned upon him, rivetted a transfixing eye on his face, adjusted the folds of his tattered night-gown, erected the curve of his body, then extended in pathetic action his single arm, and with a pitch of voice little less than theatric, harangued him as follows:

[1] Tyrant in ancient Sicily (6th-century B.C.).

210

"Innumerous volumes have been written (said Alacer) in order to prove this dusky truth, that human pleasures are unsatisfactory; with good intention, doubtless, and possibly some effect; but surely it were as laudable to apprise mankind of what is comfortably, and equally true, that their miseries are not insupportable. To pass over the factitious and assumed griefs of men, which would often justify the laughter of a Democritus,

('In pitying love we but our weakness show,
And wild ambition well deserves its woe,')[1]

even the real, and unassuageable evils of humanity, and the severest of these, are not insuperable to a magnanimous patience. You look on me, Sir, I know, as consummate in wretchedness; indigent as I am in a land of opulence, and imprisoned in a region of liberty, yet can I very easily imagine more intense hardships than any I endure; I can conceive an unfortunate fellow-creature turned into the uncompassionate street to starve, or driven on the highway by irresistible hunger, unsupported, unassisted, unconnected; to whom a jail itself would be an asylum;

"To whom the hell I suffer seems a heaven."[2]

Here I may amuse myself with meditation, with study; I can here converse with scholars and gentlemen, who arrive in increasing multitudes; (shame on the obdurate impolicy which finds them no subsisting employment!) and the most appalling spectre that my disturbed imagination can at this time present to me, (I with rigid veracity assure you, Sir) is that of a restless creditor mischievously armed with the compulsive clause."[3]

---

[1] From Alexander Pope's "Prologue to Mr. Addison's Tragedy of Cato."
[2] From Milton's *Paradise Lost* (IV, 50).
[3] The "compulsive clause," introduced in 1736-1737, prevented debtors to live in gaol indeterminately off income hidden from their creditors, and compelled them instead to use any and all assets to pay their debts.

ANONYMOUS

Goody Two-Shoes (1765)

The author: At the turn of the 19th century, writers as different as William Godwin and Washington Irving were quite passionate about identifying the author of "Goody Two-Shoes" and they both thought they had enough proof in favour of Oliver Goldsmith's authorship. Other names put forward in the 20th century include: Griffith Jones (1722-1786), editor and/or contributor of *The London Chronicle, Public Ledger, The British Magazine, or Monthly Repository* (the last two published by Newbery) as well as Johnson's *Literary Magazine*; his brother, Giles Jones, of whom little is known (the fact that Margery marries into the Jones family in the sequel and that another Newbery book is *Giles Gingerbread* have been considered evidence in favour of their authorship); and the publisher John Newbery.

The text: The following (illustrations included) is from *The History of Little Goody Two-Shoes. Otherwise called, Mrs. Margery Two-Shoes*. Third Edition (London: J. Newbery, at the *Bible* and *Sun* in *St. Paul's-Church-Yard*, 1766), 3-64, which sold at six pence.

Little Goody Two Shoes.

Further reading: Wilbur Macey Stone. "The History of Little Goody Two-Shoes." *Proceedings of the American Antiquarian Society* 49. 2 (October 1939): 333-370.

Jan Fergus. "Schoolboy Readers: John Newbery's *Goody Two-Shoes* and Licensed War." *Provincial Readers in Eighteenth-Century England*. Oxford: Oxford University Press, 2006. 118-154.

Sylvia Patterson Iskander. "'Goody Two-Shoes' and *The Vicar of Wakefield*." *Children's Literature Association Quarterly* 13.4 (Winter 1988): 165-168.

Part I.

Introduction. By the Editor.

All the World must allow, that *Two Shoes* was not her real Name. No; her Father's Name was *Meanwell*; and he was for many Years a considerable Farmer in the Parish where *Margery* was born; but by the Misfortunes which he met with in Business, and the wicked Persecutions of Sir *Timothy Gripe*, and an over-grown Farmer called *Graspall*, he was effectually ruined.

The Case was thus. The Parish of *Mouldwell* where they lived, had for many Ages been let by the Lord of the Manor into twelve different Farms, in which the Tenants lived comfortably, brought up large Families, and carefully supported the poor People who laboured for them; until the Estate by Marriage and by Death came into the Hands of Sir *Timothy*.

This Gentleman, who loved himself better than all his Neighbours, thought it less Trouble to write one Receipt for his Rent than twelve, and Farmer *Graspall* offering to take all the Farms as the Leases expired, Sir *Timothy* agreed with him, and in Process of Time he was possessed of every Farm, but that occupied by little *Margery*'s Father; which he also wanted; for as Mr. *Meanwell* was a charitable good Man, he stood up for the Poor at the Parish Meetings, and was unwilling to have them oppressed by Sir *Timothy*, and this avaricious Farmer.—Judge, oh kind, humane and courteous Reader, what a terrible Situation the Poor must be in, when this covetous Man was perpetual Overseer, and every Thing for their Maintenance was drawn from his hard Heart and cruel Hand. But he was not only perpetual Overseer, but perpetual Church-warden; and judge, oh ye Christians, what State the Church must be in, when supported by a Man without Religion or Virtue. He was also perpetual Surveyor of the Highways, and what Sort of Roads he kept up for the Convenience of Travellers, those best know who have had the Misfortune to be obliged to pass thro' that Parish.—Complaints indeed were made, but to what Purpose are Complaints, when brought against a Man, who can hunt, drink, and smoak with the Lord of the Manor, who is also the Justice of Peace?

The Opposition which little *Margery*'s Father made to this Man's Tyranny, gave Offence to Sir *Timothy*, who endeavoured to force him out of his Farm; and to oblige him to throw up the Lease, ordered both a Brick Kiln and a Dog-kennel to be erected in the Farmer's Orchard. This was contrary to Law, and a Suit was commenced, in which *Margery*'s Father got the better. The same Offence was again committed three different Times, and as many Actions brought, in all of which the Farmer had a Verdict and Costs paid him; but notwithstanding these Advantages, the Law was so expensive, that he was ruined in the Contest, and obliged to give up all he had to his Creditors; which effectually answered the Purpose of Sir *Timothy*, who erected those Nuisances in the Farmer's Orchard with that Intention only. Ah, my dear Reader, we brag of Liberty, and boast of our Laws: but the Blessings of the one, and the Protection of the other, seldom fall to the Lot of the Poor; and especially when a rich Man is their Adversary. How, in the Name of Goodness, can a poor Wretch obtain Redress, when thirty Pounds are insufficient to try his Cause? Where is he to find Money to see Council, or how can he plead his Cause himself (even if he was permitted) when our Laws are so obscure, and so multiplied, that an Abridgment of them cannot be contained in fifty Volumes in Folio?

As soon as Mr. *Meanwell* had called together his Creditors, Sir *Timothy* seized for a Year's Rent, and turned the Farmer, his Wife, little *Margery*, and her Brother out of Doors, without any of the Necessaries of Life to support them.

213

This elated the Heart of Mr. *Graspall*, this crowned his Hopes, and filled the Measure of his Iniquity; for besides gratifying his Revenge, this Man's Overthrow gave him the sole Dominion of the Poor, whom he depressed and abused in a Manner too horrible to mention.

Margery's Father flew into another Parish for Succour, and all those who were able to move left their Dwellings and sought Employment elsewhere, as they found it would be impossible to live under the Tyranny of two such People. The very old, the very lame and the blind were obliged to stay behind, and whether they were starved, or what became of them, History does not say; but the Character of the great Sir *Timothy*, and his avaricious Tenant, were so infamous, that nobody would work for them by the Day, and Servants were afraid to engage themselves by the Year, lest any unforeseen Accident should leave them Parishioners in a Place, where they knew they must perish miserably; so that great Part of the Land lay untilled for some Years, which was deemed a just Reward for such diabolical Proceedings.

But what, says the Reader, can occasion all this? Do you intend this for Children, Mr. NEWBERY? Why, do you suppose this is written by Mr. NEWBERY, Sir? This may come from another Hand. This is not the Book, Sir, mentioned in the Title, but the Introduction to that Book; and it is intended, Sir, not for those Sort of Children, but for Children of six Feet high, of which, as my Friend has justly observed,[1] there are many Millions in the Kingdom; and these Reflections, Sir, have been rendered necessary, by the unaccountable and diabolical Scheme which many Gentlemen now give into, of laying a Number of Farms into one, and very often of a whole Parish into one Farm; which in the End must reduce the common People to a State of Vassalage, worse than that under the Barons of old, or of the Clans in *Scotland*; and will in Time depopulate the Kingdom. But as you are tired of the Subject, I shall take myself away, and you may visit *Little Margery*. So, Sir, your Servant,

The EDITOR.

CHAP. I.

How and about Little Margery *and her* Brother.

Care and Discontent shortened the Days of Little *Margery*'s Father.—He was forced from his Family, and seized with a violent Fever in a Place where Dr. *James*'s Powder was not to be had,[2] and where he died miserably. *Margery*'s poor Mother survived the Loss of her Husband but a few Days, and died of a broken Heart, leaving *Margery* and her

---

[1] Newbery had published in 1757 *A Collection of Pretty Poems for the Amusement of Children Six Foot High.*

[2] Robert James (1703-1776) was a famous physician of the time. His "fever powder" from 1747 was one of the most popular "patent medicines" and it was sold by John Newbery.

little Brother to the wide World; but, poor Woman, it would have melted your Heart to have seen how frequently she heaved up her Head, while she lay speechless, to survey with languishing Looks her little Orphans, as much as to say, *Do Tommy, do Margery, come with me.* They cried, poor Things, and she sighed away her Soul; and I hope is happy.

It would both have excited your Pity, and have done your Heart good, to have seen how fond these two little ones were of each other, and how, Hand in Hand, they trotted about. Pray see them.

They were both very ragged, and *Tommy* had two Shoes, but *Margery* had but one. They had nothing, poor Things, to support them (not being in their own Parish) but what they picked from the Hedges, or got from the poor People, and they lay every Night in a Barn. Their Relations took no Notice of them; no, they were rich, and ashamed to own such a poor little ragged Girl as *Margery*, and such a dirty little curl-pated Boy as *Tommy*. Our Relations and Friends seldom take Notice of us when we are poor; but as we grow rich they grow fond. And this will always be the Case, while People love Money better than Virtue, or better than they do GOD Almighty. But such wicked Folks, who love nothing but Money, and are proud and despise the Poor, never come to any good in the End, as we shall see by and by.

CHAP. II.
How and about Mr. Smith.

Mr. *Smith* was a very worthy Clergyman, who lived in the Parish where Little *Margery* and *Tommy* were born; and having a Relation come to see him, who was a charitable good Man, he sent for these Children to him. The Gentleman ordered Little *Margery* a new Pair of Shoes, gave Mr. *Smith* some money to buy her Cloathes; and said, he would take *Tommy* and make him a little Sailor; and accordingly had a Jacket and Trowsers made for him, in which he now appears. Pray look at him.

After some Days the Gentleman intended to go to *London,* and take little *Tommy* with him, of whom you will know more by and by, for we shall at a proper Time present you with some Part of his History, his Travels and Adventures.

215

The Parting between these two little Children was very affecting, *Tommy* cried, and *Margery* cried, and they kissed each other an hundred Times. At last *Tommy* thus wiped off her Tears with the End of his Jacket, and bid her cry no more, for that he would come to her again, when he returned from Sea. However, as they were so  very fond, the Gentleman would not suffer them to take Leave of each other; but told *Tommy* he should ride out with him, and come back at Night. When night came, Little *Margery* grew very uneasy about her Brother, and after sitting up as late as Mr. *Smith* would let her, she went crying to Bed.

CHAP. III.

How Little Margery *obtained the Name of* Goody Two-Shoes, *and what happened in the Parish.*

As soon as Little *Margery* got up in the Morning, which was very early, she ran all round the Village, crying for her Brother; and after some Time returned greatly distressed. However, at this Instant, the Shoemaker very opportunely came in with the new Shoes, for which she had been measured by the Gentleman's Order.

Nothing could have supported Little *Margery* under the Affliction she was in for the Loss of her Brother, but the Pleasure she took in her *two Shoes.* She ran out to Mrs. *Smith* as soon as  they were put on, and stroking down her ragged Apron thus, cried out, *Two Shoes, Mame, see two Shoes.* And so she behaved to all the People she met, and by that Means obtained the Name of *Goody Two-Shoes,* though her Playmates called her *Old Goody Two-Shoes.*

Little *Margery* was very happy in being with Mr. and Mrs. *Smith,* who were very charitable and good to her, and had agreed to breed her up with their Family; but as soon as that Tyrant of the Parish, that *Graspall,* heard of her being there, he applied first to Mr. *Smith,* and threatened to reduce his Tythes if he kept her; and after that he spoke to Sir *Timothy,* who sent Mr. *Smith* a peremptory Message by his Servant, that *he should send back* Meanwell's *Girl to be kept by her Relations, and not harbour her in the Parish.* This so distressed Mr. *Smith* that he shed Tears, and cried, *Lord have Mercy on the Poor*!

The Prayers of the Righteous fly upwards, and reach unto the Throne of Heaven, as will be  seen in the Sequel.

Mrs. *Smith* was also greatly concerned at being thus obliged to discard poor Little

Margery. She kissed her and cried; as also did Mr. *Smith*, but they were obliged to send her away; for the People who had ruined her Father could at any Time have ruined them.

CHAP. IV.
How Little Margery *learned to read, and by Degrees taught others.*

Little *Margery* saw how good, and how wise Mr. *Smith* was, and concluded, that this was owing to his great Learning, therefore she wanted of all Things to learn to read. For this Purpose she used to meet the little Boys and Girls as they came from School, borrow their Books, and sit down and read till they returned; By  this Means she soon got more Learning than any of her Playmates, and laid the following Scheme for instructing those who were more ignorant than herself. She found, that only the following Letters were required to spell all the Words in the World; but as some of these Letters are large and some small, she with her Knife cut out of several Pieces of Wood ten Setts of each of these:

a b c d e f g h i j k l m n o p q r s t u v w x y z.[1]

And six Setts of these:

A B C D E F G H I J K L M N O P Q R S T U V W X Y Z.

And having got an old Spelling-Book, she made her Companions set up all the Words they wanted to spell, and after that she taught them to compose Sentences. You know what a Sentence is, my Dear, *I will be good*, is a sentence; and is made up, as you see, of several Words.

The usual Manner of Spelling, or carrying on the Game, as they called it, was this: Suppose the Word to be spelt was Plumb Pudding (and who can suppose a better) the Children were  placed in a Circle, and the first brought the Letter *P*, the next *l*, the next *u*, the next *m*, and so on till the Whole was spelt; and if any one brought a wrong Letter, he was to pay a Fine, or play no more. This was at their Play; and every Morning she used to go round to teach the Children with these Rattle-traps in a Basket, as you see in the Print. I once went her Rounds with her, and was highly diverted, as you may be, if you please to look into the next Chapter.

[1] Goody Two-Shoes had an extra letter, the "long s" (only lowercase, used at the beginning of words) which is now out of use and is not included here.

CHAP. V.

How Little Two-Shoes *became a trotting Tutoress, and how she taught her young Pupils.*

It was about seven o'Clock in the Morning when we set out on this important Business, and the first House we came to was Farmer *Wilson's*.

See here it is. Here *Margery* stopped, and ran up to the Door, *Tap, tap, tap.* Who's there? Only little goody *Two-Shoes*, answered *Margery*, come to teach *Billy*. Oh Little *Goody*, says Mrs. *Wilson*, with Pleasure in her Face, I am glad to see you, *Billy* wants you sadly, for he has learned all his Lesson. Then out came the little Boy. *How do doody Two-Shoes*, says he, not able to speak plain. Yet this little Boy had learned all his Letters; for she threw down this Alphabet mixed together thus:

b d f h k m o q s u w y z a c e g i l n p r t v x j

and he picked them up, called them by their right Names, and put them all in order thus:

a b c d e f g h i j k l m n o p q r s t u v w x y z.

She then threw down the Alphabet of Capital Letters in the Manner you here see them.

B D F H K M O Q S U W Y Z A C E G I L N P R T V X J

and he picked them all up, and having told their Names, placed them thus:

A B C D E F G H I J K L M N O P Q R S T U V W X Y Z.

Now, pray little Reader, take this Bodkin, and see if you can point out the Letters from these mixed Alphabets, and tell how they should be placed as well as little Boy *Billy*.

The next Place we came to was Farmer *Simpson's*, and here it is.

Bow, wow, wow, says the Dog at the Door. Sirrah, says his Mistress, what do you bark at Little *Two-Shoes*. Come in *Madge*; here, *Sally* wants you sadly, she has learned all her Lesson. Then out came the little one: So *Madge*! says she; so *Sally*! answered the other, have you learned your Lesson? Yes, that's what I have, replied the little one in the Country Manner; and immediately taking the Letters she set up these Syllables:

ba be bi bo bu, ca ce ci co cu, da de di do du, fa fe fi fo fu

and gave them their exact Sounds as she composed them; after which she set up the following:

ac ec ic oc uc, ad ed id od ud, af ef if of uf, ag eg ig og ug

And pronounced them likewise. She then sung the Cuzz's Chorus (which may be found in the *Little Pretty Play Thing*, published by Mr. NEWBERY) and to the same Tune to which it is there set.[1]

After this, Little *Two-Shoes* taught her to spell Words of one Syllable, and she soon set up Pear, Plumb, Top, Ball, Pin, Puss, Dog, Hog, Fawn, Buck, Doe, Lamb, Sheep, Ram, Cow, Bull, Cock, Hen, and many more.

The next Place we came to was *Gaffer Cook*'s Cottage; there you see it before you.

Here a number of poor Children were met to learn; who all came round Little *Margery* at once; and, having pulled out her Letters, she asked the little Boy next her, what he had for Dinner? Who answered, *Bread* (the poor Children in many Places live very hard). Well then, says she, set the first Letter. He put up the Letter *B*, to which the next added *r*, and the next *e*, the next *a*, the next *d*, and it stood thus, *Bread*.

And what had you *Polly Comb* for your Dinner? *Apple-pye*, answered the little Girl: Upon which the next in Turn set up a great *A*, the two next a *p* each, and so on till the two Words Apple and Pye were united and stood thus, *Apple-pye*.

The next had *Potatoes*, the next *Beef and Turnip*, which were spelt with many others, till the Game of Spelling was finished. She then set them another Task, and we proceeded.

The next Place we came to was Farmer *Thompson*'s, where there were a great many little ones waiting for her.

So little Mrs. *Goody Two-Shoes*, says one of them, where have you been so long? I have been teaching, says she, longer than I intended, and am afraid I am come too soon for you now. No, but indeed you are not, replied the other; for I have got my Lesson, and so has *Sally Dawson*, and so has *Harry Wilson*, and so we have all; and they capered about as if they were overjoyed to see her. Why then, says she, you are all very good, and GOD Almighty will love you; so let us begin our Lessons. They all huddled round her, and though at the other Place they were employed about Words and Syllables, here we had People of much greater Understanding who dealt only in Sentences.

The Letters being brought upon the Table, one of the little ones set up the following Sentence.

The Lord have Mercy upon me, and grant that I may be always good, and say my Prayers, and love the Lord my God with all my Heart, with all my Soul, and with all my Strength; and honour the King, and all good Men in Authority under him.

[1] *A Pretty Play-Thing for Children of All Denominations* (probably 1759), a Newbery book, includes "The Cuz's Chorus," filled with nonsense words.

Then the next took the Letters, and composed this Sentence.

Lord have Mercy upon me, and grant that I may love my Neighbour as myself, and do unto all Men as I would have them do unto me, and tell no Lies; but be honest and just in all my Dealings.

The third composed the following sentence.

The Lord have Mercy upon me, and grant that I may honour my Father and Mother, and love my Brothers and Sisters, Relations and Friends, and all my Playmates, and every Body, and endeavour to make them happy.

The fourth composed the following.

I pray GOD to bless this whole Company, and all our Friends, and all our Enemies.

To this last *Polly Sullen* objected, and said, truly, she did not know why she should pray for her Enemies? Not pray for your Enemies, says Little *Margery*; yes, you must, you are no Christian, if you don't forgive your Enemies, and do Good for Evil. *Polly* still pouted; upon which Little *Margery* said, though she was poor, and obliged to lie in a Barn, she would not keep Company with such a naughty, proud, perverse Girl as *Polly*; and was going away; however the Difference was made up, and she set them to compose the following

LESSONS
For the CONDUCT of LIFE

LESSON I

He that will thrive,
Must rise by Five.
He that hath thriv'n,
May lie till Seven.
Truth may be blam'd,
But cannot be sham'd.
Tell me with whom you go;
And I'll tell what you do.
A friend in your Need,
Is a Friend indeed.
They ne'er can be wise,
Who good Counsel despise.

LESSON II

A wise Head makes a close Mouth.
Don't burn your Lips with another Man's Broth.
Wit is Folly, unless a wise Man hath the keeping of it.
Use soft Words and hard Arguments.

Honey catches more Flies than Vinegar.
To forget a Wrong is the best Revenge.
Patience is a Plaister for all Sores.
Where Pride goes, Shame will follow.
When Vice enters the Room, Vengeance is near the Door.
Industry is Fortune's right Hand, and Frugality her left.
Make much of Three-pence, or you ne'er will be worth a Groat.

LESSON III

A Lie stands upon one Leg, but Truth upon two.
When a Man talks much, believe but half what he says.
Fair Words butter no Parsnips.
Bad Company poisons the Mind.
A covetous Man is never satisfied.
Abundance, like Want, ruins many.
Contentment is the best Fortune.
A contented Mind is a continual Feast.

A LESSON in Religion

Love GOD, for he is good.
Fear GOD, for he is just.
Pray to GOD, for all good Things come from him.
Praise GOD, for great is his Mercy towards us, and wonderful are all
his Works.
Those who strive to be good, have GOD on their Side.
Those who have GOD for their Friend, shall want nothing.
Confess your Sins to GOD, and if you repent he will forgive you.
Remember that all you do, is done in the Presence of GOD.
The Time will come, my Friends, when we must give
Account to GOD, how we on Earth did live.

A Moral LESSON

A good Boy will make a good Man.
Honour your Parents, and the World will honour you.
Love your Friends, and your Friends will love you.
He that swims in Sin, will sink in Sorrow.
Learn to live, as you would wish to die.
As you expect all Men should deal by you:
So deal by them, and give each Man his Due.

As we were returning Home, we saw a Gentleman, who was very
ill, sitting under a shady Tree at the Corner of his Rookery. Though ill,

he began to joke with Little *Margery*, and said, laughingly, so, *Goody Two-Shoes*, they tell me you are a cunning little Baggage; pray, can you tell me what I shall do to get well? Yes, Sir, says she, go to Bed when your Rooks do. You see they are going to Rest already: Do you so likewise, and

get up with them in the morning; earn, as they do, every Day what you eat, and eat and drink no more than you earn; and you'll get Health and keep it. What should induce the Rooks to frequent Gentlemens Houses only, but to tell them how to lead a prudent Life? They never build over Cottages or Farm-houses, because they see, that these People know how to live without their Admonition.

> *Thus Health and Wit you may improve,*
> *Taught by the Tenants of the Grove.*

The Gentleman laughing gave *Margery* Sixpence; and told her she was a sensible Hussey.

CHAP. VI.
How the whole Parish was frighted.

Who does not know Lady *Ducklington*, or who does not know that she was buried at this Parish Church? Well, I never saw so grand a Funeral in all my Life; but the Money they squandered away, would have been better laid out in little Books for Children, or in Meat, Drink, and Cloaths for the Poor.

This is a fine Hearse indeed, and the nodding Plumes on the Horses look very grand; but what End does that answer, otherwise than to display the Pride of the Living, or the Vanity of the Dead. Fie upon such Folly, say I, and Heaven grant that those who want more Sense may have it.

But all the Country round came to see the Burying, and it was late before the Corpse was interred. After which, in the Night, or rather about Four o'Clock in the Morning, the Bells were heard to jingle in the Steeple, which frightened the People prodigiously, who all thought it was Lady *Ducklington*'s Ghost dancing among the Bell-ropes. The People flocked to *Will Dobbins* the Clerk, and wanted him to go and see what it was; but

William said, he was sure it was a Ghost, and that he would not offer to open the Door. At length Mr. *Long* the Rector, hearing such an Uproar in the Village, went to the Clerk, to know why he did not go into the Church, and see who was there. I go, Sir, says *William*, why, the Ghost would frighten me out of my Wits.—Mrs. *Dobbins* too cried, and laying hold of her Husband said, he should not be eat up by the Ghost. A Ghost, you Blockheads, says Mr. *Long* in a Pet, did either of you ever see a Ghost, or know any Body that did? Yes, says the Clerk, my Father did once in the Shape of a Windmill, and it walked all round the Church in a white Sheet, with Jack Boots on, and had a Gun by its Side instead of a Sword. A fine Picture of a Ghost truly, says Mr. *Long*, give me the Key of the Church, you Monkey; for I tell you there is no such Thing now, whatever may have been formerly.—Then taking the Key, he went to the Church, all the people following him. As soon as he had opened the Door, what Sort of a Ghost do ye think appeared? Why Little *Two-Shoes*, who being weary, had fallen asleep in one of the Pews during the Funeral Service, and was shut

in all Night. She immediately asked Mr. *Long*'s Pardon for the Trouble she had given him, told him, she had been locked into the Church, and said, she should not have rung the Bells, but that she was very cold, and hearing Farmer *Boult*'s Man go whistling by with his Horses, she was in Hopes he would have went to the Clerk for the Key to let her out.

CHAP. VII.

Containing an Account of all the Spirits, or Ghosts, she saw in the Church.

The People were ashamed to ask Little *Madge* any Questions before Mr. *Long*, but as soon as he was gone, they all got round her to satisfy their Curiosity, and desired she would give them a particular Account of all that she had heard and seen.

Her TALE

I went to the Church, said she, as most of you did last Night, to see the Burying, and being very weary, I sate me down in Mr. *Jones*'s Pew, and fell fast asleep. At Eleven of the Clock I awoke; which I believe was in some measure occasioned by the Clock's striking, for I heard it. I started up, and could not at first tell where I was; but after some Time I recollected the Funeral, and soon found that I was shut in the Church. It was dismal dark, and I could see nothing; but while I was standing in the Pew, something jumped up upon me behind, and laid, as I thought, its

Hands over my Shoulders.—I own, I was a little afraid at first; however, I considered that I had always been constant at Prayers and at Church, and that I had done nobody any Harm, but had endeavoured to do what Good I could; and then, thought I, what have I to fear? yet I kneeled down to say my Prayers. As soon as I was on my Knees something very cold, as cold as Marble, ay, as cold as Ice, touched my Neck, which made me start; however, I continued my Prayers, and having begged Protection from Almighty GOD, I found my Spirits come, and I was sensible that I had nothing to fear; for GOD Almighty protects not only all those who are good, but also all those who endeavour to be good.—Nothing can withstand the Power, and exceed the Goodness of GOD Almighty. Armed with the Confidence of his Protection, I walked down the Church Isle, when I heard something, pit pat, pit pat, pit pat, come after me, and something touched my Hand, which seemed as cold as a Marble Monument. I could not think what this was, yet I knew it could not hurt me, and therefore I made myself easy, but being very cold, and the Church being paved with Stone, which was very damp, I felt my Way as well as I could to the Pulpit, in doing which something brushed by me, and almost threw me down. However I was not frightened, for I knew, that GOD Almighty would suffer nothing to hurt me.

At last, I found out the Pulpit, and having shut too the Door, I laid me down on the Mat and Cushion to sleep; when something thrust and pulled the Door, as I thought for Admittance, which prevented my going to sleep. At last it cries, *Bow, wow, wow*; and I concluded it must be Mr. *Saunderson*'s Dog, which had followed me from their House to Church, so I opened the Door, and called *Snip, snip*, and the Dog jumped up upon me immediately. After this *Snip* and I lay down together, and had a most comfortable Nap; for when I awoke again it was almost light. I then walked up and down all the Isles of the Church to keep myself warm; and though I went into the Vault, and trod on Lady *Ducklington*'s Coffin, I saw no Ghost, and I believe it was owing to the Reason Mr. *Long* has given you, namely, that there is no such Thing to be seen. As to my Part, I would as soon lie all Night in the Church as in any other Place; and I am sure that any little Boy or Girl, who is good, and loves GOD Almighty, and keeps his Commandments, may as safely lie in the Church, or the Church-yard, as any where else, if they take Care not to get Cold; for I am sure there are no Ghosts, either to hurt, or to frighten them; though any one possessed of Fear might have taken Neighbour *Saunderson*'s Dog with his cold Nose for a Ghost; and if they had not been undeceived, as I was, would never have thought otherwise. All the Company acknowledged the Justness of the Observation, and thanked Little *Two-Shoes* for her Advice.

REFLECTION

After this, my dear Children, I hope you will not believe any foolish Stories that ignorant, weak, or designing People may tell you about *Ghosts*; for the Tales of *Ghosts*, *Witches*, and *Fairies*, are the Frolicks of a

224

distempered Brain. No wise Man ever saw either of them. Little *Margery* you see was not afraid; no, she had *good Sense*, and a *good Conscience*, which is a Cure for all these imaginary Evils.

CHAP. VIII.

Of something which happened to Little Two-Shoes *in a Barn, more dreadful than the Ghost in the Church; and how she returned Good for Evil to her Enemy Sir* Timothy

Some Days after this a more dreadful Accident befel Little *Madge.* She happened to be coming late from teaching, when it rained, thundered, and lightened, and therefore she took Shelter in a Farmer's Barn at a Distance from the Village. Soon after, the Tempest drove in four Thieves, who, not seeing such a little creep-mouse Girl as *Two-Shoes*, lay down on the Hay next to her, and began to talk over their Exploits, and to settle Plans for future Robberies. Little *Margery* on hearing them, covered herself with Straw.  To be sure she was sadly frighted, but her good Sense taught her, that the only Security she had was in keeping herself concealed; therefore she laid very still, and breathed very softly. About Four o'Clock these wicked People came to a Resolution to break both Sir *William Dove*'s House, and Sir *Timothy Gripe*'s, and by Force of Arms to carry off all their Money, Plate and Jewels; but as it was thought then too late, they agreed to defer it till the next Night. After laying this Scheme they all set out upon their Pranks, which greatly rejoiced *Margery*, as it would any other little Girl in her Situation. Early in the Morning she went to Sir *William*, and told him the whole of their Conversation. Upon which, he asked her Name, gave her Something, and bid her call at his House the Day following. She also went to Sir *Timothy*, notwithstanding he had used her so ill; for she knew it was her Duty to *do Good for Evil*. As soon as he was informed who she was, he took no Notice of her; upon which she desired to speak to Lady *Gripe*; and having informed her Ladyship of the Affair, she went her Way. This Lady had more Sense than her Husband, which indeed is not a singular Case; for instead of despising Little *Margery* and her Information, she privately set People to guard the House. The Robbers divided themselves, and went about the Time mentioned to both Houses, and were surprized by the Guards, and taken. Upon examining these Wretches, one of which turned Evidence, both Sir *William* and Sir *Timothy* found that they owed their Lives to the Discovery made by Little *Margery*; and the first took great Notice of her, and would no longer let her lie in a Barn; but Sir *Timothy* only said, that he was ashamed to owe his Life to the Daughter of one who was his Enemy; so true it is, *that a proud Man seldom forgives those he has injured.*

CHAP. IX.
How Little Margery *was made Principal of a Country College*

Mrs. *Williams*, of whom I have given a particular Account in my *New Year's Gift*,[1] and who kept a College for instructing little Gentlemen and Ladies in the Science of A, B, C, was at this Time very old and infirm, and wanted to decline that important Trust. This being told to Sir *William Dove*, who lived in the Parish, he sent for Mrs. *Williams*, and desired she would examine Little *Two-Shoes*, and see whether she was qualified for the Office.—This was done, and Mrs. *Williams* made the following Report in her Favour, namely, *that Little* Margery *was the best Scholar, and had the best Head, and the best Heart of any one she had examined.* All the Country had a great Opinion of Mrs. *Williams*, and this Character gave them also a great Opinion of Mrs. *Margery*; for so we must now call her.

This Mrs. *Margery* thought the happiest Period of her Life; but more Happiness was in Store for her. GOD Almighty heaps up Blessings for all those who love Him, and though for a Time he may suffer them to be poor and distressed, and hide his good Purposes from human Sight, yet in the End they are generally crowned with Happiness here, and no one can doubt of their being so hereafter.

On this Occasion the following Hymn, or rather a Translation of the twenty-third Psalm, is said to have been written, and was soon after published in the *Spectator*.[2]

I.

The Lord my Pasture shall prepare,
And feed me with a Shepherd's Care:
His Presence shall my Wants supply,
And guard me with a watchful Eye;
My Noon-day Walks he shall attend,
And all my Midnight Hours defend.

II.

When in the sultry Glebe I faint,
Or on the thirsty Mountain pant;

---

[1] One of Newbery's first books for children, *Nurse Truelove's New-Year's Gift* (probably first published in 1750, but only advertised in 1753), includes a story of "Mrs. Williams and her Plumb Cake."
[2] This translation, attributed to Joseph Addison, appeared in *The Spectator* 441 (26 July 1712), whose theme was "Happiness of Dependance on the Supreme Being." The author might wish to suggest that his story is set in the early 1710s.

To fertile Vales and dewy Meads,
My weary wand'ring Steps he leads;
Where peaceful Rivers, soft and slow,
Amid the verdant Landskip flow.

III.

Tho' in the Paths of Death I tread,
With gloomy Horrors overspread,
My stedfast Heart shall fear no Ill,
For thou, O Lord, art with me still;
Thy friendly Crook shall give me Aid,
And guide me thro' the dreadful Shade.

IV.

Though in a bare and rugged Way,
Thro' devious lonely Wilds I stray,
Thy Bounty shall my Pains beguile:
The barren Wilderness shall smile,
With sudden Greens & herbage crown'd,
And Streams shall murmur all around.

Here ends the History of Little *Two Shoes*. Those who would know how she behaved after she came to be Mrs. *Margery Two-Shoes* must read the Second Part of this Work, in which an Account of the Remainder of her Life, her Marriage, and Death are set forth at large, according to Act of Parliament.

1765

ISAAC BICKERSTAFF

The Adventures of Ambrose Gwinett (1768)

The author: Isaac Bickerstaff or Bickerstaffe (that he had the name of the fictional author made up by Jonathan Swift and used by Richard Steele as the purported editor of *The Tatler* is pure coincidence) was born in Dublin on 26 September 1733. As a young boy, he was page to Lord Chesterfield (1694-1773), Lord Lieutenant of Ireland and later famous for his posthumous *Letters to His Son*. As early as 1745, when he was only 12 years old, he was given an ensign's commission in the army. He resigned, went on half-pay as a lieutenant in 1755, and tried to make a name for himself as a playwright. Unsuccessful, he joined the Marine Corps in 1758 and served in the Seven Years' War, being discharged in 1763. While still in the army, however, his musical plays and light operas (some with music by Thomas Arne) became extremely popular: *Thomas and Sally* (1760), *Judith* (1761), *Love in a Village* (1762), *The Plain Dealer* (1766), *The Padlock* (1768), *The Recruiting Serjeant* (1770) and others turned him into the most acclaimed English playwright of the decade. However, in 1772, he was accused of the "deed without a name" (as the 1812 edition of the *Biographia Dramatica* put it): more exactly, he appears to have propositioned a sentinel from the Whitehall Guard and thus risked being sentenced for sodomy. Bickerstaff chose to run away to France, where he probably spent most of his remaining years, although he also travelled to Germany (in January 1786 he was in Heidelberg) and various press reports had him spotted in either London or different French cities as late as 1816. However, Milhous and Hume suggest he may have died between 1792 and 1797, because he ceased to collect his officer's pension around that time. He was a close friend of many of the luminaries of 1760s London, including Goldsmith, Garrick, and Dr. Johnson (who refused to believe in his friend's "guilt" even after the latter's flight to France).

The text: The story first appeared in its entirety in the second issue (26 November 1768) of the mysterious (failed) weekly called *The Gentleman's Journal*, edited by Oliver Goldsmith, William Kenrick and Isaac Bickerstaff, assisted by Paul Hiffernan and Hugh Kelly. This second issue was also the last of the publication, of which no copies have survived. The story was soon afterwards published in two instalments in *The Gentleman's Magazine*. The first appeared in the *Supplement to the Gentleman's Magazine for the Year 1768* (December 1768) and bore the following title: "The Life and Adventures of Ambrose Gwinett, formerly well known to the Public as the lame Beggar man, who, in the year 1734, and for a long Time after, swept the Way between the Mouse-Gate and Spring-Garden, Charing Cross. Said to be taken almost literally from his own Mouth." The second instalment appeared in *The Gentleman's*

The Unparalleld ADVENTURES of Mr AMBROSE GWINETT

Printed for John Cooke at Little Mecegate, near to London Wall near Moorfields

Magazine for January 1769 and bore the much shorter title of "The Conclusion of the Life and Adventures of Ambrose Gwinett." The running title for both instalments was "Life of *Ambrose Gwinett*, a Beggar." At the end of the second instalment, the source is identified as "*Gent. Journ.*" It was then published as a chapbook, under the title *The Life, and Strange, Unparallel'd and Unheard-of Voyages and Adventures of Ambrose Gwinett, Formerly well known to the Public, as the Lame Beggar Man etc.*, in 1770 (London: John Lever, at Little Moorgate, next to London Wall, near Moorfields) or possibly as early as 1769 (London: Thomas Cadell), if one is to believe a mention made by Jean-Louis Castilhon (1730-1793), who translated the story into French and published it in three instalments (1 May, 15 May, and 1 June 1769) of the *Journal Encyclopédique*, after which he expanded it and issued it as a book entitled *Le Mendiant boiteux, ou les Aventures d'Ambrose Gwinett, balayeur du pavé de Spring Garden, d'après les notes écrites de sa main, par M. L. Castilhon, traduit d'Isaac Bickerstaffe* (Bouillon: Société typographique, 1770). A pirated edition of Castilhon's version appeared the following year in Germany, under the title *Candide Anglois*. The English version was republished many times, in England, Ireland, Jamaica, the United States and elsewhere until the early 19th century. Both the story and the 19th-century stage adaptation by Douglas Jerrold (*Ambrose Gwinett: A Seaside Story*) were so popular on both sides of the Atlantic that one of the most famous short-story writers in the United States, Ambrose Gwinnett Bierce (1842-c.1914) was named after Bickerstaff's hero. The following text is from the volume format of *The Gentleman's Magazine, and Historical Chronicle*, Vol. 38 (London: D. Henry, at St. John's Gate, 1768), 616-618; and Vol. 39 (London: D. Henry, at St. John's Gate, 1769), 9-14. The surviving 1770 John Lever edition (marked on the title page as the second edition) has been consulted for a few typos, whereas other changes from this version have been disregarded.

Further reading: Peter A. Tasch. *The Dramatic Cobbler: The Life and Works of Isaac Bickerstaff* (Lewisburg: Buckell University Press, 1971), 178-181.

Eve Tavor Bannet. "The two faces of *Ambrose Gwinett*." *Transatlantic Stories and the History of Reading, 1720-1810: Migrant Fictions* (Cambridge: Cambridge University Press, 2011), 89-92.

Judith Milhous and Robert D. Hume. "Isaac Bickerstaff's Copyrights and a Biographical Discovery." *Philological Quarterly* 83.3 (Summer 2004): 259-273.

I was born of reputable parents in the city of Canterbury, where my father, living at the sign of the Blue Anchor, dealt in slops.[1] He had but two children, a daughter and myself, and having given me a good school education, at the age of sixteen he bound me apprentice to Mr. George Roberts, an attorney in our town, with whom I staid four years and three quarters, to his great content and my own satisfaction.

My sister being come to woman's estate, had now been married something more than a twelvemonth to one Sawyer, a sea-faring man, who having got considerable prizes, my father also giving him 200*l.* with my sister, quitted his profession and set up a public-house within three miles of the place of his nativity, which was Deal, in the County of Kent.[2]

I had frequent invitations to pass a short time with them; and in the autumn of the year 1709, having obtained my master's consent for that purpose, I left the city of Canterbury on foot, on a Wednesday morning,

---

[1] Slops were clothes for sailors. Signboards like that of the Blue Anchor were very numerous and very useful for orientation at a time when houses had no numbers and about half the British population remained illiterate.

[2] Situated between Dover and Ramsgate, Deal was a fairly important English port at the time.

being the 17th day of Sept. but thro' some unavoidable delays on the road, the evening was considerably advanced before I reach'd Deal; and so tired was I, being unus'd to that way of travelling, that, had my life depended on it, I could not have got as far as my sister's that night, she living, as I have already said, three miles beyond the place. At this time there were many of her majesty queen Anne's ships lying in the harbour, the English being then at war with the French and Spaniards; besides which, I found this was the day for holding the yearly fair; so that the town was filled to that degree, that a bed was not to be gotten for love or money. I went seeking a lodging from house to house, to no purpose, till, being quite spent, I returned to the public house where I had first made enquiry, desiring leave to sit by their kitchen fire to rest myself till morning.

The publican and his wife where I put up happened unfortunately for me to be acquainted with my brother and sister, and finding by my discourse, that I was a relation of theirs and going to visit them, the landlady presently said she would endeavour to get me a bed; and going out of the kitchen she quickly after call'd me into a parlour, that led from it. Here I saw sitting by the fire side a middle aged man in a night gown and cap, who was reckoning money at a table. "Uncle," said the woman as soon as I entered, "this is a brother of our friend Mrs. Sawyer; he cannot get a bed any where, and is tired after his journey. You are the only one that lies in this house alone, will you give him part of yours?" To this the man answered, that she knew he had been out of order, that he was blooded that day,[1] and consequently a bedfellow could not be very agreeable; "however," said he, "rather than the young man shall sit up, he is welcome to sleep with me." After this we sat a while together, when having put his money in a canvas bag, into the pocket of his night gown, he took the candle, and I followed him up to bed.

How long I slept, I cannot exactly determine, but I conjectured it was about three o'clock in the morning when I awaken'd with a cholic attended with the most violent gripes: I attributed this to some bacon and cabbage I had eaten that day for dinner, after which I drank a large draught of milk. I found my chum awake as well as myself; he ask'd me what was the matter; I informed him, and at the same time begg'd he would direct me to the necessary. He told me when I was down stairs I must turn on my right hand and go strait into the garden, at the end of which it was, just over the sea, "but," adds he, "you may possibly find some difficulty in opening the door, the string being broke which pulls up the latch. I will give you a pen-knife, which you may open it with through a chink in the boards." So saying he put his hand into his waistcoat pocket which lay over him on the bed, and gave me a middling sized pen-knife.

I hurried on a few of my cloaths and went down stairs; but I must observe to you, that unclasping the pen-knife, to open the door of the necessary, according to his direction, a piece of money which stuck between the blade and the grove in the handle, fell into my hand: I did

_____

[1] Bloodletting, the withdrawal of blood from the patient, was a popular panacea.

not examine what it was, nor indeed could I well see, there being then but very faint moon light, so I put them together carelessly into my pocket.

I apprehend I staid in the garden pretty near half an hour, for I was extremely ill, and, by over-heating myself with walking the preceding day, had brought on the piles[1]; a disorder I was subject to from my youth. These seem trifling circumstances, but afterwards turned out of infinite consequence to me. When I returned to the chamber I was surprised to find my bedfellow gone: I called several times, but receiving no answer, took it for granted he had withdrawn into some adjoining closet for his private occasions. I therefore went to bed and again fell asleep.

About six o'clock I arose, nobody yet being up in the house. The gentleman was not yet returned to bed, or, if he was, had again left it. I drest myself with what haste I could, being impatient to see my sister; and the reckoning being paid over-night, I let myself out at the street door.

I will not trouble you with a relation of the kindness with which my sister and her husband received me. We breakfasted together, and I believe it might be about eleven o'clock in the forenoon, when standing at the door, my brother-in-law being by my side, we saw three horsemen galloping towards us. As soon as they came up they stopt, and one of them lighting, suddenly seized me by the collar, crying, "You are the king's prisoner." I desired to know my crime. He said I should know that, as soon as I came to Deal, where I must immediately go with them. One of them told my brother[2] that the night before I had committed a murder and robbery.

Resistance would have proved as vain as my tears and protestations of my innocence. In a word, a warrant was produced, and I was carried back to Deal attended by the three men; my brother, with another friend, accompanying us, who knew not what to say, or how to comfort me.

Being arrived in town, I was immediately hurried to the house where I had slept the preceding night, the master of which was one of the three men that came to apprehend me, tho' in my first hurry I did not recollect him. We were met at the door by a crowd of people, every one crying, "Which is he? Which is he?" As soon as I entered, I was accosted by the publican's wife in tears, "O! cursed wretch, what hast thou done? thou hast murdered and robbed my poor dear uncle, and all thro' me who put thee to lie with him! But where hast thou hid his money? and what hast thou done with his body? Thou shalt be hang'd upon a gallows as high as the May-pole." My brother begg'd her to be pacified, and I was taken into a private room. They then began to question me as the woman had done, about where I had put the money, and how I had disposed of the body. I ask'd them what money, and whose body they meant? They then said I had kill'd the person I had lain with the preceding night for the sake of a large sum I had seen with him. I fell down upon my knees, calling God to witness, I knew nothing of what they accused me. Then somebody cried,

---

[1] Hemorrhoids.
[2] A common appellation for a brother-in-law.

"Carry him up stairs," and I was brought into the chamber where I had slept. Here the man of the house went to the bed, and turning down the cloaths shew'd the sheets, pillows, and bolster dyed in blood. He ask'd me, did I know any thing of that? I declared to God I did not. Says a person that was in the room, "Young man, something very odd must have past here last night; for lying in the next chamber I heard groaning, and going up and down stairs more than once or twice." I told them the circumstance of my illness, and that I had been up and down myself, with all that pass'd between my bedfellow and me. Somebody proposed to search me, several began to turn my pockets inside out, and from my waistcoat tumbled the pen-knife and the piece of money I have already mentioned. Upon seeing these, the woman immediately screamed out, "O God! there is my uncle's pen-knife!" Then taking up the money and calling the people about her, "here," said she, "is what puts the villain's guilt beyond a doubt; I can swear to this William and Mary's guinea[1]; my uncle has long had it by way of pocket piece, and engraved the first letters of his name upon it." She then began to cry afresh, while I could do nothing but continue to call Heaven to witness that I was as innocent as the child unborn. After this they carried me down to the necessary, and here fresh proofs appeared against me. The constable, who had never left me, perceiv'd blood upon the edges of the seat, (which might probably proceed from my being troubled with the hemmorrage the night before) "Here," said he, "after having cut the throat, he has let the body down into the sea." This every body immediately assented to. "Then," said the master of the house, "it is in vain to look for the body any further, for there was a spring tide last night which has carried it off."

The consequence of these proceedings was an immediate examination before a justice of peace; after which I suffered a long and rigorous imprisonment in the county town of Maidstone.[2] For some time, my father, my master, and my relations, were inclin'd to think me innocent, and, in compliance with my earnest request, an advertisement was publish'd in the London Gazette representing my deplorable circumstances, and offering a reward to any person who could give tidings of Mr. Richard Collins, (the name of the man I was supposed to have murdered) either alive or dead. No information, however, of any kind came to hand; at the assizes therefore, I was brought to tryal, and circumstances appearing strong against me, I received sentence to be carried in a cart the Wednesday fortnight following, to the town of Deal, and there to be hang'd before the inn-keeper's door where I had committed the murder; after which I was to be hung in chains within a little way of my brother's house.

Nothing could have supported me under this dreadful condemnation, but a consciousness of my not being guilty of the crime for which I was to suffer. My friends now began to consider my declarations of innocence as persisting in falsehood to the perdition of my soul; many of them

[1] Guinea coin produced between 1689 and 1694, with the heads of the joint monarchs.
[2] Located SW of London, Maidstone is the county town (the capital) of Kent.

discontinued their enquiries after me; and those few who still came to visit me, only came to urge me to confession; but I was resolv'd I would never die with a lie of that kind in my mouth.

The Monday was now arriv'd before the fatal day when an end was to be put to my miseries. I was call'd down into the court of the prison, but I own I was not a little shock'd, when I found it was to be taken measure of for the irons in which I was to be hung after execution. A fellow prisoner appeared before me in the same woeful plight (he had robb'd the mail) and the smith was measuring him when I came down; while the gaoler, with as much calmness as if he had been ordering a pair of stays for his daughter, was giving directions in what manner the irons should be made, so as to support the man who was remarkably heavy and corpulent.

Between this and the day of my execution, I spent my time alone in prayer and meditation. At length Wednesday morning came, and about six o'clock I was put into the cart; but sure, such a day of wind, rain, and thunder, never blew out of the Heavens; it pursued us all the way; and when we arrived at Deal, it became so violent, that the sheriff and his officers, who had not a dry stitch upon them, could scarce sit their horses: for my own part, my mind (God help me) was with long agitation become so unfeeling, that I was in a manner insensible to every object about me: I therefore heard the sheriff whisper the executioner to make what dispatch he could without the least emotion, and suffered him to tuck me up like a log of wood, unconscious of what he was doing.

I can give no account of what I felt while I was hanging, only that I remember, after being turn'd off, something for a little time appeared about me like a blaze of fire; nor do I know how long I hung: no doubt the violence of the weather favour'd me greatly in that circumstance. What I am now going to tell you, I learn'd from my brother, which was, that after having hung about half an hour, the sheriff's officers all went off, and I was cut down by the executioner; but when he came to put the irons upon me, it was found a mistake had been made, and that the irons of the other man, which were much too large for me, had been sent instead of mine. This they remedied as well as they cou'd by stuffing rags between my body and the hoops that surrounded it; after which I was taken, according to my sentence, to the place appointed, and hung upon a gibbet[1] which was ready prepared.

The cloth over my face being but slightly tied, and suffering no pressure from the iron which stood a great way from it, was, I suppose, soon detach'd by the wind, which was still rather violent, and probably its blowing on my bare face expedited my recovery; certain it is, that in this tremendous situation I came to myself.

It was no doubt, a very great blessing, that I did not immediately return so perfectly to my senses as to have a feeling of things about me; yet I had a sort of recollection of what had happened, and, in some measure, was sensible where I was.

[1] The gibbet was a wooden structure similar to the gallows, from which the bodies of executed criminals were displayed to the public.

The gibbet was placed at one corner of a small common-field, where my sister's cows usually ran; and it pleased God, that about this time a lad, who took care of them, came to drive them home for evening milking. The creatures, which were feeding almost under me, brought him near the gibbet; when, stopping to look at the melancholy spectacle, he perceived that the cloth was from off my face; and, in the very moment he looked up, saw me open my eyes, and move my under jaw. He immediately ran home to inform the people at his master's. At first they made some difficulty to believe his story; at length, however, my brother came out, and, by the time he got to the field, I was so much alive, that my groans were very audible.

It was now dusk. The first thing they ran for was a ladder. One of my brother's men mounted, and, putting his hand to my stomach, felt my heart beating very strongly. But it was found impossible to detach me from the gibbet, without cutting it down. A saw, therefore, was got for that purpose; and, without giving you a detail of trifling circumstances, in less than half an hour, having freed me from my irons, they got me blooded, and put me into a warm bed in my brother's house.

It is an amazing thing, that, though upwards of eight persons were entrusted with this transaction, and I remained three days in the place after it happened, not a creature betrayed the secret. Early next morning it was known that the gibbet was cut down, and it immediately occurred to every body, that it was done by my relations, in order to put a slight veil over their own shame, by burying the body: but when my brother was summoned to the mayor's house, in order to be questioned, and he denied knowing any thing of the matter, little more stir was made about it; partly because he was greatly respected by all the neighbouring gentlemen, and in some measure, perhaps, because it was known that I continued to persist strongly in my being innocent of the fact for which I suffered.

Thus, then, was I most miraculously delivered from an ignominious death, if I may call my coming to life a delivery, after all I had endured: but, how was I to dispose of my life now I had regained it. To stay in England was impossible, without exposing myself again to the terrors of the law. In this dilemma, a fortunate circumstance occurred. There had lain, for some time, at my brother's house, one or two of the principal officers of a privateer that was preparing for a cruize, and just then ready to sail. The captain kindly offered to take me aboard with him. You may guess, little difficulty was made on our side to accept of such a proposal; and proper necessaries being quickly provided for me, my sister recommended me to the protection of God and the worthy commander, who most humanely received me as a sort of under-assistant to his steward.

We had been six months out upon our cruize, having had but very indifferent success, when, being upon the coast of Florida, then in the hands of the Spaniards, we unfortunately fell in with a squadron of their men of war; and being consequently taken without striking a stroke, we were all brought prisoners into the harbour of Havannah. I was really now almost weary of my life, and should have been very glad to have ended it in the loathsome dungeon, where, with forty others of my unfortunate countrymen, the enemy had stowed me; but, after three years close confinement, we were let out, in order to be put on board transports, to be conveyed to Pensylvania, and from thence to England. This, as you may believe, was a disagreeable sentence to me, taking it for granted, that a return home would be a return to the gallows: being now, therefore, a tolerable master of the Spanish language, I solicited very strongly to be left behind; which favour I obtained, by means of the master of the prisons, with whom, during my confinement, I had contracted a sort of intimacy; and he not only took me into his house as soon as my countrymen were gone, but, in a short time, procured me a salary from the governor, for being his deputy.

Indeed, at this particular time, the office was by no means agreeable. The coast had been long infested with pirates, the most desperate gang of villains that can be imagined; and there was scarce a month passed, that one or other of their vessels did not fall into the governor's hands, and the crew as constantly was put under my care. Once I very narrowly escaped being knocked o' th' head by one of the ruffians, and having the keys wrested from me: another time I was shot at. 'Tis true, in both cases the persons suffered for their attempt, and, in the last, I thought a little too cruelly; for the fellow, who let off the carabine, was not only put to the torture, to confess his accomplices, but afterwards broke upon the wheel, where he was left to expire, the most shocking spectacle I ever beheld with my eyes.

I had been in my office about three months, when a ship arrived from Port Royal, another Spanish settlement on the coast, with nine English prisoners on board. I was standing in the street as they were coming up from the port with a guard of soldiers, to the governor's house. I thought something struck me, in the face of one of the prisoners, that I had before been acquainted with. I could not stop them for us to speak together; however, in about an hour after, they were all brought down to prison, there to be lodged till the governor signified his further pleasure.

As soon as the poor creatures found I was an Englishman, they were extremely happy, even in their distressed situation, though, indeed they were treated with lenity enough, and only sent to the prison till a lodging could be provided for them, they having been, in the course of the war, made prisoners as well as myself, and then on their return home. I now had an opportunity of taking notice of the man whose face I thought I knew, and I was more and more confirmed that I was not mistaken. I a word, I verily thought, that this man was the person for whose supposed murder I had suffered so much in England; and the thought was so strong in my head, that I could not sleep a wink all night.

In the morning after their arrival, I told them, that if any of them had a mind to walk about the town, I would procure them permission, and go along with them. This man said he would go, and it was what I wished. Three other prisoners, that went out along with us, walked a little in advance. I now took the opportunity, and looking in his face, "Sir," said I, "was you ever at Deal?" I believe, he, at that instant, had some recollection of me; for, putting his hand upon my shoulder, tears burst into his eyes. "Sir," says I, "if you were, and are the man I take you for, you here see before you one of the most unfortunate of human kind; Sir, is your name Collins?" He answered, it was. "Richard Collins?" said I. He replied, "Yes." "Then," said I, "I was hanged and gibbeted upon your account in England."

After our mutual surprize was over, he made me give him a circumstantial detail of every thing that happened to me in England, from the moment we parted. I never saw any man express such concern as he did, while I was pursuing my melancholy adventures; but, when I came to the circumstance of my being hanged, and afterwards hung in chains, I could hardly prevail upon him to believe my relation, till backed by the most serious asseverations, pronounced in the most serious manner. When I had done, "Well," said he, "young man," (for I was then but in my five and twentieth year; Mr. Collins might be about three and forty) "if you have sustained misfortunes upon my account, do not imagine (tho' I cannot lay them at your door) that I have been without my sufferings. God knows my heart, I am most exceedingly sorry for the injustice that has been done you; but the ways of providence are unsearchable." He then proceeded to inform me by what accident all my troubles had been brought about.

"When you left me in bed," said he, "having at first wakened with an oppression I could not account for, I found myself grow exceedingly sick and weak; I did not know what was the matter; I groaned, and sighed, and thought myself going to die; when, accidently, putting my hand to my left arm, in which I had been blooded the morning before, I found my shirt wet, and, in short, that the bandage having slipped, the orifice was again opened, and a great flux of blood ensued. This immediately accounted for the condition I found myself in. I thought, however, I would not disturb the family, which I knew had gone to bed very late. I therefore, mustered all my strength, and got up, with my night-gown loose about me, to go to a neighbouring barber, who had bled me, in order to have the blood stopt and the bandage placed. He lived directly opposite to our house; but when I was crossing the way, in order to knock at his door, a band of men, armed with cutlasses and hangers,[1] came down the town, and seizing me, hurried me towards the beach. I begged and prayed; but they soon silenced my cries. At first, I took them for a press-gang, though I afterwards found they were a gang of ruffians, belonging to a privateer, aboard of which they immediately brought me. However, before I got thither, the loss of blood occasioned me to faint away. The surgeon of the ship, I suppose, tyed up my arm; for, when my senses returned, I found myself in a hammock, with somebody feeling my pulse. The vessel was then under way. I asked where I was? They said I was safe enough. I immediately called for my night-gown; it was brought

---

[1] A short sword similar to, but less broad than, a cutlass.

me: but, of a considerable sum of money that was in the pocket of it, I could get no account. I complained to the captain of the violence that had been done me, and of the robbery his men had committed; but, being a brutish fellow, he laughed at my grief, and told me, if I had lost any thing, I should soon have prize-money enough to make me amends. In a word, not being able to help myself, I was obliged to submit; and, for three months, they forced me to work before the mast. In the end, however, we met the same fate that you did. We were taken by the Spaniards; and, by adventures parallel to your own, you now see me here, on my return to our native country, whither if you will accompany me, I shall think myself extremely happy."

There was now nothing to prevent my going to England; and a ship being to sail for Europe in eight or ten days, in it Mr. Collins and I determined to embark. As soon as we returned home, I went to my master, and told him my resolution: he did not dissuade me from it, chiefly, I suppose, because it gave him an opportunity of getting the little office I held for a nephew of his, who was lately come to live with him, to whom, the very same day, I delivered up my trust. And here the providence of God was no less remarkable to me than in other particulars of my life: for, the very same night, eight or ten pirates, who were in the prison, watched the occasion, while the young man was locking up the wards, to seize him, taking the keys from him, after having left him for dead; and, before the alarm was sufficiently given, five of them made their escape, having, as it was supposed, got off the coast by means of piratical boats, which kept continually hovering about.

It was the 18th day of Novem. 1712, that, having made all my little preparations, I sent my trunk aboard the Nostra Senora, a merchant-ship, bound for Cadiz, Michael Deronza, master. The vessel was to sail that evening, and lay in the road, about three miles from the town. About seven o'clock in the evening, I being then sitting with Signor Gasper, my old friend and master, in the portico to his house, a lad came up, and said, the boat had been waiting half an hour for me at the port, and that my companion, Mr. Collins, was already on board. I ran into the house for a small bundle, and only staying to take leave of one or two of the family, made what haste I could to the quay: but, when I arrived, I found the boat had already put off, leaving word, that I should overtake them at a little bay, about a mile beyond the town. The dusk was coming on. I ran along the shore; and, as I imagined, soon had a sight of the boat, to which I hallooed as loud as I was able; they answered, and immediately put about to take me in: but we had scarce got fifty yards from land, when, on looking about for my friend Mr. Collins, I missed him; and then it was I found I had made a mistake, and, instead of getting aboard my own boat, which I now saw a considerable way a-head, I had got into a boat belonging to some of the pirates. I attempted to leap overboard, and should easily have swam ashore; but I was prevented by one of the crew, who gave me a stroke on the head, which immediately laid me senseless; and I found afterwards, they mistook me for one of their own men, whom they had sent to purchase something in the town.

237

A more infernal crew than these pirates breathed not upon the face of the earth. Their whole lives were a scene of rapine and murder, which, when they had not an opportunity of committing upon wretches that fell into their clutches, during their piratical pursuits, they committed upon one another. During the time that I remained with them, which was upwards of three years and three quarters, there was no less than eleven assassinations among themselves. There was an uninhabited island, about twelve leagues west of the gulph of Mexico, which those villains called Swallow island, from the great numbers of those birds which harboured upon it. Here they had a fortification; and the place being rendered almost inaccessible by rocks, except at one little inlet, just large enough to admit a single vessel, they defied the Spanish power.

Their captain was one Bryan Walsh, an Irishman, whom I cannot help calling a most execrable and bloody villain, tho' God Almighty put it into his heart to be a very good friend to me. When I was brought into the ship, and, immediately after, into the captain's cabin, the first person that accosted me was one of the fellows that had broke out of prison, and had formerly been under my care. He knew me directly; and, without any more ado, drawing out his hanger, aimed a stroke at me, which falling upon my neck, entered deep into the flesh, and must infallibly have put an end to my life, had not the captain prevented it, by raising his cane between him and me, which broke the force of the blow. From this moment, he seemed to take me under his protection. At his own request, I gave him a history of my life, which astonished him greatly: but, notwithstanding I pleaded hard to be set on shore again, he absolutely refused; and, in spite of all my entreaties to the contrary, brought me to the island and fortification I have already mentioned, where, finding I could read and write, two qualifications he wanted himself, he thought I might be of use to him.

I have already said, that with these people I remained upwards of three years: on land I acted as store-keeper; and, at sea, as a sort of purser to the ship. It is to be observed, that there was always a sufficient number of hands left on the island, to man the fort, which was so situated as effectually to prevent the approach of an enemy. Indeed, the office of store-keeper was a place of great trust. You would hardly credit me, was I to attempt to tell you the immense riches those robbers had amassed together. One article alone will be sufficient to give you an idea of it. Under one shed, I myself reckoned three thousand eight hundred bales of English goods; and I may safely declare, that, in other merchandize of almost every kind, they fell nothing behind: and, upon an average, there could not be less in their coffers than two hundred thousand pounds sterling in specie, besides a great quantity of gold in bars.

The continual terror that was on my mind while I remained with these people is not to be imagined; but, to give you a detail of my manner of life while I endured this worst of bondage, would be tedious, because it had no variety, and shocking to boot, as I was forced to enter into all their horrid schemes. I shall only tell you, that, in one of our cruizes, having met with a Jamaica ship, we hoisted out our black colours, and, having boarded her, because she made some resistance, and killed one of our men, the captain ordered that the whole crew should be massacred; which wicked command was executed upon the master, five seamen, and a boy, in a manner, before the cruel monster's eyes; then taking the cargo out, which proved to be rum and sugar, we scuttled the ship, and returned to our fortification.

But, to see how the avenger of wicked deed makes the fruits of our crimes our punishment, this cargo of rum, which was of a kind not many degrees short of aquafortis,[1] was drank by the men with such a furor, that, in little more than three days, not a drop of it was left; and, out of our complement of eighteen men, seven absolutely lost their lives by it, among which was the captain.

I cannot but confess I had some attachment to this man, because he always appeared particularly attached to me: when, therefore, I saw him lie senseless on the floor, overgorged with this infernal liquor, I did every thing I could to recover him, and so far succeeded, as to bring him to his senses; but the quantity he had drank had inflamed his bowels to a degree to be aswaged by no lenitives that was in my power to procure him. He was seized with intermitting convulsions, which, the next day, carried him off: but, about four hours before he died, he called to me, in presence of all the men, who stood about him in the cabin, and desiring me to sit down, with pen and ink, to draw his will, he left me sole heir to his share of the booty, signing the paper with his mark; which paper, through a series of unheard-of misfortunes, I have preserved in my custody ever since.

We buried the captain the next day; and, on inspection and partition of the treasure, I found myself worth considerably more than forty thousand pounds sterling. The persons now remaining of our company were, Joseph Wright, Andrew Van Hooten, a Dutchman, James Winter, and myself, the four principals, besides four common men, to whom we assigned five thousand pounds a-piece, which we gave to each of them in dollars; nor did I observe any discontent among them on account of the bequest the captain had made to me.

All my thoughts were immediately bent on getting off the island to some of the English settlements. I plainly perceived, that my companions wanted to be again at their old practices: but, one day, talking upon the subject of another cruize, I represented to them the danger and uncomfortable situation we all were in; that we had each of us a very ample fortune to support us in any part of the world; it was therefore my advice, that we should immediately put our treasure on board, with as much of the merchandize as we could conveniently carry off, and make the best of our way to Jamaica, where there was no doubt but we should be well received.

[1] Aquafortis (nitric acid) was sometimes, like here, confused with "aqua vitae" or "spirit of wine," a solution of ethanol.

239

They agreed to the proposal with more alacrity than I thought they would. We fell immediately to work, and, in two days, were prepared to sail. But, though we put a considerable quantity of bale-goods on board, the quantity still in the warehouses was astonishing. I warned the fellows of their rapacity, and the danger of too deeply loading the ship, but they would not give over till she could hold no more; and then the treasure, packed in chests, each man's share separate to himself, we put in the cabbin.

We weighed anchor the 3d of Aug. and, for three days, we had excellent weather; but the fourth, a storm began to threaten, and the symptoms still increasing, by midnight such a war was raised between heaven and earth, as, to that hour, I never was witness of. About three o'clock in the morning, we were obliged to heave the ship to under her bare poles; and the sea ran so exceeding high, that we could venture to keep no lights aboard, though the night was so dark that we could scarce see one another at a quarter of a yard distance: the wind still encreasing, we sprung the main mast about six feet from the deck, that nothing could save it. We now began to feel the consequence of too deeply lading the vessel. The first things we threw overboard were our guns; and, as our case became more and more desperate, every thing followed them, not excepting our chests of treasure. Thus, I was once more reduced to my original state of poverty. As day-light appeared, the storm abated. We then, as well as we were able, erected jury-masts;[1] and, in about four hours, managed with the greatest difficulty, to get the vessel again under sail.

I was now standing behind the man at the wheel, leaning against the mizen-mast,[2] returning God thanks in my own mind for our amazing escape, when the boatswain came up to me, and said, "Damme, master Gwinett, you have brought us all into a pretty hole here; if it had not been for you, we should not have taken this trip, and lost the substance we have been working for so many years; but you lop too, I assure you." I asked him what he meant; he said he would let me see; upon which he and two or three others of them that came behind him, seizing me by the nape of the neck, and the waistband of the breeches, forced me over the rails of the quarter deck, and dropt me into the sea.

The shock of the fall, and the amaze I was in from so unexpected an accident, almost bereaved me of my senses; I endeavoured, however, to keep myself above water as well as I could, though I had no manner of hopes of saving my life. My first attempt was to swim after the ship; but finding that impracticable, I turned about, and I believe might have swam about three quarters of an hour, when being very faint and weak, I began to put up my last prayer to God, and determined to commit myself to the bottom of the deep; but, at that instant, turning my head a little aside, I saw, at a small distance from me, a body, which at first I took for a barrel, but, Good Lord! what was my joy and astonishment, when

[1] Temporary masts to replace the ones that have broken off.
[2] The mizzen mast is the one at the rear on a ship with three masts.

coming near it, I perceived it to be one of our own boats, which had been washed overboard the night before; and, to complete my joy, the oars were lashed to the seat. Almost spent as I was, I made a shift to get into it; and here I saw myself freed in a miraculous manner, from the fury of the waves; but at the same time, I found myself in an open boat, at least sixty leagues from any land, without a compass, or any kind of nourishment whatsoever, unless I might count such some tobacco I had in a box in one of my waistcoat pockets; and I believe in my conscience, it afforded a nourishment that, in a great measure, helped to preserve me.

It was a very great blessing for me, that moderate weather followed the tempest, by which means I was enabled to keep the boat tolerable steady. I could not be less than thirty hours in this situation, when I was taken up by a Spanish carrack; but I can hardly reckon that among fortunate accidents; for, the same day that I entered the ship, one of the men, while I was asleep, hanging up my cloaths among the shrouds to dry, in doing it, emptied my pockets, and finding several papers relative to the pirates affairs, as soon as they arrived in Port Royal, whither they were bound, they seized me as one of that desperate gang. I must observe to you, that when I first was taken into the ship, I gave a false account of myself; which caution was my ruin: for now, confessing the truth, and telling them I had been forced into the pirate's service, with all that had happened to me among them, my prevarication made them suspect my veracity, and I was kept two years in prison; when, by what means I know not, some of the wretches, with whom I left our island, having been taken as pirates, upon the Spanish coasts in Europe, an order came to bring me over to Cadiz in Old Spain, in order to be an evidence. When I came there, I was again confined for many months; but, at length, when the pirates were brought to their tryal, instead of being made use of as an evidence, I found myself treated as a delinquent, and with two others, condemned to the galleys for life.

I worked on board them for some years; when the galley I belonged to was ordered to sea, against an Algerine rover that infested the coast: but, instead of one, we met with three of them. The issue of the engagement was fatal to us. The greatest part of the crew were killed, and the rest taken prisoners, among which last I was one, having lost the leg which you see me want, in the action.

After this, I passed a long and painful slavery in Algiers, till, with many other English captives, I was released, by agreement between the Dey of Algiers and his Britannick majesty's agent. In the year 1730, I returned to England. The first thing I did was to enquire after my relations; but all those nearest to me were dead; and I found Mr. Collins had never returned home, so I suppose he died in his passage. Though not an old man, I was so enfeebled by hardships, that I was unable to work; and, being without any manner of support, I could think of no way of getting my living but by begging.

THOMAS CHATTERTON
Tony Selwood (1770)

The author: Thomas Chatterton (1752-1770) was born in Bristol, where he began writing at an early age. He soon came up with the persona of Thomas Rowley, a 15th-century poet whose works he claimed to have discovered. These "medieval" poems were hotly debated in the following decades, with many believing in their authenticity. Chatterton came to London, where he took up journalism, but died after ingesting arsenic (whether he committed suicide or overdosed on a common drug taken against the symptoms of syphilis is another controversial matter). Chatterton's place in the history of English letters has been differently represented: he appeared as the unfortunate, yet talented forger to the commentators of the late 18th century; as the precursor of the Romantics (often bowdlerised), who could have become one of the greats had he lived a little longer, in the nineteenth and early twentieth century; as a multifaceted author, satirical and libertine, today.

The Death of Chatterton, an 1856 painting by Henry Wallis.

The text: This satire of an antiquarian was first published in *The Town and Country Magazine; or, Universal Repository of Knowledge, Instruction, and Entertainment* for August 1770. The following has been taken from the volume format of *The Town and Country Magazine* (London: A. Hamilton, Jr., St. John's-Gate, 1770), Vol. II, 409-410. The text was first identified as Chatterton's and anthologised by John Broughton in his edition of *Miscellanies in Prose and Verse; by Thomas Chatterton* (London: Fielding and Walker, Paternoster Row, 1778), 209-213. Broughton's version was then reproduced, a quarter of a century later, in the canonising three-volume edition of *The Works of Thomas Chatterton*, eds. Robert Southey and Joseph Cottle (London: T.N. Longman and O. Rees, Paternoster-Row, 1803), III, 171-176. In *The Town and Country*, the piece was untitled, though advertised on the top of the page as "A modern-antique Character." Broughton left it untitled, but called it "Tony Selwood's description of a modern antique character" in the Contents (vi) and used "Tony Selwood" as running title (210-213). In Southey and Cottle's edition, "Tony Selwood" becomes the title both in the contents and in the body of the book. In the magazine, the text appeared on two columns and in only four paragraphs. Here, the division into seven paragraphs suggested by Broughton and kept by Southey and Cottle has been preferred. The spelling and punctuation (modified in *The Works*) is here that of the original text, as it appeared in the magazine, with one exception: the full stops after the names of James I and Henry VII are followed in the magazine, in Broughton's *Miscellanies*, and in *The Works* by a lowercase: here, they are followed by an uppercase.

Further reading: Daniel Cook. *Thomas Chatterton and Neglected Genius, 1760-1830*. New York: Palgrave Macmillan, 2013. 85-87.

1770

To the Printer *of the* Town *and* Country MAGAZINE.

SIR,

Lest your Hunter of Oddities[1] should meet with me, and cook up my singularity as a dish of diversion for the town, I trouble you with a description of myself. Have you ever seen a portrait by Holbein,[2] or the figure of an old fellow in ancient tapestry? I am a laughable counter-part to either of these curiosities. I am heir to no inconsiderable estate, which has but one incumbrance on it; a plaguy, long-lived, surly dog of a father.

If I am not mistaken the Roman-catholics make longevity one of the peculiar gifts of heaven. I confess I am so irreligious as to wish heaven had been less sparing of its gifts to my honoured papa. You'll say I am an ungracious child, perhaps; but when you have got to the end of my epistle, you will excuse me. If absurdities and follies are the general attendants of age, I cannot see with what justice grey-hairs command veneration.

My father has as well furnished a wardrobe as any knight in the shire; but not an individual garment in it which has been made since the Revolution.[3]

My father dresses in the uniform of a courtier in the reign of James I. His hat is like a strawberry-basket, with the handle thrust under his chin: this piece of ornament belonged to Robert Cary,[4] who, as he was a great man in his time, and nearly related to our family, must not be out of remembrance. He wears also an enormous ruff, once the property of Sir Venison Goosepye, lord-mayor of London,[5] who, though of a younger branch of the family, established it on a more respectable footing than before, by doubling its rent-roll.[6] Gratitude obliges my sire to wear this ruff, though as full of holes as a lawyer's conscience. A flashed doublet, with slit sleeves, and a long cloak, envelopes his trunk; and a monstrous pair of trunk-hose, square shoes, and large shoe-roses, conclude his

---

[1] "The Hunter of Oddities" was an essay-series in *The Town and Country*, to which Chatterton himself contributed several pieces. It usually consisted in the sketch of an unusual "character."

[2] Hans Holbein the Younger (c. 1497-1543) was a German Renaissance painter who lived in England after 1532 under the protection of Henry VIII. He left many portraits of English aristocrats and members of the Royal Family.

[3] The English Civil War of 1642-1651.

[4] Robert Carey, first Earl of Monmouth (1560?-1639) was a cousin of Elizabeth I and a courtier of James I.

[5] The "ruff" was the round, white collar worn by both men and women in the second half of the sixteenth century and the first half of the seventeenth. Sir Venison Goosepye is, of course, fictional, but his name is probably a reference to the fact that lords mayor of London were merchants, only appointed knights upon taking office.

[6] The register of lands and buildings owned by a person or a family, and, more importantly, of the tenants paying rent.

bundle of ridiculous habiliments.[1] Could I persuade him to be contented with making himself laughed at, I should be happy in entertaining my friends with the oddity of his appearance; but when I consider that mine is equally as laughable, I sicken at the sight of his antiquated garb. I am almost ashamed to describe myself; but in hopes that he must soon set out on his journey to the other world, I make a virtue of necessity, and comply. He absolutely threatens to disinherit me, if I grumble at dressing for the memory of the departed; and an estate of six thousand per annum, is not to be lost for the sake of a full-trimmed suit, and a gold button. My hair is dressed in a very peculiar and risible manner; it is cut close on the middle of the head, and twisted like a horse's mane on each side: this my papa avers was the most polite fashion in the reign of queen Elizabeth, as appears by the portrait of his great uncle Sir Henry Dainty. This Sir Henry was the greatest beau of his time, and is thought by a learned antiquary to be the identical person for whom Shakespeare drew the character of Ostrick in Hamlet.[2] My hat is not quite so comical as my sire's; it inclines more to the shape of a close-stool-pan, pardon the simile, you will find it in another author, it is too delicate to be my own.[3] This ornament of the head once graced the caput of the profound Dr. Technicus, who had an universal nostrum which enabled him to ride in his chair; and what do you think this nostrum was? Nothing but a cataplasm of masticated bread and butter. My ruff is perfectly yellow; but as it belonged to the reverend Dr. Drouzy, my father makes it a point of conscience to oblige me to wear it. I have a large jutting coat and wide breeches, the very tip of the mode in the days of Henry VII. Mottled stockings, red and green, and shoes with monstrous pikes complete my ornamentals.

This, Mr. Printer, is a perfect representation of my externals. Do be so obliging as to give the old fellow a hint in your Magazine, that he acts very ridiculously. He has already felt the bad effects of his antiquated wardrobe. My sister was as laughable as myself; she wore a hood of unconscionable thick velvet, which projected on each side of her face

[1] The doublet was a buttoned jacket very popular from the 14th all the way to the mid-17th century; trunk hoses were tight breeches covering the hips and thighs, worn until the early 17th century; square shoes (or square-toed shoes) were a remnant of a bygone era, so much so that a "square-toed" idea meant an "old-fashioned" idea; shoe roses were rose-shaped ornaments worn on the front of the shoe in the 16th and in the early17th century.
[2] Alternately spelled "Osric": dandy courtier and comic relief in *Hamlet*, he referees the prince's fencing match against Laertes in the play's last scene. Hamlet mocks Ostrick's fancy language and countenance. Though a minor character, Ostrick was often played by a leading comedian of the time who, in David Garrick's rendition of the play (which Chatterton would have known), was sometimes billed immediately after Garrick himself.
[3] A close-stool (also, a close-stool-chair or a close-stool-pan) was a chair placed over a chamber pot or small chest with a lid concealing a hole and used as a toilet. Chatterton refers to Samuel Garth's 1699 mock-heroic epic *The Dispensary*, in which the character of Querpo (satirising Dr. George Howe, 1655-1710) is described as follows: "A Pestle for his Truncheon led the Van,/ And his high Helmet was a Close-stool pan."

1770

like a horse's blinds; her ruff was enormous, and betwixt that and her head-gear there was nothing but the tip of her nose to be seen: her stays reached down to her knees, her stockings were yellow, and her shoes square-toed. All these ornaments had in the days of their prosperity glittered on Alice Sevenoke, a maid of honour to queen Mary, who was famous for making custards, and giving eel-pies an excellent relish. My sister Biddy's gown was as heavy as a modern novel: upon a moderate computation it had above three pounds of silver in its embroidery: the colours indeed were faded, but that defect was made up in the length of the train, which afforded the cat a five minutes play while Miss Biddy was turning the corner.

A female must necessarily be worse qualified to bear this purgatory than a man; and she having fifteen thousand pounds, which an old aunt had left her to be paid at her marriage, whipped off to Scotland, at the age of sixteen, with a young fellow in the army.[1] Would I could make my escape too from the tyranny of this taylor of antiquity. I am sensible no character at Cornelys' could make so ridiculous an appearance as I do.[2]

O, dear Mr. Ham,[3] if you have any bowels of compassion, address a line or two to the old prig: shew him how barbarous it is to deprive a young fellow of all the pleasures of life, to indulge an unaccountable whim: push the matter home to him; and, if you succeed, you shall ever have the prayers of
Your humble servant,
TONY SELWOOD.

[1] "Scottish marriages" became a common form of elopement after the 1753 Marriage Act, because parental consent was not required in Scotland.
[2] Teresa Cornelys (1723-1797) hosted the most fashionable gatherings in London in the 1760s and 1770s. Guests had to buy tickets to attend.
[3] Archibald Hamilton, editor of *The Town and Country Magazine*.

JOHN AIKIN

Sir Bertrand. A Fragment (1773)

The author: John Aikin (1747-1822) studied medicine in Edinburgh, London, and later in Leyden. In the last decades of his life, he wrote widely consulted biographies and dictionaries of physicians and men of letters, but his claim to literary fame comes from his collaboration with his elder sister, Anna Laetitia Barbauld (1743-1825). Together, they published *Miscellaneous Pieces* in 1773 and, much later, the popular children's book *Evenings at Home* (6 volumes, 1792-1796). "Sir Bertrand" has been mistakenly attributed to his sister (it is so even today), although Lucy Aikin, John's daughter and Laetitia's niece, made it clear in her 1823 *Memoir* that this particular piece had been written by her father.

The text: First published in *Miscellaneous Pieces, in Prose, by J. and A. L. Aikin* (London: J. Johnson, in St. Paul's Church-yard, 1773), from where the following has been taken. It appeared under the title "On the Pleasure derived from Objects of Terror; with Sir Bertrand, a Fragment" (p. 119-137; 127-137 for the story alone). The same year it was reprinted in *The Westminster Magazine* for October (Vol. I, 592-595). A second edition of the *Miscellaneous Pieces* appeared in 1774, while a third, which updates spelling and punctuation, only saw the light of day in 1792. Some of the changes, e.g., the unfortunate "correction" of the name of a character mentioned in the opening essay, render this edition less reliable than it should have been. The story, usually without the essay, was often anthologised in the following 50 years or so. The opening essay is here reproduced in smaller font.

Further reading: Anne Toner, *Ellipsis in English Literature: Signs of Omission* (Cambridge: Cambridge University Press, 2015), 96-103.

Daniel White, "The 'Joineriana': Anna Barbauld, the Aikin Family Circle and the Dissenting Public Sphere." *Eighteenth-Century Studies* 32.4 (1999): 511-533.

That the exercise of our benevolent feelings, as called forth by the view of human afflictions, should be a source of pleasure, cannot appear wonderful to one who considers that relation between the moral and natural system of man, which has connected a degree of satisfaction with every action or emotion productive of the general welfare. The painful sensation immediately arising from a scene of misery, is so much softened and alleviated by the reflex sense of self-approbation attending virtuous sympathy, that we find, on the whole, a very exquisite and refined pleasure remaining, which makes us desirous of again being witnesses to such scenes, instead of flying from them with disgust and horror. It is obvious how greatly such a provision must conduce to the ends of mutual support and assistance. But the apparent delight with which we dwell upon objects of pure terror, where our moral feelings are not in the least concerned, and no passion seems to be excited but the depressing one of fear, is a paradox of the heart, much more difficult of solution.

The reality of this source of pleasure seems evident from daily observation. The greediness with which the tales of ghosts and goblins, of murders, earthquakes, fires, shipwrecks, and all the most terrible disasters attending human life, are devoured by every ear, must have been generally remarked. Tragedy, the most favourite work of fiction, has taken a full share of those scenes; "it has supt full with horrors"[1]—and has, perhaps, been more indebted to them for public admiration than to its tender and pathetic parts. The ghost of Hamlet, Macbeth descending into the witches' cave, and the tent scene in Richard,[2] command as forcibly the attention of our souls as the parting Jaffeir and Belvidera, the fall of Wolsey, or the death of Shore.[3] The inspiration of *terror* was by the antient critics assigned as the peculiar province of tragedy; and the Greek and Roman tragedians have introduced some extraordinary personages for this purpose: not only the shades of the dead, but the furies, and other fabulous inhabitants of the infernal regions. Collins, in his most poetical ode to Fear, has finely enforced this idea.

> Tho' gentle Pity claim her mingled part,
> Yet all the thunders of the scene are thine.[4]

The old Gothic romance and the Eastern tale, with their genii, giants, enchantments, and transformations, however a refined critic may censure them as absurd and extravagant, will ever retain a most powerful influence on the mind, and interest the reader independently of all peculiarity of taste. Thus the great Milton, who had a strong bias to these wildnesses of the imagination, has with striking effect made the stories "of forests and enchantments drear," a favourite subject with his *Penseroso*; and had undoubtedly their awakening images strong upon his mind when he breaks out,

> Call up him that left half-told
> The story of Cambuscan bold; &c.[5]

How are we then to account for the pleasure derived from such objects? I have often been led to imagine that there is a deception in these cases; and that the avidity with which we attend is not a proof of our receiving real pleasure. The pain of suspense, and the irresistible desire of satisfying curiosity, when once raised, will account for our eagerness to go quite through an adventure, though we suffer actual pain during the whole course of it. We rather chuse to suffer the smart pang of a violent emotion than the uneasy craving of an unsatisfied desire. That this principle, in many instances, may involuntarily carry us through what we dislike, I am convinced from experience. This is the impulse which renders the poorest and most insipid narrative interesting when once we get fairly into it; and I have frequently felt it with regard to our modern novels, which, if lying on my table, and taken up in an idle hour, have led me through the most tedious and disgusting pages, while, like Pistol eating his leek,[6] I have swallowed and execrated to the end. And it will not only force us through dullness, but through actual torture—through the relation of a Damien's execution or an inquisitor's act of faith.[7] When children, therefore, listen with pale and mute attention to the frightful stories of apparitions, we are not, perhaps, to imagine that they are in a state of enjoyment, any more than the poor bird which is dropping into the mouth of the rattle-snake—they are chained by the ears, and fascinated by curiosity. This solution, however, does not satisfy me with respect to the well-wrought scenes of artificial terror which are formed

---

[1] Macbeth, in Shakespeare's play, says "I have supped full with horrors" (*Macbeth*, V, iv).

[2] *Richard III*, Act V, scene 3.

[3] Jaffeir and Belvidera are the main characters of Thomas Otway's famous tragedy *Venice Preserv'd* (first staged in 1682); the fall of Cardinal Wolsey features prominently in Shakespeare and Fletcher's *Henry VIII* (probably 1613); the death of Jane Shore is the key event in Thomas Heywood's play *Edward IV* (1599-1600).

[4] From "Ode to Fear" by William Collins (1721-1759); we follow here the third edition (1792), in which "claims" was correctly changed into "claim."

[5] Both this and the previous quote are from Milton's *Il Penseroso* (1631).

[6] A character in three of Shakespeare's plays: *Henry IV Part II*, *The Merry Wives of Windsor*, and *Henry V*. He is forced to eat leek in *Henry V*.

[7] Robert-François Damiens, not Damien (1715-1757) was the last person executed in France by drawing and quartering for attempting to assassinate Louis XV. His execution was highly controversial, as he was deemed mentally unstable. The Inquisition's "act of faith" (auto-da-fé), generally an act of public penance, could also consist of torture and even execution by burning.

by a sublime and vigorous imagination. Here, though we know before-hand what to expect, we enter into them with eagerness, in quest of a pleasure already experienced. This is the pleasure constantly attached to the excitement of surprise from new and wonderful objects. A strange and unexpected event awakens the mind, and keeps it on the stretch; and where the agency of invisible beings is introduced, of "forms unseen, and mightier far than we,"[1] our imagination, darting forth, explores with rapture the new world which is laid open to its view, and rejoices in the expansion of its powers. Passion and fancy co-operating elevate the soul to its highest pitch; and the pain of terror is lost in amazement.

Hence the more wild, fanciful, and extraordinary are the circumstances of a scene of horror, the more pleasure we receive from it; and where they are too near common nature, though violently borne by curiosity through the adventure, we cannot repeat it or reflect on it, without an over-balance of pain. In the *Arabian nights* are many most striking examples of the terrible joined with the marvellous: the story of Aladdin, and the travels of Sinbad, are particularly excellent. The *Castle of Otranto* is a very spirited modern attempt upon the same plan of mixed terror, adapted to the model of Gothic romance. The best conceived, and most strongly worked-up scene of mere natural horror that I recollect, is in Smollett's *Ferdinand count Fathom*; where the hero, entertained in a lone house in a forest, finds a corpse just slaughtered in the room where he is sent to sleep, and the door of which is locked upon him. It may be amusing for the reader to compare his feelings upon these, and from thence form his opinion of the justness of my theory. The following fragment, in which both these manners are attempted to be in some degree united, is offered to entertain a solitary winter's evening.

1773

———————————————————————————————
———————————————————————————————

—— After this adventure, Sir Bertrand turned his steed towards the woulds,[2] hoping to cross these dreary moors before the curfew. But ere he had proceeded half his journey, he was bewildered by the different tracks, and not being able, as far as the eye could reach, to espy any object but the brown heath surrounding him, he was at length quite uncertain which way he should direct his course. Night overtook him in this situation. It was one of those nights when the moon gives a faint glimmering of light through the thick black clouds of a lowering sky. Now and then she suddenly emerged in full splendor from her veil; and then instantly retired behind it, having just served to give the forlorn Sir Bertrand a wide extended prospect over the desolate waste. Hope and native courage a while urged him to push forwards, but at length the increasing darkness and fatigue of body and mind overcame him; he dreaded moving from the ground he stood on, for fear of unknown pits and bogs, and alighting from his horse in despair, he threw himself on the ground. He had not long continued in that posture when the sullen toll of a distant bell struck his ears—he started up, and turning towards the sound discerned a dim twinkling light. Instantly he seized his horse's bridle, and with cautious steps advanced towards it. After a painful march he was stopt by a moated ditch surrounding the place from whence the light proceeded; and by a

[1] Aikin paraphrases a passage from Alexander Pope: "She [superstition] taught the weak, the proud to pray,/ To pow'r unseen, and mightier far than they" (*Essay on Man*, 3, 251-252).
[2] The Yorkshire Wolds, region of low hills in north-eastern England.

momentary glimpse of moon-light he had a full view of a large antique mansion, with turrets at the corners, and an ample porch in the centre. The injuries of time were strongly marked on every thing about it. The roof in various places was fallen in, the battlements were half demolished, and the windows broken and dismantled. A draw-bridge, with a ruinous gateway at each end, led to the court before the building—He entered, and instantly the light, which proceeded from a window in one of the turrets, glided along and vanished; at the same moment the moon sunk beneath a black cloud, and the night was darker than ever. All was silent—Sir Bertrand fastened his steed under a shed, and approaching the house traversed its whole front with light and slow footsteps—All was still as death—He looked in at the lower windows, but could not distinguish a single object through the impenetrable gloom. After a short parley with himself, he entered the porch, and seizing a massy iron knocker at the gate, lifted it up, and hesitating, at length struck a loud stroke. The noise resounded through the whole mansion with hollow echoes. All was still again—He repeated the strokes more boldly and louder—another interval of silence ensued—A third time he knocked, and a third time all was still. He then fell back to some distance that he might discern whether any light could be seen in the whole front—It again appeared in the same place and quickly glided away as before—at the same instant a deep sullen toll sounded from the turret. Sir Bertrand's heart made a fearful stop—He was a while motionless; then terror impelled him to make some hasty steps towards his steed—but shame stopt his flight; and urged by honour, and a resistless desire of finishing the adventure, he returned to the porch; and working up his soul to a full steadiness of resolution, he drew forth his sword with one hand, and with the other lifted up the latch of the gate. The heavy door, creaking upon its hinges, reluctantly yielded to his hand—he applied his shoulder to it and forced it open—he quitted it and stept forward—the door instantly shut with a thundering clap. Sir Bertrand's blood was chilled—he turned back to find the door, and it was long ere his trembling hands could seize it—but his utmost strength could not open it again. After several ineffectual attempts, he looked behind him, and beheld, across a hall, upon a large staircase, a pale bluish flame which cast a dismal gleam of light around. He again summoned forth his courage and advanced towards it—It retired. He came to the foot of the stairs, and after a moment's deliberation ascended. He went slowly up, the flame retiring before him, till he came to a wide gallery—The flame proceeded along it, and he followed in silent horror, treading lightly, for the echoes of his footsteps startled him. It led him to the foot of another staircase, and then vanished—At the same instant another toll sounded from the turret—Sir Bertrand felt it strike upon his heart. He was now in total darkness, and with his arms extended, began to ascend the second staircase. A dead cold hand met his left hand and firmly grasped it, drawing him forcibly forwards—he endeavoured to disengage himself, but could not—he made a furious blow with his sword, and instantly a loud shriek pierced his ears, and the dead hand was left powerless in his—He dropt it, and rushed forwards with a desperate valour. The stairs were narrow and winding, and interrupted by frequent breaches, and loose fragments of stone. The stair-case grew narrower and narrower, and at length terminated in a low iron grate. Sir Bertrand pushed it open—it led to an intricate winding passage, just large enough to admit a person upon his hands and knees. A faint glimmering of light served to show the nature of the place. Sir Bertrand entered—A deep hollow groan resounded from a distance through the vault—He went forwards, and proceeding beyond the first turning, he discerned the same blue flame which had before conducted him. He followed it. The vault, at length, suddenly opened into a lofty gallery, in the midst of which a figure appeared, compleatly armed, thrusting forwards the bloody stump of an arm, with a terrible frown and menacing gesture, and brandishing a sword in his hand. Sir Bertrand undauntedly sprung forwards; and aiming a fierce blow at the figure, it instantly vanished, letting fall a massy iron key. The flame now rested upon a pair of ample folding doors at the end of the gallery. Sir Bertrand went up to it, and applied the key to a brazen lock—with difficulty he turned the bolt—instantly the doors flew open, and discovered a large apartment, at the end of which was a coffin rested upon a bier, with a taper burning on each side of it. Along the room on both sides were gigantic statues of black marble, attired in the Moorish habits, and holding enormous sabres in their right hands. Each of them reared his arm, and advanced one leg forwards, as the knight entered; at the same moment the lid of the coffin flew open, and the bell tolled. The flame still glided forwards, and Sir Bertrand resolutely followed, till he arrived within six paces of the coffin. Suddenly, a lady in a shrowd and black veil rose up in it, and stretched out her arms towards him—at the same time the statues clashed their sabres and advanced. Sir Bertrand flew to the lady and clasped her in his arms—she threw up her veil and kissed his lips; and instantly the whole building shook as with an earthquake, and fell asunder with a horrible crash. Sir Bertrand was thrown into a sudden trance, and on recovering, found himself seated on a velvet sofa, in the most magnificent room he had ever seen, lighted with innumerable tapers, in lustres of pure crystal. A sumptuous banquet was set in the middle. The doors opening to soft music, a lady of incomparable beauty, attired with amazing splendor entered, surrounded by a troop of gay nymphs more fair than the Graces—She advanced to the knight, and falling on her knees thanked him as her deliverer. The nymphs placed a garland of laurel upon his head, and the lady led him by the hand to the banquet, and sat beside him. The nymphs placed themselves at the table, and a numerous train of servants entering, served up the feast; delicious music playing all the time. Sir Bertrand could not speak for astonishment— he could only return their honours by courteous looks and gestures. After the banquet was finished, all retired but the lady, who leading back the knight to the sofa, addressed him in these words: —————————— ———————————————————————————————————— ———————————————————————————————————— ———————————————

250

GEORGE COLMAN THE ELDER

A Country Gentleman (1775)

The author: George Colman the Elder (1732-1794) who, in the 1750s and 1760s, had been known for his collaborative work with Bonnell Thornton on publications like *The Connoisseur* and *St James's Chronicle*, became a successful playwright, the manager of the Covent Garden theatre, and then the owner of the Haymarket theatre. He continued writing essays and short fiction until 1785 when he began struggling with a mental illness; until 1789, he had lucid intervals and, during one of these, in 1787, he edited his prose works.

The text: First published in *The London Packet* on 25 October, 1775, as number 5 of his essay-series entitled "The Gentleman." The text here is from Colman's collection *Prose on Several Occasions; Accompanied with Some Pieces in Verse. By George Colman* (London: Printed for T. Cadel, in the Strand, 1787), Vol. I, 196-203. It was introduced by an epigraph from Virgil, "Proximus *huic*, *longo sed* proximus *intervallo*," which Colman translates as "The *next* 'tis true; and yet 'tis clear, / Altho' the *next*, it is not *near*" (the italics belong to the Colman); the literal translation is "next to him, but next by a long interval." It was untitled and, in the "Summary of the Contents," it was identified by a long, explanatory title, ending with the words "Character of a *Country Gentleman*." The story was preceded by a humoristic address to the reader of "The Gentleman" (not included here), explaining the long pause between the fourth essay (published on 7 August) and the fifth.

Further reading: Eugene Richard Page. *George Colman, the Elder: Essayist, Dramatist, and Theatrical Manager, 1732-1794*. New York: Columbia University Press, 1935.

My old schoolfellow and college acquaintance, Sir Jocelyn Hearty, having long importuned me to pass two or three weeks with him in the country, about the beginning of August I set out for his seat, and towards the conclusion of the second day, found myself nearly at the end of my journey. Within two or three miles of the mansion-house, I encountered several horse-men whose seat appeared uncommonly loose and unsteady; some in small parties, hanging over their horses, and seeming in earnest conversation with each other; some galloping furiously after, dropping whips, and hats, and wigs, by the way, and shouting as they past, to denote their good fellowship, and hail their acquaintance. Upon turning into the grounds, which lead directly to the house, my ears were saluted with a loud vocal chorus, which however quickly subsided, but was almost as quickly renewed, and thus rose and fell by turns, till I was arrived at the gate. Entering the hall, I found it strewed with honest rusticks, fast asleep, in their boots and great coats. A saloon on each side of the hall was filled with benches and long tables, at which a jovial company still kept their places, drinking, toasting, and singing.

My friend, it seems, was already retired. An old servant, however, took me under his protection, and provided me with every necessary accommodation till the next morning. About noon I was introduced to Sir Jocelyn, whom I found in his dressing-room, with a bowl before him, containing a composition of milk, nutmeg, and brandy, which he called *a Doctor*. This Doctor is, it seems, always called in on the morrow of these joyous festivities, and though not regular, may boast as numerous a set of patients, and a practice as extensive, as any of the Faculty. After a hearty shake by the hand, and a few other civilities, the Baronet informed me, that he and his friends of yesterday had been getting drunk *according to act of parliament*. Having formerly been a student of the law, I expressed some surprise at not being able to recollect so particular a chapter in the statute book. "It is one of the best of them all, for all that, said Sir Jocelyn: and yet it is but a new law neither, and I had the honour to assist at the passing it. The *Grenville* Bill, my friend![1] Since that Bill past into a law, we dare not give a gill of wine, or a tiff of punch, before the election; but it is fit we should entertain our friends handsomely some time after it is over, that the freeholders may see we do not forget them, and remember us hereafter accordingly." I could not help smiling at so ingenious an exposition of the statute, telling my friend that the soundness of his law put me in mind of Foigard's logick, "if you receive it before-hand it is a bribe; but if you take it afterwards, it is only a gratification."[2]

A few days after, Sir Jocelyn told me, if it was a matter of indifference to me which way I might ride that morning, he should be very glad of my company to a village at about eight miles distance. "But I must quit you at the town's end, says he, for I am engaged to dinner, and on particular business. We have a Meeting of the Justices." The chief business of this meeting, it seems, was to sign Licences for the Publick Houses for the year ensuing. This business was fortunately dispatched before dinner; fortunately, I say, because their Worships shewed themselves so sincerely well inclined to promote the interest of those, whose callings they met to authorise, that it would not have been prudent to postpone an operation for which their very zeal might disqualify them. In short, after a joyous day, Sir Jocelyn rode home rather quicker than he went, and we saw no more of him till the next morning.

In about a week more however he was again called forth to a Turnpike Meeting.[3] Sir Jocelyn, ever ready to accommodate his friends, and serve the Publick, duly attended; but the road under consideration proved so execrable, and so many difficulties occurred concerning the proposals for repairing it, that the Committee sat till midnight, and did not rise till they had debated the matter, like the antient Germans, both drunk and sober.[4]

---

[1] The Grenville Act of 1770, initially for one year, became perpetual in 1774.
[2] Foigard, a character in Farquhar's *The Beaux Stratagem*. The line is paraphrased.
[3] A meeting to decide whether tolls should be collected on a certain road.
[4] According to Tacitus, ancient Germans used to debate a matter when drunk, then decided upon it once sober.

The Races and the Assizes, being each a kind of assembly of the whole country, it was impossible for the Baronet and his family to be absent from either. On two different days of the Races were entered two horses belonging to Sir Jocelyn. Both started, but their fortune was as various as their colours. The first day, his bald-faced grey horse, North, won the odds against the field, carried off the King's Plate, and was victorious; but on the second day his brown horse, Orator, took rust,[1] ran out of the course, and was distanced. Sir Jocelyn and his friends, after the example of the Ancients, celebrated one of these events, and lamented the other, exactly in the same manner. The flowing bowls were crowned again and again in honour of the winner, and the cup of affliction ran over in sorrow for the loser.

At the Assizes, Sir Jocelyn was Foreman of the Grand Jury. So many bills were presented, that the several members of the Inquest, exhausted by their uncommon fatigue, required a more than ordinary recruit.[2] It is no wonder therefore that, having duly dispatched in sober sadness the business of the nation, the honest country gentlemen relaxed their gravity, and converting their solemn assembly to a merry meeting, protracted their sitting after supper till daylight.

An old boon companion of my acquaintance used to say, that getting tipsy was one of the pleasantest things in the world, but that nothing was so irksome and painful than its necessary consequence, getting sober again. This was exactly the case with Sir Jocelyn. The text of every evening was mirth and jollity, but the comment of the morrow-morning was sorrow and sickness. The hunting season commenced some little time before I departed. Every hare and fox that had been killed in the morning, was revived at night, and again run down in full cry. The exercise of the chase was less laborious than the festivity of the evening. Politicks took their turn also. America was floated with lakes of claret, and the blockade of Boston caused many an head-ach.[3] On one of these occasions, seeing my worthy friend in much pain, I could not refrain from a short and affectionate expostulation, regretting that an excellent understanding should be drowned in liquor, and the best of men rendered a martyr to his own hospitality and benevolence. "Ah, my dear friend, said Sir Jocelyn, with his hand pressed upon his temples, you Town Gentlemen imagine that we lead very quiet, idle, lives in the Country: but take my word for it, that it requires a very good estate, and a very good constitution, to support, as one ought to do, the character of a Country Gentleman."

---

[1] To "take rust" was a slang phrase meaning to become restive (of horses).
[2] "Recruit" sometimes meant "a fresh supply, a replenishment."
[3] The Boston Port Act of 1774, Britain's response to the Boston Tea Party, had instituted a blockade of the harbour, which remained closed to all ships.

ELIZABETH GRIFFITH

An Affecting Instance of the Effects of Love (1776)

The author: Elizabeth Griffith (1727-1793) was born in Wales, but grew up in Dublin, where her father was a theatre manager. She became an actress and married Richard Griffith (no relation). Together, they settled in London, where they published the letters of their 5-year courtship, in *A Series of Genuine Letters between Henry and Frances* (1757), the book that established her reputation as a writer. Over the following decades of penury, she published many translations and, encouraged by David Garrick, had several plays produced at the theatres in Drury Lane and Covent Garden. She later wrote novels (*The Delicate Distress* in 1769, *The History of Lady Barton* in 1771, *Story of Lady Juliana Harley* in 1776) and short stories published in *The Westminster Review*, where she assumed the persona of a middle-aged man

called Peter Tardy. She selected several of these stories in 1780 in a collection of *Novelettes*. The success of one of her plays allowed Griffith to purchase a commission in the East India Company for her son, Richard. When he returned wealthy, he bought his parents an estate in Ireland, where they retired.

   The text: First published in *The Westminster Magazine* for September 1776, untitled, but with the running title "An affecting Instance of the Effects of Love." It was soon reproduced in the November issues of *The Weekly Miscellany*, *The London Magazine*, and *The North British Intelligencer*. The following is from *The Westminster Magazine; or the Pantheon of Taste* (London: Printed for T. Wright, in Essex-Street in the Strand, and Sold by J. Bew, N°. 28, Paternoster-Row, 1776), Vol. IV, 462-463.

   Further reading: Dorothy Hughes Eshleman. *Elizabeth Griffith: A Biographical and Critical Study*. Philadelphia: University of Philadelphia Press, 1949.

To the Editor of the Westminster Magazine.
Good Mr. Editor,

   From the obliging attention you have paid to my former slight attempts in the literary way, I have no reason to doubt that you will again be glad to hear from your constant Friend, and annual Correspondent.

   According to the plan mentioned in my last address to you,[1] I set out in the spring on a tour into the West, and having passed the summer in the delightful and hospitable Counties of Somerset and Devon, I am safely

---

[1] Here, the author inserted the following note: "See the Magazine for October 1775, page 521." The reference is to "The Story of Miss Warner," which she selected for her anthology of "novelettes," in which it is signed "by Mrs. Griffith."

returned to my winter-quarters again, near Charing-cross.—This piece of intelligence, you may possibly say, is of small, or rather no consequence, to you or the public; but though I am an old man, and of course inclined both to garrulity and egotism, I should not trouble you with it, if I had not another, more interesting, to counterbalance the insignificance of this.

Well then, Mr. Editor, I have in my late travels seen a Phœnix! or something almost as rare; a being as often mentioned by the Poets as the Arabian bird,[1] and almost as seldom to be found amongst the haunts of men! I have seen a youth who died for love!—If you admit this fact, which I aver from my own personal knowledge, I think you will not be at a loss in what rank of life to place this *rara avis.*[2] His plumage was not of the scarlet dye, no gorget glittered on his gentle breast, nor golden epaulet adorned his shoulder—of course he was not of the military race. The peacock's gaudy tints were none of his; no spangled vest or gay embroidered coat had market him of the anomalous breed ycleped Macaronies.[3]

The linnet's russet brown was all the colour that ever decked his form; yet manly grace and natural elegance appeared in every motion of his limbs; his sun-burnt cheek gave lustre to his dark blue eyes, while they spoke all the language of his heart, and beamed forth sensibility. Such was the figure of our farmer's son, the gentle Richard Wilson.

In a cottage, separated only by a few fields from his father's house, there dwelt a maid of still lower rank than even the humble hero of my tale; her mother was a widow, left with three children, and without support, but what she could procure from her own industry. Richard's humanity at first attached him to this helpless family; he used to till their little garden, and furnish them with every small assistance which his not affluent means afforded.—But as the elder daughter of this lowly hut, the fair Eliza, grew towards womanhood, her opening charms made deep impressions upon Richard's heart, and quickly taught him that

"Pity is allied to Love."[4]

Nature and Fortune often are at strife, and rarely do we find their gifts united in a single object. Their quarrel now seemed risen to the height; Eliza was the subject of contention; and while deprived by one of every good within her power to give, the other lavishly poured forth her store to deck the blooming maid.

I think it is hardly necessary to say, that Eliza's heart soon became sensible of Richard's worth, and that their love was mutual.—The day,

[1] A periphrasis used twice by Shakespeare for the Phoenix: in *Antony and Cleopatra*, Agrippa exclaims "O Antony! O thou Arabian bird!" and in *Cymbeline*, the insidious Iachimo, speaking of Imogen, declares: "If she be furnish'd with a mind so rare,/ She is alone the Arabian bird, and I/ Have lost the wager." One year before, Griffith had published *Morality of Shakespeare's Drama Illustrated*, which includes a chapter dedicated to Imogen.
[2] Latin for "rare bird" (the phrase, used to denote any rare thing, was made famous by Juvenal in one of his satires).
[3] Macaronis were young fashionable men of the 1760s and 1770s, often ridiculed for their tall, powdered wigs, for their affectation and effeminacy.
[4] Although it had become somewhat of a proverb, the line is from an anonymous 1738 poem, "On a Lady playing on the Harpsichord, and singing."

the hour was fixed to make them one; their names had twice been called together in the church, no envious tongue forbidding, when, O sad state of sublunary bliss! Eliza felt the pangs of sickness seize on all her frame, and the most fatal symptoms of the small-pox, that tyrant to beauty, soon appeared. Though he had never had this foul disorder himself, no power could force her faithful Richard from the bed-side, where changed, disfigured, his Eliza lay.—She felt the King of Terror's near approach, and grasping Richard's hand in her's, implored that he would cease to grieve for her, but live to be a comfort to her aged mother. "She shall be mine, my mother (he replied), but I must follow you."

Eliza's spotless soul was fled, ere Richard's speech was ended.—I saw him lead her drooping mother to Eliza's grave, and all the village-youths and damsels mourn her loss, and her cold clay laid decent in the earth.

Each morn and eve was Richard found near his Eliza's grave; nor could Time's lenient power abate his grief; his cheek grew wan, his eyes were dimmed with tears, and he scarce seemed the shadow of himself.

Compassion prompted me to seek the youth, and try to reason down his fruitless grief.—I told him, if he persisted in indulging it, it would destroy his life, and frustrate the promise he had made to her he loved.— He calmly answered in the following words:

"You are mistaken, Sir, I will not die till I have fulfilled my promise; but when that happy hour shall come, no power on earth shall force me to stay longer here.—I thank you for your kindness, but my fate is fixed."

I did not comprehend the meaning of these words; but thought his mind disturbed by constant grief, which I, however, had no doubt but time would conquer.—This happened in the latter end of June, and some days after I went into Devonshire.

On my return to Somersetshire last August, I enquired what was become of Richard. My friend, at whose house I then was, told me, that he had pursued exactly the same course of daily visiting Eliza's grave, till he was become quite emaciated with grief and fasting.

On the second of August Richard became of age, and went that day dressed in his best attire to the next town, where he, in all due form, bequeathed his worldly wealth, his father being dead, to Eliza's mother; he then returned to the sad spot where all his treasure lay, bedewed it with its tears, and within a few days after expired.

If I had a talent for poetry, I should think these lovers, particularly the young man, as proper a subject for an elegant epitaph, as those less unhappy ones, whom Mr. Pope has immortalized from their being killed together by lightning;[1] but as I am not blessed with such talents as his, I shall content myself with sincerely regretting the hapless fate of this amiable pair, and hasten to subscribe myself, Sir,

Your most humble servant,
PETER TARDY.

---

[1] "On two lovers struck dead by lightning" is a short poem by Alexander Pope.

HENRY MACKENZIE
Louisa Venoni (1780)

The author: Henry Mackenzie was born in 1745 in Edinburgh, where he studied law. He wrote three novels: the very successful *The Man of Feeling* (1771), followed by *The Man of the World* (1773) and *Julia de Roubigné* (1776). He joined a literary club in Edinburgh and, with the other members, edited two influential periodicals: *The Mirror* (1779-1780) and *The Lounger* (1785-1787). From 1799 until his death in 1831 he was comptroller of taxes for Scotland, an office that did not allow him much time for writing.

The text: First published in *The Mirror* 108 (20 May 1780) and 109 (23 May 1780), where it was signed "V." Untitled, it was later identified in the volume format of the journal as "Inefficacy of guilty Pleasure to confer Happiness—Story of Louisa Venoni" followed by "Sequel of the Story of Louisa." In *The Works of Henry Mackenzie* published under his supervision in 1807-1808, it was entitled "The Story of Louisa Venoni" (Vol. V, 55-77). The following text is from *The Mirror. A Periodical Paper, Published at Edinburgh in the Years 1779, and 1780. In Three Volumes.* The Fifth Edition, Corrected (London: Printed for W. Strahan, and T. Cadell in the Strand; and W. Creech, at Edinburgh, 1783), Vol. III, 296-278. *The Mirror* ended with number 110, on 27 May 1780. It was introduced by an epigraph from one of William Shenstone's elegies: "Ah, vices! gilded by the rich and gay."

Further reading: Edward W. Pitcher. "On the Conventions of Eighteenth-Century British Short Fiction. Part II: 1760-1785." *Studies in Short Fiction* 12 (1975): 335-336.

If we examine impartially that estimate of pleasure, which the higher ranks of society are apt to form, we shall probably be surprised to find how little there is in it either of natural feeling or real satisfaction. Many a fashionable voluptuary, who has not totally blunted his taste or his judgement, will own, in the intervals of recollection, how often he has suffered from the insipidity, or the pain of his enjoyments; and that, if it were not for the fear of being laughed at, it were sometimes worth while, even on the score of pleasure, to be virtuous.

Sir *Edward* ——, to whom I had the pleasure of being introduced at *Florence*, was a character much beyond that which distinguishes the generality of English travellers of fortune. His story was known to some of his countrymen who then resided in Italy; from one of whom, who could now and then talk of something beside pictures and operas, I had a particular recital of it.

He had been first abroad at an early period of life, soon after the death of his father had left him master of a very large estate, which he

257

had the good fortune to inherit, and all the inclination natural to youth to enjoy. Though always sumptuous, however, and sometimes profuse, he was observed never to be ridiculous in his expences; and, though he was now and then talked of as a man of pleasure and dissipation, he always left behind more instances of beneficence than of irregularity. For that respect and esteem in which his character, amidst all his little errors, was generally held, he was supposed a good deal indebted to the society of a gentleman, who had been his companion at the university, and now attended him rather as a friend than a tutor. This gentleman was, unfortunately, seized at *Marseilles* with a lingering disorder, for which he was under the necessity of taking a sea-voyage, leaving Sir *Edward* to prosecute the remaining part of his intended tour alone.

Descending into one of the valleys of *Piedmont*, where, notwithstanding the ruggedness of the road, Sir *Edward*, with a prejudice natural to his country, preferred the conveyance of an English *hunter*[1] to that of an Italian mule, his horse unluckily made a false step, and fell with his rider to the ground, from which Sir *Edward* was lifted by his servants with scarce any signs of life. They conveyed him on a litter to the nearest house, which happened to be the dwelling of a peasant rather above the common rank, before whose door some of his neighbours were assembled at a scene of rural merriment, when the train of Sir *Edward* brought up their master in the condition I have described. The compassion natural to his situation was excited in all; but the owner of the mansion, whose name was *Venoni*, was particularly moved with it. He applied himself immediately to the care of the stranger, and, with the assistance of his daughter, who had left the dance she was engaged in, with great marks of agitation, soon restored Sir *Edward* to sense and life. *Venoni* possessed some little skill in surgery, and his daughter produced a book of receipts in medicine. Sir *Edward*, after being blooded, was put to bed, and tended with every possible care by his host and his family. A considerable degree of fever was the consequence of his accident; but after some days it abated; and, in little more than a week, he was able to join in the society of *Venoni* and his daughter.

He could not help expressing some surprise at the appearance of refinement in the conversation of the latter, much beyond what her situation seemed likely to confer. Her father accounted for it. She had received her education in the house of a lady, who happened to pass through the valley, and to take shelter in *Venoni*'s cottage (for his house was but a better sort of cottage) the night of her birth. "When her mother died," said he, "the Signora, whose name, at her desire, we had given the child, took her home to her own house; there she was taught many things, of which there is no need here; yet she is not so proud of her learning as to wish to leave her father in his old age; and I hope soon to have her settled near me for life."

[1] A horse used especially in hunting.

But Sir *Edward* had now an opportunity of knowing *Louisa* better than from the description of her father. Music and painting, in both of which arts she was a tolerable proficient, Sir *Edward* had studied with success. *Louisa* felt a sort of pleasure from her drawings, which they had never given her before, when they were praised by Sir *Edward*; and the family-concerts of *Venoni* were very different from what they had formerly been, when once his guest was so far recovered as to be able to join in them. The flute of *Venoni* excelled all the other music of the valley; his daughter's lute was much beyond it; Sir *Edward*'s violin was finer than either. But his conversation with *Louisa*—it was that of a superior order of beings!—science, taste, sentiment!—it was long since *Louisa* had heard these sounds; amidst the ignorance of the valley, it was luxury to hear them; from Sir *Edward*, who was one of the most engaging figures I ever saw, they were doubly delightful. In his countenance, there was always an expression animated and interesting; his sickness had overcome somewhat of the first, but greatly added to the power of the latter.

Louisa's was no less captivating—and Sir *Edward* had not seen it so long without emotion. During his illness, he thought this emotion but gratitude; and, when it first grew warmer, he checked it, from the thought of her situation, and of the debt he owed her. But the struggle was too ineffectual to overcome; and, of consequence, increased his passion. There was but one way in which the pride of Sir *Edward* allowed of its being gratified. He sometimes thought of this as a base and unworthy one; but he was the fool of words which he had often despised, the slave of manners he had often condemned. He at last compromised matters with himself; he resolved, if he could, to think no more of *Louisa*; at any rate, to think no more of the ties of gratitude, or the restraints of virtue.

Louisa, who trusted to both, now communicated to Sir *Edward* an important secret. It was at the close of a piece of music, which they had been playing in the absence of her father. She took up her lute, and touched a little wild melancholy air, which she had composed to the memory of her mother. "That," said she, "nobody ever heard except my father; I play it sometimes when I am alone, and in low spirits. I don't know how I came to think of it now; yet I have some reason to be sad." Sir *Edward* pressed to know the cause; after some hesitation she told it all. Her father had fixed on the son of a neighbour, rich in possessions, but rude in manners, for her husband. Against this match she had always protested as strongly, as a sense of duty, and the mildness of her nature, would allow; but *Venoni* was obstinately bent on the match, and she was wretched from the thoughts of it.—"To marry, where one cannot love,—to marry such a man, Sir *Edward*!"—It was an opportunity beyond his power of resistance. Sir *Edward* pressed her hand; said it would be profanation to think of such a marriage; praised her beauty, extolled her virtues; and concluded, by swearing, that he adored her. She heard him with unsuspecting pleasure, which her blushes could ill conceal.—Sir

Edward improved the favourable moment; talked of the ardency of his passion, the insignificancy of ceremonies and forms, the inefficacy of legal engagements, the eternal duration of those dictated by love; and, in fine, urged her going off with him, to crown both their days with happiness. *Louisa* started at that proposal. She would have reproached him, but her heart was not made for it; she could only weep.

They were interrupted by the arrival of her father with his intended son-in-law. He was just such a man as *Louisa* had represented him, coarse, vulgar, and ignorant. But *Venoni*, tho' much above their neighbour in every thing but riches, looked on him as poorer men often look on the wealthy, and discovered none of his imperfections. He took his daughter aside, told her he had brought her future husband, and that he intended they should be married in a week at farthest.

Next morning *Louisa* was indisposed, and kept her chamber. Sir *Edward* was now perfectly recovered. He was engaged to go out with *Venoni*; but, before his departure, he took up his violin, and touched a few plaintive notes on it. They were heard by *Louisa*.

In the evening she wandered forth to indulge her sorrows alone. She had reached a sequestered spot, where some poplars formed a thicket, on the banks of a little stream that watered the valley. A nightingale was perched on one of them, and had already begun its accustomed song. *Louisa* sat down on a withered stump, leaning her cheek upon her hand. After a little while, the bird was scared from its perch, and flitted from the thicket. *Louisa* rose from the ground, and burst into tears! She turned—and beheld Sir *Edward*. His countenance had much of its former languor; and, when he took her hand, he cast on the earth a melancholy look, and seemed unable to speak his feelings. "Are you not well, Sir *Edward*?" said *Louisa*, with a voice faint and broken.—"I am ill indeed," said he, "but my illness is of the mind. *Louisa* cannot cure me of that. I am wretched; but I deserve to be so. I have broken every law of hospitality, and every obligation of gratitude. I have dared to wish for happiness, and to speak what I wished, though it wounded the heart of my dearest benefactress— but I will make a severe expiation. This moment I leave you, *Louisa*! I go to be wretched; but you may be happy, happy in your duty to a father, happy, it may be, in the arms of a husband, whom the possession of such a wife may teach refinement and sensibility.—I go to my native country, to hurry through scenes of irksome business or tasteless amusement; that I may, if possible, procure a sort of half-oblivion of that happiness which I have left behind, a listless endurance of that life which I once dream'd might be made delightful with *Louisa*."

Tears were the only answer she could give. Sir *Edward*'s servants appeared, with a carriage, ready for his departure. He took from his pocket two pictures; one he had drawn of *Louisa*, he fastened round his neck, and, kissing it with rapture, hid it in his bosom. The other he held out in a hesitating manner. "This," said he, "if *Louisa* will accept of it, may sometimes put her in mind of him who once offended, who can never cease to adore her. She may look on it, perhaps, after the original is no more; when this heart shall have forgot to love, and ceased to be wretched."

Louisa was at last overcome. Her face was first pale as death; then suddenly it was crossed with a crimson blush. "Oh! Sir *Edward!*" said she, "What—what would you have me do!"—He eagerly seized her hand, and led her, reluctant, to the carriage. They entered it, and driving off with furious speed, were soon out of sight of those hills which pastured the flocks of the unfortunate *Venoni*.[1]

The virtue of *Louisa* was vanquished; but her sense of virtue was not overcome.—Neither the vows of eternal fidelity of her seducer, nor the constant and respectful attention which he paid her during a hurried journey to England, could allay that anguish which she suffered at the recollection of her past, and the thoughts of her present situation. Sir *Edward* felt strongly the power of her beauty and of her grief. His heart was not made for that part which, it is probable, he thought it could have performed: it was still subject to remorse, to compassion, and to love. These emotions, perhaps, he might soon have overcome, had they been met by vulgar violence or reproaches; but the quiet and unupbraiding sorrows of *Louisa* nourished those feelings of tenderness and attachment. She never mentioned her wrongs in words: sometimes a few starting tears would speak them; and, when time had given her a little more composure, her lute discoursed melancholy music.

On their arrival in England, Sir *Edward* carried *Louisa* to his seat in the country. There she was treated with all the observance of a wife; and, had she chosen it, might have commanded more than the ordinary splendor of one. But she would not allow the indulgence of Sir *Edward* to blazon with equipage, and show that state which she wished always to hide, and, if possible, to forget. Her books and her music were her only pleasures; if pleasures they could be called, that served but to alleviate misery, and to blunt, for a while, the pangs of contrition.

These were deeply aggravated by the recollection of her father: a father left in his age to feel his own misfortunes and his daughter's disgrace. Sir *Edward* was too generous not to think of providing for *Venoni*. He meant to make some atonement for the injury he had done him, by that cruel bounty which is reparation only to the base, but to the honest is insult. He had not, however, an opportunity of accomplishing his purpose. He learned that *Venoni*, soon after his daughter's elopement, removed from his former place of residence, and, as his neighbours reported, had died in one of the villages of *Savoy*.[2] His daughter felt this with anguish the most poignant, and her affliction, for a while, refused consolation. Sir *Edward's* whole tenderness and attention were called forth to mitigate her grief; and, after its first transports had subsided, he

[1] Here ends the first installment.
[2] Both Savoy (today mostly in France) and Piedmont (in Italy), mentioned earlier, were at the time part of the Kingdom of Sardinia.

carried her to *London*, in hopes that objects new to her, and commonly attractive to all, might contribute to remove it.

With a man possessed of feelings like Sir *Edward*'s, the affliction of *Louisa* gave a certain respect to his attentions. He hired her a house separate from his own, and treated her with all the delicacy of the purest attachment. But his solicitude to comfort and amuse her was not attended with success. She felt all the horrors of that guilt, which she now considered, as not only the ruin of herself, but the murderer of her father.

In *London*, Sir *Edward* found his sister, who had married a man of great fortune and high fashion. He had married her, because she was a fine woman, and admired by fine men; she had married him, because he was the wealthiest of her suitors. They lived, as is common to people in such a situation, necessitous with a princely revenue, and very wretched amidst perpetual gaiety. This scene was so foreign from the idea Sir *Edward* had formed of the reception his country and friends were to afford him, that he found a constant source of disgust in the society of his equals. In their conversation fantastic, not refined, their ideas were frivolous, and their knowledge shallow; and with all the pride of birth, and insolence of station, their principles were mean, and their minds ignoble. In their pretended attachments, he discovered only designs of selfishness; and their pleasures, he experienced, were as fallacious as their friendships. In the society of *Louisa* he found sensibility and truth; hers was the only heart that seemed interested in his welfare: she saw the return of virtue in Sir *Edward*, and felt the friendship which he shewed her. Sometimes, when she perceived him sorrowful, her lute would leave its melancholy for more lively airs, and her countenance assume a gaiety it was not formed to wear. But her heart was breaking with that anguish which her generosity endeavoured to conceal from him; her frame, too delicate for the struggle with her feelings, seemed to yield to their force; her rest forsook her; the colour faded in her cheek, the lustre of her eyes grew dim. Sir *Edward* saw these symptoms of decay with the deepest remorse. Often did he curse those false ideas of pleasure which had led him to consider the ruin of an artless girl, who loved and trusted him, as an object which it was luxury to attain, and pride to accomplish. Often did he wish to blot out from his life a few guilty months, to be again restored to an opportunity of giving happiness to that family, whose unsuspecting kindness he had repaid with the treachery of a robber, and the cruelty of an assassin.

One evening, while he sat in a little parlour with *Louisa*, his mind alternately agitated and softened with this impression, a *hand-organ*,[1] of a remarkably sweet tone, was heard in the street. *Louisa* laid aside her lute and listened: the airs it played were those of her native country; and a few tears, which she endeavoured to hide, stole from her on hearing them. Sir *Edward* ordered a servant to fetch the organist into the room: he was brought in accordingly, and seated at the door of the apartment.

[1] A portable organ, better known today as a hurdy-gurdy.

He played one or two sprightly tunes, to which *Louisa* had often danced in her infancy: she gave herself up to the recollection, and her tears flowed without controul. Suddenly the musician, changing the stop, introduced a little melancholy air of a wild and plaintive kind.—*Louisa* started from her seat, and rushed up to the stranger.—He threw off a tattered coat, and black patch.[1] It was her father!—She would have sprung to embrace him; he turned aside for a few moments, and would not receive her into his arms. But Nature at last overcame his resentment; he burst into tears, and pressed to his bosom his long-lost daughter.

Sir *Edward* stood fixed in astonishment and confusion.—"I come not to upbraid you," said *Venoni*; "I am a poor, weak, old man, unable for upbraidings; I am come but to find my child, to forgive her, and to die! When you saw us first, Sir *Edward*, we were not thus. You found us virtuous and happy; we danced and we sung, and there was not a sad heart in the valley where we dwelt. Yet we left our dancing, our songs, and our cheerfulness; you were distressed, and we pitied you. Since that day the pipe has never been heard in *Venoni*'s fields: grief and sickness have almost brought him to the grave; and his neighbours, who loved and pitied him, have been cheerful no more. Yet, methinks, though you robbed us of happiness, you are not happy;—else why that dejected look, which, amidst all the grandeur around you, I saw you wear, and those tears which, under all the gaudiness of her apparel, I saw that poor deluded girl shed?"—"But she shall shed no more," cried Sir *Edward*; "you shall be happy, and I shall be just. Forgive, my venerable friend, the injuries which I have done thee; forgive me, my *Louisa*, for rating your excellence at a price so mean. I have seen those high-born females to which my rank might have allied me; I am ashamed of their vices, and sick of their follies. Profligate in their hearts, amidst affected purity they are slaves to pleasure, without the sincerity of passion; and, with the name of honour, are insensible to the feelings of virtue. You, my *Louisa*!—but I will not call up recollections that might render me less worthy of your future esteem—Continue to love your *Edward*; but a few hours, and you shall add the title to the affections of a wife; let the care and tenderness of a husband bring back its peace to your mind, and its bloom to your cheek. We will leave for a while the wonder and the envy of the fashionable circle here. We will restore your father to his native home; under that roof I shall once more be happy; happy without allay, because I shall deserve my happiness. Again shall the pipe and the dance gladden the valley, and innocence and peace beam on the cottage of *Venoni*!"

---

[1] Patches were small pieces of material, usually velvet, and of various shapes, worn on the face either for decorative purposes or to conceal blemishes.

LEONARD MCNALLY

Fanny; or, The Fair Foundling of St. George's Fields (1782)

The author: Leonard McNally was born in Dublin in 1752 and studied law in London where, in the early 1780s, he became a playwright, songwriter, and editor of the newspaper *The Public Ledger*. Back to Ireland, he became a member and the official lawyer of the United Irishmen, but, uncomfortable with the radicalism of this organisation, he was, starting with 1794, a spy for the government. His confidential reports were instrumental in quelling the Irish rebellions of 1798 and 1803. His clandestine activities became a cause celebre in Ireland when they were discovered after his death in 1820.

The text: First published anonymously in *The British Magazine and Review; or Universal Miscellany* for July 1782. It was reprinted by other periodicals and, in 1786, it appeared under McNally's name, in *The New Novelist's Magazine* (V, 177-180). The following is from the volume format of *The British Magazine and Review; or Universal Miscellany* (London: Harrison & Co., No. 18, Paternoster-Row, 1782), Vol. I, 35-38.

Further reading: Edward R. Pitcher, "Leonard McNally." *Discoveries in Periodicals, 1720-1820*. Lewiston, NY: Edwin Mellen, 2000. 241-244.

It was in the month of June, at about five in the morning, when the sun having risen considerably above the horizon, his beams emanating from their source, danced over the face of the earth: they wantoned on every object; but, as if attracted by the beauty of Fanny, played and sported about her eyes, till they broke her golden slumber.

Fanny was about ten years old, and lay upon a verdant bank of a green-mantled stagnate pool, in St. George's Fields. Rubbing her eyes as she awoke, and finding herself alone, she set up a horrid shriek; which alarming a clergyman, who was taking his morning walk, he approached the wailing innocent, and enquired into the cause of her sorrow.

"Alas! your honour," said Fanny, sobbing as if her little heart would burst; "my father and my mother have left me, and I have neither house nor home to go to, nor any bread to eat."—Here grief stopped the organs of articulation, by a swell of passion, till Nature kindly opened the sluices of little Fanny's eyes, and calmed the storm by a plenteous shower of tears.

"What can be done with her!" said the honest clergyman to himself, gently rubbing his brow. "What can be done!" said the clergyman— looking towards the left, and taking the Magdalen Hospital[1] in his eye.

[1] The Magdalen Hospital for the Reception of Penitent Prostitutes was founded in 1758. Many more (usually called "asylums") were opened in the following years.

"Alas! if something be not done, the very beauty which should protect her virtue, will lead her to prostitution and ruin!—What can be done!" said the clergyman—looking towards the right. "I have it! I have it!" he exclaimed—at that instant seeing the Asylum for Female Orphans.[1] "Come, my girl," said the good man, taking Fanny by the hand; "you shall have a house and a home, and enough to eat, and enough to drink." And he led her to his lodgings, which were within the rules of the King's Bench.[2]—He had lent his security to a relation in trade; who, failing, was liberated by a commission of bankruptcy, and left his friend to answer an inexorable creditor.

Now the parents of Fanny loved her with as warm and natural an affection, as if she had been a princess royal. Her father was an itinerant tinker, and her mother was remarkable for restoring a vigorous respiration to the worn-out lungs of old bellows; their whole property consisted of a jack-ass, and the implements of their trade.

Unfortunately for this couple, the country they had travelled through for the day preceding their baiting in St. George's Fields,[3] had no culinary utensils out of repair, nor any consumptive bellows wanting wind; so that not having any opportunity to exercise their art, they were reduced to their last penny.

To dispose of this last penny, in procuring a breakfast for Fanny, they had issued to the Borough,[4] and entered a baker's shop. The hot loaves smoaked enticingly; and the mother of Fanny, considering that a pennyworth of bread would scarce give a mouthful to her child, and being impelled by her own hunger, and the hunger which she knew was gnawing the stomach of her husband, slipped a loaf under her cloak.

A pawn-broker on the opposite side of the street saw the transaction— he was a conscientious man, and informed the baker. The baker being rich, was strongly attached to strict justice: and poverty, which was urged in extenuation of the offence by the culprits, was with him an aggravation; it was, in his opinion, the worst of all crimes. The tinker and his wife were dragged before a justice: and the justice—which is not very usual with justices—knowing something of law, discharged the woman, as having committed the theft in company with her husband; but, to please the baker, with whom he kept a long tally, committed the man.

The mob finding the law insufficient to punish the woman, became the instruments of justice; they dragged her through the kennel, pelted her with filth, and plunged her into a ditch. In this deplorable situation she must have immediately perished; if the parish-officers, knowing that the expence of her burial would fall upon their treasury, had not ordered

[1] Opened in 1758, it had the official name of "The Asylum for the Reception of Friendless and Deserted Orphan Girls." Girls accepted there were trained as domestic servants. It was on Westminster Road, in Lambeth, central London.
[2] King's Bench was a prison, especially (though not exclusively) for debtors. Some prisoners were allowed to live conditionally out of its walls. It was located in Southwark, in central London, but south of the River Thames.
[3] Open area between Southwark and Lambeth. "Baiting" here means making a halt on a journey.
[4] The Borough High Street, leading south, ran close to the King's Bench.

her to be taken up, and passed to the parish adjacent—from whence she would have been passed to the next, if she had not given the overseers the slip—by making a sudden escape to that country, "from whose bourne no traveller returns."[1]

The tinker lay in gaol till the next quarter-sessions;[2] when, being fully convicted of stealing a loaf he never touched, he was ordered to be publicly whipped: and not having money to bribe the executioner, he got so severe a scourging, that a fever ensued, which sent him to the other world after his wife.

The jack-ass would have been seized by the justice's men; but some chimney-sweepers having got possession of the wretched animal, while the tinker was under examination, three of them mounted, and rode him till he fell, when they dispatched him with paving-stones.

While the tinker, his wife, and their jack-ass, were under the different preparations for the different fates which awaited them, Fanny was enjoying such ease and happiness as she had never before experienced. The clergyman's wife had her cleaned and cloathed, and she was put into the Asylum.

Here she lived in content and innocence for three years; at the expiration of which time the young wife of an old gentleman took her into her service. Fanny's old master was devoted to his bottle and his evening's club; his wife, to pleasures of another kind: and his absence in pursuit of his favourite amusements, furnished his wife with convenient opportunities to gratify herself in the enjoyment of her's.

When Fanny was about fifteen, a young gentleman, ward to her master, came on a visit from the University of Oxford. He cast an evil eye upon Fanny, and the mistress of Fanny cast an eye an infidelity upon him. Fanny defended her virtue against his attacks, like a heroine: her mistress attacked the virtue of her husband's ward, like an experienced general; and, discovering that his passion for Fanny was the great impediment to the indulgence of her own, she applied to a friend and associate, for advice how to protect the youth and inexperience of Fanny from the powerful attacks of the young Oxonian. This worthy friend of the lady's, was not wholly insensible to the charms of variety. He advised her removal to a private lodging, and offered to take upon himself the task of lecturing her on the temptations of the flesh. This was accordingly executed; and for three days did this zealous reformer paint to Fanny's imagination, in language of the warmest description, the wretched state of those who devote themselves to love. His lectures had their effect upon the mind and constitution of Fanny, but they increased her dislike to his person.

Fanny had been taught to write. She procured a note to be conveyed to her lover; he flew to her on the wings of joy, and the consequences were—such as might naturally be expected.

[1] This passage about death from Hamlet's famous soliloquy had entered popular language.
[2] Courts held four times a year for criminal cases and appeals.

Fanny lived with her lover during his minority, in rather an humble sphere; and an evening's walk, with tea at the Dog and Duck,[1] was among the highest of her amusements. But no sooner did he get into possession of his fortune, than a phaeton was purchased, and Fanny had an elegant chariot for her own particular use. They drove here and there, and every where; till at last her lover, having drove out every thing, was driven into the King's Bench Prison—whither Fanny, NOT being his wife, was permitted to follow him.

Her lover kept reflection at a distance, by a continued course of intoxication; and as he obliged Fanny to participate in his excess, she soon became a proficient in a vice destructive to all, but most to it's female votaries. A young officer, the intimate friend of her lover, having surprized her one day when wine had overpowered her reason, she surrendered to him that fidelity which for three years she had inviolably preserved; and an intrigue commenced, which was pursued with ardour on both sides, till the death of her first lover, which happened about eight months after.

Poor Fanny was now reduced to the efforts of her own genius, to procure her bread. The relations of her deceased lover seized every moveable he had left behind him; her cloaths, which were not very valuable, were the whole of her property; and her second admirer had no inclination to take her under his protection.

Being thus abandoned, she left the prison; took lodgings on Vauxhall road;[2] and, having made up weeds[3] in gratitude to the memory of her lover, they displayed her charms to such advantage, that she soon attracted a considerable train of admirers.

In this situation she remained for some time; till meeting with a misfortune which is the constant attendant on indiscriminate amours, the means of subsistence failed, and she was reduced to the last stage of indigence.

Returning one night into St. George's Fields, where she had repeatedly slept on the ground for want of a lodging, she was apprehended by the constables, and committed to Bridewell as a vagrant; and, being unable to work, repeatedly suffered the usual severities of the place; till, at length, her term of confinement being expired, she was again turned out upon the world, and consigned to all the accumulated horrors of wretchedness, poverty, and disease.

For two days the once beautiful Fanny was without food! Urged by pain and hunger, she took the desperate resolution to end her existence; and was crawling toward the very ditch where the good clergyman had formerly found her—when, on lifting up her eyes, she beheld at some distance her good genius, who was contemplating her miserable appearance.

He approached, and offered her money; and, having no recollection of her, was about to depart—when she mentioned his name, blessed him, and fainted——

[1] A tavern in St George's Fields, close to a famed mineral spring. It closed in 1799.
[2] The road to Vauxhall, still a village in the 18th century, close to Lambeth.
[3] "Weeds" could mean garments in general, but especially mourning apparel.

The clergyman, calling an old woman who was passing by to his assistance, left Fanny in her care, and hasted to procure her some refreshment. She soon revived; and was conveyed to the house of the old woman, who lived near the Halfpenny Hatch,[1] where a physician attended her, and in a few weeks perfectly re-established her health.

The good clergyman had long since quitted the rules of the King's Bench, having settled the debt by an annuity charged on his living; and now possessed a comfortable vicarage in Cornwall, from which place he had arrived in town but a few days before. His first resolution, on seeing Fanny recover, was to take her into the country; but, as his wife was a lady tenacious of domestic prerogatives, he determined, upon second thoughts, not to proceed without consulting her: however, that Fanny might be out of the way of temptation, he procured, in the mean time, her admission into the Magdalen.

In this situation she remained for eighteen months; the clergyman's wife considering that time as a necessary probation. She was here perfectly weaned from every vicious habit: her amiable conduct gained her the good opinion of the matron, who instructed her in the œconomy of house-keeping; and, by her pious conversation, instilled into her heart, the principles of morality, and the necessity of a virtuous life.

At the end of eighteen months, the clergyman being again in town, paid her a visit, accompanied by his lady. This worthy gentleman was delighted at the excellent character given her by the matron; nor was his wife less pleased with the account of her behaviour. They took her with them into the country; where she was soon after addressed by a young wealthy farmer, who solicited the interest of her protector in his favour. The good clergyman, disdaining every species of deception, frankly acquainted the honest farmer, in general terms, with so much of Fanny's story as related to her first seduction. This intelligence alarmed the young man's delicacy; but love soon prevailing, he made a formal declaration of his passion, and being favourably received, was in a short time married to her.

Fanny has proved a blessing to her husband: her industry had added to his fortune; and her modest, humble, and conscious deportment, has endeared her to his affections. The births of three little ones have added to their felicity; and as Fanny's worthy protector has no children, nor any relations whom he regards, and has been used to fondle the offspring of Fanny as if they were his own, it is not improbable but he will make the eldest, who is his favourite, the heir of his property; which, as he lives much within his income, may one day be very considerable.

---

[1] A thoroughfare in Lambeth, leading to Westminster Bridge. Here, Philip Astley had recently built the first modern circus.

HORACE WALPOLE
The King and His Three Daughters (1785)

The author: Horace Walpole (1717-1797) was the son of Sir Robert Walpole, 1st Earl of Orford, head of the British government between 1721 and 1742. Educated at Eton and then King's College, Cambridge, Walpole set on a Grand Tour of France and Italy (1739-1741), after which he was elected to Parliament and took his seat in the House of Commons (1742). In 1748, he bought an estate in Twickenham (southwest London), where he built the gothic Strawberry Hill manor. After poems, pamphlets, and contributions to *The World*, he began the mature phase of his literary career in 1762 with the first two volumes of *Anecdotes of Painting in England*. In 1764 he published *The Castle of Otranto*, generally regarded as the first Gothic novel. He then turned his attention to history, gardening, and his memoirs, but found the time to write a few "hieroglyphic tales," which were published privately in 1785 and came to the attention of a larger public after his death.

    The text: First published in a small run of six copies at Walpole's own printing press at Strawberry Hill in 1785 (some time between 27 September and 5 November). On his own proof copy (possibly the seventh), preserved at the Lewis Walpole Library, Horace Walpole dated the first tale (31 August 1766), the third (July 1771) and the fourth (23 December 1771). He also identified "The King and His Three Daughters" as "A Sensible Story," but he later crossed out this subtitle. It was not republished until 1798, when Mary Berry edited the collected works of Walpole and explained that "lord Orford always intended them for publication after his death" (I, xii). The following is from *The Works of Horatio Walpole, Earl of Orford. In Five Volumes* (London: G.G. and J. Robinson, Paternoster-Row, and J. Edwards, Pall-Mall, 1798), Vol. IV, 330-333. The "Hieroglyphic Tales" came with the following Postscript, probably written in 1785: "The foregoing Tales are given for no more than they are worth: they are mere whimsical trifles, written chiefly for private entertainment; and for private amusement half a dozen copies only are printed. They deserve at most to be considered as an attempt to vary the stale and beaten class of stories and novels, which, though works of invention, are almost always devoid of imagination. It would scarcely be credited, were it not evident from the Bibliotheque des Romans,[1] which contains the fictitious adventures that have been written in all ages and all countries, that there should have been so little fancy, so little variety, and so little novelty, in writings in which the imagination is fettered by no rules, and by no obligation of speaking truth. There is infinitely more invention in history, which has no merit if devoid of truth, than in romances and novels, which pretend to none" (352). "The King and His Three Daughters" is the original title; it was also super-titled "Tale II" in the cycle. In an unsigned review of Walpole's *Works*, published in the *Monthly Review* of October 1798, Charles Burney (1726-1814), a friend of the author, suggested that the tale, "if it means any thing, is a ridicule on the marriage of Princess Mary with the Prince of Orange—on Princess Anne—and on the Revolution of 1688" (182).

---

[1] *Bibliothèque universelle des romans* was a collection of novels published periodically in France (224 volumes appeared between 1775 and 1789), founded by two aristocrats, the Marquis de Paulmy (1722-1787) and the Count of Tressan (1705-1783). It included many translations of English novels.

Further reading: Laura Badot, "A Voyage of Undiscovery: Deciphering Horace Walpole's *Hieroglyphic Tales*." *1650-1850: Ideas, Aesthetics, and Inquiries in the Early Modern Era* 16 (summer 2009).

[Burney, Charles.] "The Works of the Earl of Orford." *The Monthly Review; or Literary Journal, Enlarged* (London: R. Griffiths, 1798), Vol. XXVII (From September to December, inclusive), 171-189. [This is the third of four instalments of the review.]

Jan Herman, "Les *Contes hiéroglyphiques* de Horace Walpole et la question du 'Nonsense,'" *Féeries: Etudes sur le conte merveilleux XVIIe-XIXe siècle* 5: *Le Rire des contours* (2008), 93-114.

There was formerly a king, who had three daughters—that is, he would have had three, if he had had one more—but some how or other the eldest never was born. She was extremely handsome, had a great deal of wit, and spoke French in perfection, as all the authors of that age affirm, and yet none of them pretend that she ever existed. It is very certain that the two other princesses were far from beauties; the second had a strong Yorkshire dialect, and the youngest had bad teeth and but one leg, which occasioned her dancing very ill.

As it was not probable that his majesty would have any more children, being eighty-seven years two months and thirteen days old when his queen died, the states of the kingdom were very anxious to have the princesses married. But there was one great obstacle to this settlement, though so important to the peace of the kingdom. The king insisted that his eldest daughter should be married first; and as there was no such person, it was very difficult to fix upon a proper husband for her. The courtiers all approved his majesty's resolution; but, as under the best princes there will always be a number of discontented, the nation was torn into different factions, the grumblers or patriots insisting that the second princess was the eldest, and ought to be declared heiress apparent to the crown. Many pamphlets were written pro and con; but the ministerial party pretended that the chancellor's argument was unanswerable, who affirmed, that the second princess could not be the eldest, as no princess-royal ever had a Yorkshire accent. A few persons who were attached to the youngest princess took advantage of this plea for whispering that *her* royal highness's pretensions to the crown were the best of all; for, as there was no eldest princess, and as the second must be the first if there was no first, and as she could not be the second if she was the first, and as the chancellor had proved that she could not be the first, it followed plainly by every idea of law that she could be nobody at all; and then the consequence followed of course, that the youngest must be the eldest, if she had no elder sister.

It is inconceivable what animosities and mischiefs arose from these different titles; and each faction endeavoured to strengthen itself by foreign alliances. The court party, having no real object for their attachment, were the most attached of all, and made up by warmth for the want of foundation in their principles. The clergy in general were devoted to this, which was styled *the first party*. The physicians embraced

270

the second; and the lawyers declared for the third, or the faction of the youngest princess, because it seemed best calculated to admit of doubts and endless litigation.

While the nation was in this distracted situation, there arrived the prince of Quifferiquimini, who would have been the most accomplished hero of the age, if he had not been dead, and had spoken any language but the Egyptian, and had not had three legs. Notwithstanding these blemishes, the eyes of the whole nation were immediately turned upon him, and each party wished to see him married to the princess whose cause they espoused.

The old king received him with the most distinguished honours; the senate made the most fulsome addresses to him; the princesses were so taken with him, that they grew more bitter enemies than ever; and the court ladies and petit-maîtres[1] invented a thousand new fashions upon his account—Every thing was to be à la Quifferiquimi. Both men and women of fashion left off rouge, to look the more cadaverous; their clothes were embroidered with hieroglyphics, and all the ugly characters they could gather from Egyptian antiquities, with which they were forced to be contented, it being impossible to learn a language that is lost; and all tables, chairs, stools, cabinets and couches were made with only three legs: the last, however, soon went out of fashion, as being very inconvenient.

The prince, who, ever since his death, had had but a weakly constitution, was a little fatigued with this excess of attentions, and would often wish himself at home in his coffin. But his greatest difficulty of all was to get rid of the youngest princess, who kept hopping after him wherever he went, and was so full of admiration of his three legs, and so modest about having but one herself, and so inquisitive to know how his three legs were set on, that, being the best-natured man in the world, it went to his heart whenever in a fit of peevishness he happened to drop an impatient word, which never failed to throw her into an agony of tears; and then she looked so ugly that it was impossible for him to be tolerably civil to her. He was not much more inclined to the second princess—In truth, it was the eldest who made the conquest of his affections: and so violently did his passion increase one Tuesday morning, that, breaking through all prudential considerations (for there were many reasons which ought to have determined his choice in favour of either of the other sisters), he hurried to the old king, acquainted him with his love, and demanded the eldest princess in marriage. Nothing could equal the joy of the good old monarch, who wished for nothing but to live to see the consummation of this match. Throwing his arms about the prince skeleton's neck, and watering his hollow cheeks with warm tears, he granted his request, and added, that he would immediately resign his crown to him and his favourite daughter.

I am forced for want of room to pass over many circumstances that would add greatly to the beauty of this history, and am sorry I must dash

---

[1] Dandies, fops.

the reader's impatience by acquainting him, that notwithstanding the eagerness of the old king and youthful ardour of the prince, the nuptials were obliged to be postponed; the archbishop declaring that it was essentially necessary to have a dispensation from the pope, the parties being related within the forbidden degrees; a woman that never was, and a man that had been, being deemed first cousins in the eye of the canon law.

Hence arose a new difficulty. The religion of the Quifferiquiminians was totally opposite to that of the papists. The former believed in nothing but grace; and they had a high-priest of their own, who pretended that he was master of the whole fee-simple[1] of grace, and by that possession could cause every thing to have been that never had been, and could prevent every thing that had been from ever having been. "We have nothing to do," said the prince to the king, "but to send a solemn embassy to the high-priest of grace, with a present of a hundred thousand million of ingots, and he will cause your charming no-daughter to have been, and will prevent my having died, and then there will be no occasion for a dispensation from your old fool at Rome."—How! thou impious, atheistical bag of drybones, cried the old king; dost thou profane our holy religion? Thou shalt have no daughter of mine, thou three-legged skeleton—Go and be buried and be damned, as thou must be; for, as thou art dead, thou art past repentance: I would sooner give my child to a baboon, who has one leg more than thou hast, than bestow her on such a reprobate corpse.—You had better give your one-legged infanta to the baboon, said the prince; they are fitter for one another. As much a corpse as I am, I am preferable to nobody; and who the devil would have married your no-daughter, but a dead body? For my religion, I lived and died in it, and it is not in my power to change it now if I would.—But for your part—A great shout interrupted this dialogue; and the captain of the guard, rushing into the royal closet, acquainted his majesty, that the second princess, in revenge of the prince's neglect, had given her hand to a drysalter, who was a common-councilman;[2] and that the city, in consideration of the match, had proclaimed them king and queen, allowing his majesty to retain the title for his life, which they had fixed for the term of six months; and ordering, in respect of his royal birth, that the prince should immediately lie in state and have a pompous funeral.

This revolution was so sudden and so universal, that all parties approved, or were forced to seem to approve it. The old king died the next day, as the courtiers said, for joy; the prince of Quifferiquimini was buried in spite of his appeal to the law of nations; and the youngest princess went distracted, and was shut up in a madhouse, calling out day and night for a husband with three legs.

[1] That is, he held in absolute possession.
[2] A drysalter was a dealer in chemical products, but also more specifically in the preservation of meats and vegetables. A common-councilman was a member of the administrative body of a corporate town (possessing municipal rights, and acting by means of a corporation, such as London was).

ALEXANDER FRASER TYTLER

A Letter from John Truman (1785)

The author: Alexander Fraser Tytler (1747-1813) was born and died in Edinburgh. He was a professor of history at the University of Edinburgh and Judge Advocate of Scotland. He wrote poetry and befriended Robert Burns; he translated poetry and drama from Italian and German; and he wrote a celebrated *Essay on the Principles of Translation* (1791). He published several volumes of history, and his last (posthumous) book was an analysis of the political state of India.

The text: First published untitled in *The Lounger* 44 (3 December 1785). When the newspaper was subsequently published as a volume, it appeared in the table of contents with the title "Narrative of the happiness of a virtuous and benevolent East Indian; in a letter from JOHN TRUMAN." The following is from the volume format of *The Lounger. A Periodical Paper, Published at Edinburgh in the Years 1785 and 1786. In Three Volumes*. Fourth Edition (London: Printed for A. Strahan, and T. Cadell in the Strand; and W. Creech, at Edinburgh, 1788), Vol. II, 70-80. The conclusion was written by Henry Mackenzie.

Further reading: Nandini Bhattaharya. *Reading the Splendid Body: Gender and Consumerism in Eighteenth-Century British Writing on India*. Newark: University of Delaware Press, 1998. 92-94.

Renu Juneja. "The Native and the Nabob: Representations of the Indian Experience in Eighteenth-Century English Literature." *The Journal of Commonwealth Literature* 27.1 (1992): 183-198.

To the LOUNGER.

SIR,

I have observed, that the greatest part of your correspondents have given you a detail of grievances and complaints. In disclosing their misfortunes, they have no doubt conveyed to your readers some useful lessons, for avoiding those errors of conduct which in general have been the cause of them: But the picture of happiness may often prove as instructive as that of calamity or distress; and, in that view, while I gratify my own feelings by the following narrative, I flatter myself it may not be unprofitable to others.

My father, Sir, inherited an estate in one of the northern counties

273

of this kingdom,[1] a property once considerable, and which had been in his family for some generations; but which, during his life and that of my grandfather, had, from a certain easiness of temper bordering upon improvidence, and their humane endeavours to assist their needy relations, been so greatly reduced, that at my father's death it was necessary to bring the estate to sale for the payment of his debts. A trifling reversion[2] remained for the support of my mother, myself, and an only sister; and with this slender provision we betook ourselves to a small farm-house, which my mother rented from the new possessor of our paternal lands. Here, by her uncommon industry, and the exertions of a spirit superior to her misfortunes, she maintained her little household decently and respectably, while she gained the esteem and admiration of the whole neighbourhood. My sister, who was some years younger than myself, was accustomed almost from infancy to bear her part in the management of the family. My mother had taught us reading, writing, and the first rudiments of arithmetic; and the clergyman of the parish was at pains to instruct me in the elements of the Greek and Latin languages, of which, in a few years, I obtained a competent knowledge. This worthy man, whose name was *Johnson*, had been the friend and companion of my father from their earliest infancy, and thus considered himself as bound by duty to be a guardian and parent to his children. He had himself an only daughter, of equal age with my sister, and whom, in those days of childhood and innocence, I regarded alike with the affection of a brother. But on this first period of my life, though the recollection is delightful, I forbear to enlarge.

I had now attained my fifteenth year, and it became necessary to think of some profession by which I might make my way in the world. My inclination led me to the study of medicine, which I had prosecuted for some time with great assiduity, when a near relation of my mother's, who warmly interested himself in our welfare, procured for me the commission of a surgeon's mate on board an Indiaman.[3] The ship to which I belonged was to sail within a fortnight after I received intelligence of my appointment. My mother prepared for me a stock of linens, and other necessaries, to which she added a purse with fifteen guineas. The worthy Mr. Johnson gave me a pocket-bible, with his blessing. My sister, and his daughter *Emmy*, gave me their tears; for that was all they had to bestow: But from the tears of the latter I felt an emotion of tenderness beyond what even the affection of a brother could produce. I had unconsciously nourished an attachment of which this parting first taught me the force, but which, at the same time, it obliged me to stifle and conceal.

After a voyage of six months, our ship arrived in the Ganges. During my stay at Calcutta, I was fortunate enough to recommend myself to a

---

[1] That is, in Scotland, sometimes called "North Britain" in the 18th century.
[2] A sum payable upon a person's death; a life insurance payment.
[3] A ship involved in trade with India, sailing under the auspices of the East India Company. The surgeon's mate was the lowest officer rank on board. He was paid 70 pounds a year.

countryman of my own, then high in the council; by whose interest, with my Captain's leave, I obtained an appointment of surgeon to a small settlement of the Company's, which bordered on the territory of the Nabob of ——. Various, Sir, are the methods of acquiring wealth in India. Of these the obvious and apparent are so well known, that they need not be mentioned: The more mysterious courses to affluence, as I never was solicitous myself to unravel, so I am not well qualified to explain. It is enough for me to say, that, with a good conscience, and during a twelve years exercise of a profession serviceable to my fellow-creatures, I acquired what to me appeared a competency.[1] In short, Sir, being now possessed of a fortune of 25,000 *l*. I began to think of returning to my native country. I had, from time to time, during the last years of my stay in India, remitted such sums to my mother as I judged might enable her to exchange her toilsome and parsimonious mode of life for ease and comfort; but she wrote to me, that industry was now become familiar, and even agreeable, that she could not relish the bread of idleness, and that it was sufficient happiness for her and for my sister to be assured of my health and prosperity. By the last opportunity that preceded my leaving India, I had acquainted my mother of my intention of returning home in the following spring. This intention I put in execution; and bringing with me the best part of my fortune, landed in safety on the coast of Britain, after an absence of thirteen years and a half.

A few days travelling brought me once more to the spot of my nativity. I stopped in the afternoon within a few miles of the place, and wrote the following billet:

"Jack Truman sends the bearer, his servant, to acquaint his dearest mother and sister, that he is within a day's journey of Brookland farm, and proposes, by God's blessing, to be with them this evening."

This note was meant to give them time to prepare for our meeting; but I had not patience to wait my man's return, and set out a few minutes after him. I need not describe the emotions I felt at sight of my native fields, the recollection of which, distance of place and length of time had rather endeared than impaired. I had little leisure to indulge the remembrance: My mother and sister, equally impatient with myself, had come out to watch the road by which I was to arrive. Our meeting was such as might be expected from affection, heightened by the anxieties of absence; our joy, such as prosperity can give to those to whom prosperity has not always been known, to those whom prosperity enables to make others happy.

You will easily figure, Sir, those topics, which, after so long an absence, would naturally be the subject of our conversation. One of the first enquiries I made was about the worthy Mr. Johnson and his amiable daughter. My mother informed me that this good man was then in the last stage of a painful disease, under which he had languished above three years, and which his constitution could not thus long have resisted but

---

[1] Sufficiency (of fortune).

for the tender care and dutiful attention of his daughter Emmy; but this affectionate child had, as was thought from that motive alone, rejected several advantageous offers of marriage. To this my sister added, that she was one of the loveliest and most accomplished of women.

On my way to the farm, I had remarked the ruinous appearance of the mansion-house, which had been the seat of my forefathers. My mother informed me, that the gentleman who purchased the estate from our family had been some years dead; and that his son, by a course of extravagance, had so embarrassed his fortune, that it was thought he would soon be obliged to sell the greatest part of his landed property. An opportunity thus presenting itself of recovering my paternal estate, I determined to offer immediately to become the purchaser, and flattered myself with the prospect (I hope it was an honest pride) of re-establishing our ancient family in the domain of their ancestors.

The first visit I paid to Mr. Johnson led me to form schemes of a nature yet more delightful to my imagination. Long absence, and the bustle of an active life, had lulled asleep without extinguishing that affection with which his lovely daughter had inspired me in my early years. The sight of the beautiful Emma revived that passion in its utmost force, and convinced me that she was the arbitress of my future happiness or misery. I thought I perceived in the tender confusion, the diffidence and modesty of her demeanor, and in the simplicity of a heart untaught to disguise its emotions, that I was far from being indifferent to her; nor was I deceived in this flattering idea. Her father's dissolution was fast approaching. He survived my return but a few months; and the last act of his public duty was the union of our hands.

Five years have elapsed since that event; and I hope, Sir, you will not think my narrative tedious, if I give a short sketch of the manner in which I have passed that happy period.

The transaction for the purchase of our estate was attended with very little difficulty; and the restoration of the family to its ancient territories was celebrated by all the tenants and cottagers with high festivity, and every mark of heart-felt satisfaction. I began immediately to repair the desolated mansion-house; and having myself some taste in architecture, contrived to render it a most commodious habitation, without injuring the antiquity of its appearance, which I venerated. The apartments were repaired in the modern fashion; and the elegance of my Emma's taste displayed itself in their furniture and decorations. In a few particulars I indulged perhaps a little caprice. The wide-extended chimney of the hall, which its late proprietor had contracted to the modern scale, and decorated with Dutch porcelain, I enlarged once more to its original dimensions. It was a venerable monument of ancient hospitality. My grandfather's oaken chair was found mouldering in a garret. It was restored to its place. The top of a square tower I fitted up into a library, lighted by a large Gothic window with leaden casements, from whence by day I command a beautiful landscape of the country, and by night

1785

can explore the heavens with my telescope; and here in my favourite studies of philosophy, general physics, and classical literature, of which I have a pretty numerous collection of the best authors, I pass many delightful hours. In another part of the building I have a small laboratory for chymical experiments, and the composition of medicines. Those researches to which I was formerly led by my profession, still furnish me with an amusing, and even an useful employment; for while Providence blesses me with health, I will always be the poor man's physician.

As I am rather unwilling to occupy myself with practical husbandry, a science which without a peculiar bent and inclination I have always thought was not rashly to be engaged in, I limit my rustic employments to planting and gardening. The fields which surround my house owe their principal beauties to nature. The upland and barren spots I have covered with wood, which in a few years will afford both beauty and shelter. Assisted by my Emma's judgment, I have laid out a large garden, which promises soon to furnish me with a profusion of the most delicate fruits. A fine trouting stream washes its border. My hills pasture my mutton, and supply my game; of which the first is excellent, and the last is plentiful.

Soon after our establishment at the mansion-house, my mother and sister quitted their habitation, and became members of our family. The farm, which had become a very profitable subject, has been transferred to an old domestic, who had remained attached to the family in all the changes of its fortune, and who merited that reward of his services and fidelity. My mother, whose active mind would languish if deprived of an object of exertion, has now found another occupation not less suited to her taste, and yet more pleasing in its nature. My Emma has brought me three children; two charming girls, and a stout healthy boy. These she has suckled herself, a part of the duty of a mother which she finds too agreeable to be relinquished to a hireling. The two eldest are now in charge to their grandmother, who has undertaken for them the same office she performed to myself; and in this the good woman flatters herself with a renewal of her years. My sister was wont for some time to share in the same occupation; but I don't know how, her disposition seems a good deal changed of late. In place of her work, she has taken to reading poetry; and borrows a good deal of time from her cares of the dairy, to bestow it on her books and her toilet. It is true, my neighbour *Hearty*'s son Tom is a scholar, and when he comes here with his family (and they are very frequent visitors of ours), my sister and he seem very solicitous to please each other; a circumstance I am not at all sorry to observe. Tom is a very worthy young man, and my sister an excellent girl: She has one quality to which Tom is a stranger; I have taken care that she shall be entitled to 1500 *l.* on the day of her marriage.

Such, Mr. Lounger, is my manner of life; and as I perceive from some of your late papers, that you can contrive to pass a few weeks in the country, without discontinuing to amuse the town, if you will do me the honour of a visit, I promise you the best bed in my house, a bottle of my

best wine, and the best welcome I can give. I am, Sir, yours, &c.
  JOHN TRUMAN.

I am aware that people are apt to be fastidious in the perusal of tales of happiness; but feeling an interest in the good family whose story is told in the foregoing letter, I have ventured to insert it, simple as it is, and not perhaps leading to any important conclusion. One lesson, however, it may serve to inculcate, that moderation in point of wealth, is productive of the greatest comfort and the purest felicity. Had Mr. Truman returned from India with the enormous fortune of some other Asiatic adventurers, he would probably have been much less happy than he is, even without considering the means by which it is possible such a fortune might have been acquired. In the possession of such overgrown wealth, however attained, there is generally more ostentation than pleasure; more pride than enjoyment: I can but guess at the feelings which accompany it, when reaped from desolated provinces, when covered with the blood of slaughtered myriads.

NATHAN DRAKE
Agnes Felton (1790)

The author: Nathan Drake (1766-1836) was born in Yorkshire and graduated M.D. from the University of Edinburgh in 1789. From 1792 until his death he practised medicine in Hadley, Suffolk. He published several volumes of essays and emerged as a leading expert on Shakespeare, his *Shakespeare and His Times* (1817) being translated in French and German. He wrote pre-Romantic poems and gothic tales; he was also one of the many who, around the turn of the 19th century, edited the periodical literature of the last hundred years (in *The Gleaner*, published in 1811, he even selected essays and stories from the minor magazines, usually avoided by the other editors).

The text: It was first published, untitled, in Nathan Drake and Edward Ash's *The Speculator* 23 (Saturday, 12 June 1790). It was later revised and reprinted in Drake's *Literary Hours or Sketches Critical and Narrative* (Sudbury: Printed by J. Burkitt, and sold by T. Cadell, Junior, and W. Davies, Strand, London, 1798) and in its subsequent editions, which appeared in two, three, and finally in four volumes. The following is from the book's first edition (517-526), in which it is identified both as the last of the "literary hours" ("Number XXX") and, in the Contents, as "Agnes Felton, a Tale."

Oh! come, my Fair-one; I have thatch'd above,
And whiten'd all around my little cot,
I've shorn the hedges leading to the grove,
Nor is the seat and willow bower forgot.
                    DOWNMAN.[1]

During the latter end of the summer of —— I made an excursion to the lakes of Cumberland and Westmoreland,[2] and fond of the wild and daring features of nature, I here met all that could gratify the eye of the painter, or the imagination of the poet. Many too were the scenes whose exquisite beauty and softness, whose charm of contrast and calm sweetness of expression, suggested the delightful, but, too often, visionary ideas of rural happiness and elegant simplicity.

---

[1] This stanza, from a relatively well-known (at the time) elegy (first published in 1768) by Hugh Downman (1740-1809), a fellow physician, is meant to be part of the text rather than just an epigraph. In the original magazine version, the story had a different epigraph, from the Latin poet Tibullus: "For treasur'd wealth, for stores of golden wheat,/ The hoard of frugal fires, I'll never call;/ A little farm be mine, a cottage neat/ And wonted couch, where balmy sleep may fall."
[2] Historic counties in Northwest England (Cumbria), which included the famous Lake District.

Whilst thus employed, my mind teeming with each romantic thought which the country around me, a peculiar cast of study, which youth and inexperience had planted there, an incident occurred, that even now, when time hath almost paled the vivid colouring of fancy, I recollect not but with renovated enthusiasm.

The red rays of the sun gleamed strong on the heights of Helvellyn, as I passed by its foot, on my road to Ambleside, and evening, with all her lovely tints, had stolen upon me by the time I reached the chapel of Wiborn.[1] Oppressed by the heat of the day, the coolness of the present hour became remarkably refreshing, and, riding gently on, I arrived at the margin of Grasmere water. Nothing can exceed the beauty of this charming lake diffused amid the bosom of the mountains, its banks exhibit the utmost variety of rock and turf, and are scooped into a number of little bays, while on a promontory which rushes far into the water, and at an inconsiderable height above the surface, stands the village of Grasmere, its parish church rising conspicuous in the centre.[2] A large quantity of fine old wood clothes the sides of the mountain, and here and there a cottage is discovered embosomed in the foliage. The verdure of the meadows, the grouping of the cattle, and the hanging shrubs which climb along the rugged projections of the crag, still further heighten this delicious Paradise. I walked for some time along the borders of the lake, wrapt in the contemplation of beauties to which even the pencil of Ruisdale[3] could not do justice. The sombre shades of evening were now fast approaching, the setting sun smiled with a farewel lustre on the summits of the hills, and the water, still as death, received a deep gloom from the lengthening shadows of the mountains. I sat myself down upon the roots of an old tree near the edge of the lake, and was listening to the distant murmur of some water falls, when suddenly the sound of village bells diverted my attention; no, never shall I forget their sweet and dying cadence, how softly they stole along the lake, now bursting loud and louder on the ear, and now faintly sinking to repose: they were in unison with the scene around and with my feelings—no, never shall I forget them.

> ————Wherever I have heard
> A kindred melody, the scene recurs
> And with it all its pleasures.——
> COWPER.[4]

[1] Helvellyn is a mountain in the Lake District, soon to be made famous by the Romantics; the chapel is close to Thirlmere (also called Wiborn or Wyburn), a lake (today reservoir) next to Helvellyn. Ambleside is the closest town.
[2] Both the lake and village are today associated with William Wordsworth, who lived in the vicinity for almost two decades.
[3] There are four Dutch landscape painters of this name, the best known of whom is Jacob van Ruisdael (c. 1629-1682).
[4] From Book VI of the poem *The Task* from 1785, by William Cowper (1731-1800), regarded as the greatest British poet of the decades before Romanticism. Drake wrote elsewhere that *The Task* "carried the reputation of its author to an unprecedented height in modern English poetry." The missing words in the last line (where there should not be a full stop yet) are "and its pains."

The night closed in ere I could tear myself away from this bewitching scenery, and my desire of once more enjoying it was so great, that I determined to sleep within the village and postpone for a day any farther progress towards Ambleside. The succeeding morning was excessively hot, but, as the evening began to approach, Nature again assumed her mellow colouring, and again the same delightful coolness regaled my languid senses. I traversed the edge of the water, and, having dwelt upon the scenes I had viewed with so much pleasure the night before, I entered the wood, which, climbing half way up the mountain's side, faces the village. The path ran in an oblique direction, gently winding up the hill; it was soft as moss, and of a vivid green, and through many little openings in the wood, the crags, the village, and the lake, were seen to great advantage. I had not proceeded far before a neat cottage, built on a little level, on the side of the hill, attracted my notice. There was an air of taste and simplicity in every thing around it, which highly excited my curiosity in regard to the inhabitants, of whom, from the scene before me, I conceived something extraordinary. It was placed in that situation, which, of all others, is the most pictoresque, that is, its point of elevation was not too great for the landscape. From the bottom of a small lawn which spread before it, the wood gradually fell to the margin of the water, and a number of gigantic oaks covered the hill behind it nearly to the summit, a broken line of moss-hung crag, however, still peeping beyond. Against the front of this cottage grew an old woodbine, whose branches, mingling with each other, crept round four neat sashed windows[1] that glowed as fire from the reflection of the sun. While I stood silently admiring the beauty of the scene, the door of the cottage was opened, and a young woman, clothed with elegant but artless taste, stepped out upon the green; on her arm there leant a man of a very interesting figure, and rather stricken in years, and who, after looking around him with an air of satisfaction, smiled with ineffable sweetness on his fair companion.

The landscape, however diversified, however pictoresque, is, unless animated by human figures, far from complete. The mind is soon satisfied with the view of rock, of wood and water, but if the peasant, the shepherd, or the fisherman be seen, or, if still more engaging, a group of figures be thrown into some important action, the heart as well as the imagination is affected, and a new sensation of exquisite delight, and scarce admitting of satiety, fills and dilates the bosom. Thus was I situated; and thus, having gratified my fancy with the scenery around, was about to return to the village, but no sooner did the two figures, I have just mentioned, appear before me, than my best and sweetest feelings were instantly occupied; the country assumed a more enchanting hue, the sun shed a mellower and more delicious tint, and every object seemed heightened with a pathetic grace; and surely, no incident could, better than the present one, have produced the effect; for an intelligence the most expressive sate on

[1] A window furnished with sashes, i.e., sliding frames.

the features of the young woman; and intelligence so divine, so mild, so graceful, that Guido Rheni[1] might have studied it with rapture. She had on a gown of white cotton, and round her waist there was a green sash; her hair, of a dark brown, hung down upon her shoulders, and from her left arm depended a small basket. The person who leaned upon her right was dressed in a scarlet coat, which seemed to have been formerly an uniform; his countenance was strongly marked, martial, but at the same time mingled with much benignity; his forehead was bold and open, his eye full and dark, his eye-brows black and thick, his nose aquiline, and his chin rather prominent; he had a staff in his right hand, and although apparently possessing some vigour and in health, he walked with difficulty, being, as I perceived, lame of one leg.

I had remained, until now, concealed beneath the shadow of some trees, but stepping forward to continue the objects of my admiration in view, a favourite dog, who ran by their side, caught a sight of me, and, beginning to bark with vehemence, they turned round. I found myself discovered, and advancing towards them, begged they would pardon my intrusion, for that invited by the beauty of the scene, I had inadvertently wandered into their grounds. They smiled at my apology, and the old gentleman, with much good nature, told me I was welcome to his farm, that it gave him pleasure to perceive I admired his situation, and that, provided I could bear to travel no faster than himself, he would shew me some parts well worth seeing, and which, probably, from my ignorance of the country, had escaped me. I thanked him, and willingly accepting of his proposal, we took another direction, returning to the cottage by a path which was altogether hid from common observation. An agreeable conversation soon took place, into which our fair companion occasionally entered with the most frank and amiable simplicity, and speedily convinced me that her heart and her understanding were as lovely as her form. As we became more and more pleased with each other, the reserve, natural to strangers, wore off, and having expressed much satisfaction, mingled with some curiosity, in regard to their mode of life, the old man told me, he had formerly served as a British officer in Germany, that his name was Felton, and that having lived long in the army without due promotion, and being very much wounded in his last engagement,[2] and indeed rendered incapable of further service, he had retired with his wife and daughter, the young lady now present, to a little estate which he possessed in the west riding of Yorkshire; that after residing a few happy years in that situation, he lost his wife, and unable any longer to endure the sight of objects which perpetually recalled her to his memory, he had left it for this romantic spot, where blest with the dutiful and affectionate attention of his lovely Agnes, nothing on this side of the grave, he thought,

[1] Guido Reni (1575-1642), Italian painter, whose name was among the most frequently mentioned by 18th-century British authors.
[2] The last engagement involving Britain on German territory in the Seven Years' War was the victorious siege of Cassel (today, Kassel), in 1762.

could add to his content. As he said this he turned towards his daughter, whose blue eyes, suffused with tears, beamed the most lively gratitude. I felt at this moment one of the sweetest transports my breast has ever known; I felt how much all sublunary bliss rests on the warmth of social feeling, and gazing on the tender features of Miss Felton, the tear that trickled down my cheek gave tribute to her goodness.

We had by this time reached the cottage, having in our short tour seen several little elegant and striking views, the fore ground of which, as sequestered and laying near the cot,[1] had been greatly improved by the genius of Felton. I would now have taken my leave, for the sun was near the horizon, but Felton begged I would step in, and, as he expressed it, grace his humble shed. I could not refuse, there was an air of gentleness and sincerity about him that would not admit of a refusal, so I stepped into a very neat little parlour, where, sitting down, the good old man desired his daughter to bring some of her best wine, "if you can excuse," he said, "what an old soldier can afford, you are welcome; heaven has not given me affluence, sir, but it has blessed me with what I value more, a lot above dependance, and a heart that is grateful for the gift." I was much affected, and, without saying a word, involuntarily stretched out my hand; he placed his in mine; we were silent: Miss Felton entered, she smiled, and throwing her blue eyes with a bewitching sweetness upon me, offered the wine: I took a glass; my hand trembled; I drank her health; it was, I thought, the most delightful wine I had ever tasted; I praised her skill, she blushed. "I am glad it pleases you," she said. At this moment, turning round to speak to her father, the bright hilt of a sword, which hung across the chimney-piece, caught my attention. Felton observed it, and rising from his chair, took it down; he drew it from the scabbard: "this," cried he, waving it round his head, "this, sir, was once my only fortune, my only friend, with this, and much good service has it done me, with this I've known the day when, shrinking from the lightning of its edge, the foes of Felton have retired." As he spoke this, a transient light flashed from his eyes, but pausing a while, an expression mild and pensive succeeded: "those days," resuming his discourse, "are past, nor do I wish them to return; turbulent they were, and marked with blood; war was never my enjoyment, I never did delight in devastation, the tears of the mournful were ever bitter to my soul." He sighed, and sheathing his sword, placed it in its former situation. "No," he continued, "though ever ready, and with a willing heart, to serve my country, yet never did I taste the sweets of happiness, till having sought retirement, I indulged the pleasures of domestic life. Here with my Agnes and a few friends, every wish is gratified. I here possess, and I am thankful for it, my share of human bliss."

During this little speech Miss Felton sate near a table, her head reclined upon her hand, her eyes were fixed upon her father, they were

[1] Here and in the introductory lines from Downman, "cot" means "cottage."

full of tears, tears of grateful rapture. Sure, thought I, if content did ever visit the abode of man, her residence is here, where virtue, and where feeling hearts, where peace and competence, combine. Ah, never, in the warmest sally of my imagination, never did I fancy aught so beauteous as this spot of ground, or aught so lovely as its gentle tenants. How to take leave of them I knew not, the sun had already set, and the moment of separation drew near, of a separation perhaps eternal. I rose, I kissed the white hand of Miss Felton; and, embracing her father, hurried out of the room, without being able to utter a single word: the night was fine, the moon had risen, and sweetly illumined the lake and distant mountains; all, except the nightingale, was mute, and struck by a scene so accordant with my feelings, it was late ere I reached the village, where, giving way to a strain of pensive enthusiasm, I wrote, before I went to rest, the following stanzas:

I go, farewel my beauteous maid!
I leave the land belov'd for thee,
From Grasmere's hills afar convey'd,
From all that whisper'd joy to me.

Though dear the little native vale
To which I turn my lingering feet,
Though dear the friends who in that dale
Expect their much-lov'd son to greet.

Yet will they hear the deep-drawn sigh,
As shuns his couch the traitor sleep,
Yet will they view his languid eye,
And o'er the love-lorn mourner weep.

Oh, had ye known the gentle maid,
How soft her accent, mild her air,
How sweet her dark-brown ringlets play'd
And trembled on her bosom fair.

Ye would not, oh my friends, admire
Why seeks your son the walk by stealth,
Why beats his pulse with fev'rish fire,
Why fades the purple glow of health.

And must I leave thee, must we part?
Ah, ruthless fortune bids to fly,
Nor heeds the pang that swells my heart,
Nor marks the tear-o'erflowing eye.

1790

Yet Hope shall soothe the bosom care,
Shall fondly prompt the tender sigh,
Shall smiling wave her golden hair,[1]
And roll her blue voluptuous eye.

Perchance when time hath stol'n away
A few dull years of toil and pain,
Ah then, perchance, may beam a day
To guide me to my Love again.

1790

---

[1] Drake inserted a note here, acknowledging his homage: "And Hope enchanted smil'd, and wav'd her golden hair. COLLINS." The line cited is from "An Ode for Music," one of the *Passions* of William Collins (1721-1759), which had been set to music in 1750.

ROBERT BURNS
Three Witch Stories (1790)

The author: Robert Burns (1759-1796) was born in Alloway (which he spelled "Aloway"), a small village close to Ayr, on the west coast of Scotland. After a difficult boyhood, he became famous in 1786, with his volume of *Poems, Chiefly in the Scottish dialect*, and especially with the songs he wrote in the late 1780s and early 1790s, which consolidated his reputation as the national poet of Scotland.

The text: He sent these stories to his friend Francis Grose, in June 1790. The letter was first published in Egerton Brydges's journal *Censura Literaria* in 1796. The second of these stories was turned into the poem "Tam o'Shanter" in 1791. The following is from the volume format of *Censura Literaria*, Second Edition (London: Longman, Hurst, Rees, Orme, and Brown, Paternoster-Row, 1815), Vol. IX, 103-106.

Further reading: Mary Ellen B. Lewis. "Burns' 'Tale o' Truth': A Legend in Literature." *Journal of the Folklore Institute* 13.3 (1976): 241-262.

Among the many Witch-Stories I have heard relating to Aloway Kirk, I distinctly remember only two or three.

Upon a stormy night, amid whirling squalls of wind and bitter blasts of hail, in short, on such a night as the devil would chuse to take the air in, a farmer or farmer's servant was plodding and plashing homeward with his plough-irons on his shoulder, having been getting some repairs on them at a neighbouring smithy. His way lay by the Kirk of Aloway, and being rather on the anxious look-out in approaching a place so well known to be a favourite haunt of the devil and the devil's friends and emissaries, he was struck aghast by discovering through the horrors of the storm and stormy night, a light, which on his nearer approach, plainly shewed itself to proceed from the haunted edifice. Whether he had been fortified from above on his devout supplication, as is customary with people when they suspect the immediate presence of Satan; or whether, according to another custom, he had got courageously drunk at the smithy, I will not pretend to determine; but so it was that he ventured to go up to, nay into the very kirk. As good luck would have it, his temerity came off unpunished. The members of the infernal junto were all out on some midnight business or other, and he saw nothing but a kind of kettle or caldron, depending from the roof, over the fire, simmering some heads of unchristened children, limbs of executed malefactors, &c. for the business of the night. It was, in for a penny, in for a pound, with the honest ploughman: so without ceremony he unhooked the caldron from off the fire, and poured out the damnable ingredients, inverted it on his head, and carried it fairly home, where it remained long in the family a living evidence of the truth of the story.

Another story which I can prove to be equally authentic was as follows.

On a market day in the town of Ayr, a farmer from Carrick, and consequently whose way lay by the very gate of Aloway kirk-yard, in order to cross the river Doon at the old bridge,[1] which is about two or three hundred yards further on than the said gate, had been detained by his business 'till by the time he reached Aloway, it was the wizard hour, between night and morning. Though he was terrified, with a blaze streaming from the kirk, yet as it is a well-known fact that to turn back on these occasions is running by far the greatest risk of mischief, he prudently advanced on his road. When he had reached the gate of the kirk-yard, he was surprised and entertained, through the ribs and arches of an old gothic window which still faces the highway, to see a dance of witches merrily footing it round their old sooty blackguard master, who was keeping them all alive with the powers of his bag-pipe. The farmer stopping his horse to observe them a little, could plainly descry the faces of many old women of his acquaintance and neighbourhood. How the gentleman was dressed, tradition does not say; but the ladies were all in their smocks: and one of them happening unluckily to have a smock which was considerably too short to answer all the purpose of that piece of dress, our farmer was so tickled that he involuntarily burst out, with a loud laugh, "Weel luppen, Maggy wi' the short sark!"[2] and recollecting himself, instantly spurred his horse to the top of his speed. I need not mention the universally known fact, that no diabolical power can pursue you beyond the middle of a running stream. Lucky it was for the poor farmer that the river Doon was so near; for notwithstanding the speed of his horse, which was a good one, against[3] he reached the middle of the arch of the bridge, and consequently the middle of the stream, the pursuing, vengeful, hags, were so close at his heels, that one of them actually sprung to seize him; but it was too late, nothing was on her side of the stream but the horse's tail, which immediately gave way to her infernal grip, as if blasted by a stroke of lightning; but the farmer was beyond her reach. However, the unsightly, tail-less condition of the vigorous steed was to the last hour of the noble creature's life, an awful warning to the Carrick farmers, not to stay too late in Ayr markets.

The last relation I shall give, though equally true, is not so well identified as the two former, with regard to the scene: but as the best authorities give it for Aloway, I shall relate it.

On a summer's evening, about the time that Nature puts on her sables to mourn the expiry of the chearful day, a shepherd boy belonging

---

[1] Carrick is a district in Ayrshire, through which flows the river Doon.
[2] "Luppen" is the Scots past participle of the verb "to leap." "Sark" is the Scottish version of "shift," the female undergarment (or smock). So, the sentence means: "Well leapt, Maggie with the short shift!"
[3] In the old sense of "before, by the time that."

to a farmer in the immediate neighbourhood of Aloway Kirk, had just folded his charge, and was returning home. As he passed the kirk, in the adjoining field, he fell in with a crew of men and women, who were busy pulling stems of the plant ragwort. He observed that as each person pulled a ragwort, he or she got astride of it and called out, "Up horsie!" on which the ragwort flew off, like Pegasus, through the air with its rider. The foolish boy likewise pulled his ragwort, and cried with the rest "Up horsie!" and, strange to tell, away he flew with the company. The first stage at which the cavalcade stopt, was a merchant's wine cellar in Bourdeaux, where, without saying by your leave, they quaffed away at the best the cellar could afford, until the morning, foe to the imps and works of darkness, threatened to throw light on the matter, and frightened them from their carousals.

The poor shepherd lad, being equally a stranger to the scene and the liquor, heedlessly got himself drunk; and when the rest took horse, he fell asleep, and was found so next day by some of the people belonging to the merchant. Somebody that understood Scotch, asking him what he was, he said he was such-a-one's herd in Aloway; and by some means or other getting home again, he lived long to tell the world the wondrous tale.

I am, &c. &c.

1790

MARY HAYS

Melville and Serena (1793)

The author: An early disciple of Mary Wollstonecraft and a radical feminist, Mary Hays was born in 1759 in South London, in a dissenting family. She published her first tale in 1786 and a volume of *Letters and Essays* in 1793. Having decided to live in London as a single woman, Hays wrote two autobiographical novels: *Memoirs of Emma Courtney* (1796) and *The Victim of Prejudice* (1799). Her *Female Biography* (1803), a six-volume work on the lives of celebrated women, was somewhat successful, and she continued to publish until 1821. She died in 1843.

The text: It was first published in *Letters and Essays, Moral, and Miscellaneous. By Mary Hays* (London: Printed for T. Knott, No. 47, Lombard-Street, 1793), 31-41 (from where the following has been selected). It appeared as the fourth letter, marked by a Roman numeral ("No. IV"), but in the table of contents it is identified as "Letter to Mrs.—— with a Sketch of the Family of Sempronia. History of Melville and Serena." In her Preface she almost immediately starts with a quote from Mary Wollstonecraft: "It is observed by the sensible vindicator of female rights—'that as society is at present constituted, the little knowledge, which even women of stronger minds attain, is of too desultory a nature, and pursued in too secondary a manner to give vigour to the faculties, or clearness to the judgment.' I feel the truth of this observation with a mixture of indignation and regret" (v).

Further reading: Miriam Wallraven. *A Writing Halfway between Theory and Fiction: Mediating Feminism from the Seventeenth to the Twentieth Century.* Würzburg: Königshausen & Neumann, 2007. 59-61.

Felicity James. "Writing *Female Biography*: Mary Hays and the Life Writing of Religious Dissent." *Women's Life Writing, 1700-1850: Gender, Genre and Authorship.* Eds. Daniel Cook and Amy Culley. New York: Palgrave Macmillan, 2012. 117-132.

To Mrs. ——.

My dear Madam,

Your eldest daughter you inform me is now entering her fifteenth year, and discovers a love of books, which gives you great pleasure, as you justly consider a taste for reading as the best foundation for moral as well as speculative improvement. Books contain the best parts of the finest human minds, in them you perceive only the excellencies of genius without those shades that must unavoidably discolour the purest human virtues. I am aware that book-knowledge has been ridiculed by many, as

289

useless in the common intercourses of life; but these sarcasms I fancy have generally been the refuge of ignorance, glorying in its shame; and that knowledge of the world which they recommend as a substitute, when analyzed, I believe frequently consists in an acquaintance with chicanery and turpitude, and "to touch pitch and not be defiled,"[1] is very difficult. It certainly is not necessary for every individual to apply himself to abstract and scientific pursuits, as this would be defeating the purposes of society, which requires hands as well as heads. "And what is above us (said Socrates) doth not concern us;"[2] but there are situations in the least degree superior to the lowest ranks of life, that do not allow of some leisure, and to fill up that leisure in a manner that may not only afford present entertainment, but also lay in stores for future improvement, is certainly highly laudable. Nothing is so much to be avoided in the education of young people, as the leaving too many hours of vacuity; by habits of indolence, the body, the mind, and the morals are endangered. Lavater justly observes, that "idleness is the crying sin of human nature."[3] It is an ancient and a true maxim, "That nothing can be accomplished without labour, and every thing with it."[4] Those to whom the care of youth is intrusted, should be particularly sedulous to guard them from this canker of every virtue, by exciting them to exercise their fancy and ingenuity, their faculties and their limbs.

I confess I am no advocate for cramping the minds and bodies of young girls, by keeping them for ever poring over needle-work (and when I see the tapestry and tent-stitch of former times, I sigh at the waste of eyes, spirits, and time); nor do I think it so very important a part of female education as has generally been supposed. In well-regulated families, where nothing is left till to-morrow, which can be done to-day, where every department is conducted with order and economy, where the business of the day is planned in the morning, and one thing concluded before another is begun; where the day is lengthened by early hours,

---

[1] Proverb originating in a passage from *Ecclesiastes* 13:1: "He that toucheth pitch shall be defiled therewith." Pitch is the dark resin of some coniferous trees.
[2] This maxim about our inability to penetrate the secrets of the heavens was attributed to Socrates by the early Christian philosopher Lactantius in his *The Divine Institutes* (written between 303 and 311 A.D.). It was often quoted by subsequent Christian authors.
[3] Johann Caspar Lavater (1741-1801), a Swiss poet and theologian, remembered today especially for his writings on "physiognomy," the pseudoscience according to which a man's character can be inferred from facial features. He was so popular in Britain that his *Aphorisms on Man* (1787-1788) appeared in English translation almost simultaneously with the German original. Hays uses a common paraphrase of the 477th aphorism: "If you ask me which is the real hereditary sin of human nature, do you imagine I shall answer pride, or luxury, or ambition, or egotism? No; I shall say indolence—who conquers indolence will conquer all the rest."
[4] This maxim is attributed to Diogenes, the Cynic philosopher of the 4th century BC. Hays may have found it in *The History of Philosophy* by Johann Jakob Brucker (1696-1770), recently translated into English by William Enfield (1741-1797), a Unitarian minister. Hays herself became Unitarian in the 1790s.

and short temperate meals, "eating to live, and not living only to eat;"[1] I am well assured there cannot be any occasion for this laborious and sempstress-like application: surely the covering of the body ought not to be the sole business of life. I doubt whether there will be any sewing in the next world, how then will those employ themselves who have done nothing else in this?

Sempronia had a large family of daughters, whom she early trained with unrelenting rigour to the duties of non-resistance and passive obedience. All attention to literature, she considered as mere waste of time, and valued herself upon being unacquainted with any other book than the Bible. The sole accomplishments which this notable lady deemed necessary to constitute a good wife and mother, were to scold and half starve her servants, to oblige her children to say their prayers, and go stately[2] to church, and to make clothes and household furniture from morning till night; while to supply them with constant employment of this nature, more money was expended, and materials wasted, than would have paid for having the work done from home, and have purchased a handsome collection of books beside. The unfortunate girls submitted to this severe discipline from hard necessity, but not without murmuring; till at length, from close confinement, and the dull uniformity of one tedious pursuit, the bloom faded from their cheeks, and the lustre from their eyes, their tempers lost their sprightliness, and their health its vigor. Their mother who really loved them, and who thought that while she was blighting the tender blossom in its spring, she was performing the duties of a prudent and good parent, was alarmed at the change she perceived; and after vainly trying the efficacy of various quack medicines recommended as infallible restoratives, accompanied the young ladies to one of the fashionable watering places, in the hope of their receiving benefit from the salubrious effects of the sea air.

During their residence at Brighthelmstone,[3] the languid charms of the elder daughter attracted the notice of the son of a wealthy citizen, who having received a liberal, though mercantile education, had been accustomed to amuse himself in the intervals of commercial business, with the study of the Belle-Letters. His imagination had acquired by these pursuits a tincture of what is commonly called romance by the generality of the trading part of mankind; he had been disgusted with the venal daughters of fashion, and the really sweet, though fading countenance of our young lady (whom I shall call Serena) the bashfulness of her manners, and the meekness of her deportment, awakened his tenderness, and flattered his vanity. The vulgar and confined notions of the mother he dignified with the name of simplicity; and as his Serena seldom

[1] Attributed to Socrates by Diogenes Laërtius, this maxim was popularised by Latin authors like Cicero and Quintilian.
[2] At fixed intervals; frequently, consistently.
[3] The official name of Brighton until 1810.

ventured to converse freely in his presence, her silence he construed into the effect of a delicate timidity. He could not but perceive that her mind had been greatly neglected, but he consoled himself with the hope of giving it improvement and polish, and exclaimed with Rousseau, "Lovely ignorance! Happy will he be who is destined to instruct her."[1] Full of these ideas he hastened their union, that he might remove his charming mistress out of a family where he conceived she was degraded, and transplant her into—

"A richer soil, where vernal suns and showers,
Diffuse their warmest, largest influence."[2]

Serena, by sea-bathing, recreation, and the attentions of her lover, which gave her thoughts a new turn, in some measure recovered her health and beauty, and in a few weeks became the wife of Melville, who now believed himself at the summit of human felicity. After the first congratulations and compliments were over, he conducted his bride to a pleasant villa, situated on the banks of the Thames, a few miles from the metropolis, intending before he introduced her to his connections (many of whom were among the polite and the literary) to devote his leisure hours to the cultivation and enlargement of her understanding.

For this purpose he furnished a commodious library with an elegant assortment of books, and when after the business of the day he returned from town, he would endeavour to entertain his Serena, by reading select passages from the best English authors, particularly the works of the Poets, and moral Essayists. But to his great mortification, when after repeating with enthusiasm some of the finest passages in Shakespear, he glanced his eyes on his lady to perceive the effect it produced; the settled vacuity of her features announced the blank within. She seemed to listen, and faintly smiled, but it was the forced smile of lassitude; she had no associations that could make her feel any interest in the glowing pictures of genius, and would interrupt the soul-harrowing scene between Hamlet and his guilty mother, to observe upon a phaeton that passed the window, or return the caresses of a favourite lap-dog. Poor Melville shuddered! the visionary scene of bliss began to fade from his imagination, he threw down his book, and to hide his chagrin, proposed to his wife a walk, as she had yet seen but little of the adjacent country. She readily agreed to accompany him, happy to be relieved from the irksome task, of giving a feigned attention to what she could not comprehend. Melville endeavoured to direct her view as they passed to every sublime and beautiful feature in nature, the wood and the water, the hill and the valley, the wild heath and the cultivated garden—

[1] Although she appreciated the freedom of some of his heroines, Hays, like Wollstonecraft, can be described as one of Rousseau's English opponents. The reference here, at least in part ironic, is to a famous passage from Rousseau's *Emile; or, On Education*.

[2] A paraphrase of a few lines from the "Palemon and Lavinia" episode in James Thomson's influential poetical cycle *The Seasons* (1726-1730): "O let me now, into a richer soil,/ Transplant thee safe! where vernal suns and showers,/ Diffuse their warmest, largest influence;/ And of my garden be the pride, and joy!"

"The sun-shine gleaming as through amber clouds,
O'er all the western sky."[1]

But alas! the varied "shews and forms"[2] of nature were lost on the sterile fancy that had never received—"fair cultures kind enlivening aid."[3] She entreated that they might return to the high road, for she was sure the path they had taken must be equally unsafe as dull and difficult, and she was every moment in terror, lest a robber should start out of the thicket. Her disgusted companion sighed as he silently acceded to her proposal, and began unwillingly to be convinced that true beauty must depend upon moral sentiment, and that the mere varnish of a fair complexion could make no amends for a weak and empty mind.

Vain was every subsequent attempt to give fire to this breathing clay, early habits had rendered the mental organs callous; the pretty insipid Serena would smile when he smiled, and weep when he frowned, but her tenderness flattered not; for there was no distinction in it. She had no will of her own (for the little energy she inherited from nature, had been quenched by the despotic discipline of the good lady her mother) and Melville wearied by the uniformity of her compliances, which gratified neither his judgment nor his heart, vainly exhorted her sometimes to have a taste of her own; for he would even have preferred opposition to the dead calm in which their days languished, and he dreaded to enliven them by society; for the gross inaccuracies, and frivolity of his lady's conversation, exposed him to the ridicule of his acquaintance, and covered him with confusion.

Nor did the domestic management of his affairs afford him any consolation. His wife sought amusement in the company of her servants, she preserved no dignity of character, and acted not upon any plan; consequently her authority was despised, nothing was conducted with regularity, and while she sat whole days in loose dishabille to supernumerary needle-work, which turned to little account, her house was filled with litter and disorder, her children ran wild, and her domestics quarrelled among themselves, and defrauded their master, as amid frequent changes, the certain consequence of mismanagement, it could not be expected that they would all be honest.

[1] The quote is from Mark Akenside's very popular 1744 poem *The Pleasures of the Imagination* (towards the end of Book III).

[2] In a note, Hays indicates the source: "'Oh! nature, all thy shews and forms,/ For pensive feeling hearts have charms.' Burn's Poems." The lines are, indeed, from Burns's 1785 poem "Epistle to William Simson," published in *Poems, Chiefly in the Scottish Dialect*, in which they appear as follows: "O Nature! a' thy shews an' forms/ To feeling, pensive hearts hae charms!"

[3] A paraphrase from Mark Akenside's poem, only a few lines after the ones mentioned above: "though Heaven/ In every breast hath sown those early seeds/ Of love and admiration, yet in vain,/ Without fair Culture's kind parental aid,/ Without enlivening suns, and genial showers,/ And shelter from the blast, in vain we hope/ The tender plant should rear its blooming head,/ Or yield the harvest promised in its spring."

The unfortunate Melville, whose mind was formed for elegant and domestic tenderness, execrated his fate in the bitterness of his soul, and desperately sought to forget his disappointment in scenes of dissipation and extravagance; and in a few years his expences abroad, and the want of order and economy at home, involved them in the miseries of insolvency.

This little history requires no comment; your Elizabeth, for whose entertainment it is intended, will perhaps be stimulated by it to new ardor in mental pursuits. That I interest myself in her happiness, you need not now be informed, and that I am affectionately, &c. yours.[1]

1793

---

[1] As the story is attached at the end of a letter to a mother, it ends with the usual farewell. In subsequent letters, Hays pursued the story of the life of Melville, whose wife Serena dies, he goes to America to find new fortunes (but this second story of Melville is concerned with religious issues); and the story of the other daughters of Sempronia.

MARIA EDGEWORTH
Tarlton (1796)

The author: Maria Edgeworth was born in Oxfordshire, on January 1, 1768, but, after her mother's death in 1773, she joined her father on his estate in Ireland. Her first published works were *Letters for Literary Ladies* (1795) and *The Parent's Assistant* (1796), the latter a collection of short stories about children. She achieved notoriety with her novels: *Castle Rackrent* (1800), *Belinda* (1801), *Lenora* (1806), *The Absentee* (1812), *Harrington* (1817), *Helen* (1834) and others. She continued to write well-received stories, such as her *Moral Tales* (1801) and *Tales of Fashionable Life* (1809), as well as books on education. She died at home in 1849.

The text: It was first published in *The Parent's Assistant; or, Stories for Children*, Part I. (London: J. Johnson, in St. Paul's Church-yard, 1796). The following is from the second edition, published the same year (19-53).

Further reading: O. Elizabeth McWhorter Harden. *Maria Edgeworth's Art of Prose Fiction*. The Hague: Mouton, 1971. 16-36.

Young Hardy was educated by Mr. Freeman, a very good master, at one of the Sunday schools in ——shire. He was honest, obedient, active, and good-natured; so that he was esteemed and beloved by his master, and by his companions. Beloved by all his companions who were good, he did not desire to be loved by the bad; nor was he at all vexed or ashamed, when idle, mischievous, or dishonest boys attempted to plague or ridicule him. His friend Loveit, on the contrary, wished to be universally liked; and his highest ambition was to be thought the best natured boy in the school:—and so he was. He usually went by the name of *poor Loveit*, and every body pitied him when he got into disgrace, which he frequently did; for though he had a good disposition, he was often led to do things, which he knew to be wrong, merely because he could never have the courage to say, *no*; because he was afraid to offend the ill-natured, and could not bear to be laughed at by fools.

One fine autumn evening, all the boys were permitted to go out to play in a pleasant green meadow, near the school. Loveit, and another boy, called Tarlton, began to play a game at battledore and shuttlecock,[1] and a large party stood by to look on; for they were the best players at battledore and shuttlecock in the school, and this was a trial of skill between them. When they had kept it up to three hundred and twenty, the game became very interesting: the arms of the combatants grew so tired,

[1] An early form of badminton ("battledore" is an old term for "racquet").

that they could scarcely wield the battledores:—the shuttlecock began to waver in the air; now it almost touched the ground, and now, to the astonishment of the spectators, mounted again high over their heads; yet the strokes became feebler and feebler; and "now Loveit!" "now Tarlton!" resounded on all sides. For another minute the victory was doubtful; but at length, the setting sun shining full in Loveit's face so dazzled his eyes, that he could no longer see the shuttlecock, and it fell at his feet.

After the first shout for Tarlton's triumph was over, every body exclaimed, "Poor Loveit!"—he's the best natured fellow in the world!— "what a pity he did not stand with his back to the sun."

"Now I dare you all to play another game with me," cried Tarlton, vauntingly; and as he spoke, he tossed the shuttlecock up with all his force: with so much force, that it went over the hedge, and dropped into a lane, which went close beside the field. "Hey-day!" said Tarlton, "what shall we do now?"

The boys were strictly forbidden to go into the lane; and it was upon their promise not to break this command, that they were allowed to play in the adjoining field.

No other shuttlecock was to be had, and their play was stopped. They stood on the top of the bank peeping over the hedge. "I see it yonder," said Tarlton; "I wish any body would get it. One could get over the gate at the bottom of the field, and be back again in half a minute," added he, looking at Loveit. "But you know we must not go into the lane," said Loveit, hesitatingly. "Pugh!" said Tarlton, "why now what harm could it do?"—"I don't know," said Loveit, drumming upon his battledore; "but—" "You don't know, man! why then what are you afraid of? I ask you."— Loveit coloured, went on drumming, and again, in a lower voice, said "*he didn't know.*" But upon Tarlton's repeating, in a more insolent tone, "I ask you, man, what you're afraid of?" he suddenly left off drumming, and looking round, said, "he was not afraid of any thing that he knew of."— "Yes, but you are," said Hardy, coming forward." "Am I," said Loveit; "of what, pray, am I afraid?" "Of doing wrong!" "Afraid *of doing wrong!*" repeated Tarlton, mimicking him, so that he made every body laugh. "Now hadn't you better say, afraid of being flogged?"—"No," said Hardy, coolly, after the laugh had somewhat subsided, "I am as little afraid of being flogged as you are, Tarlton; but I meant—" "No matter what you meant; why should you interfere with your wisdom, and your meanings; nobody thought of asking *you* to stir a step for us; but we asked Loveit, because he's the best fellow in the world."—"And for that very reason you should not ask him, because you know he can't refuse you any thing?" "Indeed though," cried Loveit, piqued, "*there* you're mistaken, for I could refuse if I chose it." Hardy smiled; and Loveit, half afraid of his contempt, and half afraid of Tarlton's ridicule, stood doubtful, and again had recourse to his battledore, which he balanced most curiously upon his fore finger. "Look at him!—now do look at him!" cried Tarlton; "did you ever in your life see any body look so silly!—Hardy has him quite under thumb; he's so mortally afraid of Parson Prig, that he dare not, for the soul of him, turn either of his eyes from the tip of his nose; look how he squints!"—"I don't squint," said Loveit, looking up, "and nobody has me under his thumb; and what Hardy said, was only for fear I should get into disgrace:—he's the best friend I have." Loveit spoke this with more than usual spirit, for both his heart and his pride were touched. "Come along then," said Hardy, taking him by the arm in an affectionate manner; and he was just going, when Tarlton called after him, "Ay, go along with its best friend, and take care it does not get into a scrape;—good by, Little Panado!"—"Who do they call Little Panado," said Loveit, turning his head hastily back. "Never mind," said Hardy, "what does it signify?"—"No," said Loveit, "to be sure it does not signify; but one does not like to be called Little Panado: besides," added he, after going a few steps farther, "they'll all think it so ill-natured.—I had better go back, and just tell them, that I'm very sorry I can't get their shuttlecock;—do come back with me."—"No," said Hardy, "I can't go back; and you'd better not." "But, I assure you, I won't stay a minute; wait for me," added Loveit; and he slunk back again to prove that he was not Little Panado.[1]

Once returned, the rest followed of course; for to support his character for good-nature, he was obliged to yield to the entreaties of his companions, and to shew his spirit, leapt over the gate, amidst the acclamations of the little mob:—he was quickly out of sight.

"Here," cried he, returning in about five minutes, quite out of breath, "I've got the shuttlecock; and I'll tell you what I've seen," cried he, panting for breath. "What?" cried every body, eagerly. "Why, just at the turn of the corner, at the end of the lane," panting. "Well," said Tarlton, impatiently, "do go on."—"Let me just take breath first." "Pugh! never mind your breath."—"Well then, just at the turn of the corner, at the end of the lane, as I was looking about for the shuttlecock, I heard a great rustling somewhere near me, and so I looked where it could come from; and I saw, in a nice little garden, on the opposite side of the way, a boy, about as big as Tarlton, sitting in a great tree, shaking the branches; and at every shake down there came such a shower of fine large rosy apples, they made my mouth water: so I called to the boy, to beg one; but he said, he could not give me one, for that they were his grandfather's; and just at that minute, from behind a gooseberry bush, up popped the uncle—the grandfather poked his head out of the window; so I ran off as fast as my legs would carry me, though I heard him bawling after me all the way."

"And let him bawl," cried Tarlton, "he shan't bawl for nothing; I'm determined we'll have some of his fine large rosy apples before I sleep to-night."—At this speech a general silence ensued; every body kept their eyes fixed upon Tarlton, except Loveit, who looked down, apprehensive

[1] Panado is a Portuguese dish consisting of boiled or macerated bread flavoured with sugar and currants. The word was also used mockingly about something weak or someone cowardly.

that he should be drawn on much farther than he intended.—"Oh, indeed!" said he to himself, "as Hardy told me, I had better not have come back!"

Regardless of this confusion, Tarlton continued, "But before I say any more, I hope we have no spies amongst us. If there is any one of you afraid to be flogged, let him march off this instant!"—Loveit coloured, bit his lips, wished to go, but had not the courage to move first.—He waited to see what every body else would do;—nobody stirred;—so Loveit stood still.

"Well then," cried Tarlton, giving his hand to the boy next to him, then to the next, "your word and honour that you won't betray me; but stand by me, and I'll stand by you."—Each boy gave his hand, and his promise; repeating "stand by me, and I'll stand by you."—Loveit hung back till the last; and had almost twisted off the button of the boy's coat who screened him, when Tarlton came up, holding out his hand, "Come, Loveit, lad, you're in for it: Stand by me, and I'll stand by you."—"Indeed, Tarlton," expostulated he, without looking him in the face, "I do wish you'd give up this scheme; I dare say all the apples are gone by this time;—I wish you would—Do, pray, give up this scheme."—"What scheme, man! you hav'n't heard it yet; you may as well know your text before you begin preaching." The corners of Loveit's mouth could not refuse to smile, though in his heart he felt not the slightest inclination to laugh. "Why I don't know you, I declare I don't know you to-day," said Tarlton; "you used to be the best natured, most agreeable lad in the world, and would do any thing one asked you; but you're quite altered of late, as we were saying just now, when you skulked away with Hardy: come, do man, pluck up a little spirit, and be one of us, or you'll make us all *hate you*." "*Hate* me!" repeated Loveit, with terror; "no, surely, you won't all *hate* me!" and he mechanically stretched out his hand, which Tarlton shook violently, saying, "*Ay, now, that's right.*"—"*Ay, now, that's wrong!*" whispered Loveit's conscience; but his conscience was no use to him, for it was always overpowered by the voice of numbers; and though he had the wish, he never had the power, to do right. "Poor Loveit! I knew he would not refuse us," cried his companions; and even Tarlton, the moment he shook hands with him, despised him. It is certain, that weakness of mind is despised both by the good and by the bad.

The league being thus formed, Tarlton assumed all the airs of a commander, explained his schemes, and laid the plan of attack, upon the poor old man's apple tree. It was the only one he had in the world. We shall not dwell upon their consultation, for the amusement of contriving such expeditions is often the chief thing which induces idle boys to engage in them.

There was a small window at the end of the back staircase, through which, between nine and ten o'clock at night, Tarlton, accompanied by Loveit and another boy, crept out. It was a moonlight night, and, after crossing the field, and climbing the gate, directed by Loveit, who now

1796

resolved to go through the affair with spirit, they proceeded down the lane with rash, yet fearful steps. At a distance Loveit saw the white-washed cottage, and the apple tree beside it: they quickened their pace, and with some difficulty scrambled through the hedge which fenced the garden, though not without being scratched and torn by the briars. Every thing was silent. Yet now and then at every rustling of the leaves they started, and their hearts beat violently. Once as Loveit was climbing the apple tree, he thought he heard a door in the cottage open, and earnestly begged his companions to desist and return home. This however he could, by no means, persuade them to do, until they had filled their pockets with apples; then, to his great joy, they returned, crept in at the staircase window, and each retired, as softly as possible, to his own apartment.

Loveit slept in the room with Hardy, whom he had left fast asleep, and whom he now was extremely afraid of wakening. All the apples were emptied out of Loveit's pockets, and lodged with Tarlton till the morning, for fear the smell should betray the secret to Hardy. The room door was apt to creak, but it was opened with such precaution, that no noise could be heard, and Loveit found his friend as fast asleep as when he left him.

"Ah," said he to himself, "how quietly he sleeps! I wish I had been sleeping too." The reproaches of Loveit's conscience, however, served no other purpose but to torment him; he had not sufficient strength of mind to be good. The very next night, in spite of all his fears, and all his penitence, and all his resolutions, by a little fresh ridicule and persuasion he was induced to accompany the same party on a similar expedition. We must observe, that the necessity for continuing their depredations became stronger the third day; for, though at first only a small party had been in the secret, by degrees it was divulged to the whole school; and it was necessary to secure secresy by sharing the booty.

Every one was astonished, that Hardy, with all his quickness and penetration, had not yet discovered their proceedings; but Loveit could not help suspecting that he was not quite so ignorant as he appeared to be. Loveit had strictly kept his promise of secresy, but he was by no means an artful boy; and in talking to his friend, conscious that he had something to conceal, he was perpetually on the point of betraying himself; then recollecting his engagement, he blushed, stammered, bungled; and upon Hardy's asking what he meant, would answer with a silly guilty countenance, that he did not know; or abruptly break off, saying, Oh nothing! nothing at all!

It was in vain that he urged Tarlton to permit him to consult his friend; a gloom overspread Tarlton's brow when he began to speak on the subject, and he always returned a peremptory refusal, accompanied with some such taunting expression as this—"I wish we had nothing to do with such a sneaking fellow. He'll betray us all, I see, before we have done with him."—"Well," said Loveit to himself, "so I am abused after all, and called a sneaking fellow for my pains; that's rather hard to be sure, when I've got so little by the job."

In truth he had not got much, for in the division of the booty only one apple, and a half of another which was only half ripe, happened to fall to his share; though, to be sure, when they had all eaten their apples, he had the satisfaction to hear every body declare they were very sorry they had forgotten to offer some of theirs to "*poor Loveit!*"

In the mean time the visits to the apple tree had been now too frequently repeated to remain concealed from the old man, who lived in the cottage. He used to examine his only tree very frequently, and missing numbers of rosy apples which he had watched ripening, he, though not much prone to suspicion, began to think that there was something going wrong; especially as a gap was made in his hedge, and there were several small footsteps in his flower beds.

The good old man was not at all inclined to give pain to any living creature, much less to children, of whom he was particularly fond. Nor was he in the least avaricious, for though he was not rich, he had enough to live upon, because he had been very industrious in his youth; and he was always very ready to part with the little he had; nor was he a cross old man. If any thing would have made him angry, it would have been the seeing his favourite tree robbed, as he had promised himself the pleasure of giving his red apples to his grand-children on his birth-day. However he looked up at the tree in sorrow rather than in anger, and leaning upon his staff, he began to consider what he had best do.

"If I complain to their master," said he to himself, "they will certainly be flogged, and that I should be sorry for; yet they must not be let to go on stealing, that would be worse still, for that would surely bring them to the gallows in the end. Let me see—oh, ay, that will do; I will borrow farmer Kent's dog Barker, he'll keep them off, I'll answer for it."

Farmer Kent lent his dog Barker, cautioning his neighbour at the same time, to be sure to chain him well, for he was the fiercest mastiff in England. The old man, with farmer Kent's assistance, chained him fast to the trunk of the apple tree.

Night came, and Tarlton, Loveit, and his companions, returned at the usual hour. Grown bolder now by frequent success, they came on talking and laughing. But the moment they had set their foot in the garden, the dog started up; and, shaking his chain as he sprang forward, barked with unremitting fury. They stood still as if fixed to the spot. There was just moonlight enough to see the dog. "Let us try the other side of the tree," said Tarlton. But to which ever side they turned the dog flew round in an instant, barking with encreased fury.

"He'll break his chain and tear us to pieces," cried Tarlton; and, struck with terror, he immediately threw down the basket he had brought with him, and betook himself to flight with the greatest precipitation.—"Help me! oh, pray, help me! I can't get through the hedge," cried Loveit in a lamentable tone, whilst the dog growled hideously, and sprang forward to the extremity of his chain.—"I can't get out! Oh, for God's sake, stay for me one minute, dear Tarlton!"

300

He called in vain, he was left to struggle through his difficulties by himself; and of all his dear friends, not one turned back to help him. At last, torn and terrified, he got through the hedge and ran home, despising his companions for their selfishness. Nor could he help observing, that Tarlton, with all his vaunted prowess, was the first to run away from the appearance of danger. The next morning he could not help reproaching the party with their conduct.—"Why could not you, any of you, stay one minute to help me?" said he. "We did not hear you call," answered one. "I was so frightened," said another, "I would not have turned back for the whole world."—"And you, Tarlton?"—"I," said Tarlton. "Had not I enough to do to take care of myself, you blockhead? Every one for himself in this world!" "So I see," said Loveit gravely. "Well, man! is there any thing strange in that"—"Strange! why yes, I thought you all loved me?" "Lord, love you, lad! so we do; but we love ourselves better."—"Hardy would not have served me so, however," said Loveit, turning away in disgust. Tarlton was alarmed.—"Pugh!" said he; "what nonsense have you taken into your brain? Think no more about it. We are all very sorry, and beg your pardon; come, shake hands, forgive and forget." Loveit gave his hand, but gave it rather coldly.—"I forgive it with all my heart," said he, "but I cannot forget it so soon!"—"Why then you are not such a good-humoured fellow as we thought you were. Surely you cannot bear malice, Loveit." Loveit smiled, and allowed that he certainly could not bear malice. "Well then, come; you know at the bottom we all love you, and would do any thing in the world for you." Poor Loveit, flattered in his foible, began to believe that they did love him at the bottom, as they said, and even with his eyes open consented again to be duped.

"How strange it is," though he, "that I should set such value upon the love of those I despise! When I'm once out of this scrape, I'll have no more to do with them, I'm determined."

Compared with his friend Hardy, his new associates did indeed appear contemptible; for all this time Hardy had treated him with uniform kindness, avoided to pry into his secrets, yet seemed ready to receive his confidence, if it had been offered.

After school in the evening, as he was standing silently beside Hardy, who was ruling a sheet of paper for him, Tarlton, in his brutal manner, came up, and seizing him by the arm, cried, "Come along with me, Loveit, I've something to say to you."—"I can't come now," said Loveit, drawing away his arm.—"Ah, do come now," said Tarlton in a voice of persuasion.—"Well, I'll come presently."—"Nay, but do, pray; there's a good fellow, come now, because I've something to say to you."—"What is it you've got to say to me? I wish you'd let me alone," said Loveit; yet at the same time he suffered himself to be led away.

Tarlton took particular pains to humour him and bring him into temper again; and even, though he was not very apt to part with his play-things, went so far as to say, "Loveit, the other day you wanted a top; I'll give you mine, if you desire it."—Loveit thanked him, and was overjoyed at the thoughts of possessing this top.[1] "But what did you want to say to me just now?"—"Aye, we'll talk of that presently—not yet—when we get out of hearing."—"Nobody is near us," said Loveit.—"Come a little farther, however," said Tarlton, looking round suspiciously—"Well now, well?" "You know the dog that frightened us so last night?"—"Yes."—"It will never frighten us again."—"Won't it? how so?"—"Look here," said Tarlton, drawing from his pocket something wrapped in a blue handkerchief.—"What's that?" Tarlton opened it. "Raw meat!" exclaimed Loveit. "How came you by it?"—"Tom, the servant boy, Tom got it for me, and I'm to give him sixpence."—"And is it for the dog?"—"Yes; I vowed I'd be revenged on him, and after this he'll never bark again."—"Never bark again!—What do you mean?—Is it poison?" exclaimed Loveit, starting back with horror. "Only poison for *a dog*," said Tarlton, confused; "you could not look more shocking if it was poison for a Christian." Loveit stood for nearly a minute in profound silence. "Tarlton," said he, at last, in a changed tone and altered manner, "I did not know you; I will have no more to do with you."—"Nay, but stay," said Tarlton, catching hold of his arm, "stay; I was only joking."—"Let go my arm, you were in earnest."—"But then that was before I knew there was any harm. If you think there's any harm?"—"*If,*" said Loveit. "Why you know, I might not know; for Tom told me it's a thing that's often done; ask Tom."—"I'll ask nobody! Surely we know better what's right and wrong than Tom does."—"But only just ask him, to hear what he'll say."—"I don't want to hear what he'll say," cried Loveit vehemently. "The dog will die in agonies—in horrid agonies! There was a dog poisoned at my father's, I saw him in the yard.—Poor creature! he lay, and howled, and writhed himself!"—"Poor creature!—Well, there's no harm done now," cried Tarlton, in an hypocritical tone. But though he thought fit to dissemble with Loveit, he was thoroughly determined in his purpose.

Poor Loveit, in haste to get away, returned to his friend Hardy; but his mind was in such agitation, that he neither talked nor moved like himself; and two or three times his heart was so full that he was ready to burst into tears.

"How good-natured you are to me," said he to Hardy, as he was trying vainly to entertain him; "but if you knew—." Here he stopped short, for the bell for evening prayer rang, and they all took their places, and knelt down. After prayers, as they were going to bed, Loveit stopped Tarlton—"*Well!*" asked he, in an inquiring manner, fixing his eyes upon him;—"*Well!*" replied Tarlton, in an audacious tone, as if he meant to set his inquiring eye at defiance;—"what do you mean to do to night?"—"To go to sleep, as you do, I suppose," replied Tarlton, turning away abruptly, and whistling as he walked off.

"Oh, he has certainly changed his mind!" said Loveit to himself, "else he could not whistle." About ten minutes after this, as he and Hardy were

---

[1] A toy, also called a "peg-top" or a "boy's top," of various shapes, which can be made to spin rapidly.

undressing, Hardy suddenly recollected that he had left his new kite out upon the grass. "Oh," said he, "it will be quite spoiled before morning!"—"Call Tom," said Loveit, "and bid him bring it in for you in a minute." They both went to the top of the stairs to call Tom; no one answered. They called again louder. "Is Tom below?"—"I'm here," answered he at last, coming out of Tarlton's room with a look of mixed embarrassment and effrontery. And as he was receiving Hardy's commission, Loveit saw the corner of the blue handkerchief hanging out of his pocket. This excited fresh suspicions in Loveit's mind; but, without saying one word, he immediately stationed himself at the window in his room, which looked out towards the lane; and, as the moon was risen, he could see if any one passed that way. "What are you doing there?" said Hardy, after he had been watching some time; why don't you come to bed?" Loveit returned no answer, but continued standing at the window. Nor did he watch long in vain; presently he saw Tom gliding slowly along a by-path, and get over the gate into the lane.

"He's gone to do it!" exclaimed Loveit aloud, with an emotion which he could not command. "Who's gone! to do what?" cried Hardy, starting up. "How cruel, how wicked!" continued Loveit. "What's cruel—what's wicked? speak out at once!" returned Hardy, in that commanding tone which, in moments of danger, strong minds feel themselves entitled to assume towards weak ones. Loveit instantly, though in an incoherent manner, explained the affair to him. Scarcely had the words passed his lips, when Hardy sprang up, and began dressing himself without saying one syllable. "For God's sake, what are you going to do?" said Loveit in great anxiety. "They'll never forgive me! don't betray me! they'll never forgive me! pray speak to me! only say you won't betray us."—"I will not betray you, trust to me," said Hardy; and he left the room, and Loveit stood in amazement: whilst, in the mean time, Hardy, in hopes of overtaking Tom before the fate of the poor dog was decided, ran with all possible speed across the meadow, and then down the lane. He came up with Tom just as he was climbing the bank into the old man's garden. Hardy, too much out of breath to speak, seized hold of him, dragged him down, detaining him with a firm grasp whilst he panted for utterance—"What, master Hardy, is it you? what's the matter? what do you want?"—"I want the poisoned meat that you have in your pocket."—"Who told you that I had any such thing," said Tom, clapping his hand upon his guilty pocket. "Give it me quietly, and I'll let you off."—"Sir, upon my word I hav'n't? I didn't? I don't know what you mean," said Tom trembling, though he was by far the strongest of the two; "indeed I don't know what you mean."—"You do," said Hardy, with great indignation, and a violent struggle immediately commenced. The dog, now alarmed by the voices, began to bark outrageously. Tom was terrified lest the old man should come out to see what was the matter; his strength forsook him, and flinging the handkerchief and meat over the hedge, he ran away will all his speed. The handkerchief fell within the reach of the dog, who instantly snapped

303

at it: luckily it did not come untied. Hardy saw a pitchfork on a dunghill close beside him, and seizing upon it, stuck it into the handkerchief. The dog pulled, tore, growled, grappled, yelled; it was impossible to get the handkerchief from between his teeth; but the knot was loosed, the meat unperceived by the dog dropped out, and while he dragged off the handkerchief in triumph, Hardy with inexpressible joy plunged the pitchfork into the poisoned meat, and bore it away.

Never did hero retire with more satisfaction from a field of battle. Full of the pleasure of successful benevolence, Hardy tripped joyfully home, and vaulted over the window-sill, when the first object he beheld was Mr. Power, the usher, standing at the head of the stairs, with his candle in his hand.

"Come up, whoever you are," said Mr. William Power in a stern voice; "I thought I should find you out at last. Come up, whoever you are!" Hardy obeyed without reply.—"Hardy!" exclaimed Mr. Power, starting back with astonishment; "is it you, Mr. Hardy?" repeated he, holding the light to his face. "Why, Sir," said he in a sneering tone, "I'm sure, if Mr. Trueman was here, he wouldn't believe his own eyes; but for my part, I saw through you long since, I never liked saints for my share. Will you please to do me the favour, Sir, if it is not too much trouble, to empty your pockets."—Hardy obeyed in silence. "Hey day! meat! raw meat! what next?"—"That's all," said Hardy, emptying his pockets inside out. "This is *all*," said Mr. Power, taking up the meat.—"Pray, Sir," said Hardy eagerly, "let that meat be burned, it is poisoned."—"Poisoned!" cried Mr. William Power, letting it drop out of his fingers; "you wretch!" looking at him with a menacing air, "what is all this? Speak." Hardy was silent. "Why don't you speak?" cried he, shaking him by the shoulder impatiently. Still Hardy was silent. "Down upon your knees this minute, and confess all, tell me where you've been, what you've been doing, and who are your accomplices, for I know there is a gang of you: so," added he, pressing heavily upon Hardy's shoulder, "down upon your knees this minute, and confess the whole, that's your only way now to get off yourself. If you hope for *my* pardon, I can tell you it's not to be had without asking for."—"Sir," said Hardy, in a firm but respectful voice, "I have no pardon to ask, I have nothing to confess, I am innocent; but if I were not, I would never try to get off myself by betraying my companions."—"Very well, Sir! very well! very fine! stick to it, stick to it, I advise you—and we shall see. And how will you look tomorrow, Mr. Innocent, when my uncle the Doctor comes home?" "As I do now, Sir," said Hardy, unmoved. His composure threw Mr. Power into a rage too great for utterance. "Sir," continued Hardy, "ever since I have been at school, I never told a lie, and therefore, Sir, I hope you will believe me now. Upon my word and honour, Sir, I have done nothing wrong."—"Nothing wrong? Better and better! what, when I catched you going out at night?"—"*That* to be sure was wrong," said Hardy, recollecting himself; "but except that—" "Except that, Sir! I will except nothing. Come along with me, young gentleman,

1796

304

your time for pardon is past." Saying these words, he pulled Hardy along a narrow passage to a small closet, set apart for desperate offenders, and usually known by the name of the *Black Hole*. "There, Sir, take up your lodging there for to-night," said he, pushing him in; "to-morrow I'll know more, or I'll know why," added he, double locking the door, with a tremendous noise, upon his prisoner, and locking also the door at the end of the passage, so that no one could have access to him. "So now I think I have you safe!" said Mr. William Power to himself, stalking off with steps which made the whole gallery resound, and which made many a guilty heart tremble. The conversation which had passed between Hardy and Mr. Power at the head of the stairs had been anxiously listened to, but only a word or two here and there had been distinctly overheard. The locking of the black hole door was a terrible sound—some knew not what it portended, and others knew *too well*; all assembled in the morning with faces of anxiety. Tarlton's and Loveit's were the most agitated. Tarlton for himself; Loveit for his friend, for himself, for every body. Every one of the party, and Tarlton at their head, surrounded him with reproaches; and considered him as the author of the evils which hung over them. "How could you do so? and why did you say any thing to Hardy about it? when you had promised too! Oh what shall we all do! what a scrape you have brought us into! Loveit, it's all your fault!"—"*All my fault!*" repeated poor Loveit, with a sigh; "well, that is hard."

"Goodness! there's the bell," exclaimed a number of voices at once. "Now for it!" They all stood in a half circle for morning prayers! they listened, "Here he is coming! No—Yes—Here he is!" And Mr. William Power, with a gloomy brow, appeared and walked up to his place at the head of the room. They knelt down to prayers, and the moment they rose Mr. William Power, laying his hand upon the table, cried, "Stand still, gentlemen, if you please." Every body stood stock still; he walked out of the circle; they guessed that he was gone for Hardy, and the whole room was in commotion. Each with eagerness asked each what none could answer, "*Has he told*?"—"*What* has he told?"—"Who has he told of?"—"I hope he has not told of me?" cried they. "I'll answer for it he has told of all of us," said Tarlton. "And I'll answer for it he has told of none of us," answered Loveit, with a sigh. "You don't think he's such a fool, when he can get himself off," said Tarlton.

At this instant the prisoner was led in, and as he passed through the circle, every eye was fixed upon him; his eye turned upon no one, not even upon Loveit, who pulled him by the coat as he passed—every one felt almost afraid to breathe.—"Well, Sir," said Mr. Power, sitting down in Mr. Trueman's elbow chair, and placing the prisoner opposite to him; "well, Sir, what have you to say to me this morning?"—"Nothing, Sir," answered Hardy, in a decided yet modest manner; "nothing but what I said last night."—"Nothing more?"—"Nothing more, Sir."—"But I have something more to say to you, Sir, then; and a great deal more, I promise you, before I have done with you"; and then seizing him in a fury,

305

he was just going to give him a severe flogging, when the school-room door opened, and Mr. Trueman appeared, followed by an old man whom Loveit immediately knew. He leaned upon his stick as he walked, and in his other hand carried a basket of apples. When they came within the circle, Mr. Trueman stopped short—"Hardy!" exclaimed he, with a voice of unfeigned surprise, whilst Mr. William Power stood with his hand suspended.—"Aye, Hardy, Sir," repeated he. "I told him you'd not believe your own eyes."—Mr. Trueman advanced with a slow step. "Now, Sir, give me leave," said the Usher, eagerly drawing him aside and whispering.— "So, Sir," said Mr. T. when the whisper was done, addressing himself to Hardy with a voice and manner, which, had he been guilty, must have pierced him to the heart, "I find I have been deceived in you—it is but three hours ago that I told your uncle I never had a boy in my school in whom I placed so much confidence; but, after all this show of honour and integrity, the moment my back is turned, you are the first to set an example of disobedience to my orders. Why do I talk of disobeying my commands, you are a thief!"—"I, Sir," exclaimed Hardy, no longer able to repress his feelings.—"You, Sir—you and some others," said Mr. Trueman, looking round the room with a penetrating glance—"you and some others—" "Aye, Sir," interrupted Mr. William Power, "get that out of him if you can—ask him."—"I will ask him nothing; I shall neither put his truth or his honour to the trial; truth and honour are not to be expected amongst thieves." "I am not a thief! I have never had any thing to do with thieves," cried Hardy, indignantly. "Have you not robbed this old man? don't you know the taste of these apples?" said Mr. Trueman, taking one out of the basket. "No, Sir, I do not; I never touched one of that old man's apples."—"Never touched one of them! I suppose this is some vile equivocation; you have done worse, you have had the barbarity, the baseness, to attempt to poison his dog; the poisoned meat was found in your pocket last night."—"The poisoned meat was found in my pocket, Sir! but I never attempted to poison the dog, I saved his life."—"Lord bless him," said the old man. "Nonsense! cunning!" said Mr. Power. "I hope you won't let him impose upon you so, Sir." "No, he cannot impose upon me, I have a proof he is little prepared for," said Mr. Trueman, producing the blue handkerchief in which the meat had been wrapped.

Tarlton turned pale; Hardy's countenance never changed.—"Don't you know this handkerchief, Sir?"—"I do, Sir?"—"Is it not yours?"—"No, Sir."—"Don't you know whose it is?" cried Mr. Power. Hardy was silent.

"Now, gentlemen," said Mr. Trueman, "I am not fond of punishing you; but when I do it you know it is always in earnest. I will begin with the eldest of you; I will begin with Hardy, and flog you with my own hands till this handkerchief is owned." "I'm sure it's not mine;" and "I'm sure it's none of mine," burst from every mouth, whilst they looked at each other in dismay, for none but Hardy, Loveit, and Tarlton knew the secret.— "My cane!" said Mr. Trueman, and Power handed him the cane—Loveit groaned from the bottom of his heart—Tarlton leaned back against the wall with a black countenance—Hardy looked with a steady eye at the cane.

"But first," said Mr. Trueman, laying down the cane, "let us see; perhaps we may find out the owner of this handkerchief another way," examining the corners; it was torn almost to pieces, but luckily the corner that was marked remained.

"J. T.!" Cried Mr. Trueman. Every eye turned upon the guilty Tarlton, who, now, as pale as ashes and trembling in every limb, sunk down upon his knees, and in a whining voice begged for mercy. "Upon my word and honour, Sir, I'll tell you all; I should never have thought of stealing the apples if Loveit had not first told me of them; and it was Tom who first put the poisoning the dog into my head: it was he that carried the meat; *wasn't it?*" said he, appealing to Hardy, whose word he knew must be believed—"Oh, dear Sir!" continued he, as Mr. Trueman began to move towards him, "do let me off—do pray let me off this time! I'm not the only one indeed, Sir! I hope you won't make me an example for the rest—It's very hard I'm to be flogged more than they!" "I'm not going to flog you."—Thank you, Sir," said Tarlton, getting up and wiping his eyes. "You need not thank me," said Mr. Trueman. "Take your handkerchief—go out of this room—out of this house—let me never see you more."

"If I had any hopes of him," said Mr. Trueman, as he shut the door after him; "if I had any hopes of him, I would have punished him; but I have none—punishment is meant only to make people better; and those who have any hopes of themselves will know how to submit to it."

At these words Loveit first, and immediately all the rest of the guilty party, stepped out of the ranks, confessed their fault, and declared themselves ready to bear any punishment their master thought proper.—"Oh, they have been punished enough," said the old man; "forgive them, Sir."

Hardy looked as if he wished to speak.

"Not because you ask it," said Mr. Trueman, though I should be glad to oblige you—it wouldn't be just—but there (pointing to Hardy), there is one who has merited a reward; the highest I can give him is the pardon of his companions."

Hardy bowed, and his face glowed with pleasure, whilst every body present sympathised in his feelings.—"I am sure," thought Loveit, "this is a lesson I shall never forget."

"Gentlemen," said the old man with a faultering voice, "it wasn't for the sake of my apples that I spoke; and you, Sir," said he to Hardy, "I thank you for saving my dog. If you please, I'll plant on that mount, opposite the window, a young apple tree, from my old one; I will water it, and take care of it with my own hands for your sake, as long as I am able.—And may God bless you! (laying his trembling hand on Hardy's head) may God bless you—I'm sure God *will* bless all such boys as you are."

HANNAH MORE

Betty Brown, the St. Giles's Orange Girl (1796)

The author: Hannah More (1745-1833) was born in Bristol. She got engaged to a man 20 years her senior, who, after postponing the wedding three times, broke the engagement in exchange for a 200-pound annuity in favour of his intended bride (he also bequeathed her a further 1000 pounds). This money allowed More to move to London at the age of 28 and pursue a literary career. She befriended Johnson and Garrick, as well as other women writers, together with whom she formed a group known as the Bluestockings. Her first successful work was the tragedy *Percy* (1777), but she then published mostly poems and essays, becoming a leading feminist (at the conservative end of the spectrum, as an opponent

of Mary Wollstonecraft) and abolitionist. The *Cheap Repository Tracts*, which she founded in 1795, were intended for the poor, both as inexpensive works of literature and as socio-political instruction in the wake of the radicalism of the period that followed the French Revolution. In the early 19th century, she was famed both for her philanthropic work and for her prose fictions, of which the most successful was the 1809 novel *Coelebs in Search of a Wife*.

The text: It was first published as one of her monthly *Cheap Repository Tracts*, entitled *Betty Brown, the St. Giles's Orange Girl: with Some Account of Mrs. Sponge, the Money-lender* (London: Sold by J. Marshall, Printer to the Cheap Repository for Religious and Moral Tracts, No. 17, Queen-Street, Cheapside, and No. 4, Aldermary Churcy-Yard; and R. White, Piccadilly, 1796), from which the following text has been taken. This was listed as the publication of 1 August 1796. Price one penny. It was signed "Z."

Further reading: Mona Scheuermann. "Economic Circumstances: More's Cheap Repository Tracts." *In Praise of Poverty: Hannah More Counters Thomas Paine and the Radical Threat*. Lexington, KY: The University Press of Kentucky, 2002. 135-174.

Betty Brown, the Orange Girl, was born nobody knows where, and bred nobody knows how. No girl in all the streets of London could drive a barrow more nimbly, avoid pushing against passengers more dexterously, or cry her "Fine China Oranges" in a shriller voice.[1] But then she could neither sow, nor spin, nor knit, nor wash nor iron, nor read, nor spell. Betty had not been always in so good a situation as that in which we now describe her. She came into the world before so many good gentlemen and ladies began to concern themselves so kindly that

[1] Also known as "sweet oranges" (as opposed to the "bitter" or "Seville oranges"); the term was also used figuratively for something of little value, a trifle.

the poor might have a little learning. There was no charitable Society then, as there is now, to pick up poor friendless children in the streets, and put them into a good house, and give them meat, and drink, and lodging, and learning, and teach them to get their bread in an honest way into the bargain. Whereas, this now is often the case in London, blessed be God for all his mercies.

The longest thing that Betty can remember is, that she used to crawl up out of a night cellar,[1] stroll about the streets, and pick cinders from the scavengers' carts. Among the ashes she sometimes found some ragged gauze and dirty ribbons; with these she used to dizen[2] herself out, and join the merry bands on the first of May. This was not however quite fair, as she did not lawfully belong either to the female dancers who foot it gaily round the garland, or to the footy tribe, who, on this happy holiday, forget their whole year's toil; she often, however, got a few scraps, by appearing to belong to both parties.

Betty was not an idle girl; she always put herself in the way of doing something. She would run off errands for the footmen, or sweep the door for the maid of any house where she was known; she would run and fetch some porter, and never was once known either to sip a drop or steal the pot. Her quickness and fidelity in doing little jobs, got her into favour with a lazy cook-maid, who was too apt to give away her master's cold meat and beer, not to those who were most in want, but to those who waited upon her, and did the little things which she ought to have done herself.

The cook, who found Betty a dextrous girl, soon employed her to sell ends of candles, pieces of meat and cheese, and lumps of butter, or any thing else she could crib from the house. These were all carried to her friend Mrs. Sponge, who kept a little shop, and a kind of eating-house for poor working people, not far from the Seven Dials. She also bought as well as sold many kinds of second hand things, and was not scrupulous to know whether what she bought was honestly come by, provided she could get it for a sixth part of what it was worth. But if the owner presumed to ask for it's real value, she had sudden qualms of conscience, suspected the things were stolen, and gave herself airs of honesty, which often took in poor silly people, and gave her a sort of half-reputation among the needy and the ignorant, whose friend she pretended to be.

To this artful woman Betty carried the cook's pilfering, and as Mrs. Sponge would give no great price for these in money, the cook was willing to receive payment for her eatables in Mrs. Sponge's drinkables; for she dealt in all kinds of spirits. I shall only just remark here, that one receiver, like Mrs. Sponge, makes many pilferers, who are tempted to these petty thieveries, by knowing how easy it is to dispose of them at such iniquitous houses.

Betty was faithful to both her employers, which is extraordinary, considering the greatness of the temptation, and her utter ignorance of

[1] A tavern (or brothel) open all night.
[2] To dress with clothes, to attire.

good and evil. One day, she ventured to ask Mrs. Sponge if she could not assist her to get into a more settled way of life. She told her, that when she rose in the morning, she never knew where she should lie at night, nor was she ever sure of a meal beforehand. Mrs. Sponge asked her what she thought herself fit for. Betty, with fear and trembling, said, there was one trade for which she thought herself qualified, but she had not the ambition to look so high. It was far above her humble views. This was, to have a barrow, and sell fruit, as several other of Mrs. Sponge's customers did, whom she had often looked at with envy.

Mrs. Sponge was an artful woman. Bad as she was, she was always aiming at something of a character; this was a great help to her trade. While she watched keenly to make every thing turn to her own profit, she had a false fawning way of seeming to do all she did out of pity and kindness to the distressed; and she seldom committed an extortion, but she tried to make the person she cheated believe themselves highly obliged to her kindness. By thus pretending to be their friend she gained their confidence, and she grew rich herself while they thought she was only shewing favour to them. Various were the arts she had of getting rich. The money she got by grinding the poor, she spent in the most luxurious living; and, while she would haggle with her hungry customers for a farthing, she would spend pounds on the most costly delicacies for herself.

Mrs. Sponge, laying aside that haughty look and voice, well known to such as had the misfortune to be in her debt, put on the hypocritical smile and soft tone, which she always assumed when she meant to *take in* her dependents. "Betty," said she, "I am resolved to stand your friend. These are sad times to be sure. Money is money now. Yet I am resolved to put you into a handsome way of living. You shall have a barrow, and well furnished too." Betty could not have felt more joy or gratitude, if she had been told that she should have a coach. "O, Madam," said Betty, "it is impossible. I have not a penny in the world towards helping me to set up." "I will take care of that," said Mrs. Sponge; "only you must do as I bid you. You must pay me interest for my money. And you will of course be glad also to pay so much every night for a nice hot supper which I get ready, quite out of kindness, for a number of poor working people. This will be a great comfort for such a friendless girl as you, for my victuals and drink are the best; and my company the merriest of any house in all St. Giles's."[1] Betty thought all this only so many more favours, and courtesying to the ground, said, "to be sure, Ma'am, and thank you a thousand times into the bargain."

Mrs. Sponge knew what she was about. Betty was a lively girl, who had a knack at learning any thing; and so well looking through all her dirt and rags, that there was little doubt she would get custom. A barrow was soon provided, and five shillings put into Betty's hands. Mrs. Sponge kindly condescended to go to shew her how to buy the fruit, for it was

[1] Formerly the parish of St Giles in the Fields, it was a slum in central London.

a rule with this prudent gentlewoman, and one from which she never departed, that no one should cheat but herself.

Betty had never possessed such a sum before. She grudged to lay it out all at once, and was ready to fancy she could live upon the capital. The crown, however, was laid out to the best advantage. Betty was carefully taught in what manner to cry her Oranges; and received many useful lessons how to get off the bad with the good, and the stale with the fresh. Mrs. Sponge also lent her a few bad sixpences, for which she ordered her to bring home good ones at night.—Betty stared. Mrs. Sponge said, "Betty, those who would get money, must not be too nice about trifles. Keep one of these sixpences in your hand, and if an ignorant young customer gives you a good sixpence, do you immediately flip it into your other hand, and give him the bad one, declaring, that it is the very one you have just received, and that you have not another sixpence in the world. You must also learn how to treat different sorts of customers. To some you may put off with safety goods which would be quite unsaleable to others. Never offer bad fruit, Betty, to those who know better; never waste the good on those who may be put off with worse; put good Oranges at top and the mouldy ones under."

Poor Betty had not a nice conscience, for she had never learnt that grand but simple rule of all moral obligation, "Never do that to another which you would not have another do to you." She set off with her barrow as proud and as happy as if she had been set up in the finest shop in Covent Garden. Betty had a sort of natural good-nature, which made her unwilling to impose, but she had no principle which told her it was a sin. She had such good success, that, when night came, she had not an Orange left. With a light heart, she drove her empty barrow to Mrs. Sponge's door. She went in with a merry face, and threw down on the Counter every farthing she had taken. "Betty," said Mrs. Sponge, "I have a right to it all, as it was got by my money. But I am too generous to take it. I will therefore only take sixpence for this day's use of my five shillings. This is a most reasonable interest, and I will lend you the same sum to trade with to-morrow, and so on; you only paying me sixpence for the use of it every night, which will be a great bargain to you. You must also pay me my price every night for your supper, and you shall have an excellent lodging above stairs; so you see every thing will now be provided for you in a genteel manner, through my generosity."

Poor Betty's gratitude blinded her so completely that she forgot to calculate the vast proportion which this generous benefactress was to receive out of her little gains. She thought herself a happy creature, and went in to supper with a number of others of her own class. For this supper, and for more porter and gin than she ought to have drank, Betty was forced to pay so high, that it eat up all the profits of the day, which, added to the daily interest, made Mrs. Sponge a rich return for her five shillings.

311

Betty was reminded again of the gentility of her new situation, as she crept up to bed in one of Mrs. Sponge's garrets, five stories high. This loft, to be sure, was small, and had no window, but what it wanted in light was made up in company, as it had three beds, and thrice as many lodgers. Those gentry had one night, in a drunken frolic, broke down the door, which happily had never been replaced; for, since that time, the lodgers had died much seldomer of infectious distempers. For this lodging, Betty paid twice as much to her good friend as she would have done to a stranger. Thus she continued, with great industry and a thriving trade, as poor as on the first day, and not a bit nearer to saving money enough to buy her even a pair of shoes, though her feet were nearly on the ground.

One day, as Betty was driving her barrow through a street near Holborn,[1] a lady from a window called out to her, that she wanted some Oranges. While the servant went to fetch a plate, the lady entered into some talk with Betty, having been struck with her honest countenance and civil manner. She questioned her as to her way of life, and the profits of her trade—and Betty, who had never been so kindly treated before by so genteel a person, was very communicative. She told her little history as far as she knew it, and dwelt much on the generosity of Mrs. Sponge, in keeping her in her house, and trusting her with so large a capital as five shillings. At first it sounded like a very good-natured thing; but the lady, whose husband was one of the Justices of the new Police,[2] happened to know more of Mrs. Sponge than was good, which led her to enquire still further. Betty owned, that to be sure it was not all clear profit, for that besides that the high price of the supper and bed ran away with all she got, she paid sixpence a day for the use of the five shillings. "And how long have you done this," said the Lady? "About a year, madam."

The lady's eyes were at once opened. "My poor girl," said she, "do you know that you have already paid for that single five shillings the enormous sum of 7l. 10s.? I believe it is the most profitable five shillings Mrs. Sponge ever laid out." "O, no, Madam," said the girl, "that good gentlewoman does the same kindness to ten or twelve other poor friendless creatures like me." "Does she so?" said the lady; "then I never heard of a better trade than this woman carries on, under the mask of charity at the expence of her poor deluded fellow-creatures."

"But, Madam," said Betty, who did not comprehend this lady's arithmetic, "what can I do? I now contrive to pick up a morsel of bread without begging or stealing. Mrs. Sponge has been very good to me, and I don't see how I can help myself."

"I will tell you," said the lady. "If you will follow my advice, you may not only maintain yourself honestly, but independently. Only oblige yourself to live hard for a little time, till you have saved five shillings

[1] A parish north of St Giles in the Fields.
[2] The New Police was officially established through the Middlesex Justices Act of 1792, when 7 new police sections were added to John Fielding's Bow Street Runners, while keeping the model of magistrates and officers in the same office.

out of your own earnings. Give up that expensive supper at night, drink only one pint of porter, and no gin at all. As soon as you have scraped together the five shillings, carry it back to your false friend, and if you are industrious, you will at the end of the year have saved seven pounds ten shillings. If you can make a shift to live now,[1] when you have this heavy interest to pay, judge how things will mend when your capital becomes your own. You will put some cloaths on your back, and by leaving the use of spirits, and the company in which you drink them, your health, your morals, and your condition will mend."

The lady did not talk thus to save her money. She would gladly have given the girl the five shillings; but she thought it was beginning at the wrong end. She wanted to try her. Besides, she knew there was more pleasure as well as honour in possessing five shillings of one's own saving than of another's giving. Betty promised to obey. She owned she got no good by the company or the liquor at Mrs. Sponge's. She promised that very night to begin saving the expence of the supper, and that she would not taste a drop of gin till she had the five shillings beforehand. The lady, who knew the power of good habits, was contented with this, thinking, that if the girl could abstain for a certain time, it would become easy to her. She therefore at present said little about the *sin* of drinking.

In a very few weeks, Betty had saved up the five shillings. She went to carry back this money with great gratitude to Mrs. Sponge. This kind friend began to abuse her most unmercifully. She called her many hard names not fit to repeat, for having forsaken the supper, by which she swore she got nothing at all; but as she had the charity to dress it for such beggarly wretches, she insisted they should pay for it, whether they ate it or not. She also brought in a heavy score for lodging, though Betty had paid for it every night, and given notice of her intending to quit her. By all these false pretences, she got from her not only her own five shillings, but all the little capital with which Betty was going to set up for herself. As all was not sufficient to answer her demands, she declared she would send her to prison, but while she went to call a Constable, Betty contrived to make off.

With a light pocket and a heavy heart, she went back to the lady, and with many tears told her sad story. The lady's husband, the Justice, condescended to listen to Betty's tale. He said Mrs. Sponge had long been upon his books as a receiver of stolen goods. Betty's evidence strengthened his bad opinion of her. "This petty system of usury," said the gentleman, "may be thought trifling, but it will no longer appear so, if you reflect, that if one of these female sharpers possesses a capital of seventy shillings, or 3l. 10s. with fourteen steady regular customers, she can realize a fixed income of 100 guineas a year. Add to this the influence such a loan gives her over these friendless creatures, by compelling them to eat at her house, or lodge, or buy liquors, or by taking their pawns, and you will see the extent of the evil. I pity these poor victims: You, Betty,

[1] To make a living, usually a hard one.

shall point out some of them to me. I will endeavour to open their eyes on their own bad management. It is one of the greatest acts of kindness to the poor to mend their œconomy, and to give them right views of laying out their little money to advantage. These poor blinded creatures look no farther than to be able to pay this heavy interest every night, and to obtain the same loan on the same hard terms the next day. Thus are they kept in poverty and bondage all their lives; but I hope as many as hear of this will get on a better plan, and I shall be ready to help any who are willing to help themselves." This worthy Magistrate went directly to Mrs. Sponge's with proper officers, and he got to the bottom of many iniquities. He not only made her refund poor Betty's money, but committed her to prison for receiving stolen goods, and various other offences, which may perhaps make the subject of another history.

Betty was now set up in trade to her heart's content. She had found the benefit of leaving off spirits, and she resolved to drink them no more. The first fruits of this resolution was that in a fortnight she bought her a new pair of shoes, and as there was now no deductions for interest or for gin, her earnings became considerable. The lady made her a present of a gown and a hat, on the easy condition that she should go to church. She accepted the terms, at first rather as an act of obedience to the lady, than from a sense of higher duty. But she soon began to go from a better motive. This constant attendance at church, joined to the instructions of the lady, opened a new world to Betty. She now heard for the first time that she was a sinner; that God had given a law which was holy, just, and good, that she had broken this law, had been a swearer, a sabbath-breaker, and had lived without God in the world. All this was sad news to Betty; she knew, indeed, before, that there were sinners, but she thought they were only to be found in the prisons, or at Botany Bay,[1] or in those mournful carts which she had sometimes followed with her barrow, with the unthinking crowd to Tyburn.[2]—She was most struck with the great truths revealed in the Scripture, which were quite new to her. She was desirous of improvement, and said, she would give up all the profits of her barrow, and go into the hardest service, rather than live in sin and ignorance.

"Betty," said the lady, "I am glad to see you so well disposed, and will do what I can for you. Your present way of life, to be sure, exposes you to much danger; but the trade is not unlawful in itself, and we may please God in any calling, provided it be not a dishonest one. In this great town there must be barrow women to sell fruit. Do you, then, instead of forsaking your business, set a good example to those in it, and shew them, that though a dangerous trade, it need not be a bad one. Till Providence points out some safer way of getting your bread, let your companions see, that it is possible to be good even in this. Your trade being carried on in

[1] Today part of Sydney, Australia; the penal colony associated with it (which was actually in nearby Sydney Cove) had been established in 1788.
[2] The place of public executions by hanging in London. The condemned were traditionally granted a last mug of ale at St Giles in the Fields.

the open street, and your fruit bought in an open shop, you are not so much obliged to keep sinful company as may be thought. Take a garret in an honest house, to which you may go home in safety at night. I will give you a bed and a few necessaries to furnish your room; and I will also give you a constant Sunday's dinner. A barrow woman, blessed be God and our good laws, is as much her own mistress on Sundays as a Duchess; and the Church and the Bible are as much open to her. You may soon learn all that such as you are expected to know. A barrow woman may pray as heartily morning and night, and serve God as acceptably all day, while she is carrying on her little trade, as if she had her whole time to spare.

To do this well, you must mind the following

RULES FOR RETAIL DEALERS.
Resist every temptation to cheat.
Never impose bad goods on false pretences.
Never put off bad money for good.
Never use prophane or uncivil language.
Never swear your goods cost so much, when you know it is false. By so doing you are guilty of two sins in one breath, a lie and an oath.

To break these rules, will be your chief temptation. God will mark how you behave under them, and will reward or punish you accordingly. These temptations will be as great to you as higher trials are to higher people; but you have the same God to look to for strength to resist them as they have. You must pray to him to give you this strength. You shall attend a Sunday School, where you will be taught these good things, and I will promote you as you shall be found to deserve.

Poor Betty here burst into tears of joy and gratitude, crying out, "What, shall such a poor friendless creature as I be treated so kindly, and learn to read the word of God too? Oh, Madam, what a lucky chance brought me to your door," "Betty," said the lady, "what you have just said, shews the need you have of being better taught; there is no such thing as chance, and we offend God when we call that luck or chance which is brought about by his will and pleasure. None of the events of your life have happened by chance—but all have been under the direction of a good and kind Providence. He has permitted you to experience want and distress, that you might acknowledge his hand in your present comfort and prosperity. Above all, you must bless his goodness in sending you to me, not only because I have been of use to you in your worldly affairs, but because he has enabled me to shew you the danger of your state from sin and ignorance, and to put you in a way to know his will and to keep his commandments."

How Betty, by industry and piety, rose in the world, till at length she came to keep a handsome Sausage-shop near the Seven Dials, and was married to an honest Hackney Coachman, may be told at some future time, in a Second Part.

CHRONOLOGY OF EVENTS

1700

➢ Tom Brown. *Amusements Serious and Comical, Calculated for the Meridian of London* (London: John Nutt).

Death of Prince William, the last surviving child of Princess Anne, heir to the throne, leaves many Englishmen fearing the return of a Catholic king ~ Spanish king Charles II dies childless; Louis XIV, King of France, proclaims his grandson Philip of Anjou King of Spain, thereby triggering the War of the Spanish Succession (1701-1714) ~ The Great Northern War begins (1700-1721); in November, Charles XII, King of Sweden, defeats the superior Russian forces in the Battle of Narva and, for the next decade, he captures the imagination of many Europeans ~ The Darien scheme, Scotland's attempt at creating its own colony on the Isthmus of Panama, is brought to an end by the Spanish army ~ Mary Astell publishes *Some Reflections on Marriage* ~ Premiere of William Congreve's last play: *The Way of the World* ~ Thomas Abney, Lord Mayor of London, forbids public posting of theatre playbills ~ The death of John Dryden (1631-1700) signals the end of an era in English literature.

1701

➢ Tom Brown et al. "Love-Letters by Several Hands," in vol. I of Voiture's *Familiar and Courtly Letters to Persons of Honour and Quality* (London: S. Briscoe).

➢ S. M. *The Female Critick: or, Letters in Drollery from Ladies to their Humble Servants* (London: E. Rumball).

The Act of Settlement is passed by Parliament: all Roman Catholic descendants of James I are excluded from succession to the throne of England; future Queen Anne is to be followed by members of the House of Hanover ~ England, Austria, and the Dutch Republic become allies against France in the War of the Spanish Succession (the allegiance of Spaniards will remain divided) ~ James II dies in France and his son James (1688-1766), later known as The Old Pretender, becomes the new claimant to the throne and leader of the Jacobite party in exile ~ Frederick I proclaims Prussia a kingdom ~ John Dunton edits *The Post-Angel* (-1702) ~ John Dennis publishes *The Advancement and Reformation of Modern Poetry* ~ Anne Finch publishes "The Spleen" in Charles Gildon's *New Collection of Poems on Several Occasions* ~ Daniel Defoe publishes *The True-Born Englishman*.

1702

➢ Tom Brown et al. *Letters from the Dead to the Living* (London, s.e.).

➢ Charles Gildon. "The Moon; or, the Cure of Jealousie. A Vision." *Examen Miscellaneum* (London: Bernard Lintott). 95-106.

William III dies after a riding accident; he is succeeded by Queen Anne (1702-1714) ~ Queen Anne names John Churchill, Duke of Marlborough (1650-1722), Captain-General of the Army as well as First Lord of the Commission of the Treasury (1702-1710), the equivalent of prime minister

~ Marlborough obtains his first victories against the French in Belgium, while the English ships defeat a French fleet ~ In North America, the War of the Spanish Succession begins in Florida and is known as Queen Anne's War (1702-1713) ~ Charles XII occupies Warsaw ~ Elizabeth Mallet founds *The Daily Courant*, the first English-language daily newspaper (-1735); it prints only foreign news ~ John Tutchin founds *The Observator* (-1712) ~ Publication of Clarendon's posthumous *The History of the Rebellion* begins (-1704) ~ Defoe publishes *The Shortest Way with the Dissenters* ~ John Dennis publishes "A Large Account of the Taste in Poetry."

1703

➤ Ned Ward. *The Rise and Fall of Madam* Coming-Sir (London: J. How).

➤ Anonymous. *Letters from the Living to the Living* (London, s.e.).

In the south of England, the Great Storm of 1703 destroys several military and merchant ships and kills thousands of people, mostly at sea ~ Peter the Great founds the city of Saint Petersburg ~ Hungary, under Francis II Rakoczi, rebels against Austria ~ Isaac Newton is elected president of the Royal Society ~ Daniel Defoe is pilloried in July, then imprisoned, for the crime of libel; he then publishes "Hymn to the Pillory" ~ Sarah Fyge Egerton publishes *Poems on Several Occasions* ~ First performance of Nicholas Rowe's *The Fair Penitent*.

1704

➤ Tom Brown. "A Looking-Glass for Married People: or, The Fantastick Adventures of Sir E— H— with his Seven Wives," in his translation of Louis de Gaya's *Marriage Ceremonies; As Now Used in All Parts of the World* (London: J. Nutt).

➤ Heliotropolis. *The Comical History of the Life and Death of Mumper, Generalissimo of King Charles II^d's Dogs* (London, s.e.).

At Blenheim, in the most celebrated battle of the War of the Spanish Succession, the English and Austrian forces, commanded by the Duke of Marlborough and Prince Eugene of Savoy, defeat the Franco-Bavarian troops led by Marshall Tallard ~ English Admiral George Rooke captures Gibraltar ~ Charles XII of Sweden installs Stanislaw Leszczynski as King of Poland ~ Richard "Beau" Nash becomes master of ceremonies at Bath ~ Defoe publishes *The Storm*, an account of the Great Storm of 1703, and founds *A Review of the Affairs of France* (-1713) ~ Charles Leslie edits *The Rehearsal* (-1709), a paper opposed to Defoe's *Review* and Tutchin's *Observator* ~ John Dunton publishes *The Athenian Spy* ~ John Dennis publishes *The Grounds of Criticism in Poetry* ~ Jonathan Swift publishes *A Tale of a Tub* and *The Battle of the Books*.

1705

➤ Tom Brown (posthumously). *A Legacy for the Ladies. Or, Characters of the Women of the Age* (London: S. Briscoe and J. Nutt).

Charles Mordaunt, Earl of Peterborough, commander of the Anglo-Dutch troops in Spain, captures Barcelona ~ Sophia of Hanover and all her descendants are naturalised British ~ Queen Anne begins negotiations for the union with Scotland ~ Edmond Halley calculates the periodicity of a comet that will later be named after him ~ Captain Richard Steele leaves the army; his play *The Tender Husband* is performed ~ Bernard Mandeville publishes *The Grumbling Hive*.

1706

- ➤ Daniel Defoe. *A True Relation of the Apparition of One Mrs. Veal* (London: B. Bragg).
- ➤ John Dunton. *The Whipping Post: or, A Satyr upon Every Body* (London: B. Bragg).
- ➤ Anonymous. *The Jilted Bridegroom: or, London Coquet* (London: s.e.).

Marlborough wins a new major battle against the French, at Ramillies ~ The Treaty of Union between England and Scotland (to take effect the following year) is agreed upon ~ George Farquhar's *The Recruiting Officer* premieres at Drury Lane ~ The first English version of *The Arabian Nights* begins serial publication.

1707

- ➤ Delarivier Manley. "The Unknown Lady's Pacquet of Letters," attached to her translation of Madame d'Aulnoy's *Memoirs of the Court of England* (London: B. Bragg). 519-616.
- ➤ Ned Ward. *The Wooden World Dissected* (London: B. Bragg).

The Act of Union is ratified by the Parliaments of England and Scotland and the two countries become the Kingdom of Great Britain ~ First major defeat in the War of the Spanish Succession: the French and Spanish troops led by the Duke of Berwick (illegitimate son of James II as well as Marlborough's nephew) defeat the Anglo-Portuguese troops at the Battle of Almansa ~ The decline of the Mughal Empire is signalled by the death of Emperor Aurangzeb, after a long reign (1658-1707) ~ Almost 1,500 sailors die in the Scilly disaster, in which four Royal Navy ships run aground ~ Charles XII of Sweden begins a campaign aiming to conquer Russia ~ Premiere of George Farquhar's *The Beaux' Stratagem* at the Theatre Royal, Haymarket ~ Penelope Aubin publishes *The Stuarts: A Pindarique Ode*.

1708

- ➤ Ned Ward. *The Modern World Disrob'd: or, Both Sexes Stript of Their Pretended Vertue* (London: G.S.); *The London Terrae-filius: or, The Satyrical Reformer* (London: s.e.) (in five parts, begun in 1707).

Marlborough and Eugene of Savoy win the decisive Battle of Oudenarde against the French ~ The British also capture Lille (in the northeast of France) and the Mediterranean island of Minorca ~ Admiral George Byng and bad weather prevent a Jacobite invasion of Scotland ~ Foreign Protestants Naturalisation Act in favour of Huguenot refugees from France ~ Death of Prince George of Denmark, Queen Anne's husband ~ St Paul's Cathedral in London is consecrated ~ Jonathan Swift publishes *An Argument against Abolishing Christianity*.

➢ Charles Gildon. *The Golden Spy in the Courts of Europe* (London: J. Woodward).

➢ Richard Steele. "[Valentine and Unnion]" (*The Tatler* 5); "[Pastorella Converted from Coquetry]" (9); "[The Dumb Fortune Teller and the Widow]" (14); "[Story of Pacolet]" (15); "[Complaint of a Lady]" (20); "[Mrs Jenny Distaff on the Treatment of the Fair Sex]" (33); "[Story of Teraminta]" (45); "[Aurengezebe]" (46); "[Cure for the Spleen]" (47); "[History of Orlando the Fair]" (50-51); "[Delamira Resigns Her Fan]" (52); "[The Civil Husband]" (53); "[Of the Government of Affection]" (54); "[Story of Clarinda and Chloe]" (94); "[History of Will Rosin]" (105); "[Case of a Lover Tormented by a Coquette]" (107).

➢ Joseph Addison. "[A Dancing Master Practising by Book]" (*The Tatler* 88).

➢ Jonathan Swift. "[Platonic Ladies—Madonella]" (*The Tatler* 32).

➢ Delarivier Manley. "[Story of Samuel Slender]" (*The Female Tatler* 28).

At Malplaquet, Marlborough and Savoy win a new major victory against the French ~ Great Frost of 1709 ~ Thousands of Germans dispersed by war, known as the "Poor Palatines," arrive in London and cause anti-immigration reactions (most of them will be transported to New York and Ireland) ~ Decisive Russian victory against Sweden in the Battle of Poltava: Charles XII is defeated by Peter the Great and forced to withdraw to Bender (Moldavia), where he remains for the next five years ~ Thin cast iron produced for the first time in Shropshire ~ Marooned sailor Alexander Selkirk (presumed model of Robinson Crusoe) is rescued from the Juan Fernandez Islands ~ Nicholas Rowe publishes the first modern edition of Shakespeare's plays ~ The first English version of Pierre Bayle's *Historical and Critical Dictionary* is published in 4 volumes ~ Richard Steele begins publication of *The Tatler* (-1711) ~ Delarivier Manley publishes *The New Atalantis* and edits *The Female Tatler* (-1710) ~ Alexander Pope publishes "Pastorals" (in Tonson's *Poetical Miscellanies: The Sixth Part*).

1710

➢ Richard Steele. "[The History of Tom Varnish]" (*The Tatler* 136); "[Story of Mr Eustace]" (172); "[Story of Caelia]" (198); "[Life of Margery, alias John Young]" (226); "[The Taming of the Shrew]" (231).

➢ Joseph Addison. "[The Great Newsmonger]" (*The Tatler* 155); "[Adventures of a Shilling]" (249).

➢ Henry Carey (?). "The Romantick Lady" (*The Records of Love; or, Weekly Amusements for the Fair Sex* 2); "The Generous Heiress" (6-7).

➢ A Person of Quality. *Serious and Comical Essays* (London: J. King).

The trial of Henry Sacheverell (who had first delivered, then published, a sermon critical of the Whig government and of the Glorious Revolution of 1688) causes riots in London ~ Tory electoral victory followed by Tory administration, led by Robert Harley, literary patron of Pope, Gay, and Swift ~ Britain occupies Nova Scotia ~ Parliament passes the first copyright legislation, popularly known as the Statute of Anne, allowing for a (renewable) 14-year term of copyright ~ George Berkeley publishes *A Treatise concerning the Principles of Human Knowledge* ~ Jonathan Swift, then Delarivier Manley, and finally William Oldisworth are the editors of the new Tory newspaper, *The Examiner* (-1714) ~ Joseph Addison writes the 5 numbers of *The Whig Examiner* ~ Michel de La Roche begins his periodical *Memoirs of Literature* (-1714; 1717; 1725-1727; 1730-1731) ~ Charles Povey begins an essay serial titled *The Visions of Sir Heister Ryley* (-1711) modelled on *The Tatler* ~ Arthur Mainwaring edits *The Medley* (-1712) with help from Richard Steele ~ Abel Boyer begins editing *The Political State of Great Britain* (-1729).

1711

- ➤ Richard Steele. "[Inkle and Yarico]" (*The Spectator* 11); "[Brunetta and Phyllis]" (80); "[Thomas Trusty]" (96); "[The Hen-peckt]" (176).
- ➤ Joseph Addison. "[Eudoxus and Leontine]" (*The Spectator* 123); "[The Vision of Mirza]" (159); "[Theodosius and Constantia]" (164); "[The Salamander]" (198).

The South Sea Company is founded to reduce national debt; it receives monopoly on trade with South America, although Britain is at war with Spain ~ A naval expedition against Quebec ends disastrously when 8 transport ships and 800 soldiers are lost in the treacherous St Lawrence river ~ The Occasional Conformity Act ends the loophole found by Nonconformists who were occasionally taking communion in the Church of England in order to be eligible for public office ~ Antoine de Guiscard, a French double agent, stabs Robert Harley, who survives; the would-be assassin is fatally wounded by members of the Privy Council ~ Charles of Habsburg, whose claim to the throne of Spain has been actively supported by British troops for a decade, becomes Holy Roman Emperor, as Charles VI, which will soon lead to the withdrawal of British support ~ Russia's Peter the Great loses the 1710-1711 war against the Ottoman Empire ~ Anthony Ashley-Cooper, Earl of Shaftesbury, publishes *Characteristicks of Men, Manners, Opinions, Times* ~ Alexander Pope publishes *An Essay on Criticism* ~ With Steele's help, Addison founds *The Spectator* (-1712; 1714).

1712

- ➤ Joseph Addison. "[Transmigration of Souls]" (*The Spectator* 343).
- ➤ Richard Steele. "[A Visit to the Bear Garden]" (*The Spectator* 436); "[Filial Piety of Fidelia]" (449).
- ➤ John Hughes. "[History of Amanda]" (*The Spectator* 375).
- ➤ Eustace Budgell. "[Correspondence between Amoret, a Jilt, and Philander]" (*The Spectator* 401).

The Duke of Ormond replaces out-of-favour Marlborough as commander in chief of British forces ~ Robert Walpole is sent to the Tower under accusation of bribery ~ A peace congress to end the War of the Spanish Succession begins in Utrecht ~ Without British support, Eugene of Savoy is defeated by the French in the Battle of Denain ~ The Stamp Act creates a duty of 1 penny per each copy of a newspaper sheet, which seriously stifles the growth of the free press (government-sponsored papers did not pay the tax); many new publications are registered as half-sheet pamphlets and pay a lower tax ~ A celebrated duel between the Duke of Hamilton and Charles Baron Mohun ends with both mortally wounded ~ John Arbuthnot publishes *The History of John Bull* ~ Alexander Pope publishes the first version of *The Rape of the Lock*.

1713

- ➢ Joseph Addison. "[Story of Miss Betty, Cured of Her Vanity]" (*The Guardian* 159); "[In Search of the Philosopher's Stone]" (166); "[Helim and Abdallah]" (167).
- ➢ Richard Steele. "[Letter from a Father to a Young Rake]" (*Guardian* 151).

First and Second treaties of Utrecht, ending the War of the Spanish Succession; peace is proclaimed and celebrated in London, Edinburgh, and Dublin ~ France recognises Britain's claims to Newfoundland, Nova Scotia, and Rupert's Land, all in present-day Canada ~ Another victory for Harley's Tory party in the general elections ~ Frederick William I becomes King of Prussia; known as "the Soldier King," he will rule until 1740 and turn his country into a military power ~ Charles VI, Holy Roman Emperor, issues the Pragmatic Sanction, allowing for his daughters to inherit the throne; in 1740, when he dies, this edict will trigger the War of the Austrian Succession ~ Richard Steele edits *The Guardian* and its sequel, *The Englishman* (-1714; 1715) ~ Richard Blackmore begins the essay serial *The Lay Monk* (-1714) ~ Pope publishes *Windsor Forest* ~ First performance of Joseph Addison's play *Cato, a Tragedy*.

1714

- ➢ Ned Ward. *Adam and Eve Stript of Their Furbelows: or, The Fashionable Virtues and Vices of Both Sexes* (London: J. Woodward and A. Bettesworth).
- ➢ Philip Horneck. "[A Prince from France]" (*The High-German Doctor* 10).

Sophia of Hanover, granddaughter of James I and the heir presumptive to the British crown, dies on 8 June ~ Queen Anne dies on 1 August; a few days before her death, the queen dismisses Robert Harley from his position as Lord High Treasurer ~ George of Hanover, Sophia's eldest son, arrives in London on 18 September and is crowned on 20 October as George I ~ His coronation is followed by riots spurred by supporters of the Tory party and of the High Church; for the remainder of his life, George will only trust the Whigs ~ The Ottoman Empire declares war against Venice ~ Swift, Pope, Gay, Arbuthnot, Harley and others form the Scriblerus Club ~ Bernard Mandeville publishes *The Fable of the Bees* ~ Steele edits *The Lover* and *The Reader* ~ First performance of Nicholas Rowe's *The Tragedy of Jane Shore*.

1715

- ➢ Joseph Addison. "[Memoirs of a Preston Rebel]" (*The Free-Holder* 3).
- ➢ Lewis Theobald. "[The Divining Wand] ("The Censor" 5, *Mist's Journal*).

The Whigs obtain an overwhelming majority in the elections and begin the so-called "Whig Supremacy" (1715-1760) ~ Jacobite rebellion in Scotland seeks to win the throne for the Old Pretender (James Edward Stuart, son of James II); the rebels are defeated in England, at the Battle of Preston, but they resist in Scotland, where the pretender arrives, but soon decides to return to France ~ Louis XIV, King of France since 1643 and supporter of the Jacobites, dies and is replaced by his 5-year-old great-grandson Louis XV; the Regency (1715-1723) begins in France ~ Richard Steele is knighted and granted a royal licence to "entertain" a company of comedians at Drury Lane ~ Addison edits *The Free-Holder* (-1716) ~ Steele writes the 9 papers of the essay serial *Town Talk* ~ Lewis Theobald writes "The Censor," an essay-series in *Mist's Weekly Journal* (with a second series in 1717) ~ Alexander Pope begins publication of his translations of Homer.

1716

➤ Joseph Addison. "[A Tort Fox-hunter]" (*The Free-Holder* 22); "[The Vision of Second-Sighted Highlander]" (27).

Leaders of the Jacobite Rebellion of 1715 are executed ~ Eugene of Savoy defeats the Ottomans at Petrovaradin, the decisive battle of the Austro-Turkish War of 1716-1718 ~ John Gay publishes the poem *Trivia, or, The Art of Walking the Streets of London*.

1717

➤ Lewis Theobald. "[Man Haters]" ("The Censor" 40, *Mist's Weekly Journal*); "[The Fountain that Restores Lost Maidenheads]" (42).

Britain, France, and the Dutch Republic sign a treaty and become the "Triple Alliance"; the Holy Roman Empire soon joins this coalition against Spain, which marks the beginning of the War of the Quadruple Alliance (1717-1720); the Jacobites in exile will fight for Spain ~ King George I and the Prince of Wales (the future George II) quarrel and the heir apparent is banished from the court ~ The Bangorian Controversy starts: it was named after Benjamin Hoadly, the Bishop of Bangor, who delivered a sermon on John 18:36 ("My kingdom is not of this world") suggesting that the Bible did not support any form of church government; one of the authors who will reply is Thomas Gordon ~ *Water Music* by G.F. Handel is performed for the first time on the River Thames ~ John Weaver creates the first ballet in Britain, *The Loves of Mars and Venus* ~ The twelfth and last volume of Antoine Galland's French translation (started in 1704) of *One Thousand and One Nights* appears posthumously; the English version of Galland's volumes appears almost simultaneously.

1718

➤ Thomas Gordon. "[A Country Entertainment]" (*The Weekly Packet* 339).
➤ Daniel Defoe (?). "[The Westphalia Hams]" (*Mist's Journal* 30 August).
➤ Ambrose Philips (?). "[Story of Florella]" (*The Free-Thinker* 80).
➤ Mary Hearne. *The Lover's Week; or, The Six Days Adventures of Philander and Amaryllis* (London: E. Curll and R. Francklin).

The Battle of Cape Passaro, the most important naval engagement in the War of the Quadruple Alliance, is a decisive victory for the British fleet of Admiral George Byng against the Spanish ~ The 1711 Occasional Conformity Act is repealed ~ The Transportation Act (introduced in Parliament in

1717) is applied for the first time: criminals, including vagrants, can now be transported to the colonies for indentured service ~ Ambrose Philips founds *The Free-Thinker* (-1721) ~ Thomas Brereton writes the 22 numbers of *The Critick* ~ Thomas Gordon writes the essay-series "The Humourist" (-1719) in *The Weekly Packet*.

1719

> Thomas Gordon. "The History of Miss-Manage" (*The Weekly Packet* 341).
> Ambrose Philips (?). "[Alfarute and Clarinda]" (*The Free-Thinker* 84); "[Mopsy and the Old Queen]" (92); "[Story of Florio]" (109-110); "[The History of Alibez]" (128-129).
> Charles Gildon. *The Post-Man Robb'd of His Mail: or, The Packet Broke Open* (London: A. Bettesworth and C. Rivington).

A small Jacobite army which included Spanish regulars, lands in Scotland, but is defeated in the Battle of Glen Shiel, in which is wounded one of the Jacobite leaders, Robert Roy MacGregor, later known as Rob Roy ~ The South Sea Company buys half of the national debt ~ Steele writes the 4 numbers of *The Plebeian*; it is answered by Addison's *Old Whig* (2 numbers) and Molesworth's *The Patrician* (4 papers) ~ Daniel Defoe publishes *The Life and Strange Surprizing Adventures of Robinson Crusoe, of York, Mariner* ~ Eliza Haywood publishes *Love in Excess; or, The Fatal Inquiry* ~ Matthew Prior's volume of *Poems on Several Occasions* becomes available.

1720

> Daniel Defoe. "[Good Men]" (*The Commentator* 28).
> Daniel Defoe (?). "[Character of Tom Oaken Plant]" (*Mist's Weekly Journal* 27 February).
> Thomas Killigrew (?). "A Description of New Athens." *Miscellanea Aurea; or, The Golden Medley* (London: A. Bettesworth and J. Pemberton).

The War of the Quadruple Alliance ends with the Treaty of Hague ~ The stock of the South Sea Company rises tenfold in the first six months of the year, only to plummet in early autumn; the South Sea Bubble ruins both individuals and institutions ~ A similar bubble occurs in France, where the Mississippi Company, led by the Scotsman John Law, goes bankrupt ~ The Haymarket Theatre opens in London ~ Thomas Gordon and John Trenchard publish "The Independent Whig" (-1721) and begin "Cato's Letters" (-1723), first in the *London Journal*, then in the *British Journal* ~ Defoe publishes *Memoirs of a Cavalier* and the 74 numbers of *The Commentator* ~ Steele (as Sir John Edgar) edits *The Theatre* ~ John Gay publishes *Poems on Several Occasions*.

1721

> Daniel Defoe (?). "[A South Sea Story]" (*Applebee's Journal* 4 March); "[Another South Sea Story]" (25 March).

Whig leader Robert Walpole begins his long tenure as prime minister (until 1742) ~ Innocent XIII, a great supporter of the Old Pretender, becomes

Pope ~ The Treaty of Nystad ends the Great Northern War ~ Montesquieu publishes the influential *Persian Letters* (trans. in 1722 by John Ozell) ~ Nicholas Amhurst publishes the 52 numbers of *Terrae Filius* ~ Penelope Aubin publishes *The Life and Amorous Adventures of Lucinda*.

1722

➤ Jonathan Swift. *The Wonder of All the Wonders That Ever the World Wonder'd at* (London: A. Moore).

➤ Jonathan Swift. *The Last Speech and Dying Words of Ebenezer Elliston* (Dublin: John Harding).

The Atterbury Plot to overthrow the House of Hanover is discovered ~ Peter the Great starts the Russo-Persian War of 1722-1723 ~ Daniel Defoe publishes *Moll Flanders*, *Colonel Jack*, and *A Journal of the Plague Year* ~ Steele's comedy *The Conscious Lovers* opens at Drury Lane ~ Eliza Haywood publishes *The British Recluse*.

1723

➤ Jane Barker. *A Patch-Work Screen for the Ladies* (London: E. Curll and T. Payne).

The Workhouse Test Act is passed: any person wishing to receive poor relief has to enter a workhouse; about 600 workhouses are built in the following 25 years ~ Louis XV attains majority; end of Regency in France ~ Philip, Duke of Wharton, edits *The True Briton* (-1724) ~ Allan Ramsay publishes the first instalment of *The Tea-Table Miscellany: or, A Collection of Choice Songs, Scots and English* (-1737) ~ Penelope Aubin publishes *The Life of Charlotta Du Pont*.

1724

➤ Aaron Hill (?). "The Power of Oratory" (*The Plain Dealer* 70).

Jack Sheppard, the notorious highwayman, is hanged ~ On a hunting trip in Hanover, King George I discovers Peter, a feral child, who will be brought to England in 1726 (all attempts, by John Arbuthnot and others, to teach him to speak will fail) ~ Aaron Hill and William Bond found *The Plain Dealer* (-1725) ~ First volume of Gilbert Burnet's posthumous *History of My Own Time* (2nd volume in 1734)~ Allan Ramsay publishes *The Ever Green, Being a Collection of Scots Poems* ~ Defoe publishes *Roxana* and the first volume of *A Tour thro' the Whole Island of Great Britain* ~ Swift begins publication of *Drapier's Letters* ~ Mary Davys publishes *The Reform'd Coquet*.

1725

➤ Eliza Haywood. "Fantomina." *Secret Histories, Novels, and Poems* (London: Dan Browne junior and S. Chapman), III, 257-291.

➤ Eliza Haywood. *The Dumb Projector: Being a Surprizing Account of a Trip to Holland Made by Mr Duncan Campbell* (London: W. Ellis et al.).

➤ Mary Davys. "Familiar Letters betwixt a Gentleman and a Lady." *The Works of Mrs Davys* (London: H. Woodfall), II, 265-308.

The treaties of Vienna and Hanover establish the new balance of power in Europe, through the military alliances between Spain, Austria, and

Russia, on the one hand, and Great Britain, France, Prussia, Netherlands, Denmark/Norway, and Sweden, on the other ~ Peter the Great dies and his wife Catherine I becomes Empress of Russia ~ Famous criminal Jonathan Wild is hanged ~ James Arbuckle edits "Hibernicus' Letters" (-1727) in the *Dublin Journal* ~ Allan Ramsay publishes *The Gentle Shepherd* ~ Matthew Concanen begins "The Speculatist" (-1728) in *The London Journal* and *The British Journal* ~ Francis Hutcheson publishes *An Inquiry into the Original of Our Ideas of Beauty and Virtue*.

1726

> Matthew Concanen. "A 'Novel'" (*The British Journal* 180).
> Erasmus Philips. "[Fine Weather]" (*The Country Gentleman* 39); "[A Woman of the Town and a Toad-eater]" (68).
> Eliza Haywood. "The Capricious Lover; or, No Trifling with a Woman." *Cleomelia; or, The Generous Mistress* (London: J. Millan). 94-104.

Allan Ramsay founds the first British circulating library, in Edinburgh ~ Voltaire begins a 3-year exile in England ~ Nicholas Amhurst (as Caleb D'Anvers) begins editing *The Craftsman* (-1730; 1732-1736) ~ Erasmus Philips writes the 84 numbers of *The Country Gentleman* ~ Eliza Haywood publishes *The Distress'd Orphan* ~ Jonathan Swift publishes *Gulliver's Travels*.

1727

> Henry St. John, Viscount Bolingbroke. "[The First Vision of Camilick]" (*The Craftsman* 16).
> Anonymous. "[Character of Myra]" (*Ladies' Journal* 5); "[Story of Myrtilla]" (15); "[Story of Juliana]" (18-19).

In the Anglo-Spanish War (1727-1729), Britain blockades Porto Bello (in Panama), but gives up after thousands of men die of tropical diseases; Spain unsuccessfully lays siege to Gibraltar for 4 months ~ George Frederick Handel is naturalised a British subject ~ King George I dies in Germany ~ George Augustus, Prince of Wales, becomes King George II ~ Handel composes *Coronation Anthems* (including the famous "Zadok the Priest") in honour of the new king ~ Mary Davys publishes *The Accomplish'd Rake*.

1728

> Elizabeth Singer Rowe. *Friendship in Death* (London: T. Worrall).

Frederick, Prince of Wales, arrives in England, where he soon becomes a noted patron of the arts ~ With Defoe's help, Henry Baker founds *The Universal Spectator* (-1746) ~ In Dublin, Thomas Sheridan and Jonathan Swift write the 19 issues of *The Intelligencer* (the 20th issue in 1729) ~ Ephraim Chambers publishes the first edition of his *Cyclopaedia, or, A Universal Dictionary of Arts and Sciences* ~ Francis Hutcheson publishes *Essay on the Nature and Conduct of the Passions* ~ The first production of John Gay's *The Beggar's Opera* ~ Alexander Pope publishes *The Dunciad*.

1729

> Henry Baker. "[Lothario and Calista]" (*The Universal Spectator* 59).
> Duncan Campbell (?). "[Eudocius and Selinda]" (*The Universal Spectator* 46-47).

326

The Treaty of Seville concludes the Anglo-Spanish War ~ Robert Samber offers the first English translation of Charles Perrault's fairy tales ~ Jonathan Swift publishes *A Modest Proposal* ~ Pope revises his 1728 poem as *The Dunciad Variorum*.

1730

➤ Henry Baker. "[Sir Peevy]" (*The Universal Spectator* 85).
➤ Anonymous. *The Millers Beautiful Daughter; or, True Love and Heroic Virtue of Polly Charlton* (London: Mrs Baily); with "The History of Bob Stevens" (14-16).

Anna, niece of Peter the Great, begins her decade-long rule as Empress of Russia ~ Street rioters depose Sultan Ahmed III and end the peaceful "Tulip period" (1718-1730) of Ottoman history; Mahmud I, nephew of his predecessor, becomes sultan ~ William Arnall edits *The Free Briton* (-1735) ~ Richard Russell and John Martyn found *The Grub-Street Journal* (-1736) ~ James Thomson completes *The Seasons* (begun in 1726 with "Winter") ~ Henry Fielding has several theatrical successes: *Rape upon Rape, The Temple Beau, The Author's Farce,* and *The Tragedy of Tragedies.*

1731

➤ Henry Baker. "[Leander and Lucy]" (*The Universal Spectator* 148).

The new Treaty of Vienna is signed by Great Britain and the Holy Roman Empire: the beginning of the Anglo-Austrian Alliance against France and Spain ~ William Hogarth paints *A Harlot's Progress* (the six paintings were destroyed in a fire, while the 1732 engravings survive) ~ *The Gentleman's Magazine* is founded by Edward Cave (-1922).

1732

➤ Thomas Gordon. "[Inconstancy and Fickleness of Man]" (*The Universal Spectator* 199).

James Oglethorpe is granted a royal charter for the new colony of Georgia ~ Benjamin Franklin begins publication of the yearly *Poor Richard's Almanack* (-1758) ~ The Covent Garden theatre opens ~ *The London Magazine* is founded (-1785) ~ *The Mock Doctor* is one of Fielding's many successes on the stage.

1733

➤ Anonymous. *The Secret History of Meadilla* (London: T. Reynolds).
➤ Lydia Grainger. *Modern Amours: or, A Secret History of the Adventures of Some Persons of the First Rank* (London: s.e.).

Augustus II the Strong, King of Poland, dies; the ensuing War of the Polish Succession (1733-1735) pits France and Spain against Russia, Austria, and Prussia (Great Britain and the Dutch Republic choose to remain neutral) ~ Eustace Budgell founds *The Bee* (-1735) ~ Alexander Pope publishes the first 3 epistles of *An Essay on Man* (with the 4th in 1734).

1734

➤ Anonymous. *The Secret History of an Old Shoe* (London: J. Dickerson).
➤ Anonymous. "[Arabella, Clerimont, and Cleanthes]" (*The Universal Spectator* 290).

The French defeat the Austrians in the Siege of Philippsburg, but their general, the Jacobite Duke of Berwick, is killed ~ In another battle of the War of the Polish Succession, the French and the Poles are defeated by the Russians in the Siege of Danzig; both the land forces and the fleet of Russia are commanded by Jacobites (General Peter Lacy and Admiral Thomas Gordon) ~ Aaron Hill and William Popple found *The Prompter* (-1736) ~ Voltaire publishes *Letters Concerning the English Nation* ~ A new English version of Bayle's *Dictionary* begins (-1741).

1735

➢ Thomas Gordon. "[Character of Flatus]" (*The Universal Spectator* 332).
➢ Anonymous. "Hypocrisy Outdone; or, The Imperfect Widow" (*The Universal Spectator* 329).
➢ Anonymous. "[Story of Peggy]" (*The Universal Spectator* 366-368).
➢ Jonathan Swift (?). "[A Letter from a Gentleman in the Country]" (*The Prompter* 119).

Robert Walpole moves into the renovated house at 10, Downing Street, a gift from George II, which he has refused, suggesting instead that it become official residence of the First Lord of the Treasury ~ The Russo-Turkish War of 1735-1739 begins in Crimea ~ Linnaeus publishes the first edition of his *Systema Naturae* ~ William Hogarth paints *A Rake's Progress* ~ Pope publishes "An Epistle from Mr Pope to Dr Arbuthnot" ~ Thomas Blackwell publishes *An Enquiry into the Life and Writings of Homer*.

1736

➢ Aaron Hill. "[The Basket-Maker. A Peruvian Tale]" (*The Prompter* 121).
➢ Eustace Budgell (?). "[Summer Expedition in a Sporting Country]" (*The Prompter* 120); "[Two Gentlemen of Distinction]" (161).

The Witchcraft Act of 1735 (actually 1736 according to the new calendar) decriminalises witchcraft and makes it a crime, instead, to pretend to have magical powers in order to take advantage of the credulous, as well as to accuse others of witchcraft ~ Riots erupt in Edinburgh: soldiers of the City Guard fire at the mob; their captain, John Porteous, is subsequently arrested and sentenced to death, but a large crowd drags him from his cell and he is lynched ~ The Gin Act of 1736 attempts to curb gin consumption ~ Maria Theresa, heir apparent to the Austrian crown, marries Francis, Duke of Lorraine ~ Eliza Haywood publishes *Adventures of Eovaai* ~ Elizabeth Singer Rowe publishes the poem *The History of Joseph*.

1737

➢ C. E. *A Letter from Mrs Jane Jones* (London: Anne Dodd).
➢ Anonymous. "A Story Strange as True" (*The Gentleman's Magazine*, April-August 1737, January, and March 1738).

King George II banishes the Prince of Wales from the court because of his critical views of the government ~ Through the Licensing Act of 1737, all plays must be submitted to the censorship of the Lord Chamberlain ~ William Warburton publishes the first part of *The Divine Legation of Moses* (2nd part in 1741) ~ George Lyttelton and Lord Chesterfield launch *Common Sense* (-1744) ~ Samuel Johnson comes to London and begins writing for *The Gentleman's Magazine*.

1738

> William Guthrie (?). "The Apotheosis of Milton, A Vision" (*The Gentleman's Magazine*, May, September-October 1738, January-February 1739).
> Anonymous. "[A Story of Modern Gallantry]" (*Universal Spectator* 514).

John Wesley founds the Methodist movement ~ David Hume publishes *A Treatise of Human Nature* ~ Samuel Johnson publishes *London, A Poem*.

1739

> Henry Fielding. "[The Palace of Wealth, A Dream]" (*The Champion*, 27 and 29 December).

The so-called War of Jenkins' Ear (1739-1748) between Britain and Spain begins; the British capture Porto Bello, in Panama ~ The Great Frost begins on Christmas Day and will continue all through the following year ~ The Foundling Hospital is created ~ *The Scots Magazine* is founded (-1826) ~ Henry Fielding edits *The Champion* (-1742) ~ Henry St John, Viscount Bolingbroke privately publishes *Letters on the Study of History*.

1740

> Thomas Gordon. "[Fashionable Education]" (*The Universal Spectator* 596); "[Story of Honoria]" (607).
> Henry Fielding. "[The Voyages of Job Vinegar]" (*The Champion*, 20 March).
> Anonymous. *The Devil of a Story. With an Introductory Preface, Relating the Odd Manner of It's Coming to the Author's Knowledge* (London: T. Cooper).
> Anonymous. *The Old Batchelor Outwitted* (London: J. Jones).

Charles VI dies and his daughter Maria Theresa inherits all Habsburg possessions ~ Frederick William I dies and his son Frederick II becomes King of Prussia ~ Frederick II invades Silesia, a Habsburg possession, starting the War of the Austrian Succession (1740-1748); France and Spain become Prussia's allies; Great Britain and Russia side with Maria Theresa's Austria ~ Commodore George Anson begins a voyage round the world, which includes the mission of capturing or destroying any Spanish ships encountered along the way ~ Colley Cibber publishes *An Apology for the Life of Mr Colley Cibber, Comedian* ~ James Thomson writes "Rule, Britannia" for the masque *Alfred* (music by Thomas Arne) ~ Samuel Richardson publishes *Pamela; or, Virtue Rewarded*.

1741

> Anonymous. "[Story of Melintha]" (*The Universal Spectator* 662-663).

The War of the Austrian Succession begins in failure: the Prussians beat the Austrians in the Battle of Mollvitz, while the British suffer a crushing defeat at the hands of the Spaniards at Cartagena de Indias (in present-day Columbia); after Cartagena, Admiral Vernon invades Cuba but is repelled by a much lower Spanish force ~ A French army led by Maurice de Saxe occupies Prague ~ Handel composes the oratorio *Messiah* ~ Two of the most influential British actors of the century, David Garrick and Charles

Macklin have their London debuts: the former as Richard III, the latter as Shylock ~ Fielding publishes *Shamela Andrews* ~ Eliza Haywood publishes *The Anti-Pamela*.

1742

➢ Owen Sedgewick (?). *The Universal Masquerade: or, The World Turn'd Inside Out* (London: J. Huggonson).

Faced with the early defeats of the War of the Austrian Succession, Robert Walpole resigns his position as First Lord of the Treasury ~ Frederick the Great defeats again the Austrians, in the Battle of Chotusitz, and Prussia annexes Silesia ~ Fielding publishes *Joseph Andrews* ~ Edward Young publishes *Night Thoughts*.

1743

➢ Henry Fielding. *Some Papers Proper to be Read before the R—l Society, Concerning the Terrestrial Chrysipus* (London: J. Roberts).

The Battle of Dettingen, against the French, is the first major British victory in the War of the Austrian Succession; King George II personally leads the troops on the battlefield ~ A British attack on La Guaira (present-day Venezuela) is repelled ~ Henry Pelham begins his 11-year tenure as First Lord of the Treasury (acting Prime Minster) ~ A new Gin Act provokes riots in London ~ Fielding publishes *Jonathan Wild* ~ Pope publishes a new version of *The Dunciad*.

1744

➢ Eliza Haywood. "[Story of Flavia]" (*The Female Spectator*, Book I); "[Amaranthus and Aminta]" (Book II); "[Leolin and Elmira]" (Book III); "[Story of Belinda]" (Book IV); "[The French Hermit]" (Book IV); "[The Reclamation of Dorimon]" (Book VI).
➢ J. W. "[Midnight Justice]" (*The Universal Spectator* 831).

A French invasion of Britain, led by Marshall Maurice de Saxe, with a mission to install James Edward Stuart (the Old Pretender) on the throne, is thwarted by a severe storm ~ The Royal Navy is defeated by a Franco-Spanish fleet in the Battle of Toulon ~ On land, the British are defeated by the Spanish and the French in the Battle of Villafranca (today in the southeast of France) ~ France and Spain also defeat the Sardinians and Austrians, most notably in the Battle of Madonna dell'Olmo, while Frederick the Great invades Bohemia and takes Prague ~ The War of the Austrian Succession reaches North America, where it is known as King George's War, and India, where it is known as the First Carnatic War ~ Samuel Foote makes his debut as Othello ~ In Dublin, William Rufus Chetwood edits *The Meddler* ~ Eliza Haywood begins writing *The Female Spectator* (-1746) ~ Mark Akenside publishes the poem "The Pleasures of the Imagination" ~ Sarah Fielding publishes *The Adventures of David Simple*.

1745

➢ Eliza Haywood. "[A Lady's Revenge]" (*The Female Spectator* Book XIV); "[Sergios and Aranthe]" (Book XVII); "[Lysetta]" (Book XVII).
➢ Henry Fielding. "[A Vision of Rebellion]" (*The True Patriot* 3).

The Battle of Fontenoy (in present-day Belgium) is a decisive French victory against the British: Maurice de Saxe defeats an army led by the Duke of Cumberland, King George's youngest son ~ Encouraged by the result of Fontenoy, the Jacobites led by Charles Edward Stuart (the Young Pretender), known also as "Bonnie Prince Charlie," land in Scotland, enter Edinburgh, and defeat government troops in the Battle of Prestonpans; in November, they enter England, besiege and occupy Carlisle, then reach Derby, but lack of support and of fresh recruits forces them to retreat back to Scotland ~ In London, the song "God Save the King" is performed for the first time ~ At Hohenfriedberg (present-day Poland), in one of the greatest battles of the War of the Austrian Succession, Prussia's Frederick the Great defeats the Austrians led by Charles of Lorraine, Maria Theresa's brother-in-law ~ Austria's greatest victory that year is that Maria Theresa's husband, Francis of Lorraine, is elected Holy Roman Emperor ~ In North America, the British capture the French fortress of Louisbourg (in present-day Cape Breton) ~ Fielding edits *The True Patriot* (-1746).

1746

➤ Henry Fielding. *The Female Husband* (London: M. Cooper).
➤ Henry Fielding. "[Story of Fanny]" (*The True Patriot* 21).
➤ John Gilbert Cooper. "On Friendship" (*The Museum* 4).

The Jacobites under Bonnie Prince Charlie occupy Stirling and obtain an important victory at Falkirk, but they are finally defeated at Culloden by the Duke of Cumberland; Prince Charlie escapes to France ~ Handel composes the oratorio *Judas Maccabaeus* to celebrate the victory ~ The Austrians defeat a French and Spanish army in the Battle of Piacenza ~ In India, the French occupy Madras, but their advances are curbed by the arrival of British reinforcements ~ The great Italian painter Canaletto comes to England, where he lives and works until 1755 ~ Robert Dodsley founds *The Museum; or Literary and Historical Register* (-1747) ~ Eliza Haywood edits *The Parrot* ~ William Collins publishes *Odes on Several Descriptive and Allegorical Subjects*.

1747

➤ Anonymous. "The Injur'd Wife's Revenge, or, The Tragical Story of Valero and Celia" (*The London Magazine*, March).

French general Maurice de Saxe defeats again the Duke of Cumberland in the Battle of Lauffeld (present-day Belgium); the French also take Maastricht, which signals the need for peace negotiations ~ The Royal Navy is more fortunate: the French are beaten twice off Cape Finisterre, by Admiral George Anson, back from his circumnavigation, and by Rear-Admiral Edward Hawke ~ Fielding edits the (ironically titled) *Jacobite's Journal* (-1748) ~ *The Universal Magazine of Knowledge and Pleasure* is founded (-1814) ~ Samuel Richardson publishes *Clarissa*.

1748

➤ Samuel Johnson. "The Vision of Theodore, the Hermit of Teneriffe, Found in His Cell." *The Preceptor* (London: R. Dodsley).
➤ Eliza Haywood. *Epistles for the Ladies* (November 1748-May 1749).

331

The Treaty of Aix-la-Chapelle ends the War of the Austrian Succession: it is status quo ante for Britain and France; Austria loses Silesia to Prussia and part of its Italian possessions to Spain, but Maria Theresa is recognised as Empress ~ David Hume publishes *An Enquiry Concerning Human Understanding* ~ John Cleland publishes the first part of *Memoirs of a Woman of Pleasure* (the second part in February 1749) ~ Tobias Smollett publishes *The Adventures of Roderick Random* ~ In France, Montesquieu publishes *The Spirit of the Laws* and La Mettrie publishes *Man, A Machine* ~ In Germany, Klopstock publishes the first cantos of *The Messiah* ~ Thomas Blackwell publishes *Letters Concerning Mythology*.

1749

➢ Anonymous. "[Story of Camillus]" (*The London Gazetteer*, 15 August).

➢ Anonymous. "The Treacherous Guardian" (*The Ladies' Magazine* I).

Halifax, Nova Scotia, is founded ~ Henry Fielding organises the Bow Street Runners, an early police force ~ First performances of Handel's *Music for Royal Fireworks* and the oratorio *Solomon* ~ Bolingbroke publishes *The Idea of a Patriot King* (correcting Pope's unauthorised edition of 1741) ~ Sarah Fielding publishes *Remarks on Clarissa* ~ Ralph Griffiths founds *The Monthly Review* (-1845) ~ Henry Fielding publishes *The History of Tom Jones, a Foundling*.

1750

➢ Samuel Johnson. "[History of Zosima]" (*The Rambler* 12); "[The Story of Eubulus]" (26-27); "[Cowardice for Elegance]" (35); "[A Marriage of Prudence without Affection]" (35); "[History of Miss May-pole]" (55); "[The Lingering Expectation of an Heir]" (73); "[Story of Melissa]" (75).

➢ Anonymous. "Distresses of a Clergyman's Family" (*The Student* 5); "The History of a Clergyman's Daughter" (8).

Two earthquakes are felt and much discussed in London ~ Thomas Warton and Christopher Smart edit *The Student* (-1751) ~ William Collins publishes *The Passions* ~ Samuel Johnson begins *The Rambler* (-1752).

1751

➢ Samuel Johnson. "[The Education of a Fop]" (*The Rambler* 109); "[The History of Hymenaeus's Courtship]" (113, 115); "[The Young Trader's Attempts at Politeness]" (116); "[The History of Almamoulin]" (120); "[The Young Trader Turned Gentleman]" (123); "[The Difficulty of Educating a Young Gentleman]" (132); "[Squire Bluster]" (142); "[The Courtier's Esteem of Assurance]" (147); "[The Treatment Incurred by Loss of Fortune]" (153); "[The Revolutions of a Garret]" (161); "[The Mischiefs of Following a Patron]" (163); "[Serotinus]" (165); "[History of Misella]" (170-171); "[History of Dicalculus]" (174); "[An Account of a Club of Antiquaries]" (177); "[The History of an Adventurer in Lotteries]" (181); "[The History of Leviculus, the Fortune-hunter]" (182); "[Anningait and Ajut, a Greenland History]" (186-187).

➢ Christopher Smart. "[A Very Curious Petrifaction]" (*The Midwife* 4); "[The Amours of Mr H. Lovewell and Miss E. Goodwill]" (4); "Survey of Bedlam—The History of Hannah" (5); "[Memoirs of a Tye-Wig]" (7); "[To the Wise Inhabitants of Tring]" (8).

➤ John Hill. "[Thyrsis and Saccharissa]" ("The Inspector" 2).

Frederick, Prince of Wales, dies and his son George becomes heir apparent ~ The British and the French East India Companies are at war, and Robert Clive, the British Commander-in-chief of British India, defeats a larger French force in the Battle of Arnee ~ The French *Encyclopédie* begins its publication ~ James Harris publishes *Hermes: or, A Philosophical Inquiry Concerning Universal Grammar* ~ John Hill writes "The Inspector," an essay-series in *The London Daily Advertiser* (-1753) ~ Christopher Smart (as Mrs. Mary Midnight) edits *The Midwife* ~ David Hume publishes *An Enquiry Concerning the Principles of Morals* ~ Henry Fielding publishes *Amelia* ~ Tobias Smollett publishes *The Adventures of Peregrine Pickle* ~ Thomas Gray publishes "Elegy Written in a Country Churchyard."

1752

➤ Samuel Johnson. "[The History of Abouzaid]" (*The Rambler* 190); "[The Busy Life of a Young Lady]" (191); "[The History of a Legacy-hunter]" (197-198).

➤ John Hawkesworth. "[Various Transmigrations Related by a Flea]" (*The Adventurer* 5); "[The History of Melissa]" (7-8); "[Story of Opsinous]" (12-14); "[Amurath, an Eastern Story]" (20-22).

➤ Bonnell Thornton. "[Project for an Auction of Manuscripts, by Timothy Spinbrain, Author]" (*The Adventurer* 6).

➤ Bonnell Thornton. "[Molly Packington]" (*The Drury-Lane Journal* 8).

The Calendar Act finally introduces the Gregorian Calendar in Britain; 25 March is no longer New Year's Day ~ The Murder Act is adopted: murderers are no longer to be buried, but rather "hanged in chains" on a "gibbet," or publicly dissected ~ The Paper War of 1752-1753 begins: Fielding, Christopher Smart, and others attack John Hill and other "hack writers" of Grub Street; Smollett joins the opposite side ~ Henry Fielding (as Sir Alex. Drawcansir) edits *The Covent-Garden Journal* ~ Bonnell Thornton edits *Have at Ye All, or The Drury-Lane Journal* ~ John Hawkesworth founds *The Adventurer* (-1754) ~ Charlotte Lennox publishes *The Female Quixote*.

1753

➤ Edward Moore. "[The Story of Mrs Wilson]" (*The World* 4-5); "[Amanda's Story of Her Seduction]" (52).

➤ John Boyle, Earl of Cork. "[Sir Josiah Pumpkin's Courage]" (*World* 47).

➤ John Hawkesworth. "[The Fatal Effects of False Apologies and Pretences: A Story]" (*The Adventurer* 54-56); "[Account of Eugenio]" (64-66); "[The History of Nouraddin and Amana]" (72-73).

➤ Hester Chapone. "The Story of Fidelia" (*The Adventurer* 77-79).

➤ Sir Charles Hanbury Williams. "[Mary Truman's Account of the Miseries of Dependence]" (*The World* 37).

➤ Philip Stanhope, Earl of Chesterfield. "[A Country Gentleman's Tour to Paris with His Family]" (*The World* 18, 29).

The British Museum is founded ~ Edward Moore begins editing *The World* (-1756) ~ Arthur Murphy edits *The Gray's-Inn Journal* (-1754) ~ Thomas Blackwell publishes the first volume of *Memoirs of the Court of Augustus* ~ Samuel Richardson publishes *The History of Sir Charles Grandison.*

1754

➢ Edward Moore. "[Forms of Rejecting Lovers by a Haughty Widow]" (*The World* 77); "[Letter from a Bride]" (85); "[The Seduction of a Young Lady]" (97).

➢ Earl of Chesterfield. "[The Drinking Club]" (*The World* 90-92).

➢ John Boyle, Earl of Cork. "[Tquassouw and Knonmquaiha, a Hottentot Story]" (*The Connoisseur* 21).

Thomas Pelham, Duke of Newcastle becomes prime minister (until 1756) ~ The Albany Congress debates and rejects Benjamin Franklin's proposal of an American Union ~ The French and Indian War (1754-1763) begins in Pennsylvania; American militia is led by Major George Washington ~ Clandestine Marriages Act: banns and/or license become mandatory, marriage has to be performed in a church, and persons under 21 need parental consent ~ Paul Hiffernan edits *The Tuner* (-1755) ~ Bonnell Thornton and George Colman launch *The Connoisseur* (-1756) ~ David Hume begins publication of *The History of England* (-1761) ~ Thomas Warton publishes *Observations on the Fairy Queen* ~ Sarah Scott publishes *A Journey through Every Stage of Life.*

1755

➢ George Colman the Elder and Bonnell Thornton. "[Supper at Vauxhall]" (*The Connoisseur* 68); "[A London Tradesman in the Country]" (79); "[Letter from a Hanger-on]" (100).

➢ Richard Owen Cambridge. "[Danger of Masquerades]" (*The World* 116); "[A Turtle Feast]" (123).

➢ John Herring. "[A Physician without Patronage]" (*The World* 122).

➢ Edward Moore. "[Distresses of a Ruined Wife and Mother]" (*The World* 144); "[Story of a Perfidious Lover]" (145).

➢ Earl of Chesterfield. "[On People of Fashion]" (*The World* 151).

➢ Soame Jenyns. "[A Visit to Sir John Jolly]" (*The World* 153).

Victory against the French in the Battle of Fort Beauséjour (New Brunswick), after which the decision is made to deport the Acadians (about 7,000 of them will thus be sent to the American colonies) ~ The great Lisbon earthquake (and tsunami) kills a large part of the population of the Portuguese capital (many intellectuals, most notably Voltaire, will write about it) ~ Samuel Johnson publishes *A Dictionary of the English Language* ~ Frances Brooke (as Mary Singleton) edits *The Old Maid* (-1756) ~ Tories Richard and William Beckford found *The Monitor* (-1765).

1756

➢ John Boyle, Earl of Cork. "[A Too Compliant Disposition]" (*The World* 161); "[A Wife Too Much Devoted to Her Father's Will]" (185).

➢ Soame Jenyns. "[A Visit to Sir Harry Prigg]" (*The World* 178).

➢ Edward Moore. "[Pride of the Family of Laycocks]" (*The World* 187).

➢ Richard Owen Cambridge. "[The Vexations of Gallantry]" (*World* 206).

➢ Frances Brooke. "[Curiosity Is Invincible]" (*The Old Maid* 24).

➢ Edward Long. "[Miss Aimwell]" (*The Prater* 2); "[History of Zulima and the Talisman]" (13, 15-16); "[Florio and Monimia, an Unhappy Story]" (24).

The Seven Years' War begins with hostilities between France and Great Britain ~ The French defeat Admiral John Byng's fleet in the Battle of Minorca; Byng is court-martialled, found guilty of negligence, and controversially executed ~ French General Montcalm captures Fort Oswego, New York (on Lake Ontario), then leaves with 1,700 prisoners ~ In Europe, the Seven Year's War begins with the Battle of Lobositz, in which Frederick the Great defeats the Austrians ~ William Cavendish, Duke of Devonshire, becomes prime minister (-1757), with William Pitt as Secretary of State ~ *The Critical Review* is founded (-1817), with Tobias Smollett as editor ~ *The Literary Magazine* (-1758) is founded, with Samuel Johnson editor ~ Christopher Smart and Richard Rolt edit *The Universal Visitor* ~ Edward Long (as Nicholas Babble) edits *The Prater* ~ Edmund Burke publishes *A Vindication of Natural Society* ~ Joseph Warton publishes the first volume of *Essay on the Genius and Writings of Pope.*

1757

➢ Thomas Francklin. "[Story of Scotus]" (*The Centinel* 46).

Robert Clive defeats the Nawab of Bengal and his French allies in the Battle of Plassey; Bengal is annexed by the British East India Company ~ In the Battle of Prague, Frederick the Great of Prussia defeats another Austrian army, but is in turn defeated in the Battle of Kolin ~ The Duke of Cumberland and his German allies are defeated by the French in the Battle of Hastenbeck ~ However, two crucial Prussian victories against the French at Rossbach and against the Austrians at Leuthen turn the tide of the war on the continent ~ Thomas Pelham, Duke of Newcastle begins his second term as prime minister (-1762) ~ Christopher Smart is confined to a lunatic asylum ~ Thomas Warton becomes Professor of Poetry at Oxford ~ Thomas Francklin edits *The Centinel* ~ Edmund Burke publishes *A Philosophical Enquiry into the Origin of Our Ideas of the Sublime and Beautiful.*

1758

➢ Samuel Johnson. "[Drugget's Retirement]" ("The Idler" 16); "[Betty Broom's History]" (26-29).

➢ Thomas Warton. "[Journal of a Fellow from College]" ("The Idler" 33).

After a 7-week siege, British forces led by Jeffrey Amherst and James Wolfe capture Louisbourg, making the conquest of New France possible ~ Anglo-German troops defeat the Austrians at Krefeld ~ Frederick the Great defeats the Russians at Zorndorg, but loses against superior Austrian forces at Hochkirch ~ Samuel Johnson begins editing "The Idler" (-1760) as an essay-series in *The Universal Chronicle* ~ Charlotte Lennox publishes the first edition of *Henrietta.*

1759

➢ Samuel Johnson. "[Molly Quick's Complaint of Her Mistress]" ("The

Idler" 46); "[Marvel's Journey]" (49); "[Dick Shifter's Rural Excursion]" (71); "[Gelaleddin and Bassora]" (75); "[Miss Heartless's Want of a Lodging]" (86).

➢ Bennet Langton. "[A Scholar's Journal]" ("The Idler" 67).
➢ Oliver Goldsmith. "A City Night-Piece" (*The Bee* 4); "Sabinus and Olinda" (7).

In the Battle of the Plains of Abraham, James Wolfe defeats Montcalm and captures Quebec City; both generals are mortally wounded ~ Two French fleets are defeated by the Royal Navy in the battles of Lagos and Quiberon Bay, which prevents France's planned invasion of Britain ~ The Anglo-German allies defeat the Austrians in the Battle of Minden, but a Russo-Austrian combined force manages to defeat Frederick the Great in the Battle of Kunersdorf ~ The British Museum opens ~ The Kew Gardens are founded ~ Voltaire publishes *Candide* ~ Goldsmith publishes *An Enquiry into the Present State of Polite Learning in Europe* ~ Adam Smith publishes *The Theory of Moral Sentiments* ~ Oliver Goldsmith writes the 8 numbers of *The Bee* ~ Edward Young publishes *Conjectures on Original Composition* ~ Samuel Johnson publishes *Rasselas* ~ Laurence Sterne publishes the first two volumes of *The Life and Opinions of Tristram Shandy*.

1760

➢ Oliver Goldsmith. "[A Reverie at the Boar's-Head Tavern in Eastcheap]" (*The British Magazine* 2-4); "[The Disabled Soldier]" (6); "[The History of Miss Stanton]" (7); "[The Adventures of a Strolling Player]" (10).
➢ Thomas Warton. "[Sam Softly's History]" ("The Idler" 93); "[Hacho of Lapland]" (96).

George II dies and George III becomes king (until 1820) ~ Jeffrey Amherst captures Montreal ~ Frederick the Great wins more hard-fought battles against Austria ~ Tobias Smollett founds *The British Magazine* (-1767) and begins his *Continuation* (post-1748) to Hume's *History of England* ~ James Macpherson publishes *Fragments of Ancient Poetry, Collected in the Highlands of Scotland* ~ James Ridley (as Helter Van Scelter) publishes "The Schemer" in *The London Chronicle* (-1762) ~ Oliver Goldsmith publishes "The Citizen of the World" in *The Public Ledger* ~ Charlotte Lennox begins serialisation of *Sophia*.

1761

➢ Alexander Kellet. "[The Man of Spirit]" (*The London Chronicle* 760).
➢ George Colman the Elder. "[Story of Patience Greenfield]" ("Genius" 9).

George III marries Charlotte of Mecklenburg; the king buys Buckingham Palace and turns it into the queen's private residence ~ Riot in Hexham (Northumberland) against a balloting system for military service; at least 45 are killed by the militia ~ The Anglo-German allies defeat a larger French force at Vellinghausen ~ France signs a treaty with Spain, bringing the latter into the Seven Years' War ~ The Afghan victory in the Battle of Panipat restores the Mughal Empire ~ George Colman writes "The Genius" essay-series (-1762) in *St James's Chronicle* ~ Frances Sheridan publishes *Memoirs of Miss Sidney Bidulph* ~ James Macpherson publishes *Fingal*.

1762

- Anonymous. "Guilt Discovered, or the Tendency of Avarice" (*The British Magazine*, June).
- Anonymous. "An Extraordinary Narrative of a Cabalist" (*The Gentleman's Magazine*, September).

The Tory Earl of Bute becomes the first Scottish prime minister of Great Britain (until 1763) ~ A new victory of the Anglo-German allies against the French in the Battle of Wilhelmsthal ~ France cedes all of New France, including Louisiana, to Spain ~ Following her coup against her husband Peter III, Catherine II (the Great) becomes Empress of Russia ~ Tobias Smollett edits *The Briton* (-1763) ~ John Wilkes founds *The North Briton* (-1763) ~ Arthur Murphy edits *The Auditor* (-1763) in opposition to Wilkes ~ Jean-Jacques Rousseau publishes *The Social Contract* and *Emile, or On Education* ~ Robert Lowth publishes *A Short Introduction to English Grammar* ~ Richard Hurd publishes *Letters on Chivalry and Romance* ~ Henry Home, Lord Kames publishes *Elements of Criticism* ~ Sarah Scott publishes *A Description of Millenium Hall and the Country Adjacent*.

1763

- Robert Lloyd (?). "[Distress of a Husband]" (*St James's Magazine*, May).

The Treaty of Paris ends the Seven Years' War; France cedes Britain the following territories: Canada and all of New France between the Mississippi River and the Appalachians (the territory west of the Mississippi had been given Spain in 1762), Dominica, Grenada, Saint Vincent, and Tobago; Spain cedes Britain the territory of Florida ~ Pontiac's anti-British rebellion begins in the Great Lakes area ~ By Royal Proclamation, settling in the newly acquired territory west of the Appalachian is restricted, which angers citizens of the American colonies ~ James Boswell is introduced to Samuel Johnson ~ John Wilkes is arrested for libel, but is released thanks to his MP privileges ~ Christopher Smart leaves the insane asylum and publishes *A Song to David* ~ Hugh Kelly edits the essay-series "The Babler" in *Owen's Weekly Chronicle* (-1766).

1764

- Anonymous. "[Opposite Female Characters]" (*London Magazine*, January).
- James Ridley (as Sir Charles Morell). *Tales of the Genii* (London: J. Wilkie).

The British East India Company defeats the Mughal Empire in the Battle of Buxar ~ Johann Joachim Winckelmann publishes *History of the Art of Antiquity* (Henry Fusseli's first English abridged translation appears the following year as *Reflections on the Painting and Sculpture of the Greeks*) ~ John Wilkes is expelled from the House of Commons under a new accusation of libel ~ Samuel Johnson and Joshua Reynolds found The Club ~ Horace Walpole publishes *The Castle of Otranto* ~ Oliver Goldsmith publishes the poem *The Traveller*.

1765

- Anonymous. *The History of Little Goody Two-Shoes* (London: J. Newbery).

The Stamp Act imposes a direct tax on the American colonies; various forms of protest follow, and the ad-hoc organisations are a rehearsal for future events ~ The Treaty of Allahabad (following the 1764 victory at Buxar) marks the beginning of the rule of the British East India Company on the subcontinent ~ Joseph II becomes Holy Roman Emperor (until 1790) ~ In a famous campaign (the "Calas Affair"), Voltaire exonerates Jean Calas (executed for murder in 1762) ~ William Blackstone begins publication of *Commentaries on the Laws of England* ~ Thomas Percy publishes his collection *Reliques of Ancient English Poetry* ~ Henry Brooke publishes the first volume of *The Fool of Quality* ~ Oliver Goldsmith publishes *Essays*.

1766

➢ Samuel Johnson. "The Fountains. A Fairy Tale," in Anna Williams's *Miscellanies in Prose and Verse* (London: T. Davies). 111-141.

The Stamp Act is repealed by the British Parliament ~ William Pitt the Elder becomes prime minister (until 1768) and accepts the title of Earl of Chatham ~ Tobias Smollett publishes *Travels through France and Italy* ~ Oliver Goldsmith publishes *The Vicar of Wakefield*.

1767

➢ J. Burton (?). "History of Philander and Clarinda" (*The Royal Magazine*, June-July; *The British Magazine*, June-July).

On a circumnavigation with HMS *Dolphin*, Samuel Wallis becomes the first European to visit Tahiti, which he names King George the Third Island ~ Daniel Boone defies the Royal Proclamation of 1763 and enters Kentucky ~ Cesare Beccaria's *On Crimes and Punishments* appears in English translation ~ Adam Ferguson publishes *An Essay on the History of Civil Society* ~ Sterne writes *Journal to Eliza* (published posthumously in 1904).

1768

➢ Isaac Bickerstaff. "[The Adventures of Ambrose Gwinett]" (*The Gentleman's Journal* 2).

James Cook departs on his first expedition on board HMS *Endeavour* ~ Corsica is ceded by Genoa to France ~ The Russo-Turkish War of 1768-1774 begins ~ Philip Astley founds the first modern circus ~ A riot, protesting John Wilkes's imprisonment, leads to the Massacre of St George's Fields, in which 7 protesters are killed by the troops ~ The Royal Academy of Arts is founded ~ William Gilpin publishes *An Essay on Prints*, in which he popularises the idea of the picturesque ~ *Encyclopaedia Britannica* begins publication in Edinburgh ~ Isaac Bickerstaff's *The Padlock*, Oliver Goldsmith's *The Good-Natur'd Man*, and Hugh Kelly's *False Delicacy* are among the biggest successes of the year on the London stage ~ Laurence Sterne publishes *A Sentimental Journey through France and Italy*.

1769

➢ John Murdoch. "The Danger of the Passions" (*The Universal Museum*, November-December).

➢ Anonymous. "[Useful Instructions to Novices in Town]" (*The Town and Country Magazine*, April-May).

James Cook arrives in Tahiti to observe the transit of Venus; later the same year he reaches New Zealand ~ Spain begins settlement of California ~

James Watt is granted a patent for a method of reducing the consumption of steam ~ David Garrick organises the first Shakespeare Jubilee at Stratford-upon-Avon ~ The Royal Academy of Arts holds its first summer exhibition; its president, Joshua Reynolds, delivers his first "Discourse" ~ The first anti-establishment "Letters of Junius" are published in *The Public Advertiser* ~ Archibald Hamilton founds *The Town and Country Magazine* (-1796) ~ Thomas Chatterton publishes his first poems attributed to medieval poet Thomas Rowley ~ Frances Brooke publishes *The History of Emily Montague*.

1770

➢ Thomas Chatterton. "[Tony Selwood]" (*The Town and Country Magazine*, August).

In what will soon be called "the Boston Massacre," British troops fire at a mob, killing 5 and wounding 6 protesters ~ Lord North becomes prime minister (until 1782) ~ Captain Cook drops anchor on the eastern coast of Australia, in a place he names Botany Bay; he soon claims the surrounding territory for Britain and calls it New South Wales ~ The Great Bengal famine of 1770, caused by crop failures and the policies of the British East India Company, causes the death of one third of the population of the province (an estimated 10 million die of starvation until 1773) ~ Russia defeats the Ottoman Empire on land, in the battles of Larga and Kagul, and at sea, in the Battle of Chesma ~ John Wheble founds *The Lady's Magazine* (-1837) ~ James Beattie publishes *An Essay on the Nature and Immutability of Truth* ~ Oliver Goldsmith publishes the poem *The Deserted Village*.

1771

➢ William Russell. *Sentimental Tales* (London: John Dixcey Cornish).

A rebellion in North Carolina, known as the War of Regulation, is quelled by British troops ~ John Smeaton founds the Society of Civil Engineers ~ Tobias Smollett publishes *The Expedition of Humphry Clinker* ~ Henry Mackenzie publishes *The Man of Feeling*.

1772

➢ Anonymous. "The History of a Milliner's Girl" (*The Covent Garden Magazine*, July-November).
➢ Anonymous. "The Way to Lose Her" (*The Town and Country Magazine*, October).

In the Panic of 1772, many British banks go bankrupt or stop payments; among those most affected by the crisis are the East India Company, whose stock plummets, and the American colonies, which rely on credit from British banks for their commercial relations ~ Samuel Adams forms the first Committee of Correspondence in the American Colonies ~ In the case of Somerset v Stewart, William Murray, Earl of Mansfield, Lord Chief Justice, establishes that slavery is unsupported by the common law of the land ~ James Cook leaves on his second expedition in the Pacific ~ In the first partition of Poland, Russia, Austria, and Prussia annex a large part of Polish territory ~ The anonymous anti-governmental *Letters of Junius* (published from 1769 to 1772 in the *Public Advertiser*) appear in volume format ~ Anna Laetitia Barbauld publishes *Poems*.

339

➢ John Aikin. "[Sir Bertrand. A Fragment]." *Miscellaneous Pieces, in Prose, by J. and A. L. Aikin* (London: J. Johnson).

➢ Oliver Goldsmith. "The History of Cyrillo Padovano, the Noted Sleep-Walker" (*The Westminster Magazine* I, February).

In an effort to save the East India Company (and to stop the smuggling of Dutch tea into America), British Parliament passes the Tea Act: the Company's tax-free tea is supposed to be bought by the American colonists, who are expected to pay taxes on it ~ In so-called "Boston Tea Party," American colonists, disguised as Mohawks, climb aboard East India Company ships and throw their cargo into Boston Harbour ~ *The Public Advertiser* publishes Benjamin Franklin's essay "Rules by which a Great Empire May Be Reduced to a Small One" ~ The Inclosure Act creates the legal foundation for the agricultural revolution and the gradual disappearance of the commons ~ John Harrison perfects his marine chronometer (now known as H5) ~ Captain Cook explores the coast of Tasmania ~ Hawkesworth publishes his edition of Cook's logs ~ First performance of Oliver Goldsmith's *She Stoops to Conquer*.

1774

➢ Elizabeth Griffith. "Story of Miss Williams" (*The Westminster Magazine* II, October).

The First Continental Congress opens in Philadelphia and decides in favour of the boycott of British goods ~ George Washington organises an independent militia in Virginia ~ Captain Cook reaches and names New Caledonia ~ Louis XV dies and his grandson, Louis XVI, becomes King of France ~ Russian General Suvorov defeats the Ottoman forces at Kozludzha; the Turks are forced to sign a peace treaty which allows Russia rights of protection for Turkey's Christian subjects ~ J. W. Goethe publishes *The Sorrows of Young Werther* (first translated in 1779) ~ Thomas Warton begins publication of his *The History of English Poetry* ~ The Earl of Chesterfield's *Letters to His Son* are published posthumously.

1775

➢ George Colman the Elder. "[A Country Gentleman]" (*The London Packet*, 25 October).

➢ Maria Susanna Cooper. "Benigna and Malevola. A Tale" (*The Sentimental Magazine*, September).

The American Revolution begins with the Battle of Lexington ~ The Second Continental Congress meets and decides in favour of raising a Continental Army and a Continental Navy ~ The British win the pyrrhic victory at Bunker Hill; King George III refuses requests for reconciliation and issues a "Proclamation for Suppressing Rebellion and Sedition" ~ Elizabeth Griffith publishes *The Morality of Shakespeare's Drama Illustrated* ~ First performance of Richard Brinsley Sheridan's *The Rivals* ~ Samuel Johnson publishes *A Journey to the Western Islands of Scotland*.

1776

➢ Elizabeth Griffith. "[An Affecting Instance of the Effects of Love]" (*The Westminster Magazine* IV, September).

The 13 American Colonies declare their independence from Britain ~ British troops lose control of Georgia, but then defeat the Americans in the Battle of Long Island and occupy New York and New Jersey ~ James Cook leaves Plymouth on his third expedition ~ Thomas Paine publishes *Common Sense* in Philadelphia and begins publishing *The American Crisis* ~ Edward Gibbon publishes the first volume of *The History of the Decline and Fall of the Roman Empire* ~ Adam Smith publishes *The Wealth of Nations* ~ James Beattie publishes *Essays* ("On Poetry and Music," "On Laughter, and Ludicrous Composition," "On the Utility of Classical Learning") ~ George Campbell publishes *The Philosophy of Rhetoric*.

1777

- ➤ John Hope. "The White Throat" (*The Lady's Magazine*, June).
- ➤ Samuel Jackson Pratt. "[Paladel and Patty]" (*The Westminster Magazine*, May-June).

British forces successfully besiege Fort Ticonderoga and win an important victory in the Battle of Brandywine, after which they capture Philadelphia ~ After another victory at Germantown, the British are defeated in the battles of Bemis Heights and Saratoga, where General Burgoyne surrenders ~ The Articles of Confederation are the first American constitution ~ First performance of Richard Brinsley Sheridan's *The School for Scandal* ~ Henry Mackenzie publishes *Julia de Roubigné* ~ Clara Reeve publishes a first version of *The Old English Baron* (titled *The Champion of Virtue*).

1778

- ➤ Anna Laetitia Barbauld. *Lessons for Children* (London: J. Johnson).
- ➤ Anonymous. "The Adventure of the Inn" (*The Town and Country Magazine*, April and June).

The United States and France sign a treaty of alliance ~ Captain Cook visits Hawaii ~ The Papists Act puts an end to anti-Catholic persecution ~ Vicesimus Knox publishes *Essays, Moral and Literary* ~ Fanny Burney publishes *Evelina*.

1779

- ➤ Henry Mackenzie. "[History of a Good-Hearted Man]" (*The Mirror* 23); "[The Story of La Roche]" (42-44).
- ➤ Robert Cullen. "[Silent Expression of Sorrow]" (*The Mirror* 27).
- ➤ David Dalrymple, Lord Hailes. "[Romancing in Conversation]" (*The Mirror* 62).

Spain becomes an ally of France and of the American colonies against Great Britain; Spain and France begin the Great Siege of Gibraltar (-1783) ~ A Franco-Spanish Armada attacks the British fleet in the English Channel, but the weather forces them to withdraw ~ British troops capture Savannah, Georgia ~ Captain Cook is killed in Hawaii ~ The Penitentiary Act allows for the foundation of a system of state prisons ~ Henry Mackenzie founds *The Mirror* (-1780) in Edinburgh ~ First performance of Richard Brinsley Sheridan's *The Critic* ~ Samuel Johnson begins publication of *Lives of the English Poets* (under the title *Prefaces, Biographical and Critical, to the Works of the English Poets*.

➤ Henry Mackenzie. "[Story of Emilia]" (*The Mirror* 101); "[The Story of Louisa Venoni]" (108-109).

➤ George Home. "[Story of Antonio]" (*The Mirror* 70-71).

➤ William Craig, Lord Craig. "[The Hardships of a Private Tutor]" (*The Mirror* 88).

➤ David "Baron" Hume. "[Letter from Simon Softly]" (*The Mirror* 103).

➤ William Beckford. *Biographical Memoirs of Extraordinary Painters* (London: J. Robson).

Admiral Rodney defeats a Spanish fleet in the Battle of Cape St Vincent ~ British troops capture Charleston, South Carolina; Cornwallis defeats colonial troops at Camden ~ French troops land in Rhode Island ~ The anti-Catholic Gordon Riots (triggered by the Papists Act of 1778) are quelled by the army, with hundreds of dead, wounded, and arrested (some of the latter will be executed) ~ First performance of Hannah Cowley's *The Belle's Stratagem*.

1781

➤ John Moir. "Samuel and Sally" (*The Westminster Magazine*, August).

A French fleet blockades Chesapeake Bay and defeats the ships of Admiral Graves ~ Surrounded by Washington on land and by the French on sea, General Cornwallis is besieged in Yorktown, Virginia, and surrenders ~ French spy de la Motte is executed in front of a large crowd ~ Immanuel Kant publishes *Critique of Pure Reason* (first translated in 1838) ~ William Ogilvie publishes *An Essay on the Right of Property in Land*.

1782

➤ Leonard McNally. "Fanny; or, The Fair Foundling of St George's Fields" (*British Magazine and Review*, July).

The Repeal Act restores the independence of the Parliament of Ireland ~ Admiral Rodney defeats a French fleet in the Battle of the Saintes ~ Preliminary peace talks begin in Paris between Great Britain and the future USA ~ First performance of Schiller's *The Robbers* (translated in 1792 by A. F. Tytler) ~ James Perry founds *The European Magazine* (-1826) ~ Fanny Burney publishes *Cecilia*.

1783

➤ William Mavor. "Memoirs of a Cornish Curate" (*British Magazine and Review*, July-August).

The Peace of Paris ends the American Revolutionary War ~ William Pitt the Younger becomes prime minister (until 1801) ~ Russia annexes Crimea ~ The eruption of the volcano Laki in Iceland creates a cloud of sulphur dioxide, killing thousands in Britain ~ The Montgolfier brothers successfully fly a hot air balloon for the first time; the Robert brothers fly a hydrogen-filled balloon in Paris ~ Thomas Day begins publication of *The History of Sandford and Merton* ~ Ellenor Fenn publishes *Cobwebs to Catch Flies* ~ George Crabbe publishes the poem *The Village* ~ William Blake privately prints *Poetical Sketches*.

1784

- Thomas Holcroft. "The Story-teller" (*The Wit's Magazine* 1-5).
- Anonymous. "The History of Amelia" (*The Lady's Magazine*, January-April).

The India Act introduced by Pitt the Younger brings the affairs of the East India Company under government control ~ Kant publishes the article "Answering the Question: What Is Enlightenment?" ~ First performance of Beaumarchais's *The Marriage of Figaro* (the English version is produced in London the same year) ~ Charlotte Smith publishes the first version of her *Elegiac Sonnets*.

1785

- William Craig, Lord Craig. "[History of Hortensius]" (*The Lounger* 9).
- Alexander Fraser Tytler. "[Letter from Jeremiah Dy-soon]" (*The Lounger* 24); "[A Letter from John Truman]" (44).
- Henry Mackenzie. "[Another Letter from Jeremiah Dy-soon]" (*The Lounger* 45).
- Horace Walpole. *Hieroglyphic Tales* (private printing).

First crossing of the English Channel in a hot-air baloon ~ Thomas Reid publishes *Essays on the Intellectual Powers of Man* ~ William Paley publishes *Principles of Moral and Political Philosophy* ~ Richard Cumberland publishes *The Observer* (augmented in 1786, 1788, and 1791), organised as an essay serial ~ Henry Mackenzie founds *The Lounger* (-1787) ~ James Boswell publishes *The Journal of a Tour to the Hebrides with Samuel Johnson* ~ Ann Yearsley publishes *Poems, on Several Occasions* ~ Clara Reeve publishes *The Progress of Romance* ~ Robert Merry edits *The Florence Miscellany* ~ William Cowper publishes the poem *The Task*.

1786

- William Craig, Lord Craig. "[Visit of Sir William Roberts to Mr Draper]" (*The Lounger* 71).
- Henry Mackenzie. "[History of Sophia M——]" (*The Lounger* 75); "[Story of Father Nicholas]" (82-84).
- Alexander Abercromby, Lord Abercromby. "[Martha Edwards' Complaint]" (*The Lounger* 92).
- Richard Graves. "The Origin of Gallantry." *Lucubrations* (London: J. Dodsley).

A plan for the creation of a penal colony at Botany Bay, Australia, is approved ~ Penang Island (today part of Malaysia) is acquired by Captain Francis Light in the name of the East India Company in exchange for military protection: the first British colony in Southeast Asia ~ John Smith, George Canning, Robert Percy Smith and John Hookham Frere found *The Microcosm* (-1787) ~ *The Pharos. A Collection of Periodical Essays* (-1787) is written by an anonymous female author (possibly Eliza Kirkham Matthews) ~ Robert Burns publishes *Poems, Chiefly in the Scottish Dialect* ~ W. T. Beckford's *Vathek* is published in French and English (as *An Arabian Tale*) ~ Hester Thrale publishes *Anecdotes of the Late Samuel Johnson*.

1787

> George Moutard Woodward. "The Castle of Erasmus; or, Bertrand and Eliza. A Legendary Tale" (*The General Magazine and Impartial Review*, November).

The First Fleet of 11 ships carrying 700 convicts leaves England for Australia (where it arrives in January 1788) ~ The Society for Effecting the Abolition of the Slave Trade is founded in London ~ Thomas Monro founds *The Olla Podrida* (-1788) ~ Mary Wollstonecraft publishes *Thoughts on the Education of Daughters*.

1788

> Thomas Bellamy (?). "A Melancholy Event" (*The General Magazine and Impartial Review*, January).
> Sarah Trimmer. "Moral Tales" (*The Family Magazine*, January 1788-June 1789).

The Australian frontier wars against the indigenous population begin (they will officially end in 1934) ~ The Association for Promoting the Discovery of the Interior Parts of Africa is founded in London ~ King George III's bout of madness causes a Regency Crisis (until April 1789) ~ Riots in Grenoble (the so-called "Day of the Tiles") foreshadow days of unrest in France the following year ~ Joseph Johnson and Thomas Christie found *The Analytical Review* (-1798) ~ Vicesimus Knox publishes *Winter Evenings* ~ Anne Francis publishes *A Poetical Epistle from Charlotte to Werter* ~ Charlotte Smith publishes *Emmeline* ~ Mary Wollstonecraft publishes *Mary: A Fiction* and *Original Stories from Real Life*.

1789

> Barbara Finch. "Myrtle-Wood. A Tale" (*The General Magazine and Impartial Review*, June-July).
> Alexander Bicknell. "Bunbury's Family Picture" (*The General Magazine and Impartial Review*, February) [Revised as "The Family Picture. By Bunbury," in *Painting Personified* (London: R. Baldwin, 1790), Vol. I, 1-31.

The French Revolution begins; France's Constituent Assembly passes the Declaration of the Rights of Man and of the Citizen ~ George Washington is elected President of the United States ~ James Madison introduces a Bill of Rights in the US House of Representatives; most of it is turned into the first 10 amendments to the Constitution ~ At Rymnik, in the largest battle of the Russo-Turkish War (1787-1792), Alexander Suvorov defeats the Turks ~ Fletcher Christian leads the famous mutiny on HMS Bounty in the Pacific Ocean ~ William Wilberforce delivers his first anti-slavery speech in the House of Commons ~ James Austen (Jane Austen's older brother) founds *The Loiterer, A Periodical Work* (-1790) ~ Jeremy Bentham publishes *An Introduction to the Principles of Morals and Legislation* ~ Olaudah Equiano publishes *The Interesting Narrative of the Life of Olaudah Equiano* ~ William Blake privately prints a first version of *Songs of Innocence* ~ William Lisle Bowles publishes *Fourteen Sonnets*.

344

1790

> Nathan Drake. "[Sir Gawen]" (*The Speculator* 10-12) [revised as "Henry Fitzowen, a Gothic Tale" in his *Literary Hours* (1798)]; "[Maria Arnold. A Tale]" (15-16); "[Agnes Felton]" (23).

> Robert Burns. "[Three Witch Stories]" (in a letter to Francis Grose); first published in *Censura Literaria* (1796).

France becomes constitutional monarchy; French monastic orders are dissolved; the territory of France is divided into departments ~ The Austrian Netherlands revolt against the Habsburgs and create the short-lived United Belgian States ~ In the Battle of Svensksund, the largest naval battle in the Baltic Sea, Sweden defeats Russia, ending a war begun in 1788; the two countries become allies ~ Suvorov captures the fortress of Izmail from the Turks ~ William Wordsworth travels to France ~ Nathan Drake writes the 26 numbers of *The Speculator* ~ Edmund Burke publishes *Reflections on the Revolution in France* ~ Mary Wollstonecraft publishes *A Vindication of the Rights of Men* ~ William Combe publishes the first volumes of *The Devil upon Two Sticks in England* ~ Archibald Alison publishes *Essays on the Nature and Principles of Taste* ~ Joanna Baillie publishes *Poems* ~ William Blake composes *The Marriage of Heaven and Hell* ~ Ann Radcliffe publishes *A Sicilian Romance*.

1791

> Anonymous. "The Pretty Villager" (*The Universal Magazine*, April).

> Anonymous. "The Atonements of Sensibility" (*The Universal Magazine*, May-June).

Louis XVI and Marie Antoinette are captured while attempting to flee France ~ The Haitian Revolution begins ~ Priestley Riots in Birmingham against Dissenters, seen as supporters of the French Revolution ~ Thomas Paine publishes *Rights of Man* ~ Francis Grose writes the 16 numbers of "The Grumbler," an essay-series published in *The English Chronicle* ~ Helen Maria Williams publishes *Letters on the French Revolution* ~ James Boswell publishes *Life of Samuel Johnson* ~ Isaac D'Israeli publishes the first volume of his *Curiosities of Literature* ~ Mary Robinson publishes *Poems* (2nd vol. in 1793) ~ Charlotte Smith publishes *Celestina* ~ Elizabeth Inchbald publishes *A Simple Story* ~ Ann Radcliffe publishes *The Romance of the Forest*.

1792

> John Aikin and Anna Laetitia Barbauld. *Evenings at Home* (London: J. Johnson).

Louis XVI is arrested, monarchy abolished, and the French Republic proclaimed ~ The French Revolutionary Wars begin with the War of the First Coalition (1792-1797); French artillery repels a Prussian army in the Battle of Valmy ~ Russia invades Poland ~ George Vancouver explores the Pacific coast of present-day British Columbia ~ William Roberts edits *The Looker-On* ~ T.F. Middleton edits *The Country Spectator* (-1793) ~ Arthur Young publishes *Travels in France* ~ Samuel Rogers publishes *The Pleasures of Memory, with Other Poems* ~ Mary Wollstonecraft publishes *A Vindication of the Rights of Woman* ~ Charlotte Smith publishes *Desmond*.

345

➢ Mary Hays. "[Melville and Serena]." *Letters and Essays, Moral and Miscellaneous* (London: T. Knott).

First Louis XVI, then Marie Antoinette, are guillotined; Reign of Terror begins ~ Royalist counter-revolution in the south of France; Republican forces crush the Vendean rebellion at Savenay and capture Toulon from Royalist and British defenders: young captain Napoleon Bonaparte's gallantry is noticed and he is promoted brigadier general ~ At Neerwinden, Austrian and Dutch troops defeat an invading French army ~ Second Partition of Poland between Russia and Prussia ~ A diplomatic mission led by George Macartney reaches China but fails to convince the imperial court of Beijing of the importance of developing commercial relations with Britain ~ Alexander Mackenzie becomes the first explorer to have crossed North America from east to west ~ In Madras, Hugh Boyd edits *The Indian Observer* (-1794) ~ Isaac D'Israeli publishes *A Dissertation on Anecdotes* ~ William Blake engraves *America a Prophecy* ~ Charlotte Smith publishes *The Old Manor House* .

1794

➢   Joseph Moser. *Turkish Tales* (London: William Lane).

In the Battle of Tourcoing, the French defeat an Anglo-Austrian army; at Fleurus, they defeat an Austro-Dutch army ~ In the largest naval battle of the French Revolutionary Wars (the Glorious First of June), the British defeat the French ~ Thomas Paine publishes the first part of *The Age of Reason* ~ Robert Alves's *Sketches of a History of Literature* appear posthumously ~ William Blake creates *Europe a Prophecy* ~ First performance of Richard Cumberland's *The Jew* ~ Coleridge and Southey publish their play *The Fall of Robespierre* ~ William Godwin publishes *Caleb Williams* ~ Ann Radcliffe publishes *The Mysteries of Udolpho*.

1795

➢ Thomas Bellamy. "Caroline Courtney" (*The Monthly Mirror*, December 1795-April 1796).

➢ Anonymous. "The Horrors of a Monastery" (*The Edinburgh Magazine*, August-September).

The Directory (a cabinet made of 5 ministers) starts ruling France (until 1799) ~ French troops enter Netherlands; the Batavian Republic is proclaimed in Amsterdam; Austrian Netherlands becomes France's "Belgian departments" ~ Royalist rebellion in Paris (13 Vendémiaire) defeated by Republican troops ~ Third Partition of Poland between Russia, Austria, and Prussia ~ Thomas Bellamy founds *The Monthly Mirror* (-1811) ~ Hannah More begins publishing Cheap Repository Tracts ~ Isaac D'Israeli publishes *Essay on the Manners and Genius of the Literary Character* ~ Maria Edgeworth publishes *Letters for Literary Ladies*.

1796

➢ Maria Edgeworth. *The Parent's Assistant; or, Stories for Children* (London: J. Johnson).

> Hannah More. *Betty Brown, the St Giles's Orange Girl* (London: J. Marshall).

Napoleon takes command of the Army of Italy and defeats the Austrians in the battles of Montenotte, Lodi, Castiglione, and Arcole; French troops capture Milan ~ Spain declares war against Great Britain ~ Scottish explorer Mungo Park reaches the Niger River ~ John Aikin begins editing *The Monthly Magazine* (-1826), founded by Richard Phillips ~ Coleridge publishes *Poems on Various Subjects* and his short-lived periodical *The Watchman* ~ Mary Wollstonecraft publishes *Letters Written in Sweden, Norway, and Denmark* ~ Fanny Burney publishes *Camilla* ~ Mary Hays publishes *Memoirs of Emma Courtney* ~ Elizabeth Inchbald publishes the novel *Nature and Art* ~ Matthew Lewis publishes *The Monk*.

1797

> Harriet and Sophia Lee. *The Canterbury Tales; or, The Year 1797* (London: G.G. and J. Robinson).

The Royal Navy defeats a Spanish fleet in the second Battle of Cape St Vincent ~ A French expeditionary force lands in Wales but is defeated by British troops ~ John Adams becomes the second American president ~ Still in Italy, Napoleon defeats the Austrians at Rivoli, then captures Mantua and Venice; the War of the First Coalition ends with the peace treaty of Campo Formio between France and Austria ~ Friedrich Hölderlin publishes the first volume of *Hyperion* ~ Sir Frederick Morton Eden publishes *The State of the Poor* ~ William Godwin publishes *The Inquirer: Reflections on education, manners, and literature, in a series of essays* ~ Hannah Webster Foster publishes *The Coquette* ~ Ann Radcliffe publishes *The Italian* ~ S.T. Coleridge composes "Kubla Khan."

1798

> William Gilpin. *Morul Contrasts* (London: T. Caddell and W. Davies).
> Anonymous. "The Maid of St Marino" (*Lady's Monthly Museum*, July-November).
> Anonymous. *Colville. A West Indian Tale* (London: G. Cawthorn).

French troops enter the Papal State and remove the pope from power; Switzerland becomes a client-state of France; the French capture Malta ~ Napoleon invades Egypt and defeats the Ottomans in the Battle of the Pyramids; the French occupy Cairo ~ Horatio Nelson defeats the French navy in the Battle of the Nile and begins a blockade against Napoleon's army in Egypt ~ Rebellion in Ireland: leaders of the Society of United Irishmen are arrested; martial law begins; French troops land in Ireland to support the revolution; after a long series of battles, General Cornwallis defeats the French and Irish troops; charismatic leader Wolfe Tone is captured and hanged ~ *The Lady's Monthly Museum* is founded (-1832) ~ William Jackson of Exeter publishes *The Four Ages: With Essays on Various Subjects* ~ Thomas Malthus publishes *An Essay on the Principle of Population* ~ Mary Wollstonecraft's *Memoirs* and her novel *Maria; or, The Wrongs of Woman* appear posthumously ~ Joanna Baillie publishes *Plays on the Passions* ~ Nathan Drake publishes *Literary Hours* ~ Samuel Taylor Coleridge and William Wordsworth publish *Lyrical Ballads*.

1799

> ➤ Anonymous. *Literary Leisure* (1-60, 26 September 1799-18 December 1800).

British and Russian forces invade French-controlled Netherlands with disastrous results ~ Napoleon manages to return to France, where he organises a coup in which the Directory is abolished and he is proclaimed First Consul ~ The successful Siege of Seringapatam ends the last Anglo-Mysore War; the British East India Company gains control of most of India ~ Mungo Park publishes *Travels in the Interior Districts of Africa* ~ The pseudonymous Solomon Saunter publishes the weekly *Literary Leisure* (-1800) ~ Isaac D'Israeli publishes *Romances* ~ Mary Hays publishes *The Victim of Prejudice*.

1800

> ➤ Anonymous. "A Cottage Tale" (*The Edinburgh Magazine*, July-August).

In the War of the Second Coalition, Austrian and British troops capture Genoa; Napoleon crosses the Alps again into Italy and defeats the Austrians in the Battle of Marengo ~ British Parliament passes the Act of Union with Ireland ~ British troops capture and hold Malta ~ Wordsworth writes the Preface to the 2nd edition of *Lyrical Ballads* ~ Thomas Moore publishes *Odes of Anacreon* ~ Mary Robinson publishes *Lyrical Tales* ~ Maria Edgeworth publishes *Castle Rackrent*.

Henry M. Wallace has a Ph.D. in literary studies.
His research interests include 18th-century and 19th-century
British literature and the theory of literary history.